The Pillars of Herakles

The Last of the Romans: IV

The Pillars of Herakles

A NOVEL OF BELISARIUS

WILLIAM HAVELOCK

First print edition May 2023

Book cover design by Dusan Markovic
Maps by Cyowari

ISBN: 978-1-7379808-4-1 (hardcover)
ISBN: 978-1-7379808-5-8 (paperback)
ASIN: B0BX89HFTQ (ebook)

www.havelockbooks.com

For Owen and Briella.
May your journeys take you to wondrous places.

Methinks I still can hear,
Sounding distinct and near,
The Vandal monarch's cry,
As, captive and disgraced,
With majestic step he paced,--
"All, all is Vanity!"

~Henry Wadsworth Longfellow (1807–1882 C.E.)

CHARACTERS

Aetius	Long-dead general of the Western Roman Empire, Attila's nemesis
Agathias	A slave to the Imperial Palace in Constantinople
Agila	A Visigothic warlord, close to Theudis
Aigan	An officer of the Hun foederati, succeeds Simmas
Alagild	A young Visigothic spearman
Alexander	Varus' son
al-Harith	Ghassanid King, brother of Mariya
Aliya	Handmaiden to Mariya
Altan	A young Herulian horseman
Amalasuntha	Queen regent of the Ostrogoths in Italy
Amalaric	Grandson of Theodoric, child-king of the Visigoths
Anastasius	Deceased Roman Emperor of Varus' Youth
Antonina	Young Roman aristocrat, daughter of Basilius, wife of Belisarius
Apollos	Captain of the expedition's flagship
Archelaus	A former excubitor and leader of the Thracian Army, killed in a trial by combat
Ascum	Alani ballista commander, serves the Cappadocian Army
Athalaric	Young king of the Ostrogoths, grandson of Theodoric, only child of Amalasuntha
Attila	Long-dead Khagan of the Hunnic Empire
Auria	A princess among the Mauri
Aya	An Egyptian slave to the Imperial Palace in Constantinople
Azarethes	Commander of all Persian armies
Baduarius	Ostrogoth, tribune of Belisarius' spearmen
Basilius	Former East Roman consul, senior minister to Justinian
Belisarius	Roman general, husband to Antonina, and military leader of the Imperial expedition to Carthage

Bessas	Armenian, leads Belisarius' cataphracts
Cassiodorus	A disgraced priest and Imperial minister
Cephalas	Greek, former spearman of the Thracian Army, aide to Varus
Chanaranges	Personal excubitor to Justinian
Conon	A half-Hun, half-Thracian officer
Dagisthaeus	Ostrogoth, brother of Baduarius, a deceased tribune under Belisarius
Domeric	A skilled Visigoth swordsman
Fulcaris	Centurion within the Herulian foederati
Gelimer	Former Vandal king, captured at Mount Papua
Germanus	Justinian's cousin, general of the Thracian Army
Godilas	Deceased general of the East Roman armies, and a close friend to Justin
Gratian	One of Solomon's centurions, slain under strange circumstances at Tricamarum
Gunderic	A young, celebrated warlord of the Vandal armies
Hakhamanish	The magus, a priest of the Zoroastrian religion
Hermogenes	Imperial minister and legate in the Persian War
Hypatius	The eldest nephew of Emperor Anastasius, secret father of Tiberius
Indulf	Ostrogothic commander
Irilar	A Herulian recruit, cousin to Fulcaris, slain at Ad Decimum
Isaacius	A Jewish soldier in the Thracian Army, killed in battle against the Avars
Itaxes	An older fisherman of Septem
Jamila	Principal handmaiden to Mariya
Joannina	Daughter of Belisarius and Antonina
John	Belisarius' second-in-command , accidentally killed by Uliaris
Justin	Deceased Roman emperor, former dominus of Varus and Samur
Justinian	Roman emperor, husband to Theodora

Kavadh	Shahanshah of the Persian Empire
Kazrig	Khan of the Avars
Khingila	Warlord of the Hephthalites, slain at Dara
Khosrow	Shahanshah of the Persian Empire
Leo	Long-dead Pope, met with Attila
Liberius	A senior advisor to the Emperor, legate to the Imperial expedition to Carthage
Marcellus	Lord of the excubitores
Marcian	Latin centurion, second-in-command to Solomon, murdered by Varus
Mariya	Princess of the Ghassanids, wife of Varus
Menelik	A young Aksumite spearman
Mundus	Tribune of the Thracian Army, Germanus' second-in-command
Narses	Theodora's chief spy and advisor
Nepotian	A wealthy Roman senator, Solomon's father
Odoacer	Ostrogoth who overthrew the last Western Roman Emperor
Opilio	Centurion of the Herulian foederati, slain at Dara
Paulus	Justinian's disgraced Minister of the Treasury
Perenus	An exiled Lazic prince, Varus' second-in-command
Petrus	An aged Roman priest
Procopius	Imperial scribe and historian
Rosamund	A captured Gepid pagan, Varus' companion and healer
Samur	A Herulian slave to Justin, eventually a senior officer of the Hun foederati, Varus' only sibling
Sembrouthes	Commander of Aksumites guarding Princess Mariya, Varus' chief bodyguard
Sergius	Latin centurion under Belisarius
Shaush	Prince of the Avars, eldest son of Kazrig, slain in battle against Belisarius
Silius	First centurion under Solomon

Simmas	A commander of the Hun foederati, slain at Callinicum
Sindual	Young centurion of the Herulian foederati
Sinnion	An officer in the Hun foederati, succeeds Sunicas
Solomon	A young Roman aristocrat and komes, son of Nepotian
Stotzas	Prefect of Carthage
Sunicas	An honored leader of the Hun foederati, slain at Callinicum
Theodora	Roman Empress, wife of Justinian
Theodoric	Late hero-king of all the Goths
Theudesgel	A Visigothic warlord, known for savagery
Theudis	Regent for the Visigoths in Hispania
Thurimuth	An Alemanni, first-spear centurion in the Thracian Army
Tiberius Constantine	Hypatius' young son, now Varus' ward
Tribonian	Justinian's disgraced Minister of Laws
Troglita	A komes in the Thracian Army
Tzazon	Brother of Gelimer, slain at Tricamarum
Uliaris	A Frank, leader of Belisarius' bodyguards, disgraced for accidentally killing John
Valerian	A komes in the Roman Empire's eastern provinces
Varus	The narrator, a Herulian, an excubitor and an officer in Belisarius' army
Vitalius	A youth of the Imperial household, slain in service to Varus at Tricamarum
Wazeba	An Aksumite spearman
Wisimar	A young warrior among the Vandals
Xerxes	Persian prince and Immortal, entrusted to Varus' care
Zenobia	Varus' daughter

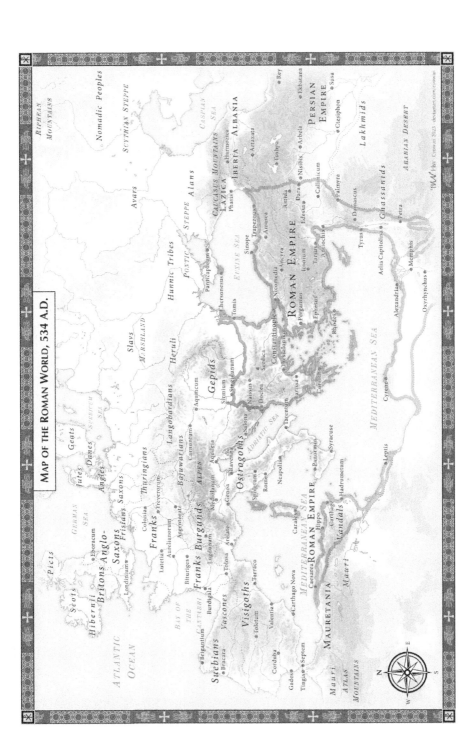

MAP OF THE ROMAN WORLD, 534 A.D.

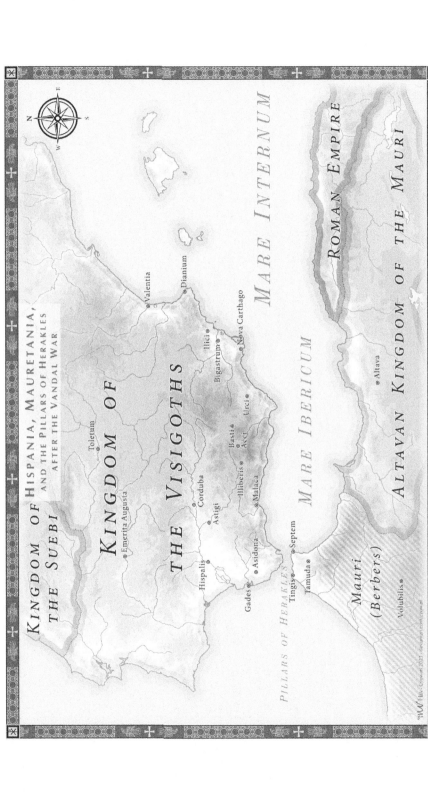

KINGDOM OF HISPANIA, MAURETANIA, AND THE PILLARS OF HERAKLES AFTER THE VANDAL WAR

KINGDOM OF THE SUEBI

KINGDOM OF THE VISIGOTHS

ROMAN EMPIRE

ALTAVAN KINGDOM OF THE MAURI

MARE INTERNUM

MARE IBERICUM

PILLARS OF HERAKLES

Mauri (Berbers)

Toletum

Emerita Augusta

Corduba

Astigi

Hispalis

Gades

Asidona

Tingis

Tamuda

Septem

Volubilis

Illiberis

Malaca

Basti

Acci

Urci

Bigastrum

Ilici

Nova Carthago

Dianium

Valentia

Altava

N E S W

PROLOGUE:
THE SENESCHAL

Gripped within a whirling maelstrom, the seneschal had little choice but to continue her duty. That was why she had been permitted to survive, and why she had endured for so long in this utterly foreign and pitiless place.

Thousands of her kinsmen, their sun-bleached bones littering the plains, could not say the same.

The seneschal had not wanted to become a subject of these conquerors; she had had little choice. An enemy band had arrived from the steppe, killing any who resisted and enslaving those who did not, and put her once-peaceful village to the torch. Initially, she assumed she'd been kept alive to labor in the wheat fields, or to warm the pillows of some rough warrior, only to discover, with surprise, that the Great King's sorcerers selected her—and only her—for the role she now occupied. Lifted from a cowering mass of filth and fear, the seneschal had soon become one of the most powerful subjects within the Great King's domain.

Unaccustomed to cruelty, the seneschal found her transition was not always smooth. Yet the Great King was charming, leaving occasional lavish gifts of gems or silks by her door and bowing to her counsel for restraint when his warlords urged impetuous action.

The seneschal offered many prayers of gratitude for her good fortune, and sought to use her status to improve the governance of the Great King's expanding realm while alleviating the crushing burdens thrust upon those tens of thousands of slaves captured as defeated enemies. She was no fool—though she did not delight in carnage herself, she did little to steer her conquerors away from their pleasures.

Even when the Great King departed for the next life, the seneschal remained hopeful that his heir would continue as an equally wise ruler. Though young, the heir had been bred for this charge, and possessed an optimism his father had not. Handsome in a wild manner, the heir was a vision of strength, wrapped in an aura that demanded obedience. The seneschal felt solemn pride to confer the Great King's remarkable sword to this deserving young man, born from war and bred to rule.

Any hope of a wise or just ruler evaporated just months after his ascension, when the heir, weakened by sickness and bested in battle, followed his father in death. In the unfamiliar aftermath of defeat, many of the Great King's men turned to the seneschal for guidance, then whispered intrigue in hopes of swinging her decision whichever way they found most favorable. She had been sorely tempted to let herself be swayed, to break with decorum and bypass the boorish wastrel of an heir that was the Great King's second son, a man lacking in any of the education, wisdom, or trappings of kingship that the Great King's people required in such dark times.

Yet the Great King's only other legitimate son was still a boy, and sidestepping the next in line to the Great King's throne would doubtlessly tear the realm asunder, fracturing the chieftains even further into their own realms and federates. And so it came to pass that the seneschal swallowed her pride and carried the Great King's blade to the wastrel, conferring it with all the power and authority that she had amassed in many years of service. The wastrel accepted such vast power with little more than a grunt, then dismissed her within moments of the hallowed ceremony. There was no sense of honor in conferring the Great King's right to rule to this accidental heir, but still the seneschal completed her duty, believing that she had made the honorable choice.

But she wept when the wastrel's men came for her that evening.

Rough hands pulled her from her feather-stuffed bed, dragging her naked into the chill of night. She demanded an audience with the new king, but her final pleas were answered with silence as she was hauled atop a nearby hill, where a lone tree cast shadows upon the vast hive of the Great King's people. She had little time to pray as they wrapped the noose around her neck, barely managing her final breaths as they lifted her high into the air. Her hangman alone showed distaste at her foreign lineage, cursing the seneschal's actions—a woman of lesser bloodlines, sitting in judgment over the king's warriors? A disgrace.

The seneschal's hands shuddered for only a heartbeat. The fall mercifully snapped her neck; the only sensation she felt was a brisk wind flowing through her hair. Her body swung there for seven days, dangling like some macabre fruit.

THE UNFORTUNATE
TIDINGS OF VICTORY

It is tempting to reduce the lives of women and men into a small collection of notable accomplishments. These sorts of tidy labels make their lives simple, easy to categorize in one of Procopius' ledgers, and easier still to remark upon with no consideration of the countless hours that led to their victories or tragedies. For in revisiting history, few desire a story of daily sweat and pain. A cleaner, less personal understanding of a life is almost always preferred.

Few are guiltier of this sin than I. Even as a palace slave, I fixated on the accomplishments of heroes, never pondering the personal toll that success requires. I cared little that Hannibal's daring march through Italy left him blind in one eye, nor did I wonder at the weeks and months of strain that my own master had suffered as a soldier in Rome's army. It is far more convenient to judge men by their achievements, as much to place their suffering out of mind as to remove any hesitation to condemn them to death, should duty require us.

Today, when citizens of the Empire recall Belisarius' conquest of the Vandals, many do speak respectfully, recognizing the victory for the staggering accomplishment that it was. Others, less moved, remark only upon the brevity of the campaign, daring to assume that the defeat of Gelimer and the Vandals was a simple and bloodless affair owing more to barbarian incompetence than Roman strategic genius. For such fools, I have only contempt. I was one of the proud few of Belisarius' men who marched along the African coastline, a living testament to the terrible truth. I bore witness to the final charge that broke Vandal power in that province forever, and I clutched a mere boy in my arms as he whimpered and cried to his death.

Not that Belisarius himself would ever remember that campaign with anything other than bitterness. Seated atop the throne of the Vandal kings, Belisarius accepted the surrender of his defeated foe readily enough, yet did so with none of the dignified warmth that had led him to victory over the Avars or the Persians. No, Belisarius' gaze was icy as he accepted Gelimer as Justinian's prisoner. Immediately thereafter, the Vandal kingdom was transformed into an Imperial prefecture, governed by military officers until pacification allowed some patrician to wield the Emperor's authority.

True, our casualties had been mercifully light. By Procopius' account, Belisarius had lost more men to bloody flux than to fighting, although even the loss of a few hundred men would leave the Roman Army perilously undermanned in such vast lands as Africa, Numidia, and Mauretania. Still, the Vandals had fared far worse, their bodies malnourished and weakened despite several days of meals that I had shared with their chieftains. Gunderic, one of Gelimer's more celebrated commanders, gave me his profuse thanks for my hospitality, niceties I awkwardly waved off as unnecessary. In those days, my thoughts often drifted back to the barren summit of Mount Papua, the mound of frozen and emaciated corpses inviting us to join their final banquet of hunger and desolation.

For a few weeks thereafter, many among the Imperial Army rejoiced. My centurions celebrated as I distributed leather pouches overflowing with silver coins, instructing that the contents be allocated evenly throughout the Herulian, Hunnic, and Gothic foederati under their—and therefore my—command. Despite warnings to guard this remuneration in store for leaner times, many—including Fulcaris and

Perenus—turned over their coins to strong drink and raucous company in Carthage's taverns. Belisarius frowned upon this unpredictable and often destructive behavior, yet even he had little real power to keep the men eternally sober and well behaved now that the Vandal War had concluded. Others, once awarded their newfound wealth, were less cheery, with Samur shrugging at his considerable fortune and Indulf grunting as his own coins were handed over.

"I had hoped," Indulf muttered, "that my men would share in the Vandal slaves as well."

"General Belisarius has forbidden the taking of any Vandal or Mauri slaves," I recited, weary of responding to the common complaint. "The Goths will be given another bonus once we leave Africa. Don't you worry."

Yet, like Belisarius, I had little appetite for celebration in the weeks after Gelimer's capitulation. I did not begrudge any who spent his hard-won silver in celebration, and encouraged the soldiers' mirth, for light spirits in the ranks begat a friendly tone with the locals in Justinian's new African province.

More than friendly, in some cases. Perenus had taken to a young Vandal woman named Hereka, whose father was a minor chieftain amongst the remaining Vandal tribes. Long-limbed and broad-shouldered, Hereka held a forceful spirit that seemed well-suited to Perenus' foibles, and it was amusing to see my wisecracking old friend suddenly tongue-tied. Even Cephalas took to joining various groups of my men in their adventures and mischief, leaving Rosamund as my sole companion throughout the long and melancholy evenings in Carthage's palace.

To an onlooker, we must have appeared as one soul—sharing most meals, visiting Carthage's merchants, or simply pacing about the coastal road to temporarily escape in favor of refreshing gusts of sea air. One of the few times we were parted was for prayers, for in this, I was still beholden to Father Petrus each morning. Beyond that, however, the lion's portion of most days I spent with Rosamund—excepting, of course, those days she sought the companionship of Antonina.

I rarely took interest in those gatherings. I had long found my former schoolmate vapid, if not cruel, and she had done little in our acquaintance to change my perception. On one occasion, however, as I escorted Rosamund to Antonina's opulently adorned quarters in the Carthaginian Royal Palace, I was all but ambushed.

"Idiots!" Antonina cried, and burst from behind closed doors, nearly knocking Rosamund and me to the floor. Behind her, two bronze-collared male slaves trailed close, then fell to their knees. One, his thinning hair and crooked back making him appear nearing forty, trembled as he begged forgiveness.

"Domina," he began, his eyes fixed upon Antonina's feet. "It was so heavy…"

Snarling, Antonina bent down and slapped the man with the back of her fingers. When she drew back, a curling cut marred the man's face where her sapphire ring had grazed his cheekbone, although he merely dipped his head in shame. Instinctively, I flinched, averting my gaze from others in the room as I hunched over. This was a scene all too familiar from the Imperial Palace, and this was not the first time I had observed Antonina in such a mood.

"Priceless!" Antonina complained. "Do you know how rare it is to find intact Punic sculptures?"

"No, domina," the injured slave answered, flinching in pain.

Looking down, Antonina kicked her feet away in disgust. "And now you're bleeding on the floor! Clean this up, or you'll find yourself sweating in a mine by week's end."

A further half dozen slaves scurried about to obey Antonina's will as she spotted me. I wanted nothing more than to depart, yet my legs felt rooted to the ground.

"Off to see my husband?" Antonina called to me. "You see him more than I do."

I shrugged. "Not true, Lady. Belisarius prefers privacy these days."

"I know," Antonina mumbled. "But you're still likely to see Belisarius before I do. Tell him that I require another purse of gold" —

she nodded toward the hustling slaves that cleaned her room—"to replace the statue of Tanit that my grease-fingered slaves decided to break."

"Of course," I replied, intent on doing no such thing. Dismissing myself with a light bow, I left Rosamund with her unlikely friend, wishing that Belisarius had been easier to access. I doubted then that Antonina had offered much support after John's death, and if anything, would have made Belisarius' worldly concerns a great deal worse. Of course, I knew little of Antonina's desires or activities, wishing to keep our interactions as few as possible. In avoiding Antonina where possible, I ignored the rumors spun by Mariya and Rosamund, whispered into my ear these past few years, feeling tainted just thinking about them.

Outside of her excursions with Antonina, it seemed as if Rosamund and I alone shared in Belisarius' melancholy—though for different reasons. While Belisarius still mourned the death of his friend now several months gone, Rosamund and I languished in my office considering our future in Justinian's army. Yet even in this, she and I were not a unified front; Rosamund pressed her demands for my freedom from the army, and by extension her own.

"Samur agrees with me. You have fulfilled your oath to Justin, Liberius, and whoever else is keeping you subjugated to the Emperor," Rosamund whispered in Heruli. "*We* have fulfilled our oaths."

"I know," I replied, my face buried in my hands. "Believe me, I know."

Yet behind my concurrence, I was hiding my exhaustion with the entire conversation. Since our earliest days together, Rosamund had bargained and pled for us to forge our own path, be it in the windswept plains of Taurus, or the sands of Mesopotamia, or the hills and mountains of Africa. Through it all, I had been insistent upon the many oaths that bound me in service. Yet now, considering the chaos I had wrought, my spirits ebbed from them. A selfish part of my soul gnashed hungrily for the release that Rosamund spoke of, and it took considerable restraint to resist that demon. Father Petrus had often warned that all men and women were born with such dark temptations, the stain of original sin that goaded us toward a less godly path. For me, it was a yearning that swelled each morning and night, fed by the intuition that any request for my retirement would ultimately be approved.

"Then why continue?" Rosamund hissed, laying a hand upon my wool-covered knee. "We can go back to Pella with your family and be in peace."

"I will consider it," I replied weakly.

Even Rosamund knew these words were lies. Despite my weakness, my longing to leave the burden of duty behind, I had come too far, and lost too much, not to see what came next.

Fool that I was. For black tidings sailed into Carthage's harbor. And, as misfortune tends to manifest, it arrived not merely from one point of origin, but two.

We were prepared for neither.

THE RED HORSEMAN

It was Cephalas who broke my malaise, rapping upon my door before slipping inside. His face pale and eyes bloodshot from yet another evening of strong drink in the city's popinae, Cephalas nevertheless bore the image of one who recently had been a warrior, a firm body marred only by a cleft jaw and an arm crippled by an Avar blade.

"A visitor, Lord," Cephalas noted, raising a hand to mask his harelipped mouth as he spoke. "Liberius wishes to speak with you urgently."

Even for Liberius, such a visit was unusual. "So late in the evening?" I asked, not that I needed his response. "Very well, I will speak with him in the atrium."

Again, Cephalas surprised me. "Liberius insists that you meet him belowground, in the cellars beneath the kitchen."

That was enough to pique my curiosity. Gathering my sword and cloak, I meandered through the kitchens, drawing curious glances from my cook and two scullions as I passed without explanation. As I descended into the cellars, my skin was cloyed by dampness, the hint of mold and earth mixing with faint traces of local garlic and rarer, exotic spices alike. It was a room built to smother the senses, and would have done so had not a single candle illuminated the abyss.

"You are alone?" Liberius whispered to me in Persian, the words laced with uncharacteristic worry.

"I received your summons," I replied. "I'm alone."

Nodding, Liberius thrust a scrap of parchment into my hands, only for it to slip clumsily through my gloves and flutter onto the floor.

"All the grace of a bullock," Liberius said.

I plucked up the note and raised it closer to Liberius' candle. It contained few words, but instantly, I understood Liberius' caution. Though the room's tapers still burned, the cellar seemed to darken, causing me to shiver.

There are spies in Carthage. All of us are in danger.

It took three passes for me to understand the fullness of Liberius' warning. Yet once I did, that dank cellar seemed to constrict my body as I realized how much every spoken syllable was a liability.

"Understand?" Liberius asked again in Persian.

As I bobbed my head in assent, Liberius stole back his note, allowing the flame of his candle to brush against a corner. The parchment blackened and curled, its dire information disappearing within heartbeats.

"You have friends you can trust in the army?" Liberius asked.

Again, I nodded. "Several, including you."

"You're either the luckiest man alive or the most naïve," Liberius said stiffly. "In time, you may share this warning. But I would ask that you not share it with others for now, beyond those who already know."

"Of course, Lord. But why? A city like Carthage is probably choked with spies and cutthroats, and has been for hundreds of years."

"Not probably. Guaranteed to be," Liberius replied. "But what we *don't* know is who in particular is involved here—who might be aiding *our* spy, whether knowingly or accidentally. The less suspicion we raise, the less likely our spidery interloper will flee. For now, keep your war plans carefully guarded, and follow me to the palace."

My head was spinning, as much from Liberius' revelation as how much these developments seemed to have shaken the usually level and laconic older man. Silently, I followed him from the cellar, squinting in the relative light as Liberius brushed the dust from his robes. A nearby scullion pretended not to see us, yet I caught the lad glancing toward Liberius from the corner of his eye.

"Trust me, boy"—Liberius grinned—"hold your tongue. You'll live longer if you lack the curiosity to ask two men what they've been doing together in a dimly lit room."

The scullion blushed and allowed us unencumbered access to an outer doorway. We swept onto Carthage's streets, welcomed by darkening skies and a rising swell of waves on the shoreline a few hundred paces off. A storm threatened, yet Carthage's stone-lined streets had only been half emptied of residents, with food merchants even now clamoring to make one last sale to an enriched Roman soldier. In fact, few feared walking the once-great city of Hannibal and Hasdrubal even in the darkness of night; the city's gutters and roadways had been thoroughly cleaned upon Belisarius' installment as overlord of the former Vandal kingdom.

However, the ravages of war and a poor autumn harvest required Belisarius to purchase copious reserves of grain from Roman Egypt, the ruinous costs of which grew ever larger as hundreds of refugees continued to pour through Carthage's repaired gates. Even then, it seemed to make little difference to morale: Though the vast wealth from Gelimer's surrendered hoard gave Belisarius enough gold to weather a hundred winters in Africa, Belisarius' spies had reported levels of dissatisfaction amongst the city's populace. After all, the Vandals had always guaranteed food and security, despotic though they were. In that respect, at least, popular opinion saw this regime as a poor substitute.

My boots clicked against the palace's worn stones. Though I normally yearned for the company of Belisarius' officers, I dreaded another baleful gathering of Belisarius' efforts to govern Carthage's recovery. Belisarius' blackened moods had done nothing to ease the task of replenishing our dwindling food supply, nor help to settle the thousands of grudges amongst the Vandals, Romans, and Mauri of the region, but this particular gathering felt, somehow, far more fraught.

The palace's Great Hall stood vacant, entirely unused, as servants escorted us to our commander. Liberius and I passed by a dozen bucellarii, the seasoned personal guardsmen whose life and loyalty depended upon their service to Belisarius alone. A notable absence was their commander, Uliaris the Frank, who still skulked in the vilest of the city brothels, wallowing in grief as he blamed himself for the death of John. Despite John's dying words absolving Uliaris of his mistake, Belisarius nonetheless could not bring himself to face the accidental slayer of his oldest and most intimate friend.

When at last we reached the cozy seaward offices that served as Belisarius' respite, we slipped through the doorway just before the creaking of iron hinges as the locks were relatched, preventing interlopers from disrupting our proceedings. Inside, I found Belisarius standing over a textured vellum scroll, its surface thinned by years of scraping it clean for reuse. Even amongst elongating shadows I could see the message had been scribbled in haste, the Latin letters sloppy and curling more and more as they progressed. Belisarius' presence was unsurprising, for I had assumed Liberius intended to share his fears with the general. However, Belisarius' companion was one I did not expect. Behind Belisarius stood Father Petrus, gazing absently out of the high window toward the crashing waves below.

"Thank you for coming, Varus."

Hearing this, Father Petrus turned his gaze and offered a stool. Reluctantly, I accepted it, and sat at the room's lavish table, which had been shaped and polished from the trees that grew along the arid African coastline.

Though I would have normally rejoiced at such company, my mind was occupied elsewhere, already wishing for a return to the quiet solitude of my private quarters. In truth, it was not even solitude I longed for, but my family; I was eager to return to Greece and seek out my wife and children in the hills of Macedonia. That I had yet to even glimpse the sweeping villa there, the home that had been the late Emperor Justin's gift, was of little matter, for I knew those surroundings would be preferable to these broken remnants of the Vandal kingdom, the daily business infinitely better than the horrors that swift and brutal conflict had incurred across the land.

My morose behavior went unremarked by Liberius or Petrus as the former poured a flask of dark-red wine into an ornate silver cup. I initially refused the cup when offered to me, though an insistent Liberius would not be denied. Draining the cup's contents, I turned my attentions to Belisarius.

"There's no benefit to disguising what has happened, Varus," Belisarius said at last, turning back toward the room's interior. "I need to know if your men are ready for another difficult campaign."

"We are at your call, Lord, always," I told him, truthful even as I was reluctant. "But our fitness for battle... that depends upon the enemy you would have us face."

"The Goths," Belisarius replied, dark and stern.

"Lord!" I could not disguise the note of fear in my voice. "Which ones?"

"The Visigoths," Liberius answered for him. "But the Ostrogoths of Italy have become a considerable threat too."

Of the dozens of tribes that spilled into the Empire in a desperate escape from Attila, none had achieved such a sweeping disruption of the old Roman Empire as the Goths. They did not invite the sort of terror that presaged the arrival of Attila and the Huns, and had little of the flair of the Vandals, yet they thrived upon the chaos of Attila's death, and consumed much of the Western Empire. Legends say that all Goths derive from a common tribe that fled in advance of Attila's ancestors. Not all were successful in the struggle, and that is about all that is known.

One section of the Goths escaped Hunnic domination, while others did not. In Hispania, the Visigoths warred with the Franks, with long-dead Visigoth warlords having previously fought alongside Aetius in the famed Battle of Châlons. In Italy, the Ostrogoths dominated, their control stretching beyond Rome and well into Illyria, even the mountain fastnesses of Raetia. A small offshoot of the Goths had settled near Cherson as well, where they provided the Empire's northernmost province with grain and slaves. Yet their numbers were always small, and their intentions—unlike those of their kinsmen—peaceful.

With a population rumored in the millions, the loosely aligned Ostrogoths and Visigoths vastly outnumbered the Vandals, though the kindred tribes nursed a centuries-old resentment of one another, borne from their positioning within opposing sides of Attila's wars.

"How is this possible?" I gaped. "Amalasuntha is a friend of Justinian, and even allowed us to resupply in Syracuse."

"Because Amalasuntha is dead." Liberius grasped for one of Belisarius' scrolls and slid it toward my outstretched hand. "Killed with her son in Lake Bolsena. The Ostrogoths fight amongst themselves now, with a half dozen men claiming the crown in Ravenna. Normally, this would be to the Empire's favor, yet an Ostrogothic force has already seized Lilybaeum, the Vandal outpost in Sicily."

The assassination of a barbarian monarch was far from unusual, even within my lifetime, yet nevertheless, I knew that Amalasuntha's death had compounded the dangers in Carthage already swirling around me. "And the Visigoths? What reason have they for war?"

"The most tempting cause of all," Belisarius answered. "Greed. Their king is a mere child, and Theudis yearns for power. With the Vandals vanquished, there are ripe provinces for Theudis to squeeze."

As confirmation, Father Petrus handed me a second scroll. The script was even cruder than the first, but its demands were plain, and the consequences of noncompliance colorfully explained.

Roman bastards, I congratulate you for removing a thorn that had pricked the skin of the Visigoths for too long. Yet you are mistaken if you believe our people will simply permit you to expand peacefully in Africa. Disband your armies, and send your perfumed boys home to Greece. We will allow your merchants to rule in Carthage, and even to keep half of the

Vandal hoard. We expect a tribute of a thousand healthy slaves each year for ten years, to commence in a month's time. Ignore this at your peril, for I, Theudis, swear that I will crucify all Romans that I find if you do not.

Though the words themselves offered no comfort, it was the promptness of the missive that I found most disconcerting. Barely more than three months had passed since our victory at Tricamarum; even accounting generously, there had simply not been enough time for Theudis to receive word of the Vandal downfall and deliver a response.

Thinking on Liberius' warning, however, I could privately guess at the cause for Theudis' efficiency. Nevertheless, I voiced the question. "How could he have known of our victory so soon?"

"He couldn't have," Father Petrus answered. "That leaves only one logical conclusion that Liberius will have already shared with you."

"Spies in Carthage," I affirmed, a sinking realization of the fullness of Liberius' worries settling over me. "Spies with the power to write in Theudis' name."

I fell silent. My eyes darted to the room's shadow-draped corners, where furniture disguised hundreds of potential vantage points to eavesdrop upon Belisarius' conversations. In my bondage to Constantinople, slaves shifted unseen between the palace walls, moving through corridors intended for the purpose of serving their masters silently, yet which provided ample opportunity to peer into more private activities of wealthy patricians. I had little doubt that Carthage had similar constructions in its palace halls, and wondered which grubby scullion or bath slave had secretly borne the might of the Visigoths.

Petrus leaned forward, whispering to me in a language I had not known him to speak. "Not only a spy," he muttered in clipped Hunnic. "But someone of letters. Someone of enough prestige and savvy to anticipate our intentions and assess our strength."

"I've written the Emperor with our assessment and request for instructions," Belisarius added, shifting us back to Latin. "But we cannot expect anything further until the seas calm in early spring. For now, we must treat both threats as imminent."

"But, Lord," I said, "if the Goths truly wish to defeat us—if they strike—then what can we even do?"

"Very little," Belisarius admitted. "Which is why we need to act decisively, and soon. Convince our would-be enemies that our strength is far greater than the few thousands we have under arms."

Drawing a stool, Belisarius sat heavily, rubbing his temples. Absent his armor, he almost appeared a common clerk, his broad chest and scarred arms the only evidence of his status as a soldier. Yet his beard had grown disheveled and cheeks sunken, a hollow and unhealthy look for a man whose whims determined the fate of thousands. Even so, as he unfurled a map and positioned a dozen wooden pieces around the African coastline, it was clear Belisarius had lost none of his acuity.

"The Ostrogoths lack the ability to transport massed forces to Africa, and it remains unclear if their new king, whoever it may be, even holds the support of his chieftains," Belisarius explained, adding additional figurine armies in Italy, Sicily, and Hispania. "So they seek softer targets like Lilybaeum as easy victories."

"What do we know of the new king?" I asked.

"Little enough, beyond rumors," Liberius replied, standing from the table for a more expansive view of Belisarius' map. "Theodahad is a former sword-bearer of the famed Theodoric, and the paramount power behind most of the clans. But Theodahad must be near sixty, allegedly bookish, and far too old for his situation."

"That never stopped you," Father Petrus chided. "Or me."

"My dear friend," Liberius said, "I've long ago given up any attempt to rule a barbarian tribe by myself. My bladder leaks, and those sorts of men do not respect anyone who cannot reach the chamber pot without groaning."

I chuckled, earning a wink from Liberius. Though both he and Petrus were likely older than this Theodahad, Liberius displayed none of the infirmity that his words suggested, his back straight and movements as limber as a youth's. Father Petrus appeared far more frail, but, though wrinkled and balding, he possessed all the sharpness of mind expected of a wizened ruler. However, with Godilas and Justin long dead, this talk of aging stoked a curious discomfort within me, and I privately convinced myself of their many years of longevity to come.

"We have yet to claim the Vandal fortresses in Corsica and Sardinia, as well as the Balearic Islands," Belisarius went on. "The former would be desolated by Tzazon's campaign, and an easy conquest for even a modest Gothic war band."

"The Balearics will be in little better condition," Liberius said. "More a nest of pirates than anything resembling civilization. They're an easy launching point for an attack on Africa and Mauretania."

I admit that I had little skill for anticipating the faraway movements of our adversaries, but I was awed by that capability in others. Belisarius seemed to keep the entire world in his mind, allocating the men and weapons needed to seize and hold everything, from a lawless island to a dust-strewn city hundreds of miles to the west. John, too, had been such a tactician, although his death at Tricamarum left a considerable void—and left me as an underqualified successor to fill it. Yet, even though the raw intelligence of Liberius and Belisarius far surpassed my own, a nagging curiosity brought me to interject.

"The Visigoths have never favored the sea, and as Liberius notes, the Balearic Islands are no prize," I reasoned. "So what advantage does Theudis gain in that sort of warfare? The Ostrogoths' gain is Theudis' loss, regardless of whatever distant kinship they share."

"None." Liberius smiled weakly. "What Theudis wants," he said while sliding pieces from Hispania to the narrow channel of water that linked the Great Ocean from the Internal Sea, "is the Pillars of Herakles. That is where he will strike."

The pillars were a place of myth, where the half-god Herakles had completed his lifelong labors. That meeting point of Africa and Europa had been a pivotal sea lane at the western extremity of the habitable world, and a place that had made many wealthy beyond imagining.

It had been, and was still, a place haunted by death, with centuries of armies fighting and dying for control of right of passage. The Vandals had most recently traversed the Pillars to reach Roman Africa and carve their kingdom from its ashes, staking outposts in their wake to prevent any who might follow their example. Yet, with Gelimer's surrender, those forts were now left rudderless, neither acknowledging Belisarius' supremacy nor declaring independence in their own right.

"If we don't take the Pillars, and especially Septem," Belisarius began, "the Visigoths will be able to invade the African coast at will, and we will have to surrender everything gained for the Emperor. That is something that I cannot allow."

"That is understandable, Lord," I said, "but how are we supposed to take Sardinia, Corsica, the Balearics, and the Pillars of Herakles, all without resupply or reinforcements? We only have five thousand men under arms, and that assumes we would take a fair number of wounded on campaign."

Liberius' brow furrowed. "You disappoint me, Varus! Of course we'll need to leave half of the army in Africa to keep the peace and seek out stubborn holdouts along the coastline."

"That may be so," I countered, unfazed by Liberius' banter, "but the question still remains."

Belisarius sighed, withdrawing another scroll from a leather satchel. "I have an answer to your concerns, Varus. But first you must answer whether you are prepared for another campaign."

"Of course, Lord... I—" I began, surprised as Belisarius interrupted my reluctant pronouncement.

"Without John, I have few others that I can rely on to lead my men." His voice was pained as he spoke the fallen soldier's name aloud. "Though I would have liked more time for you to become familiar with higher command, fortune rarely works around our schedules. I need to know if you are willing to formally serve as my second, and lead portions of the army to wherever I cannot go."

I froze. Though Belisarius' offer was not wholly unsurprising, his manner of asking stirred a strange feeling of guilt and inadequacy within me. In Belisarius' eyes, I could never hope to match John, not merely because John was a far superior strategist, but because the two had been together since the earliest years of childhood, sharing dreams of glory and grandeur that can only rise from the youthful belief that no obstacle is insurmountable, and every wish is attainable.

Though I came to know Belisarius in his younger years, I would never possess the same clarity of vision as he did with John in those early years, for our goals as men were shackled by the burdens of life and the realities of pain and loss. The memory hung over Belisarius like the thin silver cross that hung from his neck, an ornament last seen with John before he galloped into the desert in pursuit of a defeated Gelimer. None questioned the general's holding fast to such a trinket, but for me, that silver cross seemed to define my own inadequacy, a concrete reminder that Belisarius would have far preferred John's company to my own.

"My truth, Lord, is that the realities of war have changed me," I confessed. "But my loyalty and goals are unshaken. I only ask which task is to be mine to achieve, and it will be done."

Father Petrus nodded, while Liberius' expression gave over to an evanescent look of pleasure as my words became clear. So, too, did they appear to satisfy Belisarius, who reached a hand over to one of the Roman figurines, lifting it from the map and sliding it far to the west.

"Your task is the most important, and the most difficult," he said. "We must control the Pillars of Herakles, or we'll need to evacuate the region. We simply lack the numbers to defeat the Visigoths on land, but we can check and prevent their assault into Africa at the Pillars. They are also not a seafaring people, and our ships and siege engines can make up for our lacking numbers."

"It will be done, Lord," I declared, a knot forming in my throat. "But both Pillars... I'll need more than the foederati for such a task. And we'll need to see where Indulf's loyalties lie."

Belisarius nodded. "Indulf was a staunch supporter of Amalasuntha, so I cannot imagine he will be much pleased with Theodahad. But I will speak with him, and offer him and all his men safe passage back to Rome, if he so chooses. At any rate, I doubt he would refuse to lead his men against Theudis."

I shuddered, unsure of the wisdom of such decisions but unwilling to contradict the general. Such was Belisarius' will, even if it meant placing faith with one such as Indulf. The commander of our Gothic foederati had the body of an angel and the temperament of the blackest of demons, his penchant for violent revenge leading to needless losses on the battlefield. Yet I could not deny that Indulf possessed a low sort of cleverness that helped turn unfavorable engagements into victories, and such men were in high demand as our few were pitted against the Visigothic many.

"Take Baduarius and his spearmen if you'd rather not rely on Indulf as a translator," Belisarius added. "I intend to pacify Africa directly, while Valerian will command the bulk of our dromons to seize the islands. With God's favor, we will meet in Carthage three months after winter solstice."

God's favor or no, I was skeptical that I could deliver Belisarius' victory. "Baduarius' men will be most helpful, but even with them and all the foederati, I cannot hope to stand against Theudis in battle."

"I can spare you half of my spearmen, as well as Ascum's ballistae," Belisarius said. "But Varus, I will need Samur and the Huns to remain in Africa with me, because our task ahead requires swift movement."

"And not because of any lingering mistrust of the Huns?" I replied, my tone far darker than intended.

Belisarius sat a bit straighter, eyeing me curiously as he judged his response. "Not at all," he answered. "And I hope that you would trust my word on this."

"Of course, Lord." I nodded, chastened, and held my eyes downcast.

Liberius cleared his throat. "As for Varus' need for more soldiers, there are five hundred hale and eager warriors that would prove invaluable against the Visigoths. A thousand more within a month, if needed."

A thousand more? I could scarcely find the words. "From Egypt?"

"From the Vandals," Belisarius clarified. "If the chieftains can be believed, they will obey my orders, and therefore your own. I wish that I could provide you with more of my own soldiers, but we simply have none to spare."

And so, fate offered me its strangest turn. My instinct was to refuse, for Gelimer's men had been our most savage enemies a mere season prior, their influence still hated within Roman memory. Yet war rarely left a soldier with the luxury of choice, and Justinian was never an emperor to supply easy alternatives.

"I'll speak with Gunderic," I said. "We'll make preparations to leave within a week."

"Very good," Liberius replied. "Avoid open battle, and take no unnecessary risks. The point is to convince Theudis that war with the Empire is a losing proposition. If the Pillars are secure, we can defend against the greater threat posed by the Ostrogoths."

"As you command, Legate," I answered, rising to depart.

"Thank you, Varus," Belisarius said. "But two further requests, if I may."

I nodded, eager to please Belisarius. "Of course, Lord."

"First, take heed of how widely you share your intentions in the battles ahead," Belisarius cautioned. "If this spy is as well-placed as we believe, there's no telling the harm they could cause to any of us. You and I might be adept in the battlefield, but this enemy prefers shadows and deceit, which I fear we are pitifully unprepared to defend against."

Having eavesdropped on many a Roman noble in Constantinople's Imperial Palace, I knew how easily a spy might do the same, and I prayed that our precautions to secure Carthage's palace did not allow for similar opportunity for Theudis' agent. Worse, there was no lesson from childhood that I could draw upon for guidance—the realm of rumor and whispers was securely held by Narses, with few other Romans capable of harnessing vast networks of informants that spread from distant Britannia to the eastern deserts of Persia. "I'll be on my guard, Lord, although I don't know what else to do."

"Neither do I," Belisarius admitted. "Hopefully, our foe is more of a cat than a lion, casting shadows far larger than his true self."

I nodded. "And the second request?"

"Take Uliaris with you." At the mention of his disgraced bodyguard, Belisarius' tone darkened. "Other than Indulf, no others have fought against the Visigoths, and he may be of value against Theudis."

Acknowledging the order, I rose to leave the gathering, my mind awash with the evil tidings that brought us once again to the brink of war. Despite a creeping desire for peace, my oath beckoned, and I would obey. Belisarius' parting words, given as the general hustled to catch me as I slipped away from the enclosed room, added to the weight of that oath.

"You are a leader of men now, Varus," Belisarius concluded. "Few other than us understand what it's like to force starving and injured men into battle against a larger foe."

The words struck me as oddly vulnerable for a man who, until recently, had borne his duties as general with all apparent outward ease. This hint of caution only further spiked my private worries, and I wondered again whether securing the fortress of Septem would have fallen to John if he had still lived. I had no doubt that Belisarius trusted me as a friend, but until now, my role in his battles had been as a bludgeon, thumping the enemy with brute force rather than positioning thousands of warriors for victory.

Still, I gave voice to words of reassurance, though I did not believe them. "I understand, Lord, and will not fail you."

Belisarius yielded a nod. "The burden will gnaw at your confidence if you allow it to. If you intend to lead an expedition to the edge of the world, against an enemy with a hundred times your numbers, you must turn your heart to stone. Seek the advice of others, but brook no doubts in your abilities. Men will die by your orders, and it is your task to profit from their sacrifice."

I dared a reply, as imprudent as it was. "Is that what you do, Lord?"

"I believed so, once." Belisarius grimaced. "It is a lesson I am relearning painfully. You will face your own trials, in time. They will sting. Parts of you may die. But you must continue on, both for duty, and to keep those who rely upon you alive. The day you fail in that hardship is the day we are lost."

THE VANDALS OF JUSTINIAN

Poets insist that war leaders accept their duties with an inhuman grace, undeterred by hardship and unconcerned with petty dramas amongst their men. Though I received a taste of leadership at the head of Belisarius' foederati, commanding an expedition comprised of disparate warriors was something entirely foreign to me.

And so, on that first morning after I reluctantly accepted Belisarius' charge, I vomited my breakfast. It was meager fare, merely a soldier's biscuit with cuts of salted mutton, yet it sat heavily in my gut. It emerged in a brass basin in my rooms, covered in a disgorged cup of sour wine and a hint of bile. Fortunately, I had excused myself from the house's atrium in favor of a closed bedroom, and thus believed myself secure from prying eyes—until a light rap upon the door suggested otherwise.

Allowing my visitor entry with a grunt, I saw Rosamund step inside. "Ill?" she asked.

"Can't I just be sick in peace?" I muttered.

"If I allowed that, you'd be dead six times over." She grinned. "Something wrong with the mutton?"

My mind started to conjure a lie, yet I could give it no voice. Even as a longtime slave to the palace, dishonesty was a skill for which I had little use and less practice, leaving me at a grave disadvantage in this hive of liars and sycophants. "If only that were the cause."

Of all those who shared my life, Rosamund disarmed me the most. Not even Mariya could provoke such a willingness to confess my fears, for although she had proven her love many times over, some portion of my soul still felt the tug of the slave's collar, anxious that a princess would balk at any sign of inadequacy or unfitness in her common husband. In that moment, I sent forth my roiling sea of worries to Rosamund—both Liberius' warning, as well as my amplified responsibilities over Belisarius' men.

"The Vandals are easy enough to impress, as big as you are," Rosamund began. "Just puff out your chest and smack a few of them on the nose."

"You're so confident," I said flatly. "Perhaps you would perform better, were you me."

Rosamund shook her head. "I enjoy knitting bones back together and healing flesh, but that's as far as I'll ever wish to see of most men or women. A few friends and freedom are all I need. I don't envy you and I don't want your duties. I can mix a root that will calm your fears, however."

Thinking of my visions of the red-eyed horsemen, I initially balked at the offer of one of Rosamund's curious medicines, but soon relented. Rosamund skittered to her rooms, returning minutes later with a clay cup. "Drink," she commanded.

Yellowish and foul, it smelled like offal and looked like sputum. "You're certain?"

"Hold your nose and gulp it down." Rosamund rolled her eyes. "It won't dull your senses, just leave you at ease."

I complied, gagging on the viscous liquid, and handed Rosamund the empty cup.

"As to your two fears," she continued, accepting it, "there is little you can do to root out a spy. Tighten your guard, but don't allow it to nag your thoughts, otherwise you'll see enemies where your friends would normally be."

"Wise advice," I agreed. "And the other?"

"Like I said, I don't lead warriors," Rosamund said. "You gab endlessly about Belisarius and his genius, so do as he does. Emulate him however you can. Then find what each man under your thrall truly wants, and use that to gain his loyalty. Most men are simple in that way—reward them, and like a puppy, they will nestle at your feet."

Whether from the elixir or Rosamund's judgment of my sex, I heaved with laughter. "And what would they all want?"

Rosamund grinned again. "Well, most of them probably would not enjoy sleeping with you, despite the fact that your friends are mostly lust-addled animals. No," she mused, tapping her chin, "the Vandals want glory, the Ostrogoths want money, your Herulians want opportunity, and the Greeks want all the others to perform the more difficult work. Sound familiar?"

She spoke in jest, but perhaps with more truth than she realized. "And how do I lead men of such differing tastes?"

"Again, that's beyond my experience," Rosamund said. "But you have friends. Learn to use them at the opportune time, and we will all live to a ripe old age."

Our conversation left me with few explicit actions, but I at least no longer felt as if my stomach would come spurting from my mouth. Pacified, I ventured to Carthage's training yard, giddy yet terrified of how I might mold my motley charges into a singular fighting force.

What I did know, at least, was that I ought to begin with those of my warriors who were the greatest unknown. I had little desire to trust the Vandals with the success of my assignment. Unfortunately, as Liberius aptly noted, no better force lay available for the choosing.

Gunderic, on the other hand, relished the notion.

"Other than you Romans, killing Visigoths is what we live for!" he exclaimed, his off-center nose still healing from our previous bout atop Mount Papua.

Though we had crossed blades and fists in a particularly nasty duel, I could not help but like Gunderic. Utterly simple in his worldview and ferociously devoted to his loyalties, Gunderic never relinquished an opportunity for merriment, nor did he seem to care if his company included those he had tried to slaughter just months prior. As one of their main caretakers, I had found such characteristics common amongst the Vandals, save perhaps the dour and more insular Gelimer. While Gelimer retained his melancholy privacy in a small room within the Carthaginian palace, Gunderic and his people rebuilt their identity and livelihood, even if the Mauri and Romans only held distaste and fear for the Vandals, vanquished or otherwise.

Yet such resentment did not dampen Gunderic's twin desires for war and mirth, and he had led small groups of men into taverns and brothels as soon as Belisarius had permitted it after the Vandal surrender. Influenced by Hereka, his Vandal paramour, Perenus had even joined such gatherings with members of my foederati, exchanging education in lewd insults in each other's tongues.

Yet, though I found Gunderic amusing, I now feigned distaste at his enthusiastic brutality. "Then why did the Visigoths not fall to Vandals generations ago?"

"Ah, but they nearly did!" Gunderic replied. "All that saves them is their numbers, and we've simply lacked the men to take all Hispania. That's the impasse since the time of Attila, the Visigoths in Hispania and the Vandals in Africa, a fair balance for the time being."

"Until Rome returned to take back its cities," I cut back. "Yet we never understood why you Vandals had such a small force to govern such a broad area."

"Because Vandals do not abide weak children," Gunderic answered, his grin fading to a dark grimace. "Those who spawn boys and girls with twisted backs or malformed limbs have two choices— slay their young or venture into a permanent exile. Most choose murder."

"That practice will end immediately," I said.

"Aye, so much for the better," Gunderic responded. "I always liked children, filthy little worms that they are."

Xerxes shared my reservations with rearming and equipping the

Vandals for our seizure of the Pillars. Though he did not balk when I offered him command, concerns remained for the Zhayedan prince, whose insistence upon flawless discipline and unrivaled technique contrasted with the fearless, reckless, and exceedingly violent style of the Vandals.

"In Persia, we would prefer a hundred well-trained and honorable men over a thousand bloodthirsty savages," Xerxes remarked. "You would recall that I suffered greatly for that point. These men… they may not take to restraint."

I nodded, yet held firm. "For their faults, the Vandals are incredible fighters. If Gunderic tells true, they will heed Belisarius' commands, and in turn your own."

Xerxes' brow furrowed. "And if they don't?"

"Then they die," I answered, my heart deflating at the mere thought of such a massacre. "God knows I want this war to be finished, but while it continues, we cannot brook threats within our ranks. The Visigoths are enough to worry about."

Xerxes' concerns were mirrored by several officers that fell under my command. Absent Gunderic or any of the other Vandals, I called together those men which Belisarius had committed to my authority, most of whom voiced their confidence in my role. Even still, an underlying tone of caution weighted such compliments, borne by the need to challenge the collective might of the Visigoths with a mere two thousand men.

"When I was a boy, the village elders told tales of the Pillars," Baduarius recounted. "Dagisthaeus and I would listen to their stories of the far edge of the world. Yet all told the same tale: The Pillars are near impregnable, the walled cities nearest them fortified by land and sea. We need to seize them before Theudis does."

"Not concerned at all about fighting fellow Goths?" Ascum jibed, the burnt and shriveled corner of his face bringing a line of spittle down the remnants of his beard.

"I'm no kin to any Visigoth," Baduarius said, "and you lot are all the kin I have left in this world, for what good that does me."

"Poor bastard," Fulcaris muttered, earning a playful jab to the side from Baduarius.

"At any rate, Baduarius has the right of it," I cut in. "We must take both Pillars immediately, and before the Visigoths follow suit. Gunderic will convince the Vandal garrisons to surrender to us, and afterwards they should be easily defensible with just a few hundred men."

"*If* Gunderic is successful," Perenus said. "Which is no guarantee."

"Regardless," I said. "By force or by friendship, both Pillars must be taken. Mount Calpe in Hispania, and Mount Abyla in Mauretania Tingitana."

Tracing my finger upon a crudely sketched map of the region, I circled the two Pillars as our intended destination. Discussion arose about the timing and effort of each location, as well as how Theudis would likely counter any maneuver we might make.

"With good fortune, Theudis may do nothing," I offered, "but assuming the worst—"

"That's probably a good idea, given our luck," Thurimuth muttered.

"Assuming the worst," I continued, rolling my eyes, "Mount Abyla is more important. Controlling the city of Septem would make it impossible for Theudis to safely land along the coastline of Mauretania, and just might prevent a full Visigothic invasion of Africa."

Sembrouthes grunted agreement. "This all makes sense. But it all is grounded on a single bet that the Visigoths haven't already attacked the Pillars. If Theudis has overrun the lingering Vandals, we'll have a right struggle on our hands."

"Pray to God it does not come to that," I said. "But, as Belisarius insists, we plan for all possible futures."

Every man assembled looked to me, searching for answers. I will not pretend to be modest, for I did not find the experience humbling. Quite the contrary: A selfish morsel of my soul delighted in the attentions of those men, each of whom could be named in rare company amongst Justinian's heroes. I am sure neither Agamemnon nor Priam could have called upon better fighters. Yet, though I recognized and relished the deference in their gazes, another part of me shrank from my charge. And for a flicker of a moment, I wished desperately to surrender my responsibilities to someone, anyone, else.

But I did not, fool that I am. Instead, I forged on. I explained Belisarius' broader designs upon the sweeping African coastline, and doing so displayed a trust that none present could possibly be in league with the spy, nor be so careless as to let slip our designs. After all, even if I opted for mistrust amongst my friends, the movement of thousands of men, horses, ships, and a winding trail of slaves and servants would be difficult for even the ineptest of infiltrators to miss, and tightfisted control of broader strategy would leave the army wrongfooted and suspicious of one another. Given that we already knew perilous little of our enemy, my only choice was one of trust, and desperate hope that such a leap of faith would not end in tragedy.

Aside from the Vandals, I had been granted authority over four hundred Herulian and six hundred Ostrogothic foederati, Baduarius and six hundred Cappadocian spearmen, Thurimuth and a similar detachment of Thracians, Ascum's ballistae, and the sailors and crew for a requisite collection of transport ships and dromons. As always, Sembrouthes' Aksumites would accompany our expedition, serving as bodyguards rather than participants within the foederati. Likewise, Uliaris would accompany the mission, although whether sobriety would be fulfilled among his duties seemed unlikely at best. All told, it was a huge portion of Belisarius' army, yet even those numbers would be woefully inadequate against even an insignificant Visigoth chieftain capable of mustering ten thousand land-hungry spearmen.

Remaining closer to Carthage, Belisarius and Bessas would scour the countryside for remaining resistance, seeking pledges of loyalty for Emperor Justinian. Samur and the Huns would offer support, particularly for wider-ranging efforts deep into Mauritania or Tripolitana. In his stead, as the temporary commander in Carthage, Belisarius had appointed Germanus, with Solomon remaining as a city governor in Thapsus. Why that prat Solomon was granted further honors befuddled me. Worse, I could not even hope that he would embarrass himself with failure; losing Thapsus, or enraging the local populace, would imperil all of us across the former Vandal kingdom, too great a price to indulge my grudge. That fact grated upon my patience, and doubtless left Samur stewing in hatred. Solomon always found opportunity to rise, though God and all the apostles knew he did not deserve it.

Further strategy was intended to pacify regions currently beyond Belisarius' control. While Germanus tended to the endless audiences and petitions for grain and supplies, Mundus and Troglita would seize the near-anarchical Balearic Islands, and Valerian would command the expedition to take Sardinia and Corsica. Within such efforts, the greatest care would be taken to avoid any clashes with Ostrogothic ships along the Italian coastline, with Valerian's fleet cautiously vigilant for any portent of attack from Theodahad's men.

"It's bold, seizing the Pillars and pacifying the Mauri," Xerxes said as I concluded my report.

"It's not like we have a choice," Perenus remarked. "After all, we even allowed Troglita to marry one of the Mauri women, and it's made him a lovesick puppy. That should count for something, no?"

I had to smile. I could always count on Perenus to loosen even the tensest of situations with a jape. "Perhaps you might follow Troglita's example, Perenus?" I teased.

He snorted. "You're a donkey's arse, Varus."

His retort, good-natured as it was, surprisingly irked me. I knew by his tone that Perenus intended no insult, yet I found he had rankled my self-perception as a leader, as what a leader *should* be—inviting yet austere, inwardly empathetic yet unswayed by emotion, no matter the fears and urges of his men. True, Perenus was a veritable comrade of mine, the first friend I had made in the army, but his public show of familiarity made me feel weaker, a diminished version of the man I sought to emulate. How had Belisarius kept so many rogues in line without spurning any, or brewing resentments?

I stifled a grimace, turning the conversation toward my realignment of the expedition's senior leadership. Promoting Perenus to my old position, I offered him overall leadership of the combined foederati, with Fulcaris directing the Herulians and Sindual as his second. Though the change was predictable given Belisarius' wishes, all three men nonetheless beamed under the praise of their peers.

"After Mesopotamia and Carthage, we won't disappoint you," Fulcaris swore.

"Agreed," echoed Sindual. "Nor our brothers who came before and died under the banners."

Soon thereafter, I shared Liberius' warning with my officers, inspired by Rosamund's guidance. I explained Liberius' suspicions: of Amalasuntha's murder, of how the timing and tenor of Theudis' threat indicated that a spy had been well-placed to observe the activities of Belisarius' army, and of the concerning changes in the behavior of the twin Gothic kingdoms.

"We don't know how long the spy might have traveled with us—possibly since Constantinople," I said. "And it's imperative that our suspicions not be repeated outside of senior command. I have known most of you for years, and have raised each of you to leadership for a reason. If our expedition is to succeed, you must trust me, and I you."

Perenus could not resist guessing at our interloper's identity. "I'd wager my horse it's Indulf."

"Keep your horse. There's no reason to suspect Indulf," I said, echoing Belisarius' prior beliefs. "His methods are brutal, but he has served loyally. He also hates the Visigoths, and was one of Amalasuntha's most trusted chieftains."

Perenus shrugged. "He's still a slippery eel."

"An eel that you must now lead," I said stiffly, frustrated at the distraction to my plans, "so find a way to befriend him. All of us," I added to the group, "must take care of who we share our strategy with, and how often."

"Don't worry, my friend!" Baduarius chuckled. "We've emerged through tighter traps before."

Xerxes concurred. "Spies should be expected within any army, and amongst any notable town. When I led Persia's armies, we always assumed there were Roman worms slinking about in the shadows — no offense," he added with a sly smile. "What I mean to say is, be thoughtful with your daily routine, but don't allow caution to turn you into a puddle of worry."

It was an order easier spoken than obeyed, despite the fact that Xerxes was the only man other than Belisarius to understand the full weight of my charge. My mind fumbled for a response, but Ascum injected his own concerns before I could speak.

"If the Ostrogoths do attack while we're near Septem, what must we do then?"

"Nothing, for there is naught that we could do," I answered. "Our enemy is Theudis, and we must hope that the Ostrogoths would not risk an attack against a superior fleet of warships, or trust that Valerian and Belisarius could deflect any aggressive action."

Ascum scowled. "Assuming Theudis won't learn that he outnumbers us fifty to one, at least."

I sighed. "Eventually, he will. When that happens, it will be your task to block any Visigoth attempts to sail from Hispania to Tingitana. They will have fishing vessels and rowboats, but nothing to challenge our dromons."

"Something that Theudis will know as well as us, by the next moon," Ascum said pointedly.

The annoyance from Perenus' prior jokes resurged within me. Balling a fist, I glowered at Ascum but managed to keep my voice trained to a tone between yelling and casual speech. "The spy is largely out of my control, Ascum. What else would you have me do?"

Immediately, I regretted rebuking him. Ascum was one of Belisarius' few remaining senior officers from before the Tauric campaign, and his eyes narrowed as he fixed upon me, a glimpse of equal realization that he had struck a chord of irritation. "I don't mean to offend you. But as you know, Theudis did not gain his authority by sitting meekly on his arse. The Visigoths are limited in what they can do to us for now, but that doesn't mean they won't improve if we threaten their interests."

I yearned to dismiss the conversation and squash any argument but dared not toss aside Ascum's continued worries now they were voiced. More, I realized that the others remained transfixed upon me, with even Perenus having fallen silent. "I leave it to you to plan our defense of the sea channel between the Pillars," I said. "As Xerxes noted, we can't overthink what this spy may or may not do, may or may not communicate. If the Visigoths shift their plan of attack, we must be equally fluid. Unfortunately, there is no way to know what shall happen until the situation is upon us."

It was a pitifully weak answer, and one that I would have privately mocked were I listening to one of Belisarius' war councils as a mere komes. Thankfully, Ascum acceded to the point, allowing me the opportunity to close the gathering on terms that, while less than jovial, at least gave every man a clear task to complete. Others bobbed in approval, voicing no disagreement.

My concerns ebbed from the confidence of my officers—so much so that I became lulled into a dangerous sense of security. In the decades since, I have learned the perils of such a grievous mistake, where no threat or possibility should be left unaccounted for, regardless of how prepared and safe one may feel. At a minimum, never enter battle with an enemy whose intentions are poorly understood and capabilities incompletely mapped, for such limitations spell disaster for many.

At the time, however, the excitement of high command was too powerful, strong enough to mask even the gnawing anxiety that drove my desire to return home and had robbed me of restful sleep for so many weeks. Perhaps the only concern at my situation was my looming separation from Samur. It was a sensible strategy; his Huns were poorly equipped for the seaborne raids and mountainous terrain along the coastline of the Pillars of Herakles. Yet upon our initial meeting, I saw in my brother a measure of irritation at Belisarius' order that would leave him and the Huns isolated from their friends, traversing vast expanses of arid hills and deserts in Justinian's name.

"First they think we'll turn tail and run," Samur growled, "and now they want us to beat the Mauri into submission!"

"Better than rushing against a hundred thousand Visigoths," I said lightly. "Let's hope your job will be an easy one."

"I doubt that, for either of us." Samur rolled his eyes. "You haven't spent much time outside of Carthage, but I have. There's a lot of lingering resentment against the Vandals, and fear of Justinian's taxes. Belisarius is the only person keeping outright violence at bay."

"You may be right, but all we can do is try to preserve peace."

Samur snorted. "Ah, yes. Peace done the Roman way—through war."

"If needs be," I answered reluctantly. "We've won a tremendous victory against Gelimer, and now we secure it. A few more months and we can go home."

Samur gave me a dark look. "If you think that Justinian's wars are over, you are sorely mistaken," he said at last. "That man does not care if his precious God and all the angels would stand against him in combat, he'd still send the Roman Army to subjugate them. Do what you must against the Visigoths, but sacrifice nothing and come back whole. There's no reason to suffer further for their hubris."

Between Rosamund and Samur, my fortitude to contest such claims had waned to almost nothing—not because of any outright agreement with their arguments, but out of simple attrition. Their avid distaste for the army's missions sapped away all emotion in me save a desperate urge to fulfill my duty with what semblance of honor that could be mustered. Yet, in this instance, Samur's blackened mood was too much to stomach.

"You make it seem like my command is a curse," I bit out.

Samur's brow furrowed. "Isn't it?"

"It's an honor!" I roared, anger washing away any lingering anxieties. "Belisarius trusted me with hundreds of men, and you with the Huns. How many people can make similar claims?"

Samur scoffed. "You're too smart to believe these are gifts. We're slaves in all but name. Only thing missing is the collar to chafe our necks."

I should have dropped the argument, for I knew well—painfully well—that Samur had better reason than most to despise Roman leadership. But I could not. "You're wrong."

"Am I?" Samur asked, genuine surprise on his face. "I guarantee you, Justinian will get us all killed at one point or another. Even if we live long enough to retire, some street gang or another might cut our throats to steal what little plunder Justinian won't have stolen through taxes."

"You refuse to be content, even though we've come so far," I pointed out. "Perhaps you will *never* be content."

"Maybe not," Samur replied. "But you know I'm correct. Theodora, Justinian, Belisarius… they would all happily hand over our lives if it meant taking something they desired. One day you'll see the truth, Varus. And until then, know that I'm only here because *you* refuse to leave."

At that, I finally had the good sense to let the matter drop, but I left our meeting with an uncomfortable, unfulfilled sensation in my chest. Sleep came poorly, and although I met with Samur on three other occasions before departing, shamefully, I admit that I did not desire his company. As stubborn as we both were, all I wanted was for him to be happy for me with my new responsibilities. It is only from my current vantage point that I understand how impossible this was.

Our rushed preparations for the Pillars of Herakles made the days pass quickly, the rays of light growing shorter and fainter as the autumnal season waned. The already cool African coastline grew frigid in the darkest hours of the evening, the ceaseless thrumming of the waves pushing a breeze through Carthage's stone streets. Though the traditional fighting season had ended, our daily drills and preparation for a sea voyage continued day and night, with men donning thicker wool cloaks to shield prickling skin from the slow bite of the air.

The transport ships were the same as those which ferried Belisarius' army to Africa, their timbers cleaned of filth and hulls scraped of barnacles by dedicated crews of Roman sailors. Flanking them were the dromons, swift warships with a single row of twenty-five oars on each side of the craft. Their vast triangular cloth sails were engineered to catch wind in ways the more lumbering transport craft could not, allowing teams of archers and even ballistae to quickly close and fire upon adversaries at land and sea. Valerian had already taken most of Belisarius' warships to seize Corsica and Sardinia, but the general had allocated ten to guard my transports' flanks as we sailed westward. Though the prospect of sea travel had always made my stomach turn, the thought of navigating the churning waves in the rising violence of winter seemed especially daunting. Yet as the commander of my diminutive expedition, I could show no reluctance at my charge, and I gritted my teeth as I assured many under my command of the safety of our mission.

As with any period before a voyage, each moment was overloaded with unfinished work. Rosamund, who refused to be left in Carthage under any circumstances, set about spending my silver freely to procure powders, roots, and bandages to stock her healing kit. Likewise, Cephalas and a half dozen other servants acquired appropriate ringmail, weapons, and equipment for our new Vandal banda. Some, like Gunderic, shrugged off any borrowed arms and armor, preferring the spears and blades that had recently been returned by Belisarius. However, most rejoiced at the opportunity to wield professionally forged blades and mail, abandoning the crude tunics and boiled leather that the poorer Vandals carried into battle.

As the Vandals chattered excitedly about their newfound gear, Xerxes looked upon his new charges with utter disdain. Desiring respite from the clerical tedium of voyage preparations, I sat with Perenus and Fulcaris to observe one of Xerxes' training sessions. Night after night, the Zhayedan prince had drilled the Vandal warriors from before dusk through well past dawn, honing the formation's ability to respond to basic commands and obey even their lowest level dekarchos.

"In Persia, it takes a decade to make a warrior!" Xerxes yelled. "But I only have a week with you lot. You will listen, you will learn, or you will surely die."

"Persian men must grow slowly!" joked Wisimar, one of the appointed Vandal dekarchos. "I killed my first man when I was eight."

Wisimar's jest triggered rolling laughter from the Vandal gathering, which fell silent at a glowering gaze from Gunderic, leaving only sheepish grins. Xerxes, however, had no such patience. Drawing his blade from his scabbard, Xerxes marched toward Wisimar, the sword's tip angled menacingly toward the dirt.

"Dekarchos," Xerxes boomed. "You would instruct me on your prowess and skill? Draw your blade, and strike me."

"Lord Xerxes? I…" Wisimar began, an eyebrow raised.

"*Prince* Xerxes," the Zhayedan interrupted. "I am no Roman *lord*. And I insist. If you can manage to cut a single strand of cloth on my body, I shall place the right to rule upon your shoulders."

Shrugging, Wisimar stepped from the lines, drawing his blade with a swift flick of his shoulders. The mail shirt around his chest bulged with each ripple of his muscles, hinting at a savagery strong enough to decapitate a bull.

"Idiot," Fulcaris whispered.

"Don't say that," Perenus teased. "Maybe he might teach Xerxes something new."

He did not. As Wisimar raised his blade to prepare for a playful session of sparring, Xerxes rushed forward, his own sword a flurry of near-imperceptible movement. Gasping, Wisimar lifted his blade in a feeble defense, seeking only to protect his head and body from a sudden strike. The foray was over in moments, with Xerxes sending the young Vandal sprawling to the dirt amidst a roar of jeers and applause from the onlooking Vandal soldiers.

"Pathetic," Fulcaris groaned.

"You were as naïve once," I reminded Fulcaris. "We all were."

"Fair enough. We were equally as pathetic in Philippi as Wisimar is now," Fulcaris agreed. "I'll never forget Alaric's attempt to beat you in single combat."

At the sound of Alaric's name, all merriment rushed out of me, leaving only a vague image of the fallen soldier's face. Alaric had been one of the most stubborn and proud Herulians under my charge, and grew to become one of my most trusted and capable officers within the Herulian foederati. Yet he fell at Dara, along with so many others, saving my life and the lives of his comrades against a punishing onslaught of Hephthalite horsemen.

"Indeed," I muttered, my throat thick. "But Alaric served with honor. Perhaps Wisimar will learn to do the same."

Fulcaris stroked his chin thoughtfully. "Doubtful," he replied, but his tone was softer.

If such flippancy bothered Xerxes, he showed no concern, and continued his drill as though uninterrupted. Thankfully, the Vandals were as physically fit as they were reckless, requiring little conditioning to carve away the previous months of food and easy living. Instead, Xerxes focused his efforts upon the need for discipline and cooperation, insisting upon patience amongst Vandal spearmen that had long favored a headlong rush into their enemies' formations. Within the first two days, I was doubtful that Xerxes' efforts would bear fruit, yet between the lengthy drills and the constant presence of Gunderic at all exercises, my new Vandal foederati rose to the occasion. Soon, they could execute their maneuvers well, if not always elegantly, without leaving other contingents vulnerable.

Inevitably, our morning of departure arrived, and the final crates of weapons and barrels of wine and water were loaded into the ships' holds. Valerian's ships had already begun their effort to secure the outlying Vandal islands, leaving Carthage's docks far less crowded than they had become in the aftermath of our victory at Tricamarum. Though Belisarius insisted that our sojourn must be a relatively brief one, the patchwork set of troops that had become my command had nevertheless managed to procure and pack all manner of trinkets and, frankly, unnecessary comforts from Carthage's marketplace, too eager to spend the hard-won silver coin from our conquest of Africa.

Perhaps the greatest point of discord was our lack of horses. Of the combined forces lent to me, only fifty horses and twenty oxen would accompany us to the Pillars. I knew this decision was prudence on Belisarius' part, but my Herulians grumbled at being deprived of their mobility. Indulf complained most stridently, even threatening to raise the issue to Belisarius himself.

"I told Belisarius that we would remain loyal to Justinian, but that doesn't mean I'm willing to be disrespected," he barked at me.

"Belisarius needs all the horses that can be spared to secure Africa," I answered dutifully. "The boats will move us close to our destination, and the remaining terrain is too unforgiving of horse travel."

"Oh, so say you," Indulf replied, his hands raised in mock surrender. "But when we're all footsore and are being chased down by a horde of Visigoths, you'll wish you were mounted."

I made the appropriate noises to signal my understanding, but in truth there was little that could be done, by me or by anyone else. Belisarius *had* requested all available horses for his own struggles within the African interior, and our coastal fighting along Mauretania and Hispania did not demand, or even lend itself to, sweeping formations of mounted archers or lancers.

Moreover, I found myself without a dedicated mount, my own stallion Ignis now dead and burned along the hills near Tricamarum. I have little doubt that other men in the army scoffed at my sentimentality of offering a horse such an honorable funeral, but I truly did not care what they thought. Ignis had carried me through the hellish motions of Dara and our twin battles with the Vandal kingdom, and I wept when I found his heart pierced by a Vandal spear. In many ways, he was a comrade like any other, and one loyal to the death. Indeed, fortune is strange: for as I strongly resisted becoming a cavalry officer for the Herulian foederati, and never quite appreciated fighting on horseback as I did within the shield wall, Ignis' loss seemed to have shorn away a small piece of my soul.

As for Indulf's complaint, I was grateful for the continued support of his Ostrogoths, but admittedly I never became comfortable with the presence of Indulf himself. I did not understand his motivations for our journey to the Pillars, even though Baduarius had explained to me that there was little love between the two Gothic tribes, borne from their opposing allegiances to Attila. All I could surmise was that the Ostrogothic men seemed encouraged by the opportunity for further plunder, and so I selfishly did nothing to dispel the notion, even as I knew it was beyond unlikely that Theudis would forfeit gold or slaves from his vastly superior numbers.

Nevertheless, despite the swirling mixture of excitement, fear, and near-universal bluster at the lack of horses to lessen the burden of march, our departure morning began with relative ease. Detachments of the various elements of my army slowly boarded one of the transport vessels that lined the vast circle of Carthage's inner harbor, and I could not help but imagine what similar sights might have been shared by Scipio or Hannibal himself hundreds of years ago. Many men lined the edges of the transport as they moved toward the open sea, allowing another wooden hulk to take its place and continue the embarkation. I oversaw the effort from the heights of Carthage's palace, sharing a room with Belisarius.

"When you depart, take my flagship," Belisarius insisted. "It's cumbersome to change course, but a sturdier boat was never nailed together."

"Generous, Lord," I answered. "But won't Valerian require it, with as much sailing as he will undertake?"

Belisarius shook his head. "Irrelevant. You are my second, Varus. If anything were to happen to me, it would be your burden to see the army safely back to Greece. Because I won't need any ships to clear Carthage of rebels and holdouts, its ownership falls to you."

"Temporarily," I corrected, grinning.

"Temporarily," Belisarius agreed. "Enjoy its luxuries. Most of all, though, enjoy the privacy, because you won't get much once you've landed in Tingitana. Assume that someone will be watching you at all times."

"The spy?" I asked, lowering my voice.

"Perhaps, but that's not what I meant," Belisarius replied. "A leader is constantly judged based upon his words and deeds. Sleeping or awake, his fitness will be scrutinized. Camp servants will gossip about whether their leader's sneezes foretell a terrible sickness, while bodyguards gab about whether he was calm or infuriated over cups of wine. Even your friends—especially your friends—will interpret your every movement as if you were a walking omen. You will live challenging days, and will make decisions that you will later regret— that much is inevitable. Only remember that you will always be watched, and that gossip spreads faster than any fire."

Belisarius' message confused me, not least for its contrast to Rosamund's advice for boundless trust in those I had befriended. Even when John still lived, Belisarius retained a measure of aloofness. Never rude, Belisarius listened thrice as much as he spoke, but otherwise kept to himself in most moments of rest. True, in my initial leadership over the Herulian foederati, I had experienced the lidless eye of soldiers searching their commander for weakness, yet that paled in comparison to the demands of thousands of warriors, servants, and sailors.

The flagship, at least, was an expression of strength unmatched along the seas. Its deck was wide enough to support three full teams of ballistae, plus a full contingent of archers, sailors, and spearmen to fend off a boarding attempt or execute one of their own. It was among the last to depart the Carthaginian harbor, with teams of slaves and servants fulfilling final preparations as Baduarius and the Cappadocians boarded the ship. Belisarius' legendary infantry commander, Baduarius, hooted and roared with laughter as he joked with his men, yet complained noisily about the need for yet another seaward journey.

"You're getting too old for this, Baduarius!" Ascum rasped, his face twisted into a smile as he moved toward his separate transport.

"I'm not yet forty, still a young man!" the great Goth shot back. "It's just the sea I don't like."

"Or horses," I added.

"Or bowmen," Perenus put in.

"Or bathing, by the smell of you," Bessas said. "I've fought with you for years, and I can't remember ever seeing you wash."

Baduarius roared again. "I washed just after the riots ended! Once a year should be good enough for any man."

"Speak for yourself." I grinned. "Once you become used to the habit, it can be quite refreshing."

"Aye, pretty perfumed Varus!" Baduarius boomed, smirking. "Next you'll have me wearing one of your wife's gowns in the shield wall."

Soon enough, it came time for me to join the others aboard the flagship. Uliaris, his Frankish moustaches disheveled and scraggly above his stained robes, slinked aboard, with Cephalas ensuring he would not topple into the harbor's frigid waters, inebriated as he was. Equally occupied, Rosamund fretted over the final crates that were rushed aboard, chastising one group of men for their perceived carelessness as a crate's edge scraped alongside the ship's deck. I handed a lengthy scroll to one of Belisarius' servants, its contents a written explanation of my enhanced duties to Mariya. Words of love and ardor had always fallen clumsily from my pen, yet I did the best that I could to convey to her my deep longing to return home to my family. One more assignment, I promised, and it would be so. The scroll was sealed with red wax and encased in a copper tube that would carry it the hundreds of miles back toward Constantinople, joining the seemingly endless stacks of documents that detailed every bushel of grain and movement of spearmen that Belisarius oversaw in his newfound conquest.

Though most of my soldiers had set off to sea, Roman custom still dictated that a departing commander be formally charged with a duty to lead honorably within foreign lands, and to seek the blessing of God in such an endeavor. As custom of a leading family in a Roman city, Antonina led a delegation of well-wishers that waved to my departing spearmen. Robes of flawless azure wrapped her lithe torso, with sapphires woven into the fabric to catch flickers of sunlight. In such public situations, Antonina played the role of a concerned general's wife flawlessly, showing none of the snobbishness she often displayed before men and women of lower classes.

"Travel with God in your hearts!" I heard Antonina call to my men, her hand lightly waving overhead. "Through God and the Emperor, you can accomplish all things!"

Beside me, Gunderic chuckled, careful to whisper his retort into my ear. "If I had a magic monarch that granted anything I wanted, I'd have a much better imagination than to wish for the Pillars of Herakles."

"Oh?" I replied. And, stupidly, pried further. "Like what?"

Gunderic looked upon me as if I had gravely wounded him. "A thousand pretty women, and the vigor to keep all of them happy."

"Sounds exhausting," I replied.

Gunderic answered only with a vigorous scratch of his stomach and groin.

"I shall pray for all of you!" Antonina's voice soared overhead, triggering further chuckles from Gunderic.

I was unsurprised to find Antonina's bodyguard, the centurion Sergius, standing a few dozen paces away near the walls of the palace, his clothing bright and conspicuously clean next to the plainer garb of most of my soldiers. Warnings from Rosamund and Mariya entered my mind once more, yet I shook away such evil thoughts to remain focused upon the tasks set before me.

As the elected citizen-representative from Carthage, Stotzas stood to Belisarius' left, his features stern to the point it seemed he wished to be elsewhere. Stotzas had been something of a mystery to Belisarius' senior officers, for though Stotzas hailed from one of the Latin families that had inhabited the African coastline since the time of Augustus, Stotzas himself had suffered little under the succession of multiple Vandal kings. Plump and balding, he bore the trappings of his family's wealth, adding further weight to his position as a representative of the Roman people in Africa. At the time I knew little of the man and did not care to expand my knowledge, an oversight I eventually came to grievously rue.

"Carthage is in your debt, tribune," Stotzas droned, sounding almost lazy. "Return the Pillars to our province so that our citizens might sleep peacefully after a century of turmoil."

Most peculiar along the Carthaginian docks was Procopius. Flanked by more junior ink-stained scribes who took down his every dictation, Procopius muttered a ceaseless stream of words that the others would scribble and twist into a recollection of Belisarius' campaigns. Though I could not know it at the time, that history was written not to report events as they happened so much as to praise the virtues of Justinian, and to do so at Belisarius' expense.

Indeed, it was less history and more a kind of sacrilegious gospel, with the Emperor appearing the prophet of victory against a ferocious army of Vandal heathens. Of all men I have ever met, I despise Procopius the most, for though I doubt he ever took the life of a man or woman himself, his words have caused more suffering than any blade. Stretching truth and spinning tales as it suited his personal enjoyment and prospects for renumeration, he damned untold thousands to misery.

Were others from past centuries as liberal with the truth, I wonder? Doubtless some were. Kings and warlords pay poets to raise trifling accomplishments to inhuman feats, with enemy numbers puffed up and the conditions for victory rendered most dire. But which? Did Alexander's scribes exaggerate the Great King's martial prowess? Did those few scribes who lived to document Attila write plainly of the Hunnic conqueror, or did they paint Rome's enemy into a slavering beast undeservedly? Alas, we are all prisoners to the scribes and their petty jealousies, even though they be the very men who cowered from swords or spears in life.

Yet for now this was mere philosophy, easily brushed away as I boarded yet another transport craft and ordered the Imperial flags raised for our journey to the Pillars of Herakles.

Despite Stotzas' insincerity and Procopius' incessant plotting, I was determined to show a solemn dignity as I accepted my duty. However, any of my pretense was eliminated as Liberius shuffled before me, mere moments before Father Petrus would offer blessings upon our voyage. My old teacher was heavily laden with armfuls of tomes and scrolls, a half dozen palace servants panting as they hauled the legate's possessions toward the docks.

"I'm going with you," Liberius barked. "I do hope you weren't intending on claiming the large cabin aboard, Varus. I'm an old man with a bad back!"

"Lord… why?" was all I could manage.

Liberius shrugged without pausing his hurried movements. "Varus, if I must explain to you the ravages of time, I will weep at the considerable failure I have loosed upon the world in your pitiful education."

"No, Lord, I mean why are you joining us?" I said. "The campaign will be hard living on cold earth and hard marches."

"Because I've always wanted to see the Pillars!" Liberius called from over his shoulder, moving onboard the ship. "And besides, I did not think you would mind my company so much."

Liberius gave no further opportunity for me to reply. Nor, frankly, did I have the right to resist, for Liberius carried more authority than Belisarius himself, regardless of whether he wielded the Emperor's designated powers or not. But although I could not deny an Imperial legate, and Liberius' wizened mind would no doubt prove invaluable in so distant a land as the Pillars of Herakles, the thought of his constant oversight roiled my stomach. I loved Liberius, but I had no desire for my teacher to inspect my every decision, witness any failures brought on by my dim judgment. So great was my sudden panic that I turned briefly away from the crowd to gag and cough, only forcing my body to calm itself through deliberate breathing. After a few moments, I was mostly successful.

Now dumbstruck, I knelt as Father Petrus approached, the wool trousers covering my knees growing damp as they pressed into the planks of the docks. Morning mists in Carthage brought a deceptive chill that left one initially refreshed, only to set bones chattering later. Father Petrus' invocation was largely muffled in my mind as I wondered still at Liberius' presence, a dull sensation of worry and impending regret infiltrating my thoughts.

Father Petrus, on the other hand, would not allow such disruption to prevent his blessing upon our venture. His sonorous voice filled the Carthaginian harbor amidst the swell of the waves, calling upon merciful God to see the Emperor's soldiers safely returned from their righteous mission. With my head bowed, the old priest finished his ritual and placed a palm upon the top of my head, lightly ruffling my sweat-strewn hair.

As Father Petrus shuffled back to the massed crowd, Belisarius parted from his wife and strode toward the small fleet of ships that would carry my band off to the edge of the world. Though his beard remained disheveled and face gaunt, Belisarius stood straight in his ornate lamellar armor, each iron scale lined with reinforcing bronze and backed in leather. Whether he noticed Antonina's irritated glance, I strongly doubt, for the general approached with a warm smile as he summoned a nearby servant.

"As I said, Varus, don't risk open battle," Belisarius told me. "The Visigoths are stronger than anything we can muster, so you'll need to outthink Theudis."

"Yes, Lord," I replied, unable to keep my eyes from sinking to the ground.

"You will find that leadership is a lonesome vocation," he added. "None can know of your fears or doubts, yet all will look to you for guidance. Serve with honor and protect your men, and they will achieve impossible feats for you. This is a truth that all commanders come to understand, yet few embrace. It is far easier to massacre an enemy and care little for the sufferings of your men, a temptation that has become far too common in our Empire."

"Lord?" I asked, looking up to see a reassuring nod from Belisarius.

"We would not have offered you this role if you were not ready," he said firmly. "Secure the Pillars of Herakles and return safely, for I would not lose another friend in this foreign place."

As he finished, Belisarius beckoned the servant close. The stout man bowed as he offered the bundled purple cloth to the general's arms, who quickly handed the gift to me. Its deep violet was unmistakably the Imperial hue.

"Justinian gave this to me, after the Nika Riots had been quelled," Belisarius explained. "It was the only Imperial banner remaining when we retook the Hippodrome. The intent was that it would fly after our victory over the Vandals, but I just could not bring myself to do it."

"Why not, Lord?" I asked, already guessing at the answer.

"One day, you will feel comfortable addressing me by my name," Belisarius said, smiling, "but for now, take the Emperor's banner, and unfurl it when you take the Pillars. Even if it is a symbolic victory, I will be in your debt."

I made to pry further, yet a faint flash of anguish across Belisarius' tired and furrowed face kept me silent. Instead, I took the banner with two outstretched hands, the weathered cloth coarse against my fingertips. Belisarius patted the back of my wrist as he surrendered possession, quickly turning back to a distracted Stotzas and an impassive Antonina. After a moment of silence, he threw a salute that was returned by many dozens who lined the rail of my ship, their arms outstretched for a heartbeat longer than Belisarius' own.

My final farewell, and perhaps the one I dreaded most, was with Samur. Besides my brief infiltration into Nisibis against the Persians, I had never been this far from my brother since completing my training in the army, a comfort that I now realized had been taken for granted. Though I knew from our conversations earlier how much resentment Samur held at his continued service under Justinian, for now, it seemed he temporarily held such emotions in check. He offered only a tight embrace, his smaller form wrapping my far larger body with wiry strength.

"I will see you soon," Samur said.

"Only a few months," I replied. "Then it's home, and away from this place."

"Home," he grunted.

Slipping from my grasp, Samur turned and rejoined the crowd. As I ascended to the deck of my ship, his face was firm, as if carved in marble, and he stood motionless as a crowd of onlookers waved and cheered. I would like to think that such high spirits were the fruit of love for Belisarius and the Emperor, but only children and fools would see things so simply. Instead, as Liberius later told me, bread and meat had been passed amongst our well-wishers, a scheme I was surprised to find came from Belisarius himself. Regardless, whether from love or from full bellies, noises of happiness were a welcome change for my men, and likely the last we would hear for some time. I offered a final wave to Father Petrus, and to Belisarius, and finally to Samur, before worming between dozens of men to the center of the deck.

"The Pillars of Herakles," Perenus chirped. "Coming from Lazica, that's the far end of the world!"

"Same for us," Sembrouthes agreed, "although in Aksum, we place less importance on the site. There are kings and peoples farther to the south and west, beyond the vast African deserts."

"I don't believe it," Fulcaris said. "Nothing can live beyond that wasteland."

I laughed. "Well, believe it. The Empire even sent legions beyond those deserts. They found a vast lake with too many hippopotami to count, and thundering swarms of elephants and rhinoceros. The men there are dark like the Aksumites, and the place is so wealthy they wear enough gold to weigh down their limbs and bodies."

Fulcaris raised an eyebrow. "Did Liberius tell you that?"

"No, it was Justin," I answered, with a slight smile at the memory. "Before he was Emperor, Justin always said that he wanted to see the far edges of the world."

Despite everything, a feeling of warmth washed over me as I recalled a boyhood exchange with my onetime dominus. As lord of excubitores, Justin had ranged far in the service of the Emperor, but never to Africa. Never to the Pillars of Herakles, which no Roman army had trod upon in three generations, never as far as this threshold that, within days, would be overcome by a collection of Roman soldiers from a dozen different nations.

I slept well that evening, a rising swell of confidence leaving a curious sensation of hope.

It would be my last moment of unhindered peace for weeks.

JOURNEY TO THE PILLARS

Rough seas made for unpleasant sailing as we skirted the coast of Africa, Numidia, and Mauretania Caesariensis. Though the hulking transports and their brimming stacks of supplies sat low in the water, the deck rocked with each swell. Food, drink, and bodies smashed into the walls and across the planked floor. An unflagging nausea brought memories of my first sea voyage to Cherson, the tempest within the Euxine Sea lashing against our boats as if the pagan gods themselves had taken arms against our quest to relieve the province against the Avars. A far more innocent time, when others like Godilas shouldered the burden of leadership, and so many comrades remained cheerful, excited, and alive.

Instead, I found myself hating life, always at the precipice of vomiting and never released from the swirling universe of my head. Even Rosamund's treatment—a recommendation for activity, to occupy my mind during the worst of the early winter gales—did little to ease my torment. On the afternoon of our second day at sea, I called a small war council, the gathering to be held in the relatively spacious general's quarters that Liberius had commandeered without so much as a note of gratitude.

Unlike my own cabin, which was only a hair larger than the

centurion's quarters that had carried me to Cherson, Liberius' chambers included a separate bedroom, a cloakroom, a private dining area, multiple trunks for personal storage, and a simple wooden desk that had quickly become littered with a dozen pieces of ink-stained parchment. Rows of wax candles mounted upon silver cups helped brighten the room, although servants had to scrape hardened wax droplets from the floor in the aftermath of any particularly violent wave against the ship's hull. For a dreadfully enclosed space, it was as bright and clean as one could make a Roman vessel, and I was astonished to find no evidence of the rats that always seemed to find residence on any craft bearing food.

Our gathering was small, including Perenus, Fulcaris, Baduarius, Sembrouthes, and Uliaris. Though I alone held military command, I afforded Liberius the privilege of opening the gathering, his features stern as candles flickered against his bearded face and dark wool attire. Silently, he took measure of the officers present, drawing creases across his cheeks and forehead as he snorted.

The reaction was off-putting, and not how I desired to begin my command. "Something wrong, Lord?"

"The assembled lords of the Emperor's army, and only I draw lineage from Italy." Liberius chuckled. "If my father were here, he would surely choke from shock. Blessedly, I share none of his misgivings."

"You had a father?" Perenus grinned. "I assumed that you just rose up from the swamps one day, all gray and angry."

"Don't be droll. Of course I had a father," Liberius replied. "A mother too, as a matter of fact, who preferred to shower her children with more love than sense, though such behavior only earned her husband's ire."

Oddly, until that moment, I had not considered Liberius' parents, and had only rarely questioned his childhood in the Western Roman Empire. For some uncertain reason, I found the notion both unsettling and unnatural, as if it defied the natural order to think of Liberius as anything other than the wizened patrician I had known my entire life.

"At any measure, we have all agreed that Septem is the most defensible point along the Pillars, and the most important to protect our new provinces in Africa and Mauretania," I said. "What do we know about the Visigoths, and where else might we strike if Theudis contests our presence?"

"Mount Calpe is historic, of course," Liberius answered. "But it's not a significant bulwark, nor difficult to take. Taking Tingis would further protect our hold over Mauretania, while Gades would be the Visigoths' best opportunity to launch an assault from Hispania. Septem alone would achieve Belisarius' goal, although a more substantial buffer would not be unwelcome."

"What makes Septem so important?" Perenus asked.

"It's a long peninsula with a natural harbor," Liberius said. "A handful of men could defend its walls from ten thousand attackers, and no siege would find any real success without an equally vigorous attack by sea. Whoever holds Septem could easily patrol the channel between Hispania and Mauretania. With that fortress, we could easily protect against any Visigoth raid against Carthage."

"That's why we need Gunderic to convince the Vandals there to surrender it to us," I concluded. "One bloodless exchange and the Visigoths will scarcely be able to launch an assault, even if we only station a hundred men to guard the province."

The other men nodded at the plan's simplicity. Since the time of Achilles and Odysseus, all soldiers pray that fortune will bless them with a life that is glorious but uncomplicated and enemies that cower at the advance of their shield wall. Yet even in the tales, such fates are rare, and even as I held hope of rapid success and departure from the region, I resisted the urge to whisper a prayer to assuage my fears of a far more disastrous outcome.

"A remaining question," I pressed on, "is how to prepare for a fight against the Visigoths, who easily outnumber our forces ten to one."

Silence descended upon the gathering, with neither Baduarius nor even Liberius offering any retort or jibe. Instead, eyes fell upon the only living warrior within the Roman Army who had crossed blades against a Visigothic shield wall. Rubbing his temples and blinking bloodshot eyes, Uliaris seemed reluctant to participate, yet eventually surrendered to his calling.

"The Visigoths are like any other enemy we've faced," Uliaris explained in a rasp, as though his tongue were parched. "They're individually less ferocious than the Vandals, yet far more disciplined and many times again as numerous. All that makes them unique is that they can throw light spears just heartbeats before the shield walls collide, with the aim of carving holes and achieving an easy victory."

"Seems weak." Baduarius snorted. "A battle strategy like that, I mean—betting on a trick rather than skill and cunning."

"It's hardly weak if it works," I cut in, beckoning for Uliaris to continue. "Even Belisarius uses deception in battle; it's what has kept most of us alive this long."

"Aye, and Theudis cares little of honor or expectations," Uliaris went on. "I never saw him in person, but I fought under the banners of King Childebert in Septimania. After our shield wall had been joined, Theudis splashed pitch along the front, then used fire arrows to set the substance alight. You could smell burning flesh even before the men began to scream. That sticky tar would slink between iron mail and leather armor as easy as water. The tactic cost Theudis dozens of his own warriors, but it forced Childebert to leave Septimania to the Goths for another year."

"He burned his own men?" I asked skeptically. "And the Visigoths still followed him after that?"

"Theudis fought only as a sword-bearer for Theodoric then, so no Goth would have questioned such an order," Uliaris said. "But in Frankia, we always saw the Visigoths as dangerous and unpredictable, and Theudis was the most experienced warlord to come from such tribes. He might be old, but I doubt that power and time have made him gentler."

Even now, in my advanced years, men still whisper in awe of Theodoric. Though I would never have wagered against Belisarius' ability to defeat any enemy, a clash with Theodoric would have been a thing of legends for the singers, and a field of blood and suffering for thousands of soldiers. When I was still a slave, Justin had seen the wisdom in placating Theodoric with expensive symbols of friendship, leaving the united Gothic attentions focused against limiting the expansion of the Vandals in Africa or the vast Frankish kingdom spreading throughout Gaul.

Theodoric's dominion even spanned over the Visigothic kingdom, regardless of any ancestral hatred that such people held against the Ostrogoths of Italy. Though an Ostrogoth by birth, Theudis' regency over the Visigoths had been a stable one, borne from Theodoric's support and control over the child-king Amalaric, Theodoric's grandson and heir to the Visigothic throne.

Yet as we sailed westward, we knew little enough of Theudis, despite Uliaris' warnings. Every nation and tribe weaved tales of the ruthlessness of their chieftains, much of which was raw embellishment or even outright fabrication. As my stomach lurched against the heaving waves, I had a fleeting moment of disdain for the Visigoths, thinking it laughable that the victors of Dara and Tricamarum would struggle with an enemy who was both far less vicious than the Vandals and less organized, let alone well-equipped, than the Persians. Such a foolish notion passed, though, as I recalled one of Godilas' earliest lessons: never underestimate one's foe, and do not expect favorable circumstances to continue once begun.

"The moment a warrior takes the challenge before him for granted is the moment that he is already dead. The only uncertainty is which blow will bring about his end."

Head pounding, I soon concluded the gathering, thanking each man for his assessment of our plight and his contribution to our planning. Through the Vandal campaign, I had simply assumed that any war council, no matter the leader, always yielded improved morale and refined approach. I realize now that there was something special about Belisarius, something that inspired dozens of officers to stretch their imagination beyond the well-worn and predictable tactics from Roman manuals or common drill instruction. As I ventured to my cabin, I added this further deficiency to the innumerable I held compared to Belisarius or even John. My extensive education under Liberius and Godilas was no match for the general's ability to interpret the needs and will of his men.

With a woeful head and a fair touch of self-pity, I lay alone in my bunk, politely denying Cephalas or even Rosamund entry into my quarters. My quarters had little to recommend them for any kind of fraternizing, besides; the narrow wooden bed was barely long enough to support my frame. Despite my nausea, I chuckled and prayed for blessed sleep. The space was unlit by candles, and the darkness near complete. I thought of myself and Samur as children, when the thick pitch of night's blackness was such a thing of horror for my younger brother. Why he feared so intensely what he could not see, I never found out, only that he was never far parted from a set of tapers if indoors, or a bonfire if sleeping in a tent beneath the stars. And in so reminiscing in that godforsaken night, I realized that I already missed Samur, and felt a resurging desperation to abandon the pursuit of such far-flung lands and return home.

We continued for several days, the churning seas and whipping gusts propelling our transports and dromons at a favorable pace. On the second afternoon, I dared to ascend to the ship's upper deck, gaining sorely needed fresh air during a limited period of milder waves. Glancing in various directions, I was struck by the utter foreignness of the lands that we passed alongside, this country formerly peopled by a loose confederation of Carthaginian sailors and traders. Scholars had described Hispania and Mauretania as similar in climate to Greece, yet my experience—limited as it was to winter—was one of recurring chill. Rolling hills along the Mauretanian coastline were occasionally dotted with towns and villages, only some of which raised the Imperial banners as we sailed peacefully by.

"We'll pass Caesarea later tonight, Lord," said Apollos, the captain of the ship. "From there, the waves should be calmer."

"Say a prayer for that," I muttered.

"Ah, but the Balearics are almost due north—though I don't envy our comrades who have to seize such islands," Apollos replied cheerily. "Infested with a few thousand pirates, they are. The wealthier ones call themselves kings and lords." He grimaced at the ridiculousness of the assertion. "Slavers and rapists, all of them."

"If you declare yourself a king and none are nearby to contest the claim, doesn't it become truth?" I asked.

"No, Lord!" Apollos said, befuddled. "Kings and emperors are chosen by God."

"Or by slave boys." I smirked, thinking back to the days of Justin's ascension to the purple.

"Lord?" Apollos asked.

"It is nothing. Of course, you are correct," I said firmly. "See us safely to Septem, and Belisarius will surely reward you."

Apollos bobbed his head, doubtless pleased at the prospect of earning a fair bounty of silver for the transport of Belisarius' men. Keeping to the interior of the deck, I walked the length of the craft from bow to stern, gazing first to the African interior and later northward into the sea. Angry gray clouds shrouded us with little visibility, yet no rain fell, allowing teams of sailors to whoop and shout their instructions to one another in a language that seemed almost entirely foreign to the Greek that was their origin. Pausing near the front of the craft, I stared west, believing myself alone with my thoughts.

"Any regrets at taking this responsibility?"

I recognized Rosamund's voice behind me but did not turn, and kept my eyes fixed ahead.

"No," I grumbled.

Rosamund laughed. "You have always been a terrible liar. That is probably one of your nobler qualities."

"To be a bad liar?" I said, finally breaking my gaze and facing her.

"Put it this way." Rosamund smiled. "If you were skilled in that particular art, I doubt that I would have remained with you for this long."

I grunted. "Well, do you regret joining this expedition? Continuing onward?"

"Never," she replied, her pale Gepid hair flickering wildly in the sea air. "Not this, nor anything since we met in the flames of my village. It was fate, and has given me purpose in life."

"To serve those you disdain?" I asked, my tone admittedly spiteful.

At that, Rosamund grinned widely, the sparkle in her eyes a bright contrast to the dismal skies above. "You're not a Roman, Varus," she said. "You may never have ears to hear such words, but mark me anyway: you are not, and you never will be."

"And?" I prodded further, not sure I took her meaning.

"And in protecting you, my own life will have purpose," she concluded. "Just as my grandfather prophesized."

I bristled, shaking my head. "No matter who you think I am, Rosamund, I am a Christian. And I—"

Before I could finish, a wave heaved mightily against our ship, throwing icy spray onto the deck and pelting the exposed skin of my face like a thousand tiny arrows. My feet yanked from under me, I instinctively grabbed for a line of knotted rope that rose high into the air. The fibers bit into my hand as I steadied my stance, but I managed to remain upright, to Rosamund's great laughter. She playfully smacked my chin, somehow as steady and upright as ever, despite the displeasure of the sea.

"Lucky for you, then, that my beliefs don't depend on your own," she said. "Nor does my patience. I've told you for years that you're a good man, and one day you'll realize that you don't need these Romans to convince you of your worth. Until then, however, I'll stay here with you."

This did not satisfy me. "Why?" I asked, still clinging to my lifeline. "Why put yourself through this trouble?"

Rosamund sighed. "I've just told you why, Varus. It is my fate. The gods have blessed you repeatedly through your life, more than any other man I have met. I have seen their miracles work to keep you alive, and prosper. To play any part in such blessings is the greatest honor I can imagine."

"If this is their way of blessing me," I said with a grimace, wavering atop the ship, "I wish they would stop."

Rosamund gave a soft snort of disbelief. "Even beneath all the bleating and meekness of Petrus' religion, a part of you feels that I am right. Christian or otherwise."

It was true that Petrus despised me enabling Rosamund, and while I avoided her rituals and prayers, the faintest portion of my mind was curious. The nature of her faith, its gods and rituals and prophecies, remained utterly foreign despite our years together, and though it offered me little comfort, I could not deny that with whatever strength of spirit it gave her, it was Rosamund who had kept me and many of my men from death when other healers would have abandoned us to our God.

Still, I felt I must intercede on the behalf of my fellows. "Not all Romans are uncaring or bad. Like Liberius—"

"Liberius is as tolerant and understanding as Romans come, but he is still a Roman," Rosamund interrupted. "And a far better liar than you are." The smile dropped from her face. "I have no doubt that he has his reasons, but the lie is there."

The crack of such a pronouncement set my flesh prickling in fear. Though I swiftly forced myself to attribute the discomfort to the chill of the sea, I could not resist looking about the ship's deck from the corners of my eyes, childish and superstitious of any evil that might linger in dank shadow. An utterly foolish notion, to be sure, but fear rarely brings one to wisdom, preferring a course for only the terrible and the impossible.

Gradually, I brought myself back to the present moment. "Lies," I repeated. "You mean the gifts? Liberius and Father Petrus said that I would know more in time, when I am ready."

"Not about the gifts—or not entirely, anyway," Rosamund answered. "I cannot be sure of what the lies may be, or why they have come about. I just know that your interests and the interests of these

Romans are not one and the same, and that these men will sacrifice the former for the latter if you give them any opportunity to do so."

I shook my head. "I care deeply for you, Rosamund, but you are wrong in this."

"Perhaps I am." Rosamund smiled again, weakly this time. "But I think not. At any rate," she added, staring out over the waves, "it changes little of our current situation."

I offered no retort. The wet flaxen rope had grown heavy in my burning palms, and I dropped it, shuffling cautiously toward the ship's railing. While I held firmly to the worn wood, Rosamund remained as serene as ever, peering into the swirling waters of the African coastline. Though I took only a little respite from the measure, the sea air did dampen the ever-present sensation of bile in my throat, and the light spray was the closest I would come to bathing until we reached the vaunted Pillars. A few moments passed, and I felt my servant's thin yet steely fingers gripping at my elbow, less to seek support and more to impart it.

Memory fails at how long we stood at the ship's edge. It may have been but a few heartbeats or an hour; I cannot confidently say. Even a light spattering of rain did little to disrupt my concentration or convince me of the need to move from my perch. It was not until flashes of light shot across the horizon that my complacency finally surrendered. I grunted in sudden understanding.

"Godilas," I muttered, drawing a curious glance from Rosamund.

"Varus?" she asked, using a free hand to wipe thick strands of wet hair from her face.

I smiled, shaking my head—no matter to her. More lightning flickered across thick sheets of ominous gray. Nearby voices cried out in warning.

"You'd better go below, Lord!" Apollos called. "We're in for a rough evening."

I nodded, leaving the rail and accompanying Rosamund down to the relative safety of the ship's hold. A clinging stench of sweat and vomit greeted us with the peculiar heat that had grown familiar during our brief stay onboard, forcing me to grit my teeth as I trained my mind against retching. Lingering nausea returned as I reached the door to my cabin, grunting in acknowledgment of various men and officers who gambled, shared wineskins, and told bawdy tales to pass the time. Rosamund offered a final smile before leaving me to my solace, her hand falling from my arm to briefly curl around my thawing and torn fingers.

"Remember what I said," Rosamund whispered.

Slipping into my quarters, I peeled away the damp wool from my chest and torso, collapsing onto the rough wooden rectangle that served as my makeshift bed. My final thoughts before submitting to rest were of my wife and children, one of whom I had not yet met. Nor would I, should this expedition go terribly wrong.

THE PILLARS OF HERAKLES

Poor weather dogged our movement westward, our slow pace exacerbated by the need to stay south, clinging tightly to the African coastline, as the Visigothic kingdom in Hispania drew perilously close along the northern horizon. Not that our trailing line of ships was in any great danger, however; my transports were flanked by swifter yet more heavily armed dromons that would have easily swatted anything the Visigoths might put to water. It was more that our goal was stealth and surprise, our hopes to seize Septem as bloodlessly as possible. Our long column of ships proceeded in twos and threes along the Mauretanian coastline, far beyond where Bessas' or Samur's scouts had ridden within Justinian's conquest.

As the African coast began to curl northward, Liberius made it known that the southern Pillar was imminent. The walled city of Septem, which occupied Mount Abyla's protruding promontory that separated the sea from the vast and limitless ocean beyond, was less than a half day's sail by favorable winds. Once I ordered my craft to slow its pace yet further, my clerks scribbled blunt orders of what would follow next.

Ship-to-ship communication has always been a nuisance. Even in fair weather, shouting across fifty paces is hardly desirable and often indecipherable, yielding more confusion than good sense. Instead, when winds and rain permitted, a bowman could shoot a message-wrapped arrow onto an adjoining ship's mast or hull. This process had its own inefficiencies, yet all Roman ship's captains were required to be literate, and message-lined arrows were the quickest form of conversation that could be maintained at sea.

While the dromons took anchor, many of the transport ships took position near the coast. Men offloaded into smaller landing craft as they moved ashore, struggling against the current and cursing as the icy spray licked their cheeks. Amidst such activity, I ordered the various officers together, meeting fifty paces inland near an overlook of the coastline.

"I'm getting sick of these ships," Baduarius grumbled, hailing Ascum as he reached our meeting place.

"There are worse things in life," Ascum replied. "But a sea voyage in winter... perhaps not the best plan we've come up with."

I nodded vigorously. "No one agrees more than I, believe me. But it was necessary. A few weeks and we'll be on our way back to Carthage."

Baduarius groaned. "On our way, and on another ship."

A handful of servants flurried about, setting up a warped wooden table and a handful of chairs for the legate and officers present. Though Cephalas had proposed to organize an encampment of tents, I declined that sort of luxury for the time being, insisting that speed was essential for what would come next. Nevertheless, I did not begrudge Liberius his chairs, for the aging man had made a theatrical display of arthritic knees that warranted a cushioned stool. Even so, I grinned, knowing that Liberius yet had the stamina to outmarch many of Belisarius' soldiers, and only feigned weakness when it might afford him some small comforts.

"I doubt that a legate has ever been forced to suffer such indignities as sitting on a chair exposed to the elements," Liberius complained, "but we all must make sacrifices, I suppose."

"That's far from true, Lord," Xerxes answered with a sly grin, approaching the gathering with Gunderic and a half dozen Vandal officers at his flanks. "Your Emperor Julian left plenty of legates behind in Persia long ago… not by choice, of course."

"We have no time for this," I snapped, anxious to proceed. "Any losses to report on the voyage over?"

"No problems of note," Xerxes answered.

"A few were struck with the flux, but no deaths," Indulf added.

Others offered their reports, noting the moderately good fortune that no casualties were suffered in the journey from Carthage. Even with a well-fed and healthy army, when hundreds of men sleep in close quarters with one another, disease is never far. Flux has been a crippling challenge for thousands of years of Greek and Roman history, rendering once unconquerable forces weak and hopeless with sour stomachs. Other diseases like plague or the pox occasionally flared as well, yet blessedly the Empire had been spared from significant outbreaks of such pestilence. Though I could not be sure of the status of the dromons, I offered a silent prayer of thanks for such fortune, hoping it was a sign of the ease with which the expedition would unfold.

As the reports concluded, I took account of the men. Though still early in the morning, many grinned to one another, sharing sidelong jibes to pass the time. Indulf alone scowled alongside his Ostrogoth centurions, his neatly combed and oiled hair shimmering against the Mauretanian sun. None showed any reluctance to proceed nor any sense of fatigue—yet another blessing, as I myself felt mired in a curious mixture of wistfulness and pride. Our task to retake the Pillars of Herakles had finally begun.

"What do we know of the area?" I asked.

"Based upon my conversations with the ship's captain, we're near the tip of the old province of Mauretania Tingitana, and a half day's march from Tamuda," Liberius said. "The province used to hold several wealthy towns before the Vandals and Goths came, but I would be surprised if any value remains."

Though the Empire today is still organized into the provinces that had defined the accomplishments of Augustus and Trajan, many were redrawn to accommodate more defensible positions along natural bulwarks like rivers or mountains. Others still had been merged or eliminated entirely, the result of continuous loss of control to one of the innumerable barbarian nations that swarmed across the continents. I would come to learn that Mauretania Tingitana had formed within the reigns of the earliest emperors and had prospered due to trade with the nomadic Mauri and the distant nations to the south. Most of the province had been reduced to sand and rubble as the Vandals swept through Africa toward Carthage, yet a coastal Roman road still linked Septem with the two major cities of the region—Tingis and Volubilis. Neither, however, had the defensive capability or strategic positioning of Septem, and even today I doubt that more than a few thousand windswept traders call such ruins home.

Liberius continued his lecture of my officers, using a hand to smooth the wild beard that hung well into his chest. Calling for a blank scroll of papyrus, Liberius took up a thin reed pen and marked the fibers of the scroll with the dark ink dripping from its tip. Liberius strongly preferred the Egyptian method of writing and swore that if such methods could work for thousands of years of Egyptian pharaohs, it would be more than adequate for his purposes. I myself preferred the lead stylus of older Roman writing or even the feathered quill, which made for easier marking of vellum parchment. But since my clerical responsibilities were far less than Liberius' or other civilians in the army, I had little reason to deny him his preferred writing utensils, no matter their expense.

Beckoning the officers closer, Liberius asked several men to hold the papyrus flat as he scratched thin lines of ink that swept an arm's length in each direction. A crude triangle took shape, its northern point curled eastward into the sea. Liberius marked a scratch to denote Septem's position at the tip of the curled point, then added Volubilis to the south and Tingis to the west. Beyond the channel, an opposing triangle denoted the general outline of Baetica, Hispania's southernmost province. Though the larger Visigothic cities of Gades to the west and Malaca to the east framed Baetica's outline, its southern tip was marked with only the lightest indentation denoting Mount Calpe, the northern Pillar that had been among our targets.

"As you can all see, the area we're moving within is narrow and mountainous," Liberius continued. "We're likely less than a half day's march from Tamuda, which used to be a resupply depot for legionary detachments based between Septem and Volubilis. There will be a few villages nearby, but most people here are nomadic outside of the larger towns, and I doubt that even a horseless army should require more than two days of marching to reach Septem's walls."

"Wouldn't we have seen signs of the Vandal outpost already?" Sembrouthes asked.

Liberius considered, but it was Gunderic who responded first. "Unlikely," he grunted. "No Vandals would ever wish to be sent to Septem. Those men were not allowed to join in the latest raid or battle with adjoining kingdoms. Even Gelimer only posted one or two hundred riders in the entire region, with most remaining in Septem's stone fort while the Mauri collected tribute and bribes."

"Bribes from locals who hate you," Indulf scolded in his accented Latin. "Small wonder that your people were defeated by so few."

"Belisarius alone holds conquest over the Vandals," Gunderic roared. "The only Ostrogoths who've ever had any measure of victory over me is your women, for their men run with a trail of piss down their legs at the thought of battle."

Snarling, Indulf drew square to Gunderic, and the flanking Ostrogoths at his side spat insults at their looming Vandal foe. Gunderic merely boomed in laughter as he made coarse suggestions at the size of the Gothic manhood—in jest, or mostly so, yet I saw Wisimar nearby clench at the hilt of his sword, intent on Indulf's movements.

"Enough!" I cried. "Any man who draws a weapon here will lose his hand, and I will carry out the punishment myself. We are too few to squabble amongst ourselves, and too far away to accommodate unnecessary losses."

"Aye, commander." Gunderic winked.

"As you say, Lord Varus." Indulf nodded, his eyes still narrowed and fixed upon Gunderic's cheery form.

Flushing at such open and raw aggression within my expedition council, I leaned over Liberius' map to make sense of the distances between our current position and the few populated centers in the region. Grabbing a few smooth stones from the ground, I positioned them at the spot designated as our landing area, adding others to indicate the dromons that remained anchored along the shoreline.

"Indulf and Perenus will take their men and seize Tamuda, but no unnecessary violence," I ordered. "Dig trenches and repair what walls might still be standing. We need a center of operations until Septem is under our control."

"From Gelimer's reports, Tamuda has been thinly peopled for years, so there should only be a few hundred Mauri and Romans," Liberius added. "But the old town used to support stone walls that should be easily repaired from a few days' work."

"Easy pickings, then," Indulf said. "But likely a corpse picked clean of any plunder. My men have not traveled all this way to sit idly in some forgotten wasteland."

"You'll have your chance," I countered. "You and Perenus will sweep south and then west, taking Volubilis and then Tingis. Leave fifty men in Tamuda and another hundred in the other two cities, and meet me near Septem."

"Still…" Indulf began.

"Succeed, and you will be paid handsomely from my own wealth," I added, forcing myself to suppress an instinct to lash out against the Ostrogothic commander. "No unnecessary violence, for these are Justinian's and Theodora's subjects now. We need them to love us more than the Visigoths, or we'll never leave this place alive."

Indulf glowered but nodded his assent. Ignoring murmuring from the different factions amongst my officers, I moved several stones toward each of the three nearby towns.

Keeping my eyes trained upon Liberius' map, I further unfolded my plan. "Fulcaris will take what few horses we have and scout the province's coastline. If any Vandal detachments resist, or if the Visigoths cross the channel and attack, his scouts will reach the main army as well as Indulf and Perenus. We will converge on Septem if the situation warrants."

"What about Hispania?" Perenus asked. "We'd have no idea if Theudis was about to send fifty thousand men directly toward our position."

I paused, saying nothing. Similar concerns had interrupted my sleep since departing from Carthage. Mauretania was an arduous task, but a straightforward one, as its low population and limited opportunities for resistance left few chances for my forces to be struck by an ambush or harried by disgruntled natives. Hispania, however, remained as populous as ever, with several million Visigoths, Romans, and Suebi inhabiting a land that had once been famed for its silver mines and fertile valleys. Though a small segment of Theudis' lands, Baetica was a far more formidable landscape than Mauretania Tingitana, sprinkled with hundreds of villages and towns across its many rivers.

Regardless, it was a threat that could not be ignored.

"Thurimuth, you used to be a mountain fighter for the Alemanni, correct?" I asked.

"Yes, Lord, and I prefer it to skulking about in sand and dust." Thurimuth stood straighter, offering a formal salute in this otherwise informal gathering.

"With a hundred men, can you take and fortify Mount Calpe? Our reports indicate that only a small village is present along the peninsula, although the area is surrounded by a half dozen larger towns that connect to Gades."

"If that is your will, it shall be so," Thurimuth said. "Although I would be grateful for five of Fulcaris' horsemen, particularly those not shy of riding on harsh terrain."

"I would take up this responsibility for you, Lord," Sindual interjected. "Theudis won't be so much as able to belch without our knowing."

Though I was reluctant to spare any of the already limited number of available scouts, it would have been foolish to deny Thurimuth such a token force. If I had denied his request, I have little doubt that Thurimuth would have fulfilled his orders regardless of whatever resistance might be encountered, although his men would resent such harsh responsibility. In all my years, I have rarely come across one as simple and single-minded as Thurimuth, the taciturn Alemanni officer who never complained nor resisted even the most obtuse of orders.

"Granted," I affirmed. "Sindual will accompany Thurimuth on a ferry to Mount Calpe. A half dozen dromons will remain within arrowshot of the coastline, and will be given orders to extract everyone if the Visigoths descend upon your position."

"It will not come to that, Lord, although I appreciate the gesture," Thurimuth said.

I nodded, sliding a small stone across the channel and toward the northern Pillar. No sooner had my hand begun to move than a voice rasped from the periphery of our assembly.

"I would like to join Thurimuth and Sindual and head to Baetica," Uliaris said. "I know the Visigoth fighting techniques well, and can be useful if Theudis' men attack."

"No," I answered immediately. "I need you with Sembrouthes and my bodyguard. If the Visigoths invade Mauretania, we'll need your guidance soon enough."

Yet Uliaris continued. "Lord, I would very much appreciate the opportunity to—"

"The answer is no, Uliaris," I said firmly. "Your time for valor will come, but it will not be with Thurimuth."

Uliaris dropped his head as he surrendered the point. Though he appeared sober, his chapped lips and red eyes betrayed a weakened physique that hardly spoke to Uliaris' prowess as one of Belisarius' most skilled soldiers. Mercifully, he said nothing further, and I considered the matter dropped until another spoke up.

"The Visigoths would butcher a weeping drunk." Indulf smirked. "All you would do is make yourself a liability."

Uliaris did not have time to react. The bemused grin had not even left Indulf's face before Baduarius connected with an open palm, the smacking of flesh piercing the din of men's voices. Ascum followed immediately thereafter, hurling his good shoulder at one of Indulf's centurions as he launched himself from his feet. Fists and feet wrought havoc upon my makeshift camp, spreading to the Vandals who whooped at the opportunity for lighthearted violence.

"*Enough!*" I roared, drawing my sword from its scabbard. "On your knees, all of you!"

A few latent blows fell, yet the officers' scrum ended as abruptly as it began. Indulf cursed loudly as thin rivulets of blood flared from his nose, while Ascum nursed a sore hand that thankfully did not appear broken. Thurimuth was the first to kneel, followed soon thereafter by Perenus and the Herulians, leading most others to drop to the ground. Baduarius and Indulf were among the last to obey the order, leaving only Liberius and me standing amongst fifty of the expedition's leaders.

"If Belisarius were here, he would be disgusted with the example you lot put on!" I shouted, spitting into the dust. "Thousands of miles from Constantinople, and you brawl like street gangs. You disgrace me and yourselves!"

"Varus, it was Indulf who—" Baduarius began.

"I don't care if Indulf threatened to hump your mother, you will not break the peace of my camp, understand?"

Baduarius dropped his head, nodding. Thinking the men docile, I sucked in a deep breath to calm myself, yet heard a light snigger from where Indulf nursed his bloodied nose.

"And you!" I exclaimed, turning to the leader of the Ostrogothic foederati. "If you find any of what I have just said to be hilarious, please let me know."

"Commander—"

I silenced him with a plume of dirt kicked into the air. "You will not speak until I give you permission!" I ordered. "This is not some child's game. A herd of farting cattle could take down the army in its current state, let alone the thousands at Theudis' command. You have all broken my explicit order for no reason other than personal pride. In centuries past, they crucified men for such insubordination."

Eyes widened at these pronouncements, and even Baduarius allowed a flicker of fear to break through his stony, downcast visage. My chest now heaving in rage and humiliation, I took a few paces toward the center of the kneeling officers, considering my next words.

"Commander Varus," Liberius purred, his voice absent its usual mischief, "no weapons were drawn, as you requested, so there is no need for bloodshed today."

I allowed several heartbeats to pass, yet ultimately I nodded in agreement with Liberius' conclusion. In truth, I had no intention of harming any of the men, let alone institute the sort of torturous punitive death that had once been a staple of the Imperial Army, for despite my elevated role, I had no stomach for levying harsh punishment on men I called friends. Even Indulf would have been exempt from such chastisement, for his displeasure risked the wrath and abandonment of the four hundred Ostrogoths who accompanied our expedition. Such great losses would be catastrophic, and unsurvivable.

"The legate speaks wisdom," I shouted in finality. "Let the shame you feel be its own punishment. But be warned, there will be no more brawling or retaliation. Is that understood?"

"Yes, Commander," Indulf shouted. "There is no resentment from me. A foolish squabble amongst brothers, and I will make amends in some way."

"Nor me," Uliaris added, his voice sapped of vitality.

"Nor me," Baduarius added. "I am sorry, Lord Varus. I owe the army recompense for my actions."

"Yes, it's foolish and unforgiveable," Ascum added, flexing his sore wrist. "But at least now we know we're ready to bash some shit-eating Visigothic skulls."

I could not resist a chuckle. "Let's hope it won't come to that," I said simply. "Those that have not been given an assignment will accompany me along the old Roman road to Septem. Ascum will lead the remaining fleet by sea and surround the city with our warships."

"By the gods, all that because of the fight?" Ascum groaned.

I shook my head. "No. I need the ballistae fixed upon the fort's walls, and they'll be too slow to carry northward. There's no better officer for siege weapons in the Empire than you."

"Damned right," Ascum agreed. "Very well. I'll smash their walls if they resist."

"Good. Then see it done," I said, bringing the gathering to an unorthodox conclusion.

No time could be spared for rest. Frenzied activity saw men and supplies disembarked from the transports, with small portions of food, drink, and horses allocated for Thurimuth's and Sindual's journey to Baetica. Ponderous oxen were unloaded and strapped to carts of twice-baked bread and salted mutton, while other beasts hauled stacks of ladders, nails, rope, and even a transportable smithy to mend any rents or cuts in our mail and armor. To assist Ascum, all ballistae remained on the ships, their interlocking wood, iron, and twisted ropes allocated to the decks of various dromons. Yet it was his final request that caught my interest.

"I'd like all our clay pots of naphtha," Ascum said. "Even the smaller pots used to mix with wax for small fires."

I grunted in assent, yet my imagination could not begin to picture the purpose of such a request. "Why? Theudis has essentially no warships, so fire arrows would be unnecessary."

"Let's hope I'm wrong," Ascum slurred, the twisted edge of his charred cheek layered with the lightest sheen of dribble. "But I've seen what a good fire can do if the gods decide to fuck us in the ass once more."

Satisfied enough with Ascum's explanation, I allowed him to repurpose our naphtha stores, as I was otherwise unable to use the viscous pitch for my own purposes. Few grumbled at such a loss;

only Rosamund appeared visibly irritated at such an imposition, although she quickly surrendered her resistance when I explained who the supplies were destined to.

"Ascum's been blessed by fire," Rosamund explained in Heruli. "Fire reduces all to cinders, except what the gods demand be spared for another purpose. If Ascum wishes fuel for his flames, then it is for a greater purpose."

"If you say so." I shrugged, uncomfortable with Rosamund's discussion of foreign gods on a faraway land. "It keeps the pots away from my spearmen, who are as like to mistake them for wine and belch flames from their mistake."

Rosamund raised an eyebrow, a thin smile spreading across her lips. "You have no need to fear the gods, Varus."

"Who says I fear them?" I asked, with a defiance that I did not truly feel.

"Because you always make jokes about subjects that bring you worry or dread," Rosamund replied. "And your jokes are rarely any good."

Instantly, my mind swam with voices. Urgent, insistent, and terrifying, their message ending as abruptly as it began.

I saw the last of the Romans. A bride of darkness, an uncrowned king, a soiled monarch, and a windblown son would meet in the ruins of the world, and from their unholy union would be borne the damnation of the Greeks.

"Why do you care what I think?" I grumbled. Yet the hairs on my limbs prickled, and my eyes darted about the room, searching for Hakhamanish, even though the reasonable portion of my mind knew the magus was thousands of miles distant.

"Because the gods love you," Rosamund said, as though it were the most simple and obvious fact. "And they will use you as an instrument of their will, even if you don't believe in them. You are blessed, just as I am."

A voice, discernible only to me, cackled in my head. *The Great Lie is already upon you.*

I shivered. "If your gods love me, they have an ironic sense of affection."

"Hardly. We give the most challenging tests to those we love," Rosamund explained. "I knew it from our first weeks together. You have their favor and you will accomplish incredible feats."

It was too much. Despite Petrus' husbandry over my prayers, I always afforded Rosamund opportunity to freely practice her faith, though she disdained my own. Was I wrong in brooking her religion? In the darkness of night, when Hakhamanish's voice was most likely to reappear, part of me believed so. I had been the author of so much suffering that I had to wonder whether the magus had been correct. Were my actions righteous, or an insidious evil cloaked in the sweetened words of justice and civilization?

Outwardly, I allowed the topic to drop, leaving Rosamund to prepare for our northward march. Though I would have desired three times the spearmen given the objectives set before us, such a small force did bring the lone benefit of swift preparation for departure. Over a half day's march remained with the light still available to us, all facilitated by the still-reliable dressed and shaped stones of the Roman road. With a wave, I dismissed the forces under Perenus and Indulf before walking to the front of my column.

"This is either a very good idea or a truly terrible one," Sembrouthes murmured as I took my place near the front.

"But there is only one path for us to discover which it is," I replied. "Let us go."

Raising a fist, I beckoned for the march to begin, a call echoed by a dozen centurions in a mixture of coarse Latin and accented Greek. Rustling mail and slapping boots thrummed against the stones, making it near impossible to accommodate any sense of secrecy in our position. Five rows of eight men fanned forward from my location, serving as the column's vanguard and the first to receive signals from teams of scouts that ranged into the hills and thickets to search for any sign of Vandals or Visigoths.

"The edge of the world," Liberius regaled, his long legs easily keeping pace with the Aksumites. "What a time to be alive."

And so it was. The Pillars of Herakles, the farthest edge of Justinian's dominion. If we had the strength to take it.

THE CITADEL OF
THE SEVEN BROTHERS

B y Liberius' assessment, we were a mere three days' march from the walls of Septem. Compared to the circuitous route of Perenus and Indulf, it was a simple enough task, yet its end point was far more dangerous than the semi-deserted ruins of Volubilis and the less-fortified town of Tingis.

Our first day of marching commenced with relative ease, the inland roadway both temperate and comfortable compared to the chill of the sea air. The second day was little different, save for the general rise in complaints of blistered feet and strained calves from those men tasked with hauling packs of essential supplies that would not fit in the few available oxcarts.

On the third and penultimate day of our march, our scouting parties doubled in frequency, keeping close circuits with the broader column even as they sought any information about possible enemies that lay ahead. Unlike in Africa, my men were under orders not to distribute coin to passing villages or travelers, but to keep our presence muted until the province could be secured. Not that this was a terrible burden for the men, who generally despised the free distribution of silver that they themselves had to sweat and kill to possess. For those blessed few who did take solace in generosity, however, there were few natives that we encountered on our journey, finding only an occasional merchant cart whose wooden wheels bumped and scraped against the weathered stone as much as we did.

"The western coast is dotted with far more villages," Liberius explained, "yet old records show that this once was a far more populated place. Vandal pillage and Mauri raids seemed to have hollowed out signs of life."

"Blame us all you want," Gunderic said, grinning. "I say that the people here are smart. Why be pressed between two warring nations like rotting wheat under the millstone?"

"Why indeed?" I muttered, less a question and more of a statement.

While the few encounters with natives made for fewer encumbrances or opportunities to betray our position to an enemy, the empty landscape cast an eerie mood over our column. The low winter sun cast arcing shadows across the rolling landscape, leading several of our scouts to insist that they had seen figures stalking our position in the distance. Such notions were unsettling and brought cruel memories of Tauris to the fore, but I did not alter our strategy. While I doubted that any outriders had spotted our march so quickly, there was little else I could do. Our survival depended upon continuing north and taking the sweeping fortress of Septem with as little bloodshed as possible.

Though our column could have gone farther without suffering undue strain or injury, I called a halt at a half day's march from Septem, insisting that the men retain the stamina to launch an attack against the city's walls if necessary. Though it was foolish to assume that our presence had gone unnoticed, I still forbade any cookfires to be lit, fearing the plumes of a hundred fires would draw the eye of even the laziest sentry.

Huddled in my tent, I shared with Rosamund what poor fare she could muster, taking comfort in our habitual evening gatherings before returning to the mental rigors of preparing for the march. Men grumbled as they gnawed at hardened biscuits and salt mutton, the cool temperature and tough texture something that even a starving beggar would not consider a delicacy. Liberius' complaints were heard even above the most untested of my warriors, although I strongly doubt whether he truly cared that his food was near inedible.

"Nearly as despicable as the house rations Justin insisted upon eating," Liberius mused, considering his meal.

I snorted, surprised by an instinctual urge to defend my dominus after years of being separated from his yoke. Sitting alongside Liberius along a dry patch of grass, I considered the legate's words, seeking distant memories in my mind to offset what I felt to be false.

"That's not true. Samur and I always made sure that Justin received the best cuts of beef and softest bread in the palace."

"You did." Liberius smiled. "But I doubt you knew that he much preferred simple biscuits and the sour wine you soldiers love to rot your guts with."

Gunderic roared his approval, joining our gathering with a handful of officers and forming a circle of squatting men. "Aye, any soft-bodied merchant or prostitute can appreciate sweet grapes, but it takes a true man to swallow a skin full of sour red and insist upon another portion."

"True, true!" Baduarius chirped.

Liberius rolled his eyes, continuing despite the crude interjection. "Even after he became emperor, Justin always said that he wanted to return to Pella and live in simple comfort. Soldier's wine, bread, and grapes could sustain that man until the apocalypse, yet he was forced to suffer through spiced meats and lavish wines whose grapes sprouted a thousand miles distant."

Though I shook my head in feeble defiance, in my heart I understood the small revelation bore kernels of truth. My dominus had eschewed the trappings of the purple wherever possible, preferring simplicity, whereas Justinian basked in the raw power and majesty of the Imperial seat. Both men had risen to become Caesar, and though they shared blood, the difference in their approaches to governance could not have been more plain.

"In Persia, the Zhayedan rarely drink wine, and only to celebrate the birth of the Shahanshah," Xerxes added. "Clear heads always prevail, so my teachers told me."

"Another reason we hate you lot," Baduarius interjected, elbowing Xerxes playfully in the ribs. "My brother used to say that you can't ever know a man until you've gotten stinking drunk with him. If you wake up with all of your possessions and aren't in a dungeon or in a gutter, you've found a friend for life."

Liberius' face wrinkled in an expression almost like an incipient sneeze, but he let out only a rare unrestrained laugh. "Romans could never forswear the vine, although if we did, we would have conquered the world. The Immortals have the right of it: wine makes a man senseless and unthinking."

"And brave!" Baduarius roared.

"And hilarious!" Gunderic added, gulping at his wineskin for effect.

"And irritating," Sembrouthes growled.

Sharing a curious yet welcome sensation of lightness, we gnawed at our simple fare as the last rays of sunlight leaked across the western sky. All that separated us from the infinite horizon of the Great Ocean was a narrow band of Mauretania Tingitana, its reach so vast that not even the ancient Greek heroes had dared to venture beyond. Out of curiosity, I asked Liberius whether such vast ocean could truly be infinite, or whether our ships might one day take sail to conquer the mysterious lands that might rise above the violent abyss.

"Of course the ocean is not infinite," Liberius scoffed. "Our world is round! And besides, rather than playing the part of a halfwit philosopher, you should be considering the challenge of the Seven Brothers ahead."

"The Seven Brothers?" I asked.

"Ad Septem Fratres." Liberius tutted. "Really, Varus, I do wonder if you listened to any of my teachings over the years. Mount Abyla is the most famous among the city's seven hills, and used to include a complete Roman fort near its stunted summit."

"I saw it once, as a boy," Gunderic added. "Stone walls and

battlements. Not nearly as well-kept as the town, though. The early Vandal kings saw no use for the place, and did not wish to bother hauling food and weapons up the mountain each day. Still, it would be difficult for most men to scale in full armor and under arrowfire."

On the sea voyage from Carthage, we had planned meticulously for this expedition, strategizing with that mixture of ingenuity and force required to properly besiege and overwhelm the stout city walls should its defenders prove unwilling to surrender to Justinian. Even so, minor details continued to present themselves, most of which were mere rumor rather than true impediment. Others had mentioned the hilltop citadel on Mount Abyla, yet Gunderic's childhood tale made the added layer of fortification a more present concern in my mind. There was little I could do to mitigate such a threat now, yet if its walls proved as thick and durable as Septem's famed outer stone walls had been described, the casualties of such an effort would prove crippling, if not disastrous.

We reserved time for a final gathering to ensure all understood their roles in the challenge ahead. While Ascum would time his fleet to blockade Septem a day after our scheduled arrival, my men would approach from the southeast. With Perenus absent, I gave Baduarius the right of leading my vanguard opposite Septem's main gate, with Xerxes and his Vandals forming separate detachments to separate the city's northernmost gate. Relying upon a small degree of fortune and appropriate timing by Ascum and the dromons, it was a simple strategy, one that Godilas and Justin would have both approved of and appreciated.

Yet its simplicity was its blessing as well as its curse. Our men had to guard only a few hundred paces of land-facing walls, with the vast majority of Septem's winding peninsula jutting into the sea. Liberius had noted that stone seawalls had been erected to guard Septem's deep harbor along its northern edge, its battlements the height of three grown men standing on one another's shoulders. The walls were broken only by an iron-rimmed gateway that operated on a pulley system to allow even the broadest warships of the old Carthaginian era safe passage. Though we Romans held unquestioned dominance of the seas thousands of miles from Constantinople, our dromons had a daunting task to dissuade would-be supply runners and draw attention from the city's warriors away from the land-facing walls.

"Ascum will find a way to outfox our enemies," Baduarius promised. "I've never known someone more devious. He complains like a squealing pig, but he understands how to instill fear in armed men."

I grunted in interest. "How?"

"Pain," Baduarius replied. "Even mediocre warriors do not fear death when they're protecting their friends. But all men fear pain that comes from the unknown and the absurd. There's a reason why that Alani bastard has led Belisarius' ballistae for so long, when he could have risen to command armies. Whether by fire or by massive steel bolts, I've yet to meet an enemy that does not fear Ascum's clanking machines, and with fear comes the opportunity for defeat."

I shivered, mouthing a silent prayer that our trials ahead would be simple, and not require Ascum's dark art of Roman siege engines. Baduarius had the right of it, for even I dreaded the thought of facing such monstrous bolts in battle. Few retained the knowledge of building and maintaining the complicated instruments, and no barbarian tribe that I had yet encountered possessed the raw ingenuity to use gusts of wind and the shape of the soil to guide his missiles as Ascum and his fellows did.

With luck, Indulf and Perenus would peacefully liberate their various targets, while Thurimuth and Sindual would plant Justinian's flag along the northern Pillar with nary an angry word spent by Theudis' men. As we had progressed so close to our target with no resistance, I allowed a heartbeat of belief that such futures may yet hold truth, and that we would all leave this land alive and whole.

I was wrong. God help me, but even then, I was still a fool who believed that God's favor would protect me from the worst tragedies that the world's evil could muster. I was wrong, and others would pay the debt of my imprudence.

THE SIEGE OF SEPTEM

Rosamund woke me well before dawn, her slim fingers brushing firmly against my arm and shoulder. Grunting acknowledgment, I rose to a seated position, slowly gaining awareness of the wool tent that had been my evening's quarters. As Rosamund procured a clay cup of water, I felt my back groan with stiffness, the muscles slow to expand and contract after an evening spent on the hard Mauretanian ground. Though I was entitled to all the comforts of a Roman expeditionary commander, I shrugged off such niceties, insisting that our encampment would be both temporary and insignificant. Though our impending march proved my claim correct, I cursed inwardly at not accepting the wooden cot and straw mat that Cephalas offered to make available, and twisted my arms to rub at the knots in hard-to-reach places.

"Is he dressed?" Uliaris called, his voice muffled by the tent's flaps.

"Still useless!" Rosamund snickered. "Want to come in and help me?"

"Not in the slightest!" Uliaris called back, remaining outside the tent.

"Doesn't matter," I answered, drawing on trousers and a coarse shirt. "I doubt I have anything you haven't seen before."

"There's quite a bit I haven't seen, Lord." Uliaris chuckled. "And quite a bit that I'd rather not see, God willing."

To my surprise and pleasure, Uliaris' time in Mauretania Tingitana had been one of general sobriety and seriousness. Though the inability to join Thurimuth had visibly displeased him, Uliaris had taken to his responsibilities as one of my bodyguards with a grave sense of duty that had been absent since Tricamarum. Even Sembrouthes had grown grudgingly accepting of the Frank's assistance in substituting for one of the dozen Aksumites who trailed my position by no more than ten paces at all times. Still, I could tell the Aksumite commander would never grow entirely comfortable with the borrowed manpower.

"Even sober, Uliaris is still Belisarius' man," Sembrouthes had warned the day prior. "His loyalties will never be fully yours."

I waved him off. "Then we have little to fear. Besides, Uliaris is one of the most skilled and cunning soldiers we have."

On that morning of our impending arrival at Septem, once I had dressed, Uliaris opened the flaps to my tent, bringing a burning torch to illuminate the interior. Though its small embers would not leave as visible a signal as a cookfire, Uliaris had still taken precautions to light it only when I had awoken. Nodding as my eyes adjusted to the light, I caught a glimpse of the man's francisca, a weapon that had been missing since John's death, as it caught the torch's beams and gleamed.

"Ready, Lord?" Uliaris asked.

"Yes," I answered, "but let the officers know that I want the men ready to don armor once we are a mile's distance from Septem's outer walls."

With a crisp salute, Uliaris moved to execute his duties. Rosamund returned soon thereafter. Trailed by Cephalas, who distributed weapons to nearby tents that had been honed overnight by our blacksmith, Rosamund slipped into the tent and easily navigated to my side despite the dim interior. Offering a small tray of our hardened bread and dried fruit, Rosamund sat beside me and rested her head upon my shoulder as we chewed at the meager meal.

"Today is the battle?" she murmured in Heruli.

"Perhaps, perhaps not," I answered. "But we will reach Septem, either way. With luck, we'll seize the fortress without a fight."

"The Pillars of Herakles… a place of raw power," Rosamund murmured. "The footsteps of a god have a lingering memory of magic, but few have the ability to harness such force. This is a place where only the mighty can reign, and the impure will find only sorrow."

I grunted, again discomfited with her professions of faith yet reluctant to show any distaste. "And will Herakles find us wanting? Perhaps we should turn back now."

"Even if we could turn back, I'd die if I didn't get to see Mount Abyla," Cephalas remarked. "As a boy, I loved tales of Herakles. If this was his farthest trek west, I want to be able to say I witnessed it myself."

Rosamund laughed softly, her long white hair rubbing against the burly cloth atop my shoulder as her head bobbed ever so slightly. "You will not be harmed here, Varus. I will make sure of that. But whether you would wish to leave of your own will is a different matter altogether."

Finishing her meal, Rosamund departed to gather men to disassemble my tent and spread word of our looming departure. Like the others of my column, I conferred my armor, spear, and shield to the care of others minding our oxcarts, but insisted upon retaining the sword and dagger that had been priceless gifts from mentors long dead. Of the four great gifts offered to me, only the cross had a previous owner still living, and now its bronze clinked softly against the golden dragon that Mariya had given me before I had ventured north against the Avars.

In a steady and well-worn rhythm, all evidence of our camp was neatly packed and readied for the march ahead. Our column left behind only trampled ground that had been beaten by thousands of hobnailed footsteps, the only sign that a group had passed through this area. Thanks to the absence of any cookfires or deep latrine trenches that had been refilled with layers of shoveled earth, few could accurately guess how many had passed by, what allegiance such men held, or which direction they intended to follow. It was with a welcome note of confidence as we trailed along the sandblasted stones of the centuries-old Roman road, the winter sun cresting just above the eastern horizon as we snaked toward Septem and the Pillars of Herakles.

Flanked by my Aksumite guardsmen, I took my place just behind the vanguard and alongside the various banners that accompanied our journey. It was a position in the column that left me uneasy, yielding a curious sensation of wrongness as I was separated from spearmen and riders that fell under my direct instruction. Thinking of Belisarius, I chuckled under my breath. Uliaris and Sembrouthes turned their heads curiously.

"I'm wondering whether Belisarius enjoyed the commander's post within the column," I mused. "It is a role I will have to gain greater familiarity with."

Uliaris nodded. "Belisarius never complained, but I could tell that he would rather be with the common soldiers. He always seemed so melancholy until you other officers came to ride alongside him."

To some small degree, I understood Belisarius' loneliness. I held many advantages that he did not enjoy, for he had been hoisted to senior command in the early years of manhood. Until recently, I held the privilege of joining the camaraderie of the common spearmen, sharing in their travails and celebrating in their successes. When I joined the army, I longed for opportunities to rise and earn the hope and respect placed within me by Justin and Liberius. Now, as a leader of thousands, I would have happily traded the aloof existence of a senior commander for the happy mischief as a dekarchos and leader of ten.

Such dispiritedness was blessedly improved as Liberius joined our band, brushing off a thin layer of dust that formed along his blackened robes. He was followed soon thereafter by Xerxes and Gunderic, the immaculately attired Persian a solemn contrast to the thickly bearded, wine-soaked Vandal giant.

"Well, I officially don't understand how you Romans live," Gunderic complained. "A few days into a journey and I'm already footsore and shitting pellets. Why would you willingly march all day, drink weak wine, and eat the same food as rabbits?"

"Because it is how to instill discipline and good soldiering," I answered dutifully.

"Not even any women!" Gunderic exclaimed, his wicked gaze suddenly turning deferential as he met Rosamund's glare. "With present company excepted, of course. I'd never despoil your honor, kind lady."

"Like you could," Rosamund scoffed. "I've heard others tell what little you are capable of even when you're not stinking drunk, and how… inadequate the experience is."

At that, Uliaris and Sembrouthes hooted in unison, and the normally somber Xerxes flashed a grin. Even I failed to stifle a snicker as I looked toward Gunderic, though I momentarily worried that an assault on the Vandal warlord's masculinity might be too much to bear.

It was not so. Gunderic roared in laughter. Eyes watering, he clapped his hands together in three sharp bursts, his body shaking and nearly requiring a respite from the march as he repeated Rosamund's crude retort to himself. The noise drew the attention of Baduarius, who trotted enthusiastically to our minuscule gathering with a hopeful look.

"Did I miss something good?" Baduarius asked.

"Another cock joke," Liberius answered, sighing. "Something about Gunderic's relative anatomical modesty, which I am to understand is humorous given his otherwise beastly body. Not exactly the pinnacle of culture, but alas, you lot are all that is available to me."

"A cock joke!" Gunderic boomed, laughing to the brink of tears. "You hear the old man?"

Fifty Vandal voices joined the mirth, devolving into a guttural chant. Loudest among them, however, was Rosamund, echoing Gunderic's inane laughter alongside so many other Vandal warriors. "Cock joke! Cock joke! Cock joke!"

I admit, I chuckled, and a good deal. I am a warrior, not a saint. And, deprived of the comforts of family and home, it is little wonder that boorish japes about genitalia soon grow as common amongst spearmen as blades of grass on the Thracian hills.

Liberius caught my appreciation for Gunderic's chant and clicked his tongue against his teeth. "It was Socrates who chastised the manners of his younger generation." He sighed. "But if the man were alive today, I think he might have given up philosophy entirely."

I grinned. "Socrates was a hoplite during the Peloponnesian War. He probably originated many of the cock jokes we celebrate today."

Liberius flailed his hands, exasperated. "Why did I ever teach you history?"

I regret to say that his halfhearted remonstrations had no inhibiting effect upon my officers' crass humor. Not that I did much myself to discourage it, for it felt surprisingly refreshing to share pointless jokes and temporarily forget the slaughter that may yet befall us at any moment. I chuckled as Baduarius and Gunderic spurred ever more lascivious and brutish mirth that made even Rosamund blush. Liberius may have rolled his eyes as he caught a glimpse of my tolerance of it all, but he offered no more remonstrations, and we marched with the column along the dust-strewn coastal road to Septem.

That respite did not last long. Morning had not yet surrendered to midday when our progress came to a halt. Our good mood, spurred by a mixture of anxiety over encountering our enemies and hope that Septem would be easily passed into the Empire's control, evaporated into grim reality. The tidings appeared first as no more than thin pillars of dust billowing from the north.

Within moments, a Vandal sentry rushed to the gathered officers, hailing Gunderic from afar. Though his face was shrouded in a brass-ridged helmet with dented iron cheekpieces, as he came closer into view, I recognized the man as Wisimar. Gunderic summoned him yet closer, and I nodded to Uliaris and Sembrouthes to allow the interloper to pass into my presence.

Wisimar's eyes sparkled with a crude delight that I had come to understand as a common Vandal reaction to uncertainty and the looming threat of violence. "Two riders approaching, Lord," he hissed, pointing to the front of the column.

I nodded, instructing the other officers to return to their positions before leading my own guardsmen toward the column's spearhead. Gunderic's and Baduarius' shouts brought the column to a halt, allowing me to easily trot to the foremost lines of the vanguard. Wisimar followed closely behind, pointing to the thin pillar of dust that approached along the stone road to Septem.

Frowning, I turned to Uliaris. "I doubt this is an enemy force, but send word for each banda to take up their weapons, if they have not done so already. Be prepared to form lines and fight along the road."

Uliaris' eyes widened, yet he remained silent as he saluted and departed by guardsmen to deliver the order. Cacophony rose from the ranks as iron and wood clattered together, with men donning their ringmail and weapons distributed across the bandae. Ignoring the familiar sounds of battle preparation, I squinted upon twin figures slipping across the horizon that grew larger with each breath I drew.

"Horsemen," Sembrouthes growled.

I agreed. "Ours, most likely, but have a half dozen bowmen ready to strike them down if not."

Wisimar's Vandals tensed as they took two paces forward and formed a wall, the iron rims of their shields overlapping tight enough to discourage even the most experienced rider from assaulting our position. The Vandal dekarchos growled commands to keep silent, allowing us to better focus on the interlopers ahead.

We needn't have worried, for as the twin horsemen came into view, one bore a diminutive ouroboros banner that flapped in the wind. Soon thereafter, I discerned the face of Fulcaris, his helmet dangling unused from his saddle and long black hair streaming in the wind. I gave an order to stand down, curious to hear groans of disappointment from the Vandals around me. Galloping hard, Fulcaris raised an arm in salute as he cleared the final hundred paces, slowing to a halt as Wisimar's Vandals allowed Fulcaris and his Herulian companion to pass through the lines.

I returned Fulcaris' welcome before turning to Wisimar. "Bring up a waterskin, and summon a courier. Ask Xerxes and Liberius to attend me."

Wisimar puffed his chest and saluted before rushing to fulfill my commands. In the interim, Fulcaris and his partner dismounted, brushing away the thick layers of dust and grime that covered their mail and clothing. Their horses, frothy spittle lining their mouths and clearly spent from hard riding, snorted with disapproval, as no water had yet been made available for their consumption. I afforded the two scouts a moment to rest, waiting for Xerxes and Liberius before receiving a report of the road ahead. Once both men arrived, Fulcaris sucked deep breaths to regain his composure, sipping at a waterskin as he told of all that was seen along the coastline.

"I saw Septem, and Mount Abyla," Fulcaris began. "You'll be there by midday, if you march hard enough. But I would tread carefully."

Xerxes' gaze narrowed. "What did you see, precisely?"

"The city's gates are shut, and its towers fly no banners," Fulcaris rasped, pausing to drink from his waterskin again. "But I could see movement. Someone on the inside of Septem was tracking me, just the same as I was scouting them."

My heart sank at such ill fortune, but I was not yet willing to surrender my lingering hope for a bloodless victory. Even then, I knew perilously little of my enemy, yet per Fulcaris' reports, one destiny awaited me—my judgment as a leader would be put to the test. Inwardly, the thought turned my legs to glass, while outwardly I forced a stony expression and sureness of gait. I would not allow others to see my fear, for at least at the time, I believed that staunch impassiveness was as necessary of a successful commander as the meticulous planning that details every segment of a march or a battle.

Alas, I was naïve, and I pray forgiveness for those who suffered from my inexperience.

I ordered Wisimar to bring Gunderic to our gathering, and the towering Vandal sprinted forward, despite being covered in thick iron scales better suited for a Roman horseman. Gunderic wore such armor well, however, never complaining of the weight that would have suffocated a lesser-bodied spearman after the mildest of maneuvers.

I relayed Fulcaris' information, ending with a question that I both predicted yet dreaded the answer to. "Is there any reason that the Vandals would lower their banners? Some trick, perhaps?"

Gunderic smirked. "Never. We need no tricks to defeat our enemies, and would never willingly cede control over what is ours."

"We Romans have learned this all too recently," Liberius interjected. "So we must assume that the Vandal garrison is dead, or has joined with the Mauri or the Visigoths."

"Sensible," I agreed. "Gunderic, you are absolutely certain that Gelimer sent no orders to the Vandal garrison at Septem, or struck an alliance with Theudis before surrendering to Belisarius?"

Gunderic rolled his eyes, visibly irritated at being asked a question that had been thrust upon the former Vandal lords in the months since Tricamarum. Despite his warlike and scarred appearance, Gunderic also appeared offended by the intent of my question, violating the Vandal's curious sense of honesty and honor that all their warriors lived by.

"In my culture, it is rude to ask a person the same question multiple times," Gunderic said pointedly. "Gelimer and I have told you all that we know. An ambassador was sent to Gades, but no orders were sent to Septem. And the embassy was rebuffed by Theudis, who has no love for the Vandals."

"It makes no difference at this point," Liberius added. "In one form or another, the Vandal garrison no longer flies their banners. The most logical conclusion is to assume that the Visigoths control the city."

"Agreed," I concluded. "Send an advance cohort to separate the city from its outer roads. Others will signal Ascum and our dromons of our imminent arrival to Septem. Do not initiate violence unless attacked first, and be vigilant for any sign of Theudis or his warlords."

I shot a glance at Liberius, who, in his capacity as Justinian's Imperial legate, nodded assent. The officers present saluted, and only Fulcaris raised a lingering concern. Even after gulping at his waterskin, the Herulian officer's voice crackled from hard riding across Tingitana's sand-strewn hills.

"Varus, you should know Perenus and Indulf separated within a few hours into their march westward. It was a logical maneuver—the Herulians are taking Volubilis and Indulf's Goths are marching west. With your permission, I would ride out to inform them both that our army may be heading for a siege."

"Separated?" I asked as Fulcaris swallowed yet more water. A lump formed in my throat, accompanied by an urge to unsheathe my dragon-hilted sword and bury its steel into the guts of an enemy. Life is often cruel and never fair, yet in my first senior command, what ate at me was a constant irritation that progress was fleeting, with ill tidings waiting just beyond every summited hill or forded stream. In all likelihood, Fulcaris' latest revelation would bear little consequence as far as my overall designs for the province, but my officers had defied me all the same. They had disobeyed an order to keep their diminutive forces together, thereby making each band easier prey for Gothic hunters. Worse, Perenus knew better than to defy an order in enemy country, especially when leaving his commander unawares.

Perhaps there was some explanation. "Were they attacked?" I asked, clenching my fist to retain control of myself in front of my spearman.

"Not attacked, but beyond that I could not tell you for sure," Fulcaris responded. "I rode at a distance while they walked. Yet it seemed clear that the Ostrogoths and the Heruli had little desire for friendship, and that Indulf led his men toward Tingis."

I nodded, inwardly cursing Indulf's stubborn intransigence, but mostly, again, resentful that Perenus would add complication into an already uncertain circumstance. "You have ridden hard, and should gather what rest you can with my men," I told Fulcaris. "Make sure you and your mount are ready in the next day."

Whether sensing my frustration or awaiting my instruction, Liberius and my retinue stared silently on as I dismissed the outrider. Scouts had already been ordered to their intended targets as my centurions were commanded to disperse arms and armor while keeping greater attentiveness over their charges, with all men instructed to maintain readiness for any sign of assault. Yet no others were willing to speak the next order that would set our march onto the first steps to a siege—a grim duty that rested solely upon my shoulders. Only one man dared to break the silence of the moment, his low tones muffled by the whisking of the breeze and the thrumming of distant waves along the African shore.

"Varus? What are your final orders?" Liberius prodded, his usual cajoling playfulness gone.

"Forward," I grunted. "To Septem, at double pace."

A clipped roar emanated from my men as they were given the order to march. Hobnailed boots again slapped against cobblestones, the cacophony bolstered by the deep bass of the few grinding wagons that formed our column's rear. By this point, I understood that my men, much more accustomed to traversing long distances on horseback, were anxious and footsore. The chill air of the Mauretanian winter meant there was little risk of heat exhaustion, but the chill that occasionally bit at exposed faces and hands sapped vitality and left many in a mild stupor all the same. Yet we'd come too far to turn back, and we had no other choice than to complete the mission that Belisarius had entrusted to all of us.

As the column continued, most in my retinue returned to their original positions in the ranks, leaving a void of mirth or conversation as men focused upon the shrinking road ahead, upon yet another battle that doubtless awaited us. Until this moment, our pace had been leisurely; now what was a smart stroll quickened to nearly a trot. The exertion brought a note of worry to my mind as I considered how Liberius would weather the march, yet my old teacher merely brushed away my glances of concern and leaned lightly upon an age-beaten walking stick as he kept pace. The only measure of happiness came in a weak smile from Rosamund, the same look that she had offered when I joined Belisarius' army against the Avars. She, too, slipped farther down the line, falling in stride with Cephalas and awaiting any further requests from me. None would come, for there was nothing that she, or indeed anyone, could do to alleviate my fears.

Our travails were not extensive. Well before winter's midday zenith, our vanguard reported sightings of Septem's walls, and indeed, that vast stone curtain became more visible to all with each weary step. As Fulcaris had reported, no banners sailed above the ramparts, yet tiny figures seem to bob between narrow windows of the fighting platforms set in the walls, a mainstay of all major Roman fortresses that had ultimately been unsuccessful in holding back the tide of darkness. Our onlookers did not identify themselves, yet took few precautions to disguise their presence as our column drew into formation just a few hundred paces from the city's main gate.

Beyond Septem's walls, Mount Abyla towered above the city's defenses, its rounded top crowned with the interior walled citadel that Liberius and Fulcaris warned of. The southern Pillar jutted out into the sparkling, frigid sea, seeming to reach across the narrow channel of water that separated Mauretania from Hispania and all of Europa beyond. As with much of our march along the African coastline, brisk winds cut in the direction of the walls, sending our own Imperial banners flapping violently against their leather and brass constraints. The clinking of metal and wood behind me dwindled, supplanted by nervous muttering, as the Roman shield wall formed, awaiting any order from their commander or any sign of enmity from the fabled fortress that had once been a jewel of the Empire's African provinces.

Now, centuries after its initial construction, Septem still stood along the Mauretanian coastline, surrounded on three sides by crashing waves and unpredictable currents. Though only one land route remained available to our spearmen, those same few land-facing gates were also the only easy escape for Septem's inhabitants should they flee westward to Tingis. True, Septem's vast harbor provided easy access to the sea, with its thick stone and palisade seawalls protecting against vandalism or burning by an enemy warship; however, we could spot few ships of any size along the coastline, and I had full confidence that, within another day's time, my own fleet under Ascum would bottle our enemy in a trap of their own making.

Now I waited, tying the leather straps of my helmet securely underneath my chin and feeling for the reassuring lump of the bronze cross and Mariya's dragon at my throat. Though I had planned for many days for this moment, I was not confident of what I should do now that it had arrived. I had assumed, perhaps, that whoever occupied Septem's battlements would make themselves known and allow me to react accordingly. Yet no warrior obliged my secret request. The silhouettes of more bodies appeared along those vast stone walls abraded harshly by the salt air, only standing in silence, mirroring our position and making no motion to gather their weapons.

Fighting against a burning sensation of dread, I took a step forward. Uliaris and Sembrouthes both hoisted their shields and spears and moved wordlessly to guard my flanks, stopping only when I shook my head.

"Stay here for now," I said.

"I would reconsider if I were you," Sembrouthes whispered. "We do not understand who we face, and I doubt that they would hesitate to send an arrow into the throat of an enemy Roman commander."

"This is possible," I responded, selecting my words carefully to give the false impression that I did not fear such an outcome. "But if they are so foolish as to do such a thing, Belisarius will swarm this place with the entire army, sparing no warrior who may have taken part."

Sembrouthes' eyes narrowed. "Perhaps," he muttered, speaking so softly that only Uliaris and I could hear. "But you would still be dead."

I planted an additional boot forward, and then another, eventually tracing forty paces toward a wall that cast shadows even in the barest angle of the sun. The eyes of my would-be adversaries remained distant but grew discernible, all watching my approach with nary a shift in posture or resistance. The persistent wind caught my cloak and brushed its fur-lined length into a bunch behind my left leg, forcing me to straighten the material lest I trip and embarrass myself before my men. At face value, such a stumble would be inconsequential, but as a sign of our fortunes, a grave omen. Even Christian soldiers are ever superstitious, analyzing each morning or activity for moments of the day to come, and the pagans, of which there remained many within the foederati and from recruits of Justinian's outlying provinces, would spit and gaze for their own signs of evil, all muttering silent prayers that chance would remain with them once more on this day.

Upon reaching a distance where I knew Septem's sentries would clearly hear my call, I planted the butt of my spear into the ground and twisted the loops of my shield around my back so that my left arm was free. Spitting throatily on the Mauretanian dust, I raised my chin in defiance and shouted the mandate that had brought me to this far edge of the world.

"Men of Septem!" I yelled.

Nausea bubbled in my gut, and the urge to heave out my stomach surged. I suppressed it; nevertheless, I had to pause to collect my voice, my throat now constricted and breath disrupted. After a few heartbeats, I continued, clenching my fingers into a painfully tight fist as I forced my body to speak a public address—the first I had given within any independent command.

"In the name of the Emperor Justinian, his legate Liberius, and the magister militum of the Emperor's armies Belisarius…"

I paused again, sour bile lacing the back of my throat. Whoever watched us from Septem had not yet acknowledged our arrival, yet doubtless they listened to my words. God, if only I could have hit someone at that moment, the nest of knots in my gut might have unwound. Again, I held back the urge to vomit, and kept my eyes fixed upon the city's gate.

"I, Tribune Varus of the Heruli, command you to open your gates and cede to the Emperor's will."

There was no response. One or two of the figures atop the walls slipped from view, yet otherwise my command died unanswered on the periodic gusts of wind. Standing straight, I waited several more heartbeats, forcing my body still and my nervous limbs from betraying fears of what might come next. With only continued silence greeting me, in the eyes of hundreds fixed upon my figure, I roared my demands once more.

"People of Septem! You have been liberated by the army of Flavius Belisarius, who has destroyed the Vandal armies and returned the African provinces to Imperial possession. You have been liberated! Open your gates and allow our forces safe passage through your walls. You have my oath that no harm will come to any soul or piece of property in return for this peaceful end."

Once more, I detected movement along the periphery of Septem's stone ramparts, yet no voice called out to answer my own. Even in the cold, my skin felt as if it would burn away from such awkwardness and disrespect, my authority ignored as I stood before my arrayed spearmen. All I could do was take slow deliberate breaths, my gloved fist grinding against the hewn ash of my spear shaft. I waited longer, then far longer, wondering whether the city's residents within debated the appropriate response, weighing the risks of trusting a foreign army against the considerable disruption of having hundreds of bored soldiers gathered neatly along each of the city's exits. My throat clenched as if from some illness, yet I managed to stand motionless, not moving even to untangle the folds of my cloak that still caught along an occasional burst of air. Soon enough, however, I gathered my voice, and repeated my entreaty that would end this campaign in blessed peace.

This time, a response: My words were drowned out by jeers, rolling sonorously from Septem's walls. As I fixed my eyes upon the city's main gate, a thin figure loomed into clearer view, its body adorned in thick layers of dull gray ringmail. The slender soldier slid the iron skullcap from his head, revealing an unkept mane that hung a full armlength down his chest. He gestured to me, raising his voice to answer my challenge.

"You will find no friends here, Romans," the speaker roared. "Those who you expected to find are all dead, and their bodies tossed into the sea. I, Theudesgel, warlord of King Theudis, will offer you this one chance to leave Septem with your lives. Return whence you came. Learn your lesson and crawl back to Carthage, remembering that you no longer belong in this corner of the world."

As his nasal yet resounding proclamation died away, a rolling sound of thunder rose along the city's expanse. I recognized its source well enough, having heard such similar cheers of defiance along the walls of Dara, and within the earliest days of the hell-sworn Nika Riots. It was the sound of hundreds of voices all clamoring in raw hatred, their boots stomping and spear butts rattling in defiance of one who would bring death or subjugation in his wake.

For Septem had been seized by the Visigoths, with, we would soon learn, no fewer than five hundred armed warriors holding the city for Theudesgel.

This revelation should not have been surprising, especially given the nature of Fulcaris' warning. Even so, I found myself astoundingly ill at ease as the cheers of strength and hatred rose to soaring heights. Still, I knew to do nothing to provoke further reaction, and even lifted my free hand in a closed fist to signal my own forces that they should remain disciplined and silent.

After a time, the cheering dwindled to the point where I felt confident that my reply would be heard over the din. I took two steps forward, my gaze unmoving as I focused on the sickly thin outline of Theudesgel's form.

"The Visigoths have no claim to Septem," I called out, "nor do they have any interest in the ruins of Mauretania Tingitana. Moreover, a true lord of men would come look a man in the eye to speak such threats, yet you remain safely behind those high stone walls. I do not wish for bloodshed, but neither am I prepared to return to my lord and master without this city in the Emperor's control."

Theudesgel did not immediately respond. Instead, he laughed, a strange, high-pitched squeal at odds with the rumbling voice of his threats. Clapping his hands, he leaned forward from the parapet, his gangly outline seeming even larger when silhouetted against the cloud-strewn sky.

"This is no dance, Roman, and I will not allow your honeyed tongue to find its way into my arse. No, as King Theudis commands, your choice is simple: leave or die. There is no more need for talking."

As he concluded, Theudesgel swiftly raised an arm and brought his fist down with a violent jerk. A single arrow surged from atop the walls, its iron tip gleaming in the winter sun as it sailed high into the air. I had only enough time to grab my shield from my back and raise its protective bulwark above my head. That lone arrow punctured a finger length through its wooden panels and just barely above my forearm. A rush of jeers again fluttered from the city, met this time by a swirling hiss of disapproval from the spearmen behind me. Above them all, I heard Baduarius, spitting indignation at the insults levied at his commander.

"I'll skewer you cock-eaters alive!" he screamed.

"Take this as an omen," Theudesgel yelled back. "Leave now, while you still are able to walk freely."

Snarling, I spat at Theudesgel's offer, watching with ire coursing through me as the enemy warlord slipped back behind Septem's thick stones. My enemy gone, I turned my back on him and all the Visigoths, forcing myself to remain calm to show my men that I was unafraid, that I had no concern that a second arrow might succeed where its brother did not.

War is a constant display of lies and illusion, with the victor better able to mask an unappealing truth in the trappings of strength and superiority. I felt plenty of fear outside the gates of Septem—a curious thing, given all that I had suffered up to this point. Long before, Godilas had warned that all warriors, whether after one battle or a hundred, would at some point decay into a shivering mess that saw only death in every situation. I could not know whether I had reached such a jaded point; yet if I had, then I would stay intent, insistent, so that those serving beneath me would not know.

As I returned to my lines, many of my officers were visibly angry, while Sembrouthes and Uliaris retained a sense of tension that was clearly tinged with relief. Liberius alone appeared motionless and unsurprised, merely nodding to me as he had done so many times when I was a young slave child under his tutelage. Several senior officers shuffled close by, yet in truth I still had no clear vision of how our current impasse may be overcome.

"Well, at least they don't have ballistae," Sembrouthes said.

Gunderic grunted, and he, too, showed a fleeting glance of relief. "How can you be sure?"

"Because if they did, our commander would have been skewered in half by the first bolt that they could manage to launch," Sembrouthes answered.

"Aye," Uliaris agreed. "The Visigoths are not known for their intelligence or creativity. When I fought with the Franks, they rarely mustered even a cavalry, let alone siege machines."

I raised a hand, commanding silence, as I considered the options available to our forces. Though the air was still cool, the clouds had drifted apart, and the peeking sun offered a warm embrace that licked at my exposed cheeks, extinguishing some of the bite that the recurring coastal winds flushed toward the African interior. As the men looked to me for guidance, I wished that Belisarius were here to share my burden, knowing that he—along with John, God rest his soul—would have devised some stratagem to overcome even this most dire of predicaments. Despite the scouts I had sent along the coastal roads of Tingitana, I had little true notion of the forces available to Theudesgel, or whether any of Theudis' other warlords prowled broader Mauretania. Turning to Liberius, I sought the legate's wisdom in the matter, careful not to betray a creeping doubt within my gut.

"We know not whether the Visigoths can draw a bow or hurl a spear behind Septem's walls," I reasoned. "Yet we cannot leave the city untaken, especially its harbor. What would you do—assault, siege, or call for reinforcements?"

Liberius sighed, stroking his unkempt gray beard with a weathered hand. "It is not I who would do the dying, Varus. But if I were lord of war, I would understand that one does not launch an assault on a well-fortified position flippantly, yet neither does one allow the besieged to remain in comfort. If our dromons will arrive this evening or by the morrow, they will be able to pen in any ships at the Visigoths may have available, and launch bolts and stones from the siege engines on their decks. As you say, we have little choice in the long run, for if we leave here without control of the city, all of Africa will soon be overrun by Theudis' men."

"Liberius has the right of it, but I would not overly fear Theudesgel's numbers," Xerxes added. "If he came close to matching our own, there is no chance that he would willingly allow us to reach Septem's walls uncontested. We cannot drag this out for long, to be sure, but there is no reason to rush a conflict this day. Dig deep trenches, and wait for Ascum to cut the city off from any of the few sea lanes that the Visigoths may have been able to cobble together."

Such undramatic practicality played poorly with Gunderic and Baduarius. The Vandal leader insisted that his few hundred warriors would pry the Visigoths from their perch over the course of an afternoon, while Baduarius begged for the chance to repay Theudesgel's feeble attack on my person with the grotesque spectacle of blood.

"It's bad manners, it is," Baduarius insisted, his bearded face flushed red while his eyes sparkled with mischief. "If we all go around thumping leaders that we don't like, battle might become an uncivilized place to be."

I waved aside such concerns as nothing more than prideful anger, unwilling as I was to leave my army in unnecessary jeopardy when, indeed, the arrival of our dromons and ballistae would soon tip the balance of battle in our favor.

Yet something lingered at the fringes of my mind, a shapeless phantom I could have sworn I had meant never to forget—save that I could not recall what it was. As I thought again of Belisarius, realization struck: a spy. I remembered Belisarius' warning that it was such a person who had provided Theudis with the information that allowed him to react so impossibly swiftly to Gelimer's downfall at Tricamarum. And as I did, an unvoiced concern took root within me, a fear that a spy sympathetic to Visigothic goals might have planted himself somewhere amongst my soldiers.

Of course, as I considered such fears, it was Liberius' chiding that would disrupt my consternation.

"I wonder, but did any of you notice the exact words that Theudesgel used?" Liberius asked, his erstwhile impassivity given back over to his normal mischief.

"Lord?" I replied, wracking my memory for that brief exchange yet finding nothing of note.

Liberius rolled his eyes. "If you can recall, that ugly skeleton invoked *King* Theudis. Yet the Visigothic throne—so far as we know, anyway—is currently occupied by Theodoric's grandson Amalaric. Do you find such language to be odd or simply careless?"

"You mean—you're suggesting that they..." I was babbling. "That... murder?"

"It would not surprise me." This from Gunderic, who it seemed had been listening in. "As I said before, the Vandals and the Visigoths do not abide by weak children, and especially not weak kings. There is nothing worse in this life than a weak king, especially one who is a mere child. I doubt the Visigoth chieftains needed much convincing of Theudis' right to rule."

"Regicide is ugly business," Liberius remarked. "But I agree this summation of events is highly likely. And based upon our experience in Carthage, we should assume that this Theudesgel already knows everything of our forces."

Gunderic shrugged. "It wouldn't be hard to ferry a message along the coastline. Mauretania is loosely peopled and little governed. A man could slip away with little notice here."

At that moment, I had little understanding of how Theudis' advancement to the Visigothic monarchy would affect my own predicament. Nor was I particularly surprised to hear of the death of a barbarian child-king: Amalaric was not the first such young sovereign to be slain, and would certainly not be the last. Gunderic's words, despite their evil undertone, were correct—weak kings always led to the ruin of their peoples, and few made weaker kings than young children. Without the guiding influence of civilization, murder was not just an expediency, but even encouraged when its results conferred stronger leadership.

Nor, indeed, can I say that Theudis was a particularly incompetent ruler. As Amalaric's regent, Theudis governed well for a decade, keeping the vast and expanding Frankish kingdom from sweeping into Hispania and consolidating Visigothic power around the old Roman fortresses and cities. More, he had a fearsome reputation in battle, one that few of even those most ferocious Visigoths could claim. Indeed, from what smatterings of intelligence I had received of this new Visigothic king, I had little reason to doubt Gunderic's claims, and between that and Liberius' suspicions, I fully believed that Theudis had violently removed what few restrictions had stood in the way of his rise to power.

Still, all I truly knew was that such a shift in power would not be to the Empire's, nor Belisarius', advantage, especially as Justinian's African provinces remained largely undefended and chaotic in the immediate aftermath of the Vandal War.

I had to decide on a course of action. "Distribute shovels to the men and dig two concentric trenches around the perimeter of the city. If Theudesgel attacks, we will form lines and hold him. If he lacks the numbers to challenge us, however, and waits behind his walls, then we will await Ascum's arrival before mounting an assault. Regardless, once night falls, Fulcaris" —I gestured for him—"will ride out to Perenus and the Heruli, and command them to return here for reinforcement."

"And what of Indulf?" Fulcaris asked. "Who will ride to him?"

"I only have two mounted scouts," I explained, "and can send only one. Perenus' men are better trained in Roman warfare. But as soon as we are able, we will send messengers to the Ostrogothic foederati as well."

There was no further debate. Liberius nodded his assent, and orders were distributed to my centurions to carve out the crude earthen fortifications that would sever the land routes between Septem and any other Mauretanian town. To facilitate the work, I did allow most men to drop their weapons and armor in favor of the simple iron spade, although a full banda remained armed, in formation, and alert for the first sign of any sally from Septem's gates.

It was soon apparent that such an attack would not come, allowing me a silent prayer of thanks that my enemy likely had but a few men under his command. My assumptions were partially confirmed by the sparse figures that moved about Septem's battlements, raining occasional jeers and accusations of cowardice upon our soldiers. Aside from Theudesgel's previous proclamation, the Latin spoken by the Visigoths was rough to the point of incomprehensibility, with most eventually resorting to barking anger in their native Gothic tongue. I occasionally asked Baduarius the meaning of one such word or another, but he would merely shake his head and insist that we would rather not know.

Of the few practices that remained from the old legions of Marius or Caesar, the system of trenches that my men etched into the earth was one that Roman military commanders from decades, even centuries past would easily recognize. Dug down to the full height of a man, the defensive perimeter was engineered not only to dissuade would-be attackers, but also to provide staging posts for Roman spearmen to launch attacks of their own. Behind each trench, mounds of loosened clay and stone formed crude earthworks, and it was from behind these barriers that our archers or spear throwers could defend the front ranks. Such makeshift engineering could not replace the sheer advantage that thick stone walls could provide, but as our expedition's toil excavated its twin arcs around Septem, I could not help but grow more confident in our position.

Such cautious optimism was further bolstered by the continued Visigothic willingness to simply watch our labors, volleying nothing our way save the occasional insult. It was unusual: The siege of a city is by far the most uncertain and brutal of all forms of human violence, and I know of no serious military commander who would willingly allow himself to fall into such a cursed position. Ergo, given our progress, I could only assume that two scenarios were both possible. First, that Theudesgel lacked the men to even attempt halting our progress, and second, the Visigoths had other detachments in the towns and cities along the Mauretanian coast. Though I had no way of knowing for sure, I fully believed that Theudis must have sent men to seize Tingis at the same time as he dispatched this lot to Septem—a possibility that Indulf would be able to verify soon enough.

Our lines were never left undefended, with a senior officer always on duty in case Theudesgel ever mounted a sally. Yet after our defense was formed, I allowed the men double rations and the time to rest, insisting that they recover from their march and be prepared for the carnage that all but certainly lay ahead. We would do nothing until the fleet arrived, when our full strength could be brought to bear against our still mysterious enemy.

The first signs of that happy omen did not occur until the dying hours of afternoon light, which fell swiftly in these darkest days of the year. Despite the rough surf, our dromons cut their way forward, their vast cloth sails full and straining to capture the winds. Though many banners and painted shields decorated the decks of the vessels that snaked up the African coast, it was the Imperial sigil that sailed above the rest, the Chi-Rho and purple field positioned high enough that any within Septem's urban center—or, indeed, upon Mount

Abyla's summit—would clearly discern its message: At long last, the Roman Empire had returned, small in number but heavy with that craftsmanship and skill that elevated Justinian's Empire over any barbarian tribe or savage kingship in the known world.

As those sails encircled Septem's seawalls, a diminutive raft was launched from the Roman flagship, bearing a dozen men. When the boat's keel scraped against the smooth stones and layers of sand near our coastal trenches, one officer jumped overboard into waist-deep water, shivering as he helped haul the raft onto dry land. The officer held out an arm to Ascum, steadying the crippled Alani commander as he hopped from his bench and onto the shore.

With my retinue gathered, Ascum raised his unshriven arm in greeting, spat noisily, then stretched to offer a proper welcome. I clasped his forearm in my own, voicing thanks to God that the seas had not yet taken any sailors or spearmen in Ascum's voyage to Septem.

"God had nothing to do with it." Ascum grinned. "A fair bit of wine and a willingness to hold your nose, and any sea journey can become quite bearable!"

"I doubt that," I countered. "But hopefully I may soon put your suggestion to the test. I do not intend to remain here for long."

Ascum nodded. "Seems reasonable, given winter. Horrible fighting season." He glanced over at Septem, where he found no banners and only a few signs of enemy warriors along the battlements. "I don't think that those folk share your optimism, however."

At that point, Liberius inserted himself into the conversation, recounting our newfound enemy in Theudesgel, who had ventured into Vandal Africa under the orders of the now-King Theudis. Ascum nodded at these grave tidings, interrupting only to share some more favorable information.

"Thurimuth landed safely in Baetica, and we saw no sign of habitation near Mons Calpe," he reported. "It'll likely be under our control, though I'm not sure what we gain from dividing our forces."

"When Theudis discovers an armed cohort of Romans having

landed in Hispania, he will reconsider the cost of expanding into Mauretania," Liberius declared. "Theudis has an abundance of men, but few ships, while we have more than enough maneuverability to be a nuisance in his backside."

"That may be true, but it makes little matter if we cannot take the city before us," I added, glancing meaningfully at the walls of Septem. "We need to take this place from Theudesgel in one week, or we'll be bogged down for months. And I am not willing to gamble that our men have more food out here than however much is heaped up in Septem's granaries."

With that, I led my officers toward a makeshift tent that had been erected for my personal use as the expedition's commander. As with everything in this journey, it felt at once altogether familiar yet utterly foreign. Within, its thick, coarse fabric drowned out the brisk coastal winds that seemed to grow fiercer as darkness slowly consumed the horizon. Cephalas ignited several tapers, which threw a flickering light as my commanders unfurled a crudely drawn map of the surrounding region. To Ascum, I recounted Septem's considerable defenses, including the stout seawalls that provided easy advantage for Visigothic archers to fire upon any ship that drew dangerously close to the protected harbor.

"How many bolts and stones do you have?" I asked him.

"More ballista bolts than onager stones, but more than enough of both to reduce the city to smoldering ash," Ascum grunted.

"And naphtha? Pitch?"

"I warned you before the voyage," Ascum said, chuckling darkly. "I have stuffed our ships with barrels of that devil's piss. Dangerous stuff, as I would know, and easy to ignite if not stored properly."

I nodded, saying nothing; it was Xerxes who leaned forward to add an opinion. "This is the one true advantage that you Romans have in this fight," he put in. "It would be foolish to blindly assault a city when we cannot know how many defenders lie within. But these siege engines will help us get a better understanding of our enemy's strength without exposing our men to return fire."

"How do you mean?" Gunderic asked.

Xerxes gave a tight smile. "Ignite all bolts and stones. Launch an attack at night, and see how quickly the Visigoths are able to put out the fires. If they are extinguished swiftly, then they have far more men in reserves than they would have us know. If not…"

Xerxes paused, his eyes closing for a moment as if in a silent reverie. Though he made no sound, I thought I saw his lips form the words *Ahura Mazda*, then a momentary pause before he opened his eyes again to continue.

"See here: few men, savage or civilized, are willing to see their homes and possessions burned to cinders," he said. "And while little good is ever accomplished in the darkness of night, this may be our only opportunity for attack that doesn't recklessly sacrifice every man in this camp."

"Wait," Baduarius interjected. "So we aren't attacking today?"

I shook my head, thinking it through. "Xerxes' strategy has wisdom. We can give our spearmen on land an evening to rest, while Ascum's ships launch bolts and stones over Septem's walls. But," I added, "avoid any civilian areas. Try to target wherever you believe Visigothic soldiers are amassing."

"Aye, but easier ordered than carried out," Ascum cautioned. "It will be impossible to see well enough to aim properly in the dark. And even if our attack were in the noonday sun, a gust of wind could carry a flaming bolt into an unsuspecting house. There's simply no way to be sure."

"Indeed," I agreed. "Some collateral damage is unavoidable, but we must do what we can. Belisarius and the Emperor would govern this stronghold one day, which would prove an unsustainable rule if the local population associates us with wanton destruction and murder."

Ascum nodded, as did Liberius, yet neither added further words to the conversation. Nor did any other, for though the strategy was simple, it assuaged many fears that other officers felt on the eve of the siege.

Until that moment in my life, I had never fought such a siege. Those who would climb a ladder and raise a banner over an enemy's wall are unlikely to survive long, with most assaults leaving many attackers dead, and twice as many suffering horrific wounds. Septem's walls were both tall and well-kept—stouter by far than what an attacking army would normally face. I had no doubt that the Vandals under Gunderic would relish the opportunity to scale steep embankments and haul themselves toward Septem's summit, and others like Baduarius would perform well, while most of my men must have silently quivered as they gazed up at my intended target. I could only pray that Septem would surrender quickly. I was put at ease with the knowledge that, for our first night, the only offense Romans would undertake would be from a relatively safe distance.

Before breaking, Baduarius interrupted for a final time. "Ascum, do you have any extra drums aboard the ships?"

"Always," Ascum replied. "The ship's captains love the things, as annoying as they are."

"Exactly." Baduarius bared his teeth in a broad smile. "I will never forget hearing the rhythm of drums when the Avar horde closed upon my shield wall. If I were a weaker man, I would have pissed myself from fear." He cast a hopeful glance at me. "Perhaps, while Ascum's attack continues, we can have a few dozen drummers on land and at sea, making sure that Theudesgel isn't able to get a peaceful night's rest."

Laughing, I nodded at Baduarius' request, though I noted that we would need to move our own soldiers far from the lines so as to not fall victim to a similar sleepless fate. In addition, evening sentry watch would be doubled, and many torches planted, in order to avoid the surprise of any Visigothic sally. Ascum declared that a boat would first return with the drums that we requested, and then he would order the ships under his command to form a ring around Septem's seawalls and launch the flaming projectiles. They would continue for at least one hour after the final slivers of light gave way to complete and total darkness.

Thus, the first day of Septem's siege ended uneventfully. No sallies were mounted, nor any rash attacks launched against the city's fortified stone walls. With our trenches dug and a low palisade shielding our position, I instructed my centurions to make sure that the men rested, regardless of what noises they may hear in the night. Only a small contingent remained awake to protect against a potential nocturnal attack.

With each passing hour, I grew more confident—perhaps dangerously confident—that others had been correct about Theudesgel's precarious position. Though a few hundred men could easily hold Septem's walls should a much larger force attack their walls, any assault *from* those walls would be easily spotted from a distance, leaving both forces at something of a monotonous standoff. Whether Theudesgel and the Visigoths understood my pressures or not, I had little intention of remaining here for a protracted siege that would take us well into the following spring.

Night fell, but the early departure of the sun left me restless and far from eager for sleep. Instead, I sat in silence with Liberius, a low fire warming our rations of salt mutton until a blackened crisp formed around their tough exterior, and then we ate. We waited, saving all words and vitality for what we knew would come not long after darkness fell. And, as the appointed hour arose, Cephalas beckoned for my attention.

"Signals from the fleet, Lord. Ascum is in position."

I turned my gaze once again to the outline of the city. Far smaller than Constantinople or even Carthage, Septem had few of the illuminating lights that made such massive cities appear lively even in the darkest blackness of the evening. A single fiery beacon remained lit along the top of the interior citadel of Mount Abyla, while smaller torches along Septem's walls helped its defenders keep a trepidatious watch over any Roman movement. Just enough light, as it happened, to mark Ascum's targets.

"Sound the horn," I replied. "Let's see whether Theudesgel might change his mind."

Within moments, the horn blared. Its deep croon pierced through the sporadic crashing of waves, soon joined by the rhythm of no fewer than a half dozen of the massive drums that normally lined our ship's decks, positioned at different points along my lines so that their sound would carry through Septem's gates. Even after the horn faded, our landward drummers continued their harsh music for further minutes, until at last the final drum fell into a curious silence. Along the walls, I spotted further detachments of Visigoths line the battlements, their shields ready for what they assumed was an impending assault.

Along the waterfront, the short staccato notes were acknowledged by the lighting of fires that rolled with each passing wave, roughly illuminating the sails and decks of our dromons. Though my view was obscured by the city just ahead, I was still able to make out several of our outermost ships that had formed into a half-circle around Septem's harbor. Flames danced around those wooden decks, growing yet higher as lit torches touched ballistae bolts and catapult stones covered in the viscous naphtha that had long been used to ignite Roman arrows. With little knowledge of sea-battles, I initially worried aloud that such flames would spread along the wooden hull or flaxen ropes that gave each ship its figure, until Liberius put my concerns at ease.

"Men have been fighting at sea well before the time of Odysseus and Agamemnon," he explained. "If there is one thing that I have confidence in, it is the ability of our sailors to fire upon an enemy without sending their own vessels to damnation."

For several heartbeats, those lit fires stood as if at attention, their only movements in tune with the rhythm of the sea. Then, a great procession of drums boomed from each ship in response to my own call not long before, filling the air around Septem with a sensation of all-encompassing suffocation, entrapment from all sides. As the drumming grew ever more feverish, I saw a single flaming arrow flying high in the air, its light a mere pinprick against the blackness of the sky. It disappeared into Septem's harbor, signaling Ascum's command for the attack to begin.

Even at a distance, the sounds of groaning wood and creaking iron echoed mightily as the siege engines unleashed their missiles. Most ships held just two or three such devices, allowing appropriate distance for their operators to maintain and load each ballista or catapult without any concern of bumping into one another. Though I could not see it, I knew our flagship held far more ballistae, and were overseen personally by Ascum.

For the briefest moment, the flaming projectiles streaked across the sky, marvelous and stark, like orange paint splashed across a vast black canvas. Though I had seen many a battle, had witnessed the destructive power of siege engines against tender flesh and bone, until that point, I had never witnessed their true power, their intended use in a siege, and was admittedly entranced by the trails of flame and smoke that followed each fiery rock or bolt—so much so that in that moment I had no eyes for the Visigoths, only for Ascum's artistry in the art of destruction.

That trance ended abruptly as the first bolts slapped hard into Septem's sea-drenched stone walls. Those initial missiles fell far from their intended mark, the hoped-for targets being either one of the towers that provided both a commanding view and fighting platforms at regular intervals along the land and sea barrier, or else the military buildings that lined the city's inner harbor. That initial rumbling thud was almost immediately joined by the pattering of several dozen others, most of which also dashed against the city's walls or sailed well beyond their intended targets.

A rare few did find their mark, however, piercing wooden roofs and spilling a naphtha-fueled inferno onto the buildings and men below. Once a darkened urban expanse illuminated by scant torchlight, Septem's barracks and battlements were now brilliant with fire and smoke. And it was not long after that initial volley came to a halt that the truth became apparent: Theudesgel and the Visigoths had little capability and even less hope to stave off anything but perhaps the very worst of the damage.

As I watched from afar, tiny human figures rushed atop the walls, hurling buckets of water onto patches of burning oil. Those efforts eventually yielded some measure of success, only for the dromons' drums to announce that a second volley was imminent. In such profound darkness, and despite the smoldering of the first missile targets, many stones and bolts again fell wildly off their marks. It hardly mattered. Even those ill-aimed spilled the near-liquid naphtha flames onto Septem's walls and streets. Beside me, Xerxes hissed, watching as one Visigothic soldier was brushed by an exploding stone ball, his exposed arms and face sprayed viciously with naphtha.

"Of all the ways to die, I have always been told that fire is the very worst," Liberius muttered. "Give fire but an hour and it will render to ash what took a century to build."

"Fire is sacred to my people." Xerxes was all but gaping, his eyes tracking the flame-covered Visigothic soldier who flailed his arms and cried out for assistance that had no possibility of relieving his pain. "But there is nothing holy about naphtha."

"No," I agreed. "But it may save hundreds of our men from having to scale that bulwark. Ascum knows better than any man alive that a naphtha flame can be the decider between victory and defeat."

There was no response. I have little doubt that Xerxes, or any other officer, agreed with my sentiment, yet that did not change the innate sense of revulsion that any soldier felt at witnessing the fiery suffering of other warriors. The Visigoths were our dread and sworn enemies, the entire reason for our expedition. Even so, I felt a specter of human pity curl its icy fingers around my heart. Internally, I crushed such notions, for if there is anything that I have learned about being a military commander, it is that pity for an enemy will only lead to suffering and loss for my own men. War is an awful thing, but it is one that, once kindled, cannot be pursued in half measures.

For a full hour, the rhythm of the drums continued. And for that full hour, the dromons rained hellfire upon Septem, which billowed out vast clouds of smoke that choked the air immediately above the city. Most of my men had been under strict orders to sleep and rest, yet I wonder if any managed to do so, given how those on duty hooted and cheered as each bolt connected with its target, and as the Visigoths fruitlessly attempted to control the spreading flames.

I also noted that some stray missiles did connect with the civilian interior, yet blessedly, such instances were few, and those fires less violent. My concern that we should not engender hatred amongst the people of Septem was born from a critical lesson of Belisarius, who instructed each of his officers that it was far better to earn the love of those civilians on lands that we would join into Justinian's empire rather than subjugate them to the all-too-familiar routine of brutalization and fear. Septem had once been a Roman city, and I would see it return to such hands again with the least destruction and death possible.

Satisfied, I signaled my horns for Ascum to cease his assault. Both Gunderic and Baduarius begged for the privilege of leading an assault on Septem's walls, and both I swiftly denied.

"No. There is too much risk in a night assault," I explained. "Besides, Theudesgel may yet peacefully leave after seeing no future where he survives this siege."

I could tell that many others shared my optimism. And why should they not? We knew now that the Visigoths were few in number, and hopelessly outmatched by our arrows and siege machines. As flames danced over that city, the siege of Septem seemed likely to conclude almost as quickly as it had begun. Tomorrow, we reasoned, the expedition would conclude, and we could all return home.

As with so many other times in my youth, I was wrong. Our army had won the day, but the Visigoths had not yet lost the war.

THEUDESGEL'S REVENGE

At Rosamund's prodding, I awoke at dawn. Others followed my example, with weary sentries exchanging shifts with their rested comrades as the great majority of my army rose for another day of orders, exercise, and whatever else that fate may hold. After dressing, I ventured out of my tent, expecting to see the labors of Ascum's attack in the form of Visigothic disarray.

I was not entirely disappointed. Great pillars of smoke still swept upward, and a dull roar of shouting slipped past Septem's walls as dozens of sweat-streaked and ash-covered men stamped out lingering fires. Yet despite blackened roofs and smoldering fires, Septem's thick walls remained intact. Worse, Ascum's assault had claimed few victims, with Visigothic soldiers standing at the ready to receive any attack that I might mount. None showed any willingness for surrender, and no emissary signaled a desire to negotiate away the punishment I had wrought the evening prior.

"Looks like they want to fight," Baduarius said, approaching with a sagging wineskin in his arm.

"It would appear so," I answered. "But the morning is still young."

I had no intention of rushing an engagement. Many options were available, including a further barrage from our dromons under the guiding light of the sun. Time was precious, yet the advantage was clearly ours—an advantage that would grow only greater once Perenus and the Herulian foederati joined their strength to my own.

The Visigoths, however, would not wait passively for their demise. For as my men awoke from their evening's respite, the smoke-blackened walls let forth a roar that definitively signaled that Theudesgel remained unbowed. The cacophony of Visigothic voices grew loudest near the main city gate, spitting vituperation that few in my army, other than Baduarius, could understand. Dozens of armored figures leaned over that portion of the wall, and I could make out Theudesgel's disproportionately long-limbed and richly attired frame standing just above the gate's entrance. What I did not immediately comprehend, however, was the shackled figure that hunched beside the Visigothic warlord.

"An attack?" I asked.

From nearby, Liberius' voice rose above the din. "No. But what we are about to see will likely cause one."

It took me several more moments to understand his meaning. Standing in silence as other officers gathered around, we watched Theudesgel raise his wiry arms toward the sky, gyrating his hips lewdly at the captive man standing before the gate. Then, with the swift gesture for silence, Theudesgel placed two hands around the man's waist, leaning from behind and whispering something into his ear. With a single motion, the captive was thrust from the battlements, screeching with terror as the heavy chains weighed his body down. The screeching came to a sudden halt as the chain reached its maximum length a mere cubit from the African turf, jerking the captive's body and snapping his spine in a merciful note of mortality.

Brutality is a prerequisite in the art of war. Though older men like Justin and Godilas had lectured that it had not always been so, and that some measure of honor and discipline had once ruled the battlefields of our legions centuries ago, Attila changed all that, his scourge demonstrating that any hesitancy to instill dread in an adversary was a weakness, and one easily exploited. The Visigoths had learned Attila's lesson well, and though I had known of Theudis' predilections for wanton violence, such foreknowledge did little to quench the rage that flared deep in my gut right then. Even then, after seeing so much, I could still be taken by surprise.

Theudesgel laughed as his men roared their approval, the limp body of his victim swaying against the breeze. A thin trail of piss followed the swinging corpse, the muscles of the dead man already easing their grip on his bodily functions. Feigning disgust with sweeping arcs of his arms, Theudesgel tugged hard against the iron chain that connected the body to the city walls, sending it swinging ever more aggressively.

"He called himself Altan of the Herulians, and he offered to suck my cock to stay alive!" Theudesgel cackled. "But he smelled of sheep dung and moaned like a whore at night. He makes a good lesson for you Romans—leave Septem! Or swing from its walls like your catamite scout!"

Furious shouting rose from my camp, led most of all by Baduarius, who cursed Theudesgel in their shared Gothic language. I shared their disgust. Altan was one of my men, who saved the Emperor amidst the Nika Riots, and fought with honor against both of our battles against the Vandals. Altan held the naivety of youth, equally strong and clumsy. I wanted to hop forward, demand Theudesgel face me like a man, and gore that bastard with my sword.

Liberius, calm as ever, moved closer and whispered in Heruli, "Altan was one of yours?"

I nodded, remembering the young Herulian warrior marching through Africa on Belisarius' conquest of Carthage. "He fought with me at Dara and Ad Decimum, and volunteered as an outrider. I should never have sent such tiny scouting parties into Tingitana."

"This is no time to doubt yourself," Liberius insisted, calming my outward revulsion.

And it wasn't. For as more of my spearmen gathered in armored mobs, Theudesgel hitched his trousers, spraying a thick stream of urine atop Altan's corpse. The Visigothic leader laughed as he readjusted himself, then turned his back to the Roman expedition at his gates.

For Baduarius, this was an insult too far. He stormed over to me, his chest heaving in fury, "Varus, allow me to lead the attack. I'll have this bastard's head on a spear point by nightfall."

I had little time to react. Even as Baduarius voiced his urge for bloodshed, many of my centurions had already organized and armed their men for battle, with some going so far as to pass ladders toward the front of the ranks. One group of Cappadocians even hauled a fire-hardened log to our lines opposite Septem's main gate, its rounded edge capped in a thin bronze veneer capable of shattering the city's portcullis given enough time.

"This is a disorganized rabble, Varus," Liberius whispered in Heruli.

Panic streamed through my veins, rushing up my neck and flushing my face with uncomfortable heat despite the early dawn chill. Frantically surveying my army, I became acutely aware of the growing number of eyes watching my every movement, awaiting a decision that would release the expedition from its impotent fury. Their cheering grew more feverish still as Gunderic and the Vandals joined the disorganized frenzy.

"Geld the bastards!" Gunderic bellowed nearby. "The Visigoths have no need for their cocks! Ten gold Roman coins to the first man over the wall!"

Baduarius turned to me, his expression a silent plea to be free of my restrictions. "Varus, I've seen this before. Either we lead an attack now and in good order, or later as a disorganized mob. But if we do not respond, the men will take indecision as a sign of weakness, and a terrible omen."

Every instinct told me to refuse. We still knew precious little of our enemy, and even less of their ability to protect the narrow landward expanse of stone walls that enabled a far smaller force to defend its battlements. A glance at Liberius showed him ever silent, though the briefest flicker of a disapproving gaze betrayed his emotions.

In the end, it was Xerxes who countered Baduarius' claim. "Theudesgel *wants* us to rush the walls. But if we are patient, Septem will open its gates after a few further nights of fire and siege. I doubt the Visigoths have earned much love from the city's populace."

I trusted Xerxes' instincts, his words aligning with every lesson I had learned from Godilas long ago. Yet what Godilas, Justin, and Liberius had not taught me was the raw pressure of command, where a leader's obvious choice is weighted and dissembled against the unbridled passions of those who would follow. And, young and unready as I found myself, I surrendered to those fixed on carnage and revenge.

"Xerxes' point is sound," I reasoned aloud, "but we cannot show weakness to our enemy or our own soldiers, either. Baduarius, gather the men in good order and prepare for an assault. I will signal Ascum and the fleet to recommence their missiles. With God's help, we will take this city today."

Whooping with pleasure, Baduarius saluted before sprinting away, his heavy boots sounding loud thuds as they carried his massive frame over the hardened soil. As expedition commander, my duty was merely to form a strategy, with the risk of death shouldered by others on the lines. It was a discomforting notion, and privately shameful, for until that moment I had never asked my men to accept the potential of maiming, capture, or death that I was not equally privy to. More, whether from Altan's murder or the impending fight, I could feel my heart throbbing and my throat twisting into a painful knot as I glanced at a silent Xerxes and an impassive Liberius. Though neither contradicted my assessment, their sudden deference signaled disapproval.

Safeguarded by Uliaris, Sembrouthes, and my Aksumite guardsmen, I trotted toward a makeshift guard post that had been erected for exactly this purpose. Before climbing its ladder, I sent dispatches to signal instructions to our fleet, and allowed Xerxes to join the Vandal spearmen that remained nominally under his control. Liberius remained behind, grabbing my arm for stability as he ascended the platform beside me. Though my guardsmen remained on the ground, Rosamund followed closely behind the legate, her mail-covered form drawing none of the curious glances as she had in our campaign in Mesopotamia.

Standing the height of three men, the watch post could have easily fit an additional three or four armored soldiers, the wooden panels of its floors tightly nailed together and reinforced with thick beams.

Chuckling to himself, Liberius leaned heavily on his staff. "Far too old for this," he muttered.

I shook my head and attempted a grin. "You'll outlive us all, Legate."

"That may be so, for I am not rushing headlong into conflict with the Goths," Liberius retorted.

The nascent smile died on my lips, and I drew the cheek pieces of my helmet closer together to hide my reddening face. Somewhere within me, remnants of childhood deference urged me to call back the attack and return to my place within Liberius' favor, mortified that the elder counselor thought ill of my first major decision at the head of an army. Yet such vacillation would certainly be scoffed at. Men would say that Varus was both indecisive and incompetent. Hardening my heart, I committed myself anew to the assault, nodding with approval as the first ballista bolts sailed from our dromons and toward defenseless targets in the city.

The strategy, one of many discussed in prior meetings amongst my officers, was blindingly simple. With the Goths lacking the numbers to sufficiently man each section of Septem's walls, small contingents of my forces would rush to each possible staging point, raising the bottom-heavy wooden ladders that would allow thirty or forty men to ascend within short order. Simultaneously, a larger group of Cappadocians would haul our ram to Septem's main gate, forcing Theudesgel to either spread his forces painfully thin or allow one threat against his city to manifest while warding off others deemed more imminently dangerous.

Its simplicity gave me confidence that there were few opportunities for failure. No intricate timing of an attack was required, such as those favored so often by John, nor did we depend upon breaking a single point in our enemy's defenses to succeed. Yet, as Xerxes well noted, it was exactly the tactic that even a halfwit commander would expect after taunting his adversary into retaliation. I could only hope that Theudesgel was either a grossly incapable leader or was so deprived of men that there was little he could do to blunt such an obvious course of action.

To his credit, Baduarius wasted no time in his preparations, barking orders and harnessing his men's thirst for Visigothic blood and unmitigated revenge. After four volleys of siegefire spat iron and flame onto multiple defensive positions along the city, Baduarius turned back to face my tower, raising a spear in recognition.

Leaning over the railing, I called for Uliaris. "Sound the horn and allow Baduarius to commence his attack."

Men cheered as the three clipped notes sounded to permit their assault, with Baduarius screaming for them to charge the walls. Rather than remain with the main party that manned our siege ram, Baduarius instead joined a smaller group of ladder-bearers, pushing his place to the front of the team and hoisting a ladder rung to his shoulder level. Diminutive shield walls protected their advance, although at such a swift pace, it proved impossible for even our most disciplined spearmen to keep their shields tightly overlapping in defense of any projectile.

Yet none came. Dozens of armed Visigoths stood watch over our progress, and from my height I spotted a handful of bowmen in their ranks, but no arrows sailed from their strings, allowing the Romans unimpeded access to Septem's walls.

"There's something wrong about this," Rosamund whispered in Heruli.

"It is odd," I agreed, nevertheless attempting to sound confident.

One by one, the ladder teams arrived at their assigned targets outside the walls. Several were met by a hail of stones from overhead, yet even those attacks appeared halfhearted, unlikely to cause serious injury. It was not until most of the ladders were put in place, and the ram positioned just paces from its target, that Rosamund's creeping doubt came to bear in the worst of omens. Worse, I was too late to stymie the damage.

"Sembrouthes! Signal Baduarius and the men to retreat immediately!"

"Lord?" Sembrouthes' voice rose with a note of surprise.

"Do it now!" I yelled.

The Aksumite leader offered naught in reply. Though he sprinted to my banners and shouted for the horn blower, Sembrouthes' rustling seemed perilously slow in comparison to the frenzied rush of Roman spearmen that climbed the narrow ladders, several waving swords at would-be defenders. Baduarius was paramount among them, shoving a Visigothic soldier from his perch as he became the first Roman to scale Septem's battlements. A team of Vandals followed suit on the far end of the wall, their manic laughter and taunts flowing above the booming of ballista bolts and exchange of blows along the city wall. My horns blared the signal for retreat just as those carrying the ram struck the first blow along Septem's gates, the brass covering rattling against iron hinges and worn timber.

"Run!" I screamed. "Run!"

Xerxes was one of the few who heard me, and I saw him use his spear to push back the Vandals who had yet to climb their ladder and shove them in retreat toward the Roman trenches. Other slowly recognized the threat, yet by the time Baduarius, already atop Septem's walls, acknowledged my order, there was little he could do.

Theudesgel's own horn sounded opposite my own, a single confident note that echoed throughout the expanse. The Visigothic warlord's sword rose and fell, bringing with it its own wave of destruction.

Looking back on that part of the siege, our most desperate weakness was not our desire to end such difficult conflict quickly, but instead our inability to properly scout our enemy, to understand its strengths, weaknesses, and intentions. Not that proper scouting had even been possible—I could do only so much, given my position, with only what few horses were not conscripted to Belisarius' own need in the vast deserts and hills of Numidia and Tripolitana. Without the quick mobility of cavalry, we were hard-pressed to assess any Visigothic activity along the city walls. Worse, Theudesgel knew it.

Atop my watch post, I could scarcely make out the darkened outline of the mass along the ground. It was unlike any rock or grass that I have seen in the many lands I had traversed; I can only assume it had been laid there in the depths of night, for even in the glaring light of morning it was difficult to discern properly, and I prayed it was not what I thought I saw. Yet my fears were confirmed when Theudesgel's command brought forth a dozen archers with flaming arrows, their bowstrings loosed upon the slick, darkened target at the feet of my spearmen.

"Run, curse you!" Rosamund yelled. "Quickly!"

Their arrows could not miss; their target was too close. As each shaft was buried into the turf, the weak flicker along each arrowhead blossomed into a thick flame. Though most of my forces had been hardened by the shield wall and survived many a bout with certain death, I had never seen a single man face conflagration, the burning kiss that singed beards and scorched flesh of friend and foe alike, with that same calm assurance. Any semblance of discipline in my rearward ranks evaporated as men sprinted and lunged away from spreading fire, although blessedly, most retained their weapons and shields despite the rising panic.

It was then, into the thick of such disorder, that the Visigoths struck. Bowmen traded their flaming arrows for iron-tipped mankillers, firing uncoordinated shots into the swirling mass of Roman soldiers below. Other Visigoths brandished swords and spears as they surrounded the few Romans who pushed their way to the top of the walls, forcing at least a half dozen to fall painfully to the turf. Gripping hard at the rail, I watched as Baduarius bashed his shield at the nearest Visigoth before making his own escape back to friendly lines, serving as the last Roman atop Septem's walls in our pitiful assault. It seemed, as he retreated, that even between the bowmen and the brief skirmishes, the Visigoths had done little enough damage—an encouraging portent that our siege wasn't utterly doomed.

Until I realized the extent of the fire. The thin line of flames seethed along our ladders, causing the blaze to snake along each rung and leaving the once-vital equipment charred and useless. Both Baduarius and Gunderic bellowed commands to save what ladders remained unburnt, yet most were abandoned to the small scorching fires that ringed Septem's landward walls. Worst of all, our battering ram, abandoned in a fearful retreat of arrow-riddled Cappadocians, was soon reduced to blackened timbers. A month of preparations had been ruined in less than an hour, leaving our expedition with laughably little to show for it.

"Order Ascum to cease firing," I barked to a courier, glowering.

There were no words appropriate for such a situation. I had failed, and failed miserably, falling prey to an obvious and clumsy trap out of a fear of looking cowardly before my men. I wanted little more than to disappear, to jump upon the wings of some vast eagle and fly far away where nothing—not the raw embarrassment of failure, not the painstaking and laborious duty of reorganization—would find me.

Alas, the power of self-rapture belongs only to God, although Rosamund insists that there are those of her religion who can evaporate like water. And so I remained, listening to Theudesgel's jeers and the cursing of dozens of men who complained of burns, sprains, and the occasional injury by an unlucky arrow.

It was not until later in the afternoon that the angry chaos of defeat had at last been put to order. Rosamund and Cephalas summoned each of the senior officers into my tent, a command obeyed with far less enthusiasm or mischief than any under the leadership of Belisarius. Even after Callinicum, there had been a belief of moral victory, an understanding that only Belisarius could have devastated the Persians so thoroughly that even in emerging triumphant, Azarethes had been utterly ruined. What would they say of Varus, I wondered? A poor specter of John, who would never have allowed vital siege equipment to be destroyed on some foolish gambit? Or worse, just another headstrong barbarian, plunging ignorantly into an ambush like the basest animal?

It was all I could do to avoid any outward show of self-pity or bleated plea for forgiveness. Instead, with the officers assembled, I channeled my best imitation of Belisarius as could be mustered, unfurling a freshly detailed map of Septem onto a low table for all to see.

"What are our losses?"

"Five dead, and another eleven seriously wounded," Liberius recited.

"Aye, and no Vandals among them!" Gunderic boomed, a look of disdain framing his features.

"That's because the Vandals took the easiest assignment!" Baduarius snapped. "You cunts aren't disciplined enough to take on a real task!"

Two Vandals at Gunderic's side rushed forward, gloved fists squeezing the hilts of their swords. Likewise, Baduarius' hand lowered to his belt, his eyes locked with Gunderic's all the while. If any blade were drawn, bloodshed was inevitable—either directly by Baduarius or Gunderic or by my guardsmen to restore order. No man could draw a weapon in anger in his commander's tent and expect to leave unscathed. Likewise, no warlord could ignore such behavior and remain respected.

Though some decried their behavior, cooler heads were few in number as men shouted blame, flinging accusations of cowardice upon those deemed to have executed their assignments poorly. The frantic rustling grew to the point of bumping the table that bore my map, sending the parchment sliding onto the floor.

"Enough!" I shouted. "Gunderic, Baduarius, on your knees!"

In a heartbeat, Uliaris, Sembrouthes, and three other Aksumites flooded into my tent, their spears lowered with deadly purpose. Sembrouthes remained as calm as ever, his chest barely rising even as his curved spearpoint moved fluidly before his body. Uliaris, on the other hand, rushed to the center of the array, placing his body before my own.

"You heard your commander!" the Frank spat. "On your knees!"

"I will handle this, Uliaris," I murmured, my skin prickling from shame.

After the display from my guards, however, neither Gunderic nor Baduarius put up any resistance. Heads bowed, both warriors knelt, caked in a layer of dust and ash that painted their once gray mail into a soot-colored black. Around them, order was restored as remaining squabbles and other portents of bloodshed faded, and I considered my words carefully in fear, now more than ever, that the slightest display of incompetence would send the less loyal of those present back into a frenzy of distrust and fear. God help me, but in that moment, I raged against Belisarius for placing me at the lead of this expedition.

"Five dead, and eleven seriously wounded," I repeated. "Please gather their names, ranks, and units. I will include them in my report to Belisarius and the Empress. But further, what equipment have we lost?"

The hairs of my neck and arms stood on end as I awaited the final count from my officers. Xerxes was first to reply, his voice firm, flat, and absent any hint of his casual drawl.

"The siege ram is gone, as are fourteen of the ladders."

"And how many ladders do we have remaining?"

Xerxes sighed. "Seven."

So it was not an unmitigated disaster, but certainly a debilitating setback. In any case, the question remained about what it would take to overcome such a loss. I considered a solution for the problem, avoiding the gazes of the still-kneeling Gunderic and Baduarius for fear that I might lash out at either man.

"Can more be fashioned?" I asked, my words clipped and formal as if addressed to all present, yet no one at the same time.

"It will not be easy," Rosamund called out, her soft, hollow voice nevertheless drawing curious glances of the sweat-stained officers.

"The trees along the coastline here are brittle and inflexible. Good for battering at a gate, but unlikely to carry the weight of several men at a sharp angle."

Despite the tension, I could not help but smile. If anyone could be trusted to have a keen observation of the local natural resources, it was Rosamund. Her words brought no reassurance of a simple solution to my predicament, yet even knowing that I had such ingenuity at my disposal served to shore up some measure of confidence in my thinking.

"We know little of the interior, however," Rosamund added. "Perhaps that may be host to your needs."

I nodded. "Gunderic, you will lead fifty Vandals to scout one mile inland and return with any suitable lumber to fashion a ram and as many ladders as possible. You will do this and return by nightfall."

Gunderic cleared his throat, raising his eyes as he spoke. "Lord, night comes early this late in the year—"

"That is a command, Gunderic," I barked. Gritting my teeth, I nearly bit my tongue as I finally turned to face the kneeling Vandal giant. Curiously, Gunderic's face was absent malice, his brow furrowed in worry. I had expected a wild unruliness, and my frustration with the Vandals slaked somewhat at Gunderic's deference. "Do you understand?"

The massive Vandal lord sank from the rebuke. "Yes, Lord, I will do this."

"Excellent. You are dismissed, and may leave promptly. But if you cause any further acrimony in my camp, you will wish I had left you atop Mount Papua."

Gunderic rose slowly to his feet, his shoulders and head bowed in the posture of a chastised puppy. He stole a glance at the nearest Aksumite spearman, and I can only imagine that he was wondering whether I intended to slay him as some dishonorable trick. I would not, though his taunts infuriated me, yet I cannot begrudge him his wariness; he had sworn an oath of service to the Roman Empire, but only months ago he was just as loyal to a different kingdom, a different king. No, I could not appear weak or conciliatory, not if I intended to leave this land with my life, and with the victory that Belisarius demanded of me.

Gunderic edged his way from the tent, leaving his Vandal officers behind who had not been afforded the same dismissal as their leader. Only Baduarius remained kneeling, scowling as he stared at the floor.

"Can the walls be taken with the ladders that we do have?" I pressed on.

"Anything is possible, Lord," Wisimar offered. "But even with a narrow set of walls like Septem's, having too few ladders makes easy targets of men that would climb them. Especially with no ram. A handful of bowmen could pick away each attacker before he rose halfway up the rungs."

Xerxes stepped forward once more, his Zhayedan armor glittering amongst the unpolished iron links and scales of his Vandal wards. "As Rosamund said, a ram can be constructed. Theudesgel's trick is spent, and it will not succeed a second time. To Wisimar's concern, if each ladder team can be equipped with a few javelins alongside their normal spear, the Visigothic archers would have far more difficulty in making such easy prey of our men. Septem's walls are formidable, but even the most expert bowman cannot avoid exposing some side of his body when firing an arrow. Given their small numbers, even a few Visigoth casualties would be a significant boon to us."

"Your point is well taken," I replied. "Reorganize the ladder teams to your liking. Have the swiftest ready to scale the walls, and those less nimble at climbing stand by ready to launch a dart at any would be Visigothic attacker. Requisition any weapons that you need for this task, and do so immediately."

Xerxes saluted, beckoning for Wisimar and the other Vandals to follow him out of the tent. The situation eased, Uliaris and Sembrouthes raised their spears, their posture relaxed as I issued orders to the other present Cappadocian and Thracian officers. Through it all, both Baduarius and Liberius remained silent. The former still knelt at my feet, while the latter stood conspicuously off to the side of the tent, staring as though lost in a daydream yet surely following every command I uttered.

As more and more officers filed out of my tent—to attempt to retrieve discarded equipment or whatever other tasks would bring our expedition back to heel—Baduarius lifted his head but once, his cavernous hazel eyes drooping, empty of their usual mirth. Soon, the only souls remaining in my presence were Liberius, Rosamund, Cephalas, and a still-kneeling Baduarius. I allowed him to remain there in silence, watching each twitch of his head with curiosity. Eventually, it was Baduarius who broke the silence.

"Varus, I—"

"I did not give you leave to speak, *Dux*," I growled.

Baduarius, unlike Gunderic, had been a friend for years. We had bled together and wept together upon the death of his brother Dagisthaeus. While I could excuse Gunderic's misbehavior as intractable Vandal wiliness, Baduarius was well versed in Roman military life. And because he had become one of my closest comrades in Belisarius' army, his display of disrespect was impossible for me to brush aside.

"I-I'm sorry…"

Seething, I moved two paces closer to the man. Dropping to my own knees, I met him at eye level. "Do you have no respect for me as your commander?"

"Of course, Varus!"

"Then why do you put me in positions that jeopardize my rule, and in front of all of the other officers?"

"Varus, I don't mean—"

I interrupted once more, lowering my face yet nearer to his. "Would you behave this way if it were Belisarius leading you?"

Baduarius hung his head, his chest heaving, eyes hidden behind dense bushy brows. "Of course not, Lord."

"Then why do you reserve such disrespect for me?"

I had not intended such an uncontrolled outburst, but as I gazed upon my kneeling friend, I found myself burning with shame too powerful to contain. Belisarius would not have erupted in anger—but then again, Belisarius would never have been subject to such disharmony.

"Lord…" Baduarius began, sucking a deep breath as he allowed that single word to die amidst the tent's walls. "Gunderic and his Vandals insulted my men, and yours. I should have held my tongue, but… but I suppose the frustration of the attack was hot upon me."

I shook my head. "Gunderic and the Vandals have been in this army for only a matter of weeks. I trust you to be a civilizing influence, not one that starts tavern brawls at the most dangerous point of my expedition."

Baduarius stiffened. "I can't just let those Vandals run roughshod over us!"

"That is not your responsibility!" I all but spat. "Your actions jeopardize us, all of us, for men follow the example of their commanders." A dark thought entered my mind, and I lowered my voice to a fierce whisper. "And do you not suppose that the spy from Carthage might very well be stalking through our camp as we speak? If he were to discover that the units within my army might be cleaved apart so easily, threatening to butcher one another…"

"Varus, you know I would never do anything to hurt you," Baduarius whispered back. "We have shared too much, and are of the same cause."

It was then that I felt my resolve breaking. I wanted to lift Baduarius to his feet, clap him hard on the shoulder, box his ears playfully for insolence, and laugh together as if all was well. Even then, as commander, I felt the tug of camaraderie over everything else, and had I been in a different role, I most certainly would have yielded to it. Yet Baduarius' actions, however unthinking and fleeting, had stoked discord within my army. And if there was one lesson that I had learned from Belisarius, it was that leadership and loneliness are like twin horses of the same chariot—one is always harnessed with the other. Though I craved friendship, I settled for discipline.

Now, as a man who has seen far too many years and has lost far too many friends, I wish I had chosen differently.

Instead, I grunted. "You would do nothing to harm me?" I asked Baduarius. "Then prove it."

With that, I rose to my feet and slipped from the tent into what daylight remained. Only hours had passed since the battle commenced, yet my mind swam with weariness, with the longing for rest, even the dreamless sleep that I knew that Rosamund's potions might afford me. Rosamund and Cephalas followed closely behind, leaving a still-kneeling Baduarius and an aloof legate behind as the sole remnants of my war council.

We planned to fight again the next day. That much was certain. For in war, one can never allow an adversary to become too contented in his success, nor wait too long to press an advantage, however slim. The violence of Septem had hardly begun.

A TEST OF ADVERSITY

Gunderic returned just before nightfall, his body drenched in salty sweat and chest heaving from exertion. As his Vandals rested, a contingent of Cappadocians fashioned yet another crude siege ram, while others attempted to fashion the lumber of the African interior into a usable ladder. Most were poor things, as brittle as Rosamund had warned, yet two or three showed sufficient promise that they would not immediately break when placed into service on the battlefield.

The following dawn, Ascum resumed his barrage of the city's military quarters, the flying bolts and stones from his dromons splitting stones along the walls and spilling naphtha-borne flames onto rooftops. From my observation post, I watched teams of Visigoths splash ponderous wooden buckets of water onto several rising fires as before. Unique to this day, however, was the number of civilians brought into such labor, many of whom undertook the more onerous task of fetching water. I pitied them, those brought into this war through no fault of their own, yet even their suffering could not deter me from my task.

Amidst the thrumming of the ballistae, sections of my expedition wormed their way through our network of trenches, ferrying the few precious ladders remaining to predetermined positions opposite Septem's walls. None of the unbridled confidence remained from the prior morning, with each spearman moving a half step slower and far more cautiously, even at a safe distance from the Visigothic archers. Only the Vandals sang songs and screamed defiance, drumming spear shafts against the iron bosses of their shields and cheering Gunderic on with each sweeping gesture of his massive arms. Collective laughter arose from their ranks as the Vandal warlord dropped his trousers and shined his bare arse to the enemy, displaying it a good long moment for effect.

Other than my designated couriers, few approached me to offer any casual banter or offer comments of optimism. Even Rosamund remained silent when we shared a meal, while Liberius merely nodded as I approved the order for a morning attack. Xerxes suggested waiting for additional reinforcements from the Herulians, yet by this point such a delay would only worsen the tension and low morale that dogged my camp.

Nonetheless, the relative silence offered a unique moment for concentration and thought, nearly an hour where few obligations or customary demands were required of me. That happy reprieve was only broken when I was finally approached by Uliaris, begging a private word that even the legate would not be privy to. Curious, I agreed, and led the guardsman into my tent. Uliaris ignored any polite conversation, preferring instead to make his intentions plain.

"Lord, give me a fast ship and a bag of gold coins, and I will end this conflict for you," Uliaris said.

"A fast ship going where? Back to Carthage?" I asked, perhaps with more venom than I had intended. "Belisarius can't spare any men to reinforce our position, even if you offer them additional pay."

Uliaris shook his head. "Not Belisarius, and it will not place our men at risk. I will recruit men for you in my own way, with your permission. All you need to send is me, for if there is any small chance of risk, I wouldn't place others in danger from my own ideas."

Skeptical, my instinct was to refuse Uliaris yet again. Though his behavior was much improved during our expedition, there was still a general wariness of his judgment, my own fears were amplified by Sembrouthes' concerns. Yet as Uliaris pleaded for his opportunity to expunge his self-condemnation for the tragedy of John's death, I relented.

"Where?" I demanded.

"Frankia."

Uliaris' admission should not have been surprising. The man had strong connections to that mighty kingdom of his birth, and he'd been a youthful warrior of some renown before finding service in Justin's Imperial Army. But I myself knew little of the Franks, only that they governed a vast land far greater than any of the other barbarian tribes that swept across the Western Empire, and were far more numerous than even both Gothic kingdoms. I recalled from my lessons that their society was rumored to be vastly more warlike than our Empire, preferring to solve disputes with the swift elegance of single combat rather than any discordant political strife.

Regardless of whether those tales of half-naked and painted savages bore any semblance of truth, I was still skeptical about the costs in lives or influence that assistance from the Franks might bear upon Belisarius or the Emperor, even if Uliaris were successful. If I were a wagering man, I would have bet not, for Uliaris had been absent from his kin for many years. But as I weighed the options and opportunities before me, I knew I did not have the luxury of resisting such an opportunity, whatever the future costs may hold.

"Why would the Franks support our war?" I asked carefully. "They have no reason to love Justinian. Dead Romans would only help their cause, in fact."

Uliaris shrugged. "The Franks don't like the Greeks, that's true. But they hate the Goths more, and with a few concessions, we might bait one Frankish chief or another into invading Hispania and distracting Theudis."

His point was a sensible one; the Franks had warred continuously with the Visigoths and Ostrogoths since Ravenna's fall to Odoacer. I still doubted whether their intervention could tip the scales of battle in our favor, but with time short and Uliaris insistent, not allowing him to seek their aid seemed foolhardy.

"One ship," I said. "And I need you back in one month. Winter will end not long after, and we need to conclude this campaign soon, one way or another."

Uliaris bobbed his head, his moustaches swaying as they brushed against his lamellar chest armor. "Thank you, Lord. You will not regret it."

Though solemn in his gratitude, Uliaris could not help but flash a broad grin as he saluted and sprinted from my command tent. A selfish flicker of doubt took hold as I wondered whether Uliaris would take the gold and establish himself as one of thousands of hinterlands chieftains made wealthy and fat from stolen riches, or one of the semi-independent pirates who had nested along the coast and islands of Hispania. That flicker of doubt continued to smolder as I considered an even worse possibility: that Uliaris might be the spy that Liberius warned of.

I soon shrugged away such thoughts as ridiculous. In truth, I could never question Uliaris' personal devotion to Belisarius. His past conflicts with Hermogenes demonstrated the Frank held little love for the Emperor, and, as a Frank, likewise held no sense of Imperial identity, yet in the shield wall, Uliaris was devastating to behold. He had risked his life for me and others under my command, and for that I granted him the opportunity to save us all from the butchery of a prolonged siege or the drawn-out subjugation of a people who remembered little of the virtues of Roman civilization or Imperial peace.

Besides, I reasoned, no man would trust Uliaris as a spy: he favored strong drink and chose a coarse tongue when honeyed words were called for.

Uliaris' departure was expedient, leaving Sembrouthes in sole command of my bodyguards. The Aksumite showed no emotion at such an abrupt change, though I have little doubt that he felt some relief, for he, too, had little trust for a man with such a taste for drink. Sembrouthes' only mission was to see that I return to Constantinople hale and whole—a task that I made recklessly difficult with each passing battle—and of all present, the Aksumites alone bore no loyalty to Justinian or Theodora, following along on this expedition solely out of personal fidelity to Mariya, and by extension to myself. I made a private note that, should I survive Tingitana, I should give Sembrouthes and his men a much overdue reprieve and reward, although whether the impassive Aksumite would accept as much I could not say.

So it was that we were committed to battle once more. After ascending my watchtower with a polite nod to Liberius, I observed final preparations for our attack, all the while gaping at the hailstones that still fell upon defenseless Visigothic targets from Ascum's fleet. How so many of Theudesgel's men survived that barrage I will never know, but I remain grateful that his position and my own were not reversed.

As the sun rose above the eastern horizon and marked our appointed hour, Roman horns aboard Ascum's ship called for a cessation in the seaborne assault. Our freshly hewn siege ram was hauled onto the road leading to its assigned gate, that bulwark which bore a few signs of prior assault from the day before. Far more cautious and deliberate in our organization now, I took heart seeing the lines of our forces, with the Vandals occupying the left and the more numerous Cappadocians under Baduarius spread across the right and center. As with yesterday, a thickly armored Baduarius stood with one of the ladder teams, barking orders at his men for final preparations.

Yet when I was nearly ready to give the order, a Visigothic horn sounded once again from inside Septem's walls. Again, Theudesgel and his spearmen appeared along the walls, their deep-green shields reflecting little light from the winter sun. And again, the Visigothic leader raised his arm to signal yet another terrible onslaught.

When their commander's arm fell, the Visigoths flung projectiles—

not weapons, but grimy, fluid-soaked sacks, flying over the battlements and landing a good ten to fifteen paces before the city walls. Seeing no explosion of naphtha and hearing no thud of iron, I strained to make out the contents, and realized in horror what lay within: severed heads and limbs, hewn from the unlucky Cappadocian and Thracian spearmen whose retreat had not been swift enough. With a lurch inside me, I watched a man's head roll forth. Blackened blood caked his disheveled hair, flecks of filth spraying nearby as the skull skipped several paces along the road leading to our army, and I at last recognized the features: it was Altan, the captive Herulian scout who had hung in chains just prior to the start of fighting.

My spearmen, poised mutely just moments before, turned borderline riotous. Cappadocians bellowed curses at their Visigothic enemies, with Baduarius leaping from the defensive trench and condemning Theudesgel to a bottomless hell where night demons would gnaw at his intestines for pleasure. Even the Vandals, who held little regard for their Cappadocian comrades, joined in Baduarius' indignity, with Gunderic grabbing a stray bow from a nearby rack and launching an arrow toward Septem's battlements. Though the arrow reached its target thanks to his unmatched strength, the arrow's force was fully spent by the time it dropped onto the nearest Visigothic spearman, who easily deflected the wobbling missile with a toss of his shield.

"Hold!" I yelled, cupping gloved hands over my mouth and repeating the order twice over as I leaned to each section of my lines.

Ever observant, Xerxes was the first to echo the command, followed soon thereafter by a cacophony of Greek and Vandal centurions in three different languages. Baduarius hopped back into his trench, continuing his barrage of insults. Thankfully, discipline reigned, if only for a moment.

Then, for the first time since we had arrived at the outskirts of this accursed peninsula, Septem's main gate opened. Iron hinges groaned and creaked from their labor, yet ever so slowly, the portal drew open, revealing a tantalizing glimpse of the smoke-riddled city beyond. That view was soon blocked by a lone figure who, riding clumsily atop a squat pony, sauntered onto the battlefield. He did not travel far, pulling the reins taught just as the horse's front hooves came to rest adjacent to Altan's severed head. That unfamiliar soldier swung one leg from around the saddle, hopped down into the dust, and levied a lazy kick at the filth-crusted head.

"Hail, vaunted Romans!" the Visigothic rider called out, the sarcastic Latin barely comprehensible in his heavy Germanic accent. "You cower in holes like sheep! Come, and die!"

With that, the Visigothic champion sprinted forth, layers of mail and leather armor bouncing against a battle-hardened body. Then, with a forceful kick, he sent Altan's head sailing a full thirty paces closer to our trench lines, its owner's features now unmistakable in proper view.

Though my men were far warier of Visigothic trickery than the prior morning, these latest insults proved too much to stomach. Even in its earliest years as a kingdom, Rome and its soldiers had never shied from the ritual of single combat prior to a battle—even if its result would have little influence on a battle's outcome. And to my knowledge, such events rarely did cause one army to surrender to another, yet the unmistakable omen that the duel's outcome yielded would have a clear impact upon the soldiers' belief in the righteousness of their cause. In my own life, I had seen Belisarius' men stand taller after such preliminary victories outside the walls of Dara, and understood that the Visigothic champion's offer could not be ignored.

"Cephalas, prepare my sword."

"Varus..." Rosamund began to protest.

"No," Liberius declared. "In this, I will deny you."

"Lord—"

"Varus, the answer is no," Liberius growled, with a note of both finality and anger that I had rarely heard in our years together. A bare fist gripped hard at the coarse wooden railing, his tall, elegant figure stiff, as if carved from marble and not made of flesh and breath, and when I stole a look at his face, I thought I saw his eyes widen.

At first, I did not respond. I had never defied Liberius, not even in the earliest mischief of youth. As I gazed over my furious army, I was sorely tempted to do so. Yet, when Cephalas returned with my sword after a brief interlude with the whetstone, another glance at Liberius' strangely cold eyes disintegrated my need to rebel.

I nodded to the legate's will. Liberius swiftly unclenched the railing and returned to his erstwhile calm demeanor. Before us, with no challenger to meet him, the Visigothic champion unstrapped the shield from his left arm and danced toward Altan's head, stopping to lift the gruesome ball of pulp and stare into the swollen eye sockets. He bounded back to his horse and jumped back into the saddle, lifting the head high with a free hand.

"Xerxes!" I yelled.

Already watching for any command, Xerxes snapped to attention, lifting his spear high in recognition of my voice. The Visigoth began to trot slowly toward our lines, and I drew my sword and gestured aggressively before shouting out my intentions.

"Kill that bastard!"

Raising his spear in salute, Xerxes donned and fastened his helmet once more, beginning his slow trot to the center of our lines. The Visigothic champion, however, kicked his horse into a canter, rushing down the cobbled Roman road. In a sweeping arc, his mount curled within fifteen paces of our foremost spearmen, pausing only for a moment as he raised his arm and projected the severed head toward his Roman adversaries.

And directly into Baduarius' chest.

"Cowards, all Romans!" he yelled in his guttural Latin, trotting back to his prior position outside Septem's walls. "Led by a motherfucking Ostrogoth!"

Baduarius roared in anger, wiping the gruesome sludge from his armor. I had less than a heartbeat to react before Baduarius was dropping his spear to the ground and unsheathing a massive blade that he had long carried into combat. Hopping out of the trench,

Baduarius raised his arms to accept the challenge, yet cocked his head in curious recognition of the warning coming from behind him.

"Xerxes!" I all but screamed, wincing as I strained my throat. "Replace Baduarius!"

"I fear it is too late for that," Liberius replied softly.

That Baduarius was again disobeying my command brought me close to screaming. Liberius may have held the truth of the moment, but truth is not always good medicine for a bruised sense of self-worth. "Xerxes, go!"

For a long moment, Baduarius' eyes fixed upon my watch tower, undoubtedly finding his richly plumed commander at its center. Though over the years I have tried to convince myself that Baduarius did not fully hear my words, nor took much meaning by them, I know what I saw. Even beneath his iron half-helm, Baduarius' mouth fell agape, his head bobbing as I favored another to assume the duties he had long taken pride in—indeed, to defend his own honor. Immediately, I knew I had spoken poorly, yet as many a wise person has observed, words once spoken cannot be undone.

Xerxes took up a sprint for the Visigothic swordsman, but with a deep sigh, Baduarius nevertheless shifted his posture to face the stranger who had besmirched his honor as a soldier. Baduarius himself had been a considerable instigator of similar taunts, especially against the Avars, yet I doubt that his warlord's mind was much concerned with such quid pro quo. By his own report, Baduarius was neither a tactician nor a commander, not one like Belisarius, John, or myself. No, his pride was within the shield wall, or opposite the enemy's best brawler, where his raw strength and unrivaled determination had seen him through so many duels.

I saw the Visigoth smile, dismount his horse, refasten his shield, and jog forward to meet Baduarius. At this, Xerxes halted, unwilling to disrupt the sacred practice of single combat—even if it meant open defiance of my order.

The Visigoth struck the first blow. It was swift, and saw the long edge of the sword blade rattle against the wooden boards of

Baduarius' shield, yet lacked any serious force. Baduarius countered with two thrusts of his own, the first striking only air, but the second dug ever so slightly into a wooden panel just outside the Visigoth's shield boss, where his sword tip stuck. Baduarius yanked hard to free his weapon, sending a wooden shard splintering off of the shield and revealing a slight yet noticeable gap in the Visigoth's aegis.

In all of the duels I had seen Baduarius fight, this one was by far his most masterful. Despite his size, Baduarius moved deftly, his footwork as nimble as a dancer's, shifting his great weight side to side with no pause or opportunity for the Visigoth to counterstrike. He rained blows upon the enemy champion, with nary a pause to adjust his stance as he slashed his blade relentlessly forward. This Visigoth, to his credit, was no common fighter, evident by his lithe frame, his movements as fluid as an ornery cat. Yet he was a far smaller man, and lacked the Ostrogoth's strength or reach. His only tactic with any promise at all was to avoid Baduarius' attacks altogether, to merely watch as the man's sword sliced through air perilously close to his head, arms, and chest. Only when Baduarius thrust closer did he ever lift his shield, and each time the blade chewed another piece away.

In truth, I do not know what else the Visigoth might have done differently. Even his blade was far smaller than the one Baduarius bore, and unless his sword's iron was of uncommonly good stock, the size and force of a direct blow with Baduarius' own would easily bend or even shear it. Thus the Visigoth levied his sword only to deflect the occasional lunge, yet Baduarius was careful not to overextend his position and leave any opportunity for his enemy.

As the pair slid ever closer to Septem's walls, Theudesgel emerged once more atop the walls. His words came out in an angry rasp, and though his shouts were unintelligible to me in their coarse Gothic tongue, they caught the attention of his champion below, who took two paces backward and raised his sword in recognition of his master's command. Seeing such, Baduarius sought to press his advantage onward, yet a whistling arrow from Septem's walls sent him jumping back in surprise and confusion.

"Cheat!" Gunderic roared, infuriated at the dishonor of the distraction.

My eyes widened as I tore my gaze away from the duel and back onto the city's walls. An archer stood at Theudesgel's side, already reaching for a second arrow to follow the first. Theudesgel nodded, and the archer pulled the bowstring back to his ear, the wooden ends curling backward as the archer found his target. He loosed, sending Baduarius scurrying back to put distance between himself and the second attacker.

It was difficult to hear above the din that followed. I doubt that a single Roman throat was not screaming with indignity, from the low fury of Rosamund's curses to the thunderous booms from Gunderic's square jaw. Quickly taking measure of the moment, I noticed that the archer's arrow did not sail directly at Baduarius' retreating form, but rather slightly off to the side. A third missile followed, and then a fourth, allowing the Visigothic champion time to trot forward and rain his own flurry of blows as Baduarius drew back onto the defensive. Now, rather than powerful overhead slashes, he jabbed and thrusted, using his sword's tip to push Baduarius repeatedly onto his back foot, and eventually back along a straight path toward the Roman lines. They were feeble enough attacks—a stab to the eyes easily dodged, or a jab to the waist even a child could parry with a flick of the shield—yet still they demanded Baduarius' attention, and whenever it appeared that he might reclaim the advantage once more, an arrow sailed from Septem's walls to force a swift block or retreat.

"Should I call one of our own bowmen?" I asked Liberius.

He shook his head. "You're just as likely to skewer your own man. Theudesgel has the advantage—from the walls, his archer can easily hit Baduarius with minimal risk."

"Then why isn't he?"

If Liberius possessed an answer, he did not share it. I drew heart when the edge of Baduarius' sword nicked a thin gash along the Visigoth's hip, a superficial wound that nonetheless poured dark blood over sliced leather and pooled around his thigh. The enemy champion winced, finally ceding the attack and slightly changing direction to avoid Baduarius' blows. No arrows sailed to halt our champion's progress, and at last we Romans smelled vengeance and victory.

It was then, backing away from Baduarius' furious exchange of cuts and slashes, that the Visigoth finally made a mistake. While the enemy champion had moved gracefully on stone road and thin grasses alike, the heel of his boot now glanced atop one of the many severed heads that littered the land, a slick and unstable landing. Shrieking in fear and surprise, the Visigoth tumbled to the dust, his sword flung into muck and gore.

Baduarius did not hesitate. He twirled the hilt of his sword, pointed his blade downward at his exposed enemy, and, roaring in hatred and triumph, drove it directly at the Visigoth's heart.

Yet he found only the Visigoth's shield, a stubborn block to the killing blow. And that battered shield splintered before the thrust, leaving the iron blade stuck around the ruined remnants of the shield's wooden panels.

Someone screamed. Like most others, I started in surprise, at first not comprehending the fearful Persian voice screaming toward the duel.

"Baduarius, back away!" Xerxes called out again.

Though I did not see the cause of Xerxes' alarm in the moment, I understand now what he meant. In hindsight, it is clear that the Visigoth did not truly slip, but merely feinted to draw Baduarius close, where his great size would count for less.

Baduarius roared in frustration as he kicked a heavy boot toward his opponent. Then, leaning down, Baduarius gripped hard on the hilt of his blade, starting to saw his sword free of its wooden trap. A glint of steel flickered from the Visigoth as he drew a dagger from behind one of his bronze greaves. With a crunch, Baduarius at last disentangled his sword and raised it above his head for a killing stroke once more. But it was not to come. Instead, he shuddered, the

Visigoth's dagger piercing through an armpit crease in his armor, the blade buried to the hilt in his flesh.

Baduarius jerked upright, his fingers numbly allowing his sword to clatter against the ground. Stumbling, he choked up a glob of thick blood, an ominous sign of a punctured lung. Falling to a knee, Baduarius raised an arm in feeble defiance, but his strength was too sapped to deflect the incoming lunge from his enemy.

A paralyzing pain rose to my throat, making it difficult to breathe. "No!" I choked.

The Visigoth's sword, useless in sparring against Baduarius' hulking weapon, now pierced easily through the scales and leather above Baduarius' abdomen, carving through his viscera. For as skilled as Baduarius was, the Visigothic champion was far better. Dishonorable, and physically weaker, but with a mind to fell a far larger and stronger opponent with just a single blow. And in war, dishonorable cunning is far swifter and more successful than the rigid confines of honest combat.

Deaf to any words from Liberius or Rosamund, I half slid down my watch-post ladder, my gloves growing uncomfortably hot as they rubbed too quickly against the coarse wood. I did not even pause to inform my bodyguard of my intentions, simply gathered my feet at the base of the tower and sprinted as fast as my legs would take me to where Baduarius had fallen. Ranks of Roman spearmen parted as I first hopped into the trench and then crawled my way out onto the other side, only vaguely aware that Sembrouthes and the Aksumites were trailing closely behind. It was only when I had fully cleared my defenses that my perception returned, and I heard Theudesgel laugh, heard the Visigothic champion whoop with joy at his victory, dancing and hopping around the fallen Roman soldier, heard the sea of angry roars swelling behind me, with only one voice calling for strategy.

It was Xerxes. "Fall on your commander!"

I had failed. Not only in losing control of the opening duel outside Septem, but in the inability to keep a dispassionate mind. Even now, if I close my eyes, I can still see that sword piercing through Baduarius' gut, its tip glinting and bloody. In that moment, I hated Baduarius for ignoring my command, but I hated myself more for pushing my friend to take on unreasonable risks. I never knew the joy of an older brother, but if I had, I would have envisioned him to be something like Baduarius, that bawdy, gregarious oaf who aided me through the slaughter of Taurus and the darkest nights of Mesopotamia. Now that I had witnessed Baduarius fall, I cleared all thoughts of command from my mind, and only rushed forth from the lines, starving for the death of Baduarius' attacker.

Ignoring my bodyguards' attempts to wrestle me to safety, I drew my sword and closed in on the Visigothic champion. Being a leader meant nothing now. A lifetime of lessons leaked from my mind as I drew upon Baduarius' killer. Recognizing a second attacker, the man stopped his celebration, squaring his shoulders for another clash of swords. Seething, I rushed ever closer, closer, until my boot found a slick, spongey patch of earth, lost purchase, and sent me toppling to the ground.

Above, Theudesgel cackled with laughter as I tangled with my cloak, struggling to my feet. I backed away in revulsion as I realized that the hazard underfoot was the head of yet another of my slain spearmen, the skull now compressed and dark fluid oozing from the open neck from holding the weight of my body. The Visigothic champion shrugged, grinning to himself as he backed away to the safety of Septem's gate. Once he stood within, he waved, and the gate closed, leaving me alone a mere fifty paces from Septem's walls.

I cared little for the immediate danger that I found myself in. Sprinting the remaining distance to Baduarius' prone form, I found him still alive, blood streaming from the twin gashes underneath his right arm and just below his rib cage. Kneeling, I surveyed Baduarius' injuries with urgent horror, knowing full well what such blows brought to their victim.

I unstrapped his helmet, gingerly lifting his massive skull with my gloved hand, as Baduarius sputtered thick bubbles. In my concentration, I only vaguely noticed the Aksumites forming a barrier of shields around us, with Sembrouthes' bulwark absorbing an arrow that easily would have buried itself deep into my ear. I had eyes only for Baduarius, who huffed and choked as he opened his eyes to a universe of pain.

He could not speak, but he saw me. His stained crimson lips broke into a sad smile, the grin impossibly wide as endless red leaked from the corners of his mouth. I gripped Baduarius' palm into my own, and he in turn kept his eyes locked firmly upon my own, despite a light shudder from the pain in his chest. He did not moan or complain, but a single tear cut through the dirt and gore that clung to his bearded cheeks. His face had now turned the slightest tinge of blue.

"Go to Dagisthaeus," I whispered into his ear. "Tell him of all the incredible things you have seen."

Baduarius did not live for more than a dozen further heartbeats. A final choke, and a convulsion of his uninjured shoulder, and Belisarius' Ostrogothic champion perished on the outskirts of Septem. To this day, I swear that I felt the soul depart his body, something that the priests assure me was a sign that Baduarius had been taken into God's embrace. Of that, I cannot be certain—all I knew was the fresh wound of grief, of yet another friend taken in the Empire's battles. Only this time, the fault fell squarely on my own shoulders.

Rage and guilt sent all reason fleeing from my mind and poured a thirst for vengeance in their place. In that moment, it was as though I had shrunk back into the body of the boy who fought Solomon on the training sands of the Imperial Palace to take vengeance for all the pain and suffering my hated rival had brought to my younger brother.

Face burning and vision blurred, I placed Baduarius' head carefully onto the ground and rose to my feet. Somewhere in my mind, Liberius' voice urged me upright, to take hold of the situation before more wasted death befell my army along Septem's walls. Yet with Baduarius' blood slick upon my gloves, I could not do it. I could not do anything. I lacked the raw power to martial my senses into any state of calm or rationality. I wanted revenge, but equally wanted to toss aside the burdens that Belisarius had rendered onto me. In that moment, I knew acutely how much I had disappointed so many who had placed their hopes upon me, yet could not bring myself to rectify that wrong. No, truthfully, I did not even know how. In my younger years, I had rarely disappointed my teachers or my masters. Failure of this magnitude was an unwelcome stranger.

Scores of Roman spearmen had already flooded by me, many of whom joined Sembrouthes and the Aksumites to form a protective barrier from the accelerating Visigothic barrage. Close by, I found Xerxes, hailing me with a desperate wave as he ran close.

"Varus!" he screamed, his voice cracking. "We need to fall back!"

I shook my head. "Take the walls, as we planned!"

Xerxes let out a sigh of exasperation. "As you command."

I nodded, turned around, and faced Septem's walls. "Get me a fucking ladder, now!"

A nearby centurion obeyed, calling forward ladder carriers led by Baduarius until just now. "Spread the order, take these walls!"

Sharing in my rage, pockets of approval sped through the ranks. Other groups hustled to the front, dodging occasional boulders or grass-covered gullies. One group was not so lucky—their lead ladder carrier overextended a foot at full sprint, not anticipating the hand-length drop concealed by a patch of grass and weeds. Cursing, the soldier toppled over as he rolled his ankle, sending his comrades scattering fearfully aside as they fought to retain control of the ladder. Thankfully it neither dropped nor broke, though the spearman had to be carried from the battle as he limped painfully back to the safety of our trenches.

"Ladder!" I screamed again, and the team finally reached my position.

Pushing the frontmost carrier out of the way, I hoisted the heavy rung atop my own shoulder. Eyeing the wall, I quickly adjusted the ladder for a more appropriate angle, and began to push forward, stopped only momentarily by a tug at my soiled cloak.

"Your shield!" Sembrouthes yelled, offering the ouroboros-covered bulwark.

Slinging the shield about my back, I screamed aimlessly as other ladder teams reached their appointed positions at the base of the walls. All trappings of command or burdens of leadership dropped away. I ran from the embarrassment and fault of my friend's death and returned to my place as the rawest recruit in a Roman siege. Aksumite shields guarded our steady advance as the rearmost ladder carrier boomed a cadence to guide our pace and steps, keeping we six men in good alignment despite falling arrows and stones that shivered from Aksumite and Cappadocian shields. Reaching the wall at last, we hoisted the ladder high into the air, one man assigned to hold its wooden rungs in place despite any Visigothic attempts at dislodging. One archer did lean down for a quick shot at our men, yet scurried behind a stone protruding from the wall as a Cappadocian propelled a javelin a finger's length from the archer's face.

"Take the walls!" I screeched, grabbing the first rungs of the ladder and preparing for my ascent.

Then a forceful hand tugged hard at my shoulder, preventing further motion. Turning to meet the challenger, I found Sembrouthes snarling in anger.

"Varus, don't be a lunatic! Wait for others to clear the way!"

"Follow me or don't!" I called back, the heat of guilt and embarrassment creeping back. "I release you from your oath to me."

"*Varus!*"

I had no time for debate. An Aksumite shield blocked yet another stone falling from the walls above, rattling my senses alert and attuned to the task at hand. I thought of nothing else—not Baduarius, not Mariya, nor even my children—just of the need to slaughter every Visigoth in my way, to seize some real control of a task entrusted to me and execute it to the fullest.

I gripped the ladder's rungs yet again, and rose from the earth.

The climb could not have taken me more than two score heartbeats, yet each cubit seemed an eternity. The sparse allotments of enemy archers loosed down upon each of the ladder teams, and the farther I rose from the ground, the less I could depend upon any Roman spearman to come to my defense. Worse, climbing left me vulnerable to attack as I ascended the rungs, unable to keep balance and hoist my shield skywards as I progressed up the ladder. All I could do was to pray that God would brush enemy stones and arrows away from their targets, and hope that the short-shafted javelins wielded behind me would dissuade any Visigoth from a focused attack to my head or chest.

Through God's grace or blind fortune, I was not struck. Others were not so fortunate, with falling stones especially accurate. Though lacking in the deadly barbed force or accuracy of an iron arrowhead, a stone could be lofted from behind the safety of the walls, with the attacker trading the ability to target any one foe for the relative guarantee that he would rest safe from Roman javelins. Halfway up the ladder, I saw another climber thirty paces away flung from his perch, his face bashed in a mist of blood and bone as a well-placed stone crashed upon his head. Others at the foot of the walls were struck, by falling men as much as by stones and debris, their bones splintered from nothing more than poor fortune.

A tiny shred of doubt entered my heart, but I squashed away my weakness with a mindless scream. I redoubled my pace, timing my vault atop the battlements as two Roman javelinists launched their darts at would-be Visigothic attackers. Then, holding my breath, I hauled myself upright.

The scene upon the other side of the walls was nothing short of chaos. Smoke, flying stones, and manic Visigothic soldiers rushed to meet the orders of their officers, leaving the streets of Septem awash with armored bodies and smoldering flames. The closest Visigothic defender rushed at me, spear drawn and lowered to my guts. I did not have time to draw my sword or unsling my shield.

Yet he was slow and, whether from poor training or considerable lack of sleep in the preceding nights, clumsy in his movements. Effortlessly, I sidestepped his spear thrust, grabbed the hem of his leather chest armor, and used his momentum to propel him from the battlements and onto the stone ground inside Septem's walls.

Immediately thereafter, I unslung the shield from my back and drew my sword for the battle ahead.

It was at this moment that the enormity of my error struck me fully. Absent the protection of a Roman shield wall, and with no other Romans nearby to distract the Visigothic defenders, all I could do was cover my body with my iron-rimmed shield, deflecting attacks and slashing mindlessly to dissuade any attacker from drawing too close. But the shield was itself a liability; its ouroboros insignia soon drew the attention of other Visigothic archers, with one arrow burying its iron tip into my shield and sending me temporarily off balance.

As a second arrow sailed into the wooden panels of my shield, Sembrouthes hauled himself up onto Septem's walls, thrusting his lengthy spear at a nearby Visigoth and cutting through the layers of mail and flesh as though the man's abdomen were soft cheese. Hot blood and intestines spilled onto the floor, and the man dropped his weapon and fell painfully to his knees. I warded off another would-be attacker, linking my shield with Sembrouthes' and forming a tiny shield wall to fend off our attackers.

"The attack is failing!" Sembrouthes screamed. "Theudesgel set fire to the ram, and none of our ladders are breaking through."

"Hold!" I called back.

Yet with the primal danger of combat honing my mind, I quickly realized Sembrouthes was correct. As if to prove his point, a Thracian spearman climbing to the highest rungs of our ladder was impaled seconds later by a returned javelin, the iron point puncturing his neck and jutting cleanly out the other side. The man fell from the ladder, but only halfway; his calves and knees caught upon a rung while his body dangled upside down, blood rushing from the gaping wound below his chin.

Immediately, I recognized his attacker as the Visigothic champion. Slashing wildly, I cut at the champion's throat, shuffling forward to press my advantage. My progress was minimal, however, for Sembrouthes yanked hard at my belt and slammed his iron shield rim into my own.

"You want to make your wife a widow?" Sembrouthes screamed, any pretense of calm burned into fury. "We leave now!"

Sensing our hesitancy, the Visigothic champion pressed closer, and we sparred before backing further against the Roman edge of the wall.

"Down!" Sembrouthes yelled to me. "I will follow!"

Sembrouthes nudged his way forward, shoving me hard with an armored hip that nearly sent me tumbling below. Eyeing the encroaching Visigoths, I screamed in frustration before surrendering to Sembrouthes' will, hoisting my shield along my back and hopping onto the blood-soaked rungs below. True to his word, Sembrouthes followed close behind, shouting for javelins to shelter his escape. Our retreat was far more hurried than the ascent, and at times I worried that my boots would slip on the slick rungs, yet somehow, I managed to find my way back to the soil below.

We ran. The army was already in something of a rout, eager to avoid opportunistic arrows and the low fire that spread from the remnants of our second ram. God help me, but I joined them, my gore-drenched cloak flying behind me as I did so. Somehow, I had the acuity to order the wounded and dead to be carried back to our trenches, and personally saw to Baduarius' own removal, yet there was little solace in such mercies. I ran away, and behind all that could be heard the laughing of Theudesgel.

THE REMEDY FOR ANGER

Flames licked the bodies of our fallen brothers, turning hair and clothing into ash. The pyres' heat lathered the living in an uncomfortable sweat, and blurred my vision. Rosamund alone seemed unaffected, even as many shuffled back to safety from the sizzling fat roasting in the pyres. I joined them, stumbling in my prayers, my gaze fixed upon the dead so that I would not have to meet the eyes of their surviving friends. It was a ritual I had observed too many times before, yet this was the first carried out under my leadership and caused by my foolishness.

Baduarius occupied the highest platform, built from lumber of a dozen trees that grew in the Mauretanian hills. Men saluted their fallen commander and former champion as his body blackened and crisped in a fiery inferno, his life's achievements recited and celebrated by a grieving Ascum. More so the better, for I doubt whether I had the strength to give honor to the man. It was all I could do to keep from weeping, for in my heart I knew that I had killed Baduarius the same as any Visigothic marauder.

I had Christian prayers chanted for the dead, yet did not deny the pagans in my expedition the right to beseech their gods to care for the souls of the lost. Several who died were known pagans from the rugged interior of Cappadocia, while Baduarius seemed to have professed faith in Christianity and paganism alike.

"How can a man be a Christian, but seek the protection of pagan gods?" I asked Ascum.

He shrugged. "It's Christianity that has all the rules. Baduarius just wanted to make sure he would be victorious in whichever afterlife took him. If anything, it's a smart way to defend one's wager."

"Faith isn't a wager," I muttered.

"But life is," Ascum shot back. "Especially how we warriors spend it."

At the request of several pagan warriors, Rosamund led many men in prayer, although whether her gods were the same as theirs, I cannot be certain. And though I had studiously avoided any familiarity with her pantheon up to then, I found that in my mourning, I was nevertheless temporarily spellbound by Rosamund's half song, half prayer.

"Years ago, when the world was young, the first god rose from the earth. With his hands, he shaped mountains and forests, and from his blood were created the rivers and seas, while his breath drove the winds. From the god Tuisto come all beasts which stalk the lands, and fish that swim the seas, and winged creatures of the air."

In a way, the myth was not dissimilar to the story of Genesis, the earliest tales of God's creation of the world. For a brief moment, my grief abated as I fixed upon Rosamund, my curiosity overcoming any fear that I might displease Petrus or God.

"Tuisto shaped his mate, Nehalennia, from the soils of the earth and the waters of the seas, and together they built the first village. Through them, their firstborn son Mannus fathered all the tribes, his hundreds of children living in peace."

As Rosamund chanted, Baduarius' fire rose, igniting his beard before spreading across his hulking body. Crouching down, Rosamund dug one hand into the soil, then tossed a handful of dirt into the flames. Thereafter, she unstopped her waterskin, sprinkling droplets that instantly evaporated amidst the heat.

"The gods lived in peace for thousands of years. However, greed took hold as the seventh generation of gods was born, over who should have dominion over all the earth. And so, the gods separated into their war bands, creating the tribes to fight and kill. Over centuries, the old gods were killed in war, and their descendants became mortal, a punishment for sullying the harmony of Tuisto's creation. From their wrath came storms, and famine, and disease, and all manner of suffering."

Rosamund paused then to pluck jars of powders from her nearby medicine chest. Drawing out their corks, Rosamund paced toward Baduarius' platform.

"When we die, we return to the gods' original peace," Rosamund chanted, her gaze fixed upon Baduarius. "But one day, all rivalries will cease, and the unnatural urge to dominate all others will be quenched. Until that day, we sing in memory of Baduarius, and all others who have departed with him. They who descend from Mannus know only peace in death, for they already know that one day soon, harmony will return to this world."

With that, Rosamund hurled the jars into Baduarius' fire. And for several heartbeats, nothing happened.

Then the blaze burst skyward, twice as high as before. More, the flames flickered blue and green and every shade of pink and red, dancing about as if painted from the brush of a fresco artist. Their brightness stung my eyes, requiring a moment to adjust. Rosamund, however, was unperturbed.

"Weep not for Baduarius, for he is already in joy!" Rosamund screamed. "Pray only that the day of our liberation comes soon, and that Tuisto returns to start anew."

Many stamped their spears into the ground, rumbling the earth. Others spoke low prayers in various languages, their only agreement being a tone of praise. All seemed pleased with Rosamund, who turned to watch Baduarius' fire retreat back to a normal orange glow, revealing a pyre stripped of its fuel from the overpowering heat.

My trance snapped; the ritual was too much for me to bear. I stood aloof, wishing to leave, yet dared not be seen retreating by my men. I only moved after Rosamund walked to my side and squeezed my forearm.

"Varus..." she whispered.

"Not now," I grunted, shrugging fruitlessly against her grip.

Rosamund's voice was little more than a hum. "It isn't a weakness to be consoled by your friends."

"Go away!" I snarled.

Yet even as I did, every morsel of my soul wanted to reach out to Rosamund and wrap her in an embrace. I nearly did, and would have, had she not swiftly obeyed. "I'll be here when you need me."

If there is anything worse than a fool, it is a proud fool. My very identity had been wounded, and I lacked the humility to seek Rosamund's comfort, or anyone else's. As Rosamund departed, Sembrouthes and my Aksumite guards prevented any from entering into my presence for the dying hours of the first evening after our battle, allowing the sun to die without even Cephalas to ferry my meals.

In my head, insidious whispers guessed at what my men uttered around the evening campfires—that Varus was nothing more than an upjumped favorite of a celebrated general, appointed only in a deficit of good officers, and that they were likely to perish on this insane mission to seize this windswept fortress at the godforsaken ends of the earth. They had cheered when they first saw the Pillars of Herakles, yet now there was only grief. Twenty Romans lay slain and another dozen wounded after my foolhardy assault, with the greatest loss being Belisarius' greatest soldier.

I did not sleep. I felt neither hunger nor the soreness of a day's labor, my thoughts wandering far away, imagining the disdain that my loved ones would have for such failure. What would Mariya think? The Empress? Father Petrus? Belisarius? Each face I pictured only amplified my grief. Yet most of all, in the rare moments when I did close my eyes, I saw the shade of Baduarius, still trying to prove his friendship and loyalty after being humiliated before his friends and fellow commanders.

In such a stupor, and the uncertain darkness of night, I heard my tent flap unknot and open. I could see little, for no candles were lit in the pitch darkness of my quarters, yet a hazy veneer of torchlight illuminated the world just beyond.

"Leave!" I shouted. "I gave no permission for any to enter!"

"Nor do I require any," Liberius answered, slipping through the gap in my tent and resting a torch in an iron holster.

Rising to a seated position, I felt my eyes adjust to the unwelcome light, which cast a vast shadow from Liberius' cloaked body as he drew closer. His eyes were sunken from lack of sleep, yet showed little of the fatigue that many must have felt on this evening.

"May I sit?"

I nodded, before realizing Liberius could hardly see any movement in the darkness. "Of course, Lord," I said, my throat cracked and dry.

Finding a stool, Liberius dragged his perch to my bedside, such as it was. He sat heavily, exhaling a long sigh as he rubbed his forearms against the night chill. I offered no conversation, sensing he had his own purposes for arriving unannounced. We both sat in silence for several heartbeats, our only company the dancing embers atop Liberius' torch.

"Today will be a day that you shall never forget," Liberius began. "And believe me, I know this lesson far too well."

"How is that?" I answered, my throat a throbbing knot of shame.

"Because today, your first real role as a leader has ended in failure. You may even be questioning whether you ever were capable for the position, or if you will ever improve."

I grunted, unable to give a proper reply. Liberius scowled but continued.

"Men died because of your error in judgment. Many more will do the same in the years to come. This is only a tragedy if you allow yourself to surrender to self-doubt, and if you fail to emerge from these terrible lessons a better leader, and a better man."

I groaned. "I shouldn't have charged at the walls."

"No," Liberius concurred, "that was bull-headed, and played to your enemy's strengths."

My face burned, and I desired to crawl into a ball, hiding away in some corner of my tent. Yet speaking my grief and anxiety to my longtime teacher was something of a relief. "I shouldn't have humiliated Baduarius."

Again, Liberius agreed. "Another mistake, borne of a lack of confidence. Harsh discipline is often needed, yet sometimes, too, is soft speech. It is critical to understand when each is necessary, and which one might offer the best outcomes for all. Never speak when uncertain of one's intended outcomes."

And finally, I unleashed my greatest burden of all.

"I killed Baduarius," I blubbered. "If I hadn't been so stubborn..."

"On this, I disagree," Liberius answered. "Do not cheat Baduarius of his own will in life. Baduarius was a man who made his own decisions, including the one that led him into a duel that should have been avoided. If you would honor your friend, you cannot place the blame of his death at your own feet."

"But—"

"*But nothing!*" Liberius shot upright, startling me. "More friends will die in the years ahead. Some by your command. But even if the skies part and a naked angel descends from the heavens bearing every imaginable temptation, you must keep a calm mind and clear vision. In a way, you are like a father to your army, and they depend upon you for instruction and protection, like children."

Once more, for a brief time, neither of us spoke. For me, the sound of Liberius' fury was terrifying—I doubt I had ever heard him raise his voice thus. Likewise, however, the logic of his teaching sank through my thoughts, and while they did not remove the gnawing of grief in my stomach, they did lessen its sting. Liberius allowed me to grieve and collect my emotions, not deigning to push any further. His words offered little solace, yet even so, the undiluted guilt and embarrassment of such terrible failure seemed now less raw, and more closed. As my sobs grew silent, Liberius began again.

"You are a boy no longer, Varus. At times, this truth is hard for me to accept. Yet you have learned one of the surest and most terrible facts about all of life—that there is no such thing as fairness, or justice, or endless happiness. Such things are the imaginings of children—or priests."

I buried my face in my hands, still filthy from the battlefield. "Then why go on? How?"

"Because there are others who depend on us," Liberius replied. "For them, we give everything. Otherwise, we are lost and alone, without even the hope of a better tomorrow to guide our future. You, above all others, understand this notion well."

Visions of Mariya and the children, faint blurs, stole into my mind. Joining them were Theodora, and Rosamund, and Samur, and a hundred others to whom I had sworn some oath or another. They all depended upon me for something, and in turn, if Liberius could be believed, I relied upon them for purpose. Perhaps that was why my failure cut so deeply, for I believed that in my selfish shortsightedness, I had betrayed them all.

"The men will never follow me now," I moaned, my words little more than a whisper.

Liberius' eyes closed, his head tossing side to side. "Of course they will, if you have the courage to lead them. They did so for Belisarius, and his grief was far greater than what I see in this blubbering lump before me now."

Despite myself, I laughed, a bubble of phlegm gracelessly escaping a nostril. "What do you mean about Belisarius?"

Liberius chuckled. "Your brilliant general cried like a baby after Callinicum. Blamed himself for Sunicas and Simmas, and thousands of others who died on the Euphrates. And he was little bothered by Hermogenes' persecution, I might add. No, Belisarius has never been one to shrug off the deaths of his men. Indeed, that is what makes him unique, I'd wager, and infinitely more valuable to the Emperor than the procession of the Empire's failed warlords from the century before."

Where Liberius' previous lessons were simply sobering, this revelation of Belisarius' own struggles yielded a measure of understanding as well. I had glimpsed little of this sensitive and unconfident general Liberius spoke of, always seeing Belisarius as a figure of calmness, empathy, and unrivaled competence.

Liberius continued. "It is different when you are in command. Leadership is lonely business, and doubly so in war. Men second-guess each decision, and it is perilously easy for their doubts to infect your own sense of purpose. But what separates a good leader from a great one is not the ability to win battles, but to lose them graciously. Accept that you will fail, and relish the lessons that each failure brings. After that, ensure you shall never repeat the same mistakes again. If you can succeed in that, no man in all the world can stand against you."

"Lose graciously?" I repeated shakily. "Truly?"

Liberius nodded. "That skill is what makes Belisarius great, and what men will remember of you as well should you learn it. But you will do so only if you share that unbreakable will—to rise from this self-pity, strap your helmet upon your head, and lead your men to complete the task that the Emperor demands of them."

Rubbing my face, I turned to meet Liberius' shadow-cast eyes. "I will, Legate, I promise you."

Liberius gave me a weak smile. "I have no doubt. Even when you were a young boy, I had no doubt in you. Neither did Justin. And that is why we crafted seven gifts for you, in the knowledge that they would bring you closer to your destiny, and that of the Empire."

The gifts. I clutched at the cross that dangled from my neck, knowing that the dagger and sword rested close by. Those three, along with the great wealth that Justin bestowed to me upon his death, were four of the seven that had been initially promised when I was a simple bronze-helmeted recruit in Rome's armies. Much time had passed since receiving that fourth gift, and Liberius had been loath to discuss their contents or even the timing of delivery.

"Lord, will I still receive the other three?"

"In due time," Liberius responded. "But be wary, these last three are far less enjoyable, but considerably more important. Expect the fifth when you return to Constantinople."

I nodded. "Is it the scrolls you were searching for in Nisibis?"

Liberius chuckled. "Very good, Varus, but no. This will come later. You are correct in assuming it is something I intend to confer to you, but only when the time is right."

I sighed, again confronted with the same confusion and uncertainty that had nagged every step of my youth. Why had Justin placed so much favor onto me? Why so many privileges? Why so much forgiveness, when my failures would have earned condemnation or even death if borne by another? It made me want to scream, for I yearned for an answer to a lifetime of not knowing who I was.

"What are the gifts designed to do? What is their purpose?"

"Their purpose, you already know," Liberius replied. "To make you aware of who you are, and what you may become. But as I told you after Dara, do not rush their delivery. Allow me to carry this burden for you as long as my ancient bones are able. Beyond that, abandon this self-pity, and work to become better from your mistake."

There would be no answer to my lingering questions this evening. Instead, I surrendered to Liberius' rebuke and enjoyed the familiarity of his company in the privacy of my command tent. He called for servants to deliver an evening meal, and though it was a meager affair of twice-baked bread and dried fruit, in that evening and with his company, it was all the feast I could have wanted. We spoke of many things, of Mariya and my family, of the Empire and Theodora, and of the accomplishments already secured. Once the torch burned low, Liberius took his leave, allowing me to chase what little sleep could be stolen before dawn.

It was three days after Baduarius' death that Perenus and the Herulians finally arrived at our siege lines. Up to that point, I had spent time speaking with each of my centurions and dekarchoi, gauging their thoughts and attempting to rebuild their confidence in a youthful commander. Privately, I levied apologies to both Xerxes and Sembrouthes, for I had placed both men in grave danger. Xerxes shrugged and batted away my attempts, insisting that all men voyage through dark periods of life. Sembrouthes, on the other hand, shook his head with a wide grin, lightly boxing my ears as if chastising a child.

"Don't you ever do that to me again!" He laughed. "If I let some unwashed savage skewer you, Mariya will peel the flesh from my face."

"I doubt that!" I replied, embracing the man all the same.

Though morale suffered from Baduarius' loss, the men were heartened at the arrival of Perenus, Fulcaris, and their Herulian veterans. Drawing experience from multiple campaigns, they bolstered my less-experienced Cappadocians and more unruly Vandals. Most importantly, however, they provided to me additional senior officers whom I could rely upon—something that I had lacked prior to Baduarius' death, and whose absence had become an emergency immediately thereafter.

Perenus and Fulcaris both mourned the passing of our Ostrogothic champion. But it was Perenus, who knew Baduarius well, who offered a measure of consolation to my lingering guilt.

"Baduarius never declined a fight," he said. "It would have broken him to be denied the opportunity. And I do know that he loved you, for that great oaf said so many times."

When asked about why the Herulian and Ostrogothic foederati parted ways early in the expedition, Fulcaris merely shrugged.

"Indulf could not be reasoned with. He insisted that his men demanded plunder, and Tingis was a far more tempting target than Volubilis."

Other than promise that I would deal with Indulf later, there was little I could do to rectify the situation. Septem remained securely in Theudesgel's control, and it was imperative for us to seize the city as quickly as possible—in order to keep my promise to Belisarius, yet also to dissuade King Theudis from sending reinforcements to permanently occupy the region. Above all else, our presence in Mauretania Tingitana was to compel the Visigoths to remain in Hispania, not daring to venture into the new Roman prefecture of Africa. My Herulian reinforcements may have tipped the scale more in my favor, but I still lacked an appropriate strategy to crack Septem's defenses. Each day that passed without such successful resolution, the greater the risk of my men growing sick or disaffected, or that other emboldened enemies would wipe our paltry numbers from the land.

And so, two days after Perenus' arrival, I summoned my officers to a final meeting that would determine our fate. Standing to address them, I acknowledged Baduarius' passing, honoring the man for the considerable duty he had rendered in service of the Empire. Then, drawing from my lesson with Liberius, I began to heal the damage that had been brought by my rash decisions.

"I take full responsibility for the failures of the previous two attacks. Such errors, great or small, are mine alone. As Belisarius would do, I am here to listen to your thoughts on how we may best proceed, even if the only realistic option that lies ahead is retreat. Though I will listen to your counsel, out of friendship I ask that we find a way to fulfill the request Belisarius levied upon us. If we leave this city in the hands of Theudis and his warlords, all of the sacrifices and risks taken to liberate Carthage will be for naught."

With a nod, I resumed my seat, my heart pounding against my rib cage. A hundred different fears swam in my thoughts, borne of the distinct awareness that I had given little reason for any present to be confident in my leadership just then. For several moments after I concluded, the silence nearly brought me to choke, for I dared not breathe as I scanned the men's faces.

Rising a full head above his peers, it was Gunderic who spoke first. "Lord, the Vandals do not run from a fight. We have pledged loyalty to your army—all you need to do is tell us who to kill, and how."

"Indeed," Xerxes added. "The previous assaults could have been far more damaging, but our losses were thankfully light. We have enough ladders to continue, and a new siege ram can be crafted, yet I am reluctant to think that this strategy alone will see us to a successful end."

Perenus' bench was kicked backward, nearly toppling over from the excessive force. "Bugger Theudis. I would never leave you to fight alone. The foederati remembers your deeds in Mesopotamia and Carthage."

"Aye," Fulcaris confirmed.

Ascum struggled to rise, his one unscarred arm leaning heavily upon the table. "I want revenge against Theudesgel. Baduarius was one of my best friends."

"You will have it, upon my oath," I swore, the skin on my face prickling at the display of trust.

Others followed, including the Cappadocians and several captains of those dromons assigned for my use. Liberius said nothing as this procession continued, yet neither did he rush such discussions, nor disturb my relief. Despite everything, I had not lost the men—yet.

"We are in agreement, then. Septem must be taken," I began. "But a frontal assault is bordering on madness. Even a few dozen Visigoths can hold back an enemy ten times their number. So what is to be done?"

"We could starve them out?" Perenus suggested.

"Your mind has been boggled by too much sun," Liberius retorted. "That would take months, and our army is far more likely to starve itself in the meantime."

Perenus shrugged, leaving Xerxes to offer a more immediate tactic. "We could dig a tunnel under the walls. Many a siege has been broken in the East by such measures."

Again, Liberius made a tutting sound. "Tingitana is not Persia. It would break the backs of a thousand men to even attempt to carve through rock. Even then, this close to the coastline, it's more likely than not that any reasonably sized tunnel would become hopelessly flooded."

Other less-effective solutions were raised, each drawing skepticism from either Liberius or myself. Privately, I began to wonder whether Uliaris' prior insistence on reinforcements were correct, for another thousand could tip the scales of even an all-out assault well into my favor. Fulcaris even suggested that dispatches be sent to Belisarius for additional men, but I dismissed this as impossible. Though I was heartened by the reaffirmed determination to fight together, I began to internally despair that few options remained to guarantee victory—until Ascum, still heavy in his grief for Baduarius, spoke above the crowd.

"Burn them all."

All chatter amongst the officers ceased. Even Liberius raised an eyebrow at such a cryptic comment, yet he offered no retort as Ascum stood to his feet.

"We have failed to take the walls by land, but the Visigoths will be hard-pressed to defend by sea as well. Give me a few hundred brave men, and we can assault the sea gate just as the main army attempts a third attack."

Liberius' initial curiosity melded into skepticism. "Septem's sea walls are twice as thick as those by land, and give safe perch to dozens of archers. Our casualties would be enormous."

Ascum shook his head. "As I said, we will burn them all. Give me leave to gather all our naphtha stores, and I will light a fire in Septem's harbor that will never be forgotten."

All eyes, even Liberius', turned to me. Ascum's intervention was intriguing, yet such a maneuver seemed more suitable in the legends of Troy than for our current predicament. Godilas had trained me to rely upon practical skill in battle, and Ascum's plan seemed anything but practical. Worse than impractical, it was wildly unpredictable.

"What exactly will you do? What do you expect to occur?"

"Exactly what happened at Callinicum," Ascum shot back. "Except to the enemy's walls, rather than our ballistae. Naphtha burns hot enough that even ancient stones would crack."

Those words seemed to resonate, for all present knew that a blazing fire would wreak havoc upon stone fortifications—though our men had little experience with the tactic, as stone is not effective kindling.

"Ascum, I'm not sure—"

"It's brilliant," Liberius interrupted.

I furrowed my brow, still wary of the many uncertainties. "Lord, what of the sea spray? Surely that would dampen any fire? And even if it didn't, how could the naphtha be spread? Our ballistae would not do so quickly enough that the Visigoths could not douse the flames."

"Not ballistae." Ascum grinned, the twisted flesh at the corner of his burned face yielding a sinister curl. "We crash a fully laden dromon into the gate. That will get Theudesgel's attention."

There was no intelligent response. I have no shame in admitting that such an idea made me gape in awe, imagining such a massive vessel colliding with a stone fortress, belching flames. Perenus grinned madly, while Liberius clapped his hands in concordance with Ascum's words.

"We can spare a single ship," Ascum went on. "Allow me to gather all the naphtha available to our fleet. For best effect, we should attack in the noonday sun, leaving plenty of time to seize the walls while keeping the sunlight from our eyes."

Others voiced questions about such a tactic—the size of the crew, the time it would take—yet Ascum had ready answers. Only a half dozen men were needed to maintain course, and they could swim away prior to impact. Further, Ascum insisted that more than enough naphtha was available to douse Septem's entire harbor front—let alone its gate and walls. He grinned as he spoke, swearing vengeance for Baduarius and an end to this accursed expedition.

God knows, I had misgivings. Creativity has its place in battle, and ingenuity can win a war, yet reckless abandon will often lead to the ruin of any who pursue it. Nevertheless, stirred by the lessons of Liberius and the longstanding example of Belisarius, I levied trust in my officers. Of the difficult options available to us, this was one where the fates were strongly undecided, and it at least gave us some chance of a quick and relatively bloodless conclusion. And so I relented, consigning one of the Emperor's ships to damnation.

THE ANCIENT HARBOR
OF SEPTEM

It took Ascum a day and a night to gather all naphtha barrels remaining to our fleet. Joining him aboard the flagship, I marveled at the sheer logistical complexity of managing such vast quantities of the sticky onyx liquid, how its bearers were so careful to avoid dropping any or abrading the iron rims in any way. Seeing my curiosity, Ascum explained more of naphtha's properties.

"It's flammable, of course, but naphtha's real value is in how viscous and undeterrable it is. Even when doused with water, flames will still catch, and burn as hot as ever. With enough of this devil's piss, you can even turn the sea alight."

"So how do you put it out?" I asked.

"By smothering it," Ascum explained, wetting his lips. "When that's even possible, anyway. We have enough naphtha here to turn all Constantinople into a bed of charcoal. I can hardly imagine what that much would do in so small an area."

I frowned. "Truly? You mean this has not been done before?"

Ascum's grin widened. "Not against a land target. But don't worry, Varus. Leave this attack to me. I will gain you access to the city—it will be up to you and your men to exploit that opportunity. We will only have one chance to make this work."

Sailing beyond eyeshot of the walls, I stood on the flagship for a few hours more, watching as a sister vessel was loaded with hundreds of darkened barrels. If that was not enough, additional barrels and clay amphorae were loaded on the ship's decks, covering any unused space until the once-proud warship seemed little more than a floating barge bursting with a merchant's wares. Even then, a small crew of soldiers still stuffed more aboard until the vessel sat low in the sea.

We also prepared a number of smaller craft that would ferry groups of twenty or thirty men into Septem's harbor. Holdovers from our initial landing at Caput Vada so many months ago, the dromons each tugged several of the small vessels behind, their smaller holds filled with weapons and climbing rope for the eventual assault.

"I promise, Varus, we will be ready," Ascum said, placing a hand upon my shoulder. "Choose the men to lead this attack wisely."

And so I did. Later that evening, Perenus voiced surprise when I insisted the Herulians would remain on the mainland.

"It's not that I relish fighting from a boat, Varus," he said, "but that the assault will be a difficult one. Shouldn't you use the most disciplined men available?"

I disagreed. "I need my most disciplined men to lead the attack on land. For the seaborne assault, I need the moonstruck, the unbarred, and those utterly without restriction. Truly… I do not know how this gambit will progress. Those attacking from the ships must prepare for everything, and nothing."

"Gunderic, then," Perenus concluded.

"Gunderic." I smiled, my following thoughts left unspoken.

After all, who better than a couple hundred howling Vandals to barge through burning gates?

When told of this new honor, Gunderic boomed with approval. "At last! You will not regret this, Varus!"

"See that I do not," I responded. "The entire expedition hinges upon the courage of your men."

Gunderic beamed. "Then the Visigoths are already lost!"

As always, we set extra pickets along our trenches, still wary of any Visigothic attack, despite Theudesgel's inferior numbers. None came, allowing my men to consume double rations and retire early. Fearful of spies — still haunted as I was by the letter Belisarius received back in Carthage — I forced the senior commanders to keep their intentions private. Even so, with our camp rife with activity, the men must have suspected another attack on the morrow. With final orders delivered, I shared a meal with Rosamund, allowing Cephalas to go join Perenus so the two friends might share tales of their experiences in Mauretania. Strangely, I found myself at a measure of peace, enjoying the refreshing night air and the rolling thunder of the sea waves as I wrote to Belisarius of my failures, and my plans to salvage victory from loss. I could only pray that he would understand.

Preparations for the seaborne attack began well before dawn. Gunderic and Xerxes led the Vandals out of view of Septem's walls and onto rafts that ferried them toward our fleet, with each man under strict orders to remain silent. On land, Perenus took charge of the remaining Cappadocian and Herulian forces that comprised the bulk of my expedition, all under the watchful eye of Liberius. I left Cephalas to tend to the legate's needs, but found that I could not easily part from Rosamund.

"If Ascum intends to light the greatest fire of our lifetimes, I intend to see it." Rosamund grinned.

Over so many decades, I have always found it difficult to reject the wishes of women. Zenobia, Theodora, Mariya, Rosamund... they all possessed an authority over me that I could never understand. Though I was loath to place Rosamund so close to the jaws of violence, she would not be denied, and I lacked the will to resist her.

Guarded by my Aksumites, Rosamund and I took the last boat from the Mauretanian shore to rejoin our fleet — a not-insignificant undertaking, for it took a full hour of rowing before we reached the flagship. And, as always, my stomach roiled with each passing swell, made worse by the knowledge that our tiny vessel had little of the protections of the larger transports and dromons.

"You will not die today, Varus," Rosamund soothed me. "The gods love you too much."

"Then tell them to calm the seas." I groaned, retching over the side of the boat, too miserable even to word a prayer to my own God.

By the time our raft tossed its way to the flagship, the morning sun had come into full view along the eastern horizon. Shrouded by dense clouds, its feeble warmth promised a chill even later in the afternoon, and I fastened my white excubitor's cloak to block out the icy sea spray. Rosamund followed, reaching into a heavy satchel and withdrawing the white wolf's pelt that had been a spoil of battle from the Avars. I grinned as she wrapped the soft fur around her shoulders, somehow making her already translucent skin and bone-white hair all the more ethereal.

"It looks good on you!" I joked.

Rosamund smiled confidently. "I know."

My nausea waned as we climbed aboard that far larger flagship, yet I heaved one further time over the rail. As a younger man, I would have died of embarrassment at such a display, yet by now I had learned to ignore the chuckles and jibes of seasoned sailors.

"Ah, Lord Varus, I thought that was you!" Apollos, captain of the flagship, greeted me.

"Aye," I muttered, grabbing a waterskin to cleanse the foul acid of bile from my throat.

Steadying myself, I took measure of the surrounding coastline, observing Septem from a careful distance. As the more southerly of the Pillars of Herakles, Mount Abyla occupied a winding promontory that allowed Septem to nestle against its base. Even from afar I could spot Septem's inner citadel, sitting like a stone diadem atop the rolling mountain. To the far north, I could make out the outline of distant Mount Calpe, and I muttered a prayer that Thurimuth and Sindual might still live, and be successful in seizing their own targets.

Septem's seafront was bisected by the mountain, with a portion of its seawalls to the south, and others on the northern sprawling edge of the coast. It was along the northern edge's beaches and sandbars that the city's massive sea gates allowed entry to friendly vessels. Yet for the past week, it had been locked and barred from our dromons. Stone and iron stood timeless against the lashing of the waves, their thickness built in a manner to resist the exact maneuver we were foolish enough to consider. With one exception—we had enough naphtha to set the entire world alight, and could only hope that it would ruin any mortar or iron fastenings and send the wall's protections crumbling harmlessly into the sea.

After allowing me further time to survey the arrayed fleet, Ascum approached with the men who would captain our burning dromon into Septem's walls. They saluted, yet remained otherwise silent to muffle any shouts that would travel across the water. Lowering my voice to a whisper, I returned their greeting.

"Which of you will lead the attack?"

One Thracian stepped forward, his dark features betraying a mixed lineage of Greek and Hun. In the aftermath of Attila's invasions, such heritage was common enough, although most offspring decamped with the Hunnic tribes far to the north rather than remain within the Empire's borders.

"My name is Conon, Lord. Dekarchos, Thracian Army."

"Of which banda, dekarchos?" I prodded in Hunnic, testing my theories of Conon's origins.

"It is my honor to serve under Troglita, Commander," Conon responded in perfect Hunnic.

I nodded, offering a thin smile of approval before resuming the more conversant Greek. "Succeed, dekarchos, and I will have you made into a centurion. We are all depending on your wits today, Conon."

Conon yielded a crisp salute in reply, beaming a smile of crooked yellow teeth. With a final dismissal, Ascum ordered the men loaded into a raft and sent over to the doomed dromon. Within an hour, the team had scaled the ship and lifted its ponderous anchors, signaling that the overladen warship was prepared for her final voyage.

With a single blow of Ascum's horn, we began our approach.

This portion of the attack was meticulously planned, allowing select vessels carrying landing parties to approach Septem while remaining a safe distance behind the naphtha-stocked vessel. As we drew closer to our assigned positions, a Visigothic sentry blew a horn from the nearest sea wall, signaling the approach of yet another Roman fleet. In response, Ascum ordered three nearby vessels to launch unfired ballista bolts at the walls, hoping the feint would convince Theudesgel that another bombardment of the seafront was all that we planned.

The suicide dromon halted its progress, signaling a request to commence the attack. Ascum leaned closer, his rasps telling of our progress.

"They're ready, Lord."

I nodded. "What's the name of the vessel?"

Ascum shrugged, turning to relay the inquiry to Apollos. The captain returned, stroking his beard thoughtfully as he bobbed at my request.

"The *Serapis*, Commander," Apollos whispered.

"Very good," I muttered. "Justinian will be pleased that we sacrificed a pagan ship in service of the Empire!"

"I wouldn't be so jovial just yet, Varus," hissed a woman's voice behind me.

Surprised by her sternness, I turned to face a scowling Rosamund. "Why not?"

"Serapis places value in the dead and the dying," she explained. "Even here, so far from his temples, Serapis will grow powerful from the sacrifice you intend to offer."

My blood froze as she spoke, drawing from hours spent with the Egyptian priest when she first arrived in Constantinople. "I offer nothing to Serapis. My intention is only to pacify Septem."

Rosamund rolled her eyes. "What is battle other than a great sacrifice of lives? If anything, you might be one of Serapis' most beloved adherents."

By her tone, I could tell Rosamund was teasing me. Nevertheless, such pagan talk brought me to shiver, and I regretted indulging in

Rosamund's interjection. I paused for a time, my skin feeling as if it were caked in the greasy naphtha that would soon ignite Septem's seawalls, until I was interrupted by Ascum.

"Do I have your permission?" Ascum asked. "God or no, I promise you a victory."

Still chilled, I nodded. "See it done."

It began with a great blast of drums, a booming percussion reminiscent of our first night camped outside of Septem, signaling a flash of flaming ballistae and catapults that rained flaming death from the skies. Though a few stone-throwers acknowledged Ascum's drums, the assault was muted, lacking in destructive force. For now.

On land, Roman horns blared in response, acknowledging the start of our attack. Though Liberius and Perenus would form our land forces into battle array, their instructions were to wait for fire to spread along Septem's horizon, at which point they would rush the landward gate just as we seized openings by sea. I prayed the strategy would work, for though we had yearned for such an outcome, not even Ascum truly knew what would happen in such an attack.

"For Baduarius," I growled, watching the *Serapis'* sails catch wind, carrying the dromon forward from its distant origins. Conon steered the vessel to catch the swirling winds, driving the ship faster and faster as it closed distance with the gates.

"Aye, for Baduarius," Ascum agreed. "May those bastards burn in whatever hell will have them."

At two thousand paces, the first glimpses of fire were seen aboard the *Serapis* as Conon's men lit the fire that would consume the ship. The torchbearers disappeared into the ship's hold, and Ascum leaned into my ear to explain what would come to pass.

"Three men are breaking open casks, spilling the liquid on the lower decks," he whispered. "They started early this morning, so it will not be long now. They'll set each deck alight, and then jump into the sea."

"How quickly will the fires catch?" I asked.

"A few minutes," Ascum replied. "Long enough for them to leave safely, and for the ship to crash into the walls."

I nodded. "Signal the boarding parties to prepare."

As my orders were executed, my eyes grew fixed upon the *Serapis*, where faint trails of smoke rose from the ship's oar locks and twirled about its masts. Half of Conon's men abandoned the ship, yet the dekarchos kept enough men on board to retain control of the ship's rudder, steering it directly for Septem's sea gate. It was not a particularly difficult target, for that swooping stone archway could fit three dromons abreast, its rusted iron bars a full cubit thick and a half cubit wide.

Those trails of smoke transformed from a thin gray to deep and ominous black as the *Serapis* came within five hundred paces of the barred gate. Small, just-visible flames flickered from the ship's hold, spreading along the sides and into its rigging.

"The flames are rising too fast!" I said.

"Have faith, Varus," Rosamund replied in Heruli. "As I have said, you will not die this day."

"I wonder if your gods feel the same about Conon," I muttered.

More Romans jumped overboard. At two hundred paces, Visigothic archers fired upon the *Serapis*, but at which targets, I was not certain. The dromon gathered speed as it moved into shallower waters along the harbor, its bow directed almost perfectly toward the gate's center. As the *Serapis* moved closer to the walls, it grew more difficult to see Conon's movements or the Visigothic response, although the Gothic horns grew more frantic as knowledge of the *Serapis'* intent dawned upon those along the sea walls.

All I know is that, with only a hundred paces to spare, Conon leapt into the frigid waters, paddling hard for a raft that had been assigned to pluck the *Serapis'* minimal crew to safety. Uncaptained, the dromon veered slightly to the left, its curved wooden bow rotating toward the gate's stone embankment. Flames rose from flaxen ropes and began to cover the canvas of the ship's sails, its Imperial regalia blackening under swelling heat. As the rigging grew brittle and snapped under the pressure of the flames, the *Serapis* collided with

Septem's outer defenses to the sound of splintering decking.

"They missed," I whispered to Ascum, watching the flaming warship shudder upon impact.

"Just wait," Ascum replied patiently. "There is much still to see."

The *Serapis* rotated, revealing an impact point to the stone walls immediately adjacent to the gate. With its bow crumpled and front hulls collapsed, the dromon began to list, blocking the still-intact iron gates from any would-be water travelers. Smoke grew ever denser as the remnants of the deck were consumed by Conon's fire, yet little damage was evident to our intended objective. We had failed, and the faint calls of laughter rose from those Visigothic defenders who watched the *Serapis* slowly founder.

Again, the suffocating heat of humiliation crept through the veins in my throat. It was like offal, and I choked in surprise and anger. My mind raced for solutions, searching the thousands of lessons from Liberius or Godilas, yet finding none that adequately fit the disaster of our current situation.

"Ascum…" I growled.

"Listen!" he called.

At first, I heard nothing untoward. Laughter from my enemies, the rolling of the sea, and the occasional belch of one of our men. I shook my head in frustration, believing Ascum to be waiting fruitlessly for a salvation that could not come. Sighing angrily, I furrowed my brow as I gazed upon the burning vessel.

"Varus, stop!" Rosamund hissed, irritated at my fussing. "I hear it!"

She clutched at my palm, digging her pointy nails into my leather glove. Her rigid grip drew me to focus, first upon her breathing, and soon thereafter upon the noise that both Ascum and Rosamund had been able to detect.

By the time I acknowledged the error of my observation, even the deaf would have noticed something changing aboard the dying remnants of the flaming *Serapis*. The warship emitted a groan as if it were pleading for assistance, an ominous death rattle that pulsed along the sea. I felt the *Serapis* dying, and with it, my humiliation and dread of failure transfigured into confusion and awe. As the fires of *Serapis* magnified in their intensity, the ship's deck and masts seemed to lurch in the air, warping and splintering charred timbers into an impossible, deformed state. All grew silent as we watched the *Serapis*, its beams spewing white heat, roll ever so slightly toward Septem's sea gate. From there, the entire world burned.

When I speak to the priests of what I saw that morning, they claim it was divine retribution. That God, in his almighty and immaculate form, had descended from the heavens and smote the heathen Visigoths out of a once-proud city in the Christian Empire. But they are fools; they were not there. Though I do not understand what I saw, I know that it was not God. If anything, it was Satan, spewing forth brimstone to consume the souls of the entire world.

My eyes burned for several heartbeats, my lids lashing together to protect against the blinding flash from the *Serapis*. One arm still locked firmly upon Rosamund, I used a free hand to rub my watering eyes, prying them open at last to a blazing blur. My senses slowly flooded back to full perception, the sounds of a hundred thousand fires swirling in the chasm of a whirlwind. It seemed like the very air around us surged toward the burning emblem, feeding its insatiable hunger as it plumed toward the heavens. The seas rolled underneath us as a dry heat pulsed along our exposed skin, both warm and inviting yet also terrible in its embrace.

It was only then that I was able to fully grasp the desolation wrought by Ascum's attack. Where the *Serapis* once listed was a vacant space, no trace remaining of the once-proud dromon. Gone, too, was Septem's gate and a good four paces of stone wall, its debris scattered in all directions. Thick black naphtha coated the expanse, as though some fresco painter had mixed too many colors over it at once. Most of all, a vast plume of darkened smoke billowed above the sea walls, shrouding a hundred fires that burned atop stone, wood, dirt, and even the sea itself.

I crossed myself, gaping in awe. "Holy Mother of God…"

Standing close, Rosamund muttered in the indecipherable language of her Gepid ancestors, yet by the tone of her voice I could sense the desperation in her prayers as she beseeched the ancient pagan deities. Others stood dumbstruck, spat, or prayed at the sight, with only Ascum standing firm, snarling with hatred at his work.

"For Baduarius," Ascum muttered. "Burn in a thousand hells."

Xerxes whistled lightly, his eyes unblinking as he gaped at the pillar of light that would have been most pleasing to the priests of his religion. "You may get your wish, Ascum," Xerxes said, "for I cannot imagine many surviving the thunderbolt of a god."

Even as many gawked at the destruction of Septem, still others dove into the water to rescue those who had toppled helplessly into the sea due to the rolling waves of the attack. Yet it was not until I saw one team rescue Conon that my own sense of awe evaporated, our moment to seize victory finally having arrived. And with that, a giddiness overtook my senses, fueled by the realization that victory was finally within my grasp.

"To the boats!" I yelled, releasing myself from Rosamund's grip.

"Lord, perhaps you should stay and—" Sembrouthes began.

I denied him. "No, Sembrouthes. Today, I lead my men into battle."

Sembrouthes was right, of course. Only a fool of a commander charges headlong into battle, risking the very leadership core of his army in return for the rush of violence and sacrifice. As the men cheered their commander, however, my spirits soared, and I knew that I could not sit idly as hundreds risked their lives in a savage attack on this distant shore.

Ascum sounded the drums of all our ships remaining afloat, their rolling percussion signaling our success to our landward forces. Not that any confirmation was needed—it would not surprise me if the Emperor in Constantinople had seen the explosion along Septem's sea gates—yet it was a reassuring return to decorum all the same. As my Aksumites loaded themselves into my intended craft, Rosamund bade me halt one final time.

"Yes?" I called back, lifting my plumed helmet atop my head.

"Kneel down," she commanded, her hollow voice more forceful than normal.

"Yes?" I repeated dumbly, meeting her at eye level.

Rosamund lifted the rim of my helmet and planted a dry kiss on my forehead. "Survive this, and we can go home."

"Don't worry." I winked. "Today is not the day I die."

Fastening my helmet, I turned and hopped into my boat, allowing Sembrouthes to steady my stance as I boarded the hated diminutive vessel. Ascum ordered our boat lowered, with teams of sailors pulling along layers of knotted rope as we descended to the waters below. Too long thereafter, our boat ceased dangling in midair and plopped against the sea, the flagship's ropes released and allowed us to set ourselves adrift.

"Oars!" Sembrouthes boomed. "To the city!"

And so we went, at last, to seize the flaming city that had taken so much in so short a time. The Pillars of Herakles would finally be mine—for Belisarius, and for the Emperor.

RESISTANCE

There was no battle. There was only slaughter.

Grabbing the frontmost oar of our boat, I rowed alongside the Aksumite and Vandal spearmen who jostled within the narrow wooden benches. My legs stiffened as I squeezed my overlarge body into the tiny space, a discomfort made better as I watched a beefy Gunderic struggle to fit himself into an adjoining boat nearby. Behind me, a Vandal spurted booming flatulence, giggling with his kinsmen in the Vandal tongue as they whooped in their battle lust. Our order for silence broken by the destruction of Septem's harbor, we sang and cheered as we drew ever closer, forced to maneuver around occasional pillars of split stones or charred beams floating atop the sea.

Where once there had been a sea gate, I discerned only a crater of deep water. There were few hints that the *Serapis* had once floated aloft at that spot. We cut slowly through the debris-strewn interior harbor, cautious of occasional flaming timbers as well as deep pools of floating naphtha. Absent within the harbor or the shattered curtain of stone was any sign of the Visigoths, those dozens of archers who, not moments before, had mocked and cursed their Roman enemies as futile cowards. No Gothic voices were jesting now.

"Watch for movement!" Sembrouthes commanded. "Prepare for landing!"

Septem's docks were a burnt ruin, so we steered our raft to the pebble beaches that lined the harbor waterfront. Raising my oar and tying it securely to the ship's railing, I checked my shield and weapons, rose to my feet, and jumped overboard. Icy water rose to my thighs, yet I shrugged off any discomfort as another Vandal spearman and I hauled the raft to shore.

"Collect!" Sembrouthes shouted. "In formation!"

Other boats slid along the tiny stones, the ship's bow slicing onto Septem's beaches. Xerxes followed closely behind our own detachment, while Gunderic huffed and struggled a good thirty paces behind.

"Gunderic! Form the rearguard!" I shouted.

Gunderic huffed with frustration. "Goddamn it! If you Romans made boats the size of men, I'd be drinking wine in the forum by now!"

Ignoring his bluster, I signaled Xerxes and a team of some thirty Vandals to join my own forces. We unslung our shields and judged the incline that linked Septem's forum and harbor. Hefting shields and spears, Sembrouthes tested our formation for gaps or weaknesses, and grunted in approval as he found none.

"To the forum!" I yelled.

Hobnailed boots slammed once again upon dressed stone as we crested the harbor, gaining view of the city beyond. It was then that we first heard clearly the screams that permeated the city, giving voice to the destruction that followed the *Serapis'* demise and sizzled with the stench of flesh. We found chunks of stone wall and iron bars lodged deep into nearby buildings, and even found a piece of ship rigging resting along a windowsill. Dozens ran and screamed in the distance, yet hardly anything was moving on the road to the harbor. Not even the seabirds, for nearly every surface was caked in the oily-black naphtha that had torn a gaping hole into Septem's most fabled defenses.

Stepping out of formation, I walked toward a nearby building, its façade caked in oil and smelling of charred kindling. Wary of nearby fires that could easily spread with so much combustible fuel nearby, I slid my boots through the muck, nearly stumbling as the tip of one boot caught on an unseen impediment. When I threw out a hand to steady myself on the wall, my gloves came back covered with that black slime that, even when wiped against the cloth of my trousers, clung with sticky residue inside the folds of the leather palm and fingers. Looking down, I used the point of my spear to prod at the object that obstructed my progress, and its pointed tip pushed the squishy cylinder inward.

"See something?" Xerxes called.

Holding up a fist for silence, I used my spear to push the lump onto the street. Dragged from its naphtha puddle, soft, bloody sludge slipped from its interior form, revealing layers of bone and tissue underneath ragged skin. Tracing downward, I discovered three intact fingers, a metal ring still gripping the thumb of the severed arm.

"Any guards manning the walls did not survive," I whispered.

Sembrouthes grunted. "I could have told you that. Any voices inside the buildings?"

I considered ordering the column forward, driven by a rush to seize the forum and take Theudesgel prisoner. Yet I resisted, still concerned about the narrow possibility that a detachment of Visigoths lay in ambush, waiting to isolate our pocket of spearmen and pounce before the bulk of Gunderic's Vandals or our landward forces could gain entry to the city.

"Fan out!" I ordered. "Search the buildings, quickly!"

It was then that I finally began to take stock of Septem. The city's looming towers and stout walls made it appear far larger and more imposing than its interior, as if it were an eagle puffing its feathers when confronted by predators. I have little doubt that in the past century it would have been an efficient trading post, allowing merchants to exchange goods between African and European continents and gain quick access to Septem's once-bountiful and protected harbor. Its buildings were squat, rarely larger than two stories, with many built from wood and thatch rather than the mortar and stone preferred by

Roman engineers. Now, many of those utilitarian structures showed signs of charring or destruction, inflicted, no doubt, by our siege engines.

We found little enough, but more than expected. Cauterized stumps of limbs, upturned and blasted stones, and splintered lumber grew bountiful as we trod ever outward from Septem's ruined harbor, with an occasional instrument of iron or silver found shorn or melted from the heat of a nearby inferno. My men avoided any building already ablaze, for such rooms bore little risk of hidden assassins or stores of Visigothic weapons. It was not until we reached a nearby granary that two Vandals discovered anything of note, calling for assistance with excited shouts.

Inside the charred hall, I found three bodies prostrate on the floor, Vandal spears leveled against their necks. One man appeared long dead, a pool of dark blood leaking from neck wounds and collecting dust and ash as it congealed into a lumpy mass. Another moaned incoherently, his nose and upper lip mashed to ribbons, forcing his ragged breathing to come in bubbling spurts. The third sat upright, his eyes darting to each of his newfound captors as he nursed a badly broken leg that almost surely required amputation. All three wore Visigothic armor, yet only one showed any evidence of what evils had befallen Theudesgel's men.

I leaned close to the conscious man, leveling with his tear-strewn eyes. The rank stench of piss and sour wine pierced through a mask of oil and ash, and the man's jaw quivered as I drew close. He could not have been older than eighteen, and I would not have called anyone a liar for believing him a few years younger. He pleaded in the Gothic tongue in a low whisper, each syllable causing him to wince with pain.

Curiously, this was the first real chance I had to closely review a Visigothic warrior from any closer than fifty paces. His armor was flimsy, a rusted coat of mail atop boiled leather that might have saved the wearer's life from a blunted mace, but only just. The lad's helmet was in an equally sorry state, seemingly an iron pot with a broad noseguard nailed to one side. I assumed the Visigoths would closely resemble Baduarius or Indulf, yet now that I saw one, I found only a few similarities. This youth had lighter, sun-bleached auburn hair and a scraggly beard that I doubt had ever been cut or groomed. He also bore all the signs of malnutrition, with a frame only a wisp stouter than Rosamund's, and undeveloped muscles along his arms and neck. He must have been just another poor farmer's child off seeking adventure or coin, believing Theudesgel would offer both, as well as the safety to see all back to their homesteads in Hispania.

Unfortunately, this lad, like so many others who have scratched and wept through the suffering of their lives, had ended up in a private hell. His body, covered in burns and pinned by a broken leg, was now at the mercy of his hated enemies.

"Do you speak my language?" I asked in standard Greek. Seeing only confusion register, I repeated the question in Latin, enunciating each word.

Sniffling, he nodded. "Little. Not much."

Seeking to gain his trust, I offered him a smile. "Where is Theudesgel?"

He frowned, a sign of no knowledge. "I fight with Domeric, leader, until Romans come with fire."

As he spoke his leader's name, the lad gestured to the bloodied horror that twitched and sputtered on the granary floor. Dust hung like a sheet in the air, mixing with the dying man's bloodied breaths and bringing him to snort as he struggled for life. Returning my attention to the young man, my eyes fell on a shinbone jutting clean through his skin, exposed to the elements like a joint of pork for a hound.

I offered another smile, pointing at myself, and then back at my new acquaintance. "I am Varus. What is your name?"

"My name is Alagild, sworn to Domeric, of Theudesgel's tribe in Lusitania," the lad explained in painstaking Latin. "Domeric is best sword of all Visigoths."

My blood cooled. All pretense of gaining Alagild's trust evaporated as my focus returned to the dying man on the dusty floor. Cocking my head, I pored over the lines of the man's swollen and butchered face, searching my memory for Baduarius' killer. He had been fully armored that day, his face guarded by leather cheekguards and an iron helm, and had a scraggly russet beard. This figure's face had been singed hairless in many spots. Unconscious, the figure sputtered again, letting out a single gurgling moan.

I leaned closer to Alagild, pointing to Domeric. "Is he the Visigoth champion?"

Eyes widened, Alagild's breathing quickened as tears flooded the corners of his eyes. "Do not understand."

Frustrated, I reworded my question. "Domeric" —I pointed to the dying man—"did he fight in single combat?"

At first, I thought Alagild understood little, his command of Latin so thin it could not grasp much more than basic speak of traders, priests, or sailors. A twitch of the eyes, however, gave a telltale sign of fear, and I repeated my question.

"That is him," Alagild replied, his words clipped and high-pitched. "Domeric fight for Theudesgel, and win against Roman soldier."

Stepping back, I felt my mind fade into the white rage familiar to me since the training sands of the Imperial Palace. I wanted to smash the heel of my boot into the noseless, lipless horror that bled at my feet, to avenge Baduarius with the knowledge that his killer would no longer stalk the earth. Every impulse of my body screamed to fulfill that urge, driven all the more by a revulsion for the monstrosity that struggled for air below.

But I could not do it. For if I did, I would have enjoyed it far too much. Father Petrus warned that, though God permitted killing in battle in the service of Caesar, he otherwise categorically abhorred violence, and insisted that death should not be meted out for anything other than loyalty to the Emperor and my commanders. As an old man, I now understand the truth of Petrus' words, for in the darkness of the night I see the faces of every man whose life I have taken. Not just their lives, but every other life that they may give possibility to, thousands of generations wiped out with the thrust of a spear, the swing of a sword. Their faces haunt me still, and I ask forgiveness for each one.

I did not take Domeric's life—at least, not directly, not with the intimacy of a blade to the throat. And though I was often a fool, I regret nothing of that decision.

"Leave him to rot," I ordered in Latin, gesturing to Domeric's twitching body. "We need to go."

"You Romans come and summon devils! Why you do this?" Alagild wept, piteously grasping at his crippled leg as he wailed. "This is not your land. The devil ship… it take all my friends! My brother!"

In a single fluid motion, Xerxes stepped forward and thrust a spearpoint clean through Alagild's neck. The lad did not even have time to plea or scream, his soul departing his body even before his limp head struck the floor and Xerxes' spear drew back upright. From his lifeless eye, a tear mixed with Domeric's blood and a piling layer of ash, the last testament that Alagild had once been of the living.

"He was attracting too much attention with his cries," Xerxes explained, grimacing. "I know he was little more than a boy, but we cannot take prisoners now, nor can we die for him. I will light a fire and say a prayer for his soul later."

Hearing shouting in the distance, I concurred with Xerxes' assessment and muttered a brief prayer over Alagild's cooling corpse. We left Domeric to the hands of God. I was the last man to leave the granary, the moans of my suffocating enemy trailing on.

As we returned to formation, muffled cries rose from the city forum, with men and women rushing along the open expanse in fear of some unseen aggressor. My men stiffened at the warning, their shields instinctively falling into close alignment even without a disapproving remark from Xerxes.

"If there are any alive in the harbor, they're in no shape to do us any harm," I called out, allowing a brief moment for another contingent of Vandals under Wisimar to join our band. "Take the forum, and open Septem's gates!"

Against the remonstrations of their officers, the Vandals whooped at the prospect of combat, relishing an opportunity to cross blades with those hated Visigoths they did not find worthy of respect. Taking my place in the second line of our forward-facing ranks, I quickened to a trot, matching my companions as we climbed the stone streets along a rolling uphill path. After putting a hundred paces between us and the harbor, the air grew far sweeter, less clouded by ash and lingering flames. Yet at the same time, the all-too-familiar din of chaos rose to greet our arrival, and we soon realized what drove the citizens of Septem into a wild panic.

I have little doubt that those civilians in the city, no matter their opinion of Theudesgel, must have viewed us Romans with suspicion, if not outright hostility. Even though I tried to restrict our violence to the Visigoths and their commander, there was nothing I could do about those errant ballista bolts and sailing arrows that undoubtedly found their way to the homes and bodies of the innocent. Conquerors, even those bent upon liberation, are rarely beloved by those who are condemned to suffer and starve. Jogging toward the forum, I gave an order that all civilians were to be left unperturbed, and that no looting or slave-taking would be permitted. A few Vandals groaned at the diminished prospect of loot and slaves, though I trusted Xerxes to keep such men in line for the prospect of later pay and the possibility of honor from Belisarius himself.

Peering atop the shoulders of the man in front, I squinted my eyes to discern the frantic movements at the end of our street, and beyond, into the open space that was Septem's forum. There, I saw a young black-haired woman being yanked by the wrist, tripping and falling to her knees as she cried in pain and terror. Her captor, a mustachioed and armored soldier, cursed the woman's resistance to his orders and smashed the wooden shaft of his curved axe into her mouth. Recoiling, she spat a glob of blood and teeth onto the nearby gutter, her head lolling in dazed submission.

"Double pace!" I yelled, bringing our trot into a full run.

As a recruit, my reviled banda commander had berated his spearmen on the importance of endurance in the Roman Army. Archelaus insisted that a Roman soldier should be able to trot with complete kit and in full armor, for an entire day and night, neither stopping for rest nor spoiling his strength for a battle the following morning. It was a lesson that I learned well as a long-ago recruit, and had instilled into my own soldiers until they hardly felt the weight of their armor as they sprinted through Septem's streets. We swiftly reached the end of our alley, where our vision expanded across the entire expanse of the forum, replete with collapsed merchant stalls, smoldering fires, and a chaotic stream of civilians and Visigothic soldiers engaging in all acts of wanton desperation. I even caught a glimpse of Theudesgel, finding him rallying a smaller team of spearmen hauling ponderous sacks in the direction of Mount Abyla.

Raising my spear, I pointed toward Theudesgel's distant body. "That skinny shit in the fancy black leather. I'll give a hundred gold solidi to the man who strikes a killing blow!"

My Vandals roared their approval, relocking their shields as Xerxes scanned the area for opponents. Slowing our pace, we entered the forum, our presence only adding to the frantic chaos that had consumed the city. I shifted by a tannery booth, its hides reeking of urine, that vital component of softening leather that left all tanners permanently musky and sour smelling. It was there that I encountered the lone Visigoth. Still intent on hauling his female captive away, he hoisted the struggling woman over his armored shoulder.

Without even issuing an order, I moved to the rightmost edge of the ranks and raised my spear level with my eyes. The distracted Visigoth had no time to notice the flying dart rushing toward his exposed legs, where it pierced his left thigh like some haunch of tender mutton. Screaming, the Visigoth dropped his captive, rolling upon the ground as he piteously attempted to extract the spear from his pulsing leg.

Careful to watch for ambush, I left the protective cover of my formation, stepping only a couple dozen paces into the half-collapsed booth. The tannery stench grew more pungent as we traversed through smoking ruins. Drawing my axe, I chopped once into the Visigoth's neck, severing his spine, and extracted the honed edge in a pleasing arc.

"Sembrouthes, have one of your men stay with this Mauri woman," I ordered. "Column, we continue!"

Rejoining the men, we moved toward the forum's interior, our presence now noted by Visigoth and citizen alike. Many of the Visigoths rushed in the direction of Theudesgel, yet no fewer than fifty milled about in confusion at the far end of the forum's well. Each man wore interlocking layers of mail and leather, with an occasional warrior bedecked in a rich coat of scales, and all bore the crudely painted hawk that had long been a Visigothic sigil. Many carried that emblem on their shields, with others displaying the symbol or animal of any number of clans or tribes that comprised the Visigothic kingdom. Even at that distance, I could tell that the Goths favored axes and maces over swords—fearsome enough when battering a fixed enemy wall, but lacking any measure of deadly force, falling to near uselessness against the dagger or thrusting blade.

In the distance, I saw yet another detachment of Visigoths fighting along Septem's gates, hurriedly throwing stones and launching arrows as the drumming and horn-blowing of Liberius' and Perenus' forces signaled the landward Roman advance.

"Attack! Quickly!" I yelled.

Xerxes, ever patient, added a command. "Keep discipline! No chopping or bandying about like peacocks!"

Led by Wisimar, the Vandals obeyed, but in their own way, hooting and hollering, laughing manically to the point of breathlessness. To those fresh recruits with lesser training, or to any with poor discipline, the Vandals' example must have been terrifying, these dozens of massively muscled soldiers longing for a warrior's death and mocking those of lesser ability. Even to us trained Romans, it was a rush that still filled me with trepidation, my mind fluttering back to the rolling fields of Ad Decimum.

"Fucking kill them!" Wisimar screeched.

The Visigoths, absent leadership, formed a pitiable wall, as thin as it was brittle. Xerxes' charge brought Vandals to slam shields against a wavering enemy, and within a single exchange of blows, many of the rearward Visigoths broke and ran to their comrades atop the walls. One Aksumite launched a spear that pierced cleanly through a man's back, sending him toppling over and gasping for air. I also saw Xerxes lash with the speed of a desert scorpion, the sting of his spear cutting through the shoulder of one attacker and piercing the hip of another before either man was able to land a single blow. One Visigothic officer attempted a final time to restore some modicum of resistance, yet Wisimar bashed the bearded Visigoth full in the jaw with the edge of his iron-rimmed shield. Rotten teeth spewed from the Visigoth's slack mouth, his body too stunned to protect against the thrust of another Vandal spear clean through his chest and heart.

To their credit, no Visigoths surrendered meekly. Many ran, others fought with manic energy, yet none threw down his weapons and pleaded for merciful surrender. These men remembered the disgrace of Altan and the Roman dead, and knew that captives were like to be treated with less-gentle care. God willing, I did not and will never delight in the torture of prisoners, nor subject them to unnecessary punishment, but my Visigothic enemies knew little of my temperament. Besides, though I was reluctant to brutalize those willing to surrender, I cannot say that others in the army shared my scruples.

The more opportunistic of my Vandal spearmen began pillaging the bodies of their fallen adversaries even before the fighting had fully ceased. More Visigoths filed toward the winding road of Mount Abyla, yet a full hundred men had formed along Septem's walls, drawing the gate commander's attention to the incoming threat at his rear.

"Varus!" Xerxes hissed for my attention. "Theudesgel is going to the citadel!"

Indeed, the Visigothic leader had already disappeared behind rows of charred buildings, yet I could see a distant trail of men rushing up a narrow path to the mountain's summit. From this angle, it was easier to see the thin ring of stone walls atop the mountain, offering its host an unparalleled defensive view of the surrounding heights. Worse, at least for us Romans, there was only a single path to approach, and its cobbled streets were thronged with Visigothic soldiers desperate to escape to safety.

Xerxes drew closer, more urgency in his voice. "We must decide. Walls or Theudesgel? We only have the men to safely press for one."

Groaning in frustration, I instantly felt my instincts urging me to track down Theudesgel, to carry him back to our camp in irons, and to instill justice for the torture and humiliation of my men. I would like to believe that was the only raw emotion I felt, but through the wisdom of age I can now admit that I was driven by a need to alleviate the sting to my pride, the need to cast down the man who had outwitted me twice on the battlefield. Though retreating, Theudesgel was close, he was weak, and there were no more tricks that could save his surprised and overwhelmed Visigoth protectors now.

But such a move would have been grossly irresponsible. And after Baduarius, I was reluctant to surrender to passion, knowing that even a temporary lapse in control might condemn many of my men to an unnecessary death. Likewise, the Visigoths retained a sizeable force along the walls—large enough to repel Perenus' attack or instill grievous injuries. Even as shouts from the harbor signaled the arrival of yet another contingent of Vandal reinforcements, there was only one choice that I could make if I hoped to retain the respect of my men.

Turning to face our new arrivals, I waved to the thickly armored beast that stood head and shoulders above all others. There were only a hundred or so, yet coupled with the detachment under Xerxes, our strength was unquestioned.

"Hurry up! The Visigoths will die of old age by the time you're ready!" I yelled.

"Lick my arse, Varus!" Gunderic called back, a beaming grin lighting his face. "It was burned hairless by your giant candle, and is as smooth as a babe's!"

Jests aside, Gunderic bellowed at his men, who sprinted through the now-vacant forum and alongside our forces. I offered a moment for them to gather before moving on, insisting first upon a formal report of the fleet's progress in unloading our invading forces.

"Others are coming, but I could not wait at the docks any longer," Gunderic said, panting. "But you've already killed them all! There are none left for me!"

"They were poor sport." Wisimar snorted, hocking a glob of phlegm onto a mangled Visigothic corpse. "Good for feeding crows."

Gesturing for silence, I prodded Gunderic further. "We're at less than half strength. What happened to the others?"

"Gods, Varus…" Gunderic began. "But that explosion did plenty of damage. Some of our craft tipped over, and others were used to pluck careless men who fell into the sea. Others still had to navigate a labyrinth of smoking stones and literal waves of active flames. No serious casualties, but it is much harder going in the harbor than we planned."

"Understandable," I grunted. "Then we must make do. Men, we're taking Septem's walls and opening the gate. End this fight quickly!"

Gunderic lifted his spear, sparking an even more ridiculous war cry than Wisimar unleashed before our initial skirmish. We trotted along the forum's smooth stones and toward the gate, soon drawing the attention of the remaining Visigothic leaders. Teams of archers nocked arrows as we drew within a hundred paces, and fired when we were within eighty. The missiles were few and entirely ineffectual as they clattered off our layered shields, yet the attack nevertheless indicated a need for new tactics.

"Break up!" I signaled Gunderic. "Take the western stairs, and we will take the center!"

Gunderic hummed with excitement. "Dead by lunch!"

The attack started suddenly and ended briskly. Enemy archers slowed our pace, but only just, and soon we climbed the open stone stairs that linked the battlements with the ground. Jostling to the front of our narrow ascent, Wisimar impaled a would-be stone-thrower and jammed a dagger in the eye of a second. He would have attacked a third Visigoth archer, too, were that bowman not thrown backward by Xerxes' well-flung spear.

My men spread along the walls, their superior armor and furious bloodlust leaving little for the Goths to do but cower. Above all others, Gunderic terrorized the section of walls nestled closest to Mount Abyla, disemboweling one brave spearman with a single flash of the massive blade that had not long ago been a token of Gelimer's surrender. When the blade stuck in a second spearman's rib cage, Gunderic dropped its pommel, surged toward a nearby archer, and lifted the man cleanly over his head. The beastly Vandal flung his enemy over the walls, the sounds of his screams trailing until they suddenly ceased moments later.

Not long after our attack, Perenus' Herulians scaled Septem's walls, sweeping aside any resistance. Fulcaris took one such kill, yet most took the walls with dry blades and clean armor. I found myself among them, having little to do as Sembrouthes and I yanked hard upon the gate's lever, struggling until its chain finally surrendered to our efforts. Septem's gates opened, and hundreds of Romans filtered through the walls with the great cry of victory.

Nika! Nika! Nika!

And a victory it was. But it was not complete. For though we took the city, Theudesgel still held the mountain. And what a legendary mountain it was.

Avoiding the more mundane petitioners who flocked in nervous apprehension to greet their new overlords, Liberius nonetheless played the aloof Roman legate well, heeding the pleas of those impoverished by Visigoth rule or granting commendations to those who aided in Imperial governance. Most of our interactions proceeded thus, starting diplomatically and ending with general contentment that we Romans would not only mete out a measure of justice, but also pay handsomely for any supplies we required to shelter and nourish our men. Occasionally, some encounters were less pleasant.

To be honest, I expected little in the way of a happy welcome from Septem, believing its throngs would curse our footsteps and force my centurions to insist that all soldiers travel in packs to discourage hired knives in dark alleys. Within hours of Theudesgel's retreat, however, it became obvious that Septem had few enough residents to even worry about, lacking as it did the diversity of humanity so commonplace in Constantinople's wharves and various forums. Whether from centuries of neglect or forced depopulation by the raids of Vandals and Visigoths alike, Septem had hardly more than two thousand civilian souls lodged inside its protective walls.

Occasional difficulties arose as petitioners raised claims that could not be satisfied with a heavy leather bag of Justinian's silver. As it happened, one such claimant was the woman we had rescued from her would-be Visigothic captor, a man who had decapitated her betrothed and used her as his plaything during Theudesgel's occupation of the city. Missing half of her teeth and bearing a multitude of angry welts along her limbs, the woman was committed into Rosamund's care on my orders, and I promised to personally pay for any medicines and potions she might need as well as furnish ample coin and grain for her recovery.

Rosamund escorted the young woman away, her thin fingers draped along the weeping woman's shoulders, toward a vacant stone apothecary that had been commandeered for Rosamund's personal use.

In another case, even Rosamund could not avail me a worthy

solution to resolve a local man's grievances. Worse, the man howled indignantly as he grew impatient of waiting his turn in the winding avenue of petitioners, resisting calls for calm and peace by my men. Wisimar, tiring of the man's display, hoisted the smaller fellow by the collar and threatened to instill silence in his own manner. Though it may have been consistent with Vandal custom, I could not sanction such force.

"There is no need for violence, Wisimar," I lectured. "Allow this good citizen to come forward."

Growling, Wisimar released his prisoner, allowing the older man to fall harmlessly to his feet. Brushing the creases in his wool tunic, the complainant glowered at Wisimar, yet dared not show any real sign of contempt despite the thin veneer of protection my own word as Roman overlord offered in such a place.

Walking forward, I gathered a better view of this unhappy figure. Cleanshaven, with the hair atop his head thinning and sprinkled with silvery gray around his temples. His skin was tanned from days spent in the sun, yet his body was absent the colorful tunics and scarves of the Mauri. As such, I presumed his ancestors hailed from the distant tribe of Alans that had once settled this area a century prior. Indeed, with his high cheekbones and a raised brow, he even looked vaguely similar to Ascum, although while Ascum's tribe had taken residence along the Caspian Sea, other Alani clans fled westward from Attila's advancing horde, eventually reaching the continent of Africa under the dominance of the Vandals. Despite this, the man spoke passable Latin, his slurred words not dissimilar from the vulgar tongue practiced by many peasants in Justinian's Empire.

There was no pretense of deference as he addressed me, spitting at his feet before speaking. "I see your whoremaster's gold flows to buy the love of those who live in Septem, but no amount of metal can bring our port back. I know not which devils you struck bargains with, but there is nothing you can do to convince even the greediest farmer here that what you have done is unaltered evil."

"Friend—"

"You have doomed us all! And I, for one, will not sell ownership of my soul for thirty pieces of Greek silver!"

Deep creases lined the man's eyes, no doubt witness to much suffering and poor harvests. No woman or children stood anxiously nearby, suggesting he was alone in a world that punished prideful independence. More, his beefy fingers were layered with calluses, meaning he either tilled the soil or drew fish from Septem's once-proud sea lanes. Given the magnitude of his despair over the port's destruction, I guessed the latter.

I looked to Liberius and found his brows raised, but his eyes sparkled with the same note of happy mischief that I had known since I was a boy. Shrugging, Liberius responded to me in Hunnic, the only language with which we could speak privately in the current company.

"He's got a point. We have quite a bit to answer for." Liberius chuckled. "Let him voice his complaints, but don't attempt to buy this one. He may take your gold, but he'll still curse you in his meals, and others will think less of the Empire."

Nodding, I turned back to the complainant. "You would prefer Visigothic rule to that of Rome?" I asked in Latin.

"Better them than the Vandals!" the man shouted, a careful eye going to a growling Wisimar.

I shook my head. "The Emperor and the General Belisarius have subjugated Gelimer and brought all Africa back to the Empire. The men you see here are not of the Vandal kingdom, but soldiers of the Empire, just as any Greek, Latin, or Heruli that you see in my ranks. So I ask again—do you prefer the Empire or the Visigoths?"

The man moved forward, making it just two paces before Sembrouthes leveled his weapon in warning, leering at the disgruntled civilian. Shuddering, the man halted his advance, even stifling his complaints as he began to back away from his aggressor. Lifting a hand, I nodded to Sembrouthes to rest at ease. The burly Aksumite returned his spear, though no assurance or command could have brought him, or any other Aksumite, to rest at ease entirely. Wary but deferent, the civilian continued his petition.

"Theudesgel was a thief, and was cruel. There is no doubt of that, although you have yet to demonstrate that Romans are much different. But the Visigoths opened ample trade to Hispania. They even reduced tariffs to the court in Gades! And for that, Septem prospered. Now, trade is evaporated—fast as droplets of water on the dunes of the Great Desert. And what will Rome replace it with?"

"The center of the world," I shot back. "Constantinople, and all the trade it warrants from Persia, India, and even the vast uncharted lands to the east, whose streets are paved with jade and silver and whose meanest beggars are clothed in silk. Have patience. Allow Emperor Justinian's servants to rebuild your harbor, and that city will be like a dear friend to your people."

Rolling his eyes, the man raised his hands in surrender. "Constantinople? Might as well be the fucking moon!" He jabbed a finger. "But Theudesgel is still here, atop Herakles' mountain. And when you leave, the Visigoths will return and punish those who lay with perfumed Greeks."

At that, Wisimar and his growling team of Vandals reached for their weapons, eager to splatter the unimposing fisherman's brains along the stones of the forum. Again, I raised a hand for calm, aware that no fewer than a hundred city residents were watching my every move. Even the slightest violence would lose whatever favor I had gained in a morning's work, and leave my soldiers exposed to poisoned waterskins or knives in the dark. Belisarius was correct: if our army was to remain alive on such far-flung lands, we had to win the love of a people who had long forgotten the promise of the Empire.

"You are correct about much," I granted him, "but not about devils. We used naphtha to blow an opening in Septem's gates, though God knows I tried less gruesome methods of liberating this city. But you have my oath to God and the Imperial family: a Roman garrison will always remain to protect your trade routes and guard from marauders and highwaymen."

It was a small enough thing, but my promise elicited gasps from the crowd. Many had likely assumed that our stay would be short-lived, a stop long enough only to gain suzerainty over the city and plant a puppet governor to manage in the Emperor's stead. Doubtless, some must have groaned at the prospect of a permanent detachment of Roman soldiers in their midst, but most must have drawn some relief, for our presence dissuaded devastating land or sea raids that had been a fixture of life in Mauretania since the time of Hannibal and Scipio. Even my unhappy fisherman remained silent, his features softening as he listened for my next words.

"You have the courage to stand before those who could easily cause your death, but you speak honestly," I addressed him. "What is your name?"

"Itaxes, Lord."

An Alani name, I noted. "Well, Itaxes, your words may have gotten the better of you."

Itaxes' eyes widened as he swallowed hard. "Lord…"

"Itaxes, only the Emperor has the divine authority to appoint a provincial governor," I began. "One will arrive in time. But until then, the Empire requires Septem to have a harbormaster—an honest man with a clear knowledge of the needs of his city. It is troubling work, but I would have that role lain at your feet."

More gasps. It was not a noble position, nor one that entitled its bearer to any hereditary rights. Yet for a backwater city on the edge of the world, harbormasters might as well have controlled the tides and fed the masses, for their power to allow and deny trade held fast from Constantinople all the way to Londinium in the distant isles of Britannia. Neither did I lie: such a vocation made for difficult work, yet also for considerable honor, and the chance for real advancement from the miserable toiling of olive trees or fish traps.

Itaxes choked. For a moment I feared the man might be suffocating until a nearby Vandal slapped him hard on the back and spurred a coughing fit. His jaw slack, Itaxes moved his gaze from me to Liberius to a half dozen other soldiers, as though he could not think but that my offer was some sort of a trick.

"Lord, harbormaster..." He gaped in astonishment. "But I am illiterate!"

"All the better!" I exclaimed. "Then I need not worry about forged accounts or notes of conspiracy. We will pay a scribe's wages to assist with your ledgers and other duties."

"Lord... I..." Itaxes sputtered, triggering another coughing fit. His new Vandal friend moved closer for another friendly smack, yet Itaxes raised an arm to fend him off. "I have no family, nor children. None to help with the labor."

I smiled, waving a hand to suggest such matters were trivial. "I have confidence that you will find a deserving woman to provide you with hearth and kin. Until such happy days come to pass, you may pay a small staff to support your office, and the Emperor will donate to the cost."

At last, Itaxes bowed. It was a clumsy thing, lacking the fluid grace of a courtier or the dramatic flattery of a eunuch; Itaxes simply placed his gnarled fingers upon stiff knees before falling prostrate before my chair. I dared not show it, but elation rose in my heart at the gesture, for I feared what might occur should Itaxes insist upon hatred for the Emperor. I turned my head briefly to Liberius, who nodded once, closed his eyes, then offered a final assessment in Hunnic.

"Deftly handled. Theodora may have had a beneficial effect upon you after all."

Stifling a laugh, I turned back to a prostrate Itaxes, whose muffled voice echoed from the cobbled streets. "Lord, you honor me. I swear to serve Septem well... and the Emperor in Constantinople."

"That is all I can ask," I replied. "Your first duty will be to reclaim the sea lanes you love so much. Gather teams in small boats, clear what debris you can, and dredge new channels where you cannot. I expect Septem's harbor to be functional in a week, and will begin rebuilding its sea walls in a month. See it done."

We addressed other petitioners in turn. Some were combative, yet none as much as Itaxes. To be sure, we doubtlessly had enemies within

Septem's populace, yet even those would have a grudging acceptance of our presence. I had promised order and safety, and to a people that had known only brutalization and fear, those were popular prospects indeed. I did the best I could with what little I had, but even with small offerings at my disposal, God knows I enjoyed the respite of being a gift-giver and peacemaker rather than an instrument of slaughter.

In a brief interlude between petitions, I gave a missive that Rosamund's injured ward should be taken to the household of Itaxes, with strict instructions that she retain possession of the gifts of silver I had placed into her care. She was free to refuse such an offer, yet I believed that both would benefit from the other's company and protection—one an aging man encountered with the sudden loneliness of high office, and the other a woman who had been mistreated and cast aside in a society that looked poorly upon victims, no matter how undeserving.

Even after a full day of settling squabbles and assuaging Septem's troubled minds, my labors that day were not complete. Just as I collapsed into bed, Liberius glided unceremoniously into my private quarters. It took my last reserves of patience not to groan at the imposition.

"Not sleeping already, were you?" Liberius asked. "I've found that age is the best cure for fatigue. A few hours of rest, and my mind races!"

"I'll let you know when I reach that point," I said flatly, sitting upright.

Joints popping, I rose and joined Liberius at an adjoining bench. After setting down his candle, he slid a ponderous stack of parchments along the table and into my grasp.

More monotony—the exact reason I had rejected the life of a clerk long ago. I sighed. "Can this wait?"

"It could, as with all things." Liberius shrugged. "But it shouldn't. Do you think I would waste your time, and my own, if this were not sensitive?"

Upon reflection, it was indeed intriguing that Liberius would want to discuss any Imperial business at night—unless it were of dire importance, of course. Selecting the first parchment from Liberius' stack, I dragged the candle closer, wax droplets just beginning to pool along a silver basin. Aromas of smoke and the sea emanated from the paper, evidence that they had survived a voyage from Carthage, and beyond.

"Belisarius comes first," Liberius explained, eyeing the parchment in my hands. "Dispatched before we seized Septem, of course."

The note was brief, and etched in Belisarius' own hand. Each Latin letter was clearly printed, yet stocky and strong, quite unlike the elegant script of Procopius and his army of scribes. Each word rang with Belisarius' voice—at least, what I remembered of the confident and warm man prior to John's death.

You will come to question your fitness as a leader, the strength of your friendship, and even your worthiness of trust. All entrusted with such terrible responsibility struggle with these doubts. God knows, I have, and still do.

I mourn for Baduarius. He and Dagisthaeus were among my first recruits, and oldest friends. Even if, as you claim, your actions led to Baduarius' death, you cannot allow that loss to consume you. What separates good leaders from the insufficient is their ability to press forward despite the doubt. I selected you for this command because I trust your judgment, and because I believed you were ready for the challenge. I still do.

You will think of Baduarius for all the remaining days that you draw breath. I do so for Dagisthaeus, and Sunicas, and Simmas, and John. So many died for me, or by my command. You and I walk a lonesome path, but it is a path we must walk if our dreams are to become real. Know that, even in your darkest hours, neither I nor many others will ever forsake you.

"See?" Liberius teased. "You're not the first blubbering young man I've had to console in a difficult moment."

"Thank you." I blushed, pushing Belisarius' note aside and saving it for later. "No indication that Carthage might send reinforcements, though."

Liberius shook his head. "And I assume you've heard nothing

from Uliaris on his mission to recruit his countrymen?"

"Nothing," I answered. I was worried for my friend, yet the worry was tinged with suspicion that he might have simply traveled far away to spend my gold in some brothel or another until excessive wine or a cutthroat's knife ended his life. Even if I wished to seek him out for an update, Frankia was enormous, encompassing the former provinces of Gaul and beyond, and I had no notion of how to search for Uliaris, or indeed where.

"Dispatches from Constantinople are next," Liberius declared. "A bundle arrived for us in Carthage, although these are all three months old."

The second note, like the first, was uplifting. Unlike Belisarius' workmanlike hand, this script was a precise and delicate Greek text, lengthy where Belisarius preferred concision. A faint scent of rosewater rose from the parchment, tugging me back to my days as a centurion.

"Mariya." I smiled.

Her letter was chiefly an account of her life at Pella, as well as news of the children's well-being. I skimmed the text, eager to read yet preferring to pore over each word in privacy, and with the luxury of freer time away from Liberius. Yet it was evident that Mariya was pleased, using our household funds and buildings in Pella to care for the many children and crippled veterans that otherwise would have withered in Constantinople's gutters.

Come back to me, she concluded. *You've done enough for one lifetime. Come to Pella, to your children, and to my bed. I look south every morning, praying that you will be aboard the ships that ferry goods to our inland port. Don't let me wait too much longer.*

At the bottom of the letter were the traced outlines of two hands— one clearly that of a babe, and another of a small child. I raised the letter from the table and pressed it to my lips, absorbing the faint traces of my wife's perfume. And, though I fought for control of my emotions, my heart shattered at the realization of how many, many months separated me from my family. Perhaps Mariya was correct—I had seen enough and done enough. I was tired, and lonesome, and homesick for a house that I had never seen, for it sheltered my wife and children. In that moment, I knew that I wanted to retire.

But at the time, I merely voiced gratitude to Liberius and delved further into his messages. Others were informative missives from Procopius—progress toward pacifying the Balearic Islands of their piracy, of training further Vandals in Carthage for the foederati, and of a lack of men to reinforce my needs. Even mentions of Solomon made it to my evening's reading, with reports that my boyhood rival was constructing defensive fortifications between Carthage and Thapsus.

"I hear that Solomon might even be showing some competence," Liberius remarked as I finished reading. "Though, more likely, he has slaves organize everything for him."

"It wouldn't be the first time," I grumbled.

I perused a few additional letters, including a brief note of congratulation from Marcellus of my appointment to the Septem expedition. As the stack of parchment thinned, Liberius reached for his belt, where he withdrew another paper from a small brass tube. Its seal, displaying Theodora's crowned head as the Imperial Augusta, was already broken.

"Normally, I would be *horrified* at the idea of intercepting the Empress' letters," Liberius began, winking with insincerity. "But I knew Theodora would write in a cipher. I've spared you the effort of decoding it, and have written her message for you."

Ciphers were rare, but not unknown. There was generally little point in bothering with any sort of code, for the general illiteracy of our world made even plain language a safe enough respite for private thoughts. Yet some, such as the Imperial family, were known to use this layer of protection; indeed, Caesar was famous for employing them, worried that enemies might capture his couriers and anticipate the deployment of his vaunted legions.

Liberius handed me Theodora's original message, as well as a second paper that contained his interpretation of Theodora's script. Though he did not explain how he had cracked Theodora's cipher,

Liberius assured me the translation was correct. The note was brief, but unmistakably from Theodora.

I write these letters myself, for I wonder to what degree I can trust Narses. He professes loyalty, yet he visits my husband's chambers more often than my own these days.

"Not good," I mumbled.

"Not good," Liberius agreed.

Reconstruction is upon us, with most of the damage from the riots resolved. Yet ill humors brew amongst the populace. Village zealots, initially in twos and threes, have occupied entire buildings in Constantinople. They claim to want nothing other than to defend the Emperor from gaudy display and heresy, whatever that means. Those that Marcellus have questioned claim that Cassiodorus leads them, although that gluttonous sycophant hasn't been seen in months.

"Cassiodorus?" I echoed.

Liberius frowned. "You ask the wrong questions. Why heresy? Why the religious fervor?"

"Why now?" I added.

Liberius nodded. "And who truly enables them? Cassiodorus was powerful once, yes, but never possessed the resources for such a movement. No, someone else gives this movement time to build its strength and learn to fly."

Justinian, I thought. Even privately, speaking nothing aloud, I felt myself fearful as an excubitor to be accusing my oath-lord of inciting further discord. More, it made no sense.

They pose no threat to my control of the city—for now. I pray for the safe completion of your expedition. Keep a close watch upon Belisarius, and return to Constantinople as soon as you are able. I fear that I have need of friends, for whatever comes next.

The order stuck in my throat. "Watch Belisarius..."

"The worst for last, I'm afraid." Liberius sighed, pointing to the final scroll.

Of all the parchment before me, the final selection was mutilated. Rather than written in ink, the Latin letters appeared burnt into the skin, as if an infernal hand had etched the message from brimstone.

"Basilius never trusted ciphers," Liberius explained. "Ever since he learned of invisible ink, he only ever prefers to send sensitive messages that way. With spies running about, perhaps Basilius' method is best?"

"In-invisible..." I stammered.

"I thought you would ask!" Liberius plucked at a small parchment at his waist. "So I prepared a demonstration."

After pressing the creased parchment onto a flat surface, Liberius passed it atop my candle, just grazing its underside with the flame. Though I expected the parchment to burn, Liberius gently shifted its surface to catch only the heat and none of the spark. Slowly, burnt letters identical to Basilius' own emerged, and Liberius tossed the result into my possession for me to read.

Privately, I felt a fool, my thoughts self-deprecating. *"How do you not know about invisible ink?"*

"Ink from pressed oak gall." Liberius grinned, accurately guessing my inner conversation. "Made in old Byzantium, by Philo, perhaps, oh, seven hundred years ago? The advantage is twofold, for if the message's contents are intercepted, we would know. Once burned, the letters cannot disappear again."

Nodding, I grasped for Basilius' note, and the message proved far more dire than the others. Liberius' grin disappeared as I traced each revealed line, the text half as large as usual to fit more text onto the page.

Justinian no longer heeds my guidance. He follows Theodora's wishes but stews his own plots. Our government is safe for now, but I cannot guarantee that peace will reign in Constantinople for long.

"Why would Justinian..." I began, thinking of Theodora's letter.

"Keep reading," Liberius urged.

Theodora has permitted a known apostate, Jakob bar Addai, known in Greek as Jakob Baradaeus to take residence in the Imperial Palace. This Jakob, known for his poor appearance and ragged clothing, was born in the eastern provinces, and claims to have worked miracles. Theodora will not explain to me why she has done this, although Narses claims that Jakob ministers to the Empress personally.

The Imperial government has rejected these eastern apostates since Justin's reign. Justinian takes this threat with grave concern, and has whipped up his own mob to counter Jakob's influence. Justinian claims ignorance, although I am certain that he sends money to Cassiodorus.

"Cassiodorus again," I wondered aloud. "The same fat priest who the crowd tossed rotten vegetables at before the riots?"

"The same," Liberius explained.

I have jailed or exiled the worst of Cassiodorus' thugs, but cannot control Justinian or Theodora. If Justinian were not smitten with her, I should think they would be mortal enemies. The threat of violence is real. I expect many to die in the city. Pagans, Jews, Arians, and any who reject Justinian's faith.

Pagans. A direct threat to Rosamund, let alone the hundreds of others who served loyally in Belisarius' army. I had already witnessed the unnecessary slaughter of my Jewish comrade, Isaacius, and fully believed Basilius' warning.

The stakes have never been higher. Justinian keeps private councils while Theodora governs. Ostrogoths and Lombards visit the palace, while Narses coordinates them all. I do not know what to do. Our plans are unraveling.

"Basilius was always the confident one amongst my colleagues," Liberius put in sadly. "Ever practical. Emotionless. But ruthlessly effective."

"Perhaps he's wrong about Theodora?" I ventured, realizing that the Empress had made no mention of her newfound confidante in her own letter.

"I doubt it very much," Liberius said. "I do not know why, but Theodora has granted patronage to a Christian apostate. The people will never accept that."

It seemed an odd choice by a calculated Theodora, though not one that I saw as a grave threat. True, many in the Empire reviled those who did not follow the Emperor's religion, though beyond the Jews, many such creatures had been afforded Imperial favor without incident. "Is this truly a problem? Not just court gossip, easily forgotten?"

Liberius shook his head. "There's nothing we can do about this now, but hear my lesson for today. Of all the reasons to kill a man, religion is the most pervasive. Zealots never exhaust their supply of enemies, and gods have the annoying tendency to reject compromise. And with the Blues and the Greens eradicated, it was only a matter of time until another set of gangs took their places."

TINGIS

Though aiding the people of Septem had given some peace to my soul, the dark tidings of Liberius' missives stripped me back to exhaustion—exhaustion beyond the ability for restorative sleep.

I longed to be back home. Back to Mariya, to a daughter who knew little of me and a son who knew nothing. That life seemed suddenly closer, yet simultaneously as though it had never been farther away, for we still had a Pillar to seize and an entire Visigothic kingdom to bring to heel. My bones ached, and my mind felt like it was mired in a sticky paste. After years of service, the allure of the warrior's life had tarnished. I would have given anything for an easy passage home, rather than an indefinite deployment heading a pitifully small expedition at the far edge of the world.

Though I no longer felt much concern over Theudesgel, King Theudis was another matter entirely, for he was a man whose military reputation was exceeded only by his cruelty. He was far more experienced than his unlucky warlord, and had far more to gain from a conquest of Tingitana and the vast African lands beyond. I had nearly evicted his forces from Septem, yet if Perenus was correct, Theudis' men lingered in Tingis. A city facing the endless ocean, beyond which resided only fables and mystery.

And though we had gained time through a quick seizure of Septem's city walls, we still had to move with haste. Our expedition would soon be called back to Carthage, leaving behind only a token force to maintain order and dispense justice until a larger detachment could be permanently stationed in the region. Pacifying Tingis now became an urgency, although we knew perilously little of the nature of our Visigothic enemies in that salt-strewn town.

There was little enough to discuss. We spent three days putting Septem to order, clearing the streets of ballista bolts and debris from collapsed buildings. Teams of laborers were drawn up from Septem's residents and assigned to various tasks, while others from the sparsely populated countryside soon ventured to the forum, just as Liberius predicted, to take advantage of Justinian's gold and join in on the reconstruction.

To my pleasure, Itaxes threw himself into his work as harbormaster, his small frame still imposing as it barked orders at teams of sailors as they cleared the port of fallen stones, shattered lumber, and lingering pools of sticky naphtha. Somberly, I also overcame my reluctance to send missives back to Carthage, scratching letters to Belisarius that told of our partial success, yet also of the enormous cost in Baduarius' death. Companion letters were crafted for the Empress and Mariya—the former to sate her unquenchable desire for more information on the army's exploits, and the latter to express nothing more than love and longing. Curiously, I found it difficult to picture Mariya's face, yet had little such trouble outlining the Empress' strong chin and deceptively wiry figure. Exhaustion, I assumed, mixed with a crippling concoction of loneliness and deprivation.

We also stacked and burned the dead—Visigoths, mostly, yet also a number of civilians and a few unlucky Cappadocians who struggled to climb their ladders and take Septem's landward walls. We gave proper honors to all, and I even showed mercy to the corpse of Domeric, whose butchered face was impossible for others to identify and I knew only from acquaintance with his gruesome injuries. Swearing my men to secrecy, we burned Domeric's body, offering a prayer to the all-but-anonymous soul who was released from its decaying corporeal prison.

One of the townspeople complained that all the bodies should be buried, so as to better await the promised Resurrection, but I had precious few men disposable for gravedigging, and moreover feared the pestilence that earthbound corpses inevitably bring in a war-torn region.

Last of all, Ascum dispatched several dromons to patrol the narrow channel of water between the Pillars of Herakles. Critically, I did so not only to inform Thurimuth of my intentions, but also so that Ascum might garner knowledge of he and Sindual's well-being and success in taking Mount Calpe. Further, I needed to safeguard against additional Visigothic landings. Once Theudis discovered our partial victory in Septem, he would face a tempting choice to send a more powerful invading force to encircle our expedition. Ascum's dromons, I believed, might prevent that terrible fate.

Then, with recovery commenced, I left Liberius with two hundred Cappadocians to continue our labors and keep a watchful eye on Theudesgel's movements. Without Baduarius, the Cappadocians remained leaderless, and I lacked the time to fully install a dependable successor. I further intended to leave Rosamund in the relative safety of Septem, but when she heard of my plan, she all but puffed in anger.

"I have traveled half a world away to be with you," Rosamund insisted, red-faced, "and have seen you through storm and siege and fire. Yet you still think I am so delicate? Why leave me behind now when you need me more than ever? You'll take Cephalas to Tingis—"

"Yes, as my courier," I interjected.

"—but leave me here to wait sleeplessly for news like I'm some useless painted princess!"

The accusation stung, and nearly broke my resolve. For in our expedition to Carthage, and especially Septem, Rosamund had provided the only sense of comfort that I could pluck amidst the violence in such windswept lands. Not just from her oversight of my household, either, but indeed for a sense of reassurance that, despite everything, I remained a righteous man. From waking nightmares to bouts of paralyzing anxiety, Rosamund alone could be trusted to alleviate my ails, even if she sometimes invoked her blasphemous pantheon to do so. Liberius might guide my decisions, and Petrus my prayers, but it was Rosamund who offered me peace. No other possessed similar power to guide the meandering river of my life, though her talk of the gods never ceased to leave me uneasy.

"There are a great many here who require your healing and attention," I explained. "This sojourn will be a brief one, and hopefully bloodless. With luck, we will return in a couple of weeks, the region pacified and ready to return home."

Rosamund crossed her arms but said nothing. Though small in stature, Rosamund appeared downright imposing in her anger—features that one would not suspect of a healer who had mended thousands of sore feet, stinging cuts, and shattered bones. Expressionless, Rosamund merely nodded, returning to her apothecary to assist yet another injured peasant. There was nothing I could say to shift her attitude—I could only hope that the prospect of the end of our voyaging may bring the same measure of happy peace that it already offered to me.

Leaving a detachment of Cappadocians with Conon to protect Septem—under Liberius' careful eye—I gathered my other officers and commenced a march westward, where Indulf's Ostrogoths battled for control of Tingis' walls. With swift travel of the utmost importance, we took none of the oxen that had hauled vital goods on our initial march to Septem, their footsteps too ponderous and their forms too prone to injury at such a grueling pace. Instead, each man overstuffed their kits with rations of twice-baked bread and hardened beef, which would keep the army nourished if not altogether happy.

Perenus, as usual, complained bitterly about the fare, attempting vainly to sneak more sumptuous fruits that would inevitably spoil after a few days on the road. While I chastised him for such foolishness, I pretended to not notice the many wineskins that each dekarchos purchased for their spearmen. Wine would find its way back to my army; even as food grew painfully scarce, no Roman army had ever exhausted its supplies of wine. Such a fate was as unthinkable as it was impossible.

Liberius had gifted us a number of scrolls that mapped the area and detailed its defining characteristics and population counts. Far less militaristic than Septem, Tingis prospered as a trading port, although it had suffered a similar fate as the rest of Mauretania due to the frequent raids from Vandals, Visigoths, and an occasional tribe from the African interior.

Sprawling upon low hills, Tingis lacked the natural defenses of Mount Abyla or a winding promontory, and should have been easy enough to seize by storm. Privately, however, I hoped that such foolhardy attacks would prove unnecessary, for I had perilously few spearmen to protect such a vast area, and any losses would be sorely felt if Theudis pressed his advantage with a sudden assault.

Lashing winds blew along the coastal road of Tingitana that linked Septem with the province's namesake in Tingis. There was little complaining, however, for though the wind bit into exposed skin, so, too, did it push at our backs, easing the progress of our march. More, despite darkened skies that forewarned of a coming storm, fortune held the rains at bay. Even in these temperate regions, winter was never a preferred fighting season, so such mild discomforts were welcome against far more inhospitable conditions that could have befallen our expedition.

Marching sapped the men and forced us to draw camp three nights in a row. I insisted upon all the conventional requirements of Roman encampment, from deep trenches surrounding our rows of neatly arrayed tents to teams of interlocking pickets watching for any sign of a roving Visigothic force. Cephalas was constantly rushing between different elements of our force as dusk approached each evening, ensuring that my orders were sufficiently relayed to the Thracians, the Cappadocians, the Vandals, and the Herulians under Perenus and Fulcaris. No Roman soldier ever took pride in shoveling latrines or digging ditches, yet it was precisely such work that separated our cosmopolitan force from the unwashed masses of the tribes and kept our men safe and hale. For that, none dared shirk any duty under the watchful eyes of my senior officers.

Our brisk pace bore fruit on the fourth day, as Tingis finally drew within our reach. One of my precious few mounted scouts galloped ahead to inform Indulf of our arrival, with others on foot ordered to survey the nearby terrain and scout for villages or orchards that populated the sparse coastline. They found little enough, and I felt more acutely the need for a rapid resolution to whatever standoff had befallen our Ostrogoths in their quest to seize Tingis from the Visigoths.

As we neared Tingis, the Mauretanian hills grew broader yet no more challenging as we progressed along the deftly hewn stone road. That pathway wound along the coastline, offering views of vacant beaches, forbidding bluffs, and a distant, churning surf. Waves pounded into rock and sand alike, muffling our progression and lulling the men's nervous excitement into a more tractable calm. The stiff breezes continued, although occasional beams of sunlight pierced through overcast skies and yielded some measure of warmth. It was peaceful enough, allowing me a rare chance to enjoy the company of friends, and to share in their talk of wine and women without the nagging worry of enemy threats on the horizon. Regardless, I never fully fell into a carefree ease, with every move colored by the knowledge that the war in Tingitana might explode beyond my capabilities and force me to retreat to Carthage in shame. The mere thought of inadequacy, of begging for Belisarius' forgiveness, caused my hands to quiver.

My concerns were not allayed as Tingis came into view. Like Septem, it was a compact walled town, yet lacked the looming battlements that made Septem so dangerous to assault with ladders and rams. Positioned along the waterfront, it boasted a wide harbor where a multitude of crafts rowed in and out, carrying plentiful caches of fish that schooled along the shallow African reefs. No dromons could be seen amidst such seaborne traffic, allowing unfettered passage of Tingis' boats to whatever destination they pleased. It seemed almost idyllic: a temperate climate, relatively safe defenses, a city that could easily feed and shelter two thousand without much difficulty. It may have been so, if not for the hundreds of Ostrogoths arrayed along Tingis' main gate.

Theudis' hawk banners fluttered in the stiff winds, with dozens of Visigothic soldiers standing vigil atop narrow wooden fighting platforms, substitutions for the broad stone pathways of Septem. Curiously, even from a distance, I could tell such men stood silently, absorbing all manner of curses and abuse from their Ostrogothic enemies. It was only as we drew closer that I could decipher that unbalanced exchange of words, with much in the harsh Gothic tongue and occasional snippets in Latin.

"... you hear me, Agila! If you cower behind your walls, I will cut pieces from Theudis' precious nephew. You have already lost, so open your gates and leave with your lives and weapons. Resist, and this slip of goat shit will bleat for his mother."

Indulf. The voice, as well as the cruelty, was unmistakable. Such a tactic was both common and detestable, un-Christian yet brutally, undeniably effective. Few can turn their hearts to stone against the slow suffering of their kinsmen, especially when the victim is youthful, and immediately following Indulf's decree, a high-pitched voice screeched in pain, calling out in the same Gothic tongue used by Visigoths and Ostrogoths alike.

Signaling for Cephalas, I rushed a bevy of orders to my commanders. "Tell Perenus to position his Herulians along the northern coastline, and Xerxes and Gunderic to move to the south. I will take personal charge of the remainder."

"Will there be an attack? The men are eager, Varus, but also tired."

Smiling, I laid a hand upon Cephalas' shoulder. So much time had passed since the muscles on his arm were cut to ribbons in our fight against the Avars, and it was concerningly easy to forget that he was a soldier first, and a household member second. A lifetime of enduring taunts for his harelip had given Cephalas an unmatched ability to absorb doubt and show no weakness to the world, yet I knew that he would give anything to strap on a shield and return to the front of the shield wall. If our roles had been reversed, I do not know if I could have meekly accepted my new lot in life, watching my friends risk their lives while I fetched meals and carried letters. God only knows why, despite my many wounds, I had been preserved for something different.

"No battle today, most likely," I replied. "But tell me what you hear in the camp nonetheless. I'm depending on you to keep me aware of morale, and their impression of this new batch of Visigoths."

Smiling, Cephalas saluted with his one hale arm before sprinting away to execute my will. Before long, our column had broken into different segments, with my own veering toward Indulf's position. I ordered our horns to sound the advance of friends, the notes telling of an Imperial Army on the march.

Ostrogothic horns returned our greeting, welcoming our advance. As we trudged closer, the guttural squeals of a boy ranged once again across the horizon, piercing above the sounds of a thousand boots stamping along a stone road and the crash of the waves. As harsh winds swirled along Tingis' outskirts, pushing thin columns of dust across the Ostrogothic encampment, Indulf, his front spattered with fresh blood, strolled leisurely toward my banner, offering his own crisp salute once he recognized my plume.

"About time!" Indulf called, a full forty paces separating us. "Septem is ours?"

Delaying my reply, I waited until the distance of a whisper remained between us. "Nearly. The city is ours, but the citadel remains. I have come to ascertain why your foederati separated from the Herulians, and why you lingered here despite clear orders that your assistance was required in Septem's assault."

Indulf grunted, his relaxed demeanor shifting to one far warier of his current position. He waved for me to follow him to his private tent, the equipment borrowed from Belisarius' stores that marked the

Ostrogoths as direct extensions of the Imperial Army. Lacking the trappings of a senior commander that defined my own field quarters, Indulf's tent was identical to those shared with his men, although his was reserved for private use while most others housed five to ten warriors and their kits. Ducking inside, I found two stools and an uneven table.

"May I sit?"

Indulf nodded. "You are displeased with me. This is surprising."

"*Displeased* is perhaps premature," I corrected. "And the Empress knows that I myself have ignored many orders when opportunity or necessity called for it. It's more that I am interested in understanding why you are here, and what progress you have made."

Before Indulf could begin, another cry rang out from the center of the Ostrogothic camp. It was followed by a trail of weeping, the sobs of a boy with an unbroken voice. He called for one word, over and over, as if it was the only speech his body was capable of emitting.

"And I do not make war on children," I added. "Please explain how this poor boy has come to deserve torture."

Indulf grunted again. "I've warned you about this before, but your enemies do not share your misgivings. I take no joy from hurting a child, but I will do it if it means I can end a battle without losing a single man."

I did not interrupt as Indulf explained the course of events that led him to camp outside the stone walls that lined Tingis. Within a day of departing our initial landing along the African coastline, Indulf had captured and questioned a local farmer: Tingis had been seized from a Vandal garrison, and its walls flew the hawk banner of Theudis. Believing Volubilis an easy target, Indulf allowed Perenus to continue south, while he led his Ostrogothic foederati northwest toward Tingis—a tantalizing target that, while not as critical to securing the province as Septem, would prove a nuisance to Roman authority if allowed to linger in Theudis' hands.

"Your enemy is Agila, a particularly snakelike warlord within Theudis' retinue," Indulf added, his voice laced with derision. "Not the strongest, but certainly the most cunning. If he is allowed free, he will terrorize all Roman possessions from here to Tripolitana."

I nodded but kept my gaze fixed upon him. "And the boy?"

"Theudis' nephew by some bastard half sister," Indulf explained. "Some twelve years of age, and bastard-born himself, but they say that Theudis adores the lad. Agila stormed our camp in a nighttime sally two days ago. We captured the boy before beating those cowards back behind their walls. Since then, all has been peaceful from Agila and his cabal."

It was a foolish gambit, of course. One of the largest contingents of my expedition tied down against the target of little immediate value, fighting an enemy less than half its size. Indulf was correct that I benefitted from Agila's lack of mobility, yet in truth I doubted that such a small force could be anything more than a nuisance to the coastal villages. If anything, Agila depended upon the safety of Tingis far more than we required its pacification, for that town served as the only major port available to Theudis while my dromons circled Septem's walled harbor.

Indulf, as always, possessed an instinct for survival, yet I still could not see the wisdom of his encampment. Worse, I was unsure of how to proceed, for although a second seat was unthinkable, I dared not give the Visigoths any hope that we Romans would allow them to roam freely, or that Roman soldiers feared the confrontation of the vast numbers of Gothic warriors. However, in one small manner, my mind was decided.

"Free the boy," I commanded. "If he brought weapons into this camp, see that they are safely returned. But allow him safe passage back into Tingis."

Indulf sat straighter, his eyes widening. "Lord! He is my prisoner!"

"And therefore mine as well," I replied. "And though I commend your need to preserve the safety of your men, I do not make war upon children. Call it weakness or whatever you like, but I will not do it."

Indulf would not be cowed so easily, however. "But Varus, we are besieged against Agila and his men! This boy forces them to good behavior, and may even bring them to surrender! We are so close, Varus!"

I tried. Truly, I did. I entertained Indulf's machinations, even accepting his flimsy justification for rushing headlong into a separate attack with his mortal enemies. I even understood why, for the Ostrogoths and Visigoths have long despised one another. Despite deep kinship and even a union under the once-great King Theodoric, ill blood remained amongst the clans and the warlords. It hearkened back to when the Visigoths ran from Attila, leaving their kin, the Ostrogoths, to stand and fight against the overwhelming tide of the Hunnic horse archers. The Ostrogoths were subjugated, breaking free only after the Scourge of God died of a nosebleed on his wedding night.

Despite it all, I lost my temper. Fool that I was, and fool that I am.

"Besieged?" I roared. "They have complete freedom of movement by sea!"

"So?" Indulf shrugged.

"Tingis is surrounded on three sides by water!" I yelled, resisting the urge to strike Indulf in the jaw. "What good is a siege?"

"It kept these men bottled in a small place, where they wouldn't jeopardize your taking of Septem." Indulf rolled his eyes as though his logic was obvious. "Some call that a strategic victory. Give me five dromons, and Tingis will starve in a week."

I laughed, but not from mirth. No, it was a deliberately cruel tone, mocking Indulf's intransigence. "Yes, dromons will circle the harbor. But I do not have enough to prevent Theudis from landing elsewhere, or running my blockade under the cover of night."

"Varus—"

I raised a hand for silence. "What you have done is force my hand. Rather than a single victory at Septem, you have compelled me to fight a second battle at Tingis. And yes, Agila has few men. But Theudis has tens of thousands, while I have hardly two. We are hundreds of miles from safety, and the only thing keeping all of us from slaughter is Theudis' fear of the sea. Once he realizes how laughable my numbers really are, he will come in force. Tingis was *nothing*, not once we had Septem. But now, Agila knows we lack the force to even destroy a few hundred, and he will be sure to inform his master of our weakness."

A heartbeat passed. "So you say," he growled, submitting to my judgment, though hardly meekly. "But if we kill them all now, no tongues will be able to wag to the courts in Gades. Give me command, and I will place Tingis under your thrall in a day."

"No," I said with finality. "Free the boy. The men will rest for an evening. Tomorrow, we will take the measure of your Agila."

To my surprise, Indulf did not reply. Nor did he offer any visible emotion at my rebuke, staring blankly onward as if he had been deaf to such remonstrations. It was only after several moments of tense silence that he nodded, his tone strained and robbed of its vitality.

"We will free the boy. I await your instructions."

Standing, I nodded in approval. "Have your officers provide mine with reports of the region, and Agila's strength. If we must pry them from their defenses, we will not make the careless mistake of miscalculating our enemy's intent."

And so I left Indulf, slipping from his modest tent and into the biting sea air that drifted through the Ostrogothic camp. Satisfied, I did not reflect overmuch on our encounter, nor did I much care that Indulf's personal sense of leadership had been called into question. Our shared travails in the Vandal War yielded little that would bring me to value Indulf's friendship, and though he was a more-than-capable fighter, I did not trust him and his independence of movement as I would Perenus, Xerxes, or even Gunderic. I worried little at the consequences of such chastisement, and even hoped that some measure of good may come from them.

I would not discover until much later that my assessment was gravely wrong. And by then, it was far too late. At Tingis, however, the Ostrogoths fell back into line, and I began to seek answers that would extract my expedition from this increasingly overstretched position. We would have little time, for Theudis had no intention of leaving our weakness unexploited.

THE TURNING OF THE FATES

Compared to all the bluster of Septem, our encampment outside Tingis seemed almost sleepy. Theudis' nephew was released the same afternoon of my arrival, cut from his bonds and allowed to walk fearfully toward Tingis' gates. I would like to report that the boy was returned unharmed, but as he limped home with two fewer toes and a great number of cuts lacing his arms and chest, I would only be lying to claim as much. The boy would never again be a swift runner, nor traverse the stony faces of mountains, and for that I mourned. It was a curious sense of regret, for so many had been torn apart under my watch, yet I felt a profound shame that a young lad who posed no real threat could now no longer share the careless joys of his peers. Briefly, I thought of Vitalius' fearful sobs as he shuddered along the hills of Tricamarum, and wished I had arrived sooner to spare the boy such pain. At least, I reasoned to myself, he escaped with all his limbs and both eyes, for I had no doubt those would have been the next parts to fall victim to Indulf's hatred of our Visigothic enemy.

Yet after the freeing of our prisoner, little enough happened as we carved trenches and settled in for yet another siege of a sea-facing city. Herulians occasionally launched arrows over the city walls, more to keep the enemy wary of our presence rather than to do any real harm. In return, Visigothic sentries launched spears at any archers that drew too close to the walls, yet in comparison to the carnage of Septem, their counters were halfhearted. Indulf assured me that Agila's men must be running low on weapons, and in this, at least, I agreed with him.

A half dozen dromons arrived late on the first morning after our arrival. Most of Tingis' fishing boats scurried for safety well before the warships came into shouting distance, yet at least two were quilled with arrows as Roman archers lined the decks of each incoming vessel. It was a pitiful blockade, but effective during the light hours, for Agila possessed no craft that matched the speed or fighting ability of the fabled dromons. Lacking naphtha, the Visigoths had no real hope of setting our ships alight, and thus the Visigoths could do little but watch as the Roman ships took anchor along Tingis' seaward outskirts.

By night, however, the harbor was frenzied with activity. All torches along Tingis' sea walls were extinguished, making it impossible for the dromon captains to discern vulnerable targets without risking an unacceptably close encounter with coastal shoals. On land, we saw equally little, hearing only the occasional thrum of a ballista and the angry shouts of a crew. We only learned of the nighttime struggles in the early hours of dawn, tales of a greedy fishing vessel that shattered on the end of a fortunate bolt or of a trading hulk boarded and scuttled as it floated in the direction of Gades. These tales heartened the men, yet I quickly understood that for every Visigothic craft that capsized, another three or four successfully escaped Roman clutches to retrieve hauls from fishing traps or run northward to Hispania. Whether Theudis would respond was impossible to know, although it was a foregone conclusion that the Visigothic king learned of our disposition and weakness in guarding the narrow channel of water that separated the Pillars of Herakles.

Worse, the looming clouds that stalked our advance from Septem finally tore asunder, lashing down a torrent of stinging rains that made it difficult to see so much as an outstretched hand before one's face. Early on, its pattering drops were welcome, for they filled our waterskins and sent forth an agreeable scent from the thin soil of coastal Tingis, yet such pleasantness was fleeting. Soon, rivers of mud oozed through the disparate Roman camps, filling our latrines and soaking the cloth tents to the point of collapse. No fires were possible, regardless of how much Cephalas cursed and struggled with flint, leaving officers and spearmen alike shivering and miserable, gnawing at sodden crusts and slimy beef. A lone note of good fortune was that no vessels could launch into such awful seas. Yet even as our own dromons took shelter in the shallower and protected waters of a nearby bay, the thought of Agila's men nestled warm and dry before a hearth was almost too much to bear.

These soaking rains continued for a full two days, leaving the Ostrogoths near mutinous and even my Herulians begging to return to Septem's comforts. Despite Cephalas' remonstrations, I insisted upon weathering my fair portion of suffering, sacrificing what few specks of dry space that I had to protect my weapons and armor from an all-consuming rust. Pools of water squelched in my boots, and deep sores along my heels brought pain with each step.

Worse, even with the constant torrent, our camp soon stank of piss and dung, the latrines rendered useless and indifferent to the natural needs of men. Fights erupted when men defecated too close to the shared living spaces in the muck, forcing centurions to mete out occasional lashes to the instigators. I commuted all punishments to the minimum number of stripes, knowing full well that the wet morass and sickly miasmas around such men left them prone to a poisoning of the blood and a slow death. Our suffering was enough without the bloody flux.

We still assigned pickets, and kept careful watch on Tingis' gate and walls, fearful that Agila might use such a turn of fate to rush our camp and send its various segments into a disorganized rout. But that was all that could be mustered. Bowstrings were sapped of their killing force, and ladders would have sank in the soft earth before Tingis' walls. In truth, our siege had deteriorated into huddled filth and aimless moaning, with the more desperate of my spearmen stripping sodden shirts and trousers and walking about in nothing more than their wilted leather boots. In a conventional battle, such a display would warrant the harshest punishment possible short of death, yet our situation outside Tingis warranted leniency. No man deserted, and none shirked their duties, and for that I was grateful.

By the time the rains passed, however, there was little to be grateful for. A full half of my men were nursing injuries, with a handful suffering through yellowed and foul-smelling toes that could carry no weight without terrible pain. Others spent hours crouching over shallow ditches that served as makeshift latrines, their stomachs knotted and resisting any nourishment.

Worst of all were tidings from the sea: One of my dromons had foundered against hidden rocks as it tossed against swirling waves, and its hull was breached beyond simple maintenance. With no craftsmen available and Septem's harbor far too distant to effect repairs, all that could be done was to abandon the ship, tasking its sailors and archers to render it thoroughly inoperable should an opportunistic Visigoth attempt to refloat the dromon for his own men's navigation.

A half dozen sailors smashed axes into the side of their former home, the ship's captain weeping as its timbers were ripped from their moorings. After a half day of work, the dromon tilted upon its side as seawater flooded its deck and hold, releasing the ship into the shallow waters below. The other five ships remained afloat, yet two others had taken so much damage that they could only be called seaworthy by comparison. I dismissed their captains and ordered them to make course for Septem, urging Ascum to dispatch reinforcements to fortify our meager three dromons remaining to protect a full fifty miles of sea lanes.

Without fighting a single battle, our army slipped to the precipice of utter defeat. Even Gunderic's Vandals moved slowly, their lust for combat muted from vomiting and the rising threat of flux. Taking advantage of the drier air, Perenus led teams of archers to fire upon the Visigothic sentries, but their volley took no victims. In a moment of privacy, Xerxes approached my tent, seeking a word of warning as he addressed me in Persian.

"Another week, and a hundred men in your camp may be dead. Another month, and it may be half of them gone. I've seen flux and exposure many times in Persia, and it always leads to one end. We must attack now, or leave before we are encumbered by those too sick to walk."

I frowned, believing the truth of Xerxes' words even as I was cautious of their prescription. "Can we take Tingis?"

Xerxes paused, his head cocked and brow furrowed. Running a hand through his uncharacteristically disheveled beard, he slowly nodded. "Agila lacks men, more so than Theudesgel ever did. If we can break through at any point along Tingis' walls, all resistance will crumble."

"That's a considerable *if*," I added.

"It is," Xerxes admitted. "But it is one of two choices you have: fight or leave. We cannot remain on the wet ground any longer."

With that, I agreed, and gave Xerxes the freedom to prepare an assault on the following afternoon. In the meantime, I shared a sodden loaf with the Zhayedan, a fare not dissimilar from what we shared in the slime-ridden holds of Barbalissus. Xerxes laughed at our shifting fortunes, freed from a Roman prison and propelled to the heights of success in the army.

"An Immortal leading Roman soldiers into battle." He chuckled. "Such is the stuff of poetry or legends. What my father would think, if only he were alive!"

"No less incredible than a slave commanding an expedition," I countered, beaming at my friend's contentment.

Xerxes nodded, struggling to tear a chunk from his meal. "Do you believe in fate, Varus?"

The question surprised me, for it was one that echoed so many conversations with Belisarius, with Perenus, with Rosamund, and so many others who had shaped my strange journey through life. It was perhaps the most important question in all creation, and it was one that guided my path, regardless of its many failures and blemishes.

"Yes," I replied. "God has shaped my path, as he has for all others. How it will end, though? I couldn't begin to say. All I know is that there is no guarantee for happiness, only that we may choose to continue or not."

Wincing from stiffness and waterlogged clothing, Xerxes sat upright, his spine popping as he stretched for relief. "As do I. For there is no sense in how I have arrived in my current predilection. But I would change nothing, for I am thankful that the Ahura Mazda has delivered me into a far better life than I had long known."

With that, we shared a swallow of wine. After warming his hands atop the torch in my tent, Xerxes rose and saluted, slipping from my tent to deliver orders to the other officers. Later, I ordered double rations given to each man, and furthermore insisted that roaring bonfires be lit in regular intervals along our various encampments. Joining the long-absent company of Perenus and Fulcaris, we sang around a blessedly warm fire. Sembrouthes rolled his eyes as the Herulians told tales of their exploits, exaggerating each detail to the point of ridicule.

Many still suffered, and illness sapped the life force of many whom I had come to trust and love, yet they still celebrated in what may be their final night together, cursing the bitter food while toasting their comrades in arms. Most of all, we cheered the roaring flames, howling as wet logs were tossed into the inferno and sizzled before catching alight.

Many of the fires still smoldered the following morning. Rows of leather and wool had dried throughout the evening, allowing the men the first opportunity in days to don less-damp shirts and trousers. Iron mail was brushed and weapons honed as men broke their evening fast with simple fare. Predictably, Perenus voiced his discontentment with our increasingly moldy bread, offering ten gold pieces to the first man to steal Agila's roast chickens inside Tingis' walls. Sharing in the deprivation, I was tempted to join in that wager.

There was little urgency to our preparations, for there was no possibility of surprise in our movements. While Septem's hills had offered some barriers to disguise the repositioning of a besieger, Tingis had no such characteristics, leaving all Roman forces painfully visible to even the most careless of Visigoth sentries. Enemy archers shuffled along the walls with each movement of our bandae, contesting each skirmish with Herulian bowmen to disallow even the slightest advancement toward the walls. Our three remaining dromons had better fortune, yet their ballistae had little effect even when fired in concert with one another.

One ill-fated Visigoth was blown from a watch post, sending the man toppling into the sea and showering those nearby with slivers of wood and shattered sections of stone wall. However, his was the only casualty I could count, with the other bolts clattering near the base of the walls or hurtling well beyond their targets. Through it all, no Visigoth leader rose to defy our movements; Agila seemed not to share in the cruel bravado of Theudesgel.

By late morning, our lines had formed around ladder teams, and a ram had been fashioned from hewn trees lashed together with heavy flaxen rope. Only the Ostrogoths screamed hatred and mockery of their despised kin, for others in my arrayed forces too well remembered the struggles around Septem's land and seaward gates. In hindsight, such worry was overwrought, for Agila likely had only two to three hundred men at his command, with a full thousand paces of landward wall to protect. By then I wholly trusted Xerxes' judgment, and knew that if any part of Tingis' walls could be seized, the entire city would fall to our control.

Horns blared, summoning camp stragglers into formation and into their respective detachments. Perenus and Fulcaris lead my northmost spearmen, their mud-stained shields still displaying the ouroboros that had been my sigil since returning from Tauris. Gunderic and Xerxes occupied the south, their men shifting into a growling and singing mass as the looming Vandal warlord summoned primal fury that had long been the fear of the Vandals' conquests. Indulf's Ostrogoths remained in the center under my watch, joined by scattered groups of Cappadocian and Thracian infantry. Our banners, though still sodden and filthy, flew proudly: the standards of Belisarius, the Emperor, and a half dozen others who had won the right to fly their own device in their command of men on the battlefield.

Summoning Cephalas, I nodded toward the Vandal banda. "Tell Xerxes he has the right to commence the attack. Once he acknowledges, sound our horns for the assault to begin. Perenus and I will follow."

Cephalas grinned. "Aye, Lord. Can't wait to be out of this shithole."

"It was not always thus," Indulf muttered. "But war corrupts even the greenest orchards."

Not knowing the Ostrogoth to be much for poetry, I raised an eyebrow at the unexpected emotion and honesty, but waited until Cephalas sprinted toward the Vandals before offering a reply. "Well said, and true."

"My father always lectured on the need to pull corpses from wells, or keep the dead well away from fields we would plow," Indulf added. "Nothing grows from death. We Goths know this better than most. That's why I would kill all my enemies, because otherwise they would sever us root and stem. And I do not plan for me and my men to be tossed aside in the generations to come."

Ever more curious, I smiled again. "My dominus told my brother and me the same. Your father was a wise man."

Indulf grunted. "He was prudent, and knew how to survive. That is all that matters in life."

Within moments, I caught a glimpse of bronze-plated lamellar amidst a sea of Vandals, raising an arm in salute toward my position. It was followed by blaring Roman horns, their rims tipped with silver, calling long rolling notes that echoed from the city walls. A great shout rose from the Vandal ranks, led by Gunderic, mixed with the unsettling noise of cackling laughter. As the Vandal battle lust grew feverish, irrespective of any illness or fear of yet another siege, Xerxes raised his arm once more, then allowed it to fall.

"Forward!" Gunderic boomed, his voice carrying easily through the massed cheers.

It was Wisimar who jumped first, navigating his ladder through treacherous holes in the soil that could have snapped an ankle or broken a toe. Other Vandals surged forward, raising shields to protect both themselves and the ladder carriers from a thickening hail of arrows that poured from Tingis' makeshift towers. Iron-tipped shafts struck many of those upturned shields, burying into wooden panels with each strike, yet none found a careless or luckless target, and I grew heartened as Wisimar planted his ladder in the soil, thrusting the ladder toward Tingis' walls. Finding firm purchase, the ladder neither slid nor buckled, and the first Vandal spearman began to scale the walls.

"Signal Perenus," I said to Indulf. "We will attack the gate, and the Herulians will launch their own ladders."

Indulf nodded, relaying a message for the remainder of our forces to commit to the attack. Perenus responded immediately, setting aside his spear and drawing a sword before triggering a war cry from my countrymen. Their progress slow yet disciplined, the impenetrable wall of Herulian shields betrayed no vulnerability for Agila's archers to exploit. Meanwhile, Fulcaris screamed orders to keep their advance orderly, using his spear to push the slow or clumsy back into line and maintain a coherent front.

"All right, lads!" I yelled, drawing my runed blade. "Smash this gate down and end this war!"

Indulf offered his own translation, lashing his Ostrogothic kinsmen to a frenzy in their own tongue. The Goths grew even more bold from such a display, dancing before the lines and shouting curses to those guarding Tingis' primary gate. One man sprinted a bit too far, his footsteps ragged and motions clearly slurred by drink. Dropping his trousers, the man bared his arse to the enemy, smacking the pale flesh with a gloved hand before cackling with glee. His cheers were cut short, however, when an arrow pierced through the unguarded flesh and buried itself deep to the man's hip bones. Yelping and disconsolate, the man stumbled, neither able to run nor sit as a second arrow sailed into his abdomen.

"Back in line!" Indulf spat. "No more foolishness!"

While others still danced and jeered, no others deigned to follow their drunk comrade's example. None dared to even retrieve the man's twitching body, nor to shed a tear when a third arrow buried itself in the man's chest. His jerking stopped as he sank in the thick mud, the churned earth around his prone form turning crimson.

Perenus reached the walls before we did. Our progress slowed to a crawl as Indulf's men dragged the ram through sucking mud amidst an accelerating torrent of Visigothic projectiles. Arrows were soon joined by stones that clattered against our shields, the largest of which managed to temporarily break the cohesion of my lines and required our centurions to reknit the severed links.

Yet the Herulians, at least, continued their steady progress, even as my own bandae were forced to halt with each disruption. Hundreds of boots were making the sucking mud soft and nigh impassable, with few firmer paths available for the frontward ranks to signal a trail. We were in no grievous danger, yet neither did we make significant progress, with a journey of three hundred paces passing about as quickly as a crawling babe. Indulf roared in frustration, yet no quantity of insults or bullying could force the army forward. Not, at least, without making each man an easy target for an opportunistic Visigoth wall archer.

From behind the floating wall of shields, I caught glimpses of the Vandals' progress. Three ladders rested against Tingis' outer walls, with two more being ferried along by cautious yet jubilant Vandal warriors. Even with such successes, however, no Vandals had yet ascended to the top, with those daring to haul themselves to the upper rungs greeted with a barrage of heavy stones. A particularly weighty boulder crashed down and snapped the topmost rung of one ladder clean in two, rendering it unreliable to hold the weight of multiple armored men atop pliant mud, and therefore useless.

Amidst it all, cheers rose among Tingis' defenders. At first the sound was muted, small pockets of emotion contrasting with the prior week's solemnity. Soon, however, a hundred voices roared in defiance, their volleys of arrows and stones growing denser and ever more dangerous.

"We need to close the gap!" I screamed, urging the men forward.

Indulf leaned close, his words nearly drowned out by the thrumming of Visigoth arrows. "We could drop the ram, rush the wall with ladders. It's like this damned thing wants to be planted in the earth, as much mud as it is sucking up."

Despite my impatience, such a strategy would be ruinous. "No, we must put pressure on the gate. Keep Agila spread thin and unable to put all his men atop the walls!"

Nearby, a rolling Vandal cheer swarmed over the din of their Visigoth enemies. Stealing a glance from behind the curtain of shields over my head, I saw Gunderic brush aside several of his men, vaulting up the wooden ladder and gaining purchase on its middle rungs. Though bulky, Gunderic had all the agility of a street cat, moving nimbly even with only one hand on each rung, the other hoisting his massive shield against falling debris. His progress slowed as he reached the peak, yet he surged upward, flailing the iron-rimmed shield into the throats and faces of nearby Visigoth defenders. As Gunderic mounted the nearest tower, he unsheathed his sword, chopping hard onto an archer's shoulder with a force that tore the blade clean into the man's abdomen. Pulling his blade free, Gunderic kicked the butchered man from his perch, the first confirmed Visigoth casualty of the battle.

I watched each of Gunderic's movements with rising hope and burning apprehension. For no Vandal had joined their lord atop the walls, their progress stunted by stubborn resistance from nearby defenders. "Gunderic is taking the walls! We must move now! Push, men!"

All battles have moments, however fleeting, when men are willing to overcome physical limitations, either from a sheer will to survive or to spite impending injury or death. For the Ostrogoths, that moment was now. All impediments to our progress seemed to be suddenly removed. More hands grasped for the siege ram to pull it free from the muck, while small teams rushed forward to launch their spears at the Visigoth defenders. One of those darts found its mark in the chest of a careless archer, piercing the man's shoulder and throwing him over the walls and near the base of the gate. An Ostrogoth danced forward, smashing his axe into the dying archer's face and abruptly ending his cries.

Just before we reached the gate, a horn sounded from the Herulian camp. We could not see what prompted such an urgent signal, as the curvature of the walls made it impossible, but Indulf's men cheered all the same.

"Break this fucking door open!" Indulf shouted.

Lacking the latticed wood and iron of Septem's entrance, the gate at Tingis was laughably weak. Indeed, the doorway to the Imperial Palace was more formidable than our intended target, for its frame was supported by thin straps of pig iron that were bolted to a thin but solid layer of worn lumber. Doubtless, the gate's interior was reinforced with wooden crossbeams on the other side, but ultimately all was powerless to halt the ram's progress—doubly so given that the Visigoths had no oil nor even a perch to fire arrows or stones down upon our heads.

Indulf ordered the ram's first blasts to commence. "Heave!"

Our ram was a sorry thing, crudely constructed and honed to a ragged point. Even so, it bore all the necessary weight to batter its target, especially when the enemy could not repel our attack. I half expected the gates to open and for Agila's men to rush headlong into the breach in some desperate surprise attack, yet no such foolish bravado ensued.

"Heave!"

Again and again and again. Nearby, Herulian horns blared, and Vandal shouts grew louder and more frequent. Curiously, so, too, did the Visigoth cries, their tone suggesting some strange joy rather than any fear or suffering. And I knew they must have suffered, for the exchange of iron nearby signaled a rising fight for the walls. With no room to maneuver feet and weapons, those foolish or clumsy would easily be cast down, breaking hips and limbs if they were lucky, and spines if they were not.

"Heave!"

At last, Tingis' gate cracked. The initial fracture was a tiny thing, mere splinters around a poorly crafted iron hinge, but what followed was more devastating, an angry gash rent into the heart of the panel. A third blow drove a hole clean through the gate, a thin beam of light piercing through to offer a tantalizing glimpse of the city on the other side. I was so focused upon our progress that I did not mind the sounds of shouting to the north, any concerns drowned by Indulf's ravenous anger.

"Heave!" Indulf shouted one final time. "Blow this fucker down!"

With a final blow, the Ostrogoths obeyed. Tingis' gates burst forth, splitting the wooden panels and supporting crossbar underneath, and opened the city to conquest and the inward rush of my men. There was no command, only a visceral urge by the Ostrogoths to seize what had been long denied them.

Pushing aside the broken gate, our frontward spearmen passed through Tingis' threshold—only to be met immediately by staunch resistance. An enemy advance, with Theudis' hawk decorated upon each of their shields, stood firm. At the center was a burlier Visigoth coated in polished scales, armor that stood starkly against the worn leather and rusted mail of most other defenders. The man was cautious, ordering his men to advance in brisk yet disciplined order as they slammed into the disorganized Ostrogothic onslaught.

"Wall! Wall!" Indulf roared. "Cut through them! The man who butchers Agila will get his pick of the city!"

To their credit, the Ostrogoths did their best to obey. A crude wall formed, and the rival lines slammed together in a deafening crunch of wood and iron. Yet such efforts were hampered by many deficiencies. The Ostrogoths buckled at Agila's counterattack. Debris from the shattered walls formed obstructions in the second and third ranks of Indulf's lines, and many of our Thracian and Cappadocian reinforcements were still bogged down in viscous mud churned into a veritable swamp by hundreds of stamping boots. We simply were not able to use our superior numbers to drive a wedge through Agila, especially when forced to funnel through the narrow gate opening.

Indulf screamed at the delay, hefting his own shield and spear in preparation for joining the attack. Behind us, however, a flood of black-shielded men streamed eastward in panicked disarray. Alarm swelling in my throat, I grabbed Indulf's shoulder.

"Indulf, we need to regroup! There's something wrong with the Herulians!"

"We're so close!" Indulf shouted to be heard above the clashing of weapons and the cries of wounded men. "Give me the Cappadocians and the Thracians, and we will break their lines in the next charge!"

Temptation nagged in my gut. Even as Indulf spoke, the leading Ostrogoths began to solidify their flimsy shield wall, pushing back against Agila through the sheer weight of the massed Roman ranks surging through Tingis' shattered gates. Even without my permission, I have little doubt that the Ostrogoths would have broken through by force alone, bending the Visigoth lines inward, beyond the point of rearmament and repair. But the matter was soon immaterial, for the Herulian horns sounded far more clearly to our rear, with Perenus' voice calling desperately for relief.

"Varus! Ships incoming, flying Theudis' banner! Get out of there before we're surrounded!"

And in but a moment, my senses attuned to what unfolded beyond Tingis' gates. Our Visigothic adversaries continued to cheer, redoubling their efforts both along the shield wall and atop Tingis' walls to resist our attack. No Vandals had seized the city's wooden towers. Most of all, a sonorous horn sounded in the distance, echoing from the waters and sailing into the city to tell of the arrival of a significant force.

We were routed. There was no choice but to retreat.

"Indulf, order the men to fall back, in good order. We must retreat now, before the incoming enemy outflanks and encircles our position."

Wide-eyed, Indulf screamed in rage. "NO!"

More Herulians streamed behind, clutching their cloaks as they kicked through the softened mud. Fulcaris brought up their rearguard, blowing the banda horn once more toward our direction. After Fulcaris, no further Herulians followed, and our fate was apparent. No Roman forces remained between Tingis' gate and the sea, giving whatever forces sailed in to relieve the city unfettered access to our rear.

"Indulf, order the men to retreat, now!" I yelled. "If not, we all die!"

My words were not necessarily hyperbole, for one way or the other we had little knowledge of the strength of the incoming enemy forces. They might have been little more than teams of intrepid fishermen, flying the sweeping banners of a Visigothic warlord in some foolhardy subterfuge. But they might also have been a small detachment not dissimilar to Agila's or Theudesgel's, a mere blockade runner able to maneuver past my depleted dromons. Without clear visibility, I could not be certain, with only the sudden flight of my veteran Herulians to judge the challenge to come. And if I could trust anything on this battlefield, it was in Perenus' courage. He had never shirked from duty nor objected to a fight, and his retreat was all the convincing I needed that our siege must be abandoned. Even, unfortunately, if on the precipice of victory.

"Men!" I shouted, straining my voice to carry as loud as it could. "We go, now! Leave none behind!"

Indulf clenched his blade, his eyes fixed upon the resurgent form of the heavily armored Agila. Likely sensing our weakening resolve, the Visigoths pushed forward once more, propelling our shield wall back through Tingis' open gateway. I am proud to say that none of my forces ran aimlessly, and instead retained all the discipline of a fighting force even as each man layered his shield around the head and body of another. No opportunistic arrows were able to pluck unlucky casualties as we departed, and for that, I remain grateful to this day.

However, we did not leave unbloodied. At least a dozen men lay dead or dying under Tingis' gate arch, and our men were unable to organize relief in the need to depart as quickly as possible. Agila's men did not give chase, although several of their frontward spearmen chopped hard upon our forgotten wounded, offering a mercifully expedient departure from this life. None jeered, nor did any gesture for us Romans to return to battle. Agila himself merely stood before his men, the hawk sigil emblazoned upon his scaled chest, and stared as the enemy that had come within mere moments of conquest evacuated the battlefield. Once out of arrowshot, our thick curtain of shields dispersed, and our men were ordered to run toward the massed Herulians.

After moving a few hundred paces back from Tingis' defenses, I finally caught a glimpse of what had brought Perenus to run. After only a few heartbeats, I understood my friend's fear. Summoning Indulf's horn blower, I ordered him to signal for the attention of Xerxes and Gunderic, as their forces were still scattered outside the walls but not yet retreating from the battlefield. I spotted Gunderic, the hulking warrior having returned to the ground and the relative safety of his own men, and cupped a hand over my mouth to give him warning.

"Gunderic! Xerxes!" I shouted. "Evacuate! Back to Septem!"

Indulf's horn blew again for effect, bringing a dozen Vandals to turn and gawk at our retreating forces. Turning to face me, Gunderic raised his arms in confusion, calling out a response I could not hear. Xerxes, however, did not delay, responding with his own signal that the Vandals would uncharacteristically retreat from battle. And so they did—although reluctantly at first. Still, I am sure that, once given the correct view, even Gunderic saw the wisdom in such cowardice.

For Theudis had come to Tingitana. The flotilla that steered for Tingis' harbor was laughable and makeshift, yet even as my dromons launched all manner of arrows and bolts, they proved too few against a force so large. From fishing craft with a dozen warriors to trade cogs that carried a hundred, Theudis must have amassed three thousand

Visigoths beneath his banners, risking the brief sea journey from Gades to aid and protect his last remaining foothold upon the African continent.

Whether by ill fortune or poor strategy, we had failed. I had failed. And everything that Belisarius had gained in his journey to Africa now tipped in the balance. All we could do was cower and run.

CONTRAVALLATION

It was not until many months later that I came to understand the nature of Theudis' gambit across the sea. Liberius was certainly correct—the Visigoth king had no warships to compare with Roman dromons—and had absurdly few in number for a kingdom so vast as all Hispania. And so, we reckoned that Theudis had no ability to launch a major expedition. Even if he could, he dared not risk it, or so we thought. In our own way, all in the Roman command were wrong.

I have no love for Theudis, even decades later. But what he did required the same type of courage as had filled Odysseus and Agamemnon thousands of years prior, launching a thousand ships to a distant shore. Even within perilous waters, Theudis' court in Gades was only a two-day sail from Tingis, yet all the king had was a collection of tiny boats stinking of fish guts and ponderous cogs better suited in trading with the distant kingdoms of Britannia. I am convinced that no commander, not even Belisarius, nor even the vaunted Julius Caesar himself, would have predicted the Visigothic invasion of Mauretania with a fleet of civilian vessels—a fact that a wily Theudis must have intimately understood.

There is also little doubt that Theudis gained understanding of his narrow opportunity through contact with Agila at Tingis. Though

Indulf had superior numbers of spearmen, the Ostrogoths had no ships to force even the barest blockade of Tingis' port, allowing any ship to sail unmolested across the Pillars of Herakles and into Gades' deep harbors. Later, when Ascum's dromons were thinned to cover the vast distance between Septem to Tingis, we simply lacked the concentrated force to bludgeon the Visigoth king's flotilla. With a dozen dromons, Theudis would have drowned that day, and perhaps Belisarius might have enjoined Baetica or even all Hispania to his conquests of Vandal Africa. Alas, such fates did not come to pass.

We ran. God knows I resented the memory of Archelaus, but he was not wrong that a hardened Roman army must be equipped to run, in full kit, for an entire day and night without slowing for meal or rest. Weakened by flux and battle, my men were not so tireless, yet we continued our trot eastward along Tingitana's coastal road until well after the hour that darkness claimed the horizon. Satisfied that Theudis remained miles distant, my combined forces collapsed under the stars, with few caring that no tents protected against the nighttime chill; we had abandoned our camp and all its goods to Agila's men, leaving with only our armor and weapons in our haste to escape.

As all but the night sentries collapsed in exhaustion, I resisted the initial urge to sleep and paced along the ranks to a nearby fire. It was a poor thing, spawned by grass kindling and fed by the still-green branches of the coastal Mauretanian brush, yet its smoke offered a modicum of warmth that Gunderic seemed to enjoy. The Vandal giant grunted his welcome as I squatted beside the modest blaze, his outstretched fingers throwing another clump of leaves onto the smoldering flame. Keeping my voice a dull whisper, I drew Gunderic's attention.

"How are your men?"

Another grunt, with Gunderic rubbing his dirt-caked fingers together before the weak fire. "Sick, hungry, and tired… but alive."

No perfect words emerged in my mind to console the Vandal warrior. Instead, only hot shame crept up my throat, and I grew thankful that the cover of darkness masked the blush that must have colored my cheeks. I had commanded men and taken life, yet in that moment I felt as if transported back to the earliest days of my freedom, tongue-tied and apprehensive of how to give voice to my emotions.

"I will see them cared for," I offered clumsily. "I swear it."

Gunderic shook his head. "Theudis outwitted us, but none could have foreseen him sending hundreds of barely seaworthy rafts a hundred miles out to sea. Whatever gods Theudis prays to must favor his boldness."

More uncertainty, for I could not discern Gunderic's disposition. The man was normally jovial to the point of mischief, yet his current demeanor showed none of that mirth. "That is kind of you to say."

"It is the simple truth," Gunderic replied. "Whether pagan or Christian, man cannot fight a god. We were not victorious, but what few Vandals perished died a good death—like men, with their wounds to the front and their hands clutched tight around bloodied weapons. This is all we Vandals ask for in life—an ending worthy of a hundred toasts. One day, I hope for the same."

I could not help but find this curious. Though the Vandals had been subjugated, it was still unclear why their men offered such ready loyalty to their recent adversaries, oathsworn to kill and be killed at the command of Lord Belisarius. Not that I doubted Gunderic— the Vandals' courage and sacrifice in both Septem and Tingis was evidence of their loyalty, and his—even the most hardened Roman veterans would have balked at sailing into a naphtha-fueled inferno, howling for blood and charging into an enemy city. It was only that I did not understand *why* they would commit themselves so wholly. Truthfully, I never would; yet in that moment, I pried further.

"Gunderic, why are you willing to fight in Justinian's army? Your men have done little more than bleed and suffer since swearing their oaths."

The Vandal warlord chuckled. "Aye, but this is nothing. I was born from violence, like any Vandal, and with luck I will die in violence. And I do not serve your cockless Emperor, who sends others to scratch and bleed while he sits comfortably on his cushioned chair.

No, we serve Belisarius. He claimed our loyalty by right of conquest, and that is sacred to us."

Hearing this, I did not doubt Gunderic's sincerity. Nevertheless, the Vandals had been recently conquered, and I wondered whether Gunderic's profession of service had limits. "Even if such loyalty affords you no personal gain?"

"Even if Belisarius commanded us to rush naked into the enemy wall, armed with only knives and our wits." Gunderic grinned. "Do not misunderstand, I enjoy enemy gold and voluptuous women as much as any man who fears his gods. But such diversions are not my purpose, only to conquer everything. And Belisarius is a man who, if he were made king of the Romans, would be the greatest king in a dozen generations, submitting half the world to his will. If your Emperor were no fool, he would understand this, and tremble."

And there it was. In his own way, Gunderic had pledged his life to serve as I did, for a purpose greater than himself. Where we differed was intent—while I shared Belisarius' dream of peace and order, Gunderic prized only strength, and believed Belisarius the only Roman worthy of seizing Vandal loyalties. And yet, in Belisarius' absence, I was uncertain why Gunderic took *my* orders.

"And me?" I prodded.

Gunderic's smile evaporated. "What about you?"

"Belisarius is not here, but I am. Why take my commands, when to you I am little different than the Emperor?"

Yet another grunt. "You and I are no different. We are both warriors, sworn to life on the battlefield. No Vandal enjoys retreat, and neither do you. But even when losing, you have a way of preserving your ability to fight another day. So it is for me: I do not fear death, but neither will I throw away my life carelessly. I would die only in a battle worthy of the Vandal people, not in some nameless skirmish that's merely a foolhardy attempt to delay defeat."

Though meant as a compliment, his answer left me uneasy. My mind wandered back to my imprisonment in Nisibis—back to when the magus condemned me as a thing of evil, skilled only in death, destined to spread chaos in a dying world. I did not see Gunderic as an instrument of some devil, yet neither could I see the Vandals as righteous, for they took pride in destruction and sought nothing but war. Surely something separated me from this Vandal giant, shivering in his filthy armor and hovering over a dying flame.

"Believe me when I say it—I know what it means to lose men in defeat," Gunderic added. "Some will cast blame upon your judgment. Pay them no mind—such men are like hens, clucking for attention. But when the wolves truly come, even the weaklings will rally to you for shelter. That battle will be far more important."

I nodded. "Best steal what rest you can. Theudis will be hot on the march, and we need to reach Septem before his vanguard catches our stragglers."

Though the weather spared our scattered forces from frost or rain, the night was nevertheless a difficult one, spent upon hard ground. The rolling waves, though numbingly peaceful in their rhythm, propelled gusts of chilled air through the ranks of the men. Those not weary to the point of motionlessness unstrapped their helmets, using the upturned iron rims to dig divots into the stony earth in a vain effort to spare their bodies the worst of the biting winds. The healthy shivered, the ill moaned, and I did not condemn others for lighting what meager fires would stay lit, despite their obvious signal to any nearby enemy of our position and weakened numbers.

The following morning, however, it was hell getting my defeated forces back in order. Teeth chattering, many complained of little water and no bread from the previous evening, their vitality sapped to the point of sluggishness. My officers were not spared those deprivations, either, with Xerxes leaning heavily upon a spear and Perenus heaving in pain as the bloody flux claimed him as its latest victim, leaving Fulcaris to take leadership of the Herulians. I ordered two Aksumites to each lend a shoulder to Perenus, who weakly attempted to brush away such assistance.

"I'm not a damned child," Perenus moaned. "If I can survive an arrow from the Avars, I promise that I won't shit myself to death."

"No, but you might die from being an ox-brained fool!" Cephalas yelled. "If you don't let these men bear you back to Septem willingly, I'll smack you in the face with a spear butt."

Drawing back, Perenus gawked at his longtime friend, breaking into laughter a few heartbeats later. "I surrender, Cephalas," Perenus said with a chuckle, groaning as his pained guts robbed his once-proud legs of their strength. "Just like any morning after too much wine. Smells about the same, at least."

Sembrouthes alone seemed unaffected by any complaints, his back straight and concentration sharp as he continued to shadow my every move. Unexpectedly, the normally taciturn Aksumite was vocal in insisting that I keep away from the dozen tiny latrines that had formed at the edge of our scattered camps, worrying that the foul humors that emanated from such pits would surely spread the flux to me.

"If I could remember my mother, I'd assume she'd be quite a bit like you," I muttered in a half joke, half complaint as Sembrouthes steered me away from visiting a nearby Cappadocian camp.

Sembrouthes frowned. "If I were your mother, I'd smack some sense into you. For once, let me have an easy day in my duties."

Our trek back to Septem began well after the sun crested upon the eastern horizon. After extracting the last detachment of Thracians that had huddled together in a nearby hole for warmth, we also began to understand the rising dangers that only worsened with each passing hour. Ten men who had fallen asleep the night before did not wake to see the following morning, including four Ostrogoths, a young Herulian recruit, two Vandals, and three wounded Cappadocians who had each taken arrows in their shoulders or abdomen. Ever observant, Xerxes had been painfully correct about the rising toll of sickness, and I feared that another night in the cold would see our losses triple, or worse.

"Back to Septem today!" I yelled. "Warm beds, roast chicken, and a full night's sleep!"

"And women!" Gunderic shouted joyfully. "Sweet Jesus, but

introduce me to a gaggle of women. I've spent too long with you ugly lot."

In his way, Gunderic also had some measure of astuteness in his assessment of the battle. Few were concerned about the outcome—or, at least, there was no grumbling, and most seemed happy enough to escape relatively whole, and without losing much more than iron cookpots and a few dozen worn tents. True, many grieved, for as with any battle, dear friends had been severed from this coil. Their grief burned into promises for vengeance rather than the embers of mutiny and outrage. Even Indulf had been less troublesome, although he, too, had been stricken with a milder case of the flux and had kept to the company of his fellow Ostrogoths.

We departed camp—if the inhospitable quarters of our resting point could be called a camp—in relatively good spirits. Within hours, however, moans of pain and mutterings of fatigue and hunger grew to more than mere whispers. Worse, our pace had ground to a crawl, slowed by dozens of men requiring assistance to walk. Another Ostrogoth died of his wounds, a ragged spear thrust rent deep into his shoulder, and some of my Thracians requested the right to bury their fallen comrade.

"Absolutely not," Indulf insisted before me, preventing the delegation from convincing me of the justice of their cause. "The man is dead. His suffering is over. Ours remains, and if we do not keep moving, it will only grow like weeds around a ruined stone building."

It was a terrible thing, to leave the corpse of a brother to rot along the roadway, crows picking at his bloated and leaking innards. In a retreat, however, an army is afforded few luxuries. This would not be the first time a fallen Roman would be unceremoniously cast aside, and it almost certainly would not be the last.

"Say prayers over his body and leave him behind," I ruled. "God will care for his soul. It is up to me to keep the rest of you alive. We keep marching."

And so we trudged. Blessedly free to roam on firm ground, we strode along dressed stone that had not been unduly strewn by rivers of mud. It was a dull affair, the groans of the ill muffled only partially by the stamping feet of hundreds of spearmen. Each banda operated independently of the others, causing our once orderly column to snake in extended groups of ten and twenty. This slipshod travel was dangerous, leaving our rearward ranks vulnerable to opportunistic raiding parties, yet the only other choice was to reduce the army's pace down to the slowest, sickest man. Instead, I allowed the hardier Vandals to rush speedily toward Septem, ordering armored detachments of Thracians and Cappadocians to keep a stern eye along the rolling western hills.

Xerxes protested, but Gunderic did not balk at the opportunity to reach Septem early. With their nominal Persian commander at the center of their formation, even those Vandals with cramping legs and distended bellies doubled their pace. A half dozen of their number were left behind to hobble along with our sick and wounded, their bodies unable to force anything beyond a simple shuffle. As the overall commanding warlord, I remained with the bulk of my men, both because I was unwilling to abandon Perenus and desired direct oversight of any others on the precipice of collapse.

Twice, the rearguard sounded a call for urgent attention, signaling strangers stalking our movements along the craggy hills of the coastal shoreline. In both instances, the concern was uncalled for, the distant movements turning out to be once the swift footfalls of a she-fox and a litter of kits, and once no more than a looming tree whose leafless branches cast shadows like jerking movements of enemy warriors. Even after such reassurance, fear that a vengeful band of Visigothic hunters was steps away lingered. As the morning sun came to sink westward, it was clear our progress was manifestly insufficient, and left ample opportunity for Theudis' healthier forces to gnaw into our dwindling lead should they fall upon us.

Staring into the western horizon, I shared a brief moment alone with Sembrouthes. "Do you think they'll have horses?"

He thought a moment. "Some, but not many," he concluded. "Most of their boats were too cramped for a horse, and the seas too violent. They may have enough for a dozen scouts, but not for any mounted force."

"I pray you are correct," I muttered, careful that my words would not sail in the wind to the ears of my decaying column. "Even a dozen scouts could do considerable damage."

"Then we must keep going," Sembrouthes said firmly, "for that is all that can be done. As long as we move forward, Theudis will not reach our forces today, not when he must first disembark all his boats and assemble rations and supplies to march upon Septem."

So we marched, though many shivered, and some fainted from exhaustion and malnourishment. Worse, the putrid stench of dung clung to the air around our column, mixed with the acrid odor of sickness that even the youngest child would know to avoid. At the center of it all, Perenus grew ever more debilitated, his halfhearted jibes traded for grim silence and half-shut lids. There was no more griping at using two Aksumites to bear his weight, as each passing hour saw Perenus relying less upon his waste-crusted legs and more upon his saviors. By late afternoon, Perenus' feet hardly lifted from the stone road at all, his boots dragging lightly as the two huffing Aksumite spearmen hauled their ponderous weight forward.

"Wake up, you sack of shit!" I yelled at Perenus, smacking him in the face. "You're not allowed to die on me. Rosamund would curse my innards to whatever foul gods she prays to. We'll be in Septem before sundown."

Perenus coughed, moaning as a trickle of blood stained his trousers. "You were always a bad liar," he gurgled.

"And I'm a worse gravedigger. Now stay awake, or I'll cuff your cheeks again for laziness."

Somehow, Perenus tried. I knew well how draining the flux could be, for I, too, had suffered it in childhood. With me feverish and prone to sleeping near the whole day, Liberius himself had taken to my care at Justin's urgent request, drawing queer glances that a foreign-born slave such as myself would receive such intimate care. I never discovered the costs of the potions and healers inflicted upon me, for neither man would ever tell, although I don't doubt that such care would have differed little from that enjoyed by the Emperor Anastasius himself. As I writhed, consumed by one of the deadliest afflictions that God has challenged his people with, Justin watched over me with fearful concern, his fear transformed to his usual impassivity once I was able to swallow mouthfuls of warm onion soup without considerable pain or regurgitation.

But that was at the palace, equipped with all the rarest herbs and medicines at the center of a glorious Empire. Perenus suffered along a desolate Roman roadway, his chattering teeth blasted by gusts of cold sea air and surrounded by fifty other afflicted men. To halt meant death for many, and the grim realization that Perenus could hardly survive yet another night in the elements struck me. And so, as one of his Aksumite caretakers began to flag under the exertion of his efforts, I wrapped Perenus' arm around my neck, lifting the weighty man as we trod eastwards.

"Varus, you smell like a camel's arse," Perenus muttered into my ear. "I've no idea how you got an Arab princess to share your bed. Blackmail?"

Chuckling aloud, I nearly dropped him, yet was assisted by Fulcaris, who took control of Perenus' other shoulder. "Aye, and you smell like the droppings of a camel's arse," I shot back. "Thankfully, Hereka appears to have soft feelings for mud-rolling swine such as you."

"Careful now!" Perenus said. "Might have to challenge you to single combat if you keep it up."

"I'd wager good money to see that happen," Fulcaris boomed. "Five coins says Perenus shits himself before drawing his sword."

"God damn you both!" Perenus blustered, a wide grin under his disheveled beard.

We boasted and told tales as we clambered on, with Perenus offering trite curses or chuckles at various intervals. When he grew too silent, I pretended to drop him to the roadway, shaking him from his stupor and focusing him upon the task at hand. Nevertheless, as the last rays of daylight faded to the west, those silences grew more common.

"Varus, I just want to sleep," Perenus mumbled, his words slurred as if steeped in wine. "Just for a little. I'll march in an hour."

"Denied!" I barked. "You're making it back if I have to drive my boot up your backside every three paces to do so."

Perenus moaned. "I hate you, you bastard."

"I love you too," I grunted. "And soon, you'll be back to being the second-best chariot racer in Constantinople."

"Second-best?"

"Aye!" Fulcaris grinned. "You never beat Magnetius!"

"Sh-shit-eating Blues," Perenus grumbled. "Magnetius couldn't hold my reins, let alone beat me on the track. His teeth hang on the necklace of some street urchin now, for all we know."

We continued like this for hours, well into the darkness. More men fell from the column, too sick to even be dragged along the roadway, unconscious when hauled upright. I stationed a Cappadocian dekarchos and ten spearmen to stand guard at a waypoint with such wounded and sick, offering waterskins and the promise that messengers from Septem would sprint along the roadway to offer immediate relief.

My next comments to the dekarchos were mere whispers, the words more ominous. "If you see any Visigoths, just flee. No point in sacrificing your lives needlessly. Return to Septem with haste."

"Appreciated, Lord," the dekarchos responded. "But I'll roast in the foulest caverns of hell before abandoning my men."

There was nothing to gain by arguing, so I nodded. "Good lad. We will return as soon as the column is through Septem's walls."

The dekarchos saluted, using a collection of nearby stones and dried tree limbs to whip up a thin fire. I should have chastised the officer for such a careless signal of his location but could not bring myself to deprive the forlorn group of ten of their lone sliver of comfort. Perhaps I should have steeled my resolve, but I simply chose not to.

After hours of hauling Perenus, the man's weight had chafed my shoulders raw to the point of bleeding. Smaller than me, Fulcaris fared worse, yet he grunted with each pace and refused to surrender his responsibility. At one point, Perenus began to weep, a faint stutter of tears and moaning that allowed no discernible words to form. I did not press him further, begging God that our travails would soon come to an end.

More men collapsed. Another Thracian dekarchos volunteered to operate a makeshift camp, his ten standing watch over a full twenty exhausted and dying Roman soldiers. The young officer accepted the last of our waterskins and even accepted a swallow of wine, piling brush and sticks to form a crude bed for the suffering men. It was here that Cephalas begged to be allowed to stay and join in the care of the men.

"Rescue may not come until the morrow," I warned. "And Theudis may arrive well before we do."

Cephalas nodded. "I understand. I have not hoisted a spear in some time, but I am a Thracian soldier above all things, and there are Thracians dying in the dirt. Even a one-armed man can help in such circumstances."

Sighing, I did not resist. "Take no foolish risks. I'm coming back for you."

He nodded. "Just get Perenus back to the city," Cephalas muttered. "That's all that matters."

Yielding to Cephalas' request, I left him a spare blade, ordering him to avoid using it unless absolutely necessary. We shortly departed that camp, our pace somewhat lightened after jettisoning the slowest in our column. Even so, the remaining men were spent, and only the ingrained discipline to follow an officer's orders kept the column moving. Hoarse voices called less frequently across the lines, the rasping centurions saving their waning vigor for the journey ahead.

Eventually, blessedly, our travails were rewarded. First, lit torches, then a column of men moving westward, their Greek voices as sweet to my ears as the softest harp ever strummed in the Imperial

Palace. As we met, one of the lead torches filtered through their ranks, a calling voice snapping me to attention.

"Varus! Lord Varus?" the torchbearer cried, searching each face amidst the darkness.

"Here," I croaked, pausing with Perenus to wave my free hand.

Squinting, the glow of the torch revealed the man as Conon, the officer left in Septem to command Liberius' remnant forces, bearing a freshly cleaned plume of a Roman centurion and with five soldiers flanking him.

An involuntary sigh of relief flooded through my body. "I could kiss you, Conon. Now I am doubly in your debt."

Conon grinned. "I'm not sure about that, Lord, although I don't mind the gratitude. Xerxes has command of Liberius' men, and we've posted a double watch on the ascent to Septem's citadel. I have fifty men with me, half of whom are warriors. Where do you need us?"

My mind fogged from sore muscles and fatigue, I raised a finger, gesturing westward. "Farther along the road, there are two camps. One about two hours' march, another a half day. Both have small garrisons, with an equal number of sick or wounded. Go to the more distant camp first, but be wary."

Conon grunted in assent. "Is it true what they say about Theudis, Lord?"

"Indeed," I muttered. "Broke our blockade after a freak storm. We have a healthy head start, but we need to fortify Septem immediately."

"Already being done," Conon remarked. "Itaxes is doing what he can to protect the harbor, and Liberius is directing the fortification of Septem's outer walls. I offered to assist, but he claimed that I had the brains of a sheep."

"Take no offense, I've heard that more times than any other." I chuckled. "But do not tarry; we must bring everyone back by dawn."

Saluting, Conon departed without further conversation. Curiously, there was no joy in the ranks as the knowledge of our ending journey became apparent. If anything, the marching became all the more taxing, with each step seeming weightier, and the cost of closing the remaining miles more insurmountable. Despite it all, we continued, drained of any capacity yet to lift our feet, hardly able to call out to one another. Perenus' head bobbed every few paces, with my only option to shake the man awake and keep him going. Each time became more difficult, with Perenus resisting, moaning for sleep that could not come.

Another two torturous, throbbing, windswept, accursed hours later, we spotted the rows of torches that lined Septem's fabled walls. Atop Mount Abyla, rising above the city, I spotted faint flickering, and I wondered whether Theudesgel on his perch had suffered as we now did. In that moment of weakness, I sorely wished it were so. Certainly I am no saint, nor a priest, nor perhaps a good student of forgiveness. But neither was Theudesgel, nor any of his ilk who slinked in stubborn resistance inside Septem's defenses.

By this time, our column had decoupled, more resembling a ragged trail of vermin than an equipped and trained Roman army. In clumps of ten to a hundred, my depleted forces stumbled beneath the city's walls, greeted by a gawking crowd of onlookers despite the lateness of the hour. Standing atop the battlements was Liberius, hands clasped beneath sweeping robes, the only movement that of the breeze catching both beard and cloak. I brought up the column's rear, and he bobbed his head in recognition as I passed underneath the gates amidst sighs of relief and gasps of footsore pain rising from men desperate for a warm meal and a cozy cot.

Nearly all were dismissed as soon as they reached Septem's forum, but not me. Many awaited my arrival, the least patient of all being Rosamund. Nudging ahead of Xerxes, her eyes widened as she took sight of Perenus, quickly scanning my own body for injury or ailment.

"It's the flux," I whispered to her in Heruli. "Can you do anything? He has neither eaten nor taken rest across two full days."

"I can try, but this is not merely the flux," Rosamund hissed.

A painful knot formed in my throat. "The plague?"

Rosamund aggressively shook her head. "Not so terrible as that. But you must inform me if you feel any bone weariness or inability to swallow."

Laughing only drew pain to the raw flesh on my shoulder and the stiff muscles and tendons of my legs. "Everything hurts, and everything is terrible."

Rosamund was unamused. She slapped me hard along the jaw, the long nails of her fingers stinging any skin not shielded by the scruff of a beard. "This is no joke, Varus. The gods may love you, but even their favor is not unlimited. Take your health seriously and do not tempt them—if not for your sake or your family's, then for mine, who heals your injuries."

My head sank, the surprise at her remonstration mixed with embarrassment. "I know, Rosamund. And I am sorry. Please, just help Perenus. We can speak more intimately tomorrow."

"Of course." She nodded. "But make all of your men take willow bark in boiled water, and thick soup. You will take the same, only twice over. I will see this supplied to you directly."

Raising my hand in submission, I gave Perenus over to two townsfolk—one of whom, I realized, was the woman I had rescued from the Visigoths. Perenus moaned, muttering complaints at his limbs jostling about and bearing little of his own weight as he was guided back to Rosamund's quarters. Not a dozen heartbeats had passed from Rosamund's dismissal when Xerxes approached, dark circles ringing his eyes.

"You were right, Xerxes," I told him. "The flux would have destroyed us all."

Xerxes nodded. "Don't blame yourself. There is nothing that could be done. Theudis is far more unpredictable than I could have imagined. This makes him dangerous, but also prone to weakness."

"If there's a weakness, I'd love to know if it. Thus far, the Visigoths have anticipated each action we have taken."

"This is so, but I doubt it will last for long," Xerxes replied. "Even the greenest spearman could see that Belisarius must seize Septem and drive the Visigoths from Mauretania. Theudis gambled upon his good fortune, but even this was predicated upon that foreknowledge of what we must do. Now, he will advance upon Septem, but what comes after is unclear."

"Perhaps his luck will sustain itself?" I prodded.

"I have always found," came a third voice into our midst, "that it is only the lucky who claim that good fortune is the greatest trait." A curious yet disdainful Liberius had drawn to our side. "They are fools," he went on. "Fortune is merely whatever experience and planning allow. We have arrived at quite a predicament, Varus, but our Persian friend is correct. Theudis can no longer rely upon surprise, and will find it far more difficult to brutalize a trained and desperate enemy."

"Only if we can recover quickly enough," I countered.

Liberius sighed. "You can if you will it so. You are a commander of men, Varus. Command, and see it done." He shook his head. "But I am but a feeble old man, awake far beyond his appointed hour of rest, so what could I possibly know?"

"More than every man alive, Legate," I conceded. "And you are correct, but only after our men have been returned to the safety of the city. Until then, I leave you and Xerxes to lead our defenses and prevent any opportunistic nuisance from Theudesgel."

"See!" Liberius brightened. "Command, and weak blinkered fools like us two shall obey. Go and complete your rescue. I will ensure that Septem does not fall to bandits in the night."

A dozen volunteers joined in my efforts, including a visibly shaky Sembrouthes, who refused to be left behind. Shedding our armor and trading our filthy trousers and cloaks for clean attire, we each hoisted small packs of food and bandages upon our backs, bearing only smaller weapons appropriate for light travel. There was no griping or talking, although many of the men must have been terribly uncomfortable. I could sense blisters forming upon my overexerted feet, while my stomach groaned despite quick gulps of hot soup before departing. Our travels would only take us as far as Cephalas' camp, however, and I willed such pains aside for the brief hours it would take to reach such men.

Perhaps Liberius was right, for it was that, for the first time that evening, we enjoyed the good luck of a far simpler journey. Within an hour of our departure, a traveling band hobbled to greet us, and though their numbers were masked by the pitch black of night despite their few torches, we knew they hailed from the Empire, for a beautifully rich Greek voice sang into the horizon, setting the cadence of their ponderous yet determined footsteps, and I knew it could be only one man. I greeted Cephalas and quickly ordered the rations distributed and bandages wrapped around chafed feet and nagging wounds. Cephalas informed me that Conon had passed by not long ago, offering five of his men to assist Cephalas' group on their return journey back to Septem.

And so, rather than continue westward, we assisted the two dozen who groaned and hobbled along their path to safety, striking a slinking pace back to the warmth and relative safety of Septem's town. Upon arrival, each man was tended by a healer, offered a hot meal, and granted swift entry to sleeping quarters at an appointed portion of the city's low-hanging wooden buildings. I soon followed their example, surrendering command once more to the legate, who nodded in approval as the wounded men found respite from extended travails.

Conon, however, was not so fortunate. Starry night had blurred violet in the hours before dawn when Conon at last returned to Septem. A servant fearfully nudged me awake with the news, and though initially I shrugged away the intruder, my body unresponsive to basic commands and desperate to return to deep slumber, the servant was diligent, and soon I willed myself upright. My mind felt pickled, as if drunk, a fog dulling my senses so thoroughly that even a splash of frigid water from a basin along my chamber wall barely cut through. After dressing, I staggered into Septem's streets once more, my eyes throbbing and head sore.

Expecting to find another party of arrivals, instead all that greeted me was a small huddle of Thracian spearmen, with Conon at their center.

Rubbing my eyes, I struggled to gather my thoughts as I deciphered the unexpected result. "Report."

Conon saluted, waiting until I acknowledged his formality before continuing. "We inspected the camp but found none living," the runner panted. "Only bodies, stripped of weapons and armor."

I wanted to groan. To collapse to the ground and ignore this new threat. In a moment of weakness, I would have traded all my wealth to be freed of command. "Brigands?"

"Possibly," Conon mused, though his tone suggested he thought otherwise. "But the killing blows upon each man were far too precise for an opportunistic killer or a roving band of highwaymen. Not at this time of year, nor this time of night."

I sighed. "Visigoths, then."

"It seems so, Lord. We wanted to carry the men back, but there were twice the bodies as I had men. We dug a ditch and covered the bodies with soil, but I fear that won't protect them from a hungry jackal for more than a few nights."

Nodding, I rubbed my face again, finally understanding the loss of near thirty warriors. Armies the world over had taken far greater casualties from flux or plague; Belisarius himself had suffered considerable casualties from moldy bread along the great expedition's journey from Constantinople to Africa. Yet though such losses were to be expected, this news stung with surprising force, made worse by the already limited numbers available to fight against a far more numerous foe.

"You made the correct decision, Conon," I affirmed. "We will retrieve and burn their corpses once Theudis has been defeated. Dismiss your men for rest, for I fear their strength will be needed in the days to come."

Word of Visigothic activity near Septem spread quickly, even in the early hours of morning. Wall sentries were doubled with no additional scouting parties permitted to venture beyond Septem's walls, forcing us to rely upon the greater safety of our dromons skirting the coastline for signs of Theudis' vanguard. Some may chastise such a lack of visibility as an indication of cowardice, to whom I can only explain that they were not present upon that wearisome night that culminated in my defeat within Tingitana. Liberius was correct— there was only one destination that Theudis' army sought, both to free Theudesgel's survivors and to establish a permanent foothold in Africa through which the Vandal hordes could sweep cleanly into Tripolitana and even Alexandria beyond. But first, sleep returned longingly, my servants instructed to wake me only if the Visigothic army had begun to batter down the city gates.

A single night's rest was hardly rejuvenating, but free of wounds and sickness, I had no right to complain. Even better, Perenus had begun to slowly recover, although he snored heavily underneath two layers of thick wool blankets atop a freshly cleaned straw mat. As I was otherwise alone in Perenus' cozy quarters, Rosamund insisted I consume her potions, and I dutifully obliged, to her relief.

Without warning, she wrapped her arms around my chest, her fingertips nearly unable to meet as she buried herself within the embrace. Confused, I returned the gesture, believing Rosamund overwhelmed by the considerable injury to our friend and strained by a trying evening staving off his death. Eventually, yet not before some awkwardness, Rosamund released me, making me swear to return to continue a treatment that I was privately convinced was utterly unnecessary.

At last, I convened my officers. Most were in little better condition, bearing angry bruises and wincing from all manner of cuts and raw skin. Even Gunderic limped awkwardly, rubbing at groin muscles that he claimed were laced with painful scabs.

"That's not the worst," he moaned. "My armor rubbed against my chest the entire march back, and my nipples bled all night."

Fulcaris laughed, nursing bandaged feet. "I don't think they're supposed to do that. You might be walking incorrectly."

Rolling his eyes, Gunderic lifted a crust of bread and flung it at

Fulcaris' face. But Fulcaris caught the projectile in midair, then ripped a chunk out with his teeth, winking at Gunderic in thanks for the unintended meal.

As always, I ignored the banter. "We have arrived at a grave challenge. Within a day, perhaps two, Theudis and all his forces will arrive at Septem's gates. Extra labor has been directed to refortify each battlement, but any fighting will be desperate. Worse, we still must defend the entrance to Mount Abyla."

Though I made to continue, Liberius laughed aloud, bringing the briefing to a halt. He grinned knowingly, and for once I felt a sudden irritation of at his oft-strange behavior.

"Something amusing, Legate?"

"Indeed, Lord Varus." Liberius smirked. "For it seems we are preparing for contravallation. If this is so, Theudis is as good as defeated already."

Xerxes raised an eyebrow, while Indulf snorted in derision. "If our situation amuses you so much, perhaps you can carry a spear to the gates when the Visigoths come," Indulf put in. "I find nothing funny about being besieged while an enemy remains inside our walls."

Liberius was unperturbed. "I do not blame you for your apprehension, Indulf. But I am disappointed in Varus! Perhaps you were too busy gawking at pretty girls rather than paying attention to lessons."

I tensed my jaw, irritation rising further. "Yes, Lord."

"Such a shame. The fault is mine, of course, for I should have taken the cane to you far more often than I did. The poor girls did nothing to warrant your attentions."

"Lord, perhaps you can explain what knowledge may help improve our situation?"

"But I was just getting to that, Varus. Rudeness is also not a trait Justin or I imparted onto you."

Liberius stood, clapping his hands to summon a team of servants that carried a huge map of Septem's surroundings, as high and wide as the height of a man. Each battlement was richly decorated, even including the numbers of men positioned alongside the walls. Even the entrance to Mount Abyla was framed with additional defenses that had not been present upon my departure for Tingis. Within moments, I took my seat at the table, realizing that the legate had been preparing for the double defenses of Theudesgel and Theudis even prior to our defeated army's return.

"As I mentioned, before I was so impatiently interrupted," Liberius began, "no Roman army has ever been defeated during contravallation. Caesar prevailed against unfathomable odds at Alesia, while Lucullus conquered the hordes of Mithridates. Why is this?"

Other than Xerxes, I doubt that most in the room had been trained in such centuries-old history of battles long past. Both Gunderic and Indulf shared a confused glance, the former crossing his arms and sinking back in his chair. Tapping his fingers together, Liberius sighed with animated frustration, muttering to himself.

"Because their systems of command were far superior to their enemies," I stated, breaking the silence. "They were able to construct complex defensive structures that disrupted and overwhelmed the inner and outer attacking forces."

Liberius clapped. "Perhaps there is still hope for you! Indeed, Caesar even writes of this in his histories. A horribly conceited man, Julius Caesar, but I suppose one is allowed to be a stuffy megalomaniac after conquering half the world."

"But how does this knowledge help us?" Xerxes asked.

"Because, my dear man," Liberius said with another smirk, "we have all the walls, bows, and siege equipment needed to ward off a dedicated attack. Not only that, but I have spent the entire week preparing such defenses for you."

"It's true," Conon interjected. "We have interlocking palisade walls blocking the only entrance to Mount Abyla, so Theudesgel will have to scale spiked barriers to gain entry to the city. Outside the main walls, we've dug deep trenches and have fashioned sharpened stakes throughout. Theudis will have no clear route to advance, and every step will be marked with bloody horror."

"You see, my friend?" Liberius gestured to Indulf and set a hand proudly on his chest. "Perhaps this old fool need not hoist a spear and rush into a shield wall to show his value. But I leave it to you as my judge."

Indulf balked. "That's not what I meant…"

Liberius raised a hand for silence, then nodded to a more nourished and rested Itaxes. The Alani man nodded to me in turn before rising.

"Legate Liberius has worked tirelessly to support the defenses," he said. "At sea, the walls are not yet repaired, but we have more than enough dromons to protect the sea lanes. I can guarantee that, even in a lengthy siege, we can be easily resupplied by sea and gather fish for food."

"Horrible stuff, those sea creatures," Fulcaris groaned. "The smell, if not the taste. They swim in their own dung."

"You should feel more than comfortable around them, then," Ascum remarked.

I raised an arm for silence. "I appreciate your efforts, Itaxes, and they are reassuring. But we cannot afford a lengthy siege. We must inform Belisarius of our situation and seek guidance of what assistance may end our travails, and roughly when."

Not that Belisarius would procure a miracle solution for my present challenges. What we needed were reinforcements, yet there had been no word from Uliaris in weeks, and each passing day raising the possibility that he had been killed, captured, or simply absconded into the vastness of Gaul. Likewise, the Mauri would not avail me of troops. So I spoke of Belisarius' potential aid with a calm I did not feel, for although I yearned for his guidance, I knew too well that his undermanned army could not spare further bandae to reinforce Septem. In all honesty, my only possibility to break Theudis' encirclement was to hope that Rosamund was correct and wait for divine rescue from whatever gods had taken favor upon me. There was no other discernible option than to wait and pray.

"I will dispatch a cog today, Lord Varus," Itaxes added.

Even so, the situation was markedly better than I had initially feared. Having had no time to survey the city, nor account for Liberius' considerable attentions to the city's defenses in the darkness of the prior evening, the situation as it stood now did seem nearly palatable. I was confident that neither of the Visigothic forces would easily overwhelm our own, yet was panged by lingering concern that there was nothing my remaining forces could do to evict Theudis fully from the surrounding area.

Worse, if Belisarius was determined to end the campaign by winter's end, a lengthy siege would leave me unable to make progress in time. From Libya to Septem, Belisarius' forces had been overstretched, exhausted, and desiring a return to their homes, and few had an appetite for a prolonged war over Tingitana. The only choice we had was to utterly defeat Theudis' horde, but the only plan we had was to sit behind Septem's defenses. I gave no further voice to such concerns but probed within myself for the sort of answer that Belisarius, or the late John, would have offered had they been in command of such a situation.

Around me, the conversation continued, the men enthusiastically searching for opportunities to place more obstacles before Theudis' advance upon the city.

"We could position more ballistae along Septem's walls," Ascum offered. "I doubt Theudis will have any siege weapons, and a mounted ballista can wreak carnage upon an attacking enemy." Nodding to Xerxes, he added, "Your fellow Spahbad, Perozes, learned that lesson at Dara."

"Perozes was a fool." Xerxes frowned. "Theudis, by all accounts, is not. But nevertheless, the additional defenses cannot hurt our preparations."

I nodded. "Xerxes will organize our landward defenses, but Ascum will requisition ballistae and catapults from the ships for use upon the walls. We will only require a small number of armed dromons to guard the city—others should be dispatched to safeguard

Thurimuth, and prevent any further ships from Gades from reaching the African shore."

"We can try, but more vessels are needed," Ascum rasped. "The channel between the Pillars is far larger than these maps indicate."

"Understood, which is why we will send a message to Valerian in the Balearics," I concluded. "He will have more than enough armed crews to harry the coast of Hispania and protect our position along Mount Calpe."

Other commanders sought instructions on their duties, with each man eager to take up some responsibility along the landward walls. Under Xerxes' leadership, Gunderic took command of Septem's primary gate, with Fulcaris leading the Heruli during Perenus' absence along a smaller gate adjoining the northwestern coastline. Indulf's Ostrogoths occupied the southwest, tasked with resisting any ladder teams that Theudis would launch along the walls. Deprived of their officers, Cappadocian and Thracian spearmen would comprise my reserve under the leadership of Liberius, with a team of a hundred under Conon guarding the inner palisade against any opportunistic attack by Theudesgel. It was a tidy plan, one to make the organizationally minded giddy in its simplicity and the quick-maneuvering content with its fundamental capacity for easy adaptation should any concerns arise. We dominated the seas and populated Septem's walls with five times the soldiers that Theudesgel had brought to service, and for that I held a glimmer of confidence.

Moreover, it would have to suffice. Reviewing our granary stores and distributing spare weapons and shields at various points along the walls, ten thousand tasks were executed to better prepare our defenses, allowing us to maintain a siege upon Mount Abyla while becoming besieged ourselves. It was not a position to envy, but there was precious little choice in the manner. All I could do was pray that a solution would become available to me, or, at least, that Theudis would not storm a weakness in my walls, killing us all.

That prayer would soon be tested. For late that afternoon, with a rolling shout amidst the flutter of hawk-emblazoned banners, the Visigoth army arrived at Septem. And at its front stood a tall, gray-streaked figure adorned with a simple iron circlet about his head, his eyes fixed upon the Pillars of Herakles that rose along the horizon.

THE CAVE OF HERAKLES

Theudis did not attack that first night. Nor the second. Nor even the third. Instead, his men planted their banners into the rain-softened soil and carved a dual ring of trenches facing Septem's walls. Though we Romans had refilled our own trenches after seizing the city, the scars of upturned earth and grassless dirt gave the Visigoths an easy model to copy. Yet still they remained passive, well beyond the range of any bow or ballista, sending occasional runners to test the firmness of the soil along the outer limits of my ranged soldiers.

This is not to say that the Visigoths were idle. Each day that passed brought more such warriors, their faces covered in great nests of beards and moustaches, greased with animal fat and glimmering in the sunlight. As with we Romans, the Visigoths were a far from equitable force, with a contingent of scale-armored spearmen adorned with reinforced helmets and honed swords from the blacksmiths at Gades. However, the vast majority were encased in layers of boiled leather, their battered shields sporting faded emblems that stood in stark contrast to the freshly painted sigils of Theudis' elite band. These poorer footmen all carried heavy axes, while some also possessed short swords belted at their waists, suited for short jabs in close combat. Discipline, it seemed, ruled Theudis' army.

Even so, despite a similar array of divergent fighting styles, our enemy bore plenty of differences from our military organization. Rather than an officer command, the Visigoths followed chiefs and warlords into battle, with some leading fifty while others led two or three hundred. Atop Mount Abyla, Theudesgel was one such chieftain, and I spotted the expensively armored Agila leading a hundred men who had likely been our adversaries at Tingis. Curiously, there were few archers within Theudis' ranks, for I spotted only a handful of bows that would have been appropriate for hunting hare yet certainly not powerful enough for armored men.

The stream of Visigoth spearmen drew to a trickle upon the morning of the fourth day, yet the man I assumed to be Theudis disappeared with a small contingent of warriors to the northwest. Upon learning of such a maneuver, Xerxes ordered the dromons to be put on alert, yet no land or sea attack commenced beyond a few feinted charges by small groups of javelin throwers. A few well-placed arrows discouraged their mischief, and the fourth day appeared to continue as relatively uneventful as the three that preceded it.

Until, at the center of the Visigothic lines, Agila clambered from the trenches. Lacking a shield, he hoisted a white banner atop his spearpoint. Then Agila walked slowly toward Septem's walls, stopping a hundred paces from its gates.

"Should I put an arrow in him, Lord?" one of the Herulians asked.

"No," I responded. "That is a flag of truce. It's time to see what the Visigoths truly want from me."

Sembrouthes complained bitterly when I refused his protection, arguing that a chieftain such as Agila did not rise to power within the tribes without becoming skilled with a blade. When meeting Agila alone, however, bringing a bodyguard would be a sign of fear, and that I could not allow. Abandoning my shield, I brought only the dragon-hilted sword beyond Septem's gates, walking slowly to meet the enemy leader upon the grass-strewn roads along Septem's coast.

"Lord Varus," Agila called, his Latin stilted and oddly formal to my ears. "I have heard much of your prowess. I am Agila, chief of the Greuthungi of Septimania."

Where Theudesgel had been bitter laughter and disdain housed within a lanky body, Agila bore little menace in speech and figure. A round face bordering on plump was framed with a well-combed black beard, and shining eyes invited further welcome and discussion. He smiled as I approached, standing straight as he announced his lineage.

Though he seemed fluent in the Latin tongue, I formed my words slowly and carefully. "It seems you know much of me, but I have heard nothing of you."

Agila's smile deflated, his shoulders drooping as he huddled around his spear. "There is time enough for gossip. My king, the great Theudis, entreats you to speak with him in a nearby cave along the coastline. It is marked with a sweeping Visigoth banner, and you may bring a retinue of guards as companions, but only you may enter the cave. King Theudis alone awaits you inside."

"When?"

"Oh, today, of course!" Agila beamed, his mane of black hair swirling as he nodded his head at my curiosity. "The cave is but an hour's sailing by one of your ships, given a stiff wind and strong backs. If you leave now, you will arrive well before the sun reaches its zenith."

Frowning, I stared at Agila. "To what purpose?"

"Your edification, Lord Varus!" Agila's smile remained fixed, his head bobbing with an enthusiasm that seemed to suggest this was the greatest display of truth since the birth of Christ. "Perhaps more? It is not for me to tell. But I do promise that you will remain unharmed, and will return peacefully to Septem by nightfall. Surely this is an acceptable offer?"

I wanted to refuse, for no other reason than to watch the enthusiastic grin evaporate from Agila's fleshy face. Not from malice, either, for I doubted that there was any insincerity in Agila's words. He was clearly intelligent, though he lacked the cool etiquette of the Imperial Court, instead expressing a friendly deference that would have been mocked amongst most warriors. I had to remind myself that this was likely a rural chieftain, more familiar with the fields and the plow than the decorum of scepters and thrones. And if my time with men like Narses had taught me anything, it was how to spot someone with far more hidden knowledge than they would like the world to see.

"And if I refuse?"

"Then I will be most upset but will not blame you!" Agila answered. "But Theudis will be vexed, that is for certain. You have nothing to lose, and much to learn."

It could have easily been an ambush. Many a naïve commander had been lured under a similar guise, only to be massacred by stinking thugs lacking honor. Accepting Agila's offer was a risk, yet for some peculiar reason I felt no sense of foreboding. With his head swaying as darting eyes scanned the most intricate details of my armored body, this Agila appeared genuinely curious of his Roman enemies, and I believed Theudis would be the same. Agila's delight was palpable as I agreed, and our gathering concluded as the Visigothic chieftain sprinted back to their trench lines.

Back in Septem, however, Sembrouthes was thoroughly displeased. "A cave? Theudis could be hiding a half dozen assassins, maybe more. You're a fool to trust someone who would immediately benefit from your death."

But Liberius, his face bright with amusement at Sembrouthes' concern, shared different thoughts. "If we operated under such unwillingness to work with those who would do us harm, there would be no reason to return to Constantinople!"

"Nor any major city," Xerxes grumbled. "But Sembrouthes is correct. What little we know of Theudis is unsavory. You place yourself, and this army, at grave risk by accepting this offer."

"Friends, I do understand," I cut in. "But Theudis takes on similar peril, for he lacks warships and could easily be overrun by hidden Romans." Seeing my initial words drew skepticism from Ascum and Fulcaris, I added, "And besides, if Theudis was so foolish to slay a

Roman commander under a banner of truce, the entire Empire would come crashing upon him. Belisarius would raze every Visigoth fortress from here to Toletum."

"But you'd still be dead," Sembrouthes snarled. "This isn't some battle where you're obligated to fight. You have two young children, and a wife who is a foreigner to the Empire. Is this gamble truly worth your life?"

I drew back at the barbed question, vague visions of Mariya producing the unwelcome blanket of weariness that had gripped my spirit in the earliest days of the journey from Carthage. A deep longing for home reawakened in me, and a need to feel the skin of my wife's cheek against my own. Sembrouthes was correct: my actions jeopardized the future that seemed ever more distant, and in that moment of weakness I wanted nothing more than to order Septem's evacuation.

But it could not be so, not while Belisarius depended upon our success. "We will take every precaution necessary, and I will take guards," I concluded. "This meeting may end this conflict and prevent further suffering. It may keep us all alive, if diplomacy can prevail."

Sembrouthes bit his lip and stormed away from the battlements with a groan. Xerxes, though he also seemed to disapprove, showed none of the disgust of my bodyguard. Liberius, on the other hand, offered his own manner of approval, although he insisted upon a final word of wisdom.

"The Visigoths may seem similar to the Romans you were raised alongside," he informed me, "but in their own way they are far more savage than any plains rider or barbarian tribe. Speak carefully around Theudis, and listen to all you hear, but show no weakness. Theudis' ancestors were capable of unfathomable destruction, and if the Franks did not threaten their northern borders, Theudis would have few qualms in continuing such labors."

There was little time to tarry. Accompanied by a fully armed troop of Aksumites as well as a contingent of Cappadocian spearmen, we bounded to Septem's docks. Both Xerxes and Liberius stayed behind to keep watch against a leering Visigoth enemy, even though no signs of a coming battle emanated from the trenches. Our forces boarded Belisarius' flagship, with Apollos signaling three other dromons of our readiness to make for sea. This time, I gave silent thanks to God that our journey was a brief one, and through shallow waters, merely hugging the African coastline and scouting for a looming Visigoth banner that marked my meeting location with Theudis.

Even so, the nature of the journey left Apollos on edge, and he kept our pace deliberately slow to avoid surprise from any possible ambush. None came, yet our journey's duration was lengthened by such caution, and after an hour stewing in my thoughts, I, too, grew anxious that Agila's offer was an effort to deliberately mislead, and wondered whether the Visigoths had lured me away from Septem in order to launch an attack against a leaderless city.

Eventually, however, our patience was rewarded. It was Apollos who first spotted the swirling hawk banner, the massive cloth rich in color and bereft of wear that characterized most battle standards. Representing Hispania rather than a flag to be carried into battle. It waved, seemingly nailed into a tree overlooking a rock formation along the coastline, and there was no mistaking our destination. Apollos ordered the ships to draw into anchor and readied the smaller craft that would carry me and Sembrouthes' Aksumites to shore.

Mere moments after our boat's detachment from the flagship, our keel scraped against the sandy shoreline. Sembrouthes splashed from the boat, hauling it onto dry land as others raised their oars and joined in the labor. After regathering our weapons, I led the dozen men up a winding path to the hill's summit. It was a craggy thing, strewn with boulders and an occasional tree, laced with dense shrubs and grassless earth. Near the top, Sembrouthes beckoned for our formation to slow its approach, so that he walked two paces ahead as he scouted for danger. Thankfully, neither arrows nor knives seemed to have wormed their way behind the infinite creases in the hill's expanse, with our only adversary being the hidden stones that invariably caused stubbed toes and stumbling steps. Dirt covered yet unscathed, we scaled our way to the top, greeted by a roaring wind that rushed from the sea and through the openings in the boulders.

And a single stout figure, standing stiffly within a clearing atop the hill, stared directly at our advance. Rather than the grubby leather of a Gothic spearman, the man was adorned in the white toga of republican Rome. A violet stripe denoted his status as part of a family of wealth or power, while his cleanshaven face placed him in stark contrast to the intricate moustaches favored by many Gothic warriors. Squat and round, with thinning black hair across a mostly bald pate, the man wrapped a portion of the violet-streaked cloth about his hand and bowed deeply, pausing as the crown of his head shone against the noonday sun.

Though the man was clearly weaponless, and lacked the physique to even challenge a trained warrior in combat, Sembrouthes growled an order for the Aksumites to heft their spears in caution. At such commotion, the toga-clad man returned upright, his back straight as he raised his arms, palms open and free of hidden blades.

"You may rest at ease, excubitor," the toga-clad man said in flawless Latin. "King Theudis has no guardsmen inside, but he does not begrudge your soldiers from standing at the cave's entrance. He entreats you to enter with the knowledge that only he and I have traveled to this place, with no other Visigoths remaining within a journey of five miles."

"You are no Goth," I answered, tilting my head as I reviewed the man's polite yet self-assured disposition. "What business does a Roman have in a Visigoth court?"

"Oh, plenty, Lord Varus." The man smiled, offering a bow. "When Rome abandoned Hispania to the Goths, the Suebi, and even the Vandals, Roman citizens were left with a choice: serve a new master willingly or through suffering. As you might deduce, that is little choice indeed."

This casual confidence and easy recognition, as much as the man's Roman attire, gave me pause. Any doubts that the Visigoths possessed informers in Carthage and Septem, if not outright spies, evaporated. Though identifying me as an excubitor was not noteworthy, my face and position should have been little known so far from Constantinople; any Visigoth who could have identified me from my assault on Septem was stuck atop Mount Abyla, besieged with Theudesgel.

Speaking with forced calm, I pressed this Latin man further. "You can return with us, back to the Empire. The Emperor will reward your loyalty and repay your losses."

The Roman shrugged, his polite smile curling into a smirk. "Perhaps. But then again, perhaps not. King Theudis rewards those who are loyal. But you are not here to discuss the wrongs of history, but to meet with my lord and master."

Pointing to a narrow entrance amongst the rocks, the toga-clad Roman beckoned me inside. "Your lovely men and I will remain in the sunlight. Should you require any refreshment, all you need to do is call. The caves are certainly beautiful, but even the lightest whisper echoes into the heavens."

No sooner did he say as much than the faint stamping of a single pair of boots sounded from somewhere encased in rock far below the surface. Nodding, I ordered Sembrouthes to remain at the entrance.

His answer was curt yet firm. "Yell if you need us. Run if there is danger. Don't be a fool."

Though I felt neither regret nor fear at the decision to accept Theudis' meeting, there was a growing sense of unease within me as I approached the cave—not out of concern for any ambush, but more out of surprise at this immaculately attired Roman who would have not been out of place in the patrician gatherings of Constantinople. Of course, I had long known that many hundreds of thousands of Romans had been subjected to barbarian rule in the aftermath of Attila's invasions, yet it was odd that any would willingly serve such cruel masters—or worse, *prefer* them. That was a danger I had not anticipated, and it brought a fleeting worry of spies back in Carthage, betraying Belisarius' secrets to Theudis and any number of other barbarian chieftains and warlords that paid great caches of silver for knowledge of Rome's armies.

There was nothing that could eliminate that threat now, nor while in Tingitana. Instead, the only answer I could seek was located deep underground, inside a cave that echoed footsteps clapping against a slick stony surface. Nodding to Sembrouthes, I lowered my head and descended a clearing in the stones, slim rays of sunlight my only guide.

Step after step, that light soon became little more than a reflected glimmer. It was hard to discern the cave's shape or depth, although I must have walked a good fifty paces on a downward slope, my hands propped against overhanging stones to both keep my balance as well as my sense of direction. As the light from the surface grew nearly imperceptible, however, a new source of light emerged from a clearing in the stones, a faint flickering that illuminated a flat surface ahead. Cautiously, I slid forward, hearing only the movements of a single figure yet still wary of a potential ambush.

"I was beginning to believe you too cowardly to accept this meeting," a voice rasped a few paces away. "If I wanted to kill you, you would already be dead. You may enter."

Pushing away from the safety of the enclosed entrance, I strode into the clearing, following a narrow band of light that flickered along the gloomy limestone. A light splashing sound clattered against stone walls nearby, and my eyes fixed upon an opening that linked the cave to the sea. Broken by an outer bulwark of stones that lined much of the nearby shoreline, the trickle of water that entered the cave filled a space only a cubit deep, yet its gentle flows echoed and grew against the cave walls, creating an illusion of thunder echoing through the dank space.

"Welcome to the cave of Hercules," the rasping man said in clipped Latin. "Or Herakles, as you prefer. Some say that the hero rested here after completing his labors, if you believe such nonsense."

Up close, Theudis was entirely unlike the looming rogue I had pictured in my mind for so many weeks. With gray-streaked, bark-colored hair falling to his shoulders, Theudis lacked the beard or moustache favored by so many Visigoths I had already encountered; in the darkened space of the cave, he could have passed for a Roman. His face was far from handsome, framed by a crooked nose and wide lips, etched around with deep lines of weariness and deprivation. He bore few tokens of royalty, disdaining the purple robes favored by Roman emperors for all-black attire, belted at the waist with simple and faded hog leather. From atop the walls of Septem, it would have been easy to miss such details, yet mere paces from the Visigothic king, a startling realization arose: Theudis was an older man, worn down, seeming more a like a wizened priest than any warlike monarch. His only trinket was a coarse iron circlet that rested atop the graying mane, the metal closely resembling the iron rim of a helmet or cap.

"Is it not rude to greet your host?" Theudis continued, albeit in Hunnic.

The language caught me unawares, my sense of confidence stricken by the realization that Theudis was a learned man. "You speak the tongue of the Huns?"

"I speak the language of the Scourge of God," Theudis countered. "An individual man who nearly conquered the world. A blood enemy of the Visigoths, but a man to be admired nonetheless. We may continue in this tongue, for it will prevent any from successfully eavesdropping on what we may say to one another." Theudis paused, raising his chin and narrowing his eyes as he considered my form. "That is, if you are not fearful to come closer."

I did, selecting each step carefully, my boots still sliding against the wet stones as the streak of light piercing the cave gave minimal warning of hazardous footing. As I drew closer, Theudis came clearer into view. An angry scar ran from the base of his throat to the corner of his right eye, the tissue puckered and stretched from what must have been years of healing. Most striking, however, was the king's eyes. One was the faintest blue, not dissimilar from Rosamund's, and the lid on that piercing orb seemed stretched beyond its ability, rendering a fixed gaze of fury along Theudis' face. It was the other eye, however, that brought me, like surely all newcomers to his presence, to pause and gape, and to feel a swift urge to retreat from the demon's attentions. A deep green ringed by a noxious yellow, the eye suggested a sickness of the soul, the weight of original sin rooted far deeper in a rotten body that lorded over hundreds of thousands.

After I had drawn acceptably close, Theudis propped his body against a stone undergrowth, rubbing his hands together as he turned to gaze upon the trickling waves that snaked through the cave's opening. While I tried to use that opportunity to spy a better view of the king's face, he suddenly turned, his yellow eye fixed upon my own, and raised a hand to his neck.

Theudis grunted, pointing to the scar. "My father. A drunkard and a gambler. Such qualities never mix well, even amongst a moderately acclaimed spearman. His losses would frequently see his wife and children go hungry, and caused the death of an infant. So, one evening as he snored in a wine-addled stupor, I stole his coin pouch and buried it underneath my favorite apple tree. When he awoke, he beat each of his slaves to discover the location of his last remaining wealth, only to discover the culprit as his son. When I would not tell him the location of his coins, he drew a knife and cut me from gullet to eye."

Closing his eyes, Theudis sniffed the air. "I can still smell the wine on his breath. He never did find the coins, which he owed to a petty chieftain for a poorly played game of soldiers' dice. Neither did he gain a son's love, for after my mother sewed my throat and nursed me from the unctuous kiss of death, I found that dagger a month later and drove the length of the blade through my father's eye. They had to bury him with the blade still stuck amidst skull and brains, it was dug so far in. And do you know what I learned from that lesson?" Theudis' gaze returned onto my face, breaking my lulled mind from its stupor as I listened to the king's tale.

"I cannot know, Lord King. Although I would assume it would be to treat your own sons with far greater kindness."

Snorting, Theudis laughed, then gave in to a fit of coughs, bringing him to massage his old injury. "Oh no, Lord Varus. It taught me that if I should ever injure a person, then it is important to make sure they die soon thereafter. For otherwise, they will only revisit more pain onto me."

The Visigoth king's coughs turned to violent hacking, the echo of which surely emanated to the surface. Yet no Aksumites rushed to investigate, and instead I merely waited until Theudis had composed himself to speak my piece. And though it was easy to loathe Theudis, I found myself more curious than combative. His voice could hold men in a trance, and though I meant to taunt him, I also truly desired for him to speak further of himself, and of his intentions for the Visigoths.

At last, I spoke. "Perhaps you wish I had allowed my Ostrogothic foederati to butcher your nephew, then?"

More pained laughter. "For that, I thank you. I have known Indulf for many years, and I have little doubt that he would have skinned that boy until he was little more than a twitching husk. You'll discover, however, that gratitude and love are only poorly related cousins."

Theudis' words were too honeyed for the slavering butcher that I had imagined. How could our knowledge of the Visigoth leader be so poor, yet his knowledge of us so accurate?

Frowning, I straightened my back, using a hand to sweep folds of my cloak that had gotten caught within a hidden crack in the floor. Notwithstanding my curiosity, I dared show nothing other than contempt for the barbarian king. "Then why ask for a meeting under a banner of truce? You can save me the empty threats of destruction and death. Such tactics are for children and cowards."

Theudis rose, his eyes nearly level with my own. "I am not come here to treat with you, Lord Varus. More to inform you that you, and your General Belisarius, are fools. Catspaws. Sent to fight and die endless wars for an emperor that will replace you when you die, shedding tears only for the cost of replacing lost weapons and armor. In this, I am the dearest friend you will ever have in this short and miserable life."

I snorted. This was drivel, another predictable exchange in a war of words. Such discussion was common amongst foes, and although I had none of Liberius' wit, I still would not let an enemy mock me so.

"Some friend you are," I countered. "You threaten the Empire and seize lands that have little value to you other than to maim and torture Romans and Mauri who till the soil. Is it that you Visigoths thirst for blood so much, or do you merely enjoy the myth of Herakles?"

"Herakles was a cunt," Theudis snarled. "If I had the strength of the gods, I wouldn't waste my days on asinine quests. I'd grind the people to my rule and use the bones of my enemies to mortar the cities my people would build upon foreign lands. This is a lesson you would do well to remember, my wormy friend. I have been killing men since you slithered from your mother's belly. Do not mistake me, Roman, I would shed no tears from your death, even if you spared my nephew. I've killed far more of my own countrymen without so much as raising an arm, and I would do so again if it brought our tribe dominance over our enemies."

Even from such a brief exchange, it was clear that Theudis not only loved to talk, but had mastered the ability to keep an audience enraptured; in another life, he might have achieved fame as an actor in a nearby amphitheater. I knew Theudis to be a monster, yet I could not help but hang upon each word, for his wit was biting, and his leadership utterly dissimilar to Belisarius' and my own. Speaking forth thus must have caused him considerable discomfort, however, the scars along his throat hiding damage to the tissues underneath that give voice to our thoughts. Yet I realized that Theudis had captured the momentum of our dialogue, rendering any jabs I offered ineffective at best. Instead, I attempted one final barb to throw Theudis off balance.

"Did such wrath extend to your ward, Amalaric? Surely the strength of your nation would not be strengthened by the murder of its king?"

But Theudis did not rise to the bait, his eyes narrowing and mouth curling into a cruel and knowing grin. "Even as a young boy, Amalaric was a lunatic and a glutton." Coughing, Theudis wiped a line of spittle along his shoulder, never breaking eye contact with me. "A land with a fool for a king is destined for nothing but ruin. The

Visigoths have said prayers over Amalaric's body but do not mourn him."

"By your command?" I sneered.

"By the wisdom of the basest simpleton," Theudis sniped, his voice rasping and harsh. "I would kill him again, if I could. And if you Romans believe that you will be welcome in Hispania, you are mistaken. Constantinople is but a distant memory, and the Ostrogoths will not be so willing to suffer Justinian's pithy attempts to subjugate the provinces."

Again, a reference to the Ostrogoths of Italy and Illyria. A longstanding foe of the Eastern Empire, who vanquished its brother in the west with the capture of Romulus Augustus nearly six decades prior. Any goodwill between the Ostrogoths and the Empire had strained with the death of Amalasuntha and her son, yet Indulf's presence denoted a lack of outright hostility. Some infighting, perhaps, but nothing to spell outright war between the two peoples.

And for good reason, for though the Visigoths presented a near insurmountable military challenge for Belisarius' army, their cousins in Italy were far more militaristic, and greater in numbers. Beyond supporting Belisarius' need to secure the port of Lilybaeum in Sicily, I had no intention of extending our conflict any further, desiring to complete my mission in Septem and return home with the first ship that would allow for safe passage.

"I make no war on the Ostrogoths, and our generals even use Ostrogothic warlords in our armies. From Vandals to Persians to Avars, we have vanquished all enemies who would bring violence to my Emperor. My sole remaining enemy is you, Theudis, who would deprive the Empire of its right to govern this land, and a people who love the Empire's civilization and peace. They wish to be rejoined as the Emperor's subjects, and Belisarius is commanded to fulfill that promise."

"Do they?" Theudis grinned. "More the fool you are, then. You stumble blindly into a war that even if you claim victory, all that will be left are bone and ash. Goths are not Vandals or Avars, and if what I hear is true, your Emperor is not the conquering hero that his scribes would have us simple barbarians believe. It appears that you have far more battles ahead of you than behind you, tribune. You and your General Belisarius alike."

I drew back, curious at Theudis' turn in the conversation, but spoke forcefully nonetheless. "You speak from fear, or from foolishness. Whichever it is, I do not care." It was a brazen lie, for Theudis had little to gain from offering such a warning; if anything, he had much to lose. If the Ostrogoths did intend to attack Belisarius in Carthage, it would leave my own expedition cut off from Constantinople, and incapable of support or resupply. Easy prey for the far more numerous Visigoths, especially as more of our dromons fell to damage and disrepair.

Theudis' unblemished eye brightened with mirth as he judged my reaction. "Ah, but it seems that you do not know! You think that Amalasuntha's death was a simple murder by her own supplicants? No, tribune. Justinian made certain that his dear Ostrogothic friend would be slain, giving your rump of an Empire the slightest whisper of an excuse to invade Italy and divide the Gothic warlords. That mouse of a monarch that you follow plays with lives like you or I would play with dice."

Justinian ordering Amalasuntha slain, and merely as pretext for war? Such a possibility confounded me, but I would not show it. "And if he does, what is that to me?" I answered, forcing anger into my voice in an attempt to mask both my confusion and my eagerness to hear more of Theudis' tales. "Amalasuntha is nothing to me, and has nothing to do with our presence at the Pillars. I have taken Septem, Lord King, and I will seize far more if you do not come to terms with me now. That fate is in your hands."

Theudis scoffed. "You bleat like a shorn lamb. But you need not trust my words, for you shall see their truth soon enough. Your men fight and die over a distant scrap of land with almost no significance to Constantinople, all so they can confidently invade Italy. I will resist you, tribune, not because of personal malice against your band of misfits and tribesmen, but because you do not belong here."

An eerily pleasant breeze billowed between my nose guard and cheekpieces, relieving the sweat and heat that collected despite the chill of the winter air. My hands empty, I raised them on either side of my body, forming a crude cross that stretched in either direction.

"All this once belonged to the Empire," I said. "By rights, it will return to us soon. You Visigoths invaded, and pillaged, and uprooted Imperial citizens as you fled from the Huns. Perhaps your words are of fear, Lord King."

Theudis laughed again, deep, cruel notes as his clouded eye widened. "Yes, we conquered this land from Romans. Who took all from Carthage. Who themselves brought the Celts to heel. Territory belongs to those with the power to keep it, and you are far from your homeland, tribune. Though I thank you for showing mercy to my nephew, this meeting is now at an end. Out of a charitable spirit, I will allow you three days to depart Septem and return to Carthage, after which I will personally bleach your skull and use it as my piss pot."

Another bout of pained coughing interrupted the exchange, with Theudis hacking dark phlegm laced with traces of crimson onto the limestone floor. Spitting one last time, he turned to face the cave opening.

"Men say that the Phoenicians who predate us all by millennia carved this entrance into the shape of Africa," Theudis muttered. "But such is only talk, for we have no proof beyond the stories told by old women to our young. Phoenicians, Herakles, they are all meaningless stories to entertain children. Three days, excubitor, and then I will blast open your gates, dismember your men, rape your women, and efface any Latin text that disgraces Septem's tablets or buildings. Your men will not even be a memory, but you—you I will take, and pickle your severed head in a jar to send it as a memento to the lovely princess you have taken for a wife. The choice is yours, as are the outcomes."

And in a moment, my curiosity evaporated. "Or perhaps it will be your head decorating my wall," I shot back, seething with fury at Theudis' mention of Mariya.

"Many have tried!" Theudis mocked. "All have failed thus far. And from what I've gathered from your abilities, your men should be concerned at how foolish their commander is."

His words pained me. Theudis knew so much, and I so little. I did not doubt the truth of his threats—to Septem or to Mariya. Indeed, at the mere mention of my wife, I had wanted nothing more than to bash the older man's skull against the rocks, sending his body into the cave's inner pools to bloat and decay. There was little he could have done to stop me, too, for I neither heard nor saw any Gothic guardsmen, nor was Theudis even armed. He was weak and wizened and I was young and strong, a veteran of great battles and skilled with a blade. All that prevented me were the voices of my teachers, insistent that nothing good came from such grave dishonor, even if Theudis' death might spare thousands of innocents from fear and suffering.

Instead, I only spoke. "Hear me, Lord King," I rumbled. "I have urged my men to exercise restraint thus far. If you attack Septem's walls, your army will not leave this place. I command Vandals, and Greeks and Gepids, and Sclaveni and Heruli, and even Goths—all of whom have no desire other than your death. That is my answer. My lord commanded me to take and hold this city, and that is what I shall do."

"Then you are a fool and a wastrel," Theudis whispered, shaking his head. "Do not say that you were not warned. You are nothing more than a deathmonger, raping and pillaging a path of destruction for an Empire whose time has long passed, and does not want you now. You call me evil, but I am not the invader here."

At that, Theudis turned his back, shuffling deeper into the darkness of the cave. Echoes of his footsteps rang along the enclosure, and I wondered whether this cavern had any bottom, any end whatsoever. For the barest moment, the king's words revived the magus' prophecy, his sonorous laughter filling my mind.

In that moment, I cared little for what dark corner Theudis had left for, wishing only to escape back to the light.

Sembrouthes visibly relaxed when I reemerged from the cave. It took several moments for my eyes to adjust to the searing sun, squinting to offer some semblance of vision. As the sunlight became less painful, I saw Sembrouthes gesturing down the mound and back to our anchored ships. Though I agreed, the toga-clad man offered a final sentiment before allowing me to part.

"Do consider King Theudis' warning, excubitor. My master is many things, but a liar is not among them. If you will allow yourself to be used like a mindless tool, you shall not reap any reward—or, at least, none *I* would like to receive."

"Tell Theudis to shove his flowered words up his arse," I growled.

The man bowed, careful to wrap the hem of his toga in an outstretched hand before dipping to the ground. "And so I shall. I wish you good fortune in your endeavors, excubitor."

"What was that about? What did Theudis tell you?" Sembrouthes whispered as we traipsed downhill.

"Nothing good," I answered. "He'll give us three days to leave peacefully, but then they'll attack."

"Then that's three extra days to prepare," Sembrouthes said. "Theudis may have the bigger army, but he can't starve us into submission. The Visigoths need to storm the walls and rejoin with Theudesgel. Possible, but it will be bloody fighting."

"Then bloody fighting it is," I said listlessly. God knows, it was not the end that I had hoped for, but an end that I knew all too well would come nonetheless. We soon reached the shore, dragged our raft into the water, and rowed back to Apollos' ship, using the half day of light remaining to us to return to Septem.

Every moment of the journey back to harbor, my thoughts were consumed with premonitions of war in Italy. I did not share Theudis' warning with any others, not even Liberius. In some ways, I feared what the legate's answer might be, worrying that if Justinian truly had arranged the assassination of Amalasuntha as pretext for conflict,

Liberius must have some knowledge of the affair. He may have aided, or even led the clandestine task, for he was one of few in the Emperor's court who hailed from Italy, albeit only in his earliest years. Neither did I speak with Rosamund, for her thoughts on the matter were already plain: leave, before entanglements of duty, honor, and the need to survive overwhelmed my ability to retire in peace.

I did share Theudis' threat of invasion with my war council, noting the three days we had before violence would commence. Xerxes personally oversaw each cubit of the landward walls as well as the palisade fence that penned Theudesgel inside Mount Abyla, working closely with Ascum to engineer all manner of contraptions and weapons to repel attackers who were able to navigate the complex web of trenches and wooden spikes outside the walls. Their reassurance was heartening.

Those three days passed quickly. I busied myself with the endless array of tasks required for our defense, from helping Itaxes' crews haul naphtha-battered stones from the harbor front to regular intervals along the walls. Through it all, I was never able to disabuse myself of the truths of Theudis' premonition. It was an anxiety that only grew more intense as I pondered how the Visigoths knew so much of Belisarius' plans, as well as the actions of the Ostrogoths in the aftermath of Amalasuntha's death. It was little secret that the Empire craved the return of Italy to its control—such was a longstanding ambition of Justin and Anastasius before him.

Yet under Justinian, that noble goal was somehow different, both considerably more overwhelming and less fulfilling as the Emperor demanded Belisarius accomplish impossible tasks with precious few men. Worse, the Nika Riots had left their own bevy of unanswered questions that, to my fevered mind, seemed related to our current predicament. Truly, how did Hermogenes die? With his remaining rivals hanged or cowed to submission, what did Justinian's pledge before our departure from Constantinople mean? And more recently, who was the spy in Carthage, and to whom was he a catspaw? These questions had all been asked in turn, yet in the aftermath of the

Vandal War and amidst our conflict with Theudis, they bore only one miserable truth—though great and noble minds shaped the future, it was the common farmer or foot soldier who bled and suffered as payment for those dreams.

Now, as one who has lived far beyond his intended span of days, I understand and mourn that truth. In some ways, I have implicitly known this truth, from the starvation and crippling taxation of the plebeians prior to the Riots, to the massacre of so many innocents in Armenia, Mesopotamia, Numidia, Mauretania, and Tingitana. No hero, and no dream, is borne without sacrifice, nor unwatered by the spilt blood of others destined to be forgotten by the histories. I can imagine no greater punishment that this wretched life has to offer.

PERIPETEIA

Theudis was true to his word. Septem had its three days and three nights of relative peace, its sole disruption the burgeoning Visigoth army that severed all trade or communication by land. On the fourth day, as the sun rose heavily into the cloud-streaked skies above Septem, that peace was definitively shattered.

The Visigoths did not advance suddenly, nor with any urgency. Neither did my army, which carefully watched each movement of Theudis' chieftains for any sign of guile or unforeseen stratagems. Some, too, kept a discerning eye toward Mount Abyla, spying upon the movements inside its citadel as Theudesgel's survivors formed at the top of the mountain. Beyond observing, there was little else that could be done to prepare for the simultaneous attacks, with the only lingering uncertainty being the hour the attack would commence.

"Theudis' army will strike first, then Theudesgel once the bulk of our forces are occupied by the besiegers," I told Xerxes and Liberius in Persian. "The most important challenge we have is to keep Theudesgel penned along the mountain's slope, holding the palisade. If that breaks, even a dozen Visigoths could wreak havoc throughout the city and erode our defense."

"It will be done, Varus," Xerxes swore. "Your men have prepared well, and your decision to trust them in their labors is admirable."

Liberius grinned. "Don't congratulate Varus yet. It will make his head swell until it can no longer fit inside his helmet!"

"Thank you both." I nodded. "It will be hard fighting, but I have every confidence we will prevail."

Crude horns boomed from the interior, the sound both eerily similar to my own advance upon Septem's walls weeks prior and utterly divergent in its harsh and wavering tone. Thousands of Visigoths emerged from their earthen trenches, forming a tidy shield wall adorned with painted hawks as well as a half dozen other sigils from Theudis' more prominent chieftains. As others had noted, only a few archers fell behind the ranks of spearmen, and there was no cavalry to speak of.

There was, however, a well-hewn siege ram, a carved stump capped with an unpolished iron spike that protruded an arm's length from the log's edge. Likewise, the Goths retained at least two dozen siege ladders—more than enough to assault Septem's land walls at all major towers and battlements simultaneously. None of this was surprising; indeed, my men had drilled for a chaotic, all-out assault that intended to overwhelm Septem's defenses in a single blow.

What happened next was entirely unforeseen.

Draped in polished black iron, Theudis seemed to shine in the cloud-veiled sunlight, with only his face exposed to the air as his gray-streaked hair waved in the breeze. As we watched, the Visigoth king raised a hand to fix the iron circlet on his head, lifting the low-sitting crown from his temple and placing it more comfortably above his hairline. Beside the king, I spotted Agila and a half dozen other Gothic chieftains, their bodies similarly encased in expensive scales that signaled considerable wealth amongst the Gothic ranks. The Visigothic leaders converged, exchanging words until Theudis raised a hand to signal the laggards from their trench lines.

Soon, the Visigoth shield wall parted nearest the stone road leading to Septem's gate. Initially, I expected some hidden weapon, either a flame-belching catapult or pieces of a siege tower that Alexander's armies had used to conquer Persia. There was none of that, however. Rather than a siege weapon, it was far worse.

"Hairuwulf!" Indulf called from farther along the walls. "Hairuwulf!"

At first I did not understand. The gap had revealed only two warriors and a bound man between them, and I took Indulf's cries for some crude insult to Theudis' men. However, as the bound man was kicked and dragged to face the Visigoth king, I finally understood: Hairuwulf was the name of an Ostrogothic man sworn to Indulf's service, now captured. Squinting to see, I found his features familiar enough, although the man's beard had become particularly filthy and his face purpled and swollen from bruises.

At Theudis' signal, Hairuwulf's leather bindings were severed, and the man's ensuing feeble attempt at escape was cut short with a swift kick to the abdomen. As their prisoner retched in agony, the two Visigoth captors regained control of the man, waiting as Agila planted a ponderous wooden cross in the soil, burying its foundation a full cubit underground before packing earth against the structure. Satisfied that the beam would hold, Theudis gestured to Hairuwulf's body, and the Visigothic captors proceeded to string each of Hairuwulf's arms to a separate post while his legs were roped together.

At that, I knew what would come next. I said a prayer, both for Hairuwulf and for myself, for Theudis was about to make use of the crucifix by its original intended purpose amongst the long-disbanded Roman legions.

"Courage, Hairuwulf!" Indulf yelled. "I will free you!"

"Do not let Indulf open the gates without permission," I ordered Xerxes. "This is a lure, just as Theudesgel did to us. These Visigoths have no honor or morality."

"No," Xerxes agreed, "but they do understand your men."

"So make sure they don't make the same mistake as I did," I growled. "Keep the men sober and their wits sharp."

Another signal from Theudis, and the two Visigothic captors

drew daggers, cutting through the tattered remnants of Hairuwulf's shirt, exposing the pale and scabbed flesh underneath.

"Men, do not move, nor leave your posts!" I yelled, the order echoed by Roman centurions. "Whatever you see, you must honor Hairuwulf by not shirking your duty, nor allow the enemy an easier approach to the walls!"

Raising both hands to show he was unarmed, Theudis approached Septem's gate, stopping well within the bowshot of a relatively untrained archer. Xerxes sensed the opportunity and leaned toward my ear.

"What are your orders, Lord? Shall I instruct the men to kill the king?"

"No," I muttered. "Wait."

Arms outstretched as if in mockery of his captive, Theudis scanned the tops of Septem's walls, offering a curt nod as he drew level with my own figure atop the gate. Yet he did not address me, nor Xerxes, nor even Liberius. His words were reserved for my Ostrogothic warlord alone.

"Indulf, you coward!" Theudis yelled, his voice crackling and strained even from such a minimal exchange. "You tortured my nephew, a boy of twelve, before an army of men. You clipped several of his toes! In return, I shall revisit such pain a thousand times upon your man, for any Visigoth is worth three goat-fucking Ostrogoths!"

"So much for gratitude for saving the boy's life," Sembrouthes muttered.

"It was still the right thing to do," I muttered back.

Sembrouthes sighed. "I do not disagree, but in my country, we do not offer pain for mercy."

"Indulf offered no mercy of his own," I countered. "And the Visigoths have little sympathy for anyone unable to lift a sword or thrust a spear. They sacked Rome for three straight days, raping and pillaging for no reason other than avarice and bloodlust."

Coughing violently, Theudis lowered his arms, remaining still for a few heartbeats longer to survey the defenses arrayed against him.

No response came. The king shrugged and retreated to the friendly shield wall. Before he left, however, Theudis had one more insult to bestow.

"Indulf, I've known you since you slipped from your mother's arse. I always knew you to be a weakling, but I never thought you capable of nothing other than fighting mere boys. No wonder your fucking queen died! All she has in her employ is a bunch of boy-killing goat shaggers!"

At that, what remained of Indulf's reserve evaporated. "Theudis! You king slayer and oath breaker! Before this battle is over, I will carve out your testicles and feed them to the crabs along the harbor!"

Theudis grinned. I could not see his demonic yellow eye, but I had never seen such a look of wicked triumph as upon Theudis that day. Neither before nor since the dual sieges of Septem. I cannot fault Indulf for his outburst, for I myself had fallen victim to this kind of provocation, yet I worried about where the exchange might lead.

"Send a man to calm Indulf, now!" I whispered to Xerxes.

But Theudis seized his opening. "Testicles! Very imaginative, Indulf. I'm sure Amalasuntha could have used a real man, rather than the blathering idiots and drooling lunatics she kept as company. Come down from behind the skirts of your Roman overlords and take your prize!"

A Greek courier sprinted along the walls, rushing to Indulf's side to fulfill my command and beg him to show restraint. Theudis waited only a few moments longer before finalizing his exchange.

"To be expected from a *coward*!"

His chest heaving from the pain of speech once more, Theudis finally turned his back upon the walls, ambling out of bowshot and toward his captive prisoner. Shooting a glance down the walls, I saw Indulf arguing with several of his men, yet miraculously neither ordered the gates opened nor rushed forward.

Simultaneously, Theudis raised a hand, flicking it forward as if swatting at a troublesome gnat buzzing along his nose. The two captors nodded and set to their tasks with deft precision that betrayed their experience with such grisly work.

It was at that moment that I understood the truth behind all the dark tales that had been told about Theudis back in Carthage, and on the journey to the Pillars of Herakles. In all my years, I have known much cruelty. Sins far darker than those of Theudis, the pain caused far more devastating. Khingila was one such cruel actor, although I only witnessed the aftermath of the Hephthalites' pillage of Armenia prior to their temporary banishment by then-Prince Xerxes. Kazrig and Shaush were others, delighting in the suffering of their victims to placate the wrath of their dark gods. Far worse still awaits later in this tale, and there was little that Belisarius, Theodora, or any other figurehead could do to stem such a tide. Fear and pain ruled the known world—a lesson that Theudis understood well.

What separated him from most others, however, was how shrewdly he deployed the wanton torture of his enemies. With all my soul, I doubt that Theudis bore Hairuwulf any personal grudge. I doubt even that he knew the man's name, leaving such trifling details to the torturers within his army. Yet Theudis knew that Hairuwulf's screams would drive a wedge through the sections of my army, through any charge of spearmen, and scream Hairuwulf did. It was all I could do to keep Indulf calm as the torturers plucked each nail from their captive's fingers, used the bloodied stumps as leverage, peeled away strips of skin all the way to the palms.

I did not discover until later that Hairuwulf was Indulf's cousin. True, Ostrogoths had been raised in large clans, with wealthier warriors supporting multiple wives, each with her own gaggle of children, and entire villages could claim some relation if not by blood, then by marriage. Hairuwulf was one such half cousin, yet Indulf wept as if it were his own twin brother bleeding into the swirling dust.

I shall spare you the knowledge of what agonies Theudis' men inflicted upon Hairuwulf. The man died screaming, but no man could have hoped to fare better against such inhumanity. I thought of Petrus' lessons, wondering whether our Savior's scourging elicited similar suffering, roiling the stomachs of onlookers. After a lifetime of slaughter, I have taken in an overflowing portion of death, yet never grew comfortable with torture. Of all the beasts who roam God's creation, only man engages in torture, with those who do stretching out the screams of the damned for as long as possible. In battle, at least, blows are designed to kill, and quickly—or at least with no more suffering than is necessary.

Hairuwulf suffered a slow, horrible death, his life force leaching from dozens upon dozens of cuts, slashes, and stumps. It was not until they gelded Hairuwulf that Theudis turned back to Septem's walls, bowing his head in mock gratitude.

"You have my thanks, Indulf, for that idea! What an imagination you have!"

At that, Indulf shrieked in pain and rage. The sound was no different than that of a dying animal, merely unfathomable agony borne by the instinct to shout defiance to the heavens. Fearing the worst, I sprinted toward the Ostrogoth position and found Indulf gathering his weapons. He saw me, his teeth bared with rabid intent.

"Do not stop me, Varus!"

I raised a hand, not to resist the man, but to inject some measure of pause. "What will you do, Indulf? You cannot fight the whole army. Avenge Hairuwulf by defending these walls."

"Every man and woman in Septem can go fuck themselves in the arse!" he yelled. "I'm going to fight those bastards in single combat."

It was foolhardy, but who was I to say otherwise? I would have insisted upon the same, were our positions in life traded. Nay, I *had* done the same, for Isaacius, and many others.

"I will not stop you, Indulf," I said, hoping nevertheless to beg him for a measure of reason, "but go into this with clear eyes and a careful mind. Theudis is trying to draw you out in a rash of emotion."

Seething, Indulf nevertheless bobbed his head in acknowledgment. "You will not stop me?"

"No," I concluded. "I do not agree with you leaving your men here, but I cannot lie and say I do not understand. Do what you must."

Again, his head bobbed. Indulf hefted his shield and unsheathed his sword before trotting down the stairs that supported Septem's inner-facing walls. Xerxes gazed upon me with confusion, yet I merely raised an arm to order the gates opened.

By the time that Indulf emerged to challenge Theudis' men, Hairuwulf had screamed his last. Though I saw his mouth open and close, any sound was long gone, drained away by the man's exhaustion and drowned out by a booming roar from hundreds of Ostrogothic voices, all calling in support of their leader and champion. I could only watch as Indulf strode hurriedly toward Theudis, reaching the edge of our bowshot.

"Theudis! You're too weak to fight yourself, so send one of your pigs to fight me!"

The Visigoth king grinned, not from happiness, but from triumph. "As you wish, my dear lord!"

With a flick of his hand, Theudis called back to his chieftains. Agila stepped forward, casting aside his spear to mimic Indulf's example. As I walked back to Septem's gates, I considered Theudis' choice of a champion with puzzlement. Agila was an uninspiring figure; plenty a warrior in spirit, to be sure, with all the courage to stand in a desperate shield wall against a better equipped and more numerous foe, but in form far from an athlete, with his belt straining against a rounded belly. Even if brave and disciplined in the proper footwork of a trained swordsman, Agila was not the champion I would have chosen to face Indulf—a lean and muscular figure whose unscarred face told of prowess with shield and weapons alike. Shaking his shield and sword as he bellowed in anger, Indulf rushed the Visigoth champion, not hesitating to lash out a first blow.

To his credit, Agila did not embarrass himself. Indulf's thrusts and jabs were blocked or parried, and the stouter man pivoted and dodged Indulf's arcing blows that would have easily smashed pieces from a wooden panel had they landed. Agila even countered when Indulf overextended his attack, albeit without any aggression to advance himself. At each turn, Indulf quickly countered, drawing cheers from the Ostrogothic onlookers, who sensed their lord overpowered their hated foe.

"Indulf seems the better duelist," I muttered in Persian.

"Far better," Xerxes agreed. "And far more ruthless. But we will see if he keeps his wits about him."

It was then that Indulf swept his boot along the dust, kicking a thick cloud into his opponent's face. Sputtering, Agila paused just briefly, shaking away the detritus that clouded his vision and choked his nose and throat. He saw Indulf's lunge a half step too late, the blade surging past the iron-rimmed shield and cutting through iron and leather armor alike.

Yet in the swirling dust, Indulf missed his killing blow. His sword pierced cleanly through a narrow point in Agila's armor, cutting through skin along the man's hip and sending him reeling backward, hissing from the stinging pain—a true injury, but a superficial one, with a light stream of blood trickling from the open wound. Nevertheless, the Ostrogoths boomed their approval, stamping their spear butts against Septem's walls in thunderous applause.

Indulf thrust his sword to the skies, shouting in triumph. "Tell your man to surrender, Lord King!"

Theudis' features were drawn not with fear or surprise, but merely impatience. Rather than respond to Indulf's bravado, the Visigoth king shouted to Agila in their shared Gothic language, curling his fingers into a fist as he growled an order. Straightening, Agila nodded, wiping away the dust that had set into the sweat and spittle across his face, yet there was no panting, nor any sign of pain or sluggishness from his wound. Instead, the Visigothic chieftain raised his shield and sheathed his sword.

Sembrouthes leaned forward. "Surrender?"

For a heartbeat, I thought the same. Indulf began to laugh, clapping the flat of his blade against the wooden panels of his shield as he shouted back to his arrayed men. Weaponless, Agila stepped forward, his shield kept high and tight from knee to neck. Indulf cocked his head, shouting a taunt in the Gothic language, before recognizing that Agila had little intention of capitulation. With a final shout, Indulf raised the tip of his sword level with Agila's chest and sprinted to deliver a killing blow.

Only to discover his ruin. For Agila, using the shield to disguise his movements, withdrew a small clay jar that rested within his hand. Whether Indulf saw this unknown danger or heard Xerxes' cries to retreat, I cannot be certain, but it makes no difference. Indulf thrust forward with his sword just as Agila hurled the jar directly into Indulf's face, the brittle clay bursting into a hundred shards. And so, Indulf's attack was sapped of its force, allowing Agila to easily absorb the blow with his shield as Indulf writhed in horror.

From our vantage point atop the walls, it was difficult to discern the cause of Indulf's retreat. Yet as he stumbled and twirled in a keening agony, I glimpsed the thick oil that clung to his face.

"Naphtha," Xerxes muttered. "Theudis has learned from our example."

Burningly blind, Indulf collapsed in a heap, unable to even loosen the straps of his shield after abandoning his sword to the dust. Instead, he rolled around, begging for relief and choking for breath. Through it all, Agila considered Indulf with a curious eye, slowly withdrawing his sword from its scabbard before pacing idly forward. My Ostrogothic warlord was as good as dead, and perhaps such a killing blow would have been a mercy. Rising to his knees, Indulf wept tears masked by the vicious fluid, his screams carrying above Septem's walls. Standing over Indulf, Agila measured each motion carefully, raising his sword arm high above Indulf's head.

Behind Agila, Theudis cackled in triumph. "You were far too pretty, Indulf! You were making my nieces jealous. It seems that problem has been dealt with!"

Smirking, Agila aimed a heavy boot directly into Indulf's rear, sending the disarmed Ostrogoth tumbling back into the dirt, all sense of bearing gone. Another kick followed close behind, before Agila, too, took up the Visigoth king's laughter, and with him thousands of Visigoth spearmen, many of whom began to chant Indulf's name in mock celebration. Agila sheathed his sword, brushing away his cloak and turning back to the Visigothic lines. A slight limp marked his steps, the only evidence of his duel with Indulf before the gates of Septem.

"Send men to collect Indulf," I ordered Xerxes. "Quickly, before the battle begins."

At Xerxes' urging, Wisimar and a half dozen Vandals sprinted toward the still-twitching Indulf, lifting his body from the ground and rushing back to the safety of the gate. They had little time, for emboldened by Agila's victory, the Visigoths clamored for violence. All Theudis had to do was flick his wrist, and the frontward Gothic ranks rushed forward, their shields locked tightly around one another in anticipation of the barrage to come. There was no time to attend to Indulf directly, only to gape as his limp body was carried through Septem's gates, mewling in pain and calling out in incomprehensible Gothic as he was ferried toward the safety of Rosamund's apothecary.

Xerxes' hands gripped hard around the stone parapet, his left foot jittering up and down, fast as a butterfly's wings. He surveyed each section of Theudis' lines, muttering to himself as he noted each chieftain and ladder group that pushed their way closer to Septem's walls.

"You know what to do," I told him. "Give the signal."

All motion in Xerxes' body ceased. He nodded, his Zhayedan armor glittering in contrast to the varied Roman outfits of my force, its polished iron scales laced with thin layers of bronze and gold. His horsehair plume danced from the breeze atop the walls as he fastened his helmet for a final time, his eyes never leaving the Visigothic advance.

"*Ballistae!* Three hundred paces!"

Ascum did not dally at the order. Without naphtha, his siege weapons lacked the fire that had wrought such a devastating effect at Callinicum or earlier against Septem, but such a display was necessary. From atop Septem's walls, the Roman siege engines bore even deadlier force than normal, their bolts using the advantage of height to hurtle downward against massed opponents. There was little that Theudis' men could do: breaking their shield wall would leave them exposed to my Heruli and Greek archers, yet staying massed in a group made them ripe targets for Ascum's seasoned engineers.

The first bolts were loaded and launched within moments, the screeching of taut rope and creaking wooden beams telling of the raw power that had been unleashed against our enemies. Some sailed well above their targets, yet many connected against the frontward ranks of the Gothic walls, sending men scattering in fear as they vainly sought protection from the whistling death.

But Theudis, as others had warned, was no fool. After that initial volley, the Visigoth chiefs urged their men forward, seeking to quickly close the distance to their target and render the ballistae useless in close quarters. Many had done exactly that prior to the launching of Ascum's second volley, although slower groupings of spearmen were still victimized by two of the bolts.

But Xerxes had far more suffering to inflict upon the advancing enemy. "Archers, one hundred paces!"

Thracian and Heruli bowmen answered the call, their centurions ordering the men to nock, draw, and loose in orderly succession. Fulcaris took particular care to prevent disorder in his attack, trusting the punch of an arrow volley to knock holes in even the most organized and seasoned of shield walls. In that, he was not wrong, for many an iron tip slipped past the bulwark and dug into the flesh and bone underneath. At least a dozen Visigoths dropped from the frontmost ranks at that initial volley, and the progress of the others slowed to better guard against further arrows. Subsequent volleys were less successful, yet gave spearmen atop the walls a few precious moments to prepare the defense of those platforms likely to be stormed with ladders.

As ballistae and bowmen launched a hail of missiles upon the enemy, Xerxes had one final maneuver. It was not nearly as effective as the first set of defenses, yet for the few detachments of Visigoths abutting Septem's coastline, it was ruinous.

"Gunderic! Blow the horn, signal the dromons!"

The giant Vandal's chest heaved with a great breath before delivering Xerxes' command, signaling the captains of each ship to launch their own ballistae onto exposed spearmen upon the shore. Another dozen Visigoths fell here, forcing those remaining to choose between scattering to break up a potential ballista target or huddling behind shields to protect against the archers. Most chose the former, leaving them susceptible to grievous wounds as they took to the walls.

"Excellent work," I yelled. "But I need you to take command of the Ostrogoth foederati. Without Indulf, their officers may lose heart. Gunderic has earned the right to command the Vandals."

As Xerxes nodded in recognition, Gunderic whooped with joy. "You hear that, men? Gunderic's in charge now! And I say skewer the bastards!"

A half dozen Vandals clapped Gunderic on the shoulder, raising the first cheer from Roman lines since Indulf's unexpected defeat. Gunderic beamed, though his giddiness was cut short by the approaching Visigoths, whose frontmost ranks were now a mere fifty paces from Septem's walls. Within moments, the most eager of the Visigoths were clambering at the base of our rampart, selecting positions to place ladders for the coming attack.

"Stones!" Gunderic boomed, smashing the butt of his spear onto the battlements. "Prepare to repel the ladders!"

Nodding, I roared my own order. "All archers, focus on the siege ram! Pluck at the frontmost bearers!"

Though it had only been a few weeks since I myself had led an assault upon Septem's walls, I could not then—and still cannot— imagine the hell that the Visigoth spearmen must have felt that afternoon. Flying missiles sang through the air, darkening the skies as they flocked to their targets. Many trenches and staves arrayed in our defense forced once-disciplined shield walls to fracture as men navigated the ditch or swerved around the spiked barricade. None of these measures could deflect a determined attacker on their own, yet together they caused enough nuisance to blunt the assault, allowing our archers to claim a few more casualties and, more crucially, destroying any semblance of order in Theudis' attack.

Paralyzed by the continuous assault of bowmen, stones, and ballistae, few Visigoth climbers were able to reach the top rungs of their ladders. Yet still they came, howling despite the rising tide of wounded who cried out for relief. It was then, as the first Visigoths who'd survived long enough stood atop Septem's walls, that Theudesgel finally struck.

Conon's horn sounded five hurried blasts, signaling Theudesgel's descent from Mount Abyla's citadel, yet from such an angle near Septem's gate, it was difficult to tell the true urgency of the call for men to reinforce the makeshift palisade. Worse, the Visigoth siege ram had been dragged toward the gate entrance, its bearers somehow overcoming dozens of shafts and twin rows of spiked trenches to reach their barricaded destination. Conon's horn sounded again, once again signaling for reinforcements at the palisade.

"Gunderic!" I yelled. "I need to take my bodyguard to Conon! Can you hold?"

Gunderic howled, grinning with fevered delight. "All right, lads, Varus can't sit around wiping our asses all day! Let's show him what Xerxes prepared for our guests!"

Within moments, hooting Vandals cut at ropes that had been stretched in taut layers along the battlements nearest the gate, sending the torn flax spinning within a series of iron rings. At the far end of the ropes waited twin scythes—farming instruments for reaping wheat that wealthier peasants kept within their household rafters—their long curved blades whetted to a wicked edge and poised to strike.

And so they did, both scythes falling swiftly upon opposite ends of the gate, slicing through mail and bone as if they were the softest cheese. Unlucky spearmen did not even have the opportunity to scream as they were ripped asunder, limbs and trunks dashed askew in a great mist of blood. The twin scythes only came to rest when encountering the wooden log of the siege ram, digging a full hand's length into the bark. At least a dozen Visigoths fell within the span of a heartbeat, the souls already having departed the bodies of most of Gunderic's victims. It was hard to tell, but perhaps one or two remained alive after the attack, twitching and shuddering from the shock of parts suddenly detached from their familiar junction.

"Xerxes said he learned that in Persia," Gunderic said, whistling as he surveyed the casualties. "Clearly, it's a place I need to visit!"

"Whatever you say," I muttered, my stomach churning as I watched the Visigoths regroup in a flurry of shouts and fear at the unorthodox attack. "Can you hold?"

"Until the end of the world!" Gunderic grinned.

Leaving the Vandals to protect Septem's gate, I led Sembrouthes and the Aksumites into the city's interior, finding Conon's detachment using their shields to brace the palisade gate with whatever weight could be mustered. Others threw stones at oncoming attackers, using crudely constructed platforms to peer over the sharpened edges of each wooden log. Nearby, I saw Cephalas stalking my formation, waiting for the slightest signal to participate in the city's defense. He did not hesitate when I called to him.

"Cephalas, my bow!"

He nodded. "Shall I fetch others?"

"No time!" I yelled. "Grab me a quiver and throw your weight into the gate!"

Having prepared for such an order, Cephalas unslung Khingila's bow from his back before retrieving a quiver of arrows from a nearby Herulian wall guard. The arrows were stubby things, more appropriate for horseback than a fixed position atop the wall, yet their iron tips had been honed to a wicked point and would have more than enough force to drive a shaft clean through a man's chest at sixty paces. I ordered my dozen Aksumites to assist Conon before taking control over one wooden fighting platform, whose uneven steps proved rickety beneath my feet as I rose two full cubits into the air. Gathering my balance, I kept my body in a crouch, then peered over the edge at our attackers.

Rather than attack as a singular mass, Theudesgel's men rushed at the palisade in groups of ten apiece. They had no ram but bore plenty of axes, chopping vigorously into the palisade until deep gashes were exposed in a great mess of wooden shards. Their small numbers meant little threat of the gate being toppled by sheer force, yet the ingenuity of Theudesgel's maneuver was such that it kept the attacking Visigoths from becoming trapped in the press of their own ranks. Nimble, they danced away when struck by stones or an occasional arrow, using any weapons launched by Roman ranks to throw back at the walls' defenders.

"They're breaking through!" Conon yelled. "The gate won't last much longer!"

Though I can only imagine that they were both hungry and exhausted, the Visigoths exhibited impeccable discipline; those who were not chopping with axes held their shields carefully layered around their comrades in a near-impenetrable aegis of protection. Such shield rings were only broken when one axe team was shifted for another, offering but a few heartbeats to glimpse inside the great mass of warriors that huddled just thirty paces from Conon's position. It was in one such exchange that I finally glimpsed the walking skeleton that led them, his chest heaving with shouts in the Gothic tongue.

"Call for reinforcements!" Conon yelled.

"Not yet!" I replied. Having spotted Theudesgel, I could not easily change tactics.

Plucking an arrow from the Herulian quiver, the leather tips of my gloves brushed against the pruned feathers along my selected missile, its diminutive frame familiar from my days spent in the saddle as the original komes of the Herulian foederati. Instinct sharpened by countless hours within the previous years kept my motions true. With my left hand squeezing the grip of Khingila's bow, I squinted upon my intended target, my breathing slowing as all the chaos of Septem dissolved around me and my senses attuned only to the Visigoth shield ring that threatened to overrun the Roman rear.

It was a poor opportunity. No master-at-arms would train for such an unfavorable opening and would only chastise the naïve bowman who would attempt such a shot. Theudesgel's limbs and torso were only visible for heartbeats at a time, quickly covered by layers of Visigoth shields and overattentive bodyguards that never ventured more than a pace from the chieftain's side. Yet when we aim to strike down foes who would do grievous harm, we must take whatever chance the Lord provides. Exhaling a thin stream of air, I nocked my arrow and jerked upright, drawing and loosing just as another group of ten peeled away from the main Visigoth formation and headed toward the splintering palisade gate.

The arrow missed. At least, it did not strike Theudesgel in the heart, slipping past the temporary gaps in the shield wall. Instead, the barbed tip sliced underneath Theudesgel's sword-bearing collarbone, sending the warlord spinning. I was close enough to see a spatter of blood fleck his face, his mouth lolling open as if choking in pain. Even in the din I could hear his shriek of pain as his retinue closed ranks, only barely dodging a spear launched toward my exposed chest. I was able to steal one final glimpse of the Visigoth formation before retreating to safety, finding Theudesgel jumping to his feet and rushing up the winding path to Mount Abyla's citadel. Many Visigoths remained, yet others followed their wounded master as he stumbled atop the Pillar.

Though the thudding of axes did not entirely cease, the hinges along the gate buckled less violently, and its defenders were able to relax their press against the failing beams as the Visigothic onslaught weakened to only a moderate nuisance. This lessened offensive freed more of Conon's men to hurl rocks over the walls, occasionally striking an unlucky Goth in the head or shoulders with a sickening crack.

"Amazing, Lord!" Conon grinned. "I'm in your debt."

"Keep these walls standing, and the favor will be repaid," I shouted over a swelling howl of Vandals along the main gate. Soon thereafter, Theudis' horns blared outside the main walls, their coarse staccato echoed by Theudesgel's own battle call, which grew ever more distant as his main body of Visigoths retreated. More cheers soon arose, first amongst the Ostrogoths, and later amongst Fulcaris' Herulians. Nodding to Sembrouthes, I rushed back to Septem's gate, nearly slipping along a thin sheet of blood as I climbed the stone steps to the battlement.

I did not even need to ask the cause of such strange noise. Any questions were answered by the words of Greek voices sailing high above the walls, some waving banners as they screamed the age-old chant.

Roma Victrix! Nika! Nika!

Victory, if you could call it that. Upon that day, and those thereafter, many a Roman toasted to the victory of a tired and overstretched defending force as it held back Theudis' assault. And so did I.

It would not be for many years, however, that I understood this day as the fulcrum upon which my tale pivoted—the turn onto a new page and a new narrative. Many centuries ago, Plato had coined the notion of a peripeteia, or the moment when a hero's trajectory bends away from splendor and happiness and begins the lengthy arc to tragedy. Even now, I cannot say whether I am the hero of any person's tale—least of all my own.

Yet with our victory at Septem, I felt that peripeteia, felt as life shifted from promise to worry, from hope toward grim determination and sorely tested wills. Oh, I have certainly lived a vastly more comfortable life than most, survived to these advanced years that would have seen a peasant starve, shiver, or be slain decades prior. I pray for such poor folk, who deserve far more than the hollow meal of dying glories and ancient fables to nurse their deprivations. Yet neither do I count my survival as a testament to any kind of heroism. No, I beg forgiveness of my sins and weep for all that came next, both the sublime moments of happiness and the overwhelming burdens of loss.

UNBREAKABLE RESOLVE
AND DESPERATE LOYALTY

A s with so much in life and upon the battlefield, the full reckoning
of Theudis' losses was not quickly tallied; indeed, the total
devastation was not accounted for until well after sunset. The Visigoth
king, seeing Theudesgel's men retreat, attempted one final assault on
Septem's walls, yet was repelled by a suffocating press of Herulian
arrows, veteran ballistae engineers, and the seemingly indefatigable
braying of Gunderic's Vandals. Thwarted, Theudis called for a retreat,
with his men quick to obey.

The singers call it a marvelous victory. I do not begrudge them,
yet a few amongst the commons recall that Theudis was far from
beaten at that moment. With perhaps a hundred and fifty dead, the
Visigothic forces remained far greater than our own, especially given
the two dozen losses I had taken at various intervals down my line,
not to mention the many within the Roman expedition still suffering
from flux or overexertion, and the fair number of others shivering
from the seasonal maladies that seem to burn through any significant
gathering across the world. We had certainly driven a nail into the
Visigothic confidence, but with plenty of ladders and an intact siege
ram, Theudis retained double the force necessary to storm Septem's
defenses in the coming days.

Even so, Theudis' greatest strength had been defanged, leaving the Visigoth king no simple path toward conquering the coastal fortress. The morning after the battle, a bandaged Theudesgel could be seen peering over the citadel's crumbling walls, the fates having spared him the chance to fight again. Conon, however, had inflicted far more severe casualties upon Theudesgel's men, with at least two dozen dead or dying piled near the near-shattered palisade gate. We questioned the survivors who were healthy enough, and offered a merciful dispatch to those who would otherwise suffer slow deaths from creeping sickness that corrupted the blood and left wounds to fester.

All told, we came to understand that Theudesgel's survivors could not have numbered more than a hundred, and they had already been placed upon half rations in their isolation. This meant Theudis could no longer depend upon a secondary attack from Mount Abyla to distract my forces. Nor, however, could I send the requisite spearmen to seize the mountain, for even when ailing, the Visigoths could easily force dozens of casualties upon a narrow and rock-strewn approach to the summit. Sentries kept watch of Theudesgel's movements, but the threat from him and his men had dwindled to more annoyance than credible danger.

And so, still outnumbered, we rested inside the city, treating our wounded and bolstering towers with additional bolts or stones for a future attack. Liberius took direct charge of the city granaries, ordering Itaxes to triple the haul from the city's various fishing boats that stalked the coastline.

Militarily, Xerxes inspected each segment of wall, ordering Visigoth corpses piled and burned while deepening our trenches and affixing additional wooden stakes along Septem's roadways. Others fletched arrows or ferried buckets of water to clean the blood and gore from stretches of wall, evidence of Visigoths who had nearly been successful in capturing segments of our defenses. All men and women were given tasks, their efforts both urgent and efficient given a lingering fear that Theudis' horde could descend upon us again at any moment.

Back in the safety of his trenches, Theudis also bided his time, dispatching messengers westward each morning and evening. Guessing at Theudis' intent, I sent all the available dromons capable of an extended sea journey to harass the coastal towns of Hispania and hinder any transport between the two continents, though such efforts were in vain. My dromons were far too few, and Theudis too willing to lose whatever was necessary to reinforce his position, especially through voyages from Gades to Tingis within the darkest portions of night. And although Apollos reported many Visigoth cogs had turned back to port or had been sunk, within a week, Theudis had nevertheless amplified his ranks with another thousand hawk-shielded spearmen.

Each new arrival seemed to come laden with weapons and food, careful not to repeat Theudesgel's errors atop Mount Abyla. Blessedly, there were no catapults, although Theudis' men did construct a heavy mobile shack that housed a new iron-capped ram, which they set facing Septem's gate. Curiously, the Visigoths also brought at least a hundred hounds to their trenches, their shaggy gray fur covering stout frames and likely considerable weight.

"War dogs," Perenus explained. Though he insisted he should resume duties of command, he was still weak and shrunken from his bout with the flux. "In Lazica, the mountain clans use them to tear holes in the enemy's shield wall. The Goths surely will do the same."

Despite the obvious threat, I could not suppress a smile. Catching a curious look from Perenus, I told more of my servitude under Justin. "My dominus loved dogs. He must have owned a dozen. It didn't matter if they were to assist in battle or merely provide companionship in camp, Justin was never far from his hounds."

"Well, these dogs won't be for cuddling. Throats and groins, that's what any hound master would train them to go for. If I lose my manhood to a dog bite, I'm quitting the army."

Amidst the lull in fighting, Rosamund was moving in triple time, treating the wounds of three dozen men suffering from all manner of wounds and illness. I spared her all but the most gravely injured, not wishing to overwhelm her capacity, but it was not until one of her attendants sought me out in the night that I realized I had plunged her into an unceasing aura of death. When I followed her back to Rosamund's side, I was startled to see her weeping.

I relived her of her duties for the moment, drawing her back to the privacy of my assigned quarters to compose herself. Swallowing thickly, she finally submitted to my asking what was wrong.

"I had a Cappadocian come to me with an arrow wound to his thigh," she told me. "And he'd extracted the barb—he ought to have lived. But within two days it was festering. No ointments or unguents could do anything. I had no choice but to cut the limb free. I told him as much, and he agreed, but… but he died screaming nonetheless."

Burying her face in her hands, Rosamund broke into a shuddering fit of sobs.

Though she had clearly come to me for some measure of solace, I knew little of how to ease her anguish, for I had never been saddled with the awful burden of a healer—nor had I, until that same moment, considered the depths of its demands. Moreso, though many had called upon my aid since joining the army, Rosamund had never required anything other than respect. It made me uneasy to see her so distraught, her normal skepticism of our wartime duties in a faraway land transformed into a bitter hatred of the pain to which she had become privy to day in and day out.

Rising from her couch, she moved three paces to share my own, grasping my callused fingers in her freezing digits.

"You told me this would be our last assignment, Varus," Rosamund whispered. "Swear to me that this is so."

The familiar request sounded raw, ragged like I had never heard it. I could not bear to look her in the eye.

"You don't know what it's like," she went on, voice hoarse. "To hold men down by the dozens, screaming for their mothers, pleading with the gods to spare their lives. Of those who live, many are never the same, while others suffer a terrible death, all fever and gore. And it's me—I'm the last person most of them see, and they all look upon me with the same eyes."

"W-wha…" I stammered, my throat catching. "What do you see?"

"Terror," Rosamund replied. "Desperation. It's one thing to teach men to not fear death in the training yard. But it's another when their limbs have been hacked off, blood leaking onto the dirt. They moan and cry and vomit, but they all look to me for hope. And what can I do?"

I had no answer. But Rosamund did.

"I'll tell you," she said bitterly. "More often than not, I fail."

Only one truth came to my mind, and although it felt ungrateful, I could not help but give it voice. "You do not have to heal them, Rosamund. You do not have to heal anyone, least of all these Romans that you hate."

Rosamund's pained face curled into a scowl. "I don't hate Romans… just that they insist on taking what isn't theirs, regardless of the suffering it causes."

"Then why help them if it troubles you so?" I pried again. "You could give it up if you wanted to."

Rosamund yanked her hands away from mine, glaring at me. "Because if I did, then more would die. Needlessly, and in pain. Like it or not, I can never again be ignorant of what happens to these wounded men, and even I am not so selfish as to withhold my gifts out of spite." She exhaled hard before adding, "And because staying here helps you, whether or not you're aware of it."

"I am," I insisted.

In truth, though I instinctively dispatched to Rosamund any and all of the most grotesque injuries, I thought little about the practicalities of her profession. The salves and bandages and potions and the pagan prayers… they all felt foreign, and, if I am honest, uninteresting. For me, my challenge was to slay my adversary before he could do the same to me, and pray that I would not be crippled in the process. Only then, in that moment, did I understand the other side of war—that it was not the opposition of the adversary, but the aid of the healer, that was the true antithesis of combat. The feeblest boy could inflict a wound, but only the strong-souled healer could repair the body of its ails. Over time, that burden would crush the sturdiest mind.

We sat there for several moments, the power of Rosamund's confession rendering anything I could say hollow. "Rosamund, I'm so sorry…"

"I don't want you to be sorry!" Rosamund snarled. "All I want is an end to the killing and dying. Just friends, and children, and abundant harvests. All I want is a thatched hut and clean water, and the freedom to come and go as I please."

My throat ached as she begged, making the words difficult in coming. "Theodora has promised me the right to retire. Once we return to Constantinople, I intend to deliver that request. Then it is to Pella, and peace."

"Peace," Rosamund muttered. "That is the greatest magic of all, and the hardest to weave. I knew peace once, but I cannot recall the feeling. Justinian will never leave you alone in Pella, I know this in my very bones. We must go far beyond the Empire's borders, where only the steppe peoples graze their horses and gallop under the stars."

I shook my head. "My family is in Pella, as is the estate given to me by Justin. Theodora will honor her oath to me. We will have everything you desire."

Rosamund choked out a sound that would have been a sob had it not rung with frustration rather than despair. "So you say," she scoffed. "Theodora may set things to rights, but those around her will not. All they see is their own dreams of conquest and glory, caring little of the cost. Though you will insist otherwise, in your heart you know of whom I speak, and the truth of my words."

Again, I did not respond. Nor did Rosamund pry. Her oft-repeated opinion required no clarification, and she was exhausted besides.

Though she had been fiercely independent since our campaign in Mesopotamia, Rosamund slept in my rooms for the duration of the siege. There was little to recommend them, with unadorned walls and simple wooden furniture filling a cramped three-room enclosure. Blustering drafts from the sea helped lull the mind to sleep yet made for a shivering evening, and I requested extra blankets for Rosamund despite her insistence that freezing temperatures bore her no concern. Yet she did not deny the gift, wrapping herself tightly in the wool and horsehair in a room with a straw mattress.

Separate from the main sleeping quarters, I had cleared away the desk that had once filled the space, affording Rosamund what meager sense of privacy that could be afforded in such an environment. It wasn't much, a rare stone building in a city of wood and brick, offering an added measure of security against the recurring fear of fire. In her few hours of sleep, Rosamund often babbled in the foreign Gepid tongue, shrieking awake in such dark and unfamiliar quarters. In one particular episode, Rosamund was unable to return to rest, insisting that I sit to watch over her in the remaining hours of darkness. Though my body protested at its own disrupted sleep, I obliged Rosamund, waiting until she had returned to soft snores before sneaking away to the adjoining room.

For the men, spirits had improved considerably. While evenings were anxious affairs, with any movements in the dark interpreted as a lurking killer, different segments of the army broke into groups to share stories and cook meals when not pacing Septem's walls. Though I officially forbade excessive drink, I was not naïve enough to believe that such an order would be dutifully obeyed. Instead, Vandals, Ostrogoths, Herulians, and Greeks all bobbed their heads and saluted when commanded to sobriety, only to sneak heavy wineskins into Septem's inns. I pretended not to hear the riotous laughter or occasional fighting, instructing Gunderic and Fulcaris to simply keep any real violence to a minimum.

"Not sure I understand your meaning, Lord!" Gunderic grinned.

"Me neither," Fulcaris swore. "We're soldiers of the Empire. We don't drink or fight with our brothers!"

"Just make sure there's no murder or theft," I said, rolling my eyes. "And any man caught molesting local women will be hanged.

If your men are light on coin, inform me immediately, but anything taken must be paid for."

Though battered from the siege, most men were able to extract some measure of enjoyment in the aftermath of Theudis' initial defeat. Some, however, were unlucky enough to nurse wounds, leaving them bedridden and capable of little else than sucking thin gruel with a spoon. Of all such unfortunate souls, Indulf was their lord and master.

For three full days, Indulf required near constant care from multiple healers, his responses nonsensical to the point of delirium. Shrugging away the disapproving glances of several medics, Rosamund pressed a foul-smelling elixir through Indulf's cracked and deformed lips, dipping a rag into the mixture and straining its contents into the narrow opening of his mouth.

"For sleeping," Rosamund insisted. "I was able to wash away the worst of the naphtha, but Agila must have added something to make it particularly adhesive to the skin. Indulf's pain must be unimaginable."

I visited Indulf every afternoon. I admit, I felt nothing for the man who delighted in the very cruelty that Belisarius and I had been adamant to stamp out. We could never be friends, and I was sure that Indulf would care little for my own predicament had our fates been swapped. However, he was still a lord of foederati, among Belisarius' senior command and chieftain of a vast number of spearmen in my force. More, he was one of the key figures required to maintain peace with the Ostrogoths of Italy, his loyalties tied firmly to the deceased Amalasuntha. Indulf was my responsibility, and for that, I prayed over his slumbering body.

Indulf did not fully awaken for a week. When he did, I was the first he requested to his presence. Obliging, I reentered the sickly air of Indulf's chambers, reeking of poultices and rot. Inside, I found Indulf alone, his attendant resting in an adjoining hall while preparing another salve for Indulf's comfort. At first I thought him sleeping, for his eyes were swollen shut and his breathing slowed as he lay upon a raised straw mat. Yet soon he lifted his chin in recognition of his intruder.

His voice crackled against a mouth sapped of liquid. "Varus, you came."

Drawing closer, I sat upon a bench as near to his face as I dared. "How did you know it was me?"

"The boots," Indulf said. "A soldier's boots click against any wood or stone floor. My ears are all that remain to me, for now."

Suddenly, Indulf erupted in an aggressive spurt of coughing, his swollen tongue stretching from the crude circle that had once been his mouth. He resembled little of the perilously vain man I had encountered in Syracuse, with oiled hair and a face that would make Narcissus jealous. Days of intensive intervention by Rosamund had preserved the thin layers of flesh around his face, yet much of his lips seemed to have melted away, and his eyebrows had vanished, leaving behind red troughs of wrinkled skin. Similar deep crags lined his cheeks and brow, his nose shriveled into a hook.

"Water," he choked.

Spying a half-full bucket along the wall, I drew a rag from a table near Indulf's head. I followed Rosamund's prior example, dipping the cloth into cool liquid and dribbling it across Indulf's mouth. Groans of delight emanated from his throat as I repeated the gesture, continuing until Indulf choked a request to cease.

"That Gepid woman you keep is gifted," Indulf continued. "She says that my eyes will recover in time. That bastard Agila added some poison to the naphtha. I remember little of how the battle ended, but if I am still alive, then Theudis must have lost."

I leaned forward. "That is correct, but Theudis is not defeated. I wounded Theudesgel, yet he lives too, even if he can do no further harm."

Indulf coughed again, requesting a further dribble of water before resuming. "Don't be so sure. Theudesgel is nothing if not cunning. Theudis has no son, and Theudesgel would butcher any man who claimed to be Theudis' heir. But Goths do not place faith in fools or weaklings, a lesson learned hard from our time against Attila. Theudesgel cannot surrender to you, nor stay out of the battle—not if he wants to advance his claim."

"Wise counsel," I answered. "And will be taken seriously. For now, our position is secure, although Theudis has brought reinforcements. Dogs, too."

Indulf's withered nose crinkled. "Nasty beasts. But do we have a strategy to remove Theudis from Tingitana?"

I considered lying, as I had to many others. Perhaps the Visigoths would run low on food, or the flux would burn through their ranks. Perhaps additional rains or frigid weather would render their warriors homesick and weak. Perhaps Theudis would simply depart these lands, unable to force a conclusion that did not require the deaths of thousands of his own men. All of these suggestions found pliable ears, for they were sensible enough. Yet they were all lies, for Theudis had no intention of acceding to my will, even if it cost him every man assembled along the Visigoth trench lines. Indulf would understand such uncompromising will in the Visigoth king, and so I offered the simple truth.

"No. And I am uncertain that we can hold this position for more than another two months. Belisarius expects us back in Carthage and cannot spare any men to relieve our siege."

A bubbling sigh escaped Indulf's throat. "Then you will fight again. Theudis is also no fool, though he is a devil."

"It appears so, but your only task is to return to strength. We will have need of you soon enough."

Another sigh, broken by a heaving laughter. "As you say. Do what you must to win, Varus, otherwise Theudis will exploit your weakness."

"We will triumph," I muttered, not catching Indulf's meaning.

"I don't doubt it," Indulf replied. "And I thank you for caring for my men. I meant what I said before—I am willing to commit terrible deeds to protect my people. Theudis is more than willing and capable of doing the same. But if you are not, men like he and I can easily maneuver around your limitations. Whatever it takes, don't give Theudis the chance to continue the fight, or we'll all end up dead in this pile of dung."

Soon thereafter, I departed Indulf's company, feeling somehow soiled from the exchange. I said nothing of our conversation, not even to Liberius or Rosamund, yet pondered Indulf's intent all the same. Instead, I gave orders for preparations for another attack to continue, while writing missives to Carthage of our shifting conditions.

Blacksmith forges were lit day and night, while bakers mixed water and flour to feed the massed spearmen under my command. We did not lack for anything iron or wood, yet within another month or so, food would begin to become worryingly scarce, even with the open bounty of the sea. I spared a moment of pity for the natives of Septem, for if their winter stores of grain were depleted in this siege, many would go hungry well into the following planting season, forced to gnaw upon chaff and sour olives once the prior harvest was fully consumed. Another reason why Theudis' landward blockade must come to a quick end, with the bulk of our forces departed for Carthage in a matter of weeks, if only to allow for sustainable development as Septem was rebuilt in Justinian's name. Still, such concerns were relatively distant, and so my attentions were focused upon the daily activities of our army and its efforts to defeat Theudesgel atop Mount Abyla and the swelling ranks of Theudis in the dual rings of trenches outside Septem.

For two weeks after Theudis' initial attack, there was no pitched battle. That is not to say that peace reigned in the hills of Tingitana, for the Visigoth chieftains levied regular harassment of our walls, probing for weakness and inattentiveness. My only response was to order Fulcaris to feint an assault of Mount Abyla, only for a vigorous defense by Theudesgel and three wounded Herulians to end the assault before most of the Herulian foederati could even scale the narrow dirt path to the mountaintop. There were few enough casualties in those exchanges, for Theudis was loath to challenge our bowmen, yet one night attack did yield a dead Vandal sentry and a detachment of ten Visigoths nearly successful in scaling a darkened section of wall with ropes and hooks. Other Vandals rushed to the sudden commotion and threw two Visigoths from the tops of the walls, but the greater point was made: Theudis was transparently willing to use subterfuge, even in spite of his superior numbers.

More torches were carved to line every five cubits of wall, with an additional two torches per tower, ending the threat of night assassins for the duration of the siege. After that, the only suspicious Visigoth movements were tiny rafts floating off to sea, most of which were too small and insignificant to merit a dromon; driving a bolt into the enemy's flimsy hull and sending the sailors into the swirling waters was nearly always gross overkill. Several were sunk, yet others broke free toward Hispania, their tiny oars splashing with chaotic energy as the Gothic men strove northward for freedom and life.

It did not rain. If it had, there would have been little story to tell at this point, for the Visigoths would have devolved into a mob of shivering and sickened beasts. We knew such deprivations well from Tingis, and my silent prayers for a deluge went unanswered for the remainder of my time in Tingitana.

The nights were plenty cold, for the great desert to the south had always been frigid at night, and I could easily imagine Theudis' men suffering in their covered trenches and stolen Roman tents. Dogs brayed at passing foxes day and night, adding to the growing list of nuisances to the broader region. Yet through it all, though there was much activity, there was little to do beyond sit and wait and wonder whether today was the day that Theudis would seize the dice and roll them, wagering all upon a single toss. The waiting, as with the uncertainty, grew more unbearable by the day.

Nearing the third week after our initial fight, however, the waiting ceased. And it did not end with any grand pronouncement, with a proud call to formation with shields and banners billowing in the wind. No, it began as if by accident, with the sounds of unintelligible shouting as sections of the Visigoth trenches began to empty.

At first, I thought this yet another minor skirmish, with fifty or a hundred cocksure youngsters seeking to add their names to the lyrics of a song full of tales of incomparable valor and might. Within moments, however, that illusion was shattered, as more sections of the Visigoth trenches gave way to a hive of movement, with men rushing to don mail and leather and dirt-streaked slaves hauling ladders along the lines. Visigoth scouts scurried in all directions around Septem, an occasional rare horseman galloping hard from the coastline toward Theudis' tent at the center of the attacking formation. Sensing a looming assault, I gathered my officers to determine what, if anything, might be changed in our defense.

"If this is Theudis' attack, it makes no sense," I said to my assembled senior council.

Perenus rose above the others, insistent that his voice should be heard first. "Perhaps this is some trick? An attempt to draw us out into a sally, where some hidden force may attack a more vulnerable Roman army?"

"It's certainly possible," Xerxes added. "And we should be wary. But this feels... different. The Visigoths are not known for sound organization, but even by their own lax standards, this activity seems... scattered."

At Xerxes' prodding, a handful of officers issued crisp reports of Visigoth movements, none of which pointed to an orderly assault. Wisimar told of entire sections of the trench lines absent their chieftains, while an Ostrogoth officer described how the hundred or so war dogs had been positioned in teams of five or ten along the city's southeastern front, leaving the hounds far too diluted a force to elicit fear in any shield wall, let alone one atop battle-tested walls. Most of all, however, Fulcaris had kept a close watch upon Theudis himself, finding the king following a similar hurried routine amidst the chaos.

"He's been yelling at the Visigoth champion, Agila, for much of the morning, although I cannot know about what. They're all half dressed, with some men lacking shields and others spears. As Xerxes says, this does not appear to be a feint. Even if it were, it would be a perilously dangerous one for the Visigoths."

Gunderic, detesting displays of weakness or reluctance for battle, frowned. "Perhaps some power struggle? Fighting between the Goth chieftains? We Vandals would brawl, of course, but never in the sight of another tribe."

More discussion followed, yet our meeting did not have adequate time to decipher each and every kernel of information spied from a distance. Liberius himself drew the council to a close, tempering our excitement with icy warning.

"It seems something has disrupted our enemy," he boomed. "This changes nothing. They *must* take this city, and we *must* hold it. If Theudis is this desperate to force a battle, the causes of the impulsiveness matter little. An enemy is most dangerous when his hand is forced, and that is what we are witnessing now."

Gunderic slammed his hands together, his face tearing into a ravenous grin. "So, we kill them all!"

"Aye," I said. "Kill these bastards and send them back to Hispania. This is our chance to end this war."

After my parting words and Liberius' command, we each disbursed to our various posts along the walls. Curiously, there was no stirring within Mount Abyla's citadel, although Conon paced nervously around the repaired palisade gates all the same. Joined by Sembrouthes, I stood atop Septem's gates, peering across the chaotic Visigoth camp, the noise of their confusion drowning out the maelstrom of activity along Septem's battlements.

Their advance came suddenly. First amongst a group of two hundred ladder carriers opposite Fulcaris' Herulians, and soon thereafter a full thousand along the main gate. Each section held its own measure of order, their shields overlapping as they resisted volleys of Roman arrows. Yet there appeared no cohesion amongst each segment, with individual chieftains urging their men forward despite the ceaseless hail of missiles. They did not even pause against Ascum's ballistae, with dozens of the massive bolts slamming through shield and torso and burying their iron tips into the soil. One ballista bolt pierced through the shoulder of a frontward Visigoth and sliced through the abdomen of the spearman immediately behind, sending both men toppling to the ground while connected by the wooden post.

There was no conventional logic to Theudis' action. Rather than take solace in such disarray, however, I searched hurriedly across my defenses, seeking any deficiency that could be exploited. My officers had prepared well, but even standing ready atop stout walls, our forces were vastly outnumbered by Theudis'.

That fact mattered little to Gunderic or the Vandals, who stamped their spears and taunted the incoming enemy. Nor to Perenus, who was now hale enough to resume command of a thin yet deadly line of Herulian archers poised to launch volley after volley at the steady advance. As before, the bristling curtain of shields deflected the rain of shafts, yet more than a few snuck past Visigoth defenses and struck wounds through gaps in the shield wall.

Even so, there were simply too many of them. For every Visigoth that fell, three more swarmed behind, covering the grasses outside Septem like a hive of iron-coated ants. Xerxes' spikes and trenches stymied their progress, yet even those impediments could not fully halt the hawk-shielded enemy.

"Whatever happens, do not let them break down the gates!" Perenus yelled a dozen paces farther along the walls. "Keep their dogs outside the city!"

"Hit the ram-carriers!" Gunderic added. "Keep that giant prick away from the gate!"

Their commands were punctuated by a further storm of missiles, including their own, with Gunderic's spear personally piercing the knee of a Goth positioned at the front of the ram. The Vandals roared in victory as the man fell screaming, yet the other ram-bearers were saved from a similar fate by a ponderous wooden box that surrounded the ram. Indeed, after dragging the crippled Visigoth away from his post, one of his fellows hoisted the ram's front, pushing the machine ever forward to Septem's gates.

There is nothing glorious about a siege. Any man who says otherwise is either ignorant or a liar. Removed from the swift movements and vast terrain of open battle, a siege is little more than mud and blood and the screaming of men trampled underfoot or thrown from a high perch. Worse, where an open battle at least allows the defeated army to flee, a siege almost always ends in massacre.

Thus, Theudis' second assault upon Septem's walls was a savage, desperate affair, for both armies knew that the less-fortunate band would be butchered without quarter. Ladder teams sprinted to their assigned targets with suicidal abandon, while swifter teams of Visigoths returned our missiles with spears and javelins of their own. Rather than the raw press of men within a shield wall, the siege of Septem was nothing more than a struggle to survive, to kill, and simply end the need to fight over such a desolate place.

We held, if only just. I saw Fulcaris abandon his bow to cut at ascending Visigoths, while Wisimar and Gunderic both slashed upon defenseless enemies who hoisted their bodies up a nearby ladder. I, too, joined the fray, using Khingila's bow to target stray Goths who stumbled between our staves and trenches. Even Liberius joined Ascum in organizing our ballistae, his black cloak swirling in the stiff winds atop Septem's walls.

"Push them back!" the legate cried. "Send them all to Hell!"

Fortune, however, eventually slipped from my grasp. We simply could not prevent the Gothic ram from reaching Septem's gates, with its iron-tipped log soon battering at the layers of reinforced wood and iron. With Gunderic's men tossing stones from above, I ran to Xerxes to organize the defense of the gate. It was then, when tendrils of fear began to snake through my gut, that a horn blasted from Septem's harbor.

"Unknown arrivals!" Xerxes hissed.

"Defend the gate," I called back. "I'll lead the defense of the harbor myself."

Xerxes shook his head. "How did Theudis get warships this quickly?"

The fear in my stomach clamped down with the iron dread of realization. The spy—the one who had first stalked Carthage and now our camp. True, it was impossible to know for certain, yet I could not shake the sense that espionage alone could have enabled the Visigoths' crossing the straits. True, Theudis would still have required the means to destabilize our dromon formation, yet at a minimum, he seemed to know exactly where our warships were. More, he trailed our army outside Tingis with unbelievable timing.

The iron dread clenched tighter, and I cursed myself for carelessness, wondering in vain whether I could have done anything to avoid such a fate.

"It doesn't matter now!" I answered at last. "Just hold that gate, or we'll all be eaten in the streets by slathering hounds."

Leading a hundred Ostrogoths and Cappadocians to the gate, Xerxes braced against the steady battering. Though it felt cowardly to leave Xerxes against Theudis' onslaught, I ordered fifty Herulian bowmen to follow me to the harbor, concerned that a sudden attack from Septem's harbor could just as easily pierce our defenses as the thousands charging our landward gates. Despite Itaxes' efforts, the port's walls remained unfinished and difficult to defend. Our view obscured by rows of warehouses, we descended toward the waterfront, the clamor of the siege muffled by the increasing distance. Such noise was replaced by yet another horn from the harbor, its notes clipped and uneven.

"We can easily defend the walls, but the harbor…" Sembrouthes began.

"I know."

But Sembrouthes was undeterred. "If we don't leave now—"

"Sembrouthes, I know," I interrupted. "Our best chance to survive is to hold this harbor from any landing parties."

"Jesus Christ," Sembrouthes muttered, a rare blasphemy from the Aksumite—though I neither chastised his language nor disagreed with his assessment.

The horn blew again, with the few sentries left upon the harbor shouting with indecipherable excitement. Further horns blew, this time with the distinguishable mellow notes from Apollos' flagship, which was soon echoed by others along the fleet. At least our ships remained, as I dared to hope that Theudis had not outwitted us all.

More horns behind, coming from Septem's gates, followed by a rush of screams and the noise of a hundred men calling out in unison. There was no time, however, for we'd reached the edge of Septem's hill and the stone stairs that led to the incompletely repaired stone walls.

"Lord!" a voice called out. "Lord Varus!"

It took several moments to place its owner, distracted as I was while rushing up the hewn steps toward the top of the wall. Soon, however, I found Itaxes, alongside a half dozen archers, his chest heaving as he sprinted close to me. I raised a hand to caution the man against falling carelessly to the ground, my ears perking as horns blared along Septem's gates.

"Lord Varus, friends!"

And then, I turned to face the sea. No hawk emblems or other foreign sigils that threatened an implacable doom—indeed, no devices to tell their identity at all, at least that I could see. The vessels seemed hardly seaworthy, with hulls sitting low within the choppy waters and rocking as they drew closer and closer to the coastline. Searching the horizon for any distinguishing feature, any outward sign of loyalties, I had opened my mouth to question Itaxes when my gaze caught upon a distant warship at the edge of the horizon, and the mustachioed Frank who stood at the bow.

Now within two hundred paces of Septem's ruined seawall, the figure's Roman armor glinted against the sunlight. As I watched, the distant man unstrapped the helmet from about his chin, allowing a thick mane of long brown hair to brush the iron scales. With his free arm, he waved directly at me.

Uliaris.

Itaxes beamed, his body shuddering with excitement as he shifted his gaze from me back to the approaching fleet. "They are friends, Lord Varus! See the Imperial sigil?"

And so I did, now, at last, if only just. Along the distance, new dromons sailed closer to Septem, dipping their banners as they acknowledged my own ships that stalked along the coastline. At first only two or three, until bristling formations of a full twenty warships crested the horizon. It took all the reserve in my soul to not sink to my knees at the sight of the Chi-Rho soaring into the skies, the Emperor's personal symbol evidence that we had not been abandoned.

"We're coming!" Uliaris cried as his ship skirted beside my fighting platform. "The Franks are coming!"

And true to his word, they did. A full two thousand men, floating on craft that seemed more likely to capsize in ignominy rather than bear a small horde of warriors from Gaul to the tip of Africa. Yet here they were, true to Uliaris' word.

"Sound the horn!" I yelled across the walls. "Reinforcements coming! Tell Liberius to prepare an assault on the Visigoths!"

PACT WITH THE DAMNED

The Visigoths were routed. After navigating the rocky beaches near Septem's harbor, Uliaris' men stormed into the battle, slashing with axes and swords as soon as their feet splashed into shallow water. A hundred Visigoths attempted to prevent any beachhead by quilling the approaching Franks with spears and arrows, but such efforts were in vain.

Most Visigoths escaped, yet several hundred either threw down their weapons in frightened capitulation or were felled fighting to the last. Both Theudis and Agila escaped into the African interior, yet at least two of the Gothic chieftains had fallen to the furious surge of Franks that peeled along Septem's outer walls in quick succession.

At first glance, the Franks were difficult to discern from our Visigothic enemies. Heavily bearded and clad in boiled leather and stinking fur, they garbled an equally unintelligible tongue from bodies filthy with months of sweat and grease. Upon closer inspection, however, a more learned man would find our new allies far stockier than the typical Visigoth, their compact bodies affirming Caesar's accounts of the tribes of Gaul. Many wielded small axes similar to Uliaris' own prized weapons, while others bore small javelins that were flung at an enemy shield wall just prior to closing ranks together.

Most of all, however, the Franks were fearless to the point of lunacy. Though they lacked the raw scorn of death like the Vandals and the brutality of any Hun or Hephthalite, they nevertheless took spirit from one another, heading into combat at a near sprint yet never slackening their good formation as they collided with their undermanned and frightened Visigothic adversaries.

Returning to the landward walls, I found many a Frank gored by a stray Visigoth spear that would have been easily deflected by a more cautious man, yet the Frankish chieftains paid such losses little heed. Their assault saved our splintering gate, which I discovered later had nearly threatened to topple over from repeated blows by the Gothic siege ram.

Romans cheered at their fortune. No war hounds would run rampant through the city, nor would the city's inhabitants be butchered. Arrows fired longingly upon retreating Visigoths as we shouted praise for our mysterious saviors. The final siege of Septem had come to a sudden, blessed close.

I will never know the true course of events in the Visigoth camp that morning, yet even a fool could deduce that Theudis had gained warning of an incoming Frankish attack—even if perilously late. The Gothic chieftains were urged to mount a desperate attack to seize the city before facing a second army, and had nearly succeeded in accomplishing that task.

"I gave you my oath, Lord." Uliaris grinned beneath his moustache. "I've delivered the Franks to you. Without a day to spare, it seems. I have Valerian to thank for the timing… He lent us most of his dromons for transport after subduing the Balearics."

Laughter spilled from my lips despite the rising moans of misery and suffering at the base of the walls. It was hard to disguise my unbridled relief, even as nagging suspicion of the spy's treachery still lingered. "So it seems, and I will need to give thanks to Valerian when he arrives at Septem. But why would the Franks fight for a Roman city? Surely Visigoths and Romans killing one another is to the Franks' benefit?"

"Not as much as the Visigoths being absolutely annihilated," Uliaris said. "I told you before, I had some small standing as a leader of a hundred in the Mosan Franks near the border of Septimania. Many of my chieftains remain there still, and long to sweep the Visigoths clean from southern Gaul."

"Why would you leave Frankia if you enjoyed the trust of such men?"

Another toothy grin. "Let's just say I loved a woman I had no rights to, and she me. That's enough to make any warlord angry. I ran as far to the east as I needed to escape his assassins, and found safety and reasonable pay in a Roman outpost. Before long, Baduarius encountered our camp and encouraged me to sign into Belisarius' army." Uliaris paused, adding, "And where is that hairy bastard?"

"He... he..." I stuttered, unprepared for the question despite the weeks that had passed since that fateful duel. "Baduarius was slain."

Uliaris dropped his head, the gleam of self-assured victory washed from his face. "We must all go to our Creator one day," he said at last. "But I doubt any took so much joy in life as Baduarius, especially when his brother was still with us. When there is more time, I will toast to his memory."

"And I will gladly join you," I added, though not without a note of worry at the threat of Uliaris consuming more wine. Yet the man had more than delivered upon his promise, and for that, both trust and respect must be given. As the last vestiges of battle ceased outside Septem, I shifted our conversation back to our would-be saviors.

"So the Franks want to see Theudis defeated?"

Uliaris nodded. "Yes, but...additional promises were made."

I nodded in understanding, even as I felt the muscles on my neck tensing from the preconditions of such an alliance with a powerful yet distant kingdom. It was predictable—no Frankish warlord would join his strength with the Empire without the prospect of reward. Of all the tribes who carved into the dying Western Empire, the Franks had soared to the most demanding heights of power, instilling their will over various minor tribes of Gaul and Germania. None of the

Empire's scholars or diplomats could be sure, but it was rumored that the young Frankish king Theudebert could call upon the might of a thousand clans and a full million spearmen. It behooved the Empire to appease the distant Franks, yet all the same, I feared what promises Uliaris had made in my name.

"And these conditions are?"

"I would broker a meeting with the Frankish leader, Butilinus, to elaborate," Uliaris answered. "Butilinus is young, a nephew of Clovis, whom the Franks honor above all other fallen kings. He's a bloodthirsty brute, but honest to his word, as all Franks are."

"Do so," I said. "But surely he warned you of their demands?"

Uliaris shrugged. "Not in detail. All I know is that they want the Emperor to sanction Theudebert's dominion over the Alemanni, and to sanction the conquest of the Burgundians."

More warfare. Not surprising, but also not an immediate threat to the Empire's farthest provinces. "The Burgundians have never been friends of Constantinople," I remarked. "But I suppose the Franks want those lands in Gaul to better threaten the Goths of Hispania and Italy?"

Another shrug, this one more noncommittal. "They have no love of Theudis, nor any Visigoth or Ostrogoth warlord. When I was a boy, we constantly warred with Theodoric's armies, who threatened Frankia's survival. With Theodoric dead and the Gothic kingdoms riven, that threat is diminished, but no Frank will ever rest peacefully until control of all Septimania and southern Gaul is in their firm possession."

"Very well," I replied, even as my concerns went unanswered. "Another war amongst the tribes, and Theudebert's right to wage war on the Goths. Neither is against Justinian or Theodora's will. But inform Butilinus of my desire to meet with him, for I would know our new bedfellows more intimately."

After conferring with Liberius, I ordered vacant warehouses along Septem's harbor converted into a makeshift barracks, with a hundred men constructing cots and tables for Frankish use. The legate did voice concern at allowing a foreign power inside our defenses, yet he saw no other choice than to be hospitable to our new guests.

"We will likely need their assistance to swipe Theudesgel from his perch," Liberius reasoned. "And besides, it is the very height of rudeness to insult a traveler who has just recently saved your life. I only wonder whether our Frankish friends will have appropriate etiquette at dinner?"

As the earliest mob of Franks were granted entry through the gates, it soon became obvious that these fur-clad warriors would know little of Liberius' niceties. Unlike the Goths, the wild-haired Franks possessed no favor for Roman clothing or custom, with their bodies wrapped in stinking furs and greasy wool. Most appeared ill at ease as they entered Septem, goggling at the freshly swept streets and orderly buildings, their curiosity heightened only further after gazing upon my men. One Frank gaped at Sembrouthes, tugging a glove from gnarled fingers and reaching forward to brush against the darkened skin of the Aksumite commander's cheek. Sembrouthes tensed, looking to me for instruction.

"Easy," I whispered. "They mean no harm."

"So you say," Sembrouthes muttered. "But the first poxy hand that touches me will be severed at the wrist."

Another Frank scratched vigorously along his groin, his nearby comrade venturing toward a vacant patch of wall and dropping his trousers to urinate. Others passed along skins of an acrid-smelling liquid I later learned was beer, the preferred drink of those tribes too far to the north to harvest grapes for wine. All this grew ever more raucous as hundreds of Franks filed into Septem's forum, spreading into a disorderly semicircle as they spat, vomited, laughed, and otherwise looked around in excited confusion at the diverse peoples that populated Roman Septem.

Curiously, there was no fear to their behavior, even as various Roman centurions paraded in crisp formations along the forum's outskirts. Instead, the only thing to quiet the Franks' disarray was the arrival of a rare mounted figure trotting through the gate, his helmet adorned with feathers and thickly woven mail draped with the cavernous fur of a bear. As the man reached the center of the forum, Uliaris beckoned for me to follow, my only retinue Liberius and the normal cadre of Aksumites.

As we approached, dozens of Frankish warriors all clapped the mounted figure's back as he dismounted, clamoring in their tongue with sounds that closely resembled the war chants long professed by Rome's legions. The young man removed his helmet, revealing plump lips that parted over a smiling, mangled maw of crooked teeth. More cheers sounded despite our approach, forcing Uliaris to pause until the noise softened.

Speaking the Frankish tongue, Uliaris stepped forward, pointing first to Liberius, then to me, and lastly, in a broader wave, to the Aksumites. The young leader grinned again as he raised an empty hand, signaling a nearby Frank to toss him a skin of the foul-smelling beer, which he unstoppered and gulped at greedily before offering its contents to Uliaris. Uliaris swallowed his fill, then offered the skin to me.

"It is customary to drink with allies after a battle," Uliaris urged, seeing my wrinkling nose.

Liberius scratched his chin. "I can't say that I dislike beer, although I am no warrior. That honor is Varus' alone."

I grabbed the skin, drawing it close to my lips before whispering to Liberius in Hunnic. "This smells like goat piss."

"It may very well *be* goat piss," Liberius concurred in his own clipped Hunnic. "But you will drink all the same, and I will clap to your roaring demonstration of manhood."

And so I did, and so he did. The Frankish leader beamed again as our bond was sealed, taking the beer back and draining the skin in a long pull that suggested a desperate thirst. It was not the first time I had come across beer, for other merchants and tribesmen had traded in the sickly sour drink, but it was certainly the first time I was obligated to partake. Calling for another skin, the Frankish leader again drank his fill before making further offerings to Uliaris and myself, yet did not protest as we declined. At last, after belching, then hocking a yellowish glob of phlegm onto the ground, the Frankish leader spoke to Uliaris.

"He names himself Butilinus, son of Vadomar of the Alemanni, nephew of the mighty Clovis," Uliaris translated into Greek. "This is the man who agreed to come to your assistance on behalf of Theudebert, King of all Franks," he added in his own commentary. "I was friendly with his family before venturing to the Empire."

"Friendly?"

Uliaris offered a knowing grin. "You might say he considers me a half brother."

Thus introduced, Uliaris likewise offered additional insights to Butilinus in Frankish, which he then explained were the exploits of Liberius and myself. Butilinus' grin faded into a furrowed and serious gaze, his eyes meeting mine as he nodded in approval. Uliaris began to translate Butilinus' response, but the Frankish warlord raised a hand that curtailed the effort.

"You, me," Butilinus spoke in broken Latin, each word tumbling from his lips. "Leader of spearmen. Defeat Avars, Persians, Vandals. We drink and share tales."

I could not help but smile in surprise. "It would be my utmost honor and pleasure to do so, Lord Butilinus."

The Frankish leader looked upon me with confusion, and I cursed my flowery words drawn from a childhood of bowing and service in the Imperial Court. Uliaris translated, and Butilinus returned to his native tongue.

After dispersing, teams of Franks were instructed to sweep the battlefield for Visigoth survivors, while others granted rest were dispatched to the new barracks I had assigned for Butilinus' use. Initially, I presumed that Butilinus would seek solace and rest, but I was surprised to learn the Franks were eager to feast that evening. With little time to prepare and few spaces to stage so many hundreds of men and women, we elected to erect a sweeping bonfire in the forum's center, with rows of wooden benches and tables arrayed as neatly as possible along the stone walkways. The city's residents strained from the sudden urgency of hosting a foreign army, and I knew that many must have silently worried that filling Frankish bellies would exhaust their dwindling stores of grain, so I ordered Cephalas and Itaxes to send requests for additional winter stores from Carthage and beyond.

The feast did not commence until well after dark, with curious mobs of Franks and Romans eyeing one another from different ends of the forum. Hundreds of torches were erected to hold back the nighttime chill, while guardsmen were given strict orders to forbid any weapons at the gathering, with myself and Butilinus excepted. We would take no chance that a drunken misunderstanding might escalate into full-scale battle, especially as the lingering Visigoth detachment still remained atop Mount Abyla.

To my relief, Butilinus acquiesced to such decorum, although the Franks still attended in full furs and armor. I doubt they had a choice in the matter, for I soon discovered that the common Frankish warriors possessed little other than weapons and cookpots in life, with their women spending hours at a loom replacing soiled shirts and torn trousers that decayed quickly from the roughness of Frankish life.

Just prior to the beginning of the feast, Valerian's dromon had finally taken anchor in Septem's harbor. The victorious captain raised his arms in triumph as he came into my view, yet it was Butilinus who ran forward and playfully pushed the Roman officer before clapping his shoulders.

"As I said before," Uliaris whispered, "Valerian made the transport possible. He saw my men off the Balearics rowing for Gaul and accompanied me north to ward off any attackers. Without him, we would not have made it back in time."

Though I had first met Valerian as a younger, well-groomed Latin in Belisarius' defense of Dara, many weeks at sea had burnt the man's skin into a tough leather. I took his outstretched hand as I voiced my gratitude, finding him smelling strongly of salt and covered in clean yet faded clothing.

"Infested with pirates, those damned islands were," Valerian remarked. "But most ran quickly enough. A few too brave or too greedy to surrender were thrown into the sea, and we installed a magistrate to sort out any hidden criminals that disguised themselves amongst the local population."

Though messages had arrived from Carthage, Valerian's report was new information. The very thought of any sort of hidden criminal rankled me, for I had not yet contended with the possibilities of a spy in our midst, but I brushed that aside for the moment. "So you've succeeded? Your expedition is over?"

Valerian nodded. "As are Mundus' and Troglita's. All former Vandal territories are now under Belisarius' control. I'd celebrate with you, but we need to leave for Carthage as soon as you're able to end your conflict with Theudis."

My eyebrow raised at the thin veil of warning in Valerian's tone. "So soon?"

"Not soon enough, if anything," Valerian said grimly. "Belisarius has been getting couriers from Constantinople. The Emperor is demanding answers for the expedition's successes and is ordering the bulk of the army home. Barking madness, if you ask me."

"Agreed," I said slowly, "but how could the Emperor draw anything but encouragement of Belisarius' successes? We conquered the second-richest portion of the Western Empire in a single season!"

Valerian looked uneasily about before answering. "Someone has been sending private messages back to Constantinople—a spy," he whispered. "I can't be sure who, but Belisarius warned me directly to take care of all that I say."

Spies in Carthage for Theudis. Spies in Carthage for Justinian. Whether they were unconnected or in league with one another, I did not know—though that uncertainty added to my worries. The web grew ever more complex, and a far more formidable foe than even the deepest and most experienced shield wall. I had seen men such as Narses eviscerate the strength of a hundred thousand rioters and separatists in the Nika Riots with little more than whispers and gold, and I had little doubt that similar weapons would gnaw at the newfound loyalty of Roman citizens in Africa. Even the newer additions to Belisarius' army would happily trade dire secrets for a few gold coins from Constantinople.

I swore Valerian to secrecy, informing him that I would speak with Liberius about the matter. I could not help but fully believe that the threat of spies and disaffected traitors had come to inhabit Septem itself.

As the last slivers of daylight faded to the west, our varied groups were directed to tables around Septem's forum. Initially, I had worried that my Heruli and Vandals would refuse the company of our recent Frankish and Alamanni arrivals, yet Perenus, Fulcaris, and Gunderic all took to the meeting with a mirth reserved for drunken bouts at a city tavern. My Greeks were far more reserved, and even Xerxes stood alone in his foreign armor, silently gazing at the vast sea of stinking northerners that must have seemed as distant to a Persian as India was for the Empire. Sensing his apprehension, I summoned the Zhayedan to join Liberius and myself at a table with Butilinus and Uliaris, our ranks joined by a half dozen other minor chieftains in the Frankish horde.

There was no ceremony to the gathering, with the Frankish leader digging a dirt-creased finger deep into his nostril before plopping noisily upon a creaking wooden bench. Other Franks followed in due course, with the Romans all waiting for Liberius' instructions to be seated. Butilinus smirked as the legate offered a simple wave to dismiss any formality amongst our ranks, allowing drink to be poured into what wooden and clay cups were available.

Butilinus wasted little time in fostering conversation, patting Uliaris' hand as he chortled loudly to the other Frankish chiefs. Uliaris' head lowered, the darkness hardly masking reddening cheeks as my bodyguard chuckled in unison with the others. Seeing me frown in confusion, Butilinus leaned closer, attempting to speak without interpretation.

"I catch this one pumping my sister!" Butilinus roared in laughter.

"In fear, he run from room! I never again see him. Never a man so fast!"

Despite the broken Latin, I took his meaning clearly, and felt my eyes widen against the rising chorus of laughter, joined heartily by Liberius. Leaning toward Uliaris, I muttered my own question in Greek.

"*This* is the man whose sister you stole?"

"Aye," Uliaris admitted, sipping lightly at his wooden cup. "Don't worry. The Franks don't care overmuch about impropriety, and Butilinus has a dozen or so siblings to boot. Didn't I tell you we were something like brothers?"

"Then why run, if he sees you as a brother?"

Uliaris offered a playful shrug. "Ah, let's just say that he didn't consider me a brother *at the time*. The entire episode was something of a shock, after all."

Baskets of bread and iron cauldrons of steaming liquid were carried to each table as Uliaris and his Frankish kinsmen shared private conversation. Though early in the evening, my eyes sagged from lack of sleep, with only the thought of a long-delayed meal and a cramping stomach keeping me awake in the darkness. I strained to sit upright and maintain rapt attention, the temptation to rest my head almost overwhelming.

Thankfully, just as the feast was set forth without any pomp, so, too, was the meal a casual affair that began as soon as the closest Frank tore off a hunk of dark bread, dunking it into the cauldron for a sopping bite.

It was simple fare; there was hardly time to prepare anything more sumptuous or complicated. A thin soldier's gruel, its scant vegetables and precious morsels of fish meat suggesting that, though Septem was far from starving, its residents were limited to what food gave sufficient nourishment but could never fully fill rumbling bellies.

Thankfully, Butilinus' men supplemented our meager offerings by slaughtering a dozen fattened pigs that had been hauled in with their seafaring cargo, dressing thick cuts of bloody meat with salt and roasting them on spits near our bonfire. The wafting scent of fresh meat nearly brought tears to my eyes, the dripping fat collecting in sizzling pools of longing along the fire's edge. It took every fiber of reserve to restrain an urge to filch a chunk of cooked meat. Gunderic had no such reservations, stealing an entire hog and slamming it happily upon a table shared by Vandals and Franks. Neither group could understand the other, yet the common language of copious drink and rich food overcame any awkwardness.

Goaded by Butilinus, the other Frankish chieftains gorged themselves on beer and wine, frequently toasting their hosts and demanding I reciprocate. To my surprise and delight, Uliaris abstained from drinking to any but the most insistent of tributes. Liberius, meanwhile, drained each cup with nary a moment of hesitation.

"It may be prudent to mind your consumption," I whispered in Hunnic after a while.

Liberius hummed, his lips parting just slightly in a flit of mischief. "Truer words have never been spoken. But you will find, my dear boy, that the Franks distrust a man who won't toast whatever braggart is calling himself a chief or lord. I strive to follow custom, and I leave it to you to ensure that I survive such an ordeal."

And to his credit, Liberius did not hesitate to share cups with each of the Frankish leaders. After several rounds, Butilinus took Liberius' arm and crossed it against his own, and thus linked, the men shared a great swallow of the foul beer. Liberius did not balk and even hooted laughter at the exchange, though I did note that above his broad smile, his eyes were constantly shifting, lacking any of their usual innate sparkle and moving instead with the narrowed gaze of a hunter stalking wounded prey.

The sagging weight of fatigue grew weightier after a full meal, which I admit I partook of to the point of gluttony. I can only imagine that our example, with hundreds of men drunk and stuffed with unnecessary food, must have been a terrible insult to Theudesgel's survivors. At one point, Perenus stood atop his stool and raised a cup to Mount Abyla, swaying as he called fruitlessly to the Visigoth holdouts.

"Theudesgel! I'm drunk, but you're still ugly! Come down and fight, you horse's cock!"

Perenus drained his cup before jumping from his stool and rushing toward our table, followed closely behind by an exasperated Rosamund. After greeting Butilinus and boxing me on the ears, Perenus stumbled over to Xerxes, tugging on the man's cloak.

"Come on, you dour bastard!" Perenus grunted. "I'm going to force you to have fun if I have to beat it out of you!"

Rosamund leaned to my ear, sighing. "He's hopelessly drunk, Varus. I *told* him to be careful, lest he bring the flux back on. But oh no, woe betide any woman who tries to separate a man from strong drink." She spread her palms and rolled her eyes.

I laughed, which Rosamund did not appreciate. "Make sure he doesn't kill himself."

"I've become his mother," Rosamund complained, but she smiled, the faint aroma of wine lacing her own breath.

Rosamund attempted to guide Perenus away from the gathering. "You'll turn your guts to liquid death, you idiot." But he drunkenly and stubbornly refused to depart. Instead, he wrapped his arms around Xerxes, laughing as the Persian visibly stiffened at the gesture.

"I'm gonna force you to enjoy yourself!" Perenus slurred to Xerxes. "You could cut the wings from a fly, but you know what? I think your face'd shatter into a thousand pieces if you laughed once. You're coming with me!"

Wide eyed, Xerxes turned to me, pleading for relief. "Varus—"

"Don't look to me for help." I chuckled. "If I had the ability to refuse drunk Perenus anything, I would have suffered far less trouble through the years."

Perenus raised a finger at me—or roughly toward me, anyway—and waved his hand about. "That's right! And don't you forget it!"

Butilinus frowned, mumbling to Uliaris for explanation. After receiving Uliaris' translation, Butilinus beamed, rising from his seat before lifting a half-empty skin from our table. Striding around his seated compatriots and joining Perenus, Butilinus lifted Xerxes clean to his feet, raising the skin and tipping it near Xerxes' face.

"Bah, fuck you all!" Xerxes cried, trying to squirm out of reach. "I just want to sit in peace!"

Holding Xerxes still, Perenus offered a sloppy salute with a free arm. "We drink to honor our glorious dead and celebrate for those who cannot! Now open your mouth, or I'll pinch your nose shut!"

With a litany of curses in Persian, Xerxes eventually surrendered to the two men, swigging deep gulps as a hundred warriors chanted at the man who engineered the defense of Septem—and as they did, Xerxes could not help but smile, beads of wine dribbling from the corners of his mouth as he drained the skin's contents. Butilinus roared in approval, returning to his seat and swirling another cup into his open maw.

As Perenus and Rosamund dragged Xerxes away for further mandatory entertainment, Uliaris finally noted the need to discuss the business at hand—and soon, before the Frankish delegation became too drunk to speak or remember the night's events. Uliaris made a similar pronouncement to the Franks, who grew silent as Butilinus nodded in approval, his eyes falling upon me with expectation.

Fulfilling the role of a grateful recipient of aid, I began our negotiation. "We thank Lord Butilinus, and the Great King Theudebert of the Franks and the Alemanni, who came to the Empire's need. I understand that you have needs of your own, and that the Emperor's men may provide some solace."

The translation was sluggish, as all men at the table swayed from the influence of strong drink, yet I did not begrudge Uliaris of his need for deliberate and clear language. From my words, Butilinus nodded, offering suggestions of Frankish needs, which Uliaris nodded and spoke to me in Greek.

"As you now know, my father—Butilinus' father—was an Alamanni chief," Uliaris began. "The Alamanni are fully integrated into the Frankish kingdom, and Theudebert requests recognition of the Franks' right to rule such lands and peoples."

Stealing a glance at Liberius before responding, I nodded. "God has blessed the Franks. The Emperor, through his legate, approves this gesture of friendship."

The Frankish chiefs grunted in approval after the translation. Some grunted to their leader, who nodded before relaying his ask. "We would also seek the Emperor's sanction to invade the lands of the Burgundians. They are a despicable people, who feast upon the flesh of the slain and defy the Christian faith of your emperor and our king."

Again, I shared a glance with Liberius, who merely shrugged. "The Empire has no treaty with the Burgundians," I replied, "who have long been an enemy to the Empire. I wish you good fortune in your war to come. It brings the Emperor and his legate delight to bring satisfaction to our Frankish guests."

Butilinus offered additional grunts of appreciation, his chieftains following suit. Yet the Frankish warlord did not hesitate to seek a third request—this one far more sweeping.

"My king would make war on Theudis, and I would seek your aid."

I frowned, choosing my words carefully. "The Empire's war will finish as soon as Abyla is taken. The Emperor will likely recall the bulk of the expedition within a month."

Butilinus grinned as Uliaris spoke his interpretation, and quickly dictated his reply.

"You do not understand me," Uliaris translated. "I do not require your men to invade Hispania. All I ask for you to do is nothing at all."

I am not ashamed to admit that I did not initially understand Butilinus' meaning. Such words brought nothing but confusion, and I took them at first for an error in translation. In my silence, however, as I frowned at Uliaris, another voice spoke in Frankish—but to the Frankish chieftains, not from among them.

All eyes shot at Liberius. Butilinus was stunned, his mouth agape at the Frankish words that spilled from the legate's pursed lips. In that moment, Liberius' eyes sparkled as he repeated his pronouncement, the Frankish words translated hurriedly by Uliaris.

"He says 'nothing,'" Uliaris translated, "is not nothing.'"

The others at our table fell into an astounded silence. I, however, could not resist a question.

"You speak Frankish?" I demanded of Liberius.

Liberius winked. "You don't? Ah, Varus, my failures multiply!"

"But—"

"Tread carefully," the legate interrupted, switching to a Hunnic whisper. "These men are our guests, but do not mistake them for friends. Stay sober, if you can, and be hesitant to grant any requests asked of us."

Butilinus leaned closer, his gaze stern and his lips curved as he folded his hands atop a fresh skin of beer. He then closed his eyes, offering a single bob of his head before speaking directly to the legate. Uliaris shifted toward me, whispering a translation into my ear as the two engaged in a more rapid give-and-take.

"In Frankia, we have a saying: The man who carries a sword and spear against our enemies is one to be praised. My king offers thanks for your intervention against that child-killer Theudis, but your war is nearing its conclusion. All we ask is for you to maintain your current holdings... at least until our own conflict in Septimania is resolved."

At that, it was Liberius' turn to smirk in skepticism. "I would not presume to understand the mind of kings, but it appears that Theudebert would have the Empire sit its soldiers idly at our freshly liberated borders, tying down Visigothic forces that could otherwise be turned against your own invasion in the north?"

Butilinus shrugged. "You benefit from such an arrangement too. Your leader rules, what, some two thousand tired, ailing, and homesick men? You are a thousand miles from any hope of reinforcement, with only your ships keeping a hundred thousand vengeful Visigoths penned in Hispania. A wise man would understand when the tide is at its highest."

Liberius chuckled. "I would refer to myself as a man of many talents, but wisdom is not among them. And I absolutely trust you at your word, but my young friend here"—Liberius pointed at me—"is less trusting. He insists that the Franks recognize the Empire's claim on the Pillars, and all of Mauretania."

"Done," Butilinus blurted.

"But!" Liberius continued. "Dear Varus is also concerned that the Franks are not being fully forthright in their requests. Surely Theudebert did not allow thousands of his loyal spearmen across the sea to only ask a rival nation to simply taunt a common foe?"

Butilinus chortled in laughter, his chieftains following the young warlord's example with a cackling mirth. The tail of his unkempt beard grazed against the beer-soaked table as he laughed, the layers of pork grease causing his cheeks and mouth to glisten in the firelight.

"You are a slippery fellow, Legate." Butilinus grinned. "We do not tolerate such men in Frankia."

"Then you and I both will give thanks that I find myself elsewhere," Liberius countered. "But, simpering weakling that I am, the truth is plain. Speak your desires, before my young friends fall dead from lack of sleep."

"Theudebert requests your emperor declare a formal alliance with Frankia," Butilinus admitted. "Since the fall of the western emperor, chaos has ruled its territories. The Franks will bring order to the masses."

For once, Liberius had no quip or retort. Instead, he shuffled upon the bench, straightening his back as he leered upon his Frankish colleague. He did not turn to me, yet his Hunnic words were clearly addressed for none other.

"This is unwise, but I doubt that Uliaris has left us any choice in the matter. What say you?"

All the Franks looked about in confusion, with several muttering to Uliaris for a translation. But Uliaris merely shrugged, his eyes turned to me for instructions. I offered none, my own attention focused upon Liberius' unmoving form.

"Surely an alliance with a strong power is always a wise maneuver for the Emperor?" I asked in Hunnic.

"Powerful nations only make alliances for self-defense, or to exploit those they deem weak," Liberius answered, his eyes fixed upon Butilinus. "And the Franks require no support to defend Gaul. They likely want more, and Justinian's blessing gives them all the justification needed to seize all their desires."

By now, Butilinus had joined in the Frankish muttering, their words growing hurried and impatient. Again, all Uliaris could do was raise a hand for calm, yet I could sense our guests had begun to take offense at our Hunnic exchange. Still, I asked one final question of the legate.

"Italy? Hispania?"

Liberius' head shook. "More, but these lands are certainly coveted. This leaves us at an impasse. Will you accede to their request and give Theudebert more legitimacy than any barbarian king since Attila? Or will you reject Butilinus and send the Franks away at first light?"

I was weary. Too long deprived of the carefree rest of a full night's sleep, with no threat of waking in twitching fits and choking gasps, clamoring for respite from the painful weight upon my chest that had settled with Theudis' sweeping defeat. Now, full of greasy pork and some measure of drink, I wanted nothing to do with yet another struggle, especially against an adversary who outnumbered my Romans inside Septem's walls. So I resigned myself to such soul-draining fatigue, unthinking of the consequences that my decision would have upon the lives of millions.

"Tell him we concur. As you say, I do not believe we have any other choice."

Liberius neither moved nor spoke, and I started to repeat myself for fear that the older man had not heard my answer. Yet as I did so, Liberius flicked his wrist, offering an open palm to Butilinus. Relieved, Uliaris translated the final exchange between the two leaders.

"Emperor Justinian accepts your proposal. In return, the Emperor appreciates King Theudebert's acknowledgment of Imperial dominion not only over the Pillars, but also the provinces of Baetica, Lusitania, and all the lands within three days' ride of New Carthage."

Butilinus' face rose at the additional demand, but he did not balk. "Done. I wish you well in the wars to come."

More beer and wine were passed around the table to celebrate the treaty, with Butilinus calling for all within earshot to join in the merriment. I admit, I was overtaken by a sense of optimism that I had not felt since arriving in Africa, believing the struggle and conflict of the region nearly completed and peace restored. I even dismissed the impassive look upon Liberius' unblinking face, his eyes never parting from Butilinus as the Franks drank their fill. Blessedly, the feast soon ended, although many remained around the bonfire until the early hours of dawn, overindulging in food and drink with a near-riotous atmosphere.

As I excused myself for sleep, I did not realize that I would not share another conversation with Butilinus for many years to come. Truthfully, even had I known as much, I would not have cared, for the Franks were distant from my family in Macedonia, and my task had nearly come to completion. Fate had different intentions for Butilinus and myself, in a distant future and in a distant land. I did not yet share Liberius' silent worries, but without a doubt, I should have.

For my accord with Butilinus and the Franks would prove, eventually, to be a poor one.

FAREWELL TO HERAKLES

Butilinus and the bulk of his army departed the following morning. Escorted by twin dromons, the Franks ventured back to Septimania and the bloody war that awaited two massive hosts of armored men. A detachment of two hundred Franks remained in Septem to assist with our final conquest of Mount Abyla, which I quickly assigned to Uliaris' command.

Liberius stood beside me atop the harbor walls as we waved at the departing Franks. Once their transport hulk had vanished along the northern horizon, he escorted me back to a squat wooden building that housed several of my senior officers. Even before reaching the doorway, a clinging aroma of stale wine and pungent bile emanated in the breeze. Liberius, however, was undeterred, pushing open the unlocked door and striding inside without a moment's hesitation.

Inside was nothing short of the personification of human misery. A full dozen of my officers lay about in their own filth, reeking of vomit and moaning at the veneer of daylight that covered the room at our entrance. Fulcaris slept in a crude ball in the corner, while Rosamund lay sprawled upon a lone straw mat, her snores rumbling against the walls. Most curious of all was Xerxes, who slept in nothing but a loincloth, his clothing rolled to cushion his head during sleep.

Only Perenus was truly awake as we wafted through the repulsive stench, kicking aside Cephalas' discarded cloak, careful to sidestep Wisimar's prone form—and awake or no, Perenus appeared to wish for death.

He heaved, his bloodshot eyes leveling on Liberius' immaculate form. "Liberius, how are you still standing?"

Liberius snorted in derision. "The trick, my friend, is to regurgitate *before* falling asleep, not after."

"Waste of good wine, that is," Perenus muttered, his guts emptying heartbeats later into an overflowing bucket of sweetish stinking bile.

Liberius nodded, bending over to lift a bucket of cool water, which he summarily emptied over the Lazic prince. Perenus squealed in shock as he shot to his feet.

"Come," the legate ordered. "I have given you license to enjoy yourself, but there is still work to be done."

Stumbling about, Perenus muttered words of bitter hatred as he scrounged together a clean linen shirt and trousers and donned them in place of his current clothing. Admittedly, I, too, wondered at how Liberius appeared so hale in the morning after our feast with the Franks, with nary a complaint or even the telltale rubbed temples of an aching head. Instead, he brought the two of us briskly to the forum, offering his account of the morning's events.

"This expedition must end quickly, yet victory is in our grasp. I received a messenger from Theudis just before dawn. However, they insist upon meeting with Varus rather than me."

My eyes widened despite my hazy mind. "Theudis? How?"

Liberius beamed. "I dispatched Conon to seek the Visigoth king out even before our evening's feast. Though defeated, our enemy still skulks in the hinterlands, licking his wounds."

"But why treat with him when his force is broken? Surely he must surrender to us?" Perenus asked.

"Alas, *defeated* is not *broken*." Liberius sighed. "Theudesgel is still locked safely atop Mount Abyla, and at least a thousand Visigoths roam free in Tingitana. Even if half are crippled with wounds or lamed by foot sores, Theudis has more than enough men to make any protection force we leave behind live in constant stress. A single Visigoth chieftain can destabilize all Mauretania, leaving Theudis to return in strength to Hispania and give battle to our newfound allies."

"But…" I stopped short, fearful of insulting Liberius, before I plunged ahead. "Wouldn't a separate agreement with Theudis be a direct betrayal of Butilinus?"

Liberius nodded. "Of course. Just the same way that the Franks have no intention of remaining our friends as soon as the Gothic nations are destroyed. Theudebert does not require us to *invade* Hispania, only to keep forces deployed near Septem. We can maintain our treaty in good faith, yet end the war with the Visigoths without further bloodshed. Our paltry numbers are an insignificant threat to Theudis' horde, but our dromons are a mighty nuisance. Both parties stand to benefit."

Perenus brightened, momentarily abandoning his sickened posture. "And Theudis will command Theudesgel to relinquish Mount Abyla's citadel."

"Precisely," Liberius concluded. "We leave Theudis strong enough to resist the Frankish armies, while granting Theudebert's request all the same. Mauretania belongs to the Empire, and nearly all of us get to return to Carthage."

"Brilliant," Perenus muttered, then paused to retch again in a nearby gutter. "But Legate, why do you require me, and not just Varus?"

At that, Liberius smiled, revealing a full row of teeth. "Butilinus is not entirely a fool. His remaining men watch every move that Varus and I make, and would notice sinister negotiations with a hated enemy. But if Varus accompanies you with segments of the foederati on a western patrol…"

"The Franks won't suspect anything amiss," I finished.

Liberius laughed. "They probably will. But they'll have a hard time proving it. Especially with a party of drunken slobs guiding Varus' path. A Visigothic delegation will arrive at the Cave of Herakles in three days' time. Take fifty men of your choosing, and pack for a long march. Once you are well beyond the line of sight, boats will be anchored to ferry you the remaining distance. You have one week. Do not squander the opportunity I have afforded you."

We did not tarry. Within an hour, Perenus had kicked awake a Herulian centurion before requisitioning packs, weapons, fresh boots, and extra rations of twice-baked bread—all while pausing to empty his stomach of stale wine and sour beer now and again, yet he did so with a cheerful grin. Leaving a half-conscious Fulcaris to command the remaining Herulians, Perenus and I led our detachment through Septem's lesser coastal gate, bounding along the stone road and wrapping our cloaks over our bodies for warmth.

Liberius had planned such a maneuver well. A half dozen small transports awaited us within two hours' march, and those ferried us the short distance toward open water and two awaiting dromons. From there, favorable winds drove the warships to Herakles' Cave, its rising hills easily recognizable from our previous meeting. Though many of the Herulians rowed to shore, Perenus alone accompanied me into the cave, where we saw no sign of Visigoth activity.

Perenus gaped at the dancing lights and peaceful pools of water that echoed along the limestone walls. "In Lazica, we told tales of Herakles reaching the far end of the world, but never did I imagine I'd see it."

Though I smiled at my friend's wonderment, I brought a finger to my lips, my ears attuned to the reverberating echo from the cave's heart. Perenus acceded, yet could not help but place a hand upon the wet stone walls, whispering in wonder.

"Herakles…"

After gently smacking Perenus, I guided him through the gloom of the cave's descent, navigating through poorly lit bends and ducking to avoid overhanging rock. Soon, the graded floor leveled out, its slick veneer robbing our hobnailed boots of traction. Though I knew to anticipate this, Perenus slipped and crashed against a wall, cursing loudly as he nursed his shoulder. Though I urged Perenus to be quiet, a Latin voice echoed from the cave's interior.

"Ah, I was wondering when you Romans would arrive. I was growing concerned that the legate's request was little more than an insult."

It was a familiar voice but lacked Theudis' faint rasp. As we ventured farther into the primary antechamber, beams of light from the cave's opening to the sea illuminated a plump figure sitting near a pool of water. Neatly stacked boots rested nearby, allowing the man to kick playfully at the lapping waves that gently brushed along the cave opening.

Even without that distinctive armor of his, easily considered lavish by the standards of a Gothic tribe, Agila was immediately recognizable. "Liberius' man warned that you would not arrive alone," he remarked coolly. "Who, pray tell, is our guest?"

"Perenus of Lazica, leader of all Belisarius' foederati," I answered.

Though Perenus could recognize his own name and a few warlike Latin words, much of our exchange was lost on him, producing only a puzzled look upon his face. This did not go unnoticed by Agila, who nodded to Perenus as he hoisted himself from the pool, kicking wet shins and feet free of icy seawater.

"And does our friend Perenus speak for himself?"

"Latin is not a fluent tongue for him," I answered. "Only Greek, Lazic, and some Herulian."

Agila shook his head, raising an arm in apology. "A pity, for I speak little Greek. Offer dear Perenus my humble regards."

"I keep hearing my name," Perenus interjected in a whisper. "What's he saying?"

"That you are a donkey's arse for not knowing any Latin," I grumbled. "Tread carefully. This one is the king's closest war chief. For now, just nod and smile as if you've been given a compliment."

Perenus shrugged and fixed his face into a bland expression of greeting. As he returned Agila's bow, I insisted upon more direct progress to our talks.

"I have little time here, Chief Agila, and much to do before my

Frankish guests suspect something amiss."

Agila merely chuckled. "Even my king admits that he underestimated you, Excubitor Varus," he said, holding his head in a bow as his words finished.

Though I had met with Agila before, I still found it difficult to believe that the figure before me had bested Indulf in single combat, or had held the gate of Tingis against overwhelming force. He hardly seemed a warrior, with all the posture of a simpering flatterer. Yet I refused to allow myself to fall into complacency, for Theudis would not allow a weakling or a fool to represent him against an enemy.

"I offered Theudis peace, and he slapped my hand away," I declared, raising my voice as I towered over Agila. "And now his forces are broken on unfriendly soil, with Franks ravaging his northern lands."

Agila nodded, his eyes closed as if theatrically mourning such a decision. "So true! And my own clan will likely be subjected to the worst of the Frankish rapine. One wonders why the noble Romans would condemn themselves to a pact with such heathens."

A tear trickled along the corner of Agila's eye but was quickly cuffed away. Perenus frowned, his lips curled in disgust as he attempted to decipher our exchange, but there was no time to translate. The Visigoth continued his condemnation of the Franks, his tone dropping as he relayed words that likely spilled from Theudis' own lips.

"You need the Visigoths strong enough to keep the Franks from swallowing the world," Agila said. "Theudis is willing to make a gift of Tingitana if you Romans leave only a token garrison to maintain order. I suggest you accept, for you shall not receive a better offer, especially if some of the less hospitable chieftains convince the king that we have the strength to throw you all into the sea."

Such negotiations, like single combat, were a delicate dance. Though Theudesgel occupied Mount Abyla, he could no longer hope for reinforcement or resupply, and further resistance atop the mountain was meaningless even if my battle with Agila continued. However, for his part, Theudis could not be seen to accept the loss of a hundred battle-hardened warriors and a vaunted warlord with nothing to show in return—especially now that war with the Franks was looming. And, though weakened, the Visigoths remained a dire threat to Septem's future, making it essential for me to find an acceptable peace that would not inspire another war for at least another two or three years—hopefully longer. I would have to yield something—likely wealth to pay off the Visigoth chieftains—yet I could not accept Agila's paltry offer. As with any delicate negotiation, I could do nothing other than to insist, politely yet firmly, on further demands.

"Gift?" I scoffed, raising my chin in a pretense of disgust. "You cannot gift what I already possess. If Theudis were to order Theudesgel from Mount Abyla, and surrender control of Mount Calpe and the villages within a day's march of that Pillar, that would be an appropriate gift."

Agila chuckled, yet I forced myself to stay motionless and stern. In truth, a hidden force of Visigoths could easily have swept over Herakles' caves, butchering my few men as revenge for Butilinus' destruction of the Visigothic army. Yet negotiations, like battles, cannot be won by the timid. An underequipped bargainer may yet triumph if he presents himself brazenly, regardless of whether his threats are only impossible shadows.

Agila scowled. "Mount Abyla you shall have, whatever good such a desolate place might afford you. But Theudis cannot surrender a single grain of Visigothic beaches to you Romans. The other chiefs would never allow such a show of weakness."

"Not surrender," I corrected, offering a slim smile. "A gift to seal a truce, as you say. And in return for such generosity, Emperor Justinian and Lord Belisarius would happily gift King Theudis a discreet donation of gold in support of his valiant efforts to hold back the Franks."

Agila's scowl remained, yet his eyes widened as he considered my words. "What kind of donation?"

"Half your weight in gold," I shot back.

"Twice that," Agila countered, finally surrendering to a sly grin. "And I am not a small man."

"Then the deal is struck," I concluded. "Roman control over Mauretania Tingitana, as well as the immediate area around Mount Calpe."

Agila nodded. "I will present your offer to Theudis. I imagine he will be happy to put this unhappy business behind us, for the Franks are a far more dangerous foe. In return, I will personally meet you outside Septem's gates with a banner of truce, and will convince Theudesgel to abandon his perch."

"As long as he leaves our lands unmolested, it may stay that way," I answered. "But a single raid, a single slave taken, and the Emperor will send his entire army to sweep Theudis and his generals from Hispania. That is a promise that I intend to keep personally."

"As you say," Agila offered in surrender, though I could have sworn there was a hint of mockery lacing his reply. "We can both be thankful that our attentions lie elsewhere."

The deal thus agreed, Agila offered an outstretched arm. I grasped him by the wrist, surprised at the piercing grip with which he took my own.

Agila's eyes narrowed, a cruel smile shaping his thin lips. "My Lord King knows far more than you realize, Varus of the Heruli. And he never lies—much like yourself, Varus the truth-teller. Our cousins in Italy will be far less hospitable than we Visigoths."

I did not reply, nor did Agila appear to expect any retort. Instead, after dropping Agila's grasp, I gestured to Perenus of my desire to depart the cave. We exited in silence, interrupted only by a final call from our enemy.

"Three days, Lord Varus!" Agila boomed, plopping back into a seated position. The sound of splashing feet followed us as we left the cave, its echo still discernible as we traced the worn trail down to the coastline. Rejoining our guardsmen, we boarded the landing craft and rowed to the dromons, leaving Agila and the legend of Herakles behind.

"So Liberius' plan worked?" Perenus asked when we were safely aboard the ship. "Is it back to Septem, then?"

"Not yet," I remarked. "We have three days, and I have a mind to step foot on the shores of Hispania. Let's see what Thurimuth and Sindual have accomplished in their efforts."

The voyage was a brief one, yet dusk was not far in coming after our departure from the cave. Men rowed throughout the night as we proceeded northeast, still winds demanding their labor to propel us forward, but the calm seas were a welcome blessing. By dawn, we neared our destination, and came into view of the more famous of the Pillars of Herakles.

Words cannot adequately describe Mount Calpe. Of all the wonders that God has bestowed onto the world, this is one without true comparison. A towering wedge of stone atop a rounded promontory, it seemed less a mountain and more a great tower of earth that soared above the surrounding sea, with thin streams of clouds billowing along the craggy summit. Though Mount Abyla had been formidable with its easily defended peak, Mount Calpe could have swallowed an entire Imperial city, its looming cliff like a mighty finger of Herakles himself jutting out from the sea.

Gawking upward, my gaze fixed on the mount, I did not immediately take note of the small village at its base. It was a squat thing, perhaps a dozen thatched huts and a corral of sheep, and would not have drawn a second glance from even the most desperate band of seaborne pirates. It was not until a soaring Imperial banner came into view that I grinned at Thurimuth's success. Farther inland, I discerned the outline of a sweeping palisade fort, replete with twin layers of ditches and manned fighting platforms that defended the village from any would-be attackers. As we drew closer, I discovered other emblems flying beneath that of Justinian, with my own ouroboros faded to a deep gray yet still flapping in the wind.

I had no intention of staying longer than necessary. But all the same, I could not deprive myself of the chance to step foot on Hispania, the land of Carthage and of Caesar alike. Perenus raised an eyebrow as he caught me grinning absently as our dromons approached and took anchor.

"I'm just thinking of the tales I will tell Samur and Maryia once all this is over."

Perenus nodded. "Not a bad life, for a Lazic foundling and a Herulian slave to conquer the Pillars of Herakles. I wouldn't blame them for not believing you."

"Indeed." I laughed. "But what a tale it is."

Perenus and I took a dozen spearmen onto a raft and rowed our way to shore. True to his character, Thurimuth and a dozen of his own soldiers stood at rapt attention in greeting, their weapons honed to a savage edge and their armor polished to gleaming. Yet despite their impeccable presentation, I could not help but notice the deep rents in their shields; clean-cut Thurimuth had even begun to bear a bushy beard beneath the tight iron of his helm. With our boat nearing the shore, Perenus hopped into the shallow waves, hauling us the rest of the way ashore, and I soon joined his example, my boots crunching against the slippery pebbles of Hispania's coastline.

"Welcome to Hispania, Commander." Thurimuth saluted. "You will find that all is in order. I congratulate you on your success."

"And I do likewise for yours." I saluted in return, subsequently ordering a more casual walk back to Thurimuth's fort. "The Empire is in your debt for taking and holding such a place."

Thurimuth shrugged. "It was simple enough. It's hard to approach without reliable cogs, and the Visigoths have generally left us alone."

I gestured toward Thurimuth's men. "Your shields say otherwise."

Thurimuth's head bowed in admission. "Simple, perhaps, but not effortless. There was a skirmish the day we landed, and another around the same time when we heard of your first battle against Theudis. Otherwise, we've sent scouting teams to range deep into Hispania, and have discovered little resistance."

Before entering the fort, I drew to a sudden halt. Crouching low,

I dug my hand into the soft soil, allowing the coarse mixture of dirt, sand, and stones to flow through my fingers. Though I had traveled far in such a short time—Moesia, Tauris, Armenia, Mesopotamia, and Africa—somehow, standing upon this hallowed ground left me in stunned silence. The others stood politely in waiting, and soon I forced myself back to attention.

"There will be no further resistance," I explained. "Theudis has acceded to our demands. The Empire controls all Mauretania and a day's march around Mount Calpe."

Thurimuth's men stamped their spears in affirmation of our victory. The clattering only grew as we entered Thurimuth's fort, with a thickly bearded yet immaculately attired Sindual leading the cheer. Though Uliaris and others had mocked Thurimuth's dour nature in the years prior, none could ever deny the man's tenacity, nor his strict adherence to military doctrine. Not a single soldier had allowed his uniform to rot or armor to rust, and all seemed as battle ready as the day they departed Tingitana.

Summoning Sindual, I spoke plainly to the two officers, recounting all that had happened in the past three days. Nothing was a complete surprise, largely due to our constantly moving fleet of dromons, yet Thurimuth quickly hit upon the problem that I had long dreaded even before the end of Septem's siege.

"You will need some to remain behind to keep the peace," Thurimuth muttered.

I nodded. "Yes. Not many, for our truce with the Visigoths demands small occupying forces. But at least two dozen men here, and another fifty in Septem."

Thurimuth nodded. "Someone must stay here to honor Baduarius' memory," he rumbled. "Give me triple wages for a hundred spearmen and three dromons, and we'll keep the peace in Mount Calpe. I will visit Septem as soon as I'm able, but you'll need to appoint a commander there as well."

I winced at Baduarius' name, remaining silent for several heartbeats before I spoke. "You're sure?"

His request, in turn, was no surprise to me; I had little doubt that Thurimuth would hold this post until the skies tore open. Christ could be returned in all his glory, and even then Thurimuth would wait for orders to abandon his post.

"Absolutely. None in my detachment would disagree, although I begrudge none who wish to return home. Especially those with families."

"You will have your gold, and extensive commendation to Belisarius and the Emperor," I promised. "I will take Sindual with me, for I may require the Herulians soon enough."

Thurimuth raised a hand to his chest. "Your will, Commander. I will not fail you, the legate, the general, or the Emperor."

Only six of Thurimuth's men opted to leave with our dromons— including Sindual, although initially he did not agree willingly. Before the noonday sun, we shared a meal with Thurimuth's men and distributed much-needed food and supplies, with the promise that more would soon arrive from Septem. None complained, and many grinned at the prospect of the hefty bonuses that would be doled out in the coming months—all for a post that had quickly become one of the safest in the Empire. Soon thereafter, I directed the men back to the boats before sharing a final private word with Thurimuth.

"You knew Baduarius well?" I asked.

Offering a rare smile, Thurimuth nodded. "I believe most in Belisarius' army must have. I've never met a man with so much unashamed joy for life. I offered prayers when I heard of his passing, but I honor his sacrifice. Beneath all the brute strength and thirst for joy, Baduarius was unmatched in honor. I hope one day that I may demonstrate similar willingness to sacrifice for my friends."

"You already have," I offered.

"That's kind of you," Thurimuth continued. "It was obvious, by the way, that Baduarius loved you as a brother. I did not know Dagisthaeus well, but I cannot imagine Baduarius treating you much differently. He told me himself how proud he was to serve under you."

It was all I could do to keep from weeping. I would have traded all the wealth I possess to reach back across the veil of time and treat Baduarius more gently, for perhaps he might still be alive today if I had rewarded his friendship and trust with understanding. Though Thurimuth could not know the bite of his words, the image of Domeric sending Baduarius to the ground caused my breath to catch. Offering my farewells to Thurimuth, I turned and hid my eyes, whispering a prayer that God might safeguard Baduarius' soul. Most of all, however, I prayed for forgiveness from my fallen friend, with only silence greeting my pleas.

It appeared that I masked my resurgent grief well, for Perenus suspected nothing. As the rest of our men boarded landing craft, he shouted toward the craggy peak of Mount Calpe, beaming with delight. Curious, I plodded toward him, my boots sinking in the sea-drenched sand.

"Herakles!" Perenus roared, throwing an arm around my shoulder. "We've come for you!"

Shaking my head, I laughed aloud. I was able to cuff away a stray tear as Perenus continued his hooting, a fist thrust toward the skies.

"Nika! Nika! Nika!"

THE FINAL LIBERATION
OF SEPTEM

Choppy seas marked our passage back to Africa. Even though the journey was only a half day, I nevertheless emptied the contents of my stomach over the railing. God help me, but I despise boats, even if they have kept my army from complete and utter ruin.

Even before Agila's arrival, orders were given for the expedition to pack its equipment and prepare for a sea journey back to Carthage. The bulk of our food would remain behind—Itaxes crumpled in visible relief at such a boon, along with my promise that further stores would be ferried into Septem's harbor within a month. Few protested at our longed-for evacuation, although a handful of spearmen volunteered to remain behind. Upon prodding, I found most to have found a sweetheart amongst the townspeople, and I happily permitted their marriages, asking Rosamund to distribute coins as dowries for each of the brides-to-be.

Conon, like Thurimuth, volunteered to remain behind as the military commander of Septem. Including the newly betrothed, fifty volunteers agreed to the similar offer I had granted the men of Mount Calpe, provided their behavior remained immaculate and to the stringent standards of Belisarius himself. The promise of triple wages was extended to the two hundred Franks who would also remain lodged in Septem per our agreement with Butilinus, who all bobbed their heads happily at such easily earned pay. Lord knows, two hundred and fifty men could not hold Tingitana upon an invasion, yet it was a large enough force to discourage an assault upon Septem proper, while small enough to placate Theudis' ire.

A general atmosphere of contentment permeated our last days in Septem. The fighting had drawn to a close, while the promise of home enticed many to boast about all the wealth and women to be had for Belisarius' heroes back in Constantinople. Though Itaxes would not admit to such sentiment, even the locals of Septem appeared encouraged by the expedition's imminent departure, for even a well-behaved army has always been a significant burden. With the conversion of vacant warehouses into a functioning barracks, the billeting of Roman soldiers into private homes would soon cease.

Agila arrived at his promised hour. Rather than the carefree figure kicking pools of water in a seaside cove, the Visigothic chieftain appeared in that formidable pitch-stained armor that stood in contrast to the simple leather chest pieces of his entourage. A full fifty spearmen served as his escort, though all had reversed their shields and donned a flag of truce as they approached Septem. Roman horns blared their welcome as Agila halted his procession twenty paces before the gate, which creaked open to allow me passage.

I went alone, yet no fewer than a hundred archers were poised atop the fighting platforms should anything go awry. Agila showed no sign of animosity, with only a slight smirk as he came into eye contact with a curious Frank atop my walls. Greeting me with a deep bow, Agila formally ended conflict between our two peoples.

"Lord Varus, I greet you. Theudis, King of the Visigoths, steward of the clan of the Balti, wishes no further conflict with the Roman Empire."

"Emperor Justinian," I answered, straining as I shouted each word, "along with his legate, wish the same. Peace between our peoples."

The Visigoths all stamped their spears in agreement. Agila then selected a group of ten to accompany him through Septem's gate for their brief journey atop Mount Abyla, with the chieftain showing only a mild concern for his safety as he entered the bosom of two thousand enemy warriors. Though I will never have any love for the Visigoths, I could not help but admire Agila in that moment, for his death would have been laughably easy to bring about under such a scenario. True to his word, Agila followed Cephalas' direction toward Mount Abyla's pathway, plotted carefully to separate Agila from any Ostrogoths who might hold a blood feud with the man who had wrought so much pain upon Indulf.

Though my men did nothing to hurry Agila's progress, the Visigothic envoy rushed to Abyla's heights. I cannot be certain what words passed between the two chieftains, yet within an hour, Theudesgel emerged with his surviving men. All bore sunken cheeks and shaggy beards, with Theudesgel far gaunter than I had remembered. More, Theudesgel's arm was tightly wrapped in soiled cloth, the man wincing with each limped pace. Stinking and bloodstained, the defenders of Abyla moved in silence through Septem's streets and gate, finally surrendering total control of the fortress to the Empire.

It was not until the final trailing Visigoth slipped into the open hills that my men relaxed. Whispers slipped across the walls, met by angry growls from the centurions. I paid this prattle little mind, intent only upon completing the final formalities of this sordid war. Accompanied by Sembrouthes and Uliaris, we three once again plodded through Septem's gate, walking toward a bemused Agila and a frustrated Theudesgel. Both men had been arguing in Gothic, yet ceased their hostility as I came within ten paces.

"Excubitor." Agila nodded.

Theudesgel merely spat, his nose wrinkling, and a muffled groan slipped through his lips as his arm jerked with the sudden motion. Ignoring him, I kept my gaze upon Agila.

"I have kept my word," I said. "Your man is safely delivered. Do I have the oath of your king to honor our prior agreement?"

Another nod. "Indeed, Lord Varus. The mighty Theudis extends his regards for such, ah, *prudence* as he turns his attentions to the Frankish menace."

Snapping his fingers, Agila summoned a nearby spearman who had not joined the procession into the city. The man carried a small cage that jerked about in his hand, with brown sackcloth veiling its contents from the world.

Agila smiled at me, placing a hand over his heart as he bowed again. "It is our custom that gifts shall be exchanged to end a war. I would present you with one particularly precious to me."

I grunted. "I brought no gift, only a demand for peace."

Theudesgel scowled, yet Agila remained unperturbed. "Ah, Lord Varus, but allow me to correct you! You have delivered dear, precious Theudesgel back to us, when you might have bashed his brains against the harbor gate. I personally would have been sorely tempted to do just that... if I had been in your position, of course."

"Even so, a gift is unnecessary."

"Are you Romans all so rude?" Theudesgel snarled. "Or is that merely the simpering Greek manners that have infiltrated your culture?"

Agila raised a hand to Theudesgel's face before continuing. With a further snap of his fingers, the sackcloth was released from atop the cage, revealing a frizzy brown pup squealing underneath. It could not have been more than two or three months old, with rolls of fat piling on its face and fragile legs failing to bear the weight of its body.

"One of the king's bitches birthed a proud litter," Agila explained. "The ancestors of these dogs saved Prince Thorismod from a Hunnic ambush on the Catalaunian Plains. There are none in the world more loyal to a worthy master."

Frowning, I lacked an appropriate response. "What need have I for a Gothic war dog?"

"Endless need!" Agila beamed. "I have selected a female for you. Less aggressive than the unclipped males, but endlessly loyal. I have even named her Haeva, after a Gothic legend of a woman who mated with a half-god hero. Not dissimilar to your Hercules, no?"

I wanted to refuse. Not out of revulsion for hounds, for I had cared for many due to Justin's lifelong adoration for such beasts. More so out of a wish to sever all ties with a hated foe, with no reminder of the failures and loss I had wrought in my clumsy leadership of Belisarius' men. Yet such a refusal would have been a grave insult to Theudis himself, and tantamount to a declaration of further war. With such threats looming, I framed a grateful smile upon my face, accepting Agila's offer.

"Haeva will be honored in my personal household," I declared. The Visigoth cage bearer walked forth and handed the bundle to Uliaris, completing our transaction.

"We have peace!" Agila roared. "Provided, of course, that you maintain only a mild presence in Mauretania and along Mount Calpe."

"Agreed," I answered. "And I anticipate trade being restored between our towns and broader Hispania within a month. Though Tingis is a historic trading center, the Empire will use Septem as its base for the region."

And so, with little more than a salute from Agila and a disdainful shrug from a weary Theudesgel, the Empire's war over the Pillars of Herakles came to an abrupt end. Against Belisarius' accomplishments, it felt somehow unsatisfying. True, we had scored unlikely victories against Theudis' horde, yet even a thousand spearmen lost was but a fraction of the Visigoth kingdom's might. It was also true that Belisarius' objectives had been fulfilled, yet the cost in time and blood had been grave. There was no glorious charge, no defining conquest of an enemy warlord upon the field of battle. Instead, Theudis' chieftains merely bowed to sense, evacuating their remaining forces to ward off a more immediately concerning foe. Worse, Theudis could return to strike as soon as he felt our puny garrisons in Septem and Mount Calpe were at their weakest. In my bones, I knew this fear was fated to come true.

And so, despite Agila's theatrics and whooping celebration from the forces under my command, the victory was hollow. I had won minimal gains, yet taken more casualties than Belisarius or John had in the entire Vandal War, with Baduarius' loss striking a particular blow whose full force would not be understood for some time. Somehow, it all seemed shameful, yet I did nothing to curtail the celebrations of those under my thrall who had shivered through rain and mud in no fewer than a half dozen battles to seize a fortress by the sea. They had won, but I had lost.

Today, the scribes recall our liberation of Septem as a joyful act—one of mastery and strategy rather than blind fortune. I believe none of them, of course, for many of the stories and songs from that campaign were paid from Liberius' purse, though my mentor denied having any love for a sniveling scribe or a bombastic poet. For was I a good leader? From the perch of later years, I reject the notion out of hand. I was still young, putting on every air of the austere battle commander without true knowledge of the weight such office holds. I fell victim to multiple traps and allowed my judgment to cloud in moments of despair. My victories were either gruesome, such as the destruction of Septem's harbor, or fortuitous, such as Uliaris' return.

Later, Belisarius would remark that a good leader is often so lucky, yet I fail to see how any could be luckier than to have the sure demise of my expedition averted by chance. A good leader is defined by his actions in the darkest hours of deprivation, and I was found wanting. Perhaps Rosamund was right, for without the love of the Christian God or her pagan deities, my tale would have ended there, among the Pillars of Herakles.

Agila led his detachment along Tingitana's western road, with Fulcaris and Sindual's men discreetly monitoring their progress toward still-friendly ports in Tingis that would ferry Theudis' survivors back to his court in Gades. Tingis would nominally be transferred to the Empire's control in due course, yet I had no intention of leaving any rump force behind to maintain control. Septem and Mount Calpe were far more important, with the former close enough to intervene if any major lapse in Tingis' security arose. It was inevitable that the town's leadership would viciously cheat the Empire on its taxes, yet this was a problem for Justinian's eventual provincial governor. As long as the threat of invasion had been stymied, I had nothing left to concern me in Tingitana.

Back inside Septem's walls, another near-riotous celebration erupted, with only a handful of officers keeping their impulses in check long enough to meet with me in the forum. Even Liberius abandoned me with a nod and a clap upon the cheek, leaving Xerxes and Conon as the only senior officers available for my instructions.

Predictably, Perenus and Gunderic had led their men in a desperate race to the feasting halls, leaving behind only those unlucky enough to be assigned sentry duty atop the walls. Ascum was perhaps the worst of all, having skipped Agila's surrender entirely to distribute casks of wine and remaining cuts of Frankish pork as kindling for the feast to come. I begrudged none for their celebrations. Privately, I wished that I could join in, as I had many times before accepting Belisarius' charge.

Both Rosamund and Cephalas remained with me, although I could tell that both desired to sprint off toward Perenus and the unfolding jubilation. Along with Xerxes and my remaining bodyguard, we convened our meeting in the forum's open air, with clattering and screams of victory sailing in all directions.

Uliaris lifted the squirming cage, struggling to keep its contents still. "What do you want me to do with this dog?"

"Dirty creatures, even if joyful," Rosamund said, eyeing the pup suspiciously. "We'll all have fleas within a fortnight."

Cephalas, on the other hand, cooed as he unlocked the tiny cage and lifted its contents into the air with a single hand. The puppy— Haeva, as Agila had dubbed her—dribbled piss upon his chest, yet Cephalas seemed not to notice, or at least not to care. He planted a sloppy kiss along her tiny skull, cradling the bundle that easily fit within a man's palm.

At that, Rosamund giggled. "On the other hand, perhaps the fleas will not be so bad. We could use another loyal servant!"

"Indeed," I declared. "My dominus kept a private kennel, and was better for it. But take care—this pup is like to grow to the size of a bear if fed properly."

"Do not worry, Varus!" Cephalas insisted, his eyes locked upon Haeva's furry form. "She will be a credit to your household. You have my oath."

Xerxes gave a polite cough, seeking to turn my attentions to more urgent decisions. "But what of the city? Tingitana?"

"Prepare to leave in five days," I commanded. "Conon and Thurimuth have their orders and ample silver for their men. Once we have word that the Visigoths have departed for Hispania, we will sail for Carthage."

"Then congratulations are due to you, Commander." Xerxes smiled. "Our war is over."

I shut my eyes, attempting to muffle the rising cacophony of celebration around me. "I pray that it is."

And so I did. Fervently. But, just as the nagging sense of loss robbed any sense of joy from my achievement, so, too, did echoes of recent worries ring through my mind. Spies in Carthage. Spies in Septem. Religious fanatics in Constantinople and machinations by Narses and Justinian. Most of all, the self-assured proclamations of Theudis, who rasped in laughter as he insisted that Belisarius' wars had just begun. By that point, my soul had been drained of its vigor, and a weariness possessed my body in its stead. I wanted little more than to journey home. *Please, God*, I silently begged, *give me the blessing of peace.*

God did not listen. For, as the priests now insist, He had other designs set out for my path. All I can do now is weep.

THE CORRUPT AND
THE SUBLIME

Agila kept his word. The last Visigoths evacuated Tingis within days of our parting, giving me leave to do the same at Septem. Liberius handled many of the formalities of our final days, from empowering Itaxes with further responsibility in Septem to doling out payments to the countless households and farmers who had supplied shelter and feed to the Imperial Army during our stay in the province.

There was squabbling, of course, yet no encounters were serious enough to jeopardize the city's peace. I would like to believe this was due to a happiness at being returned into the Emperor's care, yet the promise of overpayment for all goods was the more likely explanation. Liberius had been correct: dozens of merchants had cheated me out of valuable coin, yet he nonetheless agreed that such excessive generosity was effective.

Having formally endowed Conon with leadership over our remaining spearmen in Septem, we boarded those few dromons that did not remain to safeguard trade and patrol the seas. Once aboard Apollos' flagship, I desired little more than sleep, yet neither Perenus nor Rosamund would allow it. Both hauled me to the stern of the ship as swift winds pushed our masts eastward, allowing for a final glimpse at Mount Abyla.

"The Pillars of Herakles," Rosamund whispered. "The triumph of a god. Such tales of our journey would be told amongst my people for generations."

"Mine as well," Perenus whispered, gawking at the vacated citadel. "Will we see it again?"

Standing between Perenus and myself, Rosamund threw her arms around our waists, staring off into the distance. Perenus' question remained unanswered as we peered across the rolling waves at the shrinking mountain, yet privately, I held on to a hope that Tingitana remained forever in the past. Others likely felt differently, yet little remained to welcome me back to the Pillars. Only spirits and memories of failure and worry.

Our voyage back to Carthage had few difficulties. Predictably, my stomach churned with even a mild swell, and only Rosamund was able to ease my suffering, however slight. In that condition, I could hardly stem the gambling and drunkenness that had continued unabated since Agila's surrender. Instead, I ordered Rosamund to spread the word that this behavior must cease upon reaching Carthage, allowing the men enough time to enjoy their relative freedom until disembarkation.

Rather than join in the revelry, I remained tucked inside my cabin, gazing upon the white wolf pelt and other trophies from my successes in Tauris, Mesopotamia, Africa, and now Tingitana that Rosamund had meticulously cleaned and displayed. Even through my nausea, I smiled at the memory of Justin's own arrayed achievements, the greatest prize of which was the dragon-hilted sword that now rested within my own possession. Even the pup Haeva, though oddly named, brought me to think of my dominus, wondering whether he felt as I do now regarding the mixed blessings of conquest and war.

Overall, it was a joyful voyage, driven by the knowledge that we had secured a lasting success. Though my stomach roiled and I cursed our transport ship as it rolled through each swell, I otherwise felt giddy at the prospect of returning to friends, and home.

"It's been months!" I said bluntly in a private conversation with Rosamund, who had prepared a potion to slake my seasickness. "Belisarius and Troglita, Mundus and Germanus and Petrus. God save me, but I have a child that I haven't met! And Samur—"

Rosamund flinched, and I cut myself short.

"Varus, there's something I need to tell you."

Rosamund rarely spoke out of fear, yet now her voice wavered.

"Anything," I urged her. "Do not worry."

Though I forced a smile as I scanned Rosamund's worried eyes, my mind flitted to a dozen possible causes. Had she been mistreated by one under my command? Sadly, such a fate would not be uncommon for women following an army, yet I deemed it unlikely given Rosamund's power in my household and her own favored status amongst many of my veterans as a true healer. A faded memory arose of Rosamund's accusation of Sergius and Antonina and their illicit affair, followed again by similar rumors by Mariya. I dismissed both insinuations as illogical and dangerous just by their utterance. For a moment I even girded myself for yet another tiresome plea to separate from the army for a freer life outside the Empire. Yet what came next was entirely unpredictable, sending flakes of frost swirling through my veins.

"Varus, your brother..." Rosamund began, trailing off to silence.

Her eyes fell to the floor, and though I thought she might speak again, she remained still. I grabbed for her hand. "What about Samur?"

Rosamund shook her head. "Forget it."

I squeezed her fingers in mine, my curiosity transforming into outright concern. "Tell me, Rosamund. What about Samur?"

Rosamund bit her lip. "I wanted to tell you for some time, but could not trust that we were alone."

"Go on," I growled.

"Samur's in pain," Rosamund said, "and he's dangerous. His body might have healed from Barbalissus, but his mind has not. And he feels that none recognize his suffering."

"But *I* did. *I* do!" I said, realizing I was shouting. "Did he tell you this?"

"Not in so many words," Rosamund said quickly, her wide eyes all but begging me to lower my voice. "But I've seen things... Ah!"

My vision clouded as I again squeezed Rosamund's hand, triggering her yelp. I had no mind for apologies, only for answers. "Things? What did you see?"

"During the riots..." Rosamund began, yet again shook her head. "I can't ever tell anyone, not even you..."

"Yes, you can!" I shouted again.

Rosamund jumped and raised her shoulders in alarm. "I swore a promise to the gods," she whispered. "Just... please watch out for Samur, Varus. He did not deserve any of this suffering, but I would not want to see further pain caused."

"Rosamund..."

"Please!" Now it was she who wrapped my hands with an insistent grip. Her breathing quickened as her icy blue eyes widened, stubbornly blinking back tears.

"You have my promise," I said, too stunned to refuse. "Anything you ever need—"

"Not anything," she muttered, closing her eyes to separate her gaze from my own. "But enough, I suppose."

We sat together in silence for what seemed the better part of an afternoon. It was not until later that, our stomachs churning from lack of food, Rosamund slipped from my cabin and sought a light meal of hardened bread and salt pork. She smiled as she returned, any notion of unhappiness wiped clean from her visage, yet her earlier words left me thoroughly, unshakably ill at ease. Rosamund did not broach her worries of Samur again, and neither did I goad her further, yet the topic never strayed far from my thoughts.

Whether by divine favor or fortuitous planning, we arrived at Carthage several days ahead of our initial benchmark. Often, exceeding such expectations would have brought celebration to the Empire's ministers, yet on that late morning, Carthage was far from prepared to entertain dozens of transports arriving at its buzzing harbor. Impatient to leave the wretched vessel for dry land, I realized the holdup—the significant increase in goods flowing into Carthage, many of which bore emblems from Alexandria, Tyrus, and even distant Constantinople. Though I momentarily cursed such an irritating delay, prudence ultimately prevailed, and I rejoiced at the city's sudden turn in fortune.

Given that our ship carried the Imperial legate, we were positioned to dock first, prior to all other vessels that circled Carthage's waterfront. Liberius exited at the front, yet insisted that Rosamund and I follow closely behind, while Cephalas organized my household for a return to the city.

"I want to meet with Belisarius," Liberius insisted in brisk Greek, "before every spy in Carthage eavesdrops upon the palace, anyway. I'm sure that the army of sniveling clerks has made a mockery of our work in my absence."

All I could do was nod and lumber onward with Rosamund. Though Carthage sprawled over a great tract of land, its harbor and palace were separated by only a few hundred paces, for the Carthaginians prized their seamless rule of the sea. Though the Consuls of the Republic had burnt the once-proud city to cinders, Caesar himself had rebuilt it as best as he could, honoring the defunct sacred principles of Carthage's lords while installing superior Roman organization and logistics in its streets. Palace guardsmen, comprised of Belisarius' burgeoning bucellarii, straightened as the legate approached, quickly parting to allow us entry into Belisarius' private quarters.

"What need do you have of me here?" Rosamund whispered as we passed through the doorway.

Liberius paused, his eyes scanning the hallway. "Keep out any Carthaginians who demand entry to Belisarius, however you can. Flirt, threaten, pretend to not speak their language… whatever you deem necessary."

Rosamund furrowed her brow and raised her chin toward the legate. "Why?"

"As I've said," Liberius whispered, switching to Heruli, "something rotten has taken root in this Court. Neither Belisarius nor Varus have the skill to extract it, or at least isolate it to the point of harmlessness. But you have a much keener eye for these things, girl. Report to me with any suspicions you may have, but do not allow anyone within earshot of Belisarius for now."

Rosamund shot a glance toward me, and, seeing no resistance, nodded. Turning on her heel to stay with Belisarius' guardsmen, she offered a curt wave as Liberius and I disappeared into the veritable maze of offices that comprised the general's quarters.

"Liberius," I whispered, once I hoped we were out of earshot. "Why Rosamund?"

"She is much too clever to be organizing pots and dispensing wages," Liberius said. "As I've explained, few patricians would pay much heed to a barbarian woman like her, and a pagan woman at that—an incalculable advantage for her. She's more capable than you of sniffing out those who would do harm, Varus. Counter my order if you wish, but you would do well to give Rosamund more of your responsibilities. It is obvious that she would never betray you."

Liberius allowed no time for argument.

Not waiting for the guards to pry the wooden gate apart, Liberius leaned onto a door and slipped inside. "Apologies! Came as quickly as the seas would allow, which is rarely at the hour one expects!"

"Ah, Liberius!" Belisarius' voice rang out. "And Varus! I did not expect either of you for some time yet."

"There will be more than enough time later to dawdle over pleasantries," Liberius huffed, looking about at the few other men gathered in Belisarius' presence. "You must tell me everything, even the most minute and inane detail. What did the letters say?"

"Letters?" I balked.

"Missives from Constantinople." This from Germanus, who offered a wave in greeting. "None of them good."

"Congratulations, Varus!" put in Troglita, who leaned over a table at Germanus' side. "The Pillars of Herakles... if only I could have gone with you to see it."

"Not now!" Liberius hissed. "I can safely vouch for all men present, but we have precious little time until others storm into this room and seek my attention. Listen very carefully to what I am about to say. There is a traitor in our midst. Before, we only suspected someone betraying our movements to Theudis, but now I am certain there is at least one such recreant present—likely several. Believe me, this is one of the gravest threats any of you have yet faced."

My chest pounded as Liberius spoke. Traitors. Grave threats. All fears that had slithered deep, with an icy grip upon my consciousness, robbing me of sleep. Yes, in Septem, Liberius had warned me of Constantinople's discontent, and the threats surrounding Theodora. But out at the far edge of the world, with battles and carnage so pressing upon my conscience, they seemed distant, almost philosophical.

Others in the room fell immediately silent upon hearing Liberius' warning. Besides Germanus and Troglita, there was Bessas, seated by a far wall and sipping from a cup of honeyed wine as he rasped from a seasonal cough. Across from the Armenian officer sat Mundus, who rose to his feet with a wink of welcome. Last of all was the wiry arm that threw itself around my neck, squeezing hard and leaving me gasping for air.

"Samur!" Liberius groaned. "I should have taken the whip to you more often as a child, but your antics amused me. Stop interrupting!"

Samur's lips curled in a wide grin. Though he did not reply, my brother did not release his arm from my shoulders, his hands squeezing to trap me in his embrace. He rocked along the balls of his feet, prompting irritated looks from the legate even has he nodded at our reunion and gestured for all to hark.

"What I tell you now," Liberius began, "must not leave this room. Our position, despite all the victories we have acquired, is tenuous. Private and sealed reports from Basilius have found me in Septem, detailing all the Imperial Court's dealings since our departure."

Despite Samur's unabated excitement, I felt a deep pain throbbing against my ribs. All I wanted was a peaceful return home. Instead, Liberius offered only the chilling sobriety of intrigue, spiced with a malice that only the Imperial Court could muster. And though Liberius had privately shared coded messages from Theodora and Basilius, I wondered whether he had shared everything he knew. To this day, I cannot be certain, though I doubt it.

Liberius took no heed of my emotions. "Belisarius, Varus has told me that you have received a formal letter from the Emperor and Empress. Basilius has offered a hidden interpretation to me. Please inform me of all that you know, beginning with the letter in your possession."

Eyes wide, Belisarius nodded from where he stood at the center of the wide circular table that occupied the heart of his hall. Beckoning to Troglita, Belisarius took in hand a scroll that was curled from the many weeks it had spent sealed in a courier's tube, ferried across the sea from the Imperial Palace. By appearances, the general had become even more strained by duty than he had been before my departure, his cheeks sunken and his figure lacking some measure of the vitality that had imbued him even in the more ominous moments in Mesopotamia just a year prior. Any happiness at our sudden arrival vanished as he unfurled his scroll and teased it flat upon the table. Instantly, I recognized the delicate whorls of Narses' hand.

"The Emperor says little," Belisarius began. "He congratulates us once more on our victory over Gelimer, and for extending our hold over Sardinia, Corsica, and the Balearic Islands. Of course, he does not yet know about Varus' success in the Pillars of Herakles."

Liberius waved an impatient hand. "Go on."

Belisarius cleared his throat, scratching at a beard that, while not overly unruly, had elongated well beyond the prim frame that he had stubbornly maintained for each of his campaigns. "Along with a further update of my progress, the Emperor offers two choices: remain in Carthage to spread Imperial control over any Mauri holdouts or return to Constantinople and be honored with a triumph."

Liberius nodded. "The choice is an illusion. You can either depart to meet with Justinian directly or be considered a traitor and usurper."

Belisarius gaped, horrified. "What?"

I followed in turn. "How?"

"Ridiculous!" Germanus added.

But Liberius was undeterred. "Quite the opposite. Though Basilius has sung his son-in-law's praises, others within the Court are not quite so friendly to our young general, nor do they appreciate the considerable troubles we have all gone through to liberate a massive chunk of territory. Instead, those senators not hanged after the Nika Riots all whisper that Belisarius wishes to crown himself a reborn Western emperor, and a true rival to Justinian."

Belisarius grunted in anger. "After everything that I have done, how could the Emperor believe—"

"It is not only Justinian," Liberius cut in. "Since the Riots, our Emperor does little without Theodora. It is said that a heretic monk arrived in the Imperial Court not long after our departure, and somehow gained the Empress' ear. This monk, Jakob, has earned the ire of Cassiodorus. Normally I would laugh at such infighting, but it appears the rift is spilling into real persecution of different religions and sects. Cassiodorus has directly blamed pagans and heretics for fanning the Nika Riots to flame in the first place."

"But that's ridiculous!" I cried. "How could pagans and heretics spawn a full-scale revolt amongst a hundred thousand residents of Constantinople?"

The name resonated in my memory—Jakob Baradaeus, the wayward priest that Basilius had warned me of in his previous letter—and I was as confounded in that moment as I had been reading of this man initially. Theodora had always struck me as a practical woman who, while outwardly religious, was too concerned with the worldly burdens of the Empire to worry about the minute schisms of religious doctrine. I could not see this latest maneuver as anything but uncharacteristically foolish on Theodora's part, nor did I recognize the portly Cassiodorus as a true threat.

Liberius raised his palms to the air, his eyes closing. "No more ridiculous than our Roman forefathers insisting that Christians ate the flesh of newborn babes to consecrate devotions to their Christ. Suspicion, you will find, is that common trait that links all of humanity."

"There's one further detail," Mundus interjected. "And it has all the tact of a sick ox."

Given the scale of the threat facing Belisarius' expedition, Mundus' addition was insignificant. Many today will either not remember those few simple words or dismiss them altogether. Yet to us commanders, they were all the evidence required that something foul had corrupted the innermost sanctum of the Imperial Palace.

Belisarius traced a final line upon the Emperor's missive, its characters expertly crafted by Narses' hand. "Our friend, the esteemed Senator Nepotian, wishes his beloved son Solomon well in his stay in Africa. We all watch his successes in power with great joy."

Samur, who must have already known of the letter's contents, still tensed at the name. Echoes of Rosamund's warning swirled in my mind, and I wondered at the extent of their merits. Liberius, however, offered no time to consider such worries further.

"This confirms it," Liberius said, sitting heavily upon a nearby bench. "There is no real choice. If you expect to both keep your head and remain in the Emperor's favor, Belisarius must travel back to Constantinople as soon as possible and leave Solomon in temporary command of the province."

"Bastard!" Germanus growled. "We'll be fighting a war here again within a year."

"It is temporary," Liberius insisted. "And believe me, I understand this to be a setback. But the consequences of ignoring such requests are far worse than allowing feckless braggarts to rule over a distant province."

Pausing, Liberius turned first to me, and then to Samur. My brother had grown eerily still, the only sign of life an occasional breath that slipped through his nostrils. When he spoke, his voice signaled an immediate willingness to kill. "So Solomon has been spying upon us for months, and sending letters for his father to manipulate the Emperor?"

Liberius shrugged. "Impossible to prove, but likely. Unfortunately, it gets worse."

Belisarius ran a hand through his hair, massaging multiple points along his scalp. "Liberius, you know I value your judgment. But from what you have told me, the Court has returned to disarray, persecution is likely, we have traitors in the army spilling lies to Constantinople, and through it all I am accused of despicable crimes. Why would you think it could be worse?"

"Because," Liberius began, "all of this ignores the fact that Theudis knew exactly what our forces would do even before we arrived in Tingitana. Solomon's cronies are not the only spies. There are others, with separate loyalties… and we have no idea who they may be."

"Suffering Christ," Germanus groaned.

I could not agree more with Germanus' pronouncement. Despite all our victories, danger never seemed more incipient than at that moment. It was so convoluted that it nearly brought me to laugh aloud, with months of fear culminating in an acknowledgment that many grim tidings remained for our forces. All that kept me focused was the promise of home, and that I could soon sever such cares in favor of quiet respite absent any killing or intrigue. A lesser man than our general would have buckled under such weighty concerns. Belisarius only nodded as he offered a smile for each of us.

"Then our choices are simple. I must return to Constantinople, and I would appreciate each of you accompanying me home. When the Emperor sees me humbling myself in his presence, surely his trust shall return."

"With one caveat," Liberius countered. "Though Basilius and I can learn the truth of Solomon and any other who whispers in the Emperor's ear, someone must remain behind to sniff out those traitors who would spill secrets to the Visigoths. If we are fortunate, Theudis' defeat will be the end of such squabbles, although I fear that other chieftains would use any weakness in Carthage to brew trouble for our soldiers."

"Sensible," Mundus said. As he turned his head, I detected a new scar that ran the length of his cheek, the reddish skin not yet fully healed. "But who? I would volunteer, but all I know is fighting in a wall. I've no mind for politics or deception."

"I would volunteer, Liberius," Germanus offered, "but I fear that I am far too visible to yield any benefit in catching traitors."

Liberius shook his head. "Basilius and I have other requests of you, Germanus, but all require you to return to Constantinople. Instead, I had a mind to ask Troglita to remain in Carthage."

Straightening at the mention of his name, Troglita's face showed no happiness at the sudden charge. Rather, a wrinkled brow and pursed lips demonstrated all the reluctance that I understood my friend to give, for he had long been a practitioner of the stoic teachings of Rome's long-dead emperors.

"If I must, Legate, although I, too, wish to return."

Liberius grinned. "Honorable but miserable! You are far too transparent, Troglita. So transparent, in fact, that I have already requested that Auria and Evanthes sail for Africa immediately. They travel in comfort, or at least what qualifies for comfort, and will be here within a month."

A heavy sigh escaped Troglita's throat. "Gratitude, Legate. I should not have questioned your plans."

"No indeed!" Liberius said cheerily. "But tread carefully. Solomon will retain authority, and you will be hard-pressed to blunt his more idiotic impulses. Do what you can to keep him in check, and use whatever means are available to track any unusual exchanges in the forum."

Troglita snorted, his eyes crinkling above a thin smile. "Like using Auria's relatives to detect any traitors in Carthage?"

"The idea had occurred to me." Liberius bobbed his head. "But I would never insinuate that a man manipulate his relatives for gain. Far too risky!"

"He did that all the time when we were little," Samur grumbled in my ear.

Our plans were set. With our expedition slowly gaining entry to Carthage's harbor, Belisarius was free to plan his return to Constantinople. A full five hundred spearmen would remain behind to maintain order, with an additional two thousand locals levied to assist with city watches and general security. Privately, Belisarius had commissioned the training and arming of another two thousand Vandal boys, with Troglita able to call upon their services in the event of an uprising.

Solomon would be blissfully unaware of this development. Instead, a messenger would ride for Thapsus to inform Solomon of his good fortune, his temporary promotion to tribune sealed by Nepotian's words, Justinian's command, and Narses' script. Of all the tidings we had received, only Narses' turn against Theodora had truly surprised me, for I'd firmly believed his loyalties lay with the Empress above all others. Theodora's signet ring remained securely in my possession, with Narses holding the only other copy in all the Empire. If Theodora could no longer count upon Narses' loyalty, it did not surprise me that she would turn to others to execute her will. Though she was Empress, the friendless and trustless in Constantinople were not long for this life.

Many sought my attentions at the conclusion of Liberius' gathering, yet between fatigue from the voyage and an increasing number of visitors seeking the legate's attentions, such niceties were delayed for the following morning. Instead, I bade temporary farewell to Belisarius' trusted circle, allowing Liberius to further tune his plots. Samur would not be parted from my side, and the two of us excused ourselves from the hall. Belisarius, however, had other desires.

"Varus, wait!"

Pausing, I waited for the general to weave past Liberius, Mundus, Troglita, and Germanus, their attentions now focused upon a growing stack of charts and scrolls that Troglita diligently unfurled from a nearby stack. Facing away from Belisarius, Samur rolled his eyes, yet said nothing.

Belisarius smiled as he approached. "Might I accompany you back to your lodging? Of course, I can wait if you'd prefer to be alone with your brother."

Though polite, Belisarius' eyes bore all the eagerness of a child recently reunited with a favorite plaything. He was impossible to deny, even with a near-overpowering urge to escape with my brother back to the comforts of private lodgings that did not roll with incessant waves.

"Of course, Lord, although my building is a considerable walk."

"No matter!" Belisarius grinned. "Being cooped inside with musty papers demands a bit of exercise."

Belisarius excused himself from the meeting, transferring responsibility of organization to Liberius for the afternoon before joining Samur and myself. We wormed through the palace offices to reach the outer door that veiled the general from would-be interlopers, and as we reached the doorway that connected Belisarius' chambers to the remainder of Carthage's seaside palace, muffled shouts could be heard ready to greet us on the other side.

"You have no authority over me, you Gepid witch!" a Greek voice called. "And you guards are insubordinate for deeming to follow her instruction!"

I then heard Rosamund cursing in Gepid before switching to the Greek tongue. "Say what you want, but you are not entering without explicit permission. If you think otherwise, I encourage you to try pushing your way through."

Belisarius' smile evaporated, replaced by a furrowed nose and bared teeth. Rushing forward, he pushed one of the doors open, slipping outside as Samur and I hurried to follow.

"Stotzas!" Belisarius growled. "What is the meaning of this?"

Though I had interacted with the half-Roman Stotzas several times before departing for Septem, the longstanding magistrate of Carthage had lost the appearance of a man struggling to please his

Vandal masters. An engorged gut rolled over a soft leather belt richly braided with golden thread, with his robes a soft blue that covered his body from throat to ankle. Gold rings and silver torques adorned the man's body, evidence of his rise in status as one of the most senior civilian leaders of not only Carthage, but the entire prefecture that formed in the ashes of the Vandal kingdom. Beside him, the scribe Procopius stood off to a corner. Yet where Stotzas' face had grown crimson with indignity, Procopius remained silent, keenly observant of all that happened around him.

"Lord, this heathen woman bars my way to speak with you!" Stotzas complained, a layer of fat underneath his chin shivering as he gritted his teeth. "Keeping me from performing my duties!"

Belisarius crept closer. "And so you threaten violence? Should I be concerned about your opinions over the thousands of subjects in this region that may share Rosamund's views?"

Stotzas clasped his hands together, wincing as a heavy golden ring dug into a bare knuckle. "General, I swear to God and all my ancestors that I serve the interests of you, and of the Emperor."

"Good," Belisarius offered with a single nod. "Then I suggest that you treat my subordinates with greater respect. Rosamund was asked to ensure my privacy, to which she has performed admirably."

Stotzas bowed, remaining silent. The two guardsmen traded confused glances, while Rosamund sighed in relief.

"He may enter," Belisarius murmured. "But I will depart for a short time, and do not require guards. Varus and Samur are more than proficient at keeping me alive."

Amidst a deferent Stotzas, a mute Procopius, and two bemused guardsmen, Belisarius led Samur, Rosamund, and myself out of Carthage's palace and into the streets. Against Septem and Tingis, Carthage's vast streets and soaring stone buildings left me feeling uneasy despite an intimate knowledge of the city's layout. Whereas Septem's denizens prayed in a simple wooden structure and held little else than a forum for trade and entertainment, Carthage boasted multiple looming churches for piety and no fewer than four theaters for amusement—each dedicated to a different performing art.

Along with an intricate web of cisterns and baths, Carthage maintained its own hippodrome, although that stadium was a poor imitation of the vast marble structure that had spawned the Nika Riots. Stepping along avenues as wide as four oxcarts standing abreast, I could not help but feel that Carthage was altogether too large even for me, and capable of hiding far too many unseen enemies.

Nevertheless, Belisarius' enthusiasm was infectious, and it was difficult to not smile at the unashamed happiness of a man of his stature in Roman society. Once safely fifty paces from the palace entrance, I whispered my first question to the general.

"Why do we entertain creatures such as Stotzas?"

Belisarius chuckled. "Because we always knew that our expedition would depart these lands. Stotzas, for all his bluster, knows the people of Carthage well. More importantly, Stotzas knows that he cannot hold the major cities without the support of Vandal warriors. The Emperor needs natives of his liberated provinces to maintain order… otherwise we'll be fighting a new battle every month."

Rosamund scoffed. "In my village, we would call such men lizards. They scurry about living on offal, and run in fear at the merest shadow of danger."

"Sounds like most of the courtiers we grew up serving," Samur muttered, earning a hearty laugh from Belisarius.

Though a winter breeze swept through Carthage's streets, it was nevertheless far more pleasant and refreshing than the bitter gusts around Septem and Tingis. Even better, with several months of Belisarius' leadership, the city's streets had been washed of the dense layers of human and animal dung that I can only imagine hailed from the earliest days of Vandal dominion over this unfortunate city. That, alongside the reconstruction of many aqueducts to supply further fresh water, alleviated the nagging problem of poor hygiene. Carthage had become, unlike Constantinople, that rare urban setting that was inoffensive to the senses, making it surprisingly pleasant to walk along its stone-lined streets for little reason other than personal leisure.

"When there is more time, you must tell me everything you've seen at the Pillars," Belisarius continued. "What a sight! And the Visigoths... John would have been awed at your victory. Theudis' reputation does not come from incompetence in battle."

I felt my face redden, eliciting a low chuckle from Samur. "Thank you, Lord—"

"Please, abandon these silly titles amongst friends!" Belisarius insisted, slowing his pace down to a crawl.

"Of course, Lord. I mean, Belisarius," I answered, snickering at my own instinctive reaction. "Spending one's youth with a slave's collar does not easily make for casual friendships with nobility. But as for the Pillars, it is a memory I would rather soon forget."

Rosamund and Samur lagged a few paces behind as Belisarius considered my words, sharing their own private conversation. We traveled a full twenty paces before he offered a response, moving through the city's primary forum and the chaotic activity it had recently come to house in its marketplace.

"Baduarius," Belisarius said, his tone low. "I understand this loss better than you might believe. And I appreciate your honest letters regarding his death. But an account on a page only offers a sliver of lived experience."

"He died bravely, Belisarius, but he died all the same," I said, the words reluctant on my lips yet necessary. "Cut down by a Visigoth champion who had little of his skill but more than enough wiliness to compensate. And if I had not publicly challenged his honor the day before, Baduarius might still be alive. I never intended to send him into single combat."

Belisarius nodded. "I know. Liberius wrote to me saying the same—though I would appreciate if you would not betray my trust in this. Baduarius is—was—my dear friend. I have no shame in saying that I wept at word of his death. And while I can insist that you take no personal responsibility or that you harden your heart to such circumstances, those with souls cannot help but feel hurt and shame."

"Lord..." I gulped, worried that Belisarius might judge me weak for giving voice to my lack of confidence. "How do you remain sane when orders that you give may send hundreds to their deaths?"

Belisarius sighed, his mouth twitching in a sad smile. He seemed to consider my question, a pregnant silence lasting for perhaps a minute before he replied.

"You know I was close with John?" Belisarius asked.

I nodded. "The whole army knows that, Lord." I left unsaid the rumors that Belisarius and John had been more than dear comrades, and that Belisarius might have shared a bed with the unmarried John as much as his own wife.

Belisarius chuckled. "I suppose so. But you were present when he was carried back to our camp?" Belisarius paused again, murmuring the next words. "After he was wounded?"

Another nod. "Yes, Lord. He thought of others before himself, even at the end."

"He was always that way!" Belisarius' melancholy turned to a brighter smile. "When we were boys, with little more than wooden staves to imagine ourselves soldiers in the Emperor's army, we would stay awake until nearly dawn, talking of how we could rise to become more in life."

"More than farm boys?" I asked, having difficulty picturing Belisarius as a dirt-stained farmhand.

"I wanted to be Caesar." Belisarius grinned. "Brave and determined to explore the vast world. John, however, always imagined himself Agrippa, building immortal structures and making the lives of our people more bearable. I confess, I found John's dream dull at the time, but now I understand its wisdom."

"I always wanted to be a warrior too," I admitted. "Even with my slave's collar."

"You and I are more similar than either of us knows." Belisarius gripped my shoulder, his mind's eye still fixed on his youth. "As John and I grew, we happened upon a traveling priest, who preached

God's will that the lost provinces of the Empire should be returned to the light. It was a calling that enraptured both of us, and as soon as we were old enough, we sought out a recruiter for the army. Before long, I found myself distantly connected to Justin's Imperial household. I was granted a centurion's helm when I was just sixteen, while John aided me with every decision. We eventually attracted the eye of Godilas and Liberius."

Parts of this I had learned during our Mesopotamian campaign, although not in such detail. "And you saved Justinian?"

"And Godilas too!" Belisarius beamed. "John planned our route of attack, though he seemed afraid of taking independent command of his own."

We paced about, my eyes darting from one figure to the next— fearful that each might be a spy, an assassin. I found none, of course, and Belisarius seemed untroubled by interlopers.

"Inevitably, my commands led men to their deaths," Belisarius continued. "Sometimes many. Sometimes needlessly, in hindsight. I carry their names in my heart like an anchor, and sometimes the weight gets the better of me."

I shivered, recognizing that awful ache. "But Lord, how do you live with that?"

"Dagisthaeus, Sunicas, Simmas..." Belisarius recounted. "So many more. All dead for me. But after each fight, John would allow me to wallow in pity for an hour to a day, but never longer. He insisted that we had to keep pushing onward, to seek that goal that had filled our dreams as boys, to free the Empire's lost provinces once more."

"It seems a bit unfeeling," I blurted out, realizing a heartbeat later that Belisarius might take such a retort as criticism. "Although—"

"It is unfeeling!" Belisarius agreed, surprising me. "Even at the end, John begged me to go on. To fix my mind upon the road ahead, and carry all those unable to walk it with me."

By then, we had reached Carthage's port, a light breeze flitting through the sea walls and rustling my hair and beard. Belisarius paused and turned to me, his eyes emblazoned with a fierce purpose that had been sorely missed in recent months.

"You now carry an anchor about your heart as well, Varus," Belisarius said. "It is not so ponderous as mine, at least not yet. But there are now those whose memory and honor depend upon you."

Baduarius, Irilar, and Alaric. Opilio, Vitalius, Isaacius, and so many others. Thinking of one man in that moment was painful enough, but to remember them all as a collective made it hard to breathe.

"Leadership is ugly. The singers make it seem grand and beautiful, but its only mud and tears and blood—and sooner or later, all leaders are tested. What separates those who survive and those who crumble is whether they are steadfast in purpose. John taught me to never lose sight of my dreams, regardless of what comes. My nights are not easy, but each one brings me closer to my life's dream. One day, God willing, I will see it done, and bring John and all the others with me."

There was no softness in Belisarius' answer. No miracles such as the priests regale, nor a ready-made salve for the wounds that affected my mind. Nevertheless, I understood Belisarius' answer more than any other that had been offered. A grim determination, and an unconquerable will to continue onward to victory.

This sentiment might have been even more powerful in the months prior, when I still had a stomach for fighting. Then, I privately nursed a desire to lay aside my arms and retire. In that moment, I opted to not confess such yearning to Belisarius, instead considering his wisdom and sharing our remaining walk in peace.

Alas, that was not a conversation I had intended upon having so soon, especially with my mind muddled with fatigue from an extended sea journey. As Belisarius drew alongside my flank, I caught a glimpse of Rosamund throwing an aggressive hug around Samur's chest, making my brother giggle as he fought to break free.

Our passage through the forum and onto Carthage's thronging streets did not go unnoticed. Most of the ships that followed me from Septem had not yet gained entry to either of Carthage's massive ports, leaving many in the city to nod in recognition of my return as a declared victorious commander.

Yet for every man or woman who recognized me, three others called to Belisarius, with most petitioning the general for some favor or another. One young woman, hair bound in a loose shawl, begged Belisarius for a donation, for her merchant father had been maimed when a passing cart rolled ponderously over the man's foot. Though her clean skin and well-kept linens showed none of the deprivations of poverty, Belisarius did not brush her requests aside. Instead, temporarily halting our progress, he offered a warm welcome. Withdrawing a thin slip of parchment from a tube hanging along his belt, Belisarius offered it as a gift.

"I am presently occupied, but make for the palace and seek the attentions of Germanus. Present this slip to the guards, who will allow you entry. This slip was prewritten to grant audiences of the citizens of Carthage to its governor."

Taking the parchment carefully in her fingers as if it were made of solid gold, the woman sank into full prostration at Belisarius' feet. Shaking his head, Belisarius insisted she rise before pointing her in the direction of the main entrance.

"Hurry now. The palace will close for public petitions in but a few hours."

Offering another swift bow, the woman turned to sprint toward the palace. Others pressed Belisarius for further favors or discussion, and he did his best to address each in turn. Eventually, however, the grasping hands and spirited shouts became too much for even the well-disciplined general, who insisted that each citizen's needs would be thoroughly discussed in the days ahead. Most shrugged and went back to their business in the forum, although a handful remained in hopes that their pleas may rise above all others.

"I think a faster pace may be warranted," Belisarius said.

"Agreed," I answered. "By now, the entire city will know of my return. By tomorrow evening, there will be ships sneaking away to Italy and Hispania, telling the Goths of our return to Constantinople."

"Troubling." Belisarius hummed in agreement. "We never did catch Liberius' spy, although my bucellarii have discovered figures lurking near the palace well after sunset, speaking with slaves or attendants."

"You did not question anyone?" I asked.

"Of course we did, although none ever knew a name or even a face," Belisarius answered, his tone somber. "However, there is one piece of information we did discover, known only to three people."

"Three?" I wondered aloud, at once curious and disappointed that I had not been previously included.

"Three," Belisarius whispered, leaning close. "Me, the bucellarius who discovered it, and the spy. My guard trailed an unknown man who was spotted in a closed section of the palace. He followed the intruder through the city and all the way to his abode."

"And caught him?"

"Sadly, no," Belisarius continued. "He seemed to have run. But my guard discovered several bags of old silver coins splayed about, as well as all the materials to unhinge locks. Those tools would be suspicious enough, had the coins not borne the face of King Theodoric."

No Roman would possess such coinage, I knew. "So the escaped man must have been in the pay of the Goths."

"Likely, but that discovery leads to two further questions," Belisarius said. "Which Goths, and who in Carthage's palace does this spy have a connection to?"

"And is there more than one spy?" I added, eyeing passersby suspiciously.

"I know nothing else," Belisarius said. "And I only have earned more questions than I started with. All I can be certain of is that we are being watched, and the likelihood that someone in Carthage is betraying our trust is uncomfortably high."

Leaving the forum, we passed along the Byrsa Hill and its rows of stone houses lacquered in white paint. Designed to repel heat even when the coastal winds grew mild on summer nights, such houses would have been a marvel for Constantinople's engineers, though in direct sunlight they strained the eyes of passersby. Squinting against the reflected rays, I struggled to keep pace with Belisarius, who visibly relaxed as the press of petitioners evaporated.

"You would think that life would have calmed down after months of rebuilding, but no," Belisarius whispered. "You have no idea how happy I am that you and Liberius have returned."

I shrugged. "Surely this stress will belong to Solomon soon enough?"

"Theoretically," Belisarius allowed. "But do you imagine that Solomon would take such responsibilities seriously?"

"No," I muttered bitterly.

I did not sense Samur shuffle closer behind me until he growled in hatred. "Not if every woman in this city would lift her skirts for him."

Belisarius offered a muted laugh to my scowling brother, raising his hand in surrender. "I have hope for the man, but I cannot help but agree with you, Samur. Which is why I'll petition Justinian to appoint a prefect more adept at addressing the considerable needs of the population more adroitly than Solomon or myself. Until then, I can only hope that Troglita and Stotzas will curb the worst of Solomon's urges."

Both Samur and Rosamund spat in derision, yet offered no further remark. These complaints were a waste of wind, for as I had discovered in the earliest years of my memory, notions of fairness or justice rarely applied to men such as Solomon. Almighty God knows that Solomon did not deserve the honor of ruling over Belisarius' conquest, yet between God and the Emperor, Romans served one master far more enthusiastically than the other.

Our pace slowed once more as we rounded Byrsa Hill. To our right, pillars of steam rose from Carthage's immense network of public baths, still well-kept and sparkling in the sun despite nearly four hundred years of continuous use. Even the Vandals were said to marvel at these gifts of long-dead and much-beloved Emperor Antoninus Pius, using the baths to scrape away thick layers of grime after a full day of training with all manner of weapons and horses. After an extended stay in Tingitana, I lusted after the scraping and washing of a formal Roman bath, yet I lacked the stamina to remain awake through the hours-long process. Such luxuries would have to wait for the morning.

Instead, our progress continued along Carthage's stone-lined alleyways. Switching toward more pleasant yet inane conversation, Belisarius chattered about topics entirely unrelated to the burdens of office. He spoke longingly of his daughter Joannina, who nevertheless was reported to be enjoying the care of Mariya's growing household on my Pella estate. Inevitably, praise of his daughter's progress turned to Antonina. Belisarius' eyes glimmered in the same manner I had seen after they were first married. "You, Troglita, and me... we're lucky!" He beamed.

I offered no reply, which Belisarius appeared to interpret as assent. Privately, I cringed for my friend, picturing not only countless instances of Antonina's entitled cruelty as a child, as well as the filthy rumors of her entanglement with Sergius. To be sure, I told no lie, not even by omission, a fact that did nevertheless not assuage the pangs I felt.

Belisarius went on to share gossip of activity in the Capitol, including the construction of a massive church intended to replace the ill-fated Hagia Sophia that had been rendered to a crisp in the riots. He began to speak of the endless need for horses, only to apologize as he saw what must have been a mournful expression on my face.

"No horse could ever replace Ignis, but we will find you another mount," Belisarius promised. "Perhaps another Nisean? They're expensive... but easier to find now that the Persians wish to trade coin rather than lives."

"Perhaps," I muttered, my thoughts traveling momentarily to my fallen steed. "It will likely be necessary, although in truth I never favored riding into battle. Plant two feet on solid earth, and I'll stand in any shield wall you command."

"This was plain, even after Dara." Belisarius sighed. "I intended to have you lead my spearmen, and John the cavalry. But with John gone..."

Belisarius paused a heartbeat, a dark shade temporarily passing over his otherwise warm smile. "I needed a man capable of commanding horsemen. We have become an army that wins or dies based upon its cavalry, and I needed a man capable of the task. I hope you are not too disappointed with me for placing you in this position."

"Of course not, Lord!" I stammered, desperate to shift the conversation away from future service. Belisarius chuckled at such a display, likely believing my grimace as stemming from the stubborn formality that I instinctively relied upon. "I know of no man who could have done more with so little," I added.

"That's overgenerous of you," Belisarius replied. "But all the same, my forces are painfully thin on officers. With Baduarius and John both gone to the afterlife, and many others likely to resign from injury or a simple desire to leave the army, I will need considerable help in the next year. I was already intending to ask Theodora to formally nominate you as my second even before Septem, but now, only a fool would not grant you such an opportunity."

Belisarius presented me with an immense honor. Unfortunately, it was the opposite of my desires, and would have committed me to another decade of service to the Emperor's wars. I was loath to disappoint Belisarius, but I eagerly sought any opening to reject Belisarius' offer. "But the foederati—"

"Perenus will also receive a formal promotion, although he has fulfilled such duties for several months now anyway," Belisarius interrupted. "Samur will be granted more independence over the Huns, but the Heruli and the Vandals will be his, as will one or two other cohorts that the Emperor intends to levy in the spring."

I felt deflated. Belisarius appeared to have considered all obstacles preventing me from serving as his second—reducing the opportunities I would have to disqualify myself from that role. "What of Indulf? The Ostrogoths?"

Belisarius shrugged. "Their campaign has ended, and I am sure that Indulf, from your reports, will desire to return home. Even if

Indulf were not wounded, all Italy is aflame with Amalasuntha dead."

There was no more opportune time to tell Belisarius of my misgivings. Of a desire, at least for a season, to part from the Imperial Army. My head swam as I gathered the courage to refuse his offer and beg the peace to return to Mariya and my children, and leave all the nightmares and killing behind. I have little doubt that Belisarius would have graciously acceded to that request.

But I was a coward. Perhaps a lingering desire to please my long-dead dominus remained, or to fulfill the dreams of Liberius or Father Petrus. More likely, however, I could not bring myself to swipe Belisarius' outstretched hand away. At least, not when his unhealed wounds left him vulnerable, and few remained to shoulder the weary struggles that had been thrust upon our general. Instead, I changed the subject, raising one further question rising from my prior meeting with Theudis.

"Lord, I know little of the Ostrogoths or Amalasuntha, but I've heard enough rumors to be concerned," I began. "Does the Emperor intend to send us to fight in Italy?"

"It certainly is disconcerting," Belisarius agreed. "It was always Justin's dream to retake Italy, although I'm not sure that even he considered outright war, rather than a marriage between Theodoric's daughter and our emperor. Theodora ended any hopes for that."

"But will Justinian draw us into conflict?"

"I truly do not know," Belisarius admitted. "The Ostrogoths violently seizing Lilybaeum from its Vandal garrison was as concerning a blow as Amalasuntha's murder. I have little doubt that there will be war in Italy… I just don't know whether we'll be drawn in. The Ostrogoths are simply too numerous, and too well armed, for the Empire to fight and win on foreign territory."

Samur drew closer, his interest piqued. "The Italians wouldn't help Justinian's army overthrow the Goths?"

"No," Belisarius said. "At least, not unless the risk of doing so is minimal. The Eastern Empire abandoned the Italians to their fate generations ago, and men like Liberius will tell you that resentment against Constantinople lingers. We may be linked by a common heritage, but much like the Ostrogoths and Visigoths, the Greeks and Italians nurse their resentments. Most of all, we simply do not have enough men to hold our new territories and simultaneously fight a full-scale war with hundreds of thousands of Ostrogoths. Basilius argued that Justinian should pursue such a course, but I doubt that the old consul could have foreseen a complete and total victory over Gelimer and his kingdom."

Curiously, Belisarius' words left me even more concerned, yet somehow at ease. Having been fortunate to only face a sliver of Theudis' forces, I had no desire to face a fully laden Ostrogothic horde in a battle of ridiculously lopsided proportions. However, if Belisarius was unaware of future plans to engage such a war, I doubted any of Justinian's other ministers would have pushed forth such a notion in secret. Basilius had given voice to Justin's dreams, but surely even he would voice caution as the Empire consolidated its sudden increase in territory and population. As I listened to Belisarius, however, the voices of Justin and Basilius somehow intertwined in my memory, leaving me only half-conscious of Belisarius' continuing thoughts as we ambled through Carthage's streets.

One land, one religion, one emperor!

We must rebuild our empire. We must take Carthage, we must take Ravenna, we must take Rome!

And ever so faintly, a rasping voice whispered behind both men. Unlike the others, it carried the faintest scent of burning oil. The hairs on my skin stood on end. None seemed to hear it but me.

All you are, my boy, is a creeping death that will cloak the world in blackness!

"At any rate, no decision will be made quickly," Belisarius said. "We will all enjoy a much-needed reunion with our families."

I nodded, having heard little of Belisarius' more recent statements. He continued to speak about his experiences in Carthage and all the things he wished to do with Antonina. Most of all, he wanted to purchase a simple house on a green hill, with plenty of oxen and attendants to grow wheat and grapes for harvest. "Perhaps we may find such lodging near Pella!"

"I would like that very much, Lord," I said, bringing another chuckle as Belisarius corrected my formality.

By then, we had finally neared the building that served as my home after Belisarius' liberation of Carthage. Despite such progress, Belisarius showed no intention of returning to the palace, and instead doubled his enthusiasm for idle conversation.

"I rarely get to leave the palace halls," he remarked. "It's refreshing to gain a better view of where Carthage's denizens live."

"There's little enough to view," I replied. "But I thank you for clearing the streets of refuse and dung."

Belisarius beamed. "Not an easy feat, especially to gather so much water to spill across the streets! For an entire week, the gutters ran brown with all manner of filth. It wasn't until the eighth day that washed stone showed through."

We did not hear the disturbance within—not at first. At first, the sounds were overwhelmed by the constant chatter of activity along the streets, the guttural moaning that echoed faintly from the building unable to reach my ears. Yet, as we reached the threshold, the keening sounds of the voice was unmistakable—coming somewhere from the upper floors.

Samur rushed to the doorway, bringing a finger to his lips before unsheathing his blade. Belisarius and I copied his example, save that I leaned toward Rosamund to whisper instructions.

"Move off to an alley in case the thief would draw blood," I hissed.

But Rosamund shook her head. "No. Varus, we should all leave—"

"Don't worry," I whispered back. "There's no reason to be afraid with all three of us armed."

"It's not that," Rosamund replied urgently. "It's—"

"Silence!" Samur whispered. "Let's go!"

"Varus!" Rosamund grabbed at my arm, her voice raised. "You don't understand. Don't—"

"Quiet!" I shook her off and brushed past.

There is nothing so insolent as a man convinced to take action. And God, but I was insolent. A cooler head would have taken a precious moment to heed Rosamund, who knew more of that building than Samur, Belisarius, or myself. Yet I ignored her, as I had done countless other times to my peril. And in that moment, her gods must have laughed at my folly. More, they must have reveled in the fate they cast for Belisarius.

With Rosamund's key, Samur jiggled the iron lock open and pushed the door slowly ajar. Then, raising a finger again to his lips, Samur lifted each foot gently along the carpeted floor, careful of the creaking that inevitably ensued along wooden floorboards. After reaching the interior, Samur beckoned first to me, then to Belisarius. Rather than risk alerting the intruders upstairs to our presence, Samur left the door unlocked and open, sliding his way toward the staircase that led up to the bedrooms.

As Samur crept up each step, the groans ceased, the pained sounds replaced by two voices, their words muffled by thick layers of wood and stone. Belisarius and I followed in Samur's wake to the landing, where darkness prevailed and only slivers of sunlight snuck through the cracks of unfastened windows. There were no candles, though neither was there any dust, curious given that no one ought to have been in while I was deployed to Septem. Stranger still were a few vague outlines of footprints etched in dried dirt along the floor.

The further we progressed along the narrow hallways, the fewer our sources of light became. Though my eyes adjusted to the gloom, inevitably Samur and I bumped along the walls, with Samur connecting hard against a railing as the hallway curved to the right. On cue, the faint voices ceased, replaced only by creaking boards and an occasional thump.

"Shit!" Samur hissed. "Prepare yourselves!"

Samur's pace quickened, and I struggled to follow without brushing along the walls. Belisarius struggled even more, and he was forced to hold tight to my cloak to keep from toppling over. We continued a few more paces until, cursing at the poor visibility,

Samur threw two shutters open. Light poured through, first blinding, then illuminating our path to the door that concealed the intruders. Hurried thudding sounded inside, something like footsteps carelessly slapping against the interior floor. Dropping to a crouch, Samur raised his blade level with his chest, prepared to thrust at first glance upon the thieves. With his free hand, he reached for the bedroom door, his fingers delicately sliding around its knob. Then, with a violent twist, Samur threw open the door and surged inside.

Only to be met by a woman's scream.

"Go back!" Samur shouted.

Confused, yet unwilling to abandon my brother to assault, I refused. Instead, with Belisarius lurking close behind, I burst through the doorway, blade raised, to join my brother. Once inside, I discovered the terrible error in my judgment. Lowering my blade, my jaw dropped, and I wished that I had not arrived early from Septem.

Belisarius spoke first. And never before or since, have I heard a greater sound of confusion or pain.

"Antonina?"

Half naked, the figure on the bed quivered in silence. Unable to think, I managed at least to avert my eyes, then sheathed my sword and motioned for Samur to do the same. Belisarius, however, remained fixed, his eyes impossibly wide as his chest rose and fell in a desperate hunger for air. It was then, in our stunned silence, that the second figure rushed to the doorway.

Both Samur and I, stunned by Antonina's presence, reacted too slowly. Jumping from a darkened corner, the half-dressed man knocked me aside and rammed Samur into a wall before slipping out the open door. Belisarius darted after him, yet tripped over Samur's upended boot as the man's feet pattered along the house's steps. Though the man's identity was difficult to discern in the upheaval, Antonina's weeping betrayed her lover.

"Sergius!"

She wailed, clutching a thin blanket around her bare skin, as her husband drew himself to stand.

"Out!" Belisarius roared.

At first I did not react, believing the order to be for his wife. Yet as I lifted Samur back to his feet, Belisarius repeated the order.

"Varus, please," he growled.

No argument. Samur and I stepped outside, my brother's face drained of all color. I thought of pursuing Sergius, yet a slamming front door sent my thoughts whirling to Rosamund, who stood but a few paces behind me. Besides, without clothes, weapons, or coin, there were very few places a Roman centurion could safely hide in the city, especially once all the resources of a Roman general were poured into a manhunt.

"I never did like her," Samur whispered in Hunnic as the door closed. "But what in the deepest hell was she thinking?"

I had no words. All I could do was curse my stubbornness, wishing I had acted upon the suspicions of Mariya and Rosamund sooner. What I might have done, I am still not certain. But inevitably, my inaction had enabled my lord's torment, almost as if I had become party to Sergius and Antonina's sin.

All I could do was shrug, interrupted by a shudder as a heavy crash came from the bedroom. Nodding further down the hall, we walked down the stairs just as a great cry echoed through the building, the deep rumble unmistakably from Belisarius.

"How could you do this?"

In an instant, all the joy of victory and hope for peace evaporated. There was nothing to be done to improve the situation—indeed, it would soon grow a great deal worse.

OBEDIENCE

Many today, in their cups, mock Belisarius, chuckling that a man who had conquered half the known world could not bring his patrician wife to heel. Such tales ultimately derive from a single source, yet spread like brushfire through the wagging tongues of the Imperial Court and well beyond. Ever the ink-stained clerk, Procopius' battles were fought with quills and secrecy, his fortunes paid through slander and cowardice. Of course, in those waning days of our occupation of Carthage, we knew little of Procopius' meddling, yet within days, whispers of Belisarius the cuckold were hissed in every tavern in the city.

Worse were the fantastic tales of Belisarius' reaction after catching his wife with her lover. Some claimed that Belisarius ordered Sergius' body to be riven at the chest and dumped in a nearby latrine, all identifiable features pounded with a blacksmith's hammer and caked in piss and dung. More sinister rumors contended that Belisarius dragged his wife naked through Carthage's gates and ordered her lashed to a wooden post and flogged bloody. In one version of that rumor, my brother had relished carrying out Belisarius' order upon his former classmate, with Samur's bloodlust and Belisarius' vengeance halted only by me. I can promise you that whoever crafted that fantastic lie paid me no favors, for it placed me directly at odds with both men whom I loved dearly.

The truth, as it almost always is, was far more mundane. After a time, Belisarius departed the soiled bedroom as Antonina wrapped a shift around her exposed skin. There were no threats of torture, at least not for her. I saw no broken furniture, nor did either of the two bear any new abrasions. Instead, face blotchy and wet, Belisarius walked to our open window and offered a brief exchange to me alone.

"Sergius escaped?"

"Unfortunately, Lord," I said. "We will send men to catch him before nightfall."

"See that you do," he muttered. "Do not let Antonina leave this place. See that her needs are met, within reason."

Belisarius did not pause for a reply. Instead, he strode briskly through the front door and back toward the palace. Shortly thereafter, Samur came to me, a Janus-like expression of anger and amusement on his face.

"Should we call for a magistrate?" he muttered in Hunnic. "A jailor?"

"No," I responded, though I was not confident in my answer. "Gather a party of trusted men and hunt down Sergius, but discreetly. We do not need to call unnecessary attention to this matter."

"Too late for that," Samur replied. "Half the city will know what transpired here by nightfall. If Belisarius doesn't at least place Antonina in chains, he'll be laughed at for the rest of his life."

"Perhaps," I countered. "But he only ordered us to keep Antonina here, and in relative comfort."

Samur grunted, not caring to press the matter. Of course, Belisarius said little about summoning a magistrate to levy charges against Antonina, when both Roman custom and law dictated severe punishment for directly observed adultery. If caught during or immediately after their transgression, Belisarius was well within his rights to slay both sinners without worrying about later condemnation. Though he did not order anyone killed, neither did he command Antonina be disgraced in the courts, the minimum that most were expecting. For now, she had been spared such public humiliation, merely left to sob in a dark room with little more than a soiled straw bed and disheveled clothing to comfort her. It was only then that I grew curious about how Belisarius' wife had gained access to my locked rooms, with a faint worry flickering in my mind that Belisarius might somehow believe me complicit.

It was Rosamund, standing patiently in the street as Belisarius' drama unfolded, who explained how such fates had come to pass. As Samur departed to assemble his Huns, she and I drew back into the house. "Antonina offered her servants to keep our rooms free of vermin while we ventured to Tingitana," she whispered. "I paid a blacksmith to fashion a second set of keys for her. She likely did not believe we would return for several more days."

I nodded. "And Sergius?"

"I warned you, Varus," Rosamund said, her whisper urgent. "He has an insatiable lust. I was a fool to trust Antonina's word, but I felt sorry for her."

Rosamund pursed her lips into a frown, though I disbelieved its authenticity. She was too intelligent to ignore Antonina's flimsy explanations or trust that Antonina's motives for seeking access to the building were altruistic. Not that I believed Rosamund complicit in Antonina's crimes—Rosamund was visibly concerned of the fate that awaited her friend. Still, it was unsettling, not understanding Rosamund's intentions, though I opted to swallow any suspicion I had of her in order to maintain peace in an already disrupted household.

"You feel sorry for her? How does she deserve any pity?"

"You do not know," Rosamund said, raising a hand as I began to mouth a protest, "what it is like to be possessed, and have no will of your own. Believe me, to be a woman in your Empire is nothing to envy. Little power and no respect... at least not beyond your duties to birth heirs and placate husbands."

My face grew hot with frustration. "What would you know of such a life? You move about as you wish."

For once, Rosamund stepped back in surprise, her tone deferential. "My life is better than most," she conceded, "and I am eternally grateful for all you have done for me, but until I spent my days with Antonina, I did not know how… *mundane* Roman women's lives were. How clipped they are of anything useful, interesting, meaningful. I knew there were differences with the men from what I saw in Constantinople, but to be shut away and ignored…"

My frustration simmered at the brink of my control. "Antonina is privileged beyond reckoning. If you believe her persecuted, then you should have seen her as a child."

"Whatever she did to you and Samur was cruel," Rosamund acknowledged, "but she was a child. Meanwhile, the Romans pride themselves on civility, insisting that we savage barbarians are trapped in some crude darkness. But there's nothing sophisticated about such routine indifference, such mistreatment of your sisters, wives, and daughters."

"I challenge you to name a single manner where Belisarius mistreated Antonina!" I yelled. "He *adored* her. He's always said so."

"Yes," Rosamund answered. "He adored her like a goddess. Like a *statue* of a goddess. But women are not statues. We want conversation and joy and life. Antonina is far too intelligent, and far too ambitious, to be given kisses and then left behind like some unspeaking monument."

Though I heard Rosamund's words, and at some level understood their meaning, I could reserve no affection in my heart for my childhood tormentor. Even if Antonina *had* been a kinder, more virtuous person, I still would have resented her for the raw shame she unleashed upon my general. All I saw was a spoiled child who had grown into a spoiled woman who surrendered to her basest urges. The daughter of a wealthy man who yearned for ever greater quantities of wealth and position in the Imperial Court, achievable through Belisarius' advancement.

Of all the people in the Empire, there could not be anyone who relished the responsibility of Antonina's care less than I did. But fate is both fickle and cruel, for just as Belisarius could not have foreseen the heartbreak that struck like lightning, neither would I ever have predicted that I would be the one to hold Antonina's comfort in my hands.

Samur despised her. That much was plain, and I doubted that his desire to drag Antonina to a jailor was to seek justice and defend Belisarius' honor as much as it was to inflict further embarrassment upon a rotten soul. Faint urges to toss Antonina aside flickered in my own heart, and I nearly surrendered to them if only to relieve myself of the unwanted burden of her minding. Yet Belisarius did command me to keep Antonina within my roof, although I have little doubt that he would not have begrudged me from seeking justice in a nearby dungeon. After all, this was the minimum that Imperial law called for in such heinous violations of marriage fidelity.

Alas, I did not succumb to my own cruel wishes, although it was not through any major sense of virtue. For now, I would respect Belisarius' wishes, and at least pay the friend of my wife and of Rosamund the courtesy of moderately comfortable care. I allowed Rosamund to enter the bedroom, with great wails echoing through the walls after its door was closed tight once more.

I did not venture back to Carthage's palace. Instead, stripping off my soiled traveling clothes and donning more comfortable linen, I moved to an unoccupied bedroom, placing my sword and dagger upon a nearby mantle before collapsing into sleep. I was left unmolested until dawn, my body soaking in long-denied rest.

As I slept, more of my ships drew into Carthage's harbor. Though most would depart for Constantinople in a matter of days, we were still required to empty our cargoes and restock stores of food and water for the much lengthier journey ahead. Moreover, few men would have happily embarked upon another voyage without stealing aboard purchases of wine and rich food from Carthage's bazaar. After awakening, I tasked a freshly returned Cephalas with procuring many of the items that inevitably would be required by the burgeoning ranks of foederati.

"No excessive wine," I warned him upon handing over a weighty sack of silver coins. "Most of the men need clothes, shoes, belts... I don't want them pissing away our wealth while rolling in squalor."

Cephalas offered a wide grin. "I'll tell them, and I'm sure they'll listen!"

My final days in Carthage blurred together. As Samur predicted, word of Antonina's transgression was on the lips of even the humblest of peasants by the following evening, made worse by Samur and the Huns' failure to locate a half-clothed and unarmed Sergius. The Hun foederati traipsed through the city and eventually rode around its hinterlands, finding little other than rumors and false trails. The promise of gold did little to simplify matters, for such rewards only enticed liars to spin fantastic tales of their brush against the now-infamous Roman centurion. After the fourth day, the hunt was prematurely ended, although the town watch was under strict orders to detain Sergius should he ever reappear in any city under Roman control.

A few meetings were called, with Belisarius absent even those that Liberius assembled in preparation of the army's long journey home. Nothing was said of Antonina, who had only spoken to Rosamund in the days that followed her downfall. Some, such as Perenus and Ascum, did pry for information, but I ignored their prodding.

Aside from Antonina's presence, little had changed in my temporary home. A blacksmith fashioned new locks for the door, while teams of servants gathered all manner of possessions and treasure that I had gained since arriving in Africa. This did not include my share of Gelimer's spoils—those remained under strict guard by Belisarius until the men returned home—yet dozens of chests were required to store household belongings. This was compounded by Cephalas' purchases of exotic fruits, cheese, twice-baked bread, and all manner of clothing and boots. Though nothing remained of Cephalas' budgeted coin, the wineskins were conspicuously absent, to which Cephalas pleaded ignorance. All I know is that none under my charge complained of unmet needs, and that Gunderic personally led a week of celebrations prior to his journey to Constantinople.

Antonina refused to leave her room, forcing Rosamund and other female servants to haul bedding, food, and piss pots to and from her makeshift prison. Washbasins were offered each morning, and each second day a change of clothes was pilfered from Antonina's rooms inside the palace. On the third day, I finally managed to reconvene with Father Petrus, yet Antonina flatly refused to speak with the priest.

"There are many things I've regretted in my service to God," Petrus confided in me, "but a lover is not amongst them, for I have witnessed how easily scorn turns to resentment. Though I wish I could provide comfort to your new ward. It is good to see you returned and well, nonetheless."

"I wish you had accompanied me to Septem, Father," I replied, desperate to change the subject away from my unwanted houseguest. "It was an experience I would not like to repeat again."

Father Petrus nodded. "Liberius has told me. But he also said that you handled your responsibility marvelously. You have freed thousands of people from tyranny and fear, Varus, and that is an accomplishment to be truly proud of."

I shook my head. "I never thought of the people of Tingitana, only of fulfilling my orders. And after Baduarius died, I nearly abandoned the siege and sailed for Carthage."

"But you did not!" Petrus insisted. "Such responsibility is a terrible thing, Varus, but it gives you the rare power to change the lives of so many. Justin knew you were more than capable for such a task, as did Godilas."

"Father..." I said, "I want to leave the army."

The words spilled from my heart, and I immediately wished I could recall them. Petrus cocked his head, pausing with his mouth slightly open as he considered a response.

"Your term of service has been fulfilled, and the Empress would grant your release," Petrus said. "Is this about Septem?"

"Yes... and no. Since Tricamarum, all I've felt are nightmares and doubt." I hesitated, my arm shaking as images of Mount Papua formed in my mind. "I want to be more than a killer. I want my two small children to know who their father is, and to be more to my wife than an estate and faint memories." Pausing again, I rubbed my hands together for warmth. "I don't know what I'm doing here anymore. I've done terrible things in the Emperor's name, and I'm not even sure whether it's for a greater purpose. Rosamund insists that her pagan gods favor me somehow, but…"

Petrus' nose wrinkled. "I've warned you about that woman. Does her belief find fertile ground in you now?"

"Of course not!" I protested. "I don't understand what she means, anyway."

"There's nothing to understand, for it's all superstition and nonsense," the priest insisted. Then, softening his gaze, he allowed several moments to pass as I took deep breaths before resting a cool, frail hand over my own. "I understand what it means to serve a leader who is undeserving of devotion. And you have been too long from your family, this is plain. But out of respect for my love for you, pay me one favor."

"Anything."

"Wait until Belisarius' triumph ends before making your decision. He needs you now, and there is little point in separating yourself from the army when a voyage awaits us."

There was little to argue with such logic. Rosamund protested later, yet the priest held one undeterrable arrow in his quiver—to abandon Belisarius now, in Carthage, would seem nothing less than an opportunistic betrayal of a broken man, regardless of my own motivations. I agreed to the priest's request, earning his embrace. After, we spoke of Theudis, the Pillars, and ominous warnings of Justinian's intentions for Italy. Father Petrus listened intently to all, yet offered neither judgment nor assessment of Amalasuntha, Theudis, or anything of Justinian's plans for the future.

As my final week progressed and the army continued its plans to load hundreds of transports and head to the seas, two more memorable conversations took place. The first was out of duty, for I had neglected our Ostrogothic foederati for too long, and Perenus had neither the formal standing nor the intuition to assuage Indulf's fragile honor. And so, leaving Sembrouthes guarding Antonina, I ventured to the temporary barracks that housed the hundreds of Ostrogoths that remained to Belisarius' forces.

Indulf would never fully recover from his duel with Agila. His face, once a lure to many a maid, had been shriven into a latticework of red and white scars. One eye drooped, leaving his face asymmetrical, as though permanently on the precipice of melting. Yet, whereas Ascum's injuries left the man crippled on one side of his body, Indulf otherwise remained in admirable fitness. Upon his return to Carthage, Indulf had regained his sight, and insisted that the pain of his ongoing healing had dulled to bearable discomfort.

"I thank you for all your sacrifices, Lord Indulf, in both Africa and Tingitana," I offered. "It is past time such sacrifices were rewarded. My wonder, however, is whether you intend to sail for Syracuse?"

"We're going back to Constantinople first," Indulf said. "I intend to collect my gold from your Emperor, and then petition directly for his capture of Amalasuntha's killers."

"And the nature of that petition?"

Indulf grunted. "The nature of any war. Men. Gold. Grain. My enemies impaled on spikes while still living. If you've a mind for war, your presence would be welcome."

"Perhaps," I lied. "I will speak with the Empress about your intentions."

"Justinian's keeper." Indulf snorted. "I wonder if that man will ever come out of Theodora's skirts, given what I've heard about his conduct during the Nika Riots. Yes, if you could convince Theodora of the validity of our claims, I could promise you gold and jewels beyond imagining."

"I am already a wealthy man, Lord Indulf, and a weary one. But you have sacrificed much for the Empire, so I will do you the courtesy of pursuing justice for your queen."

Indulf rolled his eyes. "Spare me your courtier's manners, excubitor. One thing I despise of you Romans is that you never speak plainly. My oathsworn master was slain with her son, and even with the killer's identity, your weakling Emperor has done nothing to avenge his supposed friend."

"Which man do you blame for Amalasuntha's murder?" I asked, now unable to disguise my irritation and desire to end such an unpleasant conversation.

"Theodahad, most likely," Indulf growled, confirming a name that Liberius had noted prior to my assault upon Septem. "He surely lacked the manhood to do the killing himself, but the fat old lecher surely hated his dear cousin. Now he calls himself king, although many of the Gothic lords deny his claim. They say he favors hairless boys, much in the same manner as your dead emperors used to."

"I will look into this manner and speak with Theodora personally," I offered. "That, and my thanks for your service, is all that I can promise to convey back to you."

"Save me your gratitude," Indulf spat. "Fight with us like a man or tuck your cock between your legs and run away like these Roman prats. It was a mistake coming here. If I had remained in Italy, Amalasuntha might still be alive."

There was little to gain by further argument. Indulf was brave, of course, and unquestionably skilled in the shield wall. Yet he was disagreeable and rash, and for that there was little to cool his mind. With a light bob of the head, I concluded my conversation with Indulf, hoping to never see such a wretched creature ever again. God knows I was thankful that my lordship over the Ostrogoth foederati had finally drawn to a close.

Yet, if my meeting with Indulf was unpleasant, what followed was unquestionably distasteful, as it was unforeseen. And, as is true with many vexing meetings, it began with a welcome from a friend.

With neither guards nor entourage, Bessas arrived fully cloaked, his features masked. At first, Cephalas denied the stranger entry, yet was eventually convinced to allow Bessas into a small dining hall on the lower level. Refusing wine, Bessas instead focused entirely on the sour business at hand.

"I'm glad it wasn't me that caught Antonina," Bessas mused, unwrapping the heavy cloak from his shoulders. "I've never seen Belisarius so despondent."

"He hasn't spoken with me since," I noted.

Bessas sighed, suddenly changing his mind about the wine. A household servant offered a clay cup that the Armenian soldier sipped before placing it gingerly upon a low table. "It isn't your fault, Varus. But you and your brother witnessed his wife with another man."

"But that isn't my f—"

"Of course it isn't," Bessas interrupted. "And Belisarius would not have sent me here if he bore you any grudge. But the man has changed, Varus. Even when he was imprisoned by Hermogenes after Callinicum, the general always remained implacable. But now, it seems like whatever happiness he had has been replaced with suspicion and anger." Bessas paused for another sip. "Sergius escaping also has not helped matters."

Running a hand through my hair, I used my fingers to whittle at a rising ache in my temples. "What else would Belisarius have me do?"

"Serve as Antonina's caretaker—she'll accompany you upon whichever ship you intend to sail back to Constantinople."

I groaned, the throbbing in my head worsening. "Caretaker? Or jailor?"

Bessas shrugged. "In this instance, one is the same as the other. Troglita and Mundus have both recommended that Antonina be handed over to Carthage's jailors and kept away from her father, while Ascum argued that we should hang her and be done with it."

Basilius. I had not truly considered the councilor, and was surprised that Father Petrus offered no support for his longtime friend's only child. True, there was little enough that the old priest might do to intervene so far from Constantinople, yet Basilius' wrath would be considerable—both upon his daughter, as well as those who might seek to punish her.

"What does Belisarius want?"

"To go back in time," Bessas said. "To keep her penned away until life makes sense. But the Emperor commands the army to return, so Belisarius is forced to make a decision. And so he's insistent that Antonina remain as your guest, at least until a decision is made. At a minimum, he trusts that Antonina will not be abused in your care."

"I do not want this burden," I grumbled. Privately, my thoughts were more colorful, and far more likely to foster trouble if repeated to Belisarius. That Antonina's actions were despicable, though I would do nothing about it. The woman was a torment in my childhood, and now I was expected to show her comfort and mercy when she deserved neither.

"I would not wish to be in your position, friend," Bessas concluded. "And Belisarius did say that he would not force you. But if you won't do this, then I can guarantee Antonina will end up in a far worse predicament. For Belisarius' conscience, I would not wish this."

Sighing, I agreed. "Nor I. Very well, send me whatever belongings Antonina may have from the palace. I'll have her ready to travel with me in three days."

"Good man," Bessas said, draining the cup. "I will tell Belisarius how helpful you have been."

"I wish he would come say that himself," I said. "I feel like I'm being punished."

Bessas nodded somberly. "One day at a time. Just remember, we have conquered far greater difficulties than this. All we can do is serve, even if our master appears rudderless on certain days."

There was little else to say on the matter. Later that day, a cart from the palace rolled to our house, bearing chests and crates not to unpack, but to join with those of my household as cargo on our journey home. Cephalas led the effort to ready our ship for departure, a task that he relished, bringing a soldier's discipline to his personal proficiency for organization and quartermastery.

We were not assigned berths upon the flagship intended for Belisarius or Liberius. Instead, a captive Gelimer and his household were allocated our places aboard Apollos' ship, intended for presentation before the Emperor himself. At first, this news offended me, yet within hours I surrendered to the cold logic of Belisarius' need to remain separate from his dishonored wife. Instead, we were granted command over the *Fides*, a smaller yet sturdy transport that had seen decades of service in the Imperial navy, which I took as a sign of confidence in her seaworthiness. Rosamund, however, complained bitterly at our assignment.

"They're putting us in some slime-riddled cog to aggravate Antonina," Rosamund argued. "We'll all be sick by the time we reach Greece."

"Belisarius wouldn't do that," I insisted—and for my sake, I hoped it was true.

Rosamund rolled her eyes. "Maybe yes, maybe no. But at a minimum, we're stuck on a smaller boat with too many people to care for."

And she was not wrong. Other than its bevy of sailors, our ship could berth only fifty, and the fifteen of my household and a dozen Aksumite guardsmen alone took up many of those places. Even Samur had to find lodgings on another ship, although he seemed unperturbed at spending additional time at sea with Sinnion, Aigan, and the other Huns that he had instructed. Still ostracized from the Carthaginian palace, Uliaris joined our numbers, leaving room only for a couple dozen Vandals under Gunderic. The Vandals' inclusion was at Xerxes' suggestion, drawing my confused glance at why the Vandals' war leader would be separated from the bulk of his men.

"The last thing I need is that giant oaf getting my ship's captain drunk." Xerxes grinned. "He's your problem until we reach dry land."

Even the ship's name—*Fides*, fidelity—felt like a sloppy attack upon Antonina's character. But nothing about the voyage could be changed, by me or anyone else, and the general's wife remained shut in her bedroom, allowing only Rosamund and recurring grief as her companions in isolation until we departed. The next two days were a flurry of nervous energy as hundreds of men and women hauled all manner of goods and treasure onto Belisarius' great fleet, unsure of whether the Empire would ever return in its glory.

The day before our scheduled departure, Solomon arrived with a retinue of fifty men to assume his seat in Carthage's palace. Though I did not witness his initial meeting with Liberius, I did catch his smug form riding stiffly upon a horse, his armor polished to catch the waning sun's rays. A small gaggle of Carthaginians flocked around the curious display, prompting Solomon to signal for his men to hand coins to beggars. As Solomon waved to the increasing crowd of onlookers, one woman slithered past Solomon's guards and toward his horse, planting a kiss upon the Roman commander's boot. Clearly confused by the gesture, Solomon shouted for the woman to retreat, with the harsh command sending his horse jerking into a gallop. The woman was driven hard to the ground, her skull connecting against the stone streets. A pool of blood matted along her thin mop as she remained prone, releasing a torrent of anger from Carthage's onlookers. One of Solomon's centurions attempted to restore order, succeeding in allowing Solomon to proceed toward the coastal palace without any further indignity.

"That's Silius," Samur growled. "Solomon's lapdog, now Marcian's dead."

"Leave them be," I warned, my skin prickling as I recalled Rosamund's warning of Samur during our final day's sail from Septem. "With any luck, both men will have their throats slit by disgruntled Carthaginians."

Later, I discovered that Belisarius delegated the transfer of authority to Liberius, leaving Solomon visibly angry at the perceived slight. Nevertheless, my boyhood rival immediately set about assigning responsibility to his cronies. Notably, Silius was granted control over the city watch, ensuring that Solomon would be able to dispense justice in a manner of his choosing. Despite Solomon's machinations, however, Troglita would not surrender his position as prefect, allowing him the authority to speak in the Emperor's name in a manner reduced but not dissimilar to that of a legate. Though

Solomon complained and threatened, Liberius added his voice to Troglita's claim, keeping a narrow window of oversight on the burgeoning province.

Nonetheless, Solomon had soared to incredible heights of power, including command over the rump Roman forces that would remain to maintain order in Africa, Mauretania, and Tripolitana. Theoretically, Solomon's command extended to the Pillars and amongst the few dromons that would remain patrolling the Balearics and Sardinia, although Valerian ordered his warships sent to sea before any official commands could be levied from the upstart commander. At least my men in the west would remain steadfast in their duties, provided that Valerian could keep such diminutive forces alive with grain and meat stores exhausted from near-constant winter sieges.

After sharing a final meal with Samur and Perenus the evening before we set sail, I and all within my household doused the candles early. Though Carthage had two vast circular harbors available to Belisarius, their docks had fallen into disrepair under Vandal rule, leaving far fewer berths available compared to Constantinople. As such, Procopius drafted a complex timetable for each ship to load and unload men, beasts, and wares—with virtually all unhappy at such unreasonably inflexible expectations for departure times. Nevertheless, the *Fides* had been successfully loaded the day prior, with our departure amongst the first wave of ships granted freedom to return to Carthage.

Well before dawn of our departure day, the last of the house was emptied. Though I considered forcing Antonina to walk Carthage's streets like some plebeian, Rosamund convinced me to relent. Instead, a chariot was readied to carry both women to the docks, with its windows screened shut to disguise the occupants within. I only caught glimpses of Antonina as she stepped aboard the coach and later the *Fides*, with her faced buried in a black shawl more appropriate for a widow than a young and healthy wife and mother.

Unlike in Constantinople, there was no ceremony or celebration at the rolling departure. Only Father Petrus awoke early to offer prayers as we boarded the ship, during which I bowed my head.

Gunderic, on the other hand, belched loudly as he climbed the stairs aboard the *Fides*. "Last night at a decent inn for months, and we definitely made the most of it, lads!" He laughed. "Be mindful of the pox now!"

Two dozen Vandals moaned in approval, many clutching sore heads while others stumbled up the stairs and nearly plummeted overboard. As Father Petrus shook his head through it all, Gunderic laughed maniacally, leading the Vandal group belowdecks.

And with little more than a farewell from the old priest, the *Fides'* captain ordered the ship decoupled from Carthage's ancient military harbor. As the first rays of light pierced through the violent curtain of night, we sailed northeast, beginning the long journey back to the Imperial Capitol. Back to Theodora and Basilius. To the vague plots of Narses and Justinian. Most importantly, back to Mariya and my children, and my deliverance.

ANTONINA

Few navigators would have been eager to chart a seaward passage from Carthage to Constantinople in winter. The once-peaceful Roman lake was subject to unpredictable seasonal tempests that rattled the courage of even the more veteran of sailors, with dozens of vessels vanishing with nary a survivor or witness. When the Emperor makes demands, however, worries of safety are pushed aside.

At times, I truly wonder if God hates me. Not that I had suffered in a manner such as Job—even as a slave, my trials were far easier than most suffered by those who lived and died within the Empire. No, I wonder more for the dark sense of humor He must have held for my life. I have not met a man with greater resentment for the sea than I, yet surely few in history have been subjected to the same extent of seaborne travel that I have. For my return to Constantinople, though our clutch of ships encountered no outright storm, stiff winds and rocking waves brought me to lurch and moan with sickness by the second day on the water.

Compared to other voyages, I should have been thankful that few true hazards could have capsized our ship. In keeping with Procopius' organization, our ship joined ten others in a loose wedge formation, our course charted to sail well clear of Syracuse and Brindisi. Remaining distant from hostile Ostrogoth pirates, our sailors maintained their duties. Uliaris joined Sembrouthes as he and his Aksumites shared stories, while Gunderic and the Vandals never truly sobered up. With no serious breaches of discipline, it was rather amusing to behold, particularly when Cephalas began to sneak hidden wineskins to the impossibly unsubtle Vandals.

If I ever had a foil at sea, it was Rosamund. Even where she detested Justinian's endless wars, Rosamund always gaped in awe as our ship cut through endlessly deep waters. Few would ever take in such a view, she once explained, especially not anyone from those tribes who stalked the forests and mountains of Europa. So it was that, beaming with happiness while never once shirking as my caretaker, Rosamund's only worry on our trip home came in the form of Antonina. After a full week at sea, Rosamund confronted me about our unwilling guest.

"She has barely eaten anything and won't stop crying," Rosamund explained in Heruli.

"Good," I muttered, heaving into a bucket.

Rosamund slapped my shoulder with stinging force. "Varus! You are better than the other brutes here. Antonina made a mistake, but she is still a person in need."

Groaning, I sat upright. "Fine, but what can I do to resolve this?"

"Talk to her," Rosamund said. "She's spoken to none but me for a week, and she might benefit from a different perspective on this predicament, particularly one that isn't from another woman."

The thought of aiding Antonina was loathsome. "Her *predicament* is that Belisarius may still have her killed."

Rosamund's eyes widened. "Do you believe that he will?"

"No," I answered truthfully. "He loves her too much, that is plain. But I can make no promises of her safety once we dock in Constantinople. Not even her father can, though Basilius will certainly try."

"I know," Rosamund said. "And for you, Antonina might deserve no peace, especially given that Belisarius is your lord and friend. But if nothing else, I would ask that you do this for me."

There was no arguing with this. I tolerated Belisarius' request out of friendship and duty, yet had no desire to assuage Antonina's guilt. When Rosamund made a request of me, however, I was bound by blood-oath to obey. There are few more compelling reasons to go against one's desires than to placate those who have saved your life on multiple occasions.

Churning seas marked the day of Rosamund's demands, and there was no begging off, despite my constant vertigo. Instead, Rosamund waited for me to get to my feet, and, beaming, exited the diminutive cabin that served as my berth, waving sluggishly to a band of drunk Vandals. Curiously, a young Aksumite named Menelik joined in the Vandals' gathering, gambling pieces of silver in some brutish game of soldiers' dice with a drunken Gunderic.

Compared to the flagship, our transport had little room to move about, forcing even those of average height to bend and dip beneath protruding wooden beams. Our quarters were separated from those of the sailors and crew, who bedded further belowdecks and in far less luxurious conditions than my men complained about. On our deck, most of the Vandals and Aksumites slept in open bunks, leaving five small berths intended for junior officers that were little different from the room I used on my journey to Tauris. Other than myself, Rosamund, Sembrouthes, and Gunderic were each granted a private room, with a fifth of these smaller berths made available on a rotating basis for the victor of Gunderic's drinking and gambling schemes.

Though the assignment was not mandated, Antonina had been relegated to the single cabin that would be acceptable to a more senior officer of the Imperial Army. Though still small, it contained a full bed, desk, and drawers for storage, and was even stocked with a dull mirror that flickered against the room's candlelight. Easily comfortable for sleep, the cabin was nonetheless far too small for any amount of exercise or relief, yet Antonina still kept herself locked away from her shipmates to Constantinople. As in Carthage, only

Rosamund slipped into her private quarters as Antonina's sole source of human contact.

Until now. Rosamund contorted her body between me and a nearby wooden beam as she reached Antonina's quarters with a light series of taps. After Rosamund disappeared behind the door, I heard a faint groan that was quickly dispersed. Moments later, the door reopened, with Rosamund returning to the deck hall.

"She's ready for you," Rosamund whispered. "Remember, whatever you're feeling, just listen."

Sighing, I nodded and made my way into Antonina's cabin. Though the hall was already marked by few sources of light, Antonina's quarters seemed as if a portal to some forgotten underworld, with the light from a single candle flickering against wood rubbed smooth from a thousand hands and feet. Sliding my feet to keep from tripping, my fingertips traced from the doorframe to an adjoining desk as my eyes adjusted to the gloom. Instantly, a waft of fragrant air billowed around my nose and mouth, contrasting heavily with the stale piss, bile, and acrid sweat that otherwise clung to the ship's walls.

"Rosewater," Antonina explained, her Latin crisp despite its low tone. "Rosamund is thoughtful, although even she cannot keep hewn flowers alive for too much longer. In another week, I shall be wafting in the same miasma as everyone else."

"Perhaps you think too little of Rosamund," I countered. "She may be able to prolong your luxuries."

"Perhaps you do as well," Antonina shot back, but she closed her eyes upon seeing my reaction. "Varus, I am sorry. I have no right to condescend to you."

"No, indeed," I muttered.

"Please close the door behind you."

"Lady?" I asked, incredulous. To be secluded in such tight quarters with Antonina at such a time…

"I insist," Antonina answered. "Believe me, Varus, neither my husband nor your wife would never suspect you of infidelity."

If nothing else than to regain command of our encounter, I still considered resisting Antonina's request, yet I knew that if I did, Rosamund would certainly chastise me, leaving me no closer to returning to the miserable comforts of my private quarters. Worse, if any of the inebriated Vandals took notice of our meeting, wagging tongues might misinterpret what transpired. So in the end I had little choice but to obey, and allowed the door to creak gently closed.

Absent the hall's light, Antonina's quarters were even more veiled in shadow than before. Shuddering, my mind faded to unpleasant memories of Nisibis, leaving a chill snaking along the exposed skin of my arms.

"I find the darkness to be edifying, although I can tell it does not agree with you," Antonina said, her voice rising from its whisper.

"No, Lady," I offered. "Most that I meet have a natural fear of the darkness."

Antonina shook her head. "Not me, although far be it from me to be rude to my host."

Rising from a bench, Antonina appeared to glide along the floor, her bare feet making nary a sound as she made her way to two hanging tapers and lowered their wicks against the lit candle. Soon, their joined light brought greater comfort to the cabin, further reflected by the mirror bolted to her far wall. Though it was still dim, I could now discern further creature comforts—that Rosamund had smuggled aboard, I was sure—from a small linen rug to a silk blanket folded neatly along a bed to a beaten silver basin filled with water. I also spotted no fewer than a dozen glass bottles full of red wine that would have been priceless against the rotgut swill that stained Gunderic's mouth and slopped against the floor outside.

"So, what has my husband said of me?"

"Nothing to me, Lady," I said. "He hasn't met with me since…" I paused, clumsily stumbling into our unwelcome conversation.

"Poor Varus," Antonina exhaled. "And my… the other?"

"Sergius? Vanished, as if swept on the wings of some great bird. None have seen him."

I meant this to speak artfully of his raw cowardice, yet my

chosen words inadvertently seemed to glorify his talents. Regardless, however she interpreted my musings, all Antonina could do was weep.

"Please sit," she said, pointing to a bench. Chest heaving as her sobs lessened, Antonina drew a second small bench from against a wall, dragging it noisily toward my intended perch.

It was only then that I caught a full view of Antonina. She was still young, having seen no more than thirty years, and possessed a straight back and unblemished skin that denoted her status as one of the wealthy few unrequired to toil in the fields or risk broken and smashed fingers at the loom. Deep russet hair fell well below her shoulders, its locks uncombed and bereft of the gold and silver baubles that she had been loath to be seen without just months prior.

Yet it was her face, the wide eyes and cruelly thin lips of my onetime tormentor, that told the full tale of Antonina's grief. Absent her kohl or paints, Antonina's face seemed somehow more honest, even if near unrecognizable. She offered a weak smile as she cuffed away tears, using one hand to pluck at the hem of her ornate sapphire dress.

"Rosamund wasn't able to find some of my simpler garments, not that I fault her," Antonina continued. "Do you think you might be able to find me something less gaudy?"

"Perhaps," I offered. "It depends where you will be kept, for the time being."

Wiping a lingering tear from the corner of her eye, Antonina leaned forward. "Do you know where?"

"That will be decided between Belisarius and your father."

Her eyes wide, Antonina used her thumb to swipe away another tear. "Will Belisarius have me hanged?"

There was no way that I could know the answer to such a question. Antonina's gaze was one of raw longing, her teeth biting deep into her lower lip. I thought about demurring, or even refusing to answer, yet I could not amass the will for such cruelty. As Antonina's hand began to tremor, I offered an assessment of Belisarius that I believed unshakably true.

"Belisarius won't punish you. He loves you too much to see you harmed."

More weeping. Antonina nodded, taking several moments to gather her words. "I believe you're correct, Varus. But will he free me?"

I thought on it. "No, Lady," I answered. "I doubt that even your father has that power, at least for now."

"Then I wish he would just let me die. I can't imagine such a fate is worse than being locked away like some unwanted trophy."

I flinched, my skin growing warm as I absorbed the criticism of my master. "Lady, you know not what you say."

"I ignored Sergius—at least at first!" Antonina cried. Then she lowered her voice. "When my father first told me of my betrothal to Belisarius, I nearly ran away. I was sure he would be some barbarian brute with a penchant for war. But when I met him, my heart soared. He was handsome, but not too comely, and spoke as gentle as a song. I always thought I'd become the plaything of a man my father deemed necessary to advance our family's power, and perhaps I was. But God help me, I wept in relief that my husband was everything that I ever wanted."

"Then why Sergius?"

"Because..." Antonina paused, her chest rising from a slow, deliberate breath. "My husband has two lovers. I am one, but duty is another. Belisarius gave me everything that a woman could want in this life, except time or affection. After I gave him a child, I thought things might be different, and that he might put aside his sword and dedicate his love to the two of us."

Rosamund's voice filled my thoughts. *He adored her like a statue of a goddess. Antonina is far too intelligent, and far too ambitious, to be given kisses and then left behind like some unspeaking monument.*

Rising from her chair, Antonina walked to a far table and grasped at one of the wine bottles. She poured the crimson liquid into a silver goblet, replacing the bottle's stopper only after the wine threatened to slosh over the curled rim. She returned to her seat, offering the cup to me.

"Please, Varus. I have no visitors other than Rosamund, and am not like to be popular in the coming weeks."

Her finger brushed against mine as I took the silver goblet into my grasp. Twitching, she nevertheless steadied her hand to keep the cup's contents from toppling over. "And what of you?" I asked. "Will you not be partaking?"

Antonina nodded. "Rosamund was only able to smuggle a single glass, so we must share."

The thought seemed repulsive, yet I continued my promise to Rosamund and sipped politely at Antonina's offering. Its sweetness was almost choking, the wine infused with the peeled skins of rare peaches. Antonina giggled as I struggled against the taste, and I carefully surrendered the goblet's stem to her slender hands.

"How I envy you, Varus."

I coughed my last and shot back as Antonina drank deeply. "I had few of your luxuries growing up, Lady."

"Oh no, Varus!" Antonina replied. "What I mean is that you are satisfied by simple tastes." After taking another sip, she added, "Except for your wife, that is. Never would I have wagered you capturing the heart of a foreign princess."

"Nor I, Lady," I agreed, not caring to delve deeper.

Antonina pried no further. "Belisarius was a changed man after returning from Tauris. Before Joannina, he rarely shared my bed, at least not for long. He would wake in the darkest hours of the night in a sweat and leave without a word. Once he was called to Mesopotamia..."

Antonina paused, taking another deep gulp before offering the goblet back to me. Stiffening my resolve, I lapped again at the oversweet wine as she continued.

"I didn't see him for months after landing in Antioch. Not knowing if he was living or dead, dreading the arrival of each messenger from some sand-cursed hole that the Persians wanted to fight over. Whether terror or frustration I cannot say, but it made me want to scream. Even with Mariya to share conversation, I would have killed to leave that place and ride for Dara."

As I listened to Antonina's tale, a grim fact became all too apparent—this woman had likely spent more days and nights with my wife than I had. How many weeks had Mariya and I spent in the same bed? Less than she and Antonina had spent as comrades in Antioch or Constantinople, leaving me to wonder whether Antonina might know more of my wife than I truly had. In that regard… was I any different than Belisarius?

"But I was a dutiful bride," Antonina continued. "I resented my father's strict rules, but I followed them nonetheless. Varus, I know that you do not care for me much, and likely never will, but as stubborn and headstrong as I am, I've always sought to honor my family… until recently, at least."

"Lady, I have no grudge with you."

"Then you are far more generous than I." Antonina smiled. "Getting caught committing a grievous wrong makes one reminisce upon many other sins they have committed. I may have been a brat, and for that I apologize, but I swear that I was faithful to Belisarius until Sergius came into my life."

"I believe you," I said—and curiously, somehow, I did.

"Sergius was so charming," Antonina recounted. "And… well, let me put it this way. Though I care for your wife as my friend, her friendship was to be expected. We were both high-ranking ladies, pregnant and isolated in a foreign city. Mariya also understood my station as Belisarius' wife and knew that her companionship with me might reflect better upon you to my husband."

The thought of Belisarius' opinion of me swayed by Antonina was sickening, although I saw no need to protest, given the circumstances. "So you wanted more than what was to be expected?"

"Something unpredictable, and uncontrollable," Antonina agreed. "Something that reminded me that I was once beautiful, someone whose opinion was unconnected from any desire for my husband's patronage."

Despite everything, I pitied Antonina in that moment. "You still are beautiful, Lady," I said, and although I knew no courtier or spy would hear my words and misconstrue them, I regretted speaking them.

"Generous!" Antonina laughed, watching me squirm in my chair. "I am not proud of my choices, but at the time, I wanted something to make me feel alive and desirable. Sergius was so patient with me, drawing upon each word of a lonely pregnant woman cast into a faraway city with few friends and no comforts. Late in my pregnancy, Sergius kissed me, but I declined those advances—too much wine, it seemed, and Sergius gave profuse apologies, which I accepted. Between Joannina and my excitement for Belisarius' triumph at Dara, I even forgot about the incident entirely. Yet when that abominable toad Hermogenes clapped manacles on my husband… that's when I knew that little would improve for me."

"I do not understand, Lady." I frowned. "Hermogenes was unjust, but he did not prevent you from meeting with your husband."

"No," Antonina growled. "But again, Belisarius' mind was with his other mistress. How he worried, and how he wept! For the Hun brothers who died at Callinicum, or for his fears of the safety of his men. To be forthright, for a day I hated you too, Varus, because all my husband could speak of in our time together was how you were performing in leadership, and later how you would be freed from bondage."

"Lady—"

"Varus, we are beyond formalities. Please call me by my name."

Taking a breath, I nodded. "Antonina, I had no notion of your frustration, nor did I ever take any action to wrest Belisarius from you."

Antonina raised a hand as I took another sip from the goblet. "Believe me, I know. But love does not spring from reason. I desperately wanted my husband, and he had nothing of himself to offer to me. He would smile and plant kisses, or bounce our daughter upon his knee, but he was and is a man with two wives, and only one can be victor. Sergius knew of my need, and of my weakness."

With a hand outstretched, Antonina took the goblet from me. Draining its contents, her speech slowed, her tone melancholy.

"Sergius found me alone, crying and desperate for someone to offer anything resembling desire. He took my mouth into his, and in the throes of weariness and wine, Sergius took me in Antioch. He did not force me, and did not have to, though I loathed myself as soon as it was over."

Hints of this I had learned from Mariya years ago, and Rosamund more recently. Still, I desired to hear the tale from Antonina directly, with my intention being to see whether she might implicate others in her tryst. "And none knew?"

"Mariya did," Antonina admitted, adding to the shame I had felt in disregarding my wife years ago. "Your wife is a steadfast friend. She convinced me to cast Sergius aside and forget the episode, and for a time I did. Yet again we reconvened in Constantinople, and again in Carthage. After John was killed…"

Antonina shuddered. Rising from her seat, she returned to the bottle of her choosing and refilled the goblet. She returned quickly, all happiness vanished from her weary features.

"I thought Belisarius might die. His heart was utterly broken, though he would never admit it. And by then, I was simply no longer the patient and dutiful wife. There was no easy healing of Belisarius' wounds. And so I returned to Sergius… although like the first time, and every time after, I hated myself a bit more for the transgression."

"Then why continue?"

Antonina shrugged. "I'll never know. I fucked Sergius so often that it became routine, a task as regular as writing letters to my father. I wanted to end it, but I just couldn't. Until our discretion became lazy, and it was too late to stop."

As she gulped more of the noxious wine, I broached the most

uncomfortable question of my life. "Lady, I must ask. Are you confident that Joannina is—"

"Yes!" Antonina hissed, a rivulet of crimson spilling from her lips. "Yes, she is my husband's daughter."

Placing the goblet upon a nearby table, Antonina bent forward, placing her head between both hands, whose fingers were naked of any ornament, and wept, wept harder than I had ever seen her, her entire body convulsing. Gasping for breath, she placed her forehead upon my knee, falling to the floor as her hot tears soaked through the wool of my trousers.

I knew not how to act. For a time, I sat frozen, hardly wanting to breathe as Antonina unraveled at my feet. From her confession, I wanted to hate this creature who willfully served treachery and pain as if some passing fancy. But as she wept, it was as if my soul overruled my mind, wanting to reach out to offer comfort. Placing a hand on the crown of her head, I remained still as Antonina grew calm and rose back to her seat.

"I love my husband, Varus! Even if he sends me to my death, I will always love him. Tell him that, won't you?"

I nodded, unsure of when, where, or even if I might have occasion to do so. Whether from rich wine, a churning gut, or a general desire to escape so much sadness, I began to excuse myself to depart. Antonina, however, asked two further boons of me.

"Varus," she began, "please visit me whenever you are able. You don't have to often, but just sometimes, until our voyage is over."

"If that is your wish." I nodded.

Antonina offered a smile in response, her eyes swollen from crying. "And, most importantly, if something where to happen to me—"

"Antonina—"

"If something were to happen to me," she continued, "please help my daughter. Belisarius loves her dearly, but I doubt he will be able to handle a child on his own, especially given her mother's choices."

"It would be my honor," I answered, realizing that I was adding to the gaggle of responsibilities that included my own two children, Hypatius' young son Tiberius, and however many orphans Mariya had boarded in Pella. That my prior eagerness to care for an orphaned Tiberius had infuriated Mariya—not because she desired to leave the poor boy destitute, but rather that I gave her no forewarning of accepting a ward whose father had been an infamous traitor.

But alas, I lacked the stoutheartedness to strike Antonina's hopes down. Instead, I trusted my instinct, and hoped that Mariya would be willing to support the child of a troubled friend. "You have my word."

"I am grateful, Varus," Antonina said. "I wish it were under better terms."

"So do I," I replied as I rose for the exit.

As I closed the door, her light keening continued, although it seemed somehow less aggressive than before our meeting. I reentered the deck hall and the wafting aroma of human filth, the noise of Gunderic's wagers still filling each nook with earsplitting noise. Ignoring rejoinders to throw the soldiers' dice, I waved to Rosamund and staggered into my private quarters, moaning as my head drew level with its straw mattress.

THE FIFTH GIFT

Though I cannot say that our remaining time at sea was pleasurable, it certainly lacked the note of tension that had made my care of Antonina so onerous up to that point. At Rosamund's urging, I met with Antonina in the evenings, occasionally sharing a brief meal of the simple fare available to those aboard the *Fides*. She never seemed truly happy, yet her tears gradually transformed into a grudging acceptance of her uncertain fate.

Within a week, Antonina had ventured so far as to leave the confines of her cabin. This took me unawares, and was not altogether welcome at first. Paradoxically, the forces most rabidly loyal to Belisarius were the Vandals, with Gunderic adamant regarding his outward displays of trust to the great Roman conqueror. As Antonina slipped from her room, Gunderic was, as always, somewhere between sloppiness and stupor, yet retained enough awareness to eye a young woman gliding into his midst. Rising from his game, Gunderic stormed into my private quarters.

"That wretched woman is on the deck," he barked, hardly attempting to lower his voice.

Groaning, I rose from my bed. "Antonina? For how long?"

"Just now."

I shrugged. "I never knew you to object to the company of women, Gunderic. Nor did I understand the Vandals to be a particularly prudish people."

He sneered. "I only object to those who dishonor my dread lord and master. An unmarried Vandal woman may hump any man she pleases with no scruple. But if any should marry a king, their loyalty is sworn in blood. When the Vandals were still a nomadic people, any queen who violated the marriage bed would be bound in leather and cast into an open flame."

"Belisarius is no king," I countered. "And there will be no burning, or beating, or maltreatment of any kind. Antonina is my ward, and by extension yours as well."

"Pfah!" Gunderic blurted, unable to assemble a more complex thought.

"Make certain your men understand my will."

To my astonishment, Gunderic behaved as requested. No crude language was directed at the general's wife, nor was any Vandal particularly exclusionary in their social settings. True, the men did not whoop and cheer at her presence, and none stooped to include her in conversation. Yet Antonina seemed content to sit and watch what must have been an utterly foreign display of debauchery that would have horrified most ladies of the Imperial Court. She did not flinch, and I even caught her stifling giggles as Gunderic roared a bawdy joke.

Unlike our initial voyage from Constantinople, we did not pause for refitting and resupply. Where Paulus had carelessly allowed underbaked bread to poison many of Belisarius' soldiers, Bessas took particular care to overstock each ship with provisions for an extended journey. Further, there was little understanding of whether any given Ostrogothic port in Italy would wave at passing Roman ships or launch arrows into their decks. Most of all, most captains wanted nothing more than to complete the voyage while the weather remained hospitable, even if such decisions yielded no break in the rolling misery of sea life.

True to Antonina's warning, the aroma of the ship soon transformed into a rank odor that would have brought even a seasoned veteran to gag within twenty paces. Thankfully, our noses had become immune to the stench, with even Antonina leveling few complaints long after the supply of rosewater in her rooms was exhausted. Instead, she watched Vandals play dice or the Aksumites tell stories, day after day, as the harshness of winter lessened into the promise of spring.

It was a standoff. Antonina would sit along the far side of the ship's hold, saying little more than a few words of greeting or departure. Likewise, the Vandals noted her presence with curiosity, speaking what I can only imagine were unkind descriptions of her in their native Vandal tongue. On multiple occasions, I found Gunderic's men nodding at Antonina and laughing over something in their native language, and although I considered asking Gunderic to cease such conversation, Antonina did not show any worries for her safety. Instead, as the voyage wore on, she would smile and wave at the Vandal warriors, and in so doing, eventually sapped the joy from their unintelligible japes, to the point where they stopped their suggestive behavior altogether.

"You do not need to sit in the hold with the warriors," I told Antonina during one of our private meetings. "I can't imagine it's stimulating."

"Oh, quite," Antonina replied offhandedly. "The Vandals have the courage to speak their minds, even if they think I can't understand their tongue. But teasing is universal… if you would remember our days in Liberius' classroom?"

"Too well," I replied, eyeing Antonina curiously. "It is your choice, of course."

As the weeks progressed, Antonina's melancholy ebbed, although it never fully disappeared. It was apparent that she hungered for conversation, or at least something to do, while I struggled to retain the contents of my stomach during our meals together. While I cannot say that I ever truly enjoyed Antonina's company, I found it increasingly bearable, now that her haughty disdain had been replaced with a yen to mingle with unwashed barbarian foederati.

It was not until our last week at sea, with the coastline of Greece now visible, that Antonina finally contributed to the Vandals' gathering. By then, many had become bloated and sluggish from continuous drink, with few exhibiting the same raucous disdain for human limitations as was present at the outset. Instead, rising from her chair, she slipped into her cabin for but a moment before returning with six green wine bottles filled to the brim with an expensive vintage. Plucking two discarded clay cups from the sticky planks of the deck floor, Antonina tipped dregs of stale wine out of the vessels, then filled them from her own bottles.

The nearest Vandal eyed Antonina curiously, saying nothing. Neither did he speak when she offered him the cup, eventually accepting it with a frown before sniffing noisily at the contents. Shrugging, he drank deeply, only to jerk backward at the sweetness.

Within moments, he chortled nearly to the point of choking. Raising the cup toward Antonina, he drank again, sucking down the sweet liquid and offering the empty cup for a second dose. Others soon followed, emptying the sour mash of their own vessels and feasting upon the privileged choice of the Empire's elite despite pounding headaches or a desperate need for water. Gunderic eyed each man with silent curiosity until, with the others served, Antonina carried a half-empty bottle toward the center of the Vandal circle, the hem of her sapphire gown collecting all manner of filth as it dragged along the ground.

Pausing two paces before the giant Vandal, Antonina offered an outstretched palm. Gunderic's eyes lowered to the soft skin, and initially made no motion other than to scan the far more delicate figure that stood before him. Yet Antonina did not budge until, satisfied, Gunderic offered his own cup. Antonina filled and returned the offering, speaking no words as Gunderic drained the wine with a single swallow. He kept his eyes fixed upon Antonina, with many leaning forward for a better angle at how the Vandal warlord might react to the soiled bride of Belisarius.

Rather than a frown or a smile, Gunderic's lips puckered despite visible attempts to keep his gaze locked. Then, a light twitch flickered on his brows, his lids slightly closing as his nose wrinkled. A small stream of air escaped chapped lips that had formed an oval, leaving a vein on Gunderic's neck to bulge as he shuddered.

"Too sweet!" he roared, wiping his face of involuntary tears.

A half dozen Vandals hooted in derision at their leader's weakness. Gunderic seized the bottle from Antonina's grasp and drained the liquid in three heartbeats, resulting only in a further pinched face, his tongue lolling at the unfamiliar taste. More cajoling in the Vandal language ensued as Gunderic, rising from his perch, rushed toward a bucket of water, tipped the vessel toward his lips, and spilled the liquid about his matted beard. Even Sembrouthes chuckled as Gunderic rushed for another bucket, his palate quenched only then.

Gunderic patted Antonina on the shoulder as he returned to his seat, ordering two of his men to draw the lady's seat closer to the Vandal circle and a mug filled with the more familiar Vandal mixture. Antonina bowed as she took her new seat, nearly able to disguise a light tremor in her free hand as she rested an empty wine bottle upon the floor before accepting her newly filled cup. Cautiously, she raised the sour liquid to her lips, lifting the cup as she drank.

She gagged but did not vomit. And as ridiculous as it may sound, she earned some measure of Gunderic's respect as she drank every drop of the foul mixture. The great Vandal stomped and cheered, and Antonina, eyes watering, nevertheless smiled at such acceptance, nodding toward Rosamund and myself as bystanders to such strange proceedings.

"You've done a kindness to her," Rosamund whispered to me.

"I'm not certain of that," I replied, watching Antonina hoot with laughter as Gunderic half slid, half hurled another cup toward her.

"Antonina won't forget it," Rosamund insisted. "And I think you both might be better off for this."

Turning to her, I frowned. "Both?"

"Both," Rosamund repeated. "Did you imagine you might share cups with Antonina when you were a boy?"

I laughed. "Not a chance."

For the week remaining, Antonina was a welcome guest to the Vandal circle, sharing tales of her father's exploits and explaining the various intricacies of the Imperial Palace to gawking Vandal listeners. Though such men thought city dwellers weak, they nevertheless soaked in all knowledge of the Hippodrome and the vast underground cisterns, with some skeptical that such vast construction could exist. Even Gunderic, who long ago had walked the streets of a small portion of the Imperial Capitol, could not convince his fellow men that Antonina's words were hardly exaggeration.

I spent the entire morning of our final day abovedeck, shuffling along the railings with Rosamund as we gained our first view of Constantinople since much of it had been reduced to cinders. Even the most casual glance revealed vast construction projects amidst the city's Thracian districts, including a thoroughly cleared space where the Hagia Sophia had fallen in the riots' blaze. In its place sat enormous stone foundations that, though still exposed to the elements, signaled an impossibly vast structure to replace Constantinople's premier church.

It was not the view that brought me to the open air, but a raw impatience to dock. After weeks of churning waves, the final hours of the *Fides*' approach were far more of an agony than any other. When our craft was finally sent to anchor, it was all I could do to keep from sprinting onto unmoving ground. Alas, I stood patiently as the dock workers carefully locked the gangway that linked the *Fides* deck to its assigned pier. Then, with Rosamund and Antonina in tow, I at last felt my boots connect with paved stone, only to find my wobbling legs struggling for purchase as I reacclimated to solid earth.

Trusting Cephalas and Uliaris with the organization of all household possessions, I gathered the Aksumites and walked toward the building that had previously been sequestered for my use prior to the African expedition. My cloak and clothing were disheveled, and I certainly must have stank of the worst of all evil humors, yet I doubt that those who worked Constantinople's docks took any particular notice. Instead, I half trotted along Constantinople's eerily unpopulated streets, trails of scorch marks and piles of lumber, stones, and nails lying in piles throughout each street and alley.

As we drew nearer to the Forum of Constantine, the cacophony of hammers grew to an unpleasant hum, their very vibrations seeming to shake the ground underneath me. Along the forum's far edge, a gathering of plebeians circled around a figure bearing the robes of a monk, his cowl faded by the sun and the length of rope at his waist frayed from overuse. I ignored such nuisances as well as the other pieces of evidence that signaled Constantinople's rebirth, stopping only to draw an iron key from my belt that unlocked my temporary sanctuary.

The Aksumite spearman Menelik was dispatched to the palace to inform them of my arrival. A faint twinge of guilt stirred in my gut for not seeking the Empress myself, yet as I donned her golden signet ring, I surrendered to the natural need to scrape away weeks of filth from the *Fides*. Several servants had maintained my rooms, ensuring that all halls and quarters were free of the rats that feasted on all manner of filth in Constantinople's gutters.

Rosamund and Antonina were guided to separate quarters as I assumed the rooms I had last shared with Mariya, marked by a rare featherbed atop a polished bronze frame. Having requested water heated from the kitchen ovens and sent to the private bathhouse that was fed directly from a local aqueduct, I nearly cried as layers of cold and warm liquid blanketed my grime-riddled skin. One servant scraped my bare flesh of its impurities before repeating the process, shortening the hours-long Roman bathing ritual into a brief yet effective wash.

Sembrouthes joined in similar luxuries as my other Aksumites sought a larger bathhouse along the forum, with the Aksumite leader peeling off his filth-strewn yellow robes and groaning in pleasure as hot water was scrubbed against his skin.

"Don't ever make me stay on a boat that long ever again," he growled.

"God willing," I answered.

With Rosamund and Antonina anxious to take our places, Sembrouthes and I soon parted from the warm confines of the bathhouse. Bare wet toes slid against polished stone as I climbed back to my private quarters, with only a soft wool cloth wrapped around my midriff. Frescoed illustrations of Homer's *Iliad* lined the walls, with each cubit easily worth five years wages of a typical spearman. Yet cost mattered little for buildings personally owned by the Imperial family, who had granted me the right to occupy the premises as a personal excubitor to Theodora and an invited guest of the Imperial Court.

Still awaiting Menelik's return, I lay slowly upon the bed, my eyes closing as my bare cheek brushed against a silken cushion. My senses blurred as my muscles craved sleep, and for a fleeting moment, I thought I could sense the distant shade of Mariya's perfume.

Sleep, however, would not be long for my enjoyment. At first, insistent noises merely plodded against my closed door, only to grow frustrated by their unanswered call. Soon, the door to my bedroom opened, with plodding sandals sliding along the floor to my bed. A soft hand gripped hard against my bare shoulder, jerking my torso until I groaned in acknowledgment.

"Welcome back, tribune," Narses purred. "My, how high you have risen in such a short time."

"Honors neither desired nor requested," I grumbled, sitting upright, "and paid for in blood. What time of day is it?"

"Well after the zenith," Narses answered. "Our mistress seemed disappointed you did not come to the palace straightaway. Information of Carthage is both pleasing… and concerning."

Another grumble. "Have you ever sailed for months without break, Narses?"

Narses folded his arms, allowing the overlarge sleeves of his silken robe to cover his skin like armor. "I have not had the privilege, although I cannot imagine it being particularly desirable."

"It isn't," I replied, rising nude and walking toward my folded woolen shirt and trousers. Narses raised an eyebrow, but otherwise kept his gaze upon me as I dressed. Though Narses was a eunuch, and I had changed clothes before hundreds of stinking, wine-sodden warriors before, Narses' unfeeling stare only added to my bubbling discomfort with the man. "Believe me, the Empress will thank me that I spared her the stink of that place."

"Naturally." Narses grinned. "Unfortunately, however, I have little time to trade jibes with you. As you may assume, others who have just returned have informed the Capitol of all that occurred in the expedition's final weeks in Africa, including much that involves you. Be thankful that your handsome Aksumite bodyguard found me before other, more insistent hands did so."

My eyes narrowed. "Speak plainly."

"As you wish." Narses bobbed his head. "By itself, Lady Antonina's alleged shame would be concerning to our mistress, but extenuating circumstances make it downright untenable."

"What circumstances?" I growled, only then realizing that I offered far too much hostility than was wise around a spymaster like Narses.

My guest put on a show of grief, closing his eyes and lowering his gaze to the floor. Long flowing silks covered Narses' plump form, while golden ornaments lined both of his wrists and hands. One included Theodora's golden signet, shared only by the brother that adorned my own finger. Narses let out a long sigh, nearly bringing me to insist the man speak. Like a trained actor, however, Narses timed his pause well.

"Basilius is dead," he whispered.

"Dead?"

"Likely not long after you departed from Carthage. He had been unwell for months, and I fear that his passing came as a surprise to few."

More professions of grief from the spymaster, his face wrinkled as a hand covered his features. It was so very believable. Only a discerning glance at Narses' shifting yet piercing eyes betrayed the act for what it was.

"Matters appear far worse for Antonina than they seem, I'm afraid," Narses continued. "Basilius willed the bulk of his vast wealth to the Empire, specifically the reconstruction of the Hagia Sophia. Of course, Antonina was reserved a sum, but it is not like to keep such a highborn lady in finery for more than a year. Good Basilius never expected the great Belisarius to want to divorce his daughter, but alas."

Black tidings indeed. "Antonina will remain in my care for now," I told him.

"The Empress' thoughts exactly!" Narses beamed.

"Belisarius' thoughts," I corrected. "For the time being."

Narses nodded, yet his face grew pinched. "You would do well to not confuse loyalties to the Imperial family with the general. His fortune waxes and wanes with the tides, I fear."

"Noted," I grunted. "This will crush Antonina, but I need to tell her nonetheless."

Narses pursed his lips as he shook his head. "No, Lord Varus. The Empress gave that responsibility explicitly to me. Perhaps she has a reason to deny you such privilege. She would like to see you privately, by the way."

I considered resisting, but quickly surrendered. To my surprise, I felt a pang of sorrow for Antonina, wishing that I were able to blunt the sting of Narses' dagger. Reasonably, however, there was little I could do except heed the Empress' instructions, which I had hardly any time to obey. As I began to plan my trip to the Imperial Palace, however, Narses did not dismiss himself.

"Something else?" I asked.

"Indeed," Narses said. "Though you remain a wealthy man, your riches are not unlimited, excubitor. Your wife's dealings in Pella drain far more than they replace, and a portion of your own wealth has been committed to the Hagia Sophia as well."

I could not say why, but I developed an urge to smash a closed fist into Narses' rounded chin. Instead, I merely grew suspicious of the man's information, with no outward gestures. "By whom?"

Narses bowed his head again. "The Empress, of course. We are awed by your boundless generosity, which God himself will honor in the afterlife."

This did little to quench my burgeoning frustration. "And what of all the gold and silver pilfered from those senators hanged for their role in the riots?"

"Our Imperial couple have a great many interests, Lord Varus, all of which require funding. Yet I caution you, though more gold is due to you from Gelimer's hoard, the costs of your household and your soldiers will eventually ruin you. Perhaps not soon, but eventually."

I shrugged. "I was born with nothing, Narses, and it would not bother me to die the same way."

"Admirable," Narses answered. "A belief I'm sure your wife shares with you."

I clenched my fist, biting my lip to keep from shoving the man out of the room. Aside from suspicions of the man's hidden disloyalty to Theodora, I hardly had good reason to make Narses the target of my anger, for he had been nothing but helpful to my cause. Yet, just as I found the clerk Procopius a meddling gossip, I discovered I had little respect for the spymaster's instruments or methods. Narses caught the gesture, raising an eyebrow before bowing his head.

"It appears I have offended you somehow, Lord Varus. I can assure you this is not my intent. We both serve a common master, after all."

"As you say," I replied, offering the man my outstretched arm as a peace offering. "Go and speak with Antonina, if you must."

"Of course." Narses smiled. "But there is one final item to dispense."

Narses' sandals brushed along the floor as he disappeared from the room. He reappeared moments later, yet he was not alone.

Instead, he was joined by Agathias, the boy's face flashing crooked teeth in the most genuine smile I have yet seen. The lad had grown in my extended absence, yet still retained the unfulfilled promise of youth with cherubic cheeks and no beard. In his hands was simple sackcloth, its opening sealed with a small leather ribbon. Despite its diminutive size, Agathias held the bundle in both hands as if it were some precious object, which Narses' eyes followed carefully.

"Lord Basilius named you in his will. This offering is yours, along with an instruction."

Of all that Narses offered, this revelation alone temporarily blunted my distaste for him; my mind swam with urgent curiosity at Basilius' offering. Though Basilius had softened in his later years, the patrician and onetime consul had rarely even acknowledged my presence when Justin was alive. "Why would Basilius bequeath anything to me?"

"Why indeed?" Narses asked, sounding genuinely curious. "Yet Basilius' instructions were as plain as peasant bread of gristle and chaff. His instruction required me to inform you that this would be your fifth gift, although it would offer you little benefit without its brothers."

Agathias stepped forward, his smile broadening; he offered the package as though cradling an egg. I snatched at the sackcloth, watching as Narses' eyes followed each movement of the bag. "That's all?"

"Likely no, but I have told you all that I know," Narses said. He stood silently for a few moments, shifting his weight from one fleshy leg to the other. His eyes remained on the satchel, yet neither Agathias nor myself made any motion to unravel its leather string.

Soon, he bowed once more and departed, presumably walking toward a lower floor where Antonina had taken residence. As his footsteps grew muffled, I nodded to Agathias.

"So, lad, have you learned all you could in the palace?"

"Yes, Lord!" he chirped, his voice stuttering between boyhood and manliness. "I've listened to all the proclamations of your expedition.

What incredible events to witness! Is it true you met with Theudis *and* Gelimer?"

"Indeed." I laughed. "Although I doubt it is as fanciful as the poets or singers say."

"But what *was* it like?" He shuffled closer.

"There will be plenty of time to discuss these things, Agathias," I replied. "But I can tell you that not a day passed that I did not wish to be back home."

The boy's head drooped, and I felt badly for him. And so, before occupying my attention with the gift before me, I offered a rare spot of pleasant information to one who, like me, had lived his youth as a slave. "Agathias, do you still have the gold I gifted you?"

He nodded. "Hidden carefully, Lord. Other palace slaves would trip over one another to steal such wealth, if only they knew I possessed it."

"Excellent work. If you believe your education is satisfactorily complete, use it to free yourself from bondage. If you like, you may join my household."

Agathias' gloom transformed into unbridled giddiness. "Oh, yes, Lord!"

"Don't show gratitude yet," I warned. "You will be free, but life is no less unforgiving to those lacking good fortune. I shall provide you wages, shelter, and board, and in return you shall assist with my correspondence. I trust you can write?"

"Latin *and* Greek, Lord!" Agathias cried. "You won't regret this."

"I believe you are correct," I concluded. "Now, run back to the palace and inform Marcellus that I shall arrive there today. After that, pay your dominus and wait for my arrival. Until then..." I hefted the sackcloth, its contents shifting inside. "I have business to attend to."

Agathias nearly stumbled as he bowed his head before sprinting down the stairs. As he reached the building's door, a great wail sang along the building's stone and marble corridors—unmistakably that of Antonina. I promised myself that, as soon as Narses left, I would console my ward—just after I unraveled the bequeathed bag that her august father had yielded to my possession.

The fifth gift. So long in coming, yet so bizarrely offered. The first three had come in quick succession—a bronze cross, an ornately decorated dagger, and a dragon-hilted sword rumored to be carved from a flaming stone of the heavens. After his death, Justin added the fourth gift, including the man's estate in Pella alongside a vast hoard of gold and silver. Justin, Father Petrus, and Godilas had all contributed to such offerings, with Liberius a common link between them all. Now, a fifth person had entered this frustratingly enigmatic cabal, with Basilius' offering coming years later. Per Father Petrus' original instructions, two further gifts remained for me, though Liberius insisted that those remaining gifts would bring little luster, and much pain.

Liberius was many things, but never a liar. Rather than excitement, a twinge of fear laced my reaction to this package, worrying that its contents would spell further suffering in my life. Even so, the human weakness for curiosity drew me to unlace the sackcloth and reach a bare hand into the contents nestled therein. My fingers reached out gingerly, cautious of a possible weapon that could be concealed inside.

Only to brush against coarse iron. Grasping the hidden contents, I withdrew what appeared to be a metal circle no wider than a man's palm, its iron covered in a thick onyx lacquer that helped disguise the metal's many imperfections. The pallor soaked up any light that would reveal its characteristics so well that I did not initially see the imprint of a tiny sigil in the circle's interior, its deep-set grooves forming the unmistakable symbol of the Imperial Chi-Rho.

"What are you?" I whispered aloud, far more confused and frustrated than before.

THE WORLD REMADE IN
THEODORA'S IMAGE

"It is not for me to tell you, Varus," the old priest later insisted as I thrust the branded circle before his wrinkled face.

Like me, Father Petrus had boarded one of the first ships from Carthage, docking an hour after the *Fides*. Once in Constantinople's harbor, and after a lengthy delay in disembarking, Petrus had learned of Basilius' passing, and immediately set for my quarters rather than gather rest in his own. Petrus' pale cheeks and swollen eyes spoke of the deep mourning he harbored at the news of his longtime friend's death, their friendship still largely unknown even to those closest to the ancient holy man.

"But who can explain it to me? When will I know?"

"In time, as all things," Petrus insisted. "Now, I would like to grieve for my dear friend and console his only daughter."

A hot wave of shame shot up my throat at the priest's remonstration. Though I myself had attempted to comfort Antonina after Narses' departure, all I'd succeeded in doing was amplifying her grief. Even Rosamund was able to offer little comfort, given the ardent Christianity of Basilius and his daughter. Though I doubted that Father Petrus knew Antonina well, he surely could not have done a less-effective job at consoling a freshly aggrieved orphan.

And so, I was granted no simple answers about my mysterious fifth gift. Nor did I expect any, though I intended to pry whatever I could from Liberius as soon as he returned to Constantinople. Instead, I obeyed Narses' relayed commands that I rush to the palace with due haste. After informing Sembrouthes and a freshly returned Uliaris of my intentions, I unpacked and donned the armor of all excubitores.

"Think Theodora will be happy to see you?" Uliaris asked.

"Delighted or furious," I answered. "It depends what she places greater value on—capturing the Pillars of Herakles or the humiliation of her friend Antonina."

Uliaris smirked. "Fortune truly shits on you, then."

Though he desired to attend, I insisted that Uliaris seek rest and refreshment while Sembrouthes shadowed me to the palace. Strapping my sword and dagger along my hip, I enlisted Sembrouthes' help in fastening my cloak and straightening my helmet before walking downstairs. Before I left, however, Cephalas passed into the main floor of my building, shouting instructions to teams of servants while carrying a curled ball of fluff in his arm. Smiling, I gave Haeva a thorough scratch. The pup sniffed curiously at the dense hog leather that lined my hands.

"Do you think we'll stay in the city, Varus, or leave for Macedonia?" Cephalas asked. "A pup like this would love the open fields."

"Macedonia, God willing," I answered. "Don't unpack too much until I return from the palace."

Leaving behind the flurry of activity, Sembrouthes and I walked briskly through Constantine's forum and toward the looming Imperial Palace. Within moments of entering the street, I could see the once-proud Hippodrome, seeming as if it had forgotten the horror it had housed just a year prior.

"If any place in this world is cursed, it's that racing track," Sembrouthes whispered. "Do you think Justinian will allow the games to return?"

"Not in the same manner," I guessed. "Justin always hated the factions—the Blues and Greens. Besides, after the riots, I doubt there are many ardent supporters left."

At first glance, any evidence of the once-mighty political groups had vanished. Many buildings along the forum had been rebuilt or renovated in dressed stone, with nary a sapphire- or emerald-colored banner to be found draped along the windows. Evidence of the riots did remain, however, for the brick dwellings of the poor were still laced with black singe marks, with many seemingly uninhabited. Closer to the palace, a far stouter stone wall had been erected along the palace's length, including a system of interlocking gates that prevented an opportunistic mob from rushing the palace guards and gaining entry to the Emperor's inner sanctum. If nothing else, Justinian and Theodora had learned these lessons of the Nika Riots well.

So much had appeared rebuilt to benefit the citizenry, however. Public fountains that had been clogged with filth and moss were now flowing with sparkling aqueduct water, while a new Imperial Barracks and Stables rose nearly to the height of the Hippodrome itself. Violet Imperial banners lined each building, with most bearing the Chi-Rho while a rare few still bore the Imperial Eagle. Most shocking was the vast space that had been cleared in the debris of the Hagia Sophia, with no fewer than a hundred laborers toiling on the construction site.

All these developments bore the implicit signature of Theodora, who had spoken for so long about applying the vast sums of gold earned in trade to the betterment of the Roman people. Even the roads had been thoroughly cleaned in some areas and reconstructed in others, fixing holes that had become dangerous for oxcart wheels or correcting slanted thoroughfares that may last have been fixed by Constantine himself. To this day, I have no idea how Theodora managed such progress to that point, or the vastly more complicated work still to come.

Only one off-putting sign could be easily detected in Constantinople streets. New graffiti had come to adorn many of the alleys leading away from the forum, the black and brown paint still crisp and even dripping in at least two places I was able to spot. Roman cities had suffered from such crude displays since the time of Romulus, yet usually the artist restricted their message to sports hooliganism or drunken nonsense. Now, the intent of the latest message could not be clearer.

BURN ALL PAGANS. KILL THE HERETICS AND APOSTATES.

SLAY THE UNBELIEVERS.

"Make sure Rosamund does not walk the streets alone," I muttered to Sembrouthes.

"I doubt my men will be much more tolerated if this opinion is widely held," he answered. "Which heretics and apostates do they speak of?"

"Liberius warned of a holy man who has gained the ear of Theodora," I said. "Jakob."

I did not expect Sembrouthes to tangle with the nuances of Christian heresies, nor did I desire to elaborate—indeed, earlier, when questioned about the importance of Jakob Baradaeus, or at least the danger posed by his presence, I had attempted to explain the differences between each faction to a pagan Rosamund and an indifferent Ascum, with little success.

"Years ago, when Attila and Pope Leo walked the earth, the leaders of Christianity attempted to gather and unite the various sects under a common understanding," I began, drawing from Petrus' teachings.

It seemed sensible to me, but not to Rosamund. "Why bother?"

"To give secretaries and clerks something to do." Ascum laughed. "Why else?"

Annoyed, I continued. "The meeting was held in Chalcedon, and the attendants agreed that Christ was of two natures in one person: mortal and divine. Both the Eastern and Western Emperor accepted this definition over time."

Rosamund's eyebrows arched. "Two people in one body?"

"No..." I began, though I struggled to find the correct words for explanation.

"I thought Jesus was one person?" Ascum asked. "You mean there were two of them?"

"Not exactly..." I continued.

Ascum turned to Rosamund. "I thought they believed in one God?"

"Don't ask me." Rosamund grinned. "Bunch of hypocrites. My head hurts just trying to make sense of this."

"*At any rate,*" I grumbled, "some Christians, scattered in Mesopotamia, Egypt, and Africa, rejected this definition. They insisted that Christ is of one nature. Jakob and his followers follow this different path, and have clashed with the Chalcedonians for years."

Rosamund frowned. "You mean, you're fighting over how you explain your God?"

In a way, her plain assessment of the situation made sense. "Something like that."

"But he's still your God?" Rosamund continued. "So why does your understanding matter?"

"B-because..." I stammered, my mind blank.

Ascum threw up his hands, bored with the opaque debate. "I've killed a lot of men, for all kinds of reasons. But that has to be one of the more pointless fights I've heard of."

"It makes more sense once you delve into the Scriptures," I insisted faithfully, convincing neither amongst my audience.

To Sembrouthes, I kept it simple and to the point. "Cassiodorus, Justinian's Minister of Churches, detests him," I explained as we made our way to the palace. "Our forces will stay clear of any and all gatherings, although I will gain what answers I can."

But no gatherings remained as we closed the remaining distance to the palace. Approaching the freshly constructed outer gate, I offered my salute to the six guardsmen that lined either side of the iron and wood portal. As I introduced myself, I recognized none of their faces as among the few palace guardsmen to survive the riots.

"Let him through," a voice called from opposite the wall. "He's an excubitor, and a servant of the Empress."

The guardsmen obeyed instantly. Both gates were unlocked and thrown open just long enough for Sembrouthes and I to slip through. Past the second gate, Sembrouthes' weapons were confiscated for storage, for only excubitores and palace guardsmen were permitted to carry weapons in the Emperor's presence. Grudgingly, Sembrouthes surrendered his spear and sword, allowing us entry into the courtyard.

"Looks like Africa couldn't kill you, Varus!" Marcellus called, walking forward to greet us.

"They tried," I answered. "Just not hard enough."

Marcellus offered an arm in greeting that was soon clasped tightly into my own. Marcellus' hair had grown even thinner from our parting after the riots, and much of the remaining black was now streaked with gray. Deep lines creased his eyes and cheeks, while a fair number of healed scars stretched the already taut skin around the excubitor commander's face.

"It's good to have you back. You wouldn't believe how difficult it is to bring new warriors into the brotherhood, especially after losing so many to the riots. Justinian personally interviews each man—a test of loyalty, he claims."

"How many do you need?" I asked.

"I'm still short forty-seven," Marcellus sighed. "I've had to bury too many of our brothers, more than any komes excubitorum that I know of. There are hundreds who would happily accept the nomination, but none meet the order's standards. The Empire is simply picked clean."

Such revelations were unsurprising yet still off-putting. The Imperial Sentinels were restricted to three hundred warriors who swore direct allegiance to the Imperial household, each donning a uniform set of lamellar armor to denote their status to the masses. My own dominus had once filled Marcellus' position as their anointed komes, and as a youth my dreams were filled with bearing that armor into battle against the Emperor's foes.

Regardless of the province that one found themselves in, the excubitores were viewed with reverence, for even a prefect or an Imperial governor could not levy orders upon such a man. In return, the excubitores were accepted to be masters of their craft, unmatched by potential foes and unflinching when sent into a battle's most desperate moment. Few excubitores died peacefully in their beds, with Justin as the only one who I personally could recall. Unless elevated to the purple, such men served for life, whatever fortune may bring.

"I may recommend candidates to you," I replied.

"Excellent." Marcellus smiled. "God, but I wish I could have gone with you to Carthage. And Septem!"

"You would have been most welcome, my friend," I said. "But tell me, what do these scribblings across the city mean?"

Marcellus groaned. "The graffiti, you mean? Nothing good." Leaning closer, he lowered his voice to a whisper. "It seems that the Blues and Greens were not the only threats to peace and safety. Cassiodorus has many of the city's Christians baying for blood, likely because he is secretly displeased at his informal setback in status over the past year. Nevertheless, I feel that our current problems would disappear if Theodora's... guest would return to whatever eastern desert birthed him."

"Jakob?" I asked.

"Jakob *Baradaeus*," Marcellus moaned, rolling his eyes. "The Man in Ragged Clothes, so he's called. There has never been a more apt name, although that isn't a sin by itself. No, this Jakob rustles about the city, declaring all this nonsense about our Savior being fully divine and fully human."

"Troubling," I agreed. "I've heard of this coming from the eastern provinces, but never paid much heed."

"Nor I," replied Marcellus. "Little better than heretic Nestorians, from my view, although at least they acknowledge the living Jesus as divine, in their own way. Regardless, they're here now, and if this Baradaeus is not careful, he's like to spark another riot in this city."

Mindful not to delay my meeting with the Empress, Marcellus

accompanied me into the Imperial Palace's grounds. His words had been concerning—calling upon a festering dispute from the time of Pope Leo and Attila himself, when the nature of Christ was decided by the Empire's leading churchmen. Indeed, in the Imperial Palace, the ministers and Marcellus alike believed the schism a true threat to Constantinople's peace.

As Marcellus and I climbed the marble steps to the palace's interior, with Sembrouthes a few steps behind, it was pleasing to see the once-splintered doorways replaced, with all signs of destruction painted, swept, and washed clean from the most important building in all the Empire. Marcellus, however, groaned as his knee popped while rising along the marble steps. "I'm getting too old for so much strife, Varus, so I hope you're here to be a peacemaker."

"Peace is already hard-won, with the Vandals and Visigoths subdued," I countered, "although I will prevail upon Theodora regarding this Jakob, if you feel these threats are that concerning."

"They are," Marcellus said, rubbing a gnarled hand at the sore joint. "I've seen enough war to last me ten lifetimes. If there are any words that you might speak to keep the soldiers in their barracks and the harvests plentiful, then I shall carry you up the palace steps myself."

"And shatter your back in the process," I teased.

After my entry was granted, Marcellus remained in the courtyard with Sembrouthes, who was instructed to wait for my return. As the doors closed, I was greeted by a half dozen excubitores who stood at guard along the inner doorway. After I waved a brisk salute, the rustling of their armor brought me back for a moment to the most desperate night of our defense of the palace, when ten thousand screaming insurrectionists shattered the palace doorway and streamed inside.

Adorned in the armor of my station and acknowledged by Marcellus, none of the hundreds of courtiers, excubitores, slaves, or attendants took any particular notice of my movements. Instead, guided by a lifetime of memories, I climbed the palace stairs and headed toward the private offices of the Emperor and Empress, seeking a private moment with Theodora. Yet upon reaching the doorway to Theodora's private hall, I found the doors closed, with a further half dozen excubitores barring the entry.

At their head was Chanaranges, whose right cheek bore a deep scar. Chanaranges hobbled with an uncomfortable limp, evidence of a grievous wound taken at the onset of the Nika Riots before being carried to Justinian's box. If I might be considered Theodora's personal excubitor, Chanaranges was the warrior closest to Justinian, going so far as to sleep in the same room as the Emperor in times of particular tension. Grimacing as he walked to greet me, his normally smooth cheeks had become covered in gray stubble, his deep-brown skin spotted and worn from excessive sunlight.

"Theodora will be happy to see you," Chanaranges remarked gruffly, leaning upon a walking stick. "Though if you expected carefree conversation, you might be mistaken."

"It delights me to see you well, Chanaranges," I replied, clutching at the man's outstretched arm. "Do your injuries still pain you?

"Every waking hour." He retracted his hand, instinctively reaching for a hip that had been struck by a blade in the earliest moments of the riots. "I'll never understand why the Emperor keeps me around when younger men are available, but here I am."

"You'll be crookbacked and gray, and the Emperor will still drag you around," I said, chuckling.

"God, but I hope not," Chanaranges grumbled. "A swift death is better than this crippled hell, growing feebler each day." He nodded at the doors. "He's inside, if you're wondering, and none too happy with your mistress."

"No?"

Chanaranges shrugged. "Well, as unhappy as an utterly smitten man can be. He's resentful of this eastern preacher, and for the colossal expense of the hundreds of projects the Empress personally leads. It leaves him with few men and little gold to pursue his own ends."

As Chanaranges spoke, the door to Theodora's hall burst open.

Each of the idling excubitores straightened as Justinian stormed from the room, his breathing labored and fists clenched. Behind him hobbled Paulus, his arms heavy with scrolls and face even more crimson than Justinian's own, and a man in ornate priest's robes. It was not until he passed closer that I recognized the latter man as Cassiodorus, his once rotund body seeming to have melted off its heavy layers of fat.

"We're leaving," he grunted.

Though each of the white-cloaked excubitores instantly encircled the Emperor, Chanaranges limped to his side and whispered into Justinian's ear. Still clenching his fist, Justinian nodded, his reddened face turning to meet mine.

"Approach," he commanded.

Unsure of his intent, I nevertheless obeyed immediately, hustling to five paces distant and dropping to my knees. Though I lacked Chanaranges' infirmity, my hurried movements nevertheless shot beams of pain up my thighs and calves. I was still a young man, but the summation of too many wounds in the shield wall was now too great to entirely ignore, and though creaking of the body worried me, for now I brushed those thoughts away like the sagging cloak I swept to the side.

I bowed my head, eyes fixed upon the marble floor. "Highness."

"You have done well, Lord Varus," Justinian mumbled. "I had thought Tingitana beyond my reach. Be sure to attend the triumph I intend for Belisarius."

"Your will, Augustus," I replied, remaining prostrate, given no command to shift into a more comfortable position.

"Convince your mistress of its value, and I shall commission your own triumph, Lord Varus," Justinian said. "Away to the gardens, I have need for additional donations of gold from our loyal senators."

I did not rise until Justinian and his entourage shuffled past my prone form, their steps echoing onto the floors below. Finding no guards around Theodora's door, I placed a palm upon the gold-plated panels, tapping gently to signal my presence.

"Enter!"

I obeyed, leaning my shoulder into the door and slipping inside. A near oppressive aroma of incense invaded my nostrils, forcing me to steady myself along the wall. Though wafting smoke left the room difficult to perceive, so far as I could tell it remained the same cramped quarters that I remembered. As I walked forward, my hip bumped into what turned out to be a table, sending a heavy stack of papers scattering to the floor.

"Clumsy oaf!" Narses snapped.

Bending down to rectify my error, I instead succeeded only in slamming my head against the same table. The damage to my person was minor, with the iron ridges of my helmet taking the brunt of the blow, yet I thought I would choke from embarrassment.

"Leave us, Narses," Theodora said, her voice crackling from hoarseness. "We will continue later."

Narses bowed and rushed from the door, not stopping to acknowledge my passing. After collecting the spilled parchment and placing it back upon its perch, I walked slowly toward the seated Empress.

Even from afar, I could tell that Theodora had aged. Narrow strands of gray shocked the tight bun of raven-black hair, while dark shadows ringed her eyes like halos. She had not grown old, only in her midthirties, perhaps a handful of years older than I. Yet, like me, the burdens of office had worn into the previously indefatigable Empress who had saved the last dying embers of Rome from total ruin. Where my weariness had been borne out on the battlefield, however, Theodora's was from becoming the true and sole ruler of millions.

Nevertheless, she was unmistakably an empress. Her fabled sapphire and emerald dresses had been replaced by one of deep violet, its hems traced with silver thread, while golden circlets snaked up her arms and a pearl-inlaid headdress made her appear a full head taller than she truly was. Bedecked in her finery, she sat upon a marble chair etched with all the trappings of the Caesars, her chin resting upon gold-bedecked fingers.

Most notably, however, Theodora was not alone.

"Varus, please meet Jakob, a monk of Fsilta Monastery in Syria, and a dear friend of mine," she said. "Many say Jakob is a miracle worker, and I would say that our Empire has need of miracles."

A figure, standing alongside Theodora's throne, bobbed a hooded head. Despite the swirling incense, I recognized him instantly as a man I had spotted in the forum earlier in the morning, his clothing bleached by lengthy days of exposure to the sun, and his shoes and belt barely more than a strip of fraying flax. The man allowed little skin to reveal itself, with even his fingers hidden behind ponderously extensive sleeves. Within the hood, however, I spied a sharp jaw and a graying beard, with curiously hollow cheeks holding both upright.

A worker of miracles. Many before Jakob claimed such power, and a great many afterward. Father Petrus assures me that all such men were liars and charlatans, for the only true magic is what comes from Christ the Savior, who conquered death and liberated Hell. In Petrus' hearing I would only ever heartily agree; however, although I have never wavered from Christianity, I did not share his conviction that other magics did not exist. In the vastness of this world, I have witnessed far too much to cast aside the possibility of another power, the antithesis of light.

Nevertheless, I suspected Jakob as little more than a strident village priest, conjuring tricks and fooling farmers and fishwives. He was amiable enough, a toothy grin and crinkled eyes ready in greeting when his face revealed itself, and I believed them sincere. Ultimately, it was not Jakob himself who left me befuddled, but rather Theodora, and her willingness to profess such bold claims on his behalf—Theodora, a calculating mind grounded in earthly tasks, who had rarely drifted toward spiritual conversation, at least in my presence.

"Jakob has my protection, Lord Varus, and I would see him well guarded," Theodora continued. "Although he refuses any armed consort in his wanderings of our Empire and Capitol."

"Your friends are mine, Highness," I responded. "And those

whom you hold with contempt should not sleep soundly."

Theodora laughed heartily. "So pretty! One would think you hadn't emerged neck-deep from the carnage of war, the way you spin words. Perhaps our dear Jakob might learn from such tact?"

"Lord Varus is far too important," Jakob answered, his voice a note higher in pitch than I would have assumed, "and far too clever to mentor one such as I, Empress. And it does not require the whispers of God to understand you both have much to discuss. I will go minister to the masses, with your leave."

"You hear God's words?" I interrupted, my words tinged with far more skepticism than I had intended.

"You do not?" Jakob countered. "Our divine savior speaks in and through all things, just as He was when He walked the earth as a man. All I do is listen, and allow Him to work through my feeble hands."

"Thank you, Jakob," Theodora said, a note of finality in her voice. "Do not stray far, and be mindful of your safety. The Empire will have need of your piety before long."

"My life is in the hands of God, Empress." Jakob bowed again. "Although I shall pray for safety, to ease your troubled mind. As I shall for you, Lord Varus."

Gathering his stained robe, Jakob unceremoniously departed from the room, shutting the ponderous door slowly behind him. With that, Theodora and I were finally alone. The Empress sipped at a nearby cup of wine before resting her face within both hands.

"Please sit, Varus," Theodora said, her words muffled by the prison of jeweled fingers.

A small bench faced the Empress' throne, which I pushed within a few paces of her seated form. Gathering my cloak and taking my seat, I waited as Theodora rubbed at her face, her chest rising and falling. For a moment, her shoulders shuddered, her fingers at the corners of her eyes, smudging the kohl and other powders that caked Theodora's face, yet I dared not speak of such blemishes in the current setting. Instead, with Narses and Jakob departed, I waited to speak until Theodora's head rose once more to meet my own.

"No guards, Highness?"

"Most of them whisper against me," Theodora said wistfully. "I've missed you terribly, Varus."

Before I could speak, Theodora jerked a finger to her lips. At that, the Empress scribbled on a small vellum square. After returning her quill to her inkpot, Theodora rose to her feet and shifted her hips square to my form, bringing me to scramble upright.

Theodora's voice was oddly stilted. "Embrace me as your friend, and tell me of your journeys."

Puzzled, I offered outstretched arms that seemed altogether improper for an Augusta, even if Theodora had been far more intimate in her friendship in years past. Perhaps it was her aged face, or her clear elevation into the true power of the Imperial leadership. Regardless, Theodora grinned as she caught my awkward hug, slipping her arms underneath my own and wrapping them tightly around my armored chest. She soon retracted the embrace, yet slipped a hand underneath the clasp of my cloak before returning to her seat.

Frowning, I raised a hand to the clasp, with my fingers brushing against Theodora's scroll. Drawing to a seated position, I unfurled the thick vellum and spied the hurried block letters scratched herein.

THEY LISTEN TO EVERYTHING. BE CAUTIOUS, WE ARE IN MORE DANGER THAN YOU KNOW. THE WALLS HEAR ALL.

"This mess with Belisarius and Antonina," Theodora began. "Is it really as bad as Procopius and Narses prattle about?"

I froze, my skin writhing from the knowledge that I had traded spies in Carthage for spies in a territory I had supposed friendly. And though the topic of Theodora's interest was inevitable, I lacked an elegant response that might satisfy her without jeopardizing Belisarius, Antonina, or myself. More, the urgency of her written message, the hint of fear it showed, nearly stopped my heart. Theodora was Justinian's beloved, after all. If she was truly unsafe, who among us could claim differently?

After a few moments, I assembled my reply, chosen from pieces of information that most of the Imperial Court would have already known. I opted for honesty, yet saw no need to reveal anything beyond a direct answer to Theodora's question, nor did I desire to volunteer more upon so unhappy a discussion. Honesty might be the most dependable armor against challenges from the mighty, yet only a fool would reveal all his knowledge unprompted.

"I do not know what Narses or Procopius quibble about, Highness, but I confess it is a difficult situation. I witnessed firsthand the lady's... transgression."

The Empress nodded, a weak smile evaporating as her chin sagged. "When we are alone, please abandon any titles. I am simply Theodora, daughter of a bear-tamer and a courtesan, and you are Varus, the son of a slave. Please afford me this small courtesy."

Finding myself with the same awkward instincts as with Belisarius, I could only nod. "Antonina is with the rest of my household now, and Belisarius has requested that she remain with me until a decision of her fate is rendered."

"Belisarius has no further rights to determine Antonina's fate," Theodora frowned. "Although I do not object to her remaining in your care. I will speak to her myself, but see that no harm befalls the lady. Basilius was one of my few loyal friends, and I will not see his daughter thrown into the streets like some gutter rat just weeks after his death. However, I must know—why has Belisarius not reported this issue to the palace directly?"

"The general's flagship was scheduled to depart a day after my own, Highness," I explained. "Provided fair weather, I'm sure the bulk of the fleet will arrive within the week, if not in the next day or two. Antonina's incident occurred only days before our journey, so there was no chance for a courier to arrive to inform you."

Theodora raised an arm in understanding. "I do not blame you, Varus, I am only asking. What befell her lover, this Sergius? Did Belisarius not have him hanged?"

"Escaped," I replied. "My brother personally led the manhunt, but there proved to be too little time to find him given our departure. Solomon and Troglita still seek information on the man's whereabouts, although if he has not yet been found…"

"Then he will not be found until he desires to be." Theodora sighed. "And I understand that Antonina has kept close to you since then. Does she wish a divorce? Does she contend that Belisarius has mistreated her in some way?"

Theodora was uncomfortably direct. My eyes darted to the shadow-draped corners that I now had to think hid spies—whether from Narses or Justinian, or from among the dozens of wealthy patrician families, I could not know. Theodora demanded an answer, one that could cause me to dishonor my friendship with Belisarius or violate my unwanted promise of protection over Antonina. Whatever I said in these Imperial chambers would echo in the dingiest popina by the morning, fodder for rumormongers.

"Antonina has said nothing of the sort," I answered. "If anything, she claims her… coupling… with Sergius was not initially her intention, but merely the regrettable result of a moment of weakness. She weeps every day, although I can only imagine that will double with the knowledge of her father's death."

"What a mess," Theodora mused. "Does Belisarius want her dead?"

The directness of the inquiry took me aback. Its answer was simple enough—although, again, many in the army wished Theodora herself to hang. Other women who had spurned their noble husbands had suffered far worse in recent years, with far less time for deliberation.

"No," I admitted. "But neither can he forgive, as broken as he is. Belisarius won't even speak to me now."

Theodora's brows rose at such an admission, leaning closer at the bitterness of my words. "You say you were there, to witness Antonina's lovemaking? Narses tells me that it took place in your very house within Carthage. Does Belisarius suspect you of wrongdoing?"

"Highness, I—"

"Theodora," she insisted.

"Theodora," I amended, "I do not know what Belisarius thinks on this matter. Antonina admitted to me that, after befriending my household servant Rosamund, she was able to gain access to my lodgings while I left for the Pillars of Herakles. I returned from the expedition several days early, and Belisarius walked back with me to that same building, when we discovered a surprised Antonina and Sergius."

Theodora nodded. "In time, I will speak with Belisarius as well. You are a loyal friend to him, Varus, although you have witnessed something so desperately private that I am uncertain whether Belisarius will ever treat you the same again. He writes highly of your skill and leadership, however, and I would hear more of your victories in distant Septem."

Grateful to move away from discussions of Antonina, I recounted an abbreviated telling of our struggles and ultimate victory both against the Vandals and later in the Pillars. Nearly unmoving, Theodora listened intently as I told of my capture of Mount Papua, Baduarius' death, and the godlike conflagration of Septem's port, her fingers crossed throughout.

"This is too much for one man to bear, Varus," Theodora whispered as I finished. "The Empire owes you an unfathomable debt." Her eyes fell to the dragon hilt at my hip. "May I see it?"

Amongst excubitores, such an action would have borne scrutiny, for not even the faintest threat to the Imperial household could be tolerated. Theodora, however, did not flinch as I dragged the sword from its scabbard, handing it hilt first toward her outstretched fingers. Grasping the handgrip, Theodora lifted the sword's tip toward the ceiling, running her free hand across its runes.

"Much lighter than I expected," she remarked. "Between Justin and yourself, this sword has seen much. Where did it come from, I wonder?"

I shrugged. "Justin never told me, although it must have been a war trophy. It could be hundreds of years old, if it truly spawned from the heavens. Justin himself told me that it was carved from a meteorite, and that it would never rust."

"Such history, even if we cannot understand the script it bears,"

Theodora said. "Liberius has told me that you may wish to place this blade in its scabbard for good. Is this true?"

The Empress' words caught the very air in my chest. I dreaded making such a request, worrying that Theodora would voice disappointment or fury—or worse, reject my demands outright, chaining me to a lifetime of endless campaigns only to die alone in some forgotten distant battlefield in Moesia or Armenia. For a heartbeat, I bore unfathomable resentment for Liberius' betrayal of my trust, its hold only broken by another unanticipated proclamation.

"Far be it from me to separate a family, even for as long as I have," Theodora said. "I will honor any request you seek of me, but I would ask a favor in return."

Burning anger evaporated into a flimsy hope that soared within my chest. "Speak it, and it shall be done."

"Remain in the excubitores at my side," Theodora said, her voice muted, almost pleading. "Bring your family to the Capitol, and you will be my most trusted servant, honored above all others. I will not force you as an Empress, but can only beseech you as a friend."

"I never intended to abandon my oath to the excubitores," I replied quickly, "nor to you. I cannot speak to Mariya's mind on leaving Pella, but I can promise to speak with her on this."

"Yes, I would caution you against making promises without speaking to your wife first!" Theodora chided me. "And certainly not before the triumph. My husband has placed considerable effort into Belisarius' reward, and promises that it will be a spectacle remembered for generations to come."

"You know not what will occur?"

Theodora closed her eyes. "Not in the slightest, although the expense is considerable. There hasn't been a triumph for one outside the Imperial family in half a millennium, so Justinian's expenditures are not entirely unfounded. He tells me nothing of his plans for this event, however. All I ask is that you wait until the celebrations cease, and I will negotiate your retirement from the comitatenses."

An urge to embrace Theodora swelled within my chest. After so many months of blood and struggle, my heart's desire had been all but granted, with nary a cost or sacrifice outside of the freedom of our Pella estate. Strangely, I nearly wept at Theodora's pronouncement, yet managed to remain calm as I voiced my commitment. I even decided not to press her for information about the Eastern heretic, this Jakob Baradaeus, out of fear that Theodora might change her mind.

"You have my word," I answered. "And my thanks. More than you might understand."

Theodora smiled once more before rubbing the corners of her darkened eyelids. Pausing for a moment, she lifted her crown and scarf free from the knotted hair piled high upon her head, placing the ponderous device upon a nearby table. Freed of such restriction, Theodora rubbed at the muscles of her neck before unknotting her tightly woven hair.

"You should thank God nightly that you were not born a woman, Varus," Theodora said, wincing as she teased at an overtaxed point along her neck and shoulders. "Even if they don't wish to hang you for having sex, you'd be condemned to wearing all manner of weighty devices for the sake of modesty and majesty. Whoever fashioned the first crown for an Augusta was no woman, I promise you."

I chuckled as Theodora removed the many rings and torques that adorned her fingers and arms, grateful for the shift in our discussion. She groaned in relief as she freed herself of the various impediments constricting her skin before turning her attentions to other matters within the city. Theodora spoke of all the difficulties of recovery from the riots, yet beamed as she mentioned developments around the Hagia Sophia. Though I bore some resentment that my estate had been applied to the building's expense without my knowledge, I did not press the matter, for I doubt that any good would have come from such a confrontation. Besides, in my absence, Mariya bore all rights and responsibilities of Justin's gifted gold, so there was no true wrongdoing in the matter.

It was when Theodora turned to more worrisome developments

that my interest escalated, including all manner of upheaval along the Empire's borders and beyond.

"Wars in distant Aksum, while the Franks have swarmed into the lands of the Burgundians, which makes better sense given what you've told me. There are rumors of a new plague ravaging Himyar, although old men prattle of plagues that come and go each year. Persia has kept its promise for peace, leaving us ample coin to finance repair and construction rather than equip thousands of men for fighting in the desert. What worries me most, however, is the Ostrogoths—too many chieftains claim leadership, and the matter of Amalasuntha's death remains unresolved."

"Do you think there will be war in Italy?" I asked.

"Amongst the Ostrogoths, there already is," Theodora replied. "Justinian has sent no fewer than a dozen ambassadors to Ravenna and has countless spies in Italy and Dalmatia, and most indicate that this Theodahad has seized the loyalty of the Gothic chiefs. That he is both a glutton and a hedonist matters little, nor that he murdered Theodoric's only legitimate child in Amalasuntha."

The earlier elation in my heart seized. "Will Justinian declare war?"

"Doubtful," Theodora said. "The cost would be immense, and although our coffers have swelled after absorbing the wealth of so many seditious senators and patricians, it would be impossible to equip and support the tens of thousands of men needed to capture and hold the Italian cities. We haven't even begun to adequately occupy all the Vandal lands, as you well know."

"You're certain?" I desperately wanted to believe her. "Even with others braying for blood?"

Theodora nodded. "My husband understands the challenges we face presently. Though Justin and Basilius called for Ravenna and Rome to return to the Empire, diplomacy remains our only realistic path forward. Perhaps we may recognize Theodahad's illegitimate rule in return for his formal subjugation to Imperial taxes?"

"God willing," I answered. And so I hoped, even with Theodora's protection. Not out of any sense of honor for the Empire, but more for the safety of so many friends who would suffer and die in another foreign adventure. After Tauris, and Mesopotamia, and Africa, and even Tingitana, many already had fallen to achieve the dreams of others, while those under Belisarius had only barely escaped the inevitable reaper of lives. I had every confidence in the general, yet even Caesar had met a terrible end when fate was pushed beyond its intended limits.

Though others knocked upon Theodora's door, the two of us spoke well into the early evening. She asked of Indulf and Gunderic, of my capture of Gelimer and a dozen others whose names would echo in the histories of Belisarius' conquest. Theodora paid particular attention to the slight details of Paulus' grievous errors, her nose wrinkling at the prospect of so many spearmen dying in a puddle of their own blood and dung from little more than spoiled and undercooked bread. By the edge of nightfall, however, Theodora issued one final request that, though it meant considerable hardship, I lacked any grounds to deny.

"When you leave for Pella, allow me to join you," she said. "I have already spoken with Justinian and Narses, and they both concur that a brief sojourn to the country would not be untoward."

"Theodora," I said, forcing myself to speak her name, "I have never visited my own estate myself. I doubt it is equipped to house the Augusta of the Empire."

A flick of her wrist tossed aside any such concern. "I was born in squalor, Varus. Cozy rooms have never been repugnant to me. All I ask is to enjoy the hospitality and conversation of your family and household, with minimal discussion of the Empire's affairs."

Such a goal seemed laughably impossible, but again, I did not have the standing to refuse. "Of course, Theodora."

"It is settled, then," she proclaimed. "We shall wait until the others of your vaunted expedition have returned, and then will depart shortly thereafter. The triumph shall take place at the beginning of summer, so only four months remain of us."

Bowing, I departed Theodora's presence, eager to escape the palace's enclosure. Aside from gruff greetings from four excubitores patrolling the palace halls, I faced no impediment to my escape until I reached the outer doorway, greeted by orange light from an aging day.

"Why are you still here?" I growled at Sembrouthes. "You've seen the writing on the streets! Marcellus worries that there might be another riot if we aren't careful."

Sembrouthes scowled, nodding toward his sole companion — Rosamund. "Don't blame me. The others went to your insulae, but she insisted on coming to the palace."

"Yes, don't blame Sembrouthes," Rosamund agreed.

"Definitely not." Sembrouthes was visibly irritated. "You're almost as bad as Varus, you know — insisting on getting yourself killed if I wasn't here to swaddle you."

"I just wanted to see the young slave that helped care for me during the riots," Rosamund explained, though she seemed uncharacteristically cowed by Sembrouthes' rebuke. "Agathias, the youth that Varus gave coins to."

"It doesn't matter now," I grumbled. "Let's get to safety before the roads become dark."

The greater distance we gained from the palace, the fewer people we encountered on Constantinople's thoroughfares. Merchants packed their wares for the day, while the first prostitutes began to stalk the city's alleys, searching for customers. Without a larger retinue, the streets felt unwelcoming, the three of us standing out as a collection of well-fed foreign curiosities. Unfastening my sheathed dagger from my belt, I offered the weapon to Rosamund.

"Just in case," I whispered.

Nearing the Forum of Constantine, the buildings that adjoined the main road shadowed our procession westward. Yet enough light remained to identify crude paintings along nearby walls, more suggestive than those I initially spotted.

SAVE THE EMPEROR. BURN THE HERETICS.

And, tucked away in a near-hidden corner of a cistern doorway, a direct insult.

THEODORA IS A WHORE

"Well, that's unfriendly," Rosamund mused as I murmured the accusation aloud.

"It's suicidal," Sembrouthes corrected. "You'd think Justinian would put a stop to this."

By words and deeds, it was plain to all that Justinian adored his wife. Yet after the riots, Basilius' warnings told of jealousies beneath that love, and of a man with grand dreams and an even bolder opinion of himself, one on the verge of being supplanted by the very spouse he depended on to survive.

"Keep going," I replied curtly.

Pacing onward, we reached Constantine's Forum, encountering the first crowd I had seen assembled in Constantinople's streets since my return from Africa. In my youth, such a rabble would be unworthy of note, perhaps ten cloaked men milling about. What brought me pause was how they hounded the figure, snarling is if he were some filthy beast.

"Go back east!"

"Syrian catamite!"

"Take your master and go die in the desert!"

None brandished weapons, although the cloaked men had gathered about their target in a circle. The man, ostensibly of the far eastern provinces, was adorned in a frayed gray tunic. At first, I thought he might be Jakob, but a quick glimpse at his face revealed a much younger man, and far less weathered by sun-bleached days spent wandering the Imperial roads. Nor did he carry himself with Jakob's self-sure demeanor, instead keeping his chin down and eyes locked upon the stones at his feet.

"We should help him," Rosamund whispered.

"Out of the question," Sembrouthes replied.

I agreed. "We don't know if these men are with Cassiodorus or if they have more friends nearby."

On the far edge of the forum, the taunting grew more vicious as the circle of thugs drew closer to their prey. Some appeared drunk from wine, swaying upon their feet, yet most seemed inebriated only by a desire to outdo one another in defense of their God.

Rosamund stopped, glaring at Sembrouthes and me. "You're two warriors in armor. You're supposed to defend your people, no?"

Sembrouthes shook his head. "My job is to keep Varus and you alive, and preferably unharmed."

"It's too dangerous to start fights here," I said. "Anyway, this is a quarrel amongst Christians. Why would you care?"

She glared at me, her disappointment plain. "You're better than that, Varus."

At that, Rosamund darted into the forum's center, striding toward the rabble. Muttering an oath, I trailed behind, to Sembrouthes' exasperation.

"I swear to God..." I heard him mumbling, the clink of iron indicating that Sembrouthes' had readied himself to pluck his sword from its scabbard.

"Leave him alone!" Rosamund yelled. Within the group, the taunting stopped as the cloaked men turned to face their challenger. Her accented Greek got their attention, as quickly as her bone-white hair identified her as a barbarian from beyond the Ister.

Rosamund sped up to a trot, while I remained barely two steps behind. Within heartbeats, we closed within ten paces of the men, all of whom wore frowns and dripped with malice.

"Is he a friend of yours, Gepid?" one of the rabble asked—his scraggly beard and grease-smothered face suggested he was hardly eighteen years of age—and nodded at the unfortunate Syrian.

"He's certainly not yours," Rosamund shot back. "Let him leave."

The man grunted. "He's a heretic, little better than beetles, and far messier."

Grasping Rosamund's arm, I urged her back, yet she shook free of my restraint. Then, glancing upon the cowed Syrian, Rosamund leveled a gaze at his tormentors. "So am I."

First surprise, and then horror, flashed over the scraggle-bearded man's face. "You're with Baradaeus?"

"No," Rosamund sneered. "My gods are far older, and far less patient of gangs of weasels like you."

"Witch!" another cloaked figure hissed, the accusation raised by others in the group. "You dare walk in God's city!"

God's city? Constantinople was many things, yet between its popinae, prostitutes, and armies of merchants seeking to swindle and cheat their way to profit, it could never be seriously considered any kind of holy city. The entire situation would have been humorous to me, had the mob not given me pause, and had Rosamund not become a new target for them in the process of deflecting their ire. Carefully watching the reactions of each man, I remained silent, searching for an opportunity to pry my party away.

The nearest man hefted his staff, lowering its head toward Rosamund. "Cassiodorus will reward me for seizing a witch."

With a flick of her wrist, Rosamund drew her dagger. "You're all fools. Return to your mothers before they spank you."

"Jesus Christ," Sembrouthes cursed under his breath.

As the nearest man raised his staff above his head, my restraint evaporated. Stepping forward, I drew my sword, the naked iron not directed at any specific man but rather toward the group.

"Try me," I growled. "If you so much as muss her shirt, you'll be wearing your bowels as a necklace."

For effect, Sembrouthes joined me, although he offered no taunts. It was as if Cassiodorus' men had been robbed of their vigor—wielding only staves, they needed only so much as look upon one excubitor and another expensively armored warrior to know further contest was futile.

"Let them all leave, Varus," Rosamund said. "They aren't worth it."

At that point, I felt the matter difficult to sweep aside. "The City Watch should jail these men, even if only for a few nights."

"No, they're just a bunch of idiots trying to impress one another,"

Rosamund replied. Stepping closer to the group, she pointed to the frightened Syrian. "Just let him leave, and you all can depart with all of your appendages. Refuse…"

Rather than complete her sentence, Rosamund drew a finger across her neck. There was no reply, nor pithy retort, only the pounding of footsteps as they sprinted away. Sembrouthes and I sheathed our swords, and my relief was palpable as Rosamund walked toward the Syrian.

"You're safe to leave now," she announced. "But you'd be smart to hire a guard."

"Stay away from me, witch!" the Syrian hissed.

Dumbstruck, Rosamund shuddered as the ungrateful man jogged away. She did not move for a time, instead staring at his departing form as shadows consumed a greater portion of Constantine's Forum.

"Insolent toad," she eventually grumbled. "I guess we can leave now."

"That was unwise, Rosamund," I said. "Cassiodorus' men—"

"Just a bunch of overzealous boys." Rosamund chuckled.

Sembrouthes was more forceful. "They won't forget this encounter, Rosamund."

"I won't walk alone at night," Rosamund promised. "And I'll be careful. But someone had to do something."

"Perhaps," I replied, unsure of the benefits of Rosamund's generosity toward the Syrian stranger.

We departed without further incident and reached our assigned building. Though that encounter gave life to Marcellus' worries of unrest, it simultaneously disarmed me, for those men lacked any of the organization, numbers, or even willingness to kill that had characterized the most strident of the Greens and Blues. Though I later instructed everyone in my household to avoid nighttime excursions and to travel in groups at all times, I disregarded Cassiodorus' thugs, believing it a threat incapable of striking me. Unimaginative fool that I was, even if the threat would dissipate for a time.

My thoughts turned toward rest, and Pella. Four months—well, four, less the time to travel. It seemed altogether too brief. Then again, with my battles completed, those precious days may become only the start of future intimacy with my family. I desperately wished it would be so, even if wishing meant turning a blind eye to the intrigue that now seemed to circle my every decision.

PELLA, THE HOME
OF ALEXANDER

Transports from Carthage arrived in a trickle at first, yet within a day swelled to a heavy stream of women and men lusting after the comforts of firm ground. Within a week, nearly all of the hundreds of vessels that set out from Carthage had returned to Constantinople—a minor miracle not only for Imperial leadership, but a testament to the logistical prowess of Procopius. Our clerk may have been a distrustful bastard, but he had an eye for organization unmatched by any except Narses himself. It was months later when we discovered that a half dozen transports went aground in Corinth, yet not a soul perished on the expedition's return journey.

Two days after my arrival in Constantinople, Samur and his Hunnic foederati slipped into Carthage's harbor and stormed into the makeshift barracks that would serve to house the men for a week. While Sinnion and Aigan led their filth-strewn and seasick comrades to the city's taverns, Samur did not tarry to meet with me. I insisted he bathe first, as he stunk even worse than I had after leaving the *Fides*, and after halfhearted grumbling, Samur complied. Once clean, he requested a private meeting with Rosamund and me alone. He demanded information into all that I had learned from the palace, though he found little to his tastes.

"Theodora wins no matter what you choose," Samur complained. "Leave the army, and she deprives Belisarius of a valued officer while gaining a trusted bodyguard. Stay, and Theodora retains a rare ally in Imperial command. They're using you like some blacksmith's hammer, Varus, and you're too trusting to see it!"

I jerked my head angrily. "Not everyone we meet is a killer or a schemer," I pointed out. "Theodora has never guided me toward an ill-fated path."

"Because she needs you," Samur insisted, "not out of love or kinship."

"Samur is correct," Rosamund put in. "So long as you remain under the thrall of these people, you will never be free of the burdens and nightmares they cause."

"But humor Theodora," Samur urged. "You cannot resist an Empress and expect to live safely, after all. But once this foolish triumph is over, we all leave for Pella. If Theodora, or the Emperor, or Belisarius, or anyone else objects, we ride for the plains. Between your fortune and all the plunder gathered from the Vandals, we are rich enough to build our own kingdom on the steppe. Sinnion's people would welcome us with our own celebration."

I slouched. It was a tiresome subject, made worse by the possibility of true freedom never being so close at hand. "I will not abandon Belisarius, nor the Empress. But Theodora has promised the end of my field deployment. That is a start, and one we can all benefit from."

"It is something," Rosamund admitted. "A start, at least."

Samur nodded. "A compromise. But make no promises to these Romans. We've all given more than our share of blood and sorrow for patrician dreams."

"Agreed," I concluded. "Will you not return to Pella with us now? My children have a need to meet their mischievous uncle!"

Samur grimaced. "I can't leave the Huns now. We're being transferred to Bithynia."

I am ashamed to tell you that I was not displeased about Samur's impending departure. In our years together, I was loath to be parted; leaving Samur as a slave in the palace while I trained as a Thracian recruit had given me a twinge of guilt each night. Yet after Rosamund's revelation on our return from Septem, I saw something in my brother I never had before. Wariness, if not outright concern. I loved him without exception, yet at times, I wondered whether following Sunicas' path had changed my brother, and I figured a few months' separation would grant me time to consider how to approach this rift with greater tact. All said, I could never let him know of my misgivings, for I had no doubt those opinions would crush Samur, whether or not he had become an adopted Hun.

"Surely you can request a month?" I pondered. "I could speak with Belisarius for you."

Samur shrugged. "Is Belisarius of a mind to listen? It isn't worth the bother, and we'll be rejoined in just a few months. Besides..."

He turned, eyeing a gathering of Huns some fifty paces distant. They shared a wineskin, the sour red staining cheeks scarred by ritual branding. "Justinian wants to enlarge the Hun foederati. Aigan is expected to journey northward and speak with a dozen Hun tribes for recruits. It seems that the Huns are good enough to die in Roman wars, but not worthy to share Roman tables."

I might have spoken in the Emperor's defense—as an excubitor, it was all but my duty to do so. Yet I knew better, having witnessed how the patricians viewed the Heruli, the Huns, and countless other tribes beyond the Empire's borders: as wild hogs, rutting about with no civilized thoughts and little ambition in life. "You know any Hun who fights under you will be honored in my camp."

"I do," Samur replied. "Offer my apologies to Mariya, and give a kiss to my niece and nephew. At least they'll have a chance at a happier life than we ever did."

Others were similarly preoccupied. Gunderic and the Vandals were all ordered to my old training fort in Constantinople's hinterlands, with Xerxes assigned to guard against their more disruptive inclinations. In this, I had few concerns regarding Gunderic, for although the Vandals were prone to all manner of drunkenness and debauchery in the tedium of a sea voyage, none within their ranks would ever take military training lightly. If anything, Gunderic would soon grow thankful for fresh air and open skies to practice their martial nature, removed from the restrictions of proper city life.

Likewise, Perenus had been ordered to lead the mounted Herulian foederati under Fulcaris and Sindual to the lowlands of Haemimontus. "Belisarius wants Fulcaris to recruit a full banda from the Heruli, so it looks like we'll soon be flooded with your kinsmen!" he cried. "I'm expected to train them all before the triumph."

"Belisarius said nothing to me of this," I muttered. The general had seemed busy even in his first hours landing in Constantinople, never calling upon me for advice or orders.

"Think nothing of it," Perenus said, not unreasonably. "If anything, it's better not to be given an order. Enjoy time with your family, but don't go soft while I'm away!"

Many others were scattered to the nearby provinces. Mundus' Thracians were given a week before being ferried to Singidunum, bolstering the limitanei against reported threats of Gepid and Sclaveni border crossings. Ascum would travel to Cappadocia in hopes of identifying further engineers to man the Cappadocian army's ballistae, for his ranks had grown perilously thin. Indulf and the Ostrogoths were allowed to remain in Constantinople's Imperial Barracks, yet were accompanied by an equivalent number of Cappadocians under the temporary care of Germanus. With Baduarius, John, and so many other Cappadocian officers having perished in battle, the Thracian general was the only senior leader available to maintain the remnants of the Cappadocian army, although replacements would soon be announced in the months ahead.

Even Liberius was placed into immediate action, with the Emperor allowing his disobliged legate only a short time to recuperate. Not only was my teacher tasked with forming more permanent prefectures and armies from the fledgling provinces in Africa and Tingitana, but also the reformation and supply of new recruits in Mesopotamia as well.

In his haste, Liberius had little patience for my distractions regarding Basilius' gift.

"You've been asking for this for a year, and Basilius granted your wish," Liberius remarked.

"But I don't even know what his gift is!"

"Then you are not looking closely enough," he responded. "In all the years I knew him, Basilius was always a detailed man. You were given exactly what was appropriate for your current situation."

"But why Basilius?" I demanded. "The man hated slaves, just as Antonina did, so why would he invest in this game you play?"

Liberius rolled his eyes. "I will allow your rudeness to pass for today. Basilius was a consul, not an apostle. Whatever wrongs he may have paid you are irrelevant now that the man is dead and his daughter is in your care. You have been given five of the seven gifts. But now you must wait, for there are no other answers that I can provide for you today."

Father Petrus was equally unhelpful. He was unwilling to sway Liberius' hand, nor did he wish to venture to Pella. "If it were for longer than a few months, I would not hesitate… but my joints are stiff, and I'm not sure I'd survive another long journey so soon. Besides, Liberius has need of what feeble services I can offer in the palace, now that Basilius has gone to God."

"What do you know of politics or governance, Father?" I asked, drawing a quizzical frown.

"A great many things, despite my distaste for the subject," Petrus answered. "Enjoy your time with your children, and write to me as often as you are able."

In some ways, the thought of separating from dozens of friends who had grunted and perspired over hundreds of miles of marching left me with an unforeseen sense of discomfort. Somehow, it seemed wrong to part from Perenus and Samur, or remove myself from Belisarius' reach, all for social reasons. A part of me desired all I cared for and about to be held close, yet life rarely affords such opportunities. Instead, Cephalas and Rosamund once again prepared my household for travel by sea, albeit a brief one, a mere sojourn to the gulf of Thessalonica. With most of our possessions still packed, the labor was minimal, although purchases from the city's forum would soon add considerable weight to our journey.

Nor did Theodora's baggage train ease our load. Though the Empress professed a desire for anonymity in Macedonia's mountain-streaked landscape, it appeared that Justinian had his own demands upon his beloved wife, for a dozen palace slaves were assigned to her care while in Pella. Three full oxcarts were required to haul Theodora's trunks onto our ship, compared to two carts for all others in my household combined.

My week in Constantinople was oddly peaceful, but it allowed for little contentment. Never once did Belisarius assemble his officers, nor did he seek my attention. With others quickly departing for adjoining provinces, there was no training or discipline for me to mete out, and few in the palace sought my presence.

Instead, Rosamund insisted that I awaken in the later hours of each morning, with my days spent walking through the city's depopulated streets. I must have spent hours tracing the length of Constantinople's walls, finding countless painted markings protesting pagans and Christian heretics, as well as skirting by occasional gatherings of Cassiodorus' acolytes, though never Cassiodorus himself. Whether from such disconcerting reminders of civil strike or from Belisarius' absence, the days passed slowly, with nothing to occupy my mind nor raise my joys.

Until Bessas, the last of Belisarius' commanders still present in Constantinople, knocked upon my door. Similar to so many others, Bessas would soon be dispatched to Armenia to purchase the bulky horses capable of bearing the full armor of a cataphract, an expensive and yearlong process of breeding and training. Before departing, however, the cavalry commander bore a message from the general's offices. Catching a fleeting glimpse of Antonina, Bessas insisted that we speak in a more private setting, and I obliged.

"Belisarius thanks you for taking Antonina to Pella, and will reimburse you for her expenses," Bessas began as soon as we were alone. His news brought me little else than anxiety.

"That will not be necessary," I countered. "Does Belisarius intend to come and speak to me in person?"

Bessas shook his head. "He hardly spent more than a few minutes with me. Antonina is to be watched carefully, and she's to return to Constantinople before the triumph. He asks that Uliaris join you as well."

Anxiety began to shift into a confused anger. "At this rate, it would be kinder to release Uliaris from his oath."

"I would agree," Bessas said, "but those powers are not in my hands. Belisarius will meet with you upon your return, and offers you his thanks."

"But won't do so himself," I muttered.

Bessas' eyebrows arched, yet he offered no reply.

Antonina, bedecked in blackened silk, seemed all the more distraught by Belisarius' dismissal of each of his oathsworn officers.

"He's sending everyone away," Antonina muttered as she learned of the army's developments. "My husband wants to brood alone."

I nodded. "It appears so, but there is nothing to be done. Perhaps isolation will calm his mind."

"It won't." Antonina grimaced before grasping at my hands. "Varus, there is nothing I can do to knit together what has been broken. Belisarius is like a tapestry riven along its seams. Even after repair, it can never truly be made whole as it once was." She paused, her baleful gaze struggling to keep square with my own. "But if you allow me to leave, I promise neither you nor he shall ever hear of me again. I'll leave the Empire forever, and Belisarius will be able to start his life fresh."

"No, Lady." I did not bother to hide the anger in my voice. "You are my guest for these months ahead, but I cannot allow you to depart."

"Then I am your prisoner, you mean," Antonina grumbled. "Please, just consider it. I know what you must think of me, and with but a single word, you can be rid of me. I ask for nothing else."

Though tempted to rid myself of such a burden, I never seriously considered Antonina's pleas. If I had, thousands of whisperers would have stalked my footsteps, wondering whether Varus the Herulian truly had a part to play in Antonina's indiscretions. There was only one path forward, its conclusion postponed and undecided.

Our departure was hardly noticed against the backdrop of Constantinople's rebuilding. Father Petrus offered prayers, while Justinian bestowed heavy kisses on his Empress along the Forum of Constantine, but no plebeians shouted abuse—or praise—as we boarded the single vessel for Pella.

Among the most enthusiastic travelers were the two most unalike individuals to board our ship. Even before she walked hesitantly aboard the narrow gangway, Theodora beamed with a renewed vigor that reminded me of our first meeting together, when I remained in bondage and Theodora had been little more than the paramour of a young patrician. Servants had toiled for multiple days to install greater comforts onto the transport, yet no measure of silk or cushioning could truly shield one accustomed to luxury from the rank odors and discomfort of sea travel. Still, not a single complaint could be heard from Theodora, who nearly skipped along the ship's deck after she drew safely aboard.

Aside from Theodora, Agathias was an image of unbridled joy. Freed from bondage and entered into my service, Agathias seemed to cling to my cloak as I walked about the forum, supervising the final loading of our ship and arranging purchases of precious food, bolts of silk, and other luxuries that would be scarcely available in the Macedonian interior. I doubt that an hour passed without my young ward seeking to aid with our preparations or searching desperately for a note of approval from me, behavior which went from charming to grating as the morning wore on. Nevertheless, I had once known Agathias' conflicted emotions as a freed slave on the precipice of a distant journey, and for that I yielded as much patience as I could muster.

Eventually, by the grace of God and a limit to my willingness to wait, our ship departed from Constantinople's harbor toward the Marmara Sea and the northern terminus of the Aegean beyond. As our ship was tugged by a smaller vessel from its pier and into deeper water, I stood at the ship's bow, seeking any glimpse that Belisarius might have tracked our departure. With Antonina, Rosamund, and my bodyguard climbing below, my only companion abovedeck was Theodora, who rubbed her hands together in delight.

"It is hard to explain how much I need this break from my labors, Varus." She grinned, cuffing lightly at the corner of her kohl-lined eye. "It's been so long…"

"In my own way, I am of kindred thoughts," I answered, my eyes set upon the city's harbor front.

Theodora clenched hard upon my hand as our ship rolled deeper into the water, her nails digging gently into my knuckles. Bouncing upon her toes, Theodora did not appear to notice my own struggles, with the tempest of joy and disappointment marrying in a toxic maelstrom in my heart. It was not until we drew a hundred paces from the pier and began to shift toward the Marmara that I, too, gripped hard at the ship's railing, leaning forward as I squinted at a lone armored figure standing on the pier's edge. Beams of sunlight glittered against his scales and reflected toward our craft, leaving me convinced of the man's identity. It was not what I had hoped, God knows, but it was something.

Our journey required less than two days, although the transport's captain insisted we drop anchor in the evening rather than risk running aground on hidden shoals or shifted rocks unseeable in the blackened waters. Morale was stirring, and bolstered by Theodora's infectious laughter as she navigated each nook and crevice of the ship's deck and hold. From the ship's captain to the humblest oarsman, all gained the Empress' company and conversation, if only for a brief time each.

Skirting along the coastline, we soon crossed into the Thermaicus, an open gulf of water that separated historic Thessaly from the city of Thessalonica. Rather than dock within Macedonia's provincial capital, however, our ship navigated toward the River Vardar. Gliding upstream, the ship's bow sliced through darkened waters clouded by a thick mud that drained from the hills of each riverbank. Unable to rest or even sit idly by, I spent that entire morning standing along the bow, scanning the horizon for the ancient Macedonian capital that perched upon the Vardar's inlets. When thin ringlets of smoke first appeared in the distance, the urge to scream for joy became nigh unbearable, and I paced hurriedly along the length of the ship.

Though I had never stepped foot in Pella nor its surrounding province, even the most poorly educated and illiterate farmer knew of the birthplace of the unconquerable Alexander. Nestled amongst verdant hills that sweltered in the summer and shivered in winter's darkness, it was a hard place that gave little succor. Remnants of its noble past lingered, however, with rows of villas and even a complex of bathhouses that serviced patricians and farmers alike.

As we carefully navigated the narrow channel of water to the town's dock, Pella slowly drew further into view, with a group of children rushing along a nearby knoll and shouting all manner of greetings. Our ship took anchor along a winding pier, received by a steady trickle of onlookers and a red-faced clerk who pushed his way alongside the ship's gangway. Admitting our captain to the dock, our ship steadied as its anchor dragged along the riverbed as crewmen readied the vessel and its cargo for disembarkation. It was then, strumming my fingers along the ship's railing, that I caught a glimpse of swirling crimson silk.

Sembrouthes had no time to react as I jostled for the ship's exit, sprinting across the walkway even before the craft was properly secured. No amount of whispers from the crowd or insistent grunts from the clerk could diminish my urgency, nor did I hear those who called behind me, my concerns levied only upon how to best weave through the crowd.

Until I saw her. Mariya beamed as she drew upon my hurried form, her crimson stola bouncing along the dirt path that connected Pella's riverfront with its narrow pier. God, but she was a beauty that wars could be fought over, though my memory of her features had blurred during my stay in Carthage and Septem.

I did not smile back—there was too much urgency simply to reach her. In my haste, I could hardly halt my legs as I wrapped my arms around Mariya's waist, lifting her feet far from the ground as I stumbled onto dry land. She planted a hungry kiss upon my lips, and all the world evaporated into a dull void.

JUSTIN'S LEGACY

Our joyous reunion, as with so much, was required to wait as the ship was cleared of people and goods. Though the unloading was left to teams of sailors and Mariya's many servants, there was no individual servant who could adequately assume the duty of care over the most powerful woman the Empire had seen in centuries.

Though Mariya had known that our arrival was imminent, there had been no warning that the Empress would be part of our traveling contingent. Tearing herself from my embrace, Mariya fell to the ground as Theodora approached, her knees brushing against churned dirt.

"My dear, as I have explained to your husband, in this sojourn I shall be only Theodora." Offering a gloved hand, Theodora motioned for Mariya to rise. "And with such a simple name, an empty bedroom dedicated for your guests shall perfectly suffice."

"Of course, Theodora." Mariya smiled. "You have my gratitude for bringing my husband home. We shall receive you in the villa's hall while your rooms are prepared."

Theodora gave a quick bob of her head. "By the way," she whispered, leaning forward with a wink. "Don't act so austere on my account. I know what I would do if I were parted from my beloved for a year."

Mariya hardly breathed until Theodora had walked at least twenty paces distant. "You could have told me the Empress of the Roman Empire would seek respite in our home!" she hissed at me.

Stealing another kiss, I offered her my own wink. "There was no time. I didn't know myself until a few days before our departure. Is it an untenable inconvenience?"

"I shall manage," Mariya replied, her lips pursed in mock anger.

Her eyes locked upon mine as she shook her head slightly from side to side, tossing strands of black hair against her sun-darkened face. No words passed as her lips spread into a broad smile, somehow transferring months of conversation in a single glance. Mariya's attention was broken only by a passing Cephalas, and the tiny yet growing puppy in his arms. My wife tore away from my grasp, snatching the bundle from Cephalas and stroking the shivering dog's neck and ears.

Despite the giddy abandon that lightened my steps, I felt a curious apprehension at walking into the estate that had been Justin's great gift upon his deathbed. Olive trees grew wild along the hills until the carefully groomed villa ground, where a small pool of shallow water faced away from the riverfront. The villa itself was a squat, two-story structure that nevertheless sprawled along a flattened expanse of earth, leaving easy access to the olives and grapes that grew nearby. Its plastered bricks and intricately decorated columns denoted it as belonging to one of rare wealth, someone capable of supplying a household of hundreds and maintaining buildings, aqueducts, and roads in a town that, despite its hallowed past, had largely been forgotten by the progress of time.

Though I owned the property, it was not my home. Passing servants addressed only Mariya, while villagers smiled and waved as she passed along the riverfront. Few knew me by sight, with any respect or greeting offered as the wedded man of the lady of the manor, who provided for those who now called Pella their home. And there were many who did so, for adjoining the villa were dozens of brick-layered houses with easy access to the riverbank, all of whom bore little sign of the elements or an age beyond a year or two.

"It seems though you've done much in a short time," I remarked, my worries drifting temporarily to Narses' warning of Pella's expenses.

"It was difficult at first," Mariya said, nodding. "Justin's villa had been largely uninhabited beyond a few servants to discourage vermin and residents to till the soil. But now, we have a separate building to care for Constantinople's orphans, and new caravans bearing food and goods we cannot find here. The river gives us water, thankfully, and occasional visitors from Corinth or Thessalonica."

"How did you convince any to give their labor to you for this?" I asked. "It is not Roman custom to care for lowborn orphans."

"It may not be Roman culture, but the Ghassanids allow no child to be without a measure of comfort." Mariya smiled as she pointed to a nearby brick building, its ceiling low yet expansive upon the plain. "There were many displaced in the riots—some of whom escaped Belisarius' final capture of the Hippodrome. Others are wounded spearmen, their bodies too broken to rejoin the Emperor's service. I allowed all to join me, on one provision."

My eyes narrowed. "Which was?"

"That they perform one of three roles. They either pay fair rent for room and board, work the farms and fields toward the interior, or provide for the dozens of children under my care." Smiling to herself, Mariya led me into the villa's hall. "You would be amazed at how quickly women and men would offer their labor if it prevents tax or tribute from being levied."

"But the cost—"

"Will be dealt with," Mariya promised. "I understand the gold this all requires. Within a year or two, the harvests from our lands will begin to draw their own earnings. Besides, my father was a frugal man, and left considerable wealth to the Ghassanid people. He even left me with a gift of silver and jewels, though my brother insists upon holding it until it is needed. When we return to Constantinople, I will write to him and insist the jewels are returned to me."

Nodding, I followed Mariya as she strode farther into the bowels of the villa. So much had happened during our separation, including her entire second pregnancy. Though still slight of form, Mariya's body appeared somehow softened, her skin emitting a new luster. To me, there had never been greater perfection in God's creation, with a torrent of memories flooding back in my mind as her perfume snaked about my mouth and nose. As she led me, Mariya tossed back a hand, her nails painted with a dark shade of crimson that matched her dress. Grabbing those delicate fingers, I followed my wife into the home that she alone had built.

Her pace quickened as she led me onto the villa's second floor and toward a secluded hall lit by thick beams of sunlight from open windows. Arriving at her destination, she dropped my hand and stole a further brief kiss, her teeth flashing wide and her eyes sparkling with enthusiasm. In other parts of the villa, the din of considerable labor echoed even to this remote annex, yet Mariya at that moment had no cares for whatever Theodora might have needed. Instead, she turned to a nearby door and rapped gently upon the wooden frame before propping it ajar.

"Jamila, Aya, Varus has returned to us and would like to greet his children."

And again, I felt my heart nearly cease its rhythm. Grabbing my hand once more, Mariya dragged me inside to where two of her handmaidens sat playing: one with a babe and one with a small girl who toddled clumsily around the room. Jamila had been known to me in Constantinople, yet it took several heartbeats to place Aya. It was only after the Egyptian girl's eyes met mine that I placed her as a onetime slave to Hermogenes, and the person who had discovered his hanged body.

Aya lifted the babe into her arms before pacing toward me. "Your son, Lord."

In fact, he was not truly a babe any longer, yet still bore the flabby limbs and jerking motions of one newly born to this life. Only a wisp of hair lined his head, foretelling he would share the dark onyx tresses of his mother. As I took him into my arms, the babe cried aloud, struggling yet unable to communicate his wants or desires.

"Alexander," Mariya explained. "My people revere the Great King, and your Justin once took residence in his home. I thought you would like it."

"A fine name," I whispered, a tear forming in my eye. I had no voice for further speech.

The second child, my Zenobia, eyed me curiously as she pushed her still-awkward body to her feet. Unafraid, she approached and tugged upon my trouser leg, her head cocked as she discerned my features as if from the fog of a distant and incomplete memory. I lifted her alongside her squirming brother before burying my face between the two, bringing Alexander to protest all the more spiritedly while Zenobia jostled for comfort.

"Please wait outside, ladies," Mariya ordered, shutting the door lightly as her command was instantly obeyed.

I take no shame in saying that I wept. Dropping carefully to the floor, I held both children as fat tears streamed down my cheeks and into my beard. Zenobia tugged against the coarse hair with a bemused curiosity. Mariya did not interrupt, yet slipped onto the floor and rested her chin upon my shoulder as she offered a hand to the bawling Alexander. In one form or another, the four of us lay there for some time, my exasperating tears ceasing only after Zenobia began to kick free of her confinement.

"This is all that gave me hope for the past year," I muttered. "You have no idea what I've seen, what I've done—"

"Whatever it is, it does not matter anymore, Varus." Mariya squeezed my arms. "You're home now, and where you belong."

I was loath to allow the moment to pass, yet all too soon Mariya and I were required to attend to those who had taken residence as our guests. Mariya cheerily recounted the feasts that would be held in honor of my return as well as all the games we would enjoy with our children, leaving me to grin and nod as I resisted the urge to wrap my arms around her body. Mariya's happiness was only cut short upon discussing Antonina's fall and subsequent abandonment into my care.

"Did you really walk in upon her and Sergius?"

I nodded. "Belisarius left her with me, although he won't meet with me about anything. I've spoken with Antonina, although she takes most of her company from Rosamund."

"An odd pair, Rosamund and Antonina." Mariya shrugged. "I will speak to Antonina as soon as I can... but I did warn you, Varus."

Raising my hands in surrender, my own smile faded into regret. "I was naïve. I should have trusted your judgment."

"You should have!" Mariya teased. "Life is not as simple as you pretend at. People break oaths and betray their friends. Whatever you learned in Liberius' tales is only half the truth of our world. The sooner you learn that fact, the easier both our lives will be."

I acknowledged Mariya with a nod, my neck burning in shame. "It is our task to keep Antonina safe and comfortable per her station, although Basilius left little gold for her comfort. After the triumph, Belisarius will decide what he wants to do with her."

"I can't imagine Belisarius in anger," Mariya mused. "Although neither can I imagine a more trusting man. Poor Belisarius, and poor Antonina."

Leaving the children with Aya and Jamila, we temporarily halted our desired reunion to resolve the punishing list of tasks required to bring Justin's villa into enough order to house Theodora, Antonina, Rosamund, and the collection of men and boys that had followed me from Constantinople. Before parting, however, Mariya and I encountered a dozen Aksumites under Sembrouthes who, after more than a year apart, had been rejoined with Wazeba and the few men I had left in Mariya's presence.

"My dearest friend, how I have missed you!" she shouted, wrapping her arms around her bodyguard's chest.

Stiffly, Sembrouthes nevertheless returned the embrace. Further, he offered a wide grin, his normally reserved features seeming to melt upon Mariya's touch. "I have kept your fool of a husband alive, though he won't seem to thank me for it."

"Well, I certainly do!"

Pulling at the collar of his shirt, Mariya pecked at Sembrouthes' cheek, bringing further smiles and the hint of embarrassment. Though haughty patricians might have gawked with disapproval at such a display, I cared little for their stuffy manners and laughed at Sembrouthes' awkward shuffling. As Mariya slipped away, Sembrouthes' stiffness evaporated.

"Do you think this will last?" he asked, gesturing at the villa's walls.

"Our respite, or Mariya's operation?"

"Both," he said. "But primarily the latter. Can such a place survive?"

"I am not sure, on either count," I admitted. "But that is a worry for another day. See the men unpacked, and be sure that Uliaris behaves himself around the village women."

It was breathtaking to witness Mariya navigate the thousands of tasks required to run a true household. I grasped clumsily at such efforts in military camp life, and even then, my own duties were restricted to little more than paying and clothing Rosamund, Cephalas, and the gaggle of servants that flitted through our lives with each sojourn. Mariya appeared ever calm as she directed dozens of servants, cooks, builders, and guardsmen about a rising array of tasks required to keep our estates at Pella from becoming overrun with vines, inhabited by rats, or incapable of meeting the basic burdens of servicing those who came to live under Mariya's control. Despite all of this, she never once ignored the call of an excited child, and particularly drew delight in pointing out the achievements of a three-year-old Tiberius.

"Does he have any memory of his riots, or his father?" I whispered as the boy passed by, waving sheepishly at Mariya. "Or me?"

"If he does, he does not allow me to know," Mariya muttered in return. "Although he wakes from nightmares, just as I have seen you do."

I nodded, guiltily feeling at Hypatius' golden ring that rested in a pouch upon my belt. "I'll have Rosamund spend time with him; she'll gain his trust. None can know his true identity."

"None," Mariya promised.

Overall, our arrival to Pella might not have been replete with all the magic of a poem, but it certainly was suffused with the kind of unhindered joy that I have experienced but rarely in this life. Mariya hosted as Theodora basked in her relative doldrums, listening attentively to Rosamund's explanations of medicine and Uliaris' tales of distant Frankia. Even Antonina had brightened upon being returned to her daughter—who, I soon discovered, spent much of her time with my own Zenobia—and brightened further still in Mariya's and Theodora's company, with the disgraced patrician even laughing and smiling during the feast upon our first night in Pella. In Justin's halls and a stone's throw from Alexander's childhood home, we toasted to friendship and fortune, believing all manner of sacrifice and sadness had been placed firmly in the miseries of the past.

Though the transition from military life to the life of a landowner was abrupt, my new duties nothing but foreign to me, Mariya's guidance ensured the villa kept all fed and sheltered through the planting season. I admit, I still awoke in the night from unseen terrors, reaching for a sword that had been safely stacked in the rafters of the villa's primary feasting hall. It took several weeks before I grew acquainted with the reassuring heat of Mariya's body, and even then, there were nights where my wife would call for Rosamund to ease my mind. From our first days together, it was plain that my affliction frustrated Mariya—either from her inability to ease my mind or from Rosamund's ability to succeed where all others failed.

On the second night after my return, dreams of Mount Papua returned. Walking corpses, their fat drained from brittle bones and sallow skin, the grounds littered in rotted meats and dung. With decayed eyes or blackened empty holes, all of those bodies fixed their attentions upon me.

"Why did you come here?" one Vandal woman asked. "Why did you butcher my children?"

My feet seemed rooted to the filth-strewn soil, and all I could do was twist my shoulders to avoid the corpse's touch. "I killed no children!"

"Oh no?" the corpse teased, her voice morphing into the taunts of Hakhamanish. "You might want to tell that to them."

A bony finger pointed toward a hut—the same hut that Rosamund had warned me not to open so long ago. God, but I wish I had not. In the dream, as in life, dozens of bodies lay stacked inside, with the emaciated limbs of a young girl resting on top.

"Why?" the girl screeched. "WHY?"

"I didn't kill you!" I yelled. "I didn't!"

"Varus, stop!" It was Mariya, yelling as I jerked upright in bed. "You're in Greece! Everything is safe!"

But I did not understand her, at least initially. Leaping from the bed, I stumbled into the darkness, seeking but failing to find my blades. Amidst my search, I felt a hand graze my shoulder, and I turned to squeeze my attacker's wrist. I could feel the tendons pulse and fingers scrambling wildly in my grip, unable to draw free.

"Varus, no!" Mariya begged. "It's me, your wife!"

On the far side of the bedroom, the door unlatched, slamming open. Two torches flickered, illuminating the armor of the Aksumites on duty. Releasing Mariya, I turned to grapple with those men, until a third figure stepped fearlessly toward me. I growled a challenge, yet the wispy voice returned only a greeting.

"Hush," Rosamund cooed. "I have no weapons. I am coming closer to you."

Sobbing, Mariya cried to her, "He doesn't recognize us! Keep back!"

"Everything will be set to rights," Rosamund replied, her voice adopting a singsong quality. With one careful step after another, she seemed to glide into the darkness, her feet throwing no sound from each footstep. "Mariya, you may wish to leave."

She slid a hand upon my bare forearm, and I felt myself unclench the muscles leading to my fist. "You're away from those evil places, far away."

My mind clearing, I collapsed onto the floor. I shivered, though my body seemed slathered in sweat. "I... I'm sorry..."

"It is the Romans who should apologize," Rosamund whispered, kneeling to the floor as she cradled my head. "They did this to you."

Mariya, still present, stepped closer. "Why can't I help him?"

"It's a type of madness that I've seen before in my village," Rosamund replied. "I will give him something to help with sleep."

Mariya nodded, but was clearly unsatisfied. "Why can't *I* help him?" she whispered.

"Only the gods know," Rosamund answered. "It's dangerous for me too, but I've been with him long enough to know how to treat it."

Even amidst the darkness, with only a trailing torchlight twenty paces away, I witnessed Mariya flinch. "Do what you must, then."

Alone together, Rosamund guided me back to the bed, propping me in a seated position. "Dreams?" she asked.

"I..." I began, sweat pooling on my brow. "I saw the children on Mount Papua."

Rosamund frowned, but nodded. "And why do they call to you from the afterlife?"

"Revenge," I choked. "They blame me for their fate."

Another nod. "Stay here, and do not move. I will return."

Rosamund slipped from the room, returning perhaps two minutes later with her wooden chest. Resting it upon a nearby bench, she withdrew a clay bowl, mixing a red powder into a foul-smelling black ichor. Satisfied, she snatched one of the two torches on the wall, plunging it into a separate bucket of water.

"No..." I wheezed.

"You fear the darkness?" Rosamund asked, seizing the second torch.

"Since Nisibis," I admitted. "Perhaps earlier. Samur always did, even when we were little."

Rosamund lowered the torch, allowing its flames to graze but not enter the water. "You hear my words, but have not listened. The gods love you, Varus, which means you have no reason to fear the darkness."

At that, she extinguished the last light of my room. Still tense, I yelped, answered by Rosamund's soothing hum.

"My grandfather prophesized my fate long ago," Rosamund continued, her voice breathy and distant. "I would mother no children and take no husband."

"I remember," I croaked, recalling the morning after we coupled in the Imperial Barracks, years prior.

The room grew still. Light shuffling emanated from the stone floor, yet otherwise the pitch blackness wrapped about my body. I could feel my heart slamming against my chest as I listened for any movement in the room, my other senses useless. A knot formed in my throat, and I wanted to raise my legs from the floor but feared making a sound.

Then, a finger swiped against my cheek. Its tip was wet, leaving behind a sticky, foul-smelling residue that reminded me of burning offal. I gagged, yet Rosamund hushed me silent.

"He told me that my fate was to guide a great lord along his journey," she cooed. "I believe that man is you, if only you would free yourself from the Empire."

More fingers brushed against my face, moving in slow whorls about my eyes and mouth. I sensed that Rosamund was drawing a pattern, yet whatever its meaning, I could not tell. I had descended into Rosamund's world, abandoning anything familiar that I knew.

"Is that why you follow me?" I asked, the question barely audible.

First, silence. Perhaps a minute, or an hour. However long it was, I felt as if made of stone, unmoving. Then, at last, a word.

"Yes."

For the first time since the fates smashed our lives together, I feared Rosamund. There was no particular reason—it is the same fear that a child feels for the deepest section of an ancient forest, the abode of beasts and monsters rather than men. Even Christians believe in malevolent spirits beyond the communion of God, for Jesus himself freed a man of a legion of evil spirits. I felt a wrongness in that conversation, although my last vestige of curiosity brought me to drive forward a final time.

"The only reason?"

Another pause, followed by a softer tone. "Not the only one."

After that, Rosamund began to sing. I recognized the syllables as the Gepid tongue even as the words slurred together in a flurry of unintelligible sounds. Withdrawing her fingers, Rosamund continued her song, her voice muted enough that I doubt any outside of our room heard. It was soothing, and soon I had relaxed the muscles in my chest and arms, slouching atop the bed. Still sitting in darkness, I felt my eyelids grow heavier as Rosamund's voice rolled onward, pausing only to emphasize what I presume were names. Ancient names, for ancient gods. Though part of me was horrified, the peace I felt drowned any urge to escape from this pagan ritual.

Until steely fingers grasped for my head. Freezing and stiff, they could not have been Rosamund's. Of this, I will be certain until I take my final breath.

The grasping hand thrust my head toward the bed. Rather than colliding into a blanket, however, my nose and mouth smashed into a frigid paste, the scent of burning offal filling my lungs and bringing me to gag. I struggled but could not free myself from the interloper's grip.

"Breathe," Rosamund urged, temporarily interrupting her song.

"I can't…" I gagged.

"You suffer so much," Rosamund said. "One more moment of hardship, and your cares will float away as if on wings."

Though Rosamund's voice was reassuring, the grasping hand at my scalp was anything but. I honestly believed that she might kill me. Yet though I struggled, my limbs seemed to melt away.

"Breathe, Varus," Rosamund murmured.

The weakness that first struck my limbs entered my torso and chest, and I quickly had no choice but to obey. Nearly vomiting, I allowed the foul paste to coat my face and fill my nostrils, until the fingers in my hair withdrew their grip. I fell backward, my face glancing up atop the bed, feeling the ooze slither along my face. I could not move, and besides an occasional twinge, could not feel.

"The dark is not an enemy," a voice called above me—Rosamund's, yet also, somehow, the voice of a hundred others. If I had control of my body, I would have shuddered, for I heard Justin in that fray, the same sternness that I remembered in my youth. "In the darkness, the gods see you for what you truly are."

I felt bodies all around me, lacking warmth. My eyes quivered shut as Rosamund continued to sing, and I realized that any trace of fear inside of me had withered away. Images formed in my mind— whether from dreams or while waking, I do not know. Perhaps both. But they put me at peace, darting from one scene to the next. Many I recognized, although some, I could not recall their provenance.

Samur and I in the palace's training yard, alone with Godilas as he recounted a tale of ancient heroes. A village on the plains, filled with laughter around a cookfire. Sitting outside with Isaacius, standing as night sentry for Archelaus' camp. Zenobia placed into my arms for the first time. Cheering for a warlord after a crushing victory, riding free. Receiving Justin's sword, its dragon hilt placed into my disbelieving fingers. Viewing my ouroboros for the first time, handed by Rosamund and Perenus.

"Sleep," Rosamund murmured. "All will be well."

And it was, mostly. The last thing I remember was the outline of the dark rider, his eyes turned toward me, rooting me to the ground.

I have searched for you.

I moved my mouth, but no sound emitted from my lips. As the rider guided his horse toward me, I reached down for my sword, my hand wrapping around Justin's hilt. Yet when I drew steel from scabbard, my weapon vanished. Instead, I found it in the hand of the other, who raised the sword's hilt to his eyes.

They deserve to burn.

"Who?" I attempted to shout, still muted.

The red-eyed rider laughed. It was ancient and cruel, a cackle as sonorous as stones smashing together. He approached, first fifty paces away, then twenty, and then five.

All who oppose us.

I shook my head, reaching for Godilas' dagger and Petrus' cross. Raising both against my enemy, I remained transfixed, awaiting the man's strike.

"There is no 'us,'" I attempted to shout. "Of whom do you speak?"

You know.

Oddly, I did not fear him. The same serene calm that yielded images of joy left me steady before the crimson-eyed rider, uncaring that the skies above him were ashen or that his mount was meat and bone.

Who are you? I mouthed.

In a single eyeblink, the man was dismounted. In another, he stood opposite me, his nose a finger length from my own.

A better question: Who are you?

I shuddered awake, my limbs still tingling and weak, realizing that torchlight illuminated the room's interior. Slowly raising a hand to my face, I found the skin clean of any debris. Indeed, the bed I rested upon seemed clean, and the room absent flaw or scent. In one corner, Rosamund lay curled into a ball, resting atop a cushion.

"You slept for the night and through the morning." Rosamund yawned and, watching me struggle upright, snapped up from her perch to pluck up a cup of water, which she lowered to my lips.

"What was that?" I asked, my voice hoarse.

"Dangerous," Rosamund answered. "For me, at least. Perfectly safe for you."

"Dangerous?" I asked.

"Again, not for you," Rosamund said. "But your mind should be at ease now."

Confused, part of me wanted answers, and the other desired

nothing more than to put this unholy episode in the past. "I dreamed…"

"What you dreamed is for you alone," Rosamund interrupted. "Your arms and legs should return to full strength soon. But I will require rest, for that ritual was a draining one."

Though not necessarily happy, and despite my befuddlement, my chest did feel lighter, and my mind carefree. "I don't know what to think of this."

"The gods' favor doesn't require your thoughts," Rosamund said, a note of teasing in her voice. "And you will inevitably have further instances of madness. But think about what you have seen, and what you have learned."

Breathing heavily, and with a deeply lined face, Rosamund dismissed herself for sleep. Thus left alone, I exchanged my garments for a fresh shirt and trousers, and escaped to find my family. Mariya and I did not speak of that episode. I had no desire to—I could not be certain of what was real and what might have been conjured by dreams. It was an unclean feeling, and not because the result was altogether pleasant. Rather, I feared that Rosamund's magic might have worked.

When I gathered the courage to apologize, Mariya brushed my words aside, fervently insisting that she understood. Thankfully, whether from Rosamund's magic or merely a growing comfort in my Pella home, such terrors abated, at least for a time.

Mariya was patient, and for that, I am a fortunate man. Without my asking, she took as many of my concerns upon herself as could be anticipated, including the care of Antonina as well as basic oversight of the warriors who accompanied me. She ensured that Rosamund prepared salves for my growing number of healed wounds, while allowing me time with our two children as well as Tiberius. She even addressed an overenthusiastic Agathias' desires by putting him to work in updating the villa's records, for her last clerk had died from the previous winter's cold.

Each night, she wrapped her body firmly around mine, interlocking our fingers and waiting patiently to sense my intentions. In those first weeks, our lovemaking was a desperate thing, for I wanted nothing more than to be consumed in the perfumes embedded within her soft skin.

With Mariya eternally busy, I found myself with little enough to do in my days other than to keep company with Theodora. True to her commitment, Theodora performed few functions normally demanded of an Empress, although a predictable stream of couriers and supplicants still managed to scurry toward Pella by the end of her second week in my care. I knew well her desire for the relaxing tedium of irresponsibility and did all within my power to shield Theodora from inconvenience, even if my duty as an excubitor insisted that I shadow the Empress' movements from dawn through dusk. Sembrouthes and Wazeba aided me in this task, yet thankfully there was little requirement for such supervision. Perhaps the only cause for alarm rose as the Empress swam along Pella's inlet each morning, with even Mariya cautioning against deceptive currents and considerable drop-offs well beyond the height of several men stacked foot to shoulder. Theodora merely shrugged aside such concerns and spent an hour paddling and drifting along the cool waters.

Though seeming to prefer solitude, Theodora occasionally was joined by Antonina, with both women whispering in tones that prevented even the most astute eavesdropper from making out any of their conversation over the rush of water lapping against rocks and coastline. Such occasions doubled my anxiety, for Antonina was no fair swimmer, and my thoughts were consumed by fears of her drowned body being hauled back to Constantinople to an already grieving Belisarius. Courteously, Theodora never ventured beyond the river's neckline when joined by company—just far enough for assured privacy. Much had troubled my mind throughout Theodora's stay, yet I kept such worldly concerns unspoken during our rest, until an unforeseen opportunity arose that was impossible to ignore.

On an unseasonably cold spring morning, just as the sun crested above the eastern hills, Mariya and I escorted Theodora toward a more isolated stream. Meandering from the main inlet, the stream drew nearly the height of a man yet was far too shallow for any serious cog to navigate, leaving it generally unused by any in the villa or the more distant village huts. For Theodora, however, it was perfectly situated for her uses.

"Join me!" she insisted. "I haven't been able to do this since I was a girl, and I've forgotten how wonderful such a morning habit is."

"Lady—" I began, horror rising in my chest.

"Theodora," she corrected, her lips pursed as she began to tease me. "I promise, I shall not seduce you, Varus. Do you not know how to swim?"

"I don't," Mariya admitted. "Little reason to learn in much of Arabia."

Theodora nodded. "Then we'll stay in a shallower portion. Think of it as a bath, Varus, for I know you insist upon washing far more often than most."

There was no convincing Theodora to abandon the request, even if her rank and title were deemed unimportant to our lives in Pella. Mariya and I watched as Theodora shrugged off a heavier fur for a thin blue stola underneath, not hesitating to wade into gently flowing water.

"Come on, then!" she called. "It really is quite pleasant."

Mariya turned to me, shaking her head lightly as she discarded her own furs. Adorned in her own crimson stola, Mariya slid the sandals from her feet before dipping a toe into the water, only to shriek from the cold. Following her example, I removed my boots and rushed into the shallower embankment, allowing the stream to reach up to my thighs. Reaching a hand back for Mariya, I half dragged her into the waters, and she yelped as the cool rush engulfed her prickling skin. Though far from freezing, such first contact was initially unpleasant, growing only further painful as we followed Theodora toward the deeper center of the stream. Water rose quickly from my torso to my chest, while Mariya was neck deep in the flowing current.

"It's all about the breathing," Theodora instructed. "A little cold is good for the body."

"If y-you insist," Mariya said, her teeth beginning to clack.

As if to display her immunity to such discomfort, Theodora gathered her air and dunked into the stream for several moments. A light steam emanated from her head as she emerged, spitting a trickle of water from her mouth and using her fingers to comb aside matted hair. Rolling her eyes, Mariya followed Theodora's example, shooting out of the water nearly as quickly as her head became submerged. I joined in Mariya's suffering, although pleasantly discovered my body would acclimate to the cold. Nevertheless, Mariya edged closer to me, wrapping her arms over her chest and leaning into my torso for warmth.

"You would swim often as a child?" Mariya asked, the kohl around her eyes streaming down her cheeks in dark rivulets.

"Oh yes," Theodora replied, kicking her feet to the surface as she floated with the current. "Near Kourion, in Cyprus. We were desperately poor, but the sea cares little about one's wealth or standing. We children swam naked, though."

Her face peeling into a mischievous grin, Theodora splashed lightly as she noted my rising discomfort. Returning upright, she gathered her hair into a dense wet bun. "So dour, Varus!"

It was then that, after weeks of speaking little of the Empire's burdens, I pried Theodora for her judgment into the matter that now afflicted me. I felt guilty, spoiling Theodora's rare moment of childish sport, yet the rustling of the water diminished the possibility of eavesdroppers. As I had reluctantly taken Antonina into my care, and knowing that my old schoolmate had retained patronage from Theodora, I yearned for answers regarding what would be done with her, and how to put these unhappy events firmly in the past.

"Theodora, you have spoken with Antonina on many occasions now. What do you believe will happen?"

"Nothing ill will befall Antonina," Theodora declared. "That is my will... and yours as well."

The response was as immediate as it was definitive. It also, while not entirely surprising, was unexpected. By Roman law, Belisarius had every right to divorce his unfaithful wife and even demand a measure of punishment. By custom, society demanded as much, with more grievous infidelity requiring an equally brutal response.

"I mean nothing untoward, of course," I replied. "I just do not understand my position, or even what I am expected to do. Antonina is welcome in my household for as long as necessary, but no one has told me what comes next."

"You have done the right thing by caring for her, Varus," Theodora said, her voice lowering in response. "And if any seek to yield punishment on Antonina, you will make sure that she remains safe, and then immediately seek my attention."

"Of course," I agreed. "But may I ask why?"

Mariya pinched my side, seeking to prevent such a foolish question from gaining traction. Theodora, however, gave no remonstration. "Because Antonina is my friend," Theodora explained, "and Belisarius is not, though he is a competent servant and a rare military mind. I would appreciate you keeping my thoughts private, but you deserve to know."

Theodora surely sought to placate my worries. Yet, more than ever, I felt my chest constrict from the tearing web of loyalties and oaths. By oath and friendship, both Belisarius and Theodora could call upon me to execute their bidding, yet I had never seriously considered what I might do if such loyalties came into conflict. For now, there was no immediate danger, for Theodora sought to avoid conflict and Belisarius had refused to speak with me for weeks. Antonina, however, threatened to bring such concerns into a festering corruption that would leave me with enemies in either Belisarius or the Empress. Though I understood the danger of that situation, I had yet to truly grasp the extent of misery it would cause.

"Thank you for your trust, Augusta," I answered dryly, the title triggering an exasperated sigh from Theodora. Before she could speak, however, I finally dared to raise questions of Theodora's mysterious prophet. "On a separate matter, I have heard of a priest who is a guest in the Imperial Palace."

"Don't ruin a pleasant moment with talk of worries," Theodora said pointedly. "I will explain to you soon enough."

Thwarted, I acceded to Theodora's request, turning the conversation to descriptions of faraway lands and peoples that we had encountered.

Thankfully, the remainder of our stay in Pella was blissful, if painfully brief. I allocated plentiful time for Zenobia, Alexander, and Tiberius, with the latter as eldest most capable of playing along with my games among Pella's fields and pools. Rosamund frequently joined our japes, and even a skittish Alexander took quickly to her soft cooing. Only once did I attempt to broach the subject of her ritual, but she cast such conversation aside.

"One day, you will see the wisdom of my beliefs," Rosamund insisted. "Everything else, all the suffering that the Empire causes, that will fade like a bad memory. The only question is when you will realize that men like Justinian, and all his cronies, are a blight upon this world."

Those sentiments were treasonous, and I should not have brooked such talk as an excubitor. Nevertheless, Rosamund had earned the right to speak freely in my presence. I owed her a life debt many times over, and believed that her words were spoken only in an attempt to better my future.

"Thank you for your aid, as always," I replied.

Other functions of my daily ritual were far more straightforward than Rosamund's mysticism. Uliaris and I trained with blunted blades each morning, while the Aksumites performed their own duties and exercises under Sembrouthes' careful gaze. Each evening, Mariya ensured all were welcome to her table for dinner, with our gatherings frequently rising to include sixty or seventy men and women. Nearing the end of our stay, a larger feast was prepared for all of Pella, its intent to provide joy and nourishment to the dozens of children that remained in her care. Many groaned when Mariya announced that she would voyage to Constantinople for the triumph, yet she did what was possible to assuage their fears.

"The villa will continue to perform all its functions, and ample coin will remain to pay for its upkeep," she explained. "Though guards will remain, I'm trusting each of you to keep this place free from violence or danger."

I can imagine that Eden would have been something like Pella. Not perfect, but sublime in all it could offer and all it lacked. Though each passing day left a greater sensation of foreboding within me, I doubt that any other than Theodora regretted the need to depart for Constantinople, although the Empress made no noises about resisting her intended duties. After a final feast, all our belongings were again packed aboard a ship that would carry us toward the capital.

The morning of our departure only sharpened the sting of leaving. A soft glow blanketed the nearby hills, promising a day of few clouds and blessed warmth in which farmers might till the soil with ease. Many, including Theodora, exited in those early hours, allowing my immediate household a few final hours to say our farewells. In the vacant feasting hall, I found Mariya fussing over Alexander, singing to the babe in Arabic. Her kohl had been misted, and without words, I could feel Mariya's sorrow like a jab to the chest.

"It's only temporary," I insisted. "We'll return soon."

Mariya smiled sadly. "I know you believe those words, and I appreciate them. But I wonder if we'll ever come back."

Her mourning left me unsettled, my confidence routed as if a shield wall had been ruthlessly battered aside. "Why say such things?"

"Because I know the minds of kings," Mariya replied bitterly. "Remember, even though I was my father's favorite, he still would have sold me to Solomon's dogs if it would have granted Ghassan guaranteed protection."

"I will retire," I insisted. "Or I can convince Theodora…"

Scooping Alexander onto her hip, Mariya strode toward me and pecked a kiss upon my hand. "You're too honest for this life, Varus. I've always admired that trait in you. No, we are caught in Justinian's wake now, and without a sail to guide us. All we can do is follow and pray he does not turn against us."

She handed me Alexander, who slapped my chest with a belly laugh. In return, I brushed my beard into Alexander's face, bringing him to squirm between giggles. Then, guided by Mariya, we paced outside, stealing one final glance upon the clearing that had been Mariya's teaching yard. The morning sun kissed Mariya's auburn skin, glinting against tears welling in her eyes. She grasped for my free hand, glancing into the verdant hills. Then, after minutes of silence, she whispered aloud, seemingly to no one.

"It was wonderful while it lasted."

THE TRIUMPH OF
FLAVIUS BELISARIUS

Our journey from Pella to Constantinople was brief, although split across two ships to account for the increased burden of Mariya's household and attendants. Within two nights, we would dock at Constantinople's towering piers, with dozens of servants ready to greet Theodora's retinue.

Though I occupied a brick insula near the Forum of Constantine, Theodora gave us little choice but to reside within a renovated and secured Imperial Palace for the duration of the triumph. "There are gardens for the children to play, and far more servants to assist with daily chores," Theodora insisted. "You've given me delicious respite these past three months, now I ask that you permit me the same courtesy."

A massive lacquered carriage waited to bear the Empress from the docks to the palace, and Theodora insisted upon my company. Reluctantly, I left Mariya, Rosamund, and Cephalas to monitor our unloading and squeezed my armor-clad shoulders through the carriage's narrow opening. Four black horses awaited their driver's whip as the door shut behind me, sending me nearly toppling onto Theodora as the wheels spurred into motion.

"Such a cumbersome way to travel," Theodora griped.

"It beats stomping your way through piss and dung on the streets," I countered. "In Constantinople, at least."

Even with Theodora's insistence upon familiarity, any ease that I acquired in Pella was quickly shed as we rolled through Constantinople streets. Theodora mused aloud about a half dozen matters that had been long delayed, her speech interrupted only as she found my hand gripped tightly about my sword's pommel. True, there were no immediate aggressors seeking to topple the Empress' chariot, but my eyes still caught the veiled threats scratched upon the walls upon many buildings.

"Varus?"

"Highness," I whispered in formal Latin, "you asked me not to bother you in Pella, but I must know more. This Jakob Baradaeus, who is he to you?"

Theodora frowned, requiring several heartbeats to fashion an answer. "A dear friend, as I have explained."

"To you, surely, but it appears many do not share your friendly convictions."

At that, I raised a finger toward bloodred paint upon a nearby fishmonger's stall, its droplets still glistening and falling to the stone-lined path as if some cruel rain. Shuffling in her seat, Theodora gripped a hand upon my shoulder as she leaned toward a nearby window. Her frown furrowed in momentary anger as the crude Greek letters became apparent, joined by other, more faded scribblings as we passed by.

SAVE THE EMPEROR. DEATH TO PAGANS AND APOSTATES.

"Save the Emperor?" I questioned aloud.

"The meaning is clear," Theodora said sharply. "A better question is: Save Justinian from whom? I find it curious that I am not included in the well-wishes of this mob."

"Theodora," I whispered, keeping my tone so low that even she had to strain over the carriage wheels to hear, "Jakob, whoever he truly is, has no love of the people. And if Cassiodorus is fueling their discontent, perhaps it is best to send him back to the East."

"Because he rejects some narrow view of Christianity that thousands of others have protested over the past century?" Theodora hissed. "Am I any less a Christian than you for having a similar mind as Jakob?"

Her hostility, so rarely levied, took me unawares. More so her admission of faith, which admittedly I knew nothing of. On instinct, a feeling of revulsion flitted through my gut, dampened only by a lifetime of discipline in scraping and serving others whose lives did not echo my own. I cared nothing for Cassiodorus, and believed the current malcontent little more than the councilor's attempt to retain relevancy in the aftermath of the riots, yet I still shared the core tenets of the Christian faith that unified the Pope and the Patriarch. Justin had seen personally to that, even in my earliest of memories, although the same harsh strictures seemed to have had less of an effect upon by younger brother.

"Of course not, Highness," I answered. "But others are less... welcoming... of religious dispute." I paused before adding, "And dispute tends to end in violence."

"Noted," Theodora replied, her eyes narrowed as she held her gaze upon the graffitied walls. "Just understand that I allow all to live in peace—even, I might add, the pagans who live in your own household."

"For which they are eternally grateful," I said, the flesh along my neck beginning to prickle as if from heat.

Her mood soured, Theodora said nothing else along our brisk journey to the palace. Nor did I broach further discussion, for between simmering concerns of religion and Antonina, there was much to occupy Theodora's attention. All I wanted was to rid myself of such anxieties, already longing to return to a simple life at Pella. That fate was an impossible one, though in my dreams to this day, I see it still.

Much of the lingering afternoon and evening was spent, once again, unpacking and reorganizing my household inside the palace grounds. Though Mariya, our two children, and Tiberius took residence in Theodora's care, Rosamund led a separate party to take up residence in my quarters along the forum. Though I cautioned Rosamund against venturing into the city without proper guard, she insisted that she was capable enough to keep safe on Constantinople's busier streets. Likewise, Rosamund desired freedom of movement that she would not be granted in the palace, where the excubitores subjected all to exceedingly intimate searches of would-be visitors. With Cephalas, Agathias, and a half dozen others joining her, I had no good argument for her to stay with me in my relative captivity.

Even as we were surrounded by family and bristling with uneasy excubitores, the palace nevertheless held far too many nightmares for any of us to truly rest carelessly. Every hall had borne witness to terror from the mob, while most rooms had given shelter to all manner of rape and murder. Father Petrus assures me that the notion of malevolent spirits is little more than pagan superstition, yet even he tread lightly upon the palace's uppermost floors. New purchases of priceless carpets and thick layers of plaster masked trails of blood, yet could not disguise the fact that Justinian's reign had come within a single room of utter conquest just a year prior. And, hanging along the Hippodrome's outskirts, all of us would have joined him in death, like so many other unfortunates guilty of imagined sedition against the foolhardy Hypatius and the now-slain senators who backed him.

Three weeks separated our arrival in the Capitol from Justinian's triumph. That stint was quickly spent, as considerable preparation was required on behalf of both Justinian's clerks as well as his soldiers. Narses and Procopius shuffled ceaselessly between the palace and the Hippodrome, barking commands in Justinian's name while commanding all manner of ludicrously expensive purchases. Perhaps a more reasonable leader would have balked at the thousands of coins spent on preparing donations of bread and wine to feed the city alongside a vast tapestry of Imperial violet that cloaked every tower and structure, yet even Liberius seemed to approve of Justinian's improvident designs.

"The triumph is perhaps the only Roman ceremony that still means anything," Liberius informed me, "and it falls to us to make sure that Belisarius receives his due. Cheer up, Varus, for you're about to witness a spectacle that would make Augustus himself jealous."

As more of Belisarius' soldiers arrived within the city, most appeared to share Liberius' confused sense of solemnity and enthusiasm. Virtually every room in the freshly constructed Imperial Barracks was overstuffed with spearmen, their sigils mixed between the varied warlords of Thrace and Cappadocia. Other structures, abandoned from the riots' destruction, were converted to house my Herulians, although it seemed that wine casks would soon occupy as much space as bedding or tables in such quarters. When lodgings grew scarce inside Constantinople's Theodosian Walls, camps were erected along the city's outskirts, including all the Huns under Sinnion, Aigan, and Samur. I was at first concerned that Samur would take offense to such treatment, but my brother merely shrugged.

"Better the clear skies than that nest of vipers and rats. You are more than welcome to join me when you tire of their squabbling."

By sea or by road, other officers arrived at Constantinople's gates with unblooded recruits and fresh horses alike. Having secured our borders along the Ister, both Germanus and Mundus arrived well before the triumph, although a full thousand Thracian veterans remained to safeguard against rumors of Sclaveni assaults or Gepid raids. Ascum and Bessas both rode into Constantinople soon thereafter, with Bessas grinning from the hundreds of mounts that had been acquired from the hilly interior of Roman Armenia. Other than those deployed to Carthage or Septem, all my living comrades gathered in a single place—save Gunderic.

"It would be imprudent to celebrate the defeat of our freshly loyal Vandal soldiers in their presence, wouldn't you agree?" Liberius explained. "A triumph has to be a victory over someone else, after all. Spare your friend and those under him the humiliation."

Despite such warnings, Xerxes resisted any attempts to restrict him from the procession. "As a boy, Hakhamanish regaled all youthful Zhayedan with the many triumphs of Caesar and Octavian." He grinned. "Perhaps his intent was to ensure that we would never allow ourselves to become a similar spectacle in defeat, although I would resent being unable to bear witness to such a celebration that I may have played some small part in."

"Not small," I countered. "Theodora herself understands your role in breaking Tzazon's lines and in holding Septem from Theudis."

"That matters little to me," Xerxes declared. "But appreciation is certainly preferable to disdain."

Many gathered for private celebration, discouraged neither by the taverns serving nothing other than thin gruel and wine that tasted of vinegar nor by the occasional protestations of black-frocked priests condemning pagans and outsiders; indeed, many tribesmen were unable to understand the flowery speech of Church-educated men in the first place. As Theodora's liaison and ever-present guard, I declined all invitations for revelry, leaving me privately resentful as others like Rosamund and Perenus freely abandoned their responsibilities for nightly excursions to raucous gatherings. Part of me desired to set down my blade and rush headlong into the night, yet such fantasies were easily squashed by the promise of stealing more time with Mariya and my children.

Though the palace hummed from near-constant activity from clerks and soldiers alike, Belisarius never mixed with any gathering that I knew of. This was not an act of obstinacy, for the Emperor never demanded the general's presence. Instead, couriers fluttered from the palace to Belisarius' lodging in Rufinianae, a budding town just opposite Constantinople along the Bosphorus. Though tantalizingly close, the general was removed from me by an expanse of sea, and the need for a voyage by ship was more than enough to dissuade me from seeking entry into his presence. Instead, along with Antonina, I remained in the Imperial Palace, counting the days until the triumph and the formal end to my enlistment in the Imperial Army.

The morning of the triumph began like many other brisk mornings along the Marmara, with cloud-veiled skies and a pleasant wind blowing from the sea. Well before dawn, however, I was awoken by the insistent hands of palace servants, urging me to wake and dress.

"Enjoy yourself," Mariya mumbled, half awake. "The children and I will meet you in the Hippodrome."

With a kiss, I arose and dressed, donning my scale-and-leather battle armor instead of the polished scales of an excubitor. Forged soon after my return from Tauris, the once-rich coat was now marked by rents and tears that had been hastily repaired between battles. Many urged me to discard such ragged armor in favor of a kit more befitting a Roman warlord and tribune—and so I would, eventually. For Belisarius' triumph, however, nothing told more tales than the torn armor of a battlefield survivor.

Though we of Belisarius' armies were instructed to gather outside Constantinople's Golden Gate along the Via Egnatia, I first jogged toward the lodgings where Rosamund, Cephalas, and the bulk of my bodyguard slept. Upon my arrival, Sembrouthes and the Aksumites were already dressed for war, with Cephalas and Rosamund not far behind in their preparations. Uliaris, however, required a full bucket of water dumped over his head before he vaulted upright, cursing to the heavens as he brushed water from his eyes.

"Remember, only the officers bear weapons," I instructed.

As we waited for Uliaris to don his mail, I ventured toward a diminutive room, likely intended for a more senior servant than a distinguished guest. Knowing Agathias to be sleeping on the other side, I rapped softly upon the door before turning its handle open. Agathias was already awake and dressed, reading a borrowed tome by a small taper.

"Quickly, don your best clothes," I whispered. "We're leaving as soon as Uliaris stumbles downstairs."

"Lord?" Agathias said, his head cocked as his eyes adjusted to my features. "I'm to watch the procession from the streets, and some of the other servants are reserving space in the Forum of Arcadius."

"Nonsense," I huffed. "This is a triumph of oathsworn warriors.

You stood for the Emperor's defense during the riots and aided Belisarius when most ran screaming. Now put on your boots and march with the rest of us."

After a moment of confusion, Agathias' eyes widened as his face broke into an unabashed grin. "At once, Lord!"

With such a distance to cover, I had ordered ponies saddled and ready for our gallop toward the Via Egnatia. We used little more than dying moonlight and the occasional smoldering torch to guide our path, trotting along the roadway and toward the vaunted Theodosian Walls that shielded Constantinople in an unbroken cocoon of stone and marble. Initially solitary, we soon joined a trickle of other mail-clad soldiers along the Forum of the Ox, a procession that thronged as the Golden Gate towered into view. Surprisingly, the movement of men and horses proceeded with minimal disruption underneath the interlocking system of open gates, revealing thousands of warriors and servants gathered upon the other side.

Per Narses' and Procopius' preparations, Belisarius would lead a proceeding column seven abreast, with Imperial and bandae banners fluttering between each group of one hundred. Such a compact formation would help limit the length of the column to a mere mile, although further space was allocated for servants and household attendants to distribute gifts and showcase Belisarius' spoils from battle. Upon arriving at the Forum of Constantine, the army would be broken into segments and led by their senior officers in a slow march along the coastal road of the Marmara. Once at the final forum, all senior officers would rejoin Belisarius at the head of the column, then march into the Hippodrome for an awaiting crowd.

Yet Belisarius was nowhere to be found. Without his immediate guard of bucellarii, the column's temporary head rested with Ascum and Bessas' Cappadocians. The Herulians, which were my assigned unit for this day, were positioned immediately behind, followed by the Huns, Ostrogoths, Corinthians, and finally the veterans of Germanus' Thracian Army. Though such organization seemed excessive, I admit I was impressed by the sweeping display of men and banners, all unified under the Imperial banner and the generalship of Flavius Belisarius.

My first surprise of the day was a mildly unpleasant one. "Lord Varus!" a voice squeaked. "Lord Varus!"

"It's that worm Procopius," Rosamund whispered to me.

Turning to meet the Emperor's trusted clerk, I found the balding Procopius puffing as he gathered his breath. "Lord Varus," he said at last, "I was worried you would be late. Once you find your place, please hand your horses over to the Emperor's slaves."

He gestured to three boys who followed closely behind, their necks shackled with the slave collar I knew too well.

"No horses?" I asked. "But it's a triumph! Belisarius himself will be on a chariot; surely ponies will do little harm other than shit on the road."

Procopius shook his head vigorously. "No horses. Belisarius will walk on foot, and none else are afforded the privilege. This is by the Emperor's command."

"No chariot?" I grumbled, signaling for my followers to dismount. "What kind of triumph is that?"

"The Christian kind, Lord Varus," Procopius sneered. "One removed of pagan filth and nonsense."

Rosamund made to approach the clerk, yet I stayed her with a hand. Instead, abandoning our mounts, we left Procopius as we walked the limited distance toward the great black banners of the ouroboros, the dark cloth soaking in the limited rays that peeked above the horizon.

"A *Christian* Triumph," Rosamund mocked. "What will Belisarius do? Weep and pity himself?"

"It need not be a harmful thing, such changes," Sembrouthes rebuffed. "Although what horses have to do with paganism, I have no understanding."

Neither did any of us, yet there was no countering Justinian's will. Instead, amidst yawns and the dew-mottled grasses trampled flat along the Via Egnatia, we found Perenus and Fulcaris crouching at the front of the Herulian ranks, with Xerxes close by, stretching stiff limbs and pacing absently toward the seafront not a hundred paces distant.

"Drink?" Fulcaris croaked, handing me a near-drained skin of wine.

"Not for me," I replied. "And keep your wits. The day will be long."

"More for me, then," Perenus said, his hand outstretched. "If the courtiers won't let me ride a horse, the least they can do is keep me good and drunk. I've never heard of a triumph on foot, Varus, although perhaps the scribes in Lazica aren't as wise as they claim to be."

"They aren't wrong," I said. "But we'll do what we must to please the Emperor."

There was little to do but wait. With the triumph's timetable secured in the greedy claws of Procopius, I ordered our men to sit and rest while such respite remained a possibility, although many shrugged off the order as mere suggestion in favor of smuggled drink and games. Soon, Samur and Aigan hailed our arrival as they joined our circle, awaiting further instructions before returning to lead the Hunnic foederati.

"I wish Sunicas was here to see this," Samur whispered. "This is all he ever wanted. To be accepted, and to honor Belisarius."

I placed an arm around his shoulders. "This day belongs to Sunicas, Simmas, Baduarius, Dagisthaeus, and so many others who died so we might live and succeed. One day, when you have children of your own, you'll tell them that you led the Huns in Belisarius' triumph and fought alongside mighty Sunicas at Dara and Callinicum."

Twin tears formed in Samur's eyes that were angrily swiped away. Before he could respond, a roaring giant bellowed greetings, jostling atop an exhausted horse before gracelessly plopping to the ground.

"Did I miss anything?"

"Gunderic!" I hissed. "You're supposed to be farther west, in your fort!"

"Aye, but with all this racket, it was hard to sleep." He grinned. "Wisimar will keep our sleeping darlings in good order, don't you worry."

"You may not like what you're about to see," Perenus warned. "A triumph is a celebration of Rome... over their conquered victims."

Gunderic shrugged. "You think we haven't paraded thousands of slaves naked and dancing along the streets of Carthage? Nay, I'd see this gathering with my own eyes."

"If you insist," I muttered, still wishing he would return to his men. Though I had never witnessed a triumph myself, I knew that conquered leaders were paraded through city streets, and Gelimer remained alive for such a purpose. "But you must remain silent and calm, no matter what you see or hear."

"On Christ's blood and bones, Varus, I swear to you!" Gunderic bowed animatedly, beating a meaty fist upon his chest.

As dawn broke, the cacophony of the triumphal column grew ever rowdier. I began to fear that all this careful organization would soon give way to drunkenness and indifference, especially when the officers had little inkling about what was to come. Like me, most only knew triumphs as pageants from a long-dead past. All we could do was watch the changing of the guard atop Constantinople's double walls and pray that this display would not end in utter humiliation.

Until, as if struck by an arrow from the heavens, the ranks grew silent. Samur and Aigan darted back to their foederati, yet none of my gathering could tell the cause of such reverence. Pacing toward the seafront, I glimpsed a single boat of some twenty men, hauling oars with silent grace. And at their bow, a figure with a snow-white plume, his lamellar armor and wolf's-head banner glistening in the sunlight that shone from the Marmara.

I, too, found no words. Belisarius may have borne much of my recent frustrations, but he was still my oath-lord, and I can think of nothing that quite compared with the general's arrival at the Golden Gate that day. A Cappadocian in front of me kneeled, followed by several others, until I, too, felt the urge to fall to the road in deference.

Within heartbeats, the entire procession knelt before the approaching boat. The foremost bucellarii hopped overboard and hauled Belisarius to the safety of shore.

I cannot recall whether a single man or woman even so much as inhaled as Belisarius' boots brushed against the stones, or as he began his gradual climb uphill to the front of the column. Behind him followed the ranks of wolf-branded bucellarii, although a curiously tall figure adorned in golden ornament followed in the center of their ranks.

It was Perenus who broke that silence. "Belisarius!" he cried, his voice straining for maximal volume. "Belisarius *Victor*!!"

"*Victor*!" Agathias echoed. "Belisarius *Victor*!!"

At first a smattering, then a swell, soon a thousand voices joined Perenus.

"Victor!"

"Victor!"

"Belisarius *Victor*!"

Not a victory for Rome or for Justinian. But for Belisarius, by acclamation by men that had bled and suffered half a world distant. And God help me, but I joined in those chants, unable to resist the idol that captured the eye of all. As the chant died down, others rammed their shields onto the turn, unable to draw upon spears or swords to add to a rumbling of approval. All told, an ocean of noise greeted the Golden Gate of Constantinople, and with a great shout of triumph, the column moved forward.

Compressed from the dense pack of men, the column ground to a halt just outside the outer gate. By then, I was a mere hundred paces from the general, his features becoming clearer. Rather than the customary purple of glorious victory, Belisarius had instead covered his armor in a cloth of purest white, reflecting the sun's rays and nearly blinding those who drew close. Gone too were the laurels of past victors, with Belisarius retaining only his plumed helmet to mark his status. He took a step forward, and awaited the call from the gate.

"Who would call upon the grace of Justinian, Caesar Augustus?"

a voice roared, amplified by a curious horn that I had seen displayed in the city's amphitheaters.

"Belisarius, Magister Militum of the Orient," the general called, his tenor steady and true. "Victor in the name of the Empire!"

At that cue, all our voices rose again in unison, proclaiming the validity of Belisarius' claims. It took several heartbeats for order to be restored, with the guardsman atop the gate waiting for his appointed moment.

"Enter, Belisarius, and be honored with the sacred triumph. The Senate and People of Rome celebrate you."

Another near-riotous cheer. With that, Belisarius took his first step into Constantinople's threshold, followed behind by a booming acclamation of thousands of spearmen and dozens of languages. Within moments, I passed through the doubled Golden Gate and into the city's expanse.

And into utter silence.

Though hundreds of sentries stood atop Constantinople's walls, there was no one along the streets adjacent to the Golden Gate—not even so much as a stray dog. No cheering crowds pressing adulation upon victors against a terrible foe.

"I don't understand," Fulcaris grumbled. "Where are all the people?"

Gunderic rocked atop his toes, using his superior height to peer above the ranks. "Did you kill them all in the riots? I have heard stories about what happened, and I cannot believe you Romans had the stones to butcher so many of your own people."

"We did," I answered curtly. "But Constantinople is a city of hundreds of thousands. The streets should be thronged with people, if for no other reason than to receive handouts."

Jubilation from the trailing ranks gradually faded into confusion as more cleared the Golden Gate's interior and beheld the empty streets. Some continued their cheers for Belisarius, yet most began to walk hesitantly forward. Our pace, expected to be little more than a crawl, soon accelerated, with some of the column rushing forward as others lagged behind the cadence of our procession. I heard Sindual roar for discipline as the Herulian disorder threatened to overlap with the Huns to our rearguard, temporarily preventing our portion of the column from spilling out of the roadway and into the adjoining alleys and depots that serviced Constantinople's more southerly gates.

"This is ridiculous," Perenus muttered. "Why would Narses not pack the streets for us?"

I should have held my tongue, but the swelling bile of resentment grew too much to choke back. "Ask Justinian. He'll have an answer."

Our first hundred paces beyond the Walls continued thus. In response, a cohort of horn-blowers blared the oft-heard announcement of the army's march, its clipped staccato emulating the hobnailed boots that slapped against worn stones of the roadway. Such was the only outpouring of noise from our column, however, for with no onlookers demanding a view of Belisarius' considerable spoils, the triumph had devolved into a sloppy jaunt through the city, and I began to fear that the Emperor's supposed insult would unleash havoc upon a city scarred by madness and destruction. Rosamund, her body bedecked in the same mail that had disguised her features in Dara and Callinicum, grew particularly suspicious.

"Are they going to punish Belisarius for allowing pagans in his army?" she whispered. "I don't even see any of the city watch on the streets."

"No," I promised. "The Emperor would have denied us entry to the city if that were so. But this is unlike any triumph I have ever heard of."

A muted chorus of hissing spread throughout the ranks as we snaked along the Studion, hugging the seaward-facing walls that blocked much of our view of the water. The discontent only grew as we passed through the outermost edges of the Xerolophos Hill, affording us a view of the River Lycus that had been channeled toward the city's peninsula and provided flowing water to Constantinople's palace and various baths. Absent the buzz and filth of daily life, the view was nearly bucolic, though it was marked by the growing shouts of centurions seeking, and failing, to keep good order. And I could not blame them, for none had expected our passage to be anything other than joyous.

It was then, as we crested a rolling slope and gained view of the abandoned walls of Constantine that had once guarded the fledgling city from attack, that all became clear.

Though half ruined by earthquakes, the Constantinian Walls still marked the beginning of Constantine's original city, and therefore the sacred heart of the Eastern Empire. It was there, amidst crumbling marble blocks, that a contingent of hundreds of city guardsmen had formed a shield wall along the Gate of Attalos, their spears pointed toward the heavens.

"Treachery!" Fulcaris hissed.

"Quiet," I shouted.

"Varus, we have no weapons," Gunderic muttered. "We'll be butchered like sheep."

"I said quiet!"

The Cappadocians before us drew to a sudden halt, forcing my own men to follow their example in swift order. Stepping from the column, I pushed my cloak off my shoulders and peered toward the column's front, finding Belisarius' plume bouncing as the general moved to greet the city's defenders.

"Halt!" a voice rasped. "Who comes to Constantine's immortal city, the heart of the world?"

Instantly, I broke into a grin. Xerxes trotted to my side for his own view.

"Liberius?" he asked, and I nodded. "That wily bastard," Xerxes said, shaking his head playfully. "I'll kill him. I could have sworn the Emperor's men were about to drive us into the sea."

"Flavius Belisarius, anointed victor!" the general's voice roared above the din.

Unharmonized chants sang out Belisarius' name once more, yet hisses for quiet soon regained control, restoring a modicum of peace in Belisarius' column while the centurions were able to regain organization amongst a churning mass of overexcited spearmen. I had no ears for such developments, however, for my whole attention was honed upon the soaring voice of my old teacher.

"The August Justinian recognizes you, citizen. Seek the blessing of God, and be rejoined with your people!"

It was nearly impossible to hear what exchange followed, although Liberius' shield wall quickly parted to allow our formation easy passage through the ruined gate. Soon a great roar from Bessas soared above our heads, echoed by a hundred others to fill Constantinople's skies.

"Soldiers, advance!"

And then, with one ponderous step after another, we entered to screams of pride so deafening they nearly brought me to cover my ears. Thousands of voices all called for Belisarius, their power so great it brought the very air around us to tremble. As we passed through the Attalos Gate, our cheers were joined by a thundering stampede of shields by the gate's guardsmen.

Any memory of fear or distrust was forgotten as we passed through the gate and soaked in the cacophonous roar upon the other side. Though I joined in the shouts of praise for our general, I felt a soft tug upon my shoulder and turned my attention temporarily away from the column.

"Incredible, isn't it?" Father Petrus said, rising on his toes to speak next to my helmet. "My father told me tales of such gatherings, but I never thought I would live to see one."

"Were you with Liberius?" I asked.

The priest nodded. "Gave Belisarius his blessing. We'll weave through all the forums, but you're to join Liberius and Belisarius at the Forum of Constantine. From there, it's the Hippodrome."

Beaming, Perenus clapped the priest on the shoulder, who jumped from surprise. "Marching with us, Father?"

Fixing his robes, Petrus nodded, prompting Perenus to scream an order back toward the Herulians. On command, four men affixed their shields to their backs before lifting Father Petrus unceremoniously into the air, forming a crude palanquin of iron and boiled leather. The priest protested, yet neither Perenus nor Gunderic had any ears for the old man's desire for solid ground.

"Petrus! Petrus! Petrus!"

Passing by the final rows of guardsmen, we were greeted by a press of humanity that yielded an intense and pungent heat. Belisarius' horns responded to their cheers, triggering yet another bout of acclamation for the general. As Father Petrus slapped at Perenus' grasping hand, the Lazic commander and his four Herulian warriors bounced the priest up and down, initiating another cry.

"Belisarius! Belisarius Victor!"

It was then that our vast baggage train was unveiled. Though no horses were permitted for our men, hulking teams of oxen bore thousands of pounds of gold, silver, and jewels that had been covered by heavy flaxen tarp. Once removed, the treasure glittered against the morning light, and tens of thousands of eyes gaped in awe at such unfathomable wealth.

"Belisarius! Belisarius Victor!"

With another blast of horns, the frontmost oxcart nearest Belisarius was unveiled. Though its contents differed little from the other wagons laden with treasure, many in the crowd nevertheless gasped. Whispers flickered within the crowd's frontmost ranks, with adults and children alike jostling for an improved view.

"That's the treasure from the Temple of Jerusalem!" a woman near me shouted—an unlikely observation by a plebeian, putting me to wonder whether the woman was secretly Jewish.

Father Petrus, still sitting uncomfortably atop his Herulian perch, shouted toward Perenus with what vigor could be mustered. Nodding, Perenus helped lower the priest, who shouted an explanation back to the onlookers.

"Liberated from the Vandals, who pillaged these treasures when they sacked Rome!"

The spoils meant little enough to me, although for many today, the Temple treasures were the most noteworthy inclusion in this unconventional triumph. Most of all was a massive golden temple menorah, its great stem bearing the seven lamps sacred to the Jews. Having only viewed it in brief passing in Carthage, I found the treasure far larger than I had initially believed, easily three cubits high.

I shouted toward Perenus. "What do you think Isaacius would do if he were here?"

"Weep, get drunk, and run screaming through the streets—the same as us!" Perenus smiled. However, I noted a shudder in his chest as his eyes clenched tightly shut, opening upon the menorah after several moments of reflection.

After an hour or more, we arrived at the Forum of the Ox. Ordinarily, the journey would have passed far more quickly, for perhaps only three or four hundred paces separated that waypoint from the Forum of Arcadius. It was one of the city's lesser gathering points, yet connected directly to the vast harbor network that established Constantinople as the foremost sea power in all the world. Here, the crowd's composition shifted from laborers and farmers to those who made their living upon the water, their skin tanned dark and hands thick with calluses from hard living. At this point, with our column turning slightly upon a juncture in a road to the forum, I stole a glance backward.

"We still have men that haven't entered the Golden Gate!"

"Don't wish your time to pass any faster than it must, Varus," Father Petrus chastised. "You'll find that its churning grows harder as you age."

As we stepped onto the Forum of the Ox, our cheers were blunted against an even louder blaring of horns, their clipped notes exchanged for extended blasts. At that, predetermined men along the column raised the banners of Belisarius' defeated enemies, while yet more oxcarts stuffed with plundered armor and foreign weapons were parted from their coverings. Snaking along the column were frayed Avar banners, their blackened cloth decorated with animal bones and torn from arrows and ballistae in Belisarius' victory against Kazrig.

There were runic sigils of the Hephthalites, the bent crosses of the Vandals, and the more recent Visigothic hawk, all carried beneath the twin emblems of the Imperial Chi-Rho and the wolf of Belisarius.

Toward the front of the formation, I glimpsed a billowing Derafsh Kaviani, the legendary Persian battle flag taken from a defeated Perozes. Nearby, a team of oxen strained against a wagon overflowing with armor from fallen Immortals, their bronze-rimmed scales denoting their owners as once-living members of Persia's elite warriors.

Muscles tensing, I involuntarily turned toward Xerxes, but he only shrugged thoughtfully. "Perozes was a fool," he said simply. "I take no offense at this display. If I had been smarter at Thannuris, this procession might be riding through Ctesiphon rather than Constantinople."

I shivered at the thought, though thankfully I detected no hostility in Xerxes' tone. There was no question that the symbolism of his fallen brothers would be painful, although it was equally apparent that the Shahanshah Khosrow would not allow the onetime Persian Spahbad to return to that vast Eastern Empire. Only a few years ago, Khosrow's emissaries promised near-immeasurable treasure should Xerxes be killed in our protection—an offer that I found repugnant, though not unforeseen. Even then, I had been drawn to protect Xerxes from our time together in the prisons of Barbalissus and Antioch, and would not sacrifice him to satisfy an anxious young king's concerns of rivals and usurpers.

With the full grandeur of conquest on display, teams of servants began to hand coins and wineskins to the senior officers of our column. Temporarily breaking ranks from the grinding procession, I followed the example of Bessas and Ascum farther ahead, and sought onlookers to offer such largesse. My handful of coins, freshly minted with the likenesses of Justinian and Theodora, were granted upon a small girl no older than seven or eight, her fingers just large enough to close upon the newfound treasure. The engravings captured Theodora's sharp jaw, yet pictured her hair wrapped in a ponderous veil that allowed only heavy, seemingly disappointed eyes to peer toward the coin bearer. In contrast, Justinian bore a cocksure gaze above his dimpled chin, his lank hair crowned with a jeweled diadem and his overlarge eyes austere and aloof as though judging his beholder.

Behind me, teams of servants tossed coins and wineskins into the crowd, whipping up a frenzy of grabbing hands and jubilant cries. Though guardsmen were posted along our route to maintain order, I did spot scatterings of fights over Belisarius' coins, though they quickly dissolved as further wealth was tossed into the fray and recaptured the attention of any disgruntled citizens.

The custom of public donation harkened back to the earliest days of the Roman kingdom, yet the raw extent of the distributed riches was numbing to behold. Thousands upon thousands of coins found their way into the pockets of Constantinople's dockworkers and merchants, while those owning slaves tasked such individuals with gathering monies upon their dominus' behalf. I witnessed several slaves shoved and struck from such efforts, although I took a small measure of relief as teams of city guardsmen quickly disrupted more serious scuffles. If nothing else, Justinian had taken all precautions against violent revolt, even if he allowed religious hatred to stew amongst the city's residents.

Slowly, we trudged from the Forum of the Ox to the Forum of Theodosius, a gathering of tanners and smithies that served the Imperial Barracks as well as the city's churchmen. Nestled at the base of Constantinople's third hill, the forum was overseen by several ancient temples looming overhead. As further donations of silver and sustenance were yielded to the public, I could not help but wonder how the city had changed as its population traded paganism for Christianity. Few records survived as reminders, yet this ancient section of old Byzantium had borne witness to much in over a thousand years of life.

More cheers. More declarations of love for Belisarius, the Victor. Many in the column began to beat closed and gloved fists against their shields, stirring the crowd into an ever greater frenzy of love and greed. Shouts for Belisarius boomed in their unison, somehow rising with each step taken.

"A year ago, they would have torn us apart," I grumbled.

"Aye, but the Empire loves a victorious general," Perenus replied. "Besides, most with a grudge from the Nika Riots haven't survived to seek vengeance. Narses and Justinian saw to that."

By that point, each step seemed to take several heartbeats, forcing our cadence to slow to an occasional short hop. As members of the crowd scurried for silver coin in the narrow confines of Theodosius' Forum, Gunderic pumped a fist into the air, roaring for the attention of a dozen Herulians around him. Pointing to me, the Vandal chieftain rushed unnaturally quickly for his great size, lifting me cleanly from my feet. Rosamund protested, yet Gunderic could only grin as I struggled for balance. Others joined his labors, throwing me a full cubit into the air as I rose and fell amidst the roar of the crowd.

"Varus! Varus! Varus!" Gunderic boomed. Even Xerxes followed suit, attempting to assist Gunderic in tossing me into the air. "Varus Veridicus! Veridicus! Herule!"

Varus the truth-sayer. Hardly a sobriquet that would instill fear on the battlefield, yet one that struck my heart a familiar sense of meaning. As a dozen Herulians gathered to throw me high into the air, they chanted the name for but a few moments alongside the general. My senses swam with dizziness, yet I nearly choked from joyous laughter all the same.

As our procession suddenly quickened its pace, Gunderic lowered me to my feet, and we proceeded toward Constantinople's historic heart. Already, the Hippodrome and Imperial Palace soared upon the horizon, while scaffolding atop the ruined Hagia Sophia suggested the sheer magnitude of the structure that would soon be developed upon the cleared and leveled site. Before all, the Forum of Constantine's vast circle held the largest gathering yet, marked at its center by the soaring column that bore the forum's name: a full twenty cubits tall and topped with a statue of Constantine bedecked in the halo of the ancient god Apollo.

Piercing into the forum, city guardsmen forced the crowd to part, offering Belisarius an unimpeded advance to the column's base. He rose atop its steps before turning to face his proceeding column, his plumed helmet held high as he absorbed chants from soldiers and citizens alike.

"Belisarius! Belisarius! Belisarius!"

"Time to go," Father Petrus instructed. "We're headed to the forum."

Leaving the others to retain control of the Herulian procession, I joined Father Petrus and Perenus as we slipped from the ranks and rushed forward. It took only moments to reach the Cappadocian front, where Ascum and Bessas both offered their greetings.

"It's like they've forgotten we killed tens of thousands of them." Ascum grinned, wiping a trickle of spittle from the burnt edge of his mouth.

We awaited arrivals from other sections of the army. Belisarius remained at the column's base as we were soon joined by Samur, Indulf, Germanus, and Mundus, along with a half dozen others afforded the honor to complete the triumphal march at the head of our parade.

Liberius winked to me as Germanus hustled to the front. "Varus Veridicus?"

"You heard that?"

He chuckled. "I hear everything, Varus. It isn't the worst honor I've heard bestowed upon a warrior."

With the final officers gathered, Belisarius stepped down from Constantine's column. Though shadows from the helmet's cheek pieces veiled the general's eyes, he nodded to each of us as he took his place at the formation's head, raising a fist to begin the march once more. We had not far to go, but two remarkable details became apparent before our arrival at the Hippodrome.

The first was a young boy who stood close behind Belisarius. Adorned in simple robes, he bore all the features of a native Italian, and carried his body with the presence of a patrician despite an age of no greater than twelve years. I was close enough to hear the boy speak to the back of Belisarius' head.

"Memento mori," he grunted. Twenty paces later, the warning was repeated. "Memento mori."

"Remember, you will die," I muttered to myself, drawing Petrus' attention.

"Perhaps the best lesson the triumphs offer," the priest replied. "Whether kings and emperors or the lowliest slave, all eventually perish to meet the Creator."

The high-pitched warning, though melodramatic, had been heard by Pompey, by Caesar, and so many others honored with the rare Roman triumph. And though Belisarius lacked Pompey's bravado or Caesar's decades-long military career, the young general had accomplished feats perhaps even more impossible than those who had once been worshipped as gods. In that moment, none paid any mind to the dishonor of Antonina's infidelity or Hermogenes' condemnation, or even that unpredictable treatment that Belisarius suffered at the hands of the Emperor. As he marched through Constantinople's streets, Belisarius was raised to the level of myth. And with that, a reminder of mortality and fallibility were prudent safeguards against a ravenous mob.

The second was far more surprising than my initial observation of Belisarius' mock soothsayer. Walking close behind the general, his head hanging against golden raiment, was Gelimer. The deposed Vandal king had grown flatter around the gut, yet had lost none of his sternness, with deep furrows lining his balding head. Though sober, he seemed to stagger between lines of grasping hands and euphoric cries for silver and wine, muttering absently to himself. As we neared the palace and began to turn into the Hippodrome's main gate, I shuffled closer to hear the words Gelimer spoke.

"Vanity of vanities," he muttered. "All is vanity."

Gelimer repeated the mantra as if a solemn oath. And I could not think less of such a pronouncement, for amidst the crushing weight of plundered gold and the distribution of ruinous amounts of coin, no declaration could have been more true than his. Gelimer continued his repetitive muttering as we reached the Hippodrome gates, where the stadium's bellowed roar washed over Belisarius' column with a force that nearly brought me to stagger the same as the Vandal king.

There were no trails of blood or stains of arson. No fires or piles of bodies, or the darkened haze of destruction. Once the hive of sedition amongst the Blues and Greens, the Hippodrome was now scrubbed and polished clean. It was rumored that Justinian had even ordered an army of slaves to scoop its sands into sackcloth and toss them into the depths of the Euxine Sea, then replace the Hippodrome's track with imported silt from the distant Nile River. Whatever the truth was, there remained not a shred of evidence that the Hippodrome had witnessed the worst horrors of humanity, with even the old pagan statues restored and the Triumphal Quadriga polished to a shine.

Other than shouts and cheers, Belisarius' men were greeted with a steady thrum of pounding shields by two hundred excubitores that lined the Hippodrome's track. At their center, standing below the Emperor's box, Marcellus held the Imperial standard, his own armor scarred with deep rents. Belisarius led his column on a great circuit across the Hippodrome's track until halting before Marcellus' still form. Though not all of the column could fit within the Hippodrome itself, thousands had joined in the triumph's culmination, raising a final booming shout before falling silent.

"Belisarius! Belisarius! Belisarius!"

Inside the Emperor's box, Justinian and Theodora stood together, their violet attire standing in contrast to all who gathered in the Hippodrome. Taking Theodora's hand, Justinian navigated to an exit and guided a small procession of dignitaries down the Hippodrome steps. More cheers initially brought Justinian to smile, until lingering shouts for the general soon erased his outward displays of pleasure. Nevertheless, the Emperor soon reached the Hippodrome's base and walked before Marcellus, his robes blowing against the wind.

"Kneel," Justinian said, his voice low.

Belisarius cocked his head, seemingly confused. So, too, did Liberius, who began to walk to the general's side, yet was stopped by the repetition of the order.

"Kneel!" the Emperor yelled.

Belisarius did not hesitate. Behind him, the army fell to its knees in a cascade, leaving only Bessas standing amongst the fray, who took Gelimer by the arm and ordered the king to kneel before joining the officers in obeisance. Even Theodora obeyed the command, when such strictures had rarely been required of her. His word honored, Justinian closed his eyes and raised his chin, breathing deeply as a hundred thousand souls focused upon his next move.

He forced all to wait for a considerable time. However, before any grumbling could arise, the Emperor summoned an attendant. "Give the blessing."

Cassiodorus, bedecked in far simpler robes than he had worn the year prior, grinned wolfishly. Both smaller in belly and quicker in step, he appeared a new man, although his whitening hair still revealed his advanced age as the Emperor's chief religious minister. Behind the Emperor stood Paulus, smirking as he clenched and unclenched a fist, a survivor despite his undoubted role as the riots' primary cause. What hold Paulus and Cassiodorus had over Justinian I cannot say—Justinian had rid the land of a less-fortunate Tribonian—although the reviled ministers remained with some semblance of power. Curiously, amongst such company stood Nepotian, the senator bearing the trappings of a senior minister.

Cassiodorus paced beside the Emperor, lifting his arms high into the air as he prayed aloud. He trumpeted all the usual blessings and praise for the Father and Son, yet ceased his proclamation with a curious addendum that brought Father Petrus to purse his lips in anger.

"We swear an oath to you, Father, to purge the land of heathens and apostates. The land of the Romans shall be pure again! We shall repent of our sins!"

Concluded, Cassiodorus retook his space with the other ministers.

None were invited to stand as Justinian strode forward, his sandals touching Belisarius' downed knee.

"Do you swear fealty to me, now and always, even if it means your death?"

"Yes, Highness," Belisarius responded.

Justinian shuffled toward Gelimer, leveling a light tap with his sandal. "And you?"

"Yes," Gelimer croaked, his eyes affixed to the ground.

"Excellent." Justinian smiled.

Moving between both men, Justinian took a deep breath before speaking to the prostrate crowd. "It occurs to me that we have long been without a consul. Flavius Belisarius shall be appointed to such a role for the next year."

There was applause and an occasional shout of the general's name, as much as could be expected from a crowd with a knee planted onto the ground. Indeed, I suspect this was Justinian's intent, for he quickly continued his speech.

"This triumph honors Belisarius, but it is a greater display of love and honor to the Imperial seat, which is ordained by God as the leader of all Christians. We gather to honor God and the Empire, to which great wealth has been bestowed. But if the Empire is to thrive, more sacrifice is needed." He paused for a heartbeat. "Far, far more."

"What in the deepest hell is he speaking of?" Samur whispered.

"Be quiet and you'll find out," I warned.

"Under Belisarius, you men have protected Tauris, defended Armenia and Mesopotamia, and have retaken all the lands sacred to Carthage," Justinian continued. "An excellent start, and the Empire honors your losses. But as I've said, far more is needed."

Justinian paced around Belisarius' prostrate form and toward we senior officers. "You men are led by the officers that will rebuild this Empire! By my will, you have Belisarius and Germanus, Mundus, and Varus, and all our valiant foederati that beckon to our call. You are invincible! So what shall you accomplish next, my titans?"

At that, Justinian's gaze seemed to fall upon me. Assuming he was looking directly into my staring face, I averted my eyes, feeling a cold sweat pool along my neck. With no response coming, however, I stole a glance back to the Emperor, and found his scrutiny placed upon one immediately behind me—Indulf. Justinian nodded, and a new voice filled the Hippodrome.

"Emperor!" Indulf screamed. "I am Indulf of the Ostrogoths, veteran of your wars, and maimed in your service. I have a boon to seek of you and this army."

Justinian bit his lip, the edges of his mouth curling upward. "Rise, Lord Indulf, and speak your mind to those gathered here."

"Highness!" Indulf responded, rising awkwardly to his feet and rustling past me. "Queen Amalasuntha, the true heir to Theodoric, gave aid to you in the Empire's great time of need. But Amalasuntha was left friendless, slain with her young son by an assassin's knife. I ask that your Empire avenge Amalasuntha's death. Bring her killers to justice!"

Indulf's words were met with a great wave of confusion, with rising noises of doubt spreading from the army and the Hippodrome's audience alike. Yet Justinian raised a hand for quiet, quickly responding to the request.

"Queen Amalasuntha was my dearest friend, and I wept at news of her passing," Justinian recounted, placing a hand over his heart. "But tell me, who is to blame for her murder? What shall be done to bring justice to her people, who have aided the Empire in its struggles?"

At that, Indulf nearly jumped as he shouted his reply. "Theodahad is the name of her killer. As a man sworn into your foederati, I beg you to send this glorious army to Italy and free Goths and Romans alike from his murderous tyranny. Only then will Amalasuntha be avenged."

My limbs turned to stone, all joy fading from my mind. For I had been a naïve fool, and Theudis had spoken the truth.

"No," I muttered, my glove closing tight around a pile of sand beneath me.

Theodora's eyes shot open, while Belisarius nearly stumbled from his kneeling position. I wanted to spring up and crawl to Justinian's feet, offering all the lands and wealth I had acquired to sway his mind. But all I could do was watch as the greatest mistake of all mankind unfolded in a scene that had been obviously planned well in advance.

"Lord Indulf, my heart is moved by your plight. Along with all my glorious officers, Belisarius shall lead the army to Italy and butcher this Theodahad as a common criminal. Then, freed from that baleful cloud, we shall join our peoples with one God, one land, and one Emperor." Justinian paced back to Belisarius and Gelimer, ignoring the grunts and discomfort of those around him. "One God, one land, one emperor! We go to Italy!"

Many cheered. And why not? They had rejoiced before at the thought of reclaiming Italy, as if such a challenge were a simple thing, when none knew the horrific cost such a war would bring. Certainly, however, they know now. Just as the magus had warned, it is a shadow that will one day consume us all.

Stunned and despairing, I wept. I have little doubt that Justinian, if he cared at all, assumed that such tears were of joy at his sacred task. Yet they were not, for it meant once again that I would be sent to do more killing, and to suffer for the Empire. True, I had once been moved by such words, yet they came from the mouth of a different man, and in a different time. Though since then I had been made enormously wealthy, covered in glories of so many campaigns, Justinian's decree meant that I still was a slave.

For the Gothic War, that hungry maw of souls, had begun. And there would be no victors.

AUTHOR'S NOTE

As with every novel in The Last of the Romans, *The Pillars of Herakles* is a work of fiction. I take considerable creative license with the characters and timeline of events in order to spin a tale, and make the sixth-century world more approachable to a general audience. The truth of the period is far more convoluted than any author can do justice, full of enough drama to fill dozens of novels. Regardless of my meddling with the historical account of Belisarius' world, my intent was to stay true to the culture, actors, and customs of the era.

The Vandal War was unexpectedly brief. Encompassing two pitched battles and a handful of skirmishes, upon its conclusion, the north African coastline was suddenly and irrevocably changed. For a time, largely while Belisarius mopped up resistance in the former Vandal kingdom's minor towns, Roman control was generally unchecked. But Belisarius, mourning the death of his dearest friend John, knew that this hard-won peace would not remain amidst such a sudden power vacuum.

Procopius tells us of many areas that presented challenges to Roman rule. Named areas requiring military response included Tripolis (modern Tripoli, in Libya's west), Lilybaeum (Marsala, on the western tip of Sicily), the whole of Sardinia (won over to the Roman side after Belisarius' envoy displayed the hated Tzazon's head, who had recently laid much of the island to waste), the Balearic Islands, and other cities northwest of Carthage. Procopius tells us that, while Belisarius' pacification efforts were largely successful, the attempt to seize Lilybaeum was met with determined resistance by the Ostrogoths. This insult would serve as fodder for the enmity to come, and one of the reasons for the Gothic War to erupt.

But in the aftermath of the Vandal kingdom's collapse, there was plenty else to occupy Belisarius' time. Other than the regions mentioned above, among the most critical points of instability was the ancient province of Tingitana. While most of Belisarius' diminutive army was required to garrison the areas around Carthage and Hippo Regius, there was fear that the Visigoths would invade Africa in the same manner as the Vandals had a century earlier.

At its narrowest point, the modern-day Strait of Gibraltar is roughly thirteen kilometers wide, and on days of fair weather and good visibility, it is possible to glimpse the opposite continent. Even for a people lacking a formidable navy, the Visigoths would have been sorely tempted to cross the Strait, seize fertile grain-bearing land, and place a greater buffer between themselves and a resurgent Empire.

Tingitana possessed several towns of note, though all had fallen on leaner trading times as Roman authority over the region declined. The greatest military prize at the time was the fortress of Septem—locally dubbed Septem Fratres, the seven-hilled city. We know Septem today as Ceuta, a Spanish exclave surrounded by Moroccan land or open water, and one of the last vestiges of overseas Spanish control. Drenched in sun, it is a beautiful place, and ancient. The area was heavily influenced by the Carthaginians—so much so that hundreds of years after Carthage's destruction, many of the local Berbers still spoke Punic in the ports and markets.

Most important to mythology, however, is Septem's proximity to Mount Abyla (today, Monte Hacho). Mount Abyla is one of the two most likely candidates for the African coast's Pillars of Hercules, flanking Gibraltar (Mount Calpe in antiquity). Ancient scholars make various claims about the Pillars of Hercules (or Herakles, to the Greeks). Pindar claimed that the mountains marked the demigod's farthest travels west, with many others describing Hercules' activities there as among his twelve labors. Others debate Hercules' modification of the local geography: Diodorus Siculus claimed that Hercules had narrowed a much wider strait to keep sea monsters from the Atlantic out of the Mediterranean, while others claimed that Hercules smashed through an isthmus to create the narrow water channel and liberate a tormented Atlas.

The Caves of Hercules, where Varus and Theudis meet along Tingitana's coastline, is a real and wonderous place. Located in present-day Cape Spartel, Morocco, the caves in myth were believed to be bottomless and endless, and were the temporary abode of the Greek god-hero Hercules before setting out to complete his eleventh Labor. Comprised of natural limestone and open in parts to the tides, the Caves are known to have been inhabited since Neolithic times. Visitors can enter, with each footstep and word echoing through the underground maze. Most notable of the Caves is the "map of Africa," a section of caves facing the sea that roughly resembles an outline of the African continent. Today, the Moroccan government carefully balances modern development and tourism with the preservation needs of the site.

Regardless of the many tales that circled the Pillars, they were and remain a place of history, mythological awe and natural beauty. For Belisarius' world, the Pillars represent "farthest west" where, beyond the strait, sailors would only find ocean and monsters. Likewise, those who held one or both Pillars possessed considerable control over trade and security in the region. With its favorable waters and easily defensible peninsula, ancient Septem was an ideal choice for any military commander in the region. Based upon Belisarius' actions in dispatching a tribune to seize Septem shortly after Tricamarum, our hero understood the strategic need to hold Septem in order to ward off future Visigoth attacks.

Not that the Visigoths peacefully accepted the Empire as their renewed neighbors. Raids spawned from Hispania shortly thereafter, transpiring throughout Theudis' campaign. Roger Collins contends that Theudis jumped at the collapse of the Vandal kingdom by occupying the African coastline along the Strait of Gibraltar, which was later rebuffed by the surging Romans. Unnamed battles occurred in AD 542 and 546, though the Visigoths were never able to permanently eject their Roman enemies from Septem's stronghold. Justinian later committed money to strengthen Septem's fortifications, and dissuaded further assaults through regular patrols by the Imperial navy.

A quick note about incendiaries and stone fortifications: While the sequence of events depicting the destruction of Septem's harbor are fictional, incendiaries like pitch and naphtha were well-known to Roman scholars and military leaders (Adrienne Mayor's *Greek Fire, Poison Arrows, and Scorpion Bombs* is an informative read on the subject). Flaming arrows were common by Belisarius' time, with Thucydides describing their use in the Peloponnesian War. The use of adhesive and caustic resins and other chemical mixtures would eventually be engineered for efficacy against stone fortifications — Apollodorus of Damascus (second century AD) added vinegar to a combination of combustibles that, when ignited, could shatter rock. Accounts of a besieger's use of fire to shatter fortifications are noted in Livy and Cassius Dio — accounts that were long ridiculed but later confirmed in the 1990s (particularly for limestone and marble, as Mayor notes, which was a favorite building material of the age).

Curious little is known of the Goths before their confrontation with the Romans. We know that Gothic peoples settled widely and had been strewn about during the Hunnic push westward — the Visigoths in southern Gaul and Hispania, the Ostrogoths in Illyria and later Italy, and even a small kingdom in present-day Crimea. Similarities in their origin myths maintained shared culture and language between the Gothic kingdoms. Indeed, the labels Visigoth or Ostrogoth appear later. They were all simply called Goths, though I use distinguishment in this and future novels to prevent confusion for the reader. The term Visigoth is of debatable origin, with Peter Heather and others suggested that the terms "vesi" or "visi" were used as colloquial tribal names, with some sources, such as Jordanes, connecting similarly named tribes of Goths known as the Thervingi as the predecessor of the Visigoths.

Likewise, tribal references to the "Greuthungi" or "Austrogothi" became the Ostrogoths. Other conflicts with nomadic tribes, like the Vandalii (Vandals) were possible, though difficult to pin down. By Belisarius' day, the Gothic peoples had been thoroughly Christianized, albeit to Arianism rather than Nicene Christianity. Per the *Lex Visigothorum* (Law of the Visigoths) distributed in the mid-seventh century, we know that the Visigoth kings gradually took steps to eliminate differences in legal treatment for Visigoths and Romans, respectively, although such practices lingered through Theudis' rule. Women maintained a measure of property rights in the Visigoth kingdom, and many Visigoth bishops and lords sponsored religious construction and goldsmithing work alike.

What is known is that, around the mid-third century AD, the Gothic tribes were violently displaced by the Huns. The Visigoths and Crimean Goths escaped, with the former pouring into the Eastern and Western Roman Empires. The Ostrogoths were less fortunate, with many subjugated under the Huns via the Amal dynasty, including, much later, Theodoric the Great, who would temporarily unite much of Illyria, Italy, southern Gaul, and Hispania in the Gothic kingship.

After extensive conflict with the Romans (including the pivotal Battle of Adrianople, which claimed the life of Emperor Valens, as well as Alaric's sack of Rome in AD 410), the Visigoths slowly entered into an on-again, off-again alliance with the dying Western Empire via their kingdom in southwestern Gaul. In the mid-fifth century, the crafty General Aetius would enlist Visigothic aid against the Hun–Ostrogoth–Gepid–Heruli army led by Attila at the famous Battle of the Catalaunian Plains—also known as the Battle of the Campus Mauriacus, the Battle of Châlons, Battle of Troyes, and the Battle of Maurica.

Over time, Western authority would wane, and Visigoth dominance over Septimania (southern Gaul) and much of Hispania would rise. Eventually, the Visigoths would find greater difficulty in warring with the resurgent Franks, which under Clovis had aggressively expanded through Gaul.

Understanding the tensions of displacement that had transpired immediately prior to Belisarius' campaigns is critical to comprehend the tension, uncertainty, and upheaval that had consumed the Western Empire. Virtually no city was untouched by war, and few peoples could claim constant friendship in the preceding century. The Goths and Vandals nursed longstanding rivalries with one another, while none of the tribes trusted the Empire (and generally resented its return to dominance) despite the presence of considerable populations of Romanized people in their conquered kingdoms that had not migrated to the east. Unsettled rivalries and longstanding mistrust would haunt Justinian and later emperors, kindling violent uprisings and outright war for much of the next century.

Many of the Visigothic characters referenced in this novel are based upon historical figures. Theudis is one—a former sword-bearer to Theodoric the Great and regent of Theodoric's grandson Amalaric. Procopius paints Theudis as a crafty figure who married a wealthy woman to pay for a private army, ultimately raising his profile as a senior leader of the Visigoth kingdom. A young Amalaric was eventually killed after a defeat by the Franks, with Isidore of Seville (late sixth-century theologian in Hispania) arguing that Amalaric was assassinated by his own warriors. Some historians implicate Theudis in this plot.

Regardless, Theudis was the prime beneficiary of Amalaric's death, and was elected king of the Visigoths shortly thereafter. Theudis would enjoy a relatively long rule, though I shall leave his history here, for we are not quite finished with the Visigoth king. We do know that the Visigoths were fierce fighters—lightly armored and preferring spears and short swords, though often adapted to the methods of their enemies over the decades. Turning back to the Empire, one of the more infamous stories of Belisarius' life was the infidelity of Antonina. I have simplified that indiscretion for the sake of storytelling, though the truth is far more lurid. Antonina was alleged by Procopius to have entered into an affair with a man named Theodosius, who had been Belisarius' godson. Belisarius had ignored signs of the infidelity, which would have been viewed as emasculating and humiliating by his warriors and Imperial society. Common tales paint Belisarius as a figure who doted over his wife to the point of foolishness, although many of these tales are spun from Procopius' openly biased account. Rumors eventually became too difficult to ignore. However, Theodora intervened to prevent Antonina from being punished or divorced, forcing Belisarius to "reconcile" with Antonina.

Belisarius' triumph would have been a spectacle, albeit entirely different from the celebrations and parades that swept through Rome in prior centuries. Procopius offers a firsthand account, while Mary Beard's *The Roman Triumph* details the day's procession. In pagan times, a Roman general granted a triumph would enter Rome on a chariot—Belisarius would do so on foot, with less distinction. No sacrifices were made to Jupiter or any other pagan gods, which was a significant departure from Roman tradition.

Ultimately, Belisarius made his way to the Hippodrome, followed by a deposed and captive King Gelimer of the Vandals. Famously, Gelimer recited Ecclesiastes 1:2 during the procession ("Vanity of vanities, all is vanity"), but did not resist his treatment. Both Belisarius and Gelimer prostrated themselves in the Hippodrome before Justinian, conferring the day's glory to the Emperor rather than the victorious general.

Amalasuntha was one of the last living descendants of Theodoric the Great, and is described by writers Cassiodorus and Procopius as having a strong will. To preserve the Amal dynasty, Amalasuntha married a blood relative named Eutheric, and had two children (Athalaric and Matasuntha). Eutheric died in AD 522, and Theodoric in AD 526, leaving a considerable power vacuum. Ten-year-old Athalaric became king of the Ostrogoths, with his mother Amalasuntha as regent.

Athalaric leaves a poor legacy, having been a heavy drinker and being pulled between Amalasuntha and a collection of Ostrogoth nobles who despised the regent's close ties to the Eastern Roman Empire. Amalasuntha attempted to strengthen her position by promoting her cousin Theodahad to co-ruler after Athalaric's death in AD 534. Amalasuntha ruled for another year but was murdered in her bath on an island in Lake Bolsena (central Italy). Theodahad, who was considered weak by many Gothic warlords and desired to appease them, is implicated in Amalasuntha's murder, though no hard proof exists.

Amalasuntha's death was shocking to contemporary observers. Many of her retainers fractured against Theodahad, creating civil tension throughout the Ostrogoth kingdom. But, as the end of *The Pillars of Herakles* notes, Amalasuntha's murder conferred Justinian with all the necessary *casus belli* to invade Italy and retake the Roman ancestral heartland. Procopius goes so far as to claim that Amalasuntha had intended to bend to Justinian's rule and merge Gothic Italy into the Eastern Empire. While Amalasuntha definitely held strong pro-Roman preferences, such a surrender would have infuriated the Gothic armies beyond the resentment they already kindled to her rule. We shall say no more for now, save that Amalasuntha's death effectively began the Gothic Wars that would devastate much of the Mediterranean world for the next two decades.

The Pillars of Herakles, like the three books that preceded it, are the result of the diligent work of many individuals. Blair Thornburgh (The Author Studio) provided the developmental and line edits—I'm grateful for her technical abilities as much as her knowledge and diligence to realism for the time period! Crystal Watanabe of Pikko's House provided the copyediting, proofreading, and formatting, and crafted beautiful interiors. The creative Dusan Markovic illustrated the book's cover. Likewise, Cyowari provided the book's maps. I am grateful to them, as well as my beta readers, for their patience and support in bringing this novel to life.

If you enjoyed *The Pillars of Herakles*, please consider leaving a review on Amazon and Goodreads. I am so thankful for your time in this—ratings and reviews are what allow the series to continue! And continue the series shall, for we have arrived at the most pivotal chapter of Belisarius' life. The Gothic War holds plenty of glory, but far greater portions of sorrow, with no person emerging better off for the experience. It is a tale of apocalypse—devastating regional war, a year without summer, terrorizing pestilence, and an unforgiving Imperial government that demanded success regardless of whatever challenges arose.

Printed in Great Britain
by Amazon

25492743R00310